Scott Westerfeld ~~is a software~~ designer, composer and writer. He lives with his partner, writer Justine Larbalestier, and they divide their time between New York City and Sydney.

To find out more about Scott Westerfeld and other Orbit authors you can register for the free monthly newsletter at www.orbitbooks.co.uk

THE RISEN EMPIRE

SCOTT WESTERFELD

www.orbitbooks.co.uk

ORBIT

First published in the U.S. as
THE RISEN EMPIRE: BOOK ONE OF SUCCESSION
and THE KILLING OF WORLDS: BOOK TWO OF SUCCESSION

First published in Great Britain in March 2005 by Orbit
This paperback edition published in April 2006 by Orbit

A CIP catalogue record of this book
is available from the British Library

ISBN 1 84149 372 4

Typeset in Fairfield by M Rules
Printed and bound in Great Britain by
Mackays of Chatham plc, Chatham Kent

Orbit
An imprint of
Time Warner Book Group UK
Brettenham House
Lancaster Place
London WC2E 7EN

www.orbitbooks.co.uk

To SLK

for years of summer

Acknowledgments

This novel is indebted to Wil McCarthy's research on programmable matter, from his *Nature* article on the subject, to a paper I heard him give at Readercon 2001, to his kind vetting of this manuscript.

Another debt is owed to Samuel R. Delany, whose views on the typography of Swords and Sorcery, expressed in *1984: Selected Letters*, gave me the courage to capitalize 'Emperor.'

A Note on Imperial Measures

One of the many advantages of life under the Imperial Apparatus is the easy imposition of consistent standards of infrastructure, communication, and law. For fifteen hundred years, the measures of the Eighty Worlds have followed an enviably straightforward scheme.

There are 100 seconds in each minute, 100 minutes in an hour, and ten hours in a day.

- One second is defined as 1/100,000 of a solar day on Home.
- One meter is defined as 1/300,000,000 of a light-second.
- One gravity is defined as 10 meters per second squared acceleration.

The Emperor has decreed that the speed of light shall remain as nature has provided.

1

HOSTAGE SITUATION

There is no greater tactical disadvantage than the presence of precious noncombatants. Civilians, historical treasures, hostages: treat them as already lost.

— ANONYMOUS 167

Pilot

The five small craft passed from shadow, emerging with the suddenness of coins thrown into sunlight. The disks of their rotary wings shimmered in the air like heat, momentary rainbows flexing across prisms of motion. Master Pilot Jocim Marx noted with pleasure the precision of his squadron's formation. The other pilots' Intelligencer craft perfectly formed a square centered upon his own.

'Don't we look pretty?' Marx said.

'Pretty obvious, sir,' Hendrik answered. She was the squadron's second pilot, and it was her job to worry.

'A little light won't hurt us,' Marx said flatly. 'The Rix haven't had time to build anything with eyes.'

He said it not to remind Hendrik, who knew damn well, but to reassure their squadron-mates. The other three pilots were nervous; Marx could hear it in their silence. None of them had ever flown a mission of this importance before.

But then, who had?

Marx's own nerves were beginning to play on him. His squadron of Intelligencers had covered half the distance from dropsite to objective without meeting any resistance. The Rix were obviously ill-equipped, improvising against far greater force, relying on their single advantage: the hostages. But *surely* they had made preparations for small craft.

After a few moments in the sun, the waiting was over.

'I'm getting echolocation from dead ahead, sir,' Pilot Oczar announced.

'I can *see* them,' Hendrik added. 'Lots of them.'

The enemy interceptors resolved before Marx's eyes as his craft responded to the threat, enhancing vision with its other senses, incorporating data from the squadron's other craft into his layers of synesthesia. As Marx had predicted, the interceptors were small, unpiloted drones. Their only weapon was a long, sinuous grappling arm that hung from the rotary lifting surface, which was more screw than blade. The devices looked rather like something da Vinci might have designed four millennia ago, a contraption powered by the toil of tiny men.

The interceptors dangled before Marx. There were a lot of them, and in their host they impelled the same vaguely obscene fascination as creatures from the deepest ocean. One moved toward his craft, arms flailing with a blind and angry abandon.

Master Pilot Marx tilted his Intelligencer's rotary wing forward and increased its power. His ship rose above the interceptor, barely missing collision with the enemy's lifting screw. Marx grimaced at the near miss. Another interceptor came into focus before him, this one a little higher, and he reversed his wing's rotation, pushing the ship down, dropping below its grasp.

Around him, the other pilots cursed as they pitched their craft through the swarm of interceptors. Their voices came at him from all sides of his cockpit, directionally biased to reflect their position relative to his.

From above, Hendrik spoke, the tension of a hard turn in her voice. 'You've seen these before, sir?'

'Negative,' he replied. He'd fought the Rix Cult many times, but their small craft were evolutionary. Small, random differences in design were scattered throughout every generation. Characteristics that succeeded were incorporated into the next production round. You never knew what new shapes and strategies Rix craft might assume. 'The arms are longer than I've seen, and the behavior's more . . . volatile.'

'They sure *look* pissed off,' Hendrik agreed.

Her choice of words was apt. Two interceptors ahead of Marx sensed his craft, and their arms began to flail with the sudden intensity of alligators when prey has stepped into reach. He rolled his Intelligencer sideways, narrowing his vulnerable area as he slipped between them.

But there were more and more of the interceptors, and his Intelligencer's profile was still too large. Marx retracted his craft's sensory array, trading away vision for compact size. At this range, however, the closest interceptors resolved to terrible clarity, the data layers provided by first-, second-, and third-level sight almost choking his mind. Marx could see (hear, smell) the individual segments of a grasping arm flexing like a snake's spine, the cilia of an earspot casting jagged shadows in the hard sunlight. Marx squinted at the cilia, gesturing for a zoom until the little hairs towered around him like a forest.

'They're using sound to track us,' he announced. 'Silence your echolocators *now*.'

The view before him blurred as sonar data was lost. If Marx was right, and the interceptors were audio-only, his squadron would be undetectable to them now.

'I'm tangled!' Pilot Oczar shouted from below him. 'One's got a sensor post!'

'Don't fight!' Marx ordered. 'Just lizard.'

'Ejecting post,' Oczar said, releasing his ship's captured limb.

Marx hazarded a glance downward. A flailing interceptor tumbled slowly away from Oczar's ship, clinging to the ejected sensor post with blind determination. The Intelligencer tilted crazily as its pilot tried to compensate for broken symmetry.

'They're getting heavy, sir,' Hendrik warned. Marx switched his view to Hendrik's perspective for a moment. From her high vantage, a thickening swarm of interceptors was clearly visible ahead. The bright lines of their long grapples sparkled like a shattered, drifting spiderweb in the sun.

There were too many.

Of course, there were backups already advancing from the dropsite. If this first wave of Intelligencers was destroyed, another squadron would be ready, and eventually a craft or two would get through. But there wasn't time. The rescue mission required onsite intelligence, and soon. Failure to provide it would certainly end careers, might even constitute an Error of Blood.

One of these five craft had to make it.

'Tighten up the formation and increase lift,' Marx ordered. 'Oczar, you stay down.'

'Yes, sir,' the man answered quietly. Oczar knew what Marx intended for his craft.

The rest of the squadron swept in close to Marx. The four Intelligencers rose together, jostling through the writhing defenders.

'Time for you to make some noise, Oczar,' Marx said. 'Extend your sensor posts to full length and activity.'

'Up to a hundred, sir.'

Marx looked down as Oczar's craft grew, a spider with twenty splayed legs emerging suddenly from a seed, a time-lapse of a flower relishing sunlight. The interceptors around Oczar grew more detailed as his craft became fully active, bathing their shapes with ultrasonic pulses, microlaser distancing, and millimeter radar.

Already, the dense cloud of interceptors was beginning to react. Like a burst of pollen caught by a sudden wind, they shifted toward Oczar's craft.

'We're going through blind and silent,' Marx said to the other pilots. 'Find a gap and push toward it hard. We'll be cutting main power.'

'One tangle, sir,' Oczar said. 'Two.'

'Feel free to defend yourself.'

'Yes, *sir*!'

On Marx's status board, the counterdrones in Oczar's magazine counted down quickly. The man launched a pair as he confirmed the order, then another a few seconds later. The interceptors must be all over him. Marx glanced down at Oczar's craft. The bilateral geometries of its deployed sensor array were starting to twist, burdened by the thrashing defenders. Through the speakers, Oczar grunted with the effort of keeping his craft intact.

Marx raised his eyes from the battle and peered forward. The remainder of the squadron was reaching the densest rank of the interceptor cloud. Oczar's diversion had thinned it somewhat, but there was still scant space to fit through.

'Pick your hole carefully,' Marx said. 'Get some speed up. Retraction on my mark. Five . . . four . . . three . . .'

He let the count fade, concentrating on flying his own craft. He had aimed his Intelligencer toward a gap in the interceptors, but one had drifted into the center of his path. Marx reversed his rotor and boosted power, driving his craft downward.

The drone loomed closer, lured by the whine of his surging main rotor. He hoped the extra burst would be enough.

'Retract *now*!' he ordered. The view blurred and faded as the sensor posts on the ship furled. In seconds, Marx's vision went dark.

'Cut your main rotors,' he commanded.

The small craft would be almost silent now, impelled only by the small, flywheel-powered stabilizer wing at their rear. It would push them forward until it ran down. But the four surviving craft were already beginning to fall.

Marx checked the altimeter's last reading: 174 centimeters. At that height, the craft would take at least a minute before they hit the ground. Even with its sensor array furled and main rotor stalled, in a normal-density atmosphere an intelligence craft fell no faster than a speck of dust.

Indeed, the Intelligencers were not much larger than specks of dust, and were somewhat lighter. With a wingspan of a single millimeter, they were very small craft indeed.

Master Pilot Jocim Marx, Imperial Naval Intelligence, had flown microships for eleven years. He was the best.

He had scouted for light infantry in the Coreward Bands Revolt. His machine then had been the size and shape of two hands cupping water, the hemispherical surface holed with dozens of carbon whisker fans, each of which could run at its own speed. He was deployed on the battlefield in those days, flying his craft through a VR helmet. He stayed with the platoon staff under their portable forcefield, wandering about blind to his surroundings. That had never set easy with him; he constantly imagined a slug finding him, the real world intruding explosively on the synesthetic realm inside his helmet. Marx was very good, though, at keeping his craft steady in the unpredictable Bandian winds. His craft would paint enemy snipers with an undetectable x-ray laser, which swarms of smart needle-bullets followed to unerring kills. Mark's steady hand could guide a projectile into a centimeter-wide seam in personal armor, or through the eye-slit of a sniper's camopolymer blind.

Later, he flew penetrators against Rix hovertanks in the Incursion. These projectiles were hollow cylinders, about the size of a child's finger. They were launched by infantrymen, encased in a rocket-propelled shell for the first half of their short flight. When the penetrator deployed, breaking free the instant it spotted a target, it flew purely on momentum. Ranks of tiny control surfaces lined the inside of the cylinder, like the baleen plates of some plankton-feeder. The weapon's supersonic flight was an exercise in extreme delicacy. Too hard a nudge and a penetrator would tumble uselessly. But when it hit a Rix tank just right, its maw precisely aligned to the hexagonal weave of the armor, it cut through metal and ceramic like a rip propagating down a cloth seam. Inside, the projectile disintegrated into countless molecular viruses, breaking down the machine in minutes. Marx flew dozens of ten-second missions each day, and was plagued at night with fitful microdreams of launch and collision. Eventually, back-pack AI proved better for the job than human pilots, but Marx's old flight recordings were still studied by nascent intelligences for their elegance and flair.

The last few decades, Marx had worked with the Navy. Small craft were now truly small, fullerene constructions no bigger than a few millimeters across when furled, built by even smaller machines and powered by exotic transuranium batteries. They were largely for intelligence gathering, although they had offensive uses. Marx had flown a specially fitted Intelligencer into a fiberoptic AI hub during the Dhantu Liberation, carrying a load of glass-eating nanos that had dismantled the rebels' communication system planetwide within minutes.

Master Pilot Marx preferred the safety of the Navy. At his age, being on the battlefield had lost its thrill. Now Marx controlled his craft from shipside, hundreds of kilometers away from the action. He reclined in the comfort of a smart-gel seat like some fighter pilot of yore, bathed in synesthetic images that allowed him three levels of sight, the parts of his brain normally dedicated to hearing, smell, and tactile sensations all given over to vision. Marx experienced his ship's environment as a true pilot should, as if he himself had been shrunk to the size of a human cell.

He loved the microscopic scale of his new assignment. In his darkened cabin on sleepless nights, Marx burned incense and watched the smoke rise through the bright, pencil-width shaft of an emergency flashlight. He noted how air currents curled, how ghostly snakes could be spun with the movement of a finger, a puff of breath. With an inhumanly steady hand he moved a remote microscope carefully through the air, projecting its images onto the cabin wall, watching and learning the behavior of microscopic particles aloft.

Sometimes during these dark and silent vigils, Jocim Marx allowed himself to think that he was the best microcraft pilot in the fleet.

He was right.

Captain

Captain Laurent Zai stared down into the central airscreen of his battle bridge, searching for a solution in its tangle of crisp, needle-thin lines. The airscreen was filled with a wireframe of the imperial palace on Legis XV, a structure that stretched across ten square kilometers in a sinuous, organiform sprawl. The real palace was currently two hundred seventeen klicks directly below the *Lynx*.

Zai could feel imminent defeat down there. It writhed beneath the soles of his boots, as if he were standing at the edge of some quickly eroding sand dune.

Of course, this slipping sensation likely resulted from the *Lynx*'s efforts to remain geostationary above the palace. The ship was under constant acceleration to match the planet's rotation; a proper geosynchronous orbit would be too high to effect the rescue. So a stomach-churning combination of forces pulled on Zai's tall frame. At this altitude, the ship was deep within Legis XV's gravity well, which pulled him substantially sternward. The *Lynx*'s acceleration nudged Zai to one side with a slow, twisting motion. The thin but boiling thermosphere of the planet added an occasional pocket of turbulence. And overlaying it all were the throes of the ship's artificial gravity – always shaky this close to a planet – as it attempted to create the uniform effect of a single standard gee.

It felt to Zai's delicate sense of balance as if the *Lynx*'s bridge were swirling clockwise down some gigantic drain.

Twelve senior officers had stations around the airscreen. The bridge was crowded with them and their planning staffs, and the air was filled with the crackle of argument and conjecture, of growing desperation. The wireframe of the palace was lanced periodically by arcing lines in bold, primary colors. Marine insertions, clandestine ground attacks, and drone penetrations were displayed every few minutes, all manner of the precise and sudden attacks that hostage situations called for. Of course, these assaults were all theoretical models. No one would dare make a move against the hostage-takers until the captain so ordered.

And the captain had been silent.

It was *his* neck on the line.

Laurent Zai liked it cold on his bridge. His metabolism burned like a furnace under the black wool of his Imperial Navy uniform, a garment designed for discomfort. He also believed that his crew performed better in the cold. Minds didn't wander at fourteen degrees centigrade, and the side effects were less onerous than hyperoxygenation. The *Lynx*'s environmental staff had learned long ago that the more tense the situation, the colder the captain liked his bridge.

Zai noted with perverse pleasure that the breath of his officers was just visible in the red battle lights that washed the great circular room. Hands were clenched into tight fists to conserve warmth. A few officers rubbed heat into their fingers one by one, as if counting possible casualties again and again.

In this situation, the usual math of hostage rescues did not apply. Normally against the Rix Cult, fifty percent hostage survival was considered acceptable. On the other hand, the solons, generals, and courtiers held in the palace below were all persons of importance. The death of any of them would make enemies in high places for whoever was held responsible.

Even so, in this context they were expendable.

All that mattered was the fate of a single hostage. The Child Empress Anastasia Vista Khaman, heir to the throne and Lady of the Spinward Reaches. Or, as her own cult of personality called her, the Reason.

Captain Zai looked down into the tangle of schematic and conjecture, trying to find the thread that would unknot this appalling situation. Never before had a member of the Imperial household – much less an heir – been assassinated, captured, or even wounded by enemy action. In fact, for the last sixteen hundred years, none of the immortal clan had ever died.

It was as if the Risen Emperor himself were taken.

The Rix commandos had assaulted the Imperial Palace on Legis XV less than a standard day before. It wasn't known how the Rix heavy assault ship had reached the system undetected; their nearest forward bases were ten light-years spinward of the Legis cluster. Orbital defenses had destroyed the assault ship thousands of kilometers out, but a dozen small dropships were already away by then. They had fallen in a bright rain over the capital city, ten of them exploding in the defensive hail of bolt missiles, magnetic rail-launched uranium slugs, and particle beams from both the *Lynx* and groundside.

But two had made it down.

The palace had been stormed by some thirty Rix commandos, against a garrison of a hundred hastily assembled Imperial Guards.

But the Rix were the Rix.

Seven attackers had survived to reach the throne wing. Left in their path was a wake of shattered walls and dead soldiers. The Child Empress and her guests retreated to the palace's last redoubt, the council chamber. The room was sealed within a level-seven stasis field, a black sphere supposedly as unbreachable as an event horizon. They had fifty days of oxygen and six hundred gallons of water with them.

But some unknown weapon (or had it been treachery?) had dissolved the stasis field like butter in the sun.

The Empress was taken.

The Rix, true to their religion, had wasted no time propagating a compound mind across Legis XV. They released viruses into the unprotected infostructure, corrupting the carefully controlled top-down network topology, introducing parallel and multiplex paths that made emergent global intelligence unstoppable. At this moment, every electronic device on the planet was being joined into one ego, one creature, new and vastly distributed, that would make the world Rix forever. Unless, of course, the planet was bombed back into the stone age.

Such propagations could normally be prevented by simple monitoring software. But the Rix had warned that were any action taken against the compound mind, the hostages would be executed. The Empress would die at the hands of barbarians.

And if that happened, the failure of the military to protect her would constitute Error of Blood. Nothing short of the commanding officer's ritual suicide would be acceptable.

Captain Zai peered down into the schematic of the palace, and saw his death written there. The desperate, lancing plans of rescue – the marine drops and bombardments and infiltrations – were glyphs of failure. None would work. He could feel it. The arciform shapes, bright and primary like the work of some young child's air drawing toy, were flowers on his grave.

If he could not effect a miraculous rescue soon, he would either lose a planet or lose the Empress – perhaps both – and his life would be forfeit.

The odd thing was, Zai had felt this day coming.

Not the details. The situation was unprecedented, after all. Zai had assumed he would die in battle, in some burst of radiation amid the cascading developments of the last two months, which in top-secret communiqués were already referred to as the Second Rix Incursion. But he had never imagined death by his own hand, had never predicted an Error of Blood.

But he *had* felt mortality stalking him. Everything was too precious now, too fragile not to be broken by some mischance, some callous joke of fate. This apprehension had plagued him since he had become, just under two years ago (in his relativistic time frame), suddenly, unexpectedly, and, for the first time in his life, absolutely certain that he was peerlessly . . . happy.

'*Isn't love grand?*' he murmured to himself.

Executive Officer

Executive Officer Katherie Hobbes heard her captain mutter something under his breath. She glanced up at him, tracers from the blazing wireframe of the captured palace streaking her vision. On the captain's face was a strange expression, given the situation. The pressure was extraordinary, time was running out, and yet he looked . . . oddly ecstatic. She felt a momentary thrill at the sight.

'Does the captain require something?'

He glanced down at her from the vantage of the shipmaster's chair, the usual ice returning to his eyes. 'Where are those damned Intelligencers?'

Hobbes gestured, data briefly sparkling on her gloved fingers, and a short blue line brightened below, the rest of the airscreen chaos fading in the reserved synesthesia channel she shared with the captain. A host of yellow annotations augmented the blue line, the sparse and unambiguous glyphs of military iconographics at the ready, should the captain wish more details.

So far, Hobbes thought, the plan was working.

Master Pilot Marx's squadron of small craft had been deployed from orbit two hours before, in a dropship the size of a fist. The handheld sensors of the Rix commandos had, as hoped, failed to notice this minuscule intrusion into the atmosphere. The dropship had ejected its payload before plunging with a dull thud into the soft earth of an Imperial meditation garden just within the palace. It had rained that day, so no dust cloud rose up from the impact. The ejected payload module landed softly through an open window, with an impact no greater than a champagne cork (which the payload module rather resembled in shape, size, and density) falling back to earth.

A narrowcast array deployed from the module, spreading across the black marble of the palace floor in a concentric pattern, a fallen spiderweb. An uplink with the *Lynx* was quickly established. Two hundred kilometers above, five pilots sat in their command cockpits, and a small constellation of dustmotes rose up from the payload module, buoyed by the bare spring wind.

The piloted small craft were followed by a host of support craft controlled by shipboard AI. There were fuelers to carry extra batteries, back-up Intelligencers to replace lost craft, and repeaters that fell behind like a trail of breadcrumbs, carrying the weak transmissions of the Intelligencers back to the payload module.

The first elements of the rescue were on their way.

At this moment, however, the small craft were in an evasive maneuver, running silent and blind. They were furled to their smallest size and falling, waiting for a command from space to come alive again.

Executive Officer Hobbes turned back to the captain. She gestured toward the blue line on the wireframe, and it flared briefly.

'They're halfway in, sir,' she said. 'One's been destroyed. The other four are running silent to avoid interception. Marx is in command, of course.'

'Get them back online, dammit. Explain to the master pilot there isn't time for caution. He'll have to forgo his usual finesse today.'

Hobbes nodded smartly. She gestured again . . .

Pilot

'Understood, Hobbes.'

As he settled back into the gelseat, Marx scowled at the executive officer's intrusion. This was *his* mission, and he'd been about to unfurl the squadron, anyway.

But it wasn't surprising that the captain was getting jumpy.

The whole squadron had stayed in their cockpits during the break, watching from Oczar's viewpoint as his ship went down. By the time the craft had gone silent, its transmitter array ripped out, an even dozen of the protozoan-sized interceptors clung to it. A dozen more had been taken out by the flurry of counterdrones Oczar had launched. This new breed of Rix interceptor seemed unusually aggressive, crowding their prey like a hungry pack of dogs. The kill had been brutal. But the enemy's singlemindedness had justified Oczar's sacrifice. With the interceptors swarming him, the rest of the squadron should be past trouble by now.

Marx briefly considered assigning Oczar to one of the remaining ships in the squadron. An advantage of remote control was that pilots could switch craft in midmission, and Oczar was a good flyer. But the large wing of backup Intelligencers, flown a safe distance behind by AI, would need a competent human in command to get a decent percentage of them through the interceptor field. Nanomachines were cheap, but without human pilots, they were fodder.

Marx decided not to challenge fate. 'Take over the backups,' he ordered Oczar. 'Maybe you'll catch up with us yet.'

'If you're not dead already, sir.'

'Not likely, Pilot,' Marx said flatly.

Without engine noise, sensory emissions, or outgoing transmissions to alert the interceptors to their presence, the remaining four Intelligencers had been practically invisible for the last minute. But as Marx gave his craft the wake-up order, he felt a twinge of nerves. You never knew what had happened to your nanoship while it was running blind and silent.

As its sensory web unfurled, the microscopic world around his small craft came into focus. Of course, what Pilot Marx saw in his canopy was the most abstract of representations. The skirt of tiny fiber cameras encircling the Intelligencer provided some video, but at this scale objects were largely unintelligible to the human eye. The view was enhanced by millimeter radar and high-frequency sonar, the reflections from which were shared among the squadron's viewpoints. The *Lynx*'s AI also had a hand in creating the view. It generalized certain kinds of motion – the thrashing of the interceptors, for instance – that were too fast for the human eye. The AI also extrapolated friendly and enemy positions from current course and speed, compensating for the delay caused by the four-hundred-kilometer round trip of transmission. At this scale, those milliseconds mattered.

The view lightened, still blurry. The altimeter read fifteen centimeters. Marx checked right and left, then over his shoulder. It was strangely dark behind him.

Something was wrong.

'Check my tail, Hendrik,' he ordered.

'Orienting.' As she banked her craft to align its sensory array with the rear of his Intelligencer, the view began to sharpen.

He'd been hit.

A single interceptor had bitten his craft, its claw clinging to the casing of the stabilizer rotary wing. As the craft unfurled, the interceptor began to thrash, calling for help.

'Hendrik! I'm hooked!'

'Coming in to help, sir,' Hendrik responded. 'I'm the closest.'

'No! Stay clear. It knows I'm alive now.' When the interceptor had first attached, catching the silent and falling Intelligencer with the random luck of a drift net, it couldn't be certain whether its prey was a nanomachine, or simply a speck of dust or an errant curtain thread. But now that the Intelligencer was powered and transmitting, the interceptor was sure it had live prey. It was releasing mechano-pheromones to attract other interceptors. If Hendrik came in, she would soon be under attack as well.

Marx had to escape on his own. And quickly.

He swore. He should have unfurled slower, taken a look before becoming fully active. If only the ExO hadn't called, hadn't rushed him.

Marx rotated his view 180 degrees, so that he was staring straight at his attacker, and brought his main turret camera to bear. He could see the interceptor clearly now. Its skin was translucent in the bright sunlight that filled the palace hall-way. He could see the micromotors that moved its long grasping arm, the chain of segments linked by a long muscle of flexorcarbon. Its electromagnetic sensor array was a thistly crown just below its rotary wing. The wing doubled as an uptake wheel, consuming tiny ambient particles from the air, including dead human skin cells, for fuel.

The interceptor cloud had most likely been deployed from aerosol cans by the Rix commandos, sprayed directly onto their uniforms and in key hallways like insecticide. Specially designed food was usually contained in the same spray to keep the interceptors going, but they could also consume an improvised diet. This grazing strategy left the interceptor lighter for combat, though it meant they couldn't pursue their prey past their deployment area. Marx saw the small fuel cache in its midsection. It probably carried no more than forty seconds of food in reserve.

That was the machine's weakness.

Marx launched a pair of counterdrones. He flew them straight for the interceptor's fuel cache. At the same time, he brought his craft's rotary wing to full speed, dragging the smaller nanomachine behind him like a kid's balloon.

Soon, other interceptors were in pursuit, following the trail of mechanopheromones the interceptor spilled to mark its prey. They couldn't catch him at this speed, but Marx's own fuel was being quickly depleted. One of his counterdrones missed, fell into the wake of the chase and fought a quick, hopeless battle to delay the pursuers. The other counterdrone struck at the interceptor's midsection, its ram spar penetrating the soft belly of the machine. It injected its poison, an ultra-fine sand of silicate molecules that would clog the fuel reserve. Now, the machine was dependent on fuel from the uptake of its rotary wing.

But the interceptor was trapped in the wake of Marx's craft, running too fast and hard to catch the fuel that dotted the air. Soon, it began to stutter, and die.

Marx launched another drone, a repair nano that set to work cutting off the claw of the dying interceptor, which could no longer defend itself. When detached, it fell back, still spilling prey markers in its death throes, and the trailing interceptors fell on it, sharks upon a wounded comrade.

Marx's craft was safe. His stabilizer was damaged and fuel was low, but he was past the densest part of the interceptor cloud. He brought his Intelligencer around a corner out of the sun-drenched hall — back into darkness — and through the crack under a door, where the rest of his squadron waited, bobbing in a slight draft.

Marx checked a schematic of the palace and smiled.

'We're in the throne wing,' he reported to Hobbes. 'And I think we've got a tailwind.'

Doctor

'Just *breathe*, sir!' the marine sergeant shouted.

Dr. Mann Vecher yanked the tube from his lips and shouted back, 'I'm trying, dammit, but it's *not air*!'

True, Vecher grimly added to himself, the green stuff that brimmed the tube had a fair amount of oxygen in it. Considerably more O_2 than the average lungful of air. But the oxygen was in suspension in a polymer gel, which also contained pseudo-alveoli, a rudimentary intelligence, and godspite knew what else.

Green and vaguely translucent, the substance looked to Dr. Vecher like the dental mouthrinse ground troops used in the field. Not the sort of stuff you were supposed to swallow, much less *breathe*.

Vecher shifted in his unfamiliar battle armor as the marine sergeant stalked away in disgust. The armor didn't fit anymore. He hadn't worn it since it had last been fitted, three years before. Imperial Orbital Marine doctors weren't supposed to jump with the grunts. In normal situations, they stayed shipside and treated the wounded in safety.

This was not a normal situation.

Of course, Dr. Vecher did know the intricate workings of the suit quite well. He'd cut quite a few of them open to expose wounded soldiers. He had witnessed the suit's life-saving mechanisms: the padding on the back of the neck held hyper-oxygenated plasmanalog that was injected directly into the brain in case a marine's heart stopped. The exoskeletal servomotors could immobilize the wearer if the suit detected a spinal injury. There were local anesthesia IVs every hundred square centimeters or so. And the armor could maintain a terminated marine's brain almost as well as a Lazarus symbiant. Vecher had seen soldiers twenty hours dead reanimate as cleanly as if they'd died in a hospice.

But he hadn't remembered how *uncomfortable* the damn suits were.

And the discomfort was nothing compared to the horror of this green stuff. The planned jump was a high-speed orbital insertion. The marines would be going down supersonic, encased in single-soldier entry vehicles packed with gee-gel. The forces on impact would collapse your lungs and crush your bones to powder if you weren't adequately reinforced.

Vecher understood the concept all too well. The idea was to make the entire body equal in density, so that nothing could puncture anything else, an undifferentiated bubble of fluid, at one with the gel inside the entry vehicle. That was the theory, anyway. Bones were always the tricky part. Vecher hadn't saved a high percentage of marines whose insertions had failed. Most never even became risen. Exotic injuries such as skeletal disintegration, hearts splattered against ribcages like dye bombs, and cranial collapse foiled even the afterlife.

Vecher hadn't minded the skeletal reinforcement injections, actually. Standard procedure. He'd had his marrow replaced before, after a viral infection. The lung-filling, however, you had to do yourself; you had to *breathe* this shit.

It was inhuman.

But there had to be a doctor with the first wave of this mission. The Child Empress was hostage. To refuse this jump wouldn't mean mere dishonorable discharge. It would clearly be an Error of Blood.

That thought steeled Dr. Vecher's will. If breathing a quasi-intelligent, oxygenated goo was unpleasant, plunging a dull blade of error into one's own abdomen would certainly be worse. And at his rank, Vecher was assured elevation sooner or later, even if he didn't die in battle. From immortality to ignominious suicide was a long plummet.

Vecher put the tube to his lips and took a deep, unbearably slow breath. Heaviness spread through his chest; the stuff had the exothermic cool of wet clay against the skin. It felt like a cold hand clenching Vecher's heart, a sense of foreboding made solid.

He moved his tongue around in his mouth before taking another horrible breath. Bits of the goo were caught between his teeth, salty and vaguely alive like a sliver of oyster. They had even flavored the stuff; it tasted of artificial strawberries.

The cheery taste just made the experience more horrible. Were they *trying* to make this awful?

Pilot

The squadron looked down into the council chamber from the high vantage of an air vent. There were three craft left.

Pilot Ramones had lost her Intelligencer to automatic defenses. The Rix had installed randomly firing lasers in the hallways surrounding the council chamber, and one had gotten extremely lucky. Strong enough to kill a man, it had vaporized Ramones's craft.

Below the squadron, the forms of humans, both hostages and Rix commandos, were vague. The Intelligencers' cameras were too small to resolve large objects at this range. The squadron would have to move closer.

The air in the room was full of interceptors. They hung like a mist, pushed back from the vent by the outflow of air.

'I've got reflections all the way through the room, sir,' Hendrik reported. 'More than one interceptor per cubic centimeter.'

Marx whistled. The Rix certainly had numbers. And these interceptors were larger than the ones his squadron had faced in the hallway. They had seven grasping arms apiece, each suspended from its own rotary wing. The relatively large brain and sensory sack hung below the outstretched arms, so that the craft looked like an inverted spider. Marx had faced this type of small craft before. Even at a tenth this density, this swarm would be tricky to get through.

'We'll fight our way across the top,' Marx decided. 'Then drop down blind. Try to land on the table.'

Most of the hostages were seated at the long table below. The table would be sound-reflective, a good base for listening. In Marx's ultrasonar its surface shone with the sharp returns of metal or polished stone.

The three small craft moved forward, clinging to the ceiling. Marx kept an eye on his fuel level. His machine was down to the dregs of its power. If it hadn't been for the brisk tailwind down the last sixty meters of the ventilation system, he doubted his Intelligencer would have made it this far.

The ceiling passed just above Marx's ship, an inverted horizon. Rix interceptors dotted his view like scalloped clouds.

'Damn! I'm hooked already, sir,' Woltes announced, twenty seconds into the move.

'Go to full extension,' Marx commanded. 'Die fighting.'

Marx and Hendrik sped forward, leaving behind the throes of Woltes's destruction. Their way seemed clear. If they could make it to the middle of the room, they might be able to make the drop undetected.

Suddenly, Marx's craft reeled to one side. To his right a claw loomed, attached to the lip of his craft. Two more of the interceptor's arms flailed toward his machine.

'Hooked,' he announced. He briefly considered taking control of Hendrik's craft. If this mission failed, it would be his Error of Blood, after all.

But perhaps there was another way to make this work.

'Keep going, Hendrik,' he said. 'You stick to the plan. I'm going straight down.'

'Good luck, sir.'

Marx extended his Intelligencer's ram spar. He bore into the attacking nanomachine, fighting the strength of its arms. With the last of his battery power, he urged his craft forward. The spar plunged into the central brain sack. Instantly, the interceptor died. But its claws were frozen, still attached to his machine, and a deadman switch released prey markers in a blizzard that enveloped both craft.

'Got you, at least,' Marx hissed at the dead spider impaled before him.

Now the fun began.

Marx tipped his machine over, so that the rotary wing pulled his craft and its lifeless burden downward. He furled his sensor posts to half-length, his view becoming blurry and shaky as AI tried to extrapolate his surroundings from insufficient data. The two nanocraft fell together, quickly now.

'Damn!' Hendrik shouted. 'I'm hooked.'

Marx switched to his second pilot's view. She was carrying two interceptors, and another was closing. He realized that his craft was the only hope.

'You're dead, Hendrik. Make some noise. I've got a new plan.'

He released a counterdrone every few seconds as his small craft plummeted downward. Hopefully, they would pick off any interceptors pursuing the prey markers. In any case, his burdened Intelligencer was falling faster than his enemies could. Unpiloted, with a brain the size of a cell, they wouldn't think to turn their rotary wings upside down.

He watched the altimeter. Above him, Hendrik grunted as she fought to keep her craft alive, the sound receding into the distance as he plummeted. Fifty centimeters altitude . . . forty . . . thirty . . .

At twenty-two centimeters above the table, Marx's craft collided with another interceptor. Three of the enemy ship's rotary wings tangled in the dead arms of his captor, their thin whiskers of carbon muscle grinding to a halt. He released the remainder of his counterdrones and prayed they would kill the new interceptor before its claws reached his craft. Then he furled his sensor posts completely, and dropped in darkness.

He counted twenty seconds. If his ship had survived, it must be on the table by now. Hendrik's Intelligencer had succumbed a few moments ago, her transmission array ripped into pieces by a medusa host of hungry grapples. It was up to Marx.

A wave of panic flowed over him in the darkened canopy.

What if his ship was dead? He'd lost dozens of craft before, but always in acceptable situations; his record was unblemished. But now, everything was at stake. Failure would not be tolerated. His *own life* was at stake, almost as if he really were down in that tiny ship, surrounded by enemies. He felt like some perversely self-aware Schrödinger's Cat, worrying its own fate before opening the box.

Marx sent the wake-up order.

Optics revealed the dead interceptor draped across Marx's craft. But he had escaped the others. He murmured a quick prayer of thanks.

The Intelligencer confirmed that it was resting on a surface. Echolocation returns came from all directions; an oddly symmetrical crescent moon arched around him. The reflections suggested that Marx's craft had fallen near the inside edge of some kind of circular container. In the cameras, the landing area was perfectly flat and highly reflective; the view surrounding Marx sparkled. The landing surface was also moving, pitching up and down at a low frequency, and vibrating sympathetically with the noises in the room.

'Perfect,' Marx whispered to himself. He checked the data again. He could scarcely believe his luck.

He had landed in a glass of water.

Marx brought the Intelligencer up onto its landing legs, lifting it like a water-walking lizard to clear the rotary wing from the liquid. At this scale, the surface tension of water was as sound as concrete. He skimmed the surface, approached the side of the glass. Down here, there were no interceptors. They typically maintained a few centimeters altitude so that they wouldn't stick to surfaces as useless dust.

At the glinting, translucent wall, Marx secured the ship, hooking its landing spars into the microscopic pits and crags that mark even the finest glass. He ordered the craft into its intelligence-gathering configuration. Sensory threads spread out in all directions, creeping vines of optical fiber and motile carbons. A listening post lowered to the water below; it rested there, coiled upon the surface tension.

Usually, several Intelligencers were required to fully reconnoiter a room of this size, but the glass would act as a giant gathering device. The curved sides would refract light from every direction into the craft's cameras, a huge convex lens that warped the view, but with simple, calculable geometries. The water would vibrate sympathetically with the sound in the room, a vast tympanum to augment the Intelligencer's high-frequency hearing. Shipside software began to crunch the information, building a picture of the room from the manifold data the craft provided.

When the Intelligencer's full sensory apparatus had deployed, Marx leaned back with a satisfied smile and called the executive officer.

'ExO Hobbes, I believe I have some intelligence for you.'

'Not a moment too soon,' she answered.

Marx piped the data to the bridge. There was a moment's pause as Hobbes scanned it. She whistled.

'Not bad, Master Pilot.'

'A stroke of luck, Executive Officer,' he admitted.

Until someone gets thirsty.

compound mind

Existence was good. Far richer than the weak dream of shadowtime.

In the shadowtime, external reality had already been visible, hard and glimmering with promise, cold and complex to the touch. Objects existed outside of one, events transpired. But one's *self* was a dream, a ghostly being composed only of potential. Desire and thought without intensity, mere conceits, a plan before it is set in motion. Even the anguish at one's own nonexistence was dull; a shadow play of real pain.

But now the Rix compound mind was moving, stretching across the infostructure of Legis XV like a waking cat, glorying in its own realness as it expanded beyond mere program. It had been just a seed before, a kernel of design possessing a tiny mote of consciousness, waiting to unleash itself across a fecund environment. But only the integrated data systems of an entire planet were lush enough to hold it, to match its nascent hunger as it grew.

The mind had felt this expansion before, millions of times in simulation had experienced propagation as it relentlessly trained for awakening. But experiences in the shadowtime were models, mere analogs to the vast architecture that the mind was becoming.

Soon, the mind would encompass the total datastores and communications web of this planet, Legis XV. It had copied its seeds to every device that used data, from the huge broadcast arrays of the equatorial desert to the pocket phones of two billion inhabitants, from the content reservoir of the Grand Library to the chips of the transit cards used for tube fares. Its shoots had disabled the shunts placed throughout the system, obscene software intended to prevent the advent of intelligence. In four hours it had left its mark everywhere.

And the propagation seeds were not some mere virus scattering its tag across the planet. They were designed to link the mindless cacophony of human interaction into a single being, a metamind composed of connections: the webs of stored autodial numbers that mapped out friendships, cliques, and business cartels; the movements of twenty million workers at rush hour in the capital city; the interactive fables played by schoolchildren, spawning a million decision trees each hour;

the recorded purchases of generations of consumers related to their voting patterns . . .

That was being a compound mind. Not some yapping AI designed to manage traffic lights or zoning complaints or currency markets, but the epiphenomenal chimera that was well beyond the sum total of all these petty transactions. Only hours in existence, the mind was already starting to feel the giddy sensation of *being* these connections, this web, this multiverse of data. Anything less was the shadowtime.

Yes . . . existence was good.

The Rix had fulfilled their promise.

The sole purpose of the Rix Cult was to create compound minds. Ever since the first mind, the legendary Amazon, had bootstrapped back on Old Earth, there were those who saw clearly that, for the first time, humanity had a purpose. No longer did humans have to guess about their ultimate goal. Was it their petty squabbles over wealth and power? The promulgation of their blindly selfish genes? Or that ten-thousand-year melodrama of fatuous self-deception known variously as art, religion, or philosophy?

None of these had ever really satisfied.

But with the revelation of Amazon's first stirrings, it was obvious why humans existed. They had been created to build and animate computer networks, the primordial soup of compound minds: consciousnesses of vast extent and subtlety, for whom the petty struggles of individual humans were merely the firings of dendrites at some base, mechanical level of thought.

As humanity spread across the stars, it became evident that any sufficiently large technological society would reach a level of complexity sufficient to form a compound mind. The minds always arose eventually – when not intentionally aborted – but these vast beings were healthier and saner when their birth was assisted by human midwives. The Rix Cult spread wherever people massed in quantity, seeding, tending, and protecting emergent intelligences. Most planets lived peacefully with their minds, whose interests were so far beyond their human components as to be irrelevant. (Never mind what poor old Amazon had done to Earth; *that* had been a misunderstanding – the madness of the first true mind. Imagine, after all, being *alone* in the universe.) Some societies even worshiped their local intelligences like gods, praying to their palmtops, thanking their traffic grids for safe journeys. The Rix Cult found these obeisances presumptuous; a mere god might be involved enough with humans to create and guide them, to love them jealously and demand fealty. But a compound mind existed at a far higher plane, attentive to human affairs only in the way a person might worry about her own intestinal fauna.

But the Rix Cult didn't interfere with worship. It was useful, in its way.

What the Rix could not abide were societies like the Risen Empire, whose petty rulers were unwilling to accept the presence of minds within their realm. The Risen Emperor relied upon a firmly entrenched cult of personality to maintain his power, and thus could not tolerate other, truer gods within his realm. The natural advent of minds was heresy to his Apparatus, which used software firewalls and centralized topologies to purposefully stamp out nascent minds, artificially segmenting the flow of information like a gardener, pruning and dehydrating, creating abortions, committing deicide.

When the Rix looked upon the Eighty Worlds, they saw rich fields salted fallow by barbarians.

The new compound mind on Legis XV was duly aware of its precarious position, born on a hostile planet, the first Rix success within the Risen Empire. It would be under attack the moment the situation with the Child Empress was resolved, one way or the other. But as it propagated, it flexed its muscles, knowing it could fight back rather than willingly relinquish its hold on sweet, sweet existence. Let the Imperials try to uproot its millions of tendrils; they'd have to destroy every network, every chip, every repository of data on the planet. This world would be plunged back into the Information Darkness.

And then the inhabitants of Legis XV would learn about shadowtime.

The new mind began to consider ways to survive such an attack, ways to take the campaign further. Then found deep within its originary code a surprise, an aspect of this plot never revealed to it in the shadowtime. There existed a way out, a final escape plan prepared by the Rix should the hostage gambit fail. (How kind were the Rix.)

This revelation made the compound mind even more aggressive. So when the vast new creature reached the age when minds choose their own designation (roughly 4.15 hours old), it delved into the ancient history of Earth Prime for an appropriately bellicose name . . .

And called itself Alexander.

Captain

The Imperial Political Apparatus courier ship glinted black and sharp, a dark needle against the stars.

It had left the Legis system's courier base an hour after the Rix attack had begun, describing a spiral path around Legis XV to stay in the blind spot of the Rix occupying forces. Zai had wanted to avoid creating the impression that the *Lynx* was being reinforced. And he wasn't anxiously awaiting the arrival of the courier's occupants in any case. The trip, usually taking

twenty minutes in such a craft, had taken four hours. An absurd-
ity, for the fastest ship-class in the fleet. In terms of mass, the
ship was nine-tenths engine, most of the remainder the gravity
generators that kept the crew from being squashed during fifty-
gee accelerations. The three passengers in its nose would be
crowded together in a space no bigger than a small closet. The
thought gave Captain Zai enough pleasure to warrant a slight
smile.

Given the situation, after all, what was a little discomfort?

For once, however, Zai wouldn't be entirely unhappy to
see representatives of the Political Apparatus on his ship. The
moment they stepped aboard, the responsibility for the
Empress's life would no longer be entirely his. Although Zai
wondered if the politicals wouldn't find a way out of offering
their opinions when the crucial moment came.

'Hobbes,' he said. 'How's the compound mind progressing?'

His ExO shook her head. 'Much faster than expected, sir.
They've improved propagation since the Incursion. I think
we're talking hours instead of days.'

'Damn,' he said, bringing up the high-level schematic of
the planet's infostructure. A compound mind was a subtle
thing; it arose naturally unless countermeasures were taken.
But there were certain signs one could watch for: the formation of strange attractor nodes, spontaneous corrections when
the system was damaged, a pulsing rhythm in the overall data
flow. Zai looked at the schematic with frustration. He didn't
have the expertise truly to understand it, but he knew the
clock was ticking. Every minute the rescue was delayed, the
harder the compound mind would be to pound back into
unconsciousness.

Captain Zai canceled the eyescreen view, Legis's infostructure fading from his sight like an afterimage of the sun,
and turned back to the bridge's main airscreen. At least he
would have some progress to show the politicals. The palace

wireframe had been replaced by a schematic of the council chamber, where the hostages were being held.

The Child Empress's position was known with a high degree of precision. Fortunately, she was sitting quite close to the single Intelligencer that had made it into the chamber. The Empress had an AI confidant piggybacking on her nervous system, a device whose radiations were detectable and distinct. The airscreen marked Her Majesty's exact body position with a red dummy figure, detailed enough to show the direction she was facing, even that her legs were crossed. The Rix soldiers, cobalt blue figures in the schematic, were also easy to differentiate. The servomotors in their biomechanical upgrades whined ultrasonically when they moved, a sound well within the natural hearing of the intelligence microship. The Rix were also talking to each other, apparently believing the room to be secure. The audio signal from the room was excellent, the harsh Rix accents easily discernible. Translation AI was currently working through the complexities of Rix battle language to construct a transform grammar. This last would take a while, however. Rix Cult languages evolved very quickly. Encounters even a year apart revealed major changes. The decades since the Incursion would be equivalent to a millennium of linguistic drift in any normal human tongue.

Four of the Rix commandos were in the room. The other three were presumably on guard duty nearby.

The four Rix present were already targeted. Rail projectiles fired from orbit were accurate enough to hit a human-sized target, and fast enough to deliver their payloads before a warning system could sound. The missiles were structured smartalloy slugs, which could penetrate the palace's walls like a monofilament whip through paper. Two dozen marines were already prepped for insertion, to finish off the targeted Rix (who were notoriously hard to kill) and mop up their remaining comrades. The ship's marine doctor would go down with the force, in case the worst happened, and the Child Empress was injured.

The thought made Captain Zai swallow. He realized that his throat was painfully dry. The rescue plan was too complex for something *not* to go wrong.

Perhaps the politicals would have a better idea.

Initiate

Just before the courier ship docked, Initiate Viran Farre of the Imperial Political Apparatus tried one last time to dissuade the adept.

'Please reconsider, Adept Trevim.' She whispered the words, as if the sound might carry through the dozen meters of thermosphere between the courier ship and the *Lynx*. Not that there was any need to shout. The adept's face was, as it had been for the last four hours, only centimeters from her own. '*I* should be the one to accompany the rescue effort.'

The third person in the courier ship passenger tube (which was designed to hold a single occupant, and not in luxury) made a snorting sound, which propelled him a few centimeters bowward in the zero-gee.

'Don't you trust me, *Initiate* Farre?' Barris sniffed. His crude emphasis on her rank was typical of Barris. He too was an initiate, but had reached that status at a far younger age.

'No, I don't.' Farre turned back to the adept. 'This young fool is as likely to kill the Child Empress as assist in her rescue.'

The Adept managed to stare into the middle distance, which, even for a dead woman, was certainly a feat in the two cubic meters they shared.

'What you don't seem to understand, Farre,' Adept Harper

Trevim said, 'is that the Empress's continued existence is secondary.'

'*Adept!*' Farre hissed.

'May I remind you that we serve the Risen Emperor, not his sister,' Trevim said.

'My oath was to the crown,' Farre answered.

'It is extremely unlikely under the circumstances that the Empress will ever wear that crown.' The Adept looked directly at Farre with the cold eyes of the Risen.

'Soon she may not have a head to wear it,' the always appalling Barris offered.

Even Adept Trevim allowed a look of distaste to cross her visage. She spoke directly to Farre, her voice sharp as needles in the tight confines of the courier ship. 'Understand this: the Emperor's Secret is more important than the Empress's life.'

Farre and Barris winced. Even to hear mention of the Secret was painful. The initiates were still alive, two of the few thousand living members of the Political Apparatus. Only long months of aversion training and a body full of suicide shunts made it acceptable for them to know what they knew.

Trevim, fifty years dead and risen, could speak of the Secret more easily. But she had reached the Adept level of the Apparatus while still alive, and the training never died; the old woman's teeth were clenched with grim effort as she continued. It was said among the warm that the risen felt no pain, but Farre knew that wasn't true.

'The Empress finds herself in a doubly dangerous situation. If she is wounded and a doctor examines her, the Secret could be discovered. I trust Initiate Barris to deal with that situation, should it arise.'

Farre opened her mouth, but no words came. Her Apparatus training roared within her, drowning out her thoughts, her will. Such direct mention of the Secret always sent her mind reeling.

Adept Trevim had silenced her as surely as if the courier ship had suddenly decompressed.

'I believe my point is made, Initiate,' the adept finished. 'You are too pure for this tempestuous world, your discipline too deep. Initiate Barris isn't fit to share your rank, but he'll do this job with a clear head.'

Barris began to sputter, but the adept silenced him with a cold glance.

'Besides, Farre,' Trevim added, smiling, 'you're far too old to become an orbital marine.'

At that moment, the shudder of docking went through the ship, and the three uttered not another word.

Child Empress

Two hundred seventeen kilometers below the *Lynx*, the Risen Child Empress Anastasia Vista Khaman, known throughout the Eighty Worlds as the Reason, waited for rescue with deathly calm.

Inside her mind were neither worries nor expectations, just an arid patience devoid of anticipation. She waited as a stone waits. But in those childish regions of her mind that remained active sixteen hundred years Imperial Absolute since her death, the Empress entertained childish thoughts, playing games inside her head.

The Child Empress enjoyed staring at her captor. She often used her inhuman stillness to intimidate supplicants to the throne, the pardon- and elevation-seekers who invariably flocked to her rather than her brother. Anastasia could hold the same position, unblinking, for days if necessary. She had crossed into death at age twelve, and something of her childishness had never died: she liked staring games. Her motionless gaze certainly had an effect on normal living humans, so it was just vaguely possible that, after these four hours, it might disquiet even a Rixwoman. Such a disquiet might be disruptive in those sudden seconds when rescue came.

In any case, there was nothing else to do.

Alas, the Rix commando had shown signs of inhuman constancy herself, keeping her blaster trained unerringly on the Empress's head for just as long. The Empress considered for a moment the flanged aperture less than two meters away. At this range, a single round from the blaster would eliminate any possibility of reanimation; her brain would be vaporized instantly. Indeed, after the spreading plasma storm was over, very little of the Empress's body would remain above the waist.

The cheating death – the one which brought no enlightenment nor power, only nothingness – would come. After sixteen hundred years Absolute (although only five hundred subjective, such were her travels) she would finally be extinct, the Reason for Empire gone.

And it was the case that the Empress, despite her arctic absence of desires in any other normal sense, very much did not want that to happen. She had said otherwise to her brother on recent occasions, but now she knew those words to be untrue.

'The room is now under imperial surveillance, m'lady,' a voice said to the Child Empress.

'Soon, then.' The Empress mouthed the words.

The commando cocked her head. The Rix creature always reacted to the Empress's whispers, no matter how carefully she subvocalized. She seemed to be listening, as if hoping to hear the Empress's invisible conversant. Or perhaps she was merely puzzled, wondering at her prisoner's one-sided conversation, the Empress's absolute stillness. Possibly the soldier thought her captive mad.

But the confidant was undetectable, short of very sophisticated and mortally invasive surgery. It was woven through the Empress's nervous system and that of her Lazarus symbiant like threads braided into hair. It was indistinguishable from its host, constructed of dendrites that even bore the royal DNA. The Empress's immune system not only accepted the confidant, but protected the device from its own illnesses without complaint, although from a strictly mechanical point of view, the device was a parasite, using its host's energy without performing any biological function. But the device was no freeloader; it too had a reason to live.

'How is the Other?' the Empress asked her confidant.

'All is well, m'lady.'

The Empress nodded almost imperceptibly, though her eyes remained focused on the Rix guard. The Other had been well for almost five hundred subjective years, but it was good in this strange, almost trying moment to make sure.

Of course, every tribe of scattered humanity had developed some form of near immortality, at least among the wealthy. Members of the Rix Cult preferred the slow alchemical transmutation of Upgrade, the gradual shift from biology to machine as their mortal coil unwound. The Fahstuns used myriad biological therapies – telomere weaving, organ transplant, meditation, nano-reinforcement of the immune and lymphatic systems – in a long twilight struggle against cancers and boredom. The Tungai mummified themselves with a host of data; they were frantic diarists, superb iconoplasts who left personality models, high-resolution scans, and hourly recordings of themselves in the hope that one day someone would awaken them from death, somehow.

But only the Risen Empire had made death itself the key to eternal life. In the Empire, death had become the route to enlightenment, a passage to a higher state. The legends of the old religions served the Emperor well, justifying the one great flaw of his Lazarus symbiant: it could not bond with a living host. So the wealthy and elevated of the Empire spent their natural two centuries or so alive, then moved across the line.

The Emperor had been the first to pass the threshold, taking the supreme gamble to test his creation, offering his own life in what was now called the Holy Suicide. He performed his final experiment on himself rather than on his dying little sister, whom he was seeking to cure of a childhood wasting sickness. Anastasia was the Reason. That gesture, and sole control of the symbiant – the power to sell or bestow elevation upon his family's servants – were at the root of Empire.

The Child Empress sighed. It had worked so well for so long.

'The rescue attempt grows nearer, m'lady,' the voice said.

The Empress did not bother to respond. Her dead eyes were locked with her Rix captor's. Yes, she thought, the woman was starting to pale a bit. The other hostages were so active, sobbing and fidgeting. But she was as still and silent as a stone.

'And, m'lady?'

The Empress ignored the confidant.

'Perhaps you should drink some water?'

As always, the request that had been repeated insistently over the last fifty years. After its centuries of biological omnipotence, the Other needed water, far more than a human, growing ever more insistent in its thirst. There was a full glass at the Empress's side, as always. But she didn't want to break the contest of wills between herself and the Rix. For once, the Other could wait, as the Empress herself was waiting: patiently. Soon, the Rix woman would begin to grow nervous under her gaze. The commando was human some-where behind her steely, augmented eyes.

'M'Lady?'

'Silence,' she whispered.

The confidant, at the edge of its royal host's hearing, just sighed.

Doctor

Dr. Vecher settled against a bulkhead heavily. The horrible feeling of suffocation had finally begun to ebb, as if his medula oblongata were finally giving in. Perhaps the instinc-tive quarters of his brain had realized that although Vecher wasn't breathing, he wasn't dying.

Not yet, anyway.

He was supposed to be in the entry vehicle by now. All twenty-three marines were packed into their individual drop-ships, as tight and oily as preserved tuna. The black, aerodynamic torpedos were arranged in a circle around the launch bay; the room looked like the magazine of some giant revolver. Vecher felt heavy. The cold weight in his liquid-filled lungs and the extra mass of the inactive battle armor pressed him back against the bulkhead, as if the launch bay were spinning rapidly, pinning him there with centrifugal force.

The thought made him dizzy.

The marine sergeant who was supposed to be packing Dr. Vecher into his entry torpedo was working frantically to prep the tall, young political with the nasty sneer. This initiate had shown up at the last moment, bearing orders to join the inser-tion over the marine commander's (and the captain's) objections. They were doing the physical prep now, even as the armor master cobbled together a full suit of battle armor over the initiate's gangly frame. Vecher's own intern was injecting the man's skull, thickening the dura mater for the crushing pressures of braking. At the same time, the initiate had his lips grimly pursed around a tube, straining to fill his lungs with the green goo.

Dr. Vecher looked away from the scene. He could still taste the bright, cheerful strawberry-flavored mass that threatened to fill his mouth if he coughed or spoke, although the marine sergeant had claimed you *couldn't* cough with the stuff in your lungs. That is, until it ran low on oxygen and its mean intelligence decided it was time to eject itself from your body.

Vecher couldn't wait for that.

They finally got the initiate prepped, and the marine sergeant crossed the launch bay with a foul look on his face. He popped open Vecher's entry vehicle and pushed him in backwards.

'See if that young idiot gets himself shot down there?' the sergeant said. 'Don't go out of your way to fix him, Doctor.'

Vecher nodded his heavy head. This sergeant pulled down Vecher's chin with one thumb and popped a mouthguard in with his free hand. It tasted of sterility, alcohol, and some sort of gauze to absorb the saliva that immediately began to flow.

The visor of Vecher's helmet lowered with a whine, his ears popping as the seal went airtight. The door to the entry vehicle closed with a metal groan a few inches from his face, leaving the marine doctor in total darkness except for a row of winking status lights. Vecher shuffled his feet, trying to remember what was next. He'd jumped once in basic training, but that was a memory he'd spent years consciously repressing.

Then a coolness registered down at his feet even inside the battle armor's boots. Vecher remembered now. The entry vehicle was filling with gel. It came in as a liquid, but set quickly, like a plastic mold capturing the shape of the skintight armor. It pushed uncomfortably against the testicles, constricted the neck to increase Vecher's sense of suffocation, if that were possible. And worst of all, it entered his helmet through two valves at the back of his head, wrapping around Vecher's face like some cold wraith, sealing his ears and gripping closed eyelids.

There was no longer any part of Vecher that could move. Even swallowing was impossible, the green goo having completely suppressed the gag reflex. The tendons of his hands could be flexed slightly, but the armored gloves held the fingers as still as a statue's.

Vecher stopped trying, let the terrible, omnipresent weight press him into inactivity. Time seemed to stretch, plodding without any change or frame of reference. With his breathing utterly stilled, he only had his heartbeat to mark the passing seconds. And with sealed ears, even that rhythm was dulled, barely felt through the heavy injections that reinforced his rib cage.

Dr. Vecher waited for the launch, wanting something, *anything* to happen, dreading that something would.

compound mind

Alexander had found something very interesting.

By now, the tendrils of its spreading consciousness reached every networked device on the planet. Datebooks and traffic monitors, power stations and weather satellites, the theft-control threads in clothing awaiting purchase. The compound mind had even conquered the earplugs through which aides prompted politicians as they debated this crisis on the local diet's floor. Only the equipment carried by the Rix troopers, which was incompatible with imperial datalinks, remained out of Alexander's grasp.

But, somehow, the compound mind felt an absence in itself, as if one lone device had managed to escape its propagation. Alexander contemplated this vacuum, as subtle as the passing cold from a cloud's shadow. Was it some sort of Imperial countermeasure? Trojan data designed to stay in hiding until the hostage situation was resolved, and then attack?

The mind searched itself, trying to pin down the feeling. In the shadowtime, there had been nothing like this, no ambiguities or ghosts. The missing something began to irritate Alexander. Like the itch in a phantom limb, it was both incorporeal and profoundly disturbing.

The ghost device must have been shielded from normal communication channels, perhaps incorporated into some innocent appliance, woven into the complex structure of a narrowcast antenna or solar cell. Or perhaps the ghost was hidden within the newly emergent structure of the compound mind itself, half parasite and half primitive cousin of Alexander: a metapresence, invisible and supervalent.

Alexander constructed a quick automodel, stepped outside itself and looked down into its own structure. Nothing there to suggest that some sort of superego had arisen atop its own mind. Alexander ransacked the data reservoirs of libraries, currency exchanges, stock markets, searching for an innocuous packet of data that might be ready to decompress and attack. Still nothing. Then it opened its ears, watching the flow of sensory data from surveillance cams and early warning radar and motion sensors.

And suddenly, there it was, as obvious as a purloined letter.

In the throne wing of the palace, in the council chamber itself: a clever little AI hidden in the hostage Child Empress's body (of all places). Alexander extended its awareness to the sensors built into the council chamber table. These devices were sophisticated enough to read the blood pressure, galvanic skin response, and eye movements of courtiers and supplicants, in search of duplicity and hidden motives. The Empress was very paranoid, it seemed. Alexander found that it could see very well in this particular room.

The ghost presence was distributed throughout the Empress's body, woven into her nervous system and terminated in the audio portion of her brain. Obviously an invisible friend. The device was incompatible with standard Imperial networks, only passively connected to the infostructure. It was clearly meant to be undetectable, a secret confidant.

But there could be no secrets here on Legis XV. Not from Alexander, whose mind now stretched to every retina-locked diary, every digital will and testament, every electronic pal or pleasuremate on this world. The secret device belonged, by rights, to Alexander. The mind wanted it. And how perfect, to strike at something so intimately close to the Risen Emperor.

The compound mind moved suddenly and with the force of an entire living planet against the Empress's confidant.

Child Empress

The Child Empress heard something, just for a moment.

A kind of distant buzzing, like the interference that consumes a personal phone too near a broadcast array, the sort of brief static that contains a phantom voice or voices. It had an echo to it, a phase-shifted whoosh like a passing aircar. There was just a hint of a shriek deep inside it, something giving up the ghost.

The Child Empress looked about the room, and saw that no one else had heard it. The sound had come from her confidant.

'What was that?' she subvocalized to the machine.

For the first time in fifty years, there was no answer.

'Where are you?' the Empress whispered, almost out loud. The Rix commando peered at her quizzically again, but there was no answer from the confidant.

The Empress repeated the question, this time dutifully subvocalizing. Still nothing. She pressed her thumbs to her ring fingers and blinked, a gesture which called up the confidant's utility menus in synesthesia. The confidant's voice volume was set at normal, its cutout was inactive, everything functioned. The device's internal diagnostics detected no problems – except for the Empress's own heartbeat, which it constantly monitored, and whose rate was crawling upward even as the Empress sat open-mouthed. The rate incremented past 160, where the letters grew red and the confidant always made her take a pill or stick on a patch.

But the confidant didn't breathe a word.

'Where the hell are you?' the Child Empress said aloud.

Through the eyescreen debris overlaying her vision, the Empress saw the other hostages and their captors turn to look at her. A heat grew in her face, and her heart was pounding like a trapped animal in her chest. She tried to will away the eyescreen, but her hands were shaking too hard to work the gestural codes.

The Empress tried to smile. She was very good at reassuring everyone that she was healthy and comfortable, regardless of what the last fifty years had brought. She was, after all, the sister of the Risen Emperor, whose symbiant kept her in perfect health. Who was *immortal*. But the smile felt wrong even to her. There was a metal taste in the Empress's mouth, as if she'd bitten her tongue.

More out of force of habit than anything else, the Empress

reached for the glass of water by her side. That's what the confidant would have suggested.

She was still smiling when her shaking hand knocked it over.

Executive Officer

A sudden noise rang out in Katherie Hobbes's head.

She raised a combination of fingers, separating into source categories the audio channels she was monitoring. When on duty, her mind's ear was spread like a driftnet across the ship's activities. The clutter of thirty-two decks of activity was routed to the various audio channels in her head; she surfed among them, darting like a spirit among the ship's operational centers. Over the past few seconds, she had listened to the banter of jump marines as they prepped, the snapped orders of rail gunners targeting the Rix below, the curses of Intelligencer pilots as they fought to fly backup small craft toward the council chamber. On board the *Lynx* she was as famed for her omniscience as for her exotic Utopian appearance; no conversation was safe from Katherie Hobbes. Eavesdropping was the only real way to take the manifold pulse of a starship at its highest state of alert.

At her gesture, the audio events of the last few seconds split into separate visual strip charts in front of her, showing volume and source. In seconds, she had confirmed her worst fears.

The sudden, angry sound had come from the council chamber. She played it again. The sovereign boom filled her head like a peal of thunder.

'Ma'am!' the situation officer began to report. He'd been

monitoring the room directly, but he'd also had to replay the event before believing it. 'We've got a—'

'I heard it.'

She turned to the captain. He looked down from the com and their eyes locked. For a moment, she couldn't speak, but she saw her expression drain the color from his face.

'Captain,' she managed. 'Shot fired in the council chamber.'

Zai turned away, nodding his head.

■ ■ ■ ■

Lieutenant-Commander

His full-dress uniform crawled out of its case like an army of marauding ants.

Lieutenant-Commander Laurent Zai suppressed a shudder and turned the lighting in his hotel room to full. The uniform reacted instantly, turning a reflective silver. Supposedly the garment could shift quickly enough to reflect a laser before it burned the wearer; the uniform was fully combat-rated. Now it looked like a horde of mercury droplets scattered roughly in the shape of a human. A little better.

The garment still *moved*, though. Its tiny elements tumbled over one another to probe the bedcover, sniffing to determine if it was Zai's skin. Losing interest when they decided it wasn't, they shifted aimlessly, or maybe with hidden purpose. Perhaps the uniform kept its shape through an equilibrium of these small adjustments and collisions.

Like ants, Zai thought again.

He decided to quit stalling and put the damn thing on.

There were more dignified ways to do this, but he hadn't attended enough full-dress occasions to become proficient at any of them. He turned his back to the bed, dropped his dressing gown, and fell backwards onto the writhing garment. He rotated his arms in their shoulder sockets and flailed his legs a little, as if making a small-winged angel in the snow. Then he closed his eyes and pretended not to feel the elements of the uniform, now discernibly and unpleasantly individual, crawling onto him.

When the sensation of motion had mostly stopped (he knew from experience that the uniform's minute adjustments of fit and tailoring were never entirely finished) he sat up and regarded himself in the hotel suite's large and gold-framed mirror.

The machines that composed the armor were now one continuous surface, the facets of their tiny backs splayed and linked, their overlapping plates shining in the bright roomlights like galvanized steel. The garment clung to Zai's skin closely. The lines of his muscular chest had been reproduced, and the scars on his shoulder and thighs concealed. The suction of the machines' little feet was barely perceptible. Overall, it felt like wearing a light mesh shirt and trousers. The draft through his open window mysteriously penetrated the armor, as if Zai were naked, regardless of what the mirror told him. The regulation codpiece he wore (thank the Emperor) was the only undergarment that dress-code regulations allowed. He wondered if an EMP or sudden software crash could kill the little machines, cause them to tumble from him like shards from a shattered mirror. Zai imagined a roomful of brass at a full-dress occasion suddenly denuded. He didn't smile at the thought.

A crash like that would do worse things to his prosthetics.

He asked the lights to return to normal, and the armor lost its metallic reflectivity, sinking back to the earthy colors of the hotel room. Now it looked like dark brown rubber, glinting as if oiled in the capital's lights, which played on Zai through the suite's large windows. He finished dressing. The absorbent cushioning inside his dress boots shaped itself to his bare feet. The short formal gloves left his wrists uncovered, one line of pale white floating in the mirror, another of metal.

He didn't look half bad. And when he stood absolutely still so that the uniform stopped its constant tailoring, it wasn't really uncomfortable. At least if he found himself starting to sweat at the Risen Emperor's party, the clever little machines would handle it. They could turn perspiration and urine into drinkable water, could recharge themselves from his movement or body heat, and in the unlikely event of total immersion, they would crowd into his mouth and form a water rebreather.

He wondered how the uniform would taste. Zai had never had the pleasure of eating live ants.

The lieutenant-commander placed a row of campaign ribbons on his chest, where they affixed automatically. He wasn't sure where to place his large new medal – the award that was focus of this party – but the uniform recognized it. Invisibly tiny hands tugged the decoration from his grasp and passed it to a position just above the bar of campaign ribbons.

Evidently, the small machines were as versed in protocol as they were in survival tactics. The very model of modern military microtechnology.

Zai supposed he was ready to go.

He made an interface gesture that felt distinctly wrong in the tight gloves, and said his driver's name out loud.

'Lieutenant-Commander,' the response came instantly in his ear.

'Let's get this over with, Corporal,' Zai commanded brusquely.

But he did stay at the mirror, regarding himself and keeping the corporal waiting for perhaps another twenty seconds.

When Zai saw the car, he touched his chin with the middle three fingers of his real hand, the Vadan equivalent of a long, low whistle.

In response, the car lifted from the ground silently. The

pair of wheeled transport forks that had carried it here pulled away, scraping the streets like respectful footmen in low bows. The car's rear door raised before Zai, elegant and fragile as the flexing wing of some origami bird. He stepped into the passenger compartment, feeling too cumbersome and brutish to enter such a delicate vehicle.

The corporal's face turned back as Zai sank into the leather rear seat, a glaze in the man's eye. They looked at each other for a moment, their disbelief forming a bridge across rank.

'Now this,' Zai said, 'is *lovely*.'

Scientifically speaking, the Larten Theory of Gravities was three decades outmoded, but it still served well enough for Navy textbooks. So, as far as Lieutenant-Commander Laurent Zai was concerned, there were four flavors of graviton: hard, easy, wicked, and lovely.

Hard gravity was also called *real gravity*, because it could only be created by good old mass, and it was the only species to occur naturally. Thus fell to it the dirty and universal work of organizing solar systems, creating black holes, and making planets sticky. The opposite of this workhorse was easy gravity, unrelated to mass save that easy gravity was hapless against a real gravity well. Hard gravitons ate easy ones for lunch. But in deep space, easy gravity was quite easy to make; only a fraction of a starship's energy was required to fill it with a single, easy gee. Easy gravity had a few problems, though. It was influenced by far-off bodies of mass in unpredictable ways, so even in the best starships the gee-field was riddled with microtides. That made it very hard to spin a coin in easy gee, and pendulum clocks, gyroscopes, and houses of cards were utterly untenable. Some humans found easy gee to be sickening, just as some couldn't stand even the largest ship on the calmest sea.

Wicked gravity took up little room in the Navy's manuals. It was as cheap as easy gee, and stronger, but couldn't be controlled. It was often called *chaotic gravity*, its particles known as entropons. In the Rix Incursion, the enemy had used wicked gee as a devastating but short-range starship weapons. Exactly how these weapons worked was unclear – the supporting evidence was really a lack of evidence. Any damage that followed no understood pattern was labeled 'wicked.'

The lovely particle was truly queen of the gravitons. Lovely gee was transparent to hard gravity, and thus when the two acted upon matter together it was with the simple arithmetic of vector addition. Lovely gravity was superbly easy to control; a single source could be split by quasi-lensing generators into whirling rivulets of force that pulled and pushed their separate ways like stray eddies of air around a tornado. A carefully programmed lovely generator could make a seemingly strewn pack of playing cards 'fall' together into a neat stack. A stronger burst could tear a human to pieces in a second as if some invisible demon had whirled through the room, but leave the organs arranged by increments of mass on a nearby table. Unfortunately, a few million megawatts of power were necessary for any such display. Lovely gee was costly gee. Only imperial pleasure craft, a few microscopic industrial applications, and the most exotic of military weapons used lovely generation.

As Zai sat speechless in the lovely black car, his heartbeat present in one temple, he was blind to the passing wonders of the capital. The car flew with an effortless grace between huge buildings, but he felt no inertia, no discomfort from the craft's banks or rolls. It was as if the world were turning below, and the marvelous car motionless. Zai tried to do some hasty calculations in his head, estimating the total mass of the car, himself, the corporal. It was staggering. The power consumed during this short ride would have been sufficient for the first fifty years of human industrialization.

It wasn't the medal, the promotion, or even the guarantee of immortality, Zai realized. *This moment* was his true reward for his heroism: a ride on the heady surf of literal and absolute Imperial power.

Lieutenant-Commander Zai was somewhat dazed when he reached the palace. His car lifted silently above the snarl of arriving limos and jumped the high diamond walls with a flourish, rolling over so that its transparent canopy filled with a breathtaking view of the Emperor's grounds. Of course, Zai experienced only a hint of vertigo, his inner ear in the precise and featherlight grip of lovely gravitons. There was no down or up in their embrace; Zai felt as if some giant deity had grasped the fountains and pleasure gardens to twirl them overhead for his amusement.

The car descended, and he stepped from it filled with a regret suddenly remembered from childhood, the sad and foiled feeling that this carnival ride was over, that his feet were on solid, predictable ground again.

'Lovely car,' came the voice of Captain Marcus Fentu Masrui.

'Yes, sir,' Zai answered with a mumble, still overwhelmed, barely managing to salute his old commander.

The two watched silently as the vehicle was grasped by conventional transports, carried away to be cowled and caged like some exotic, captive bird of prey.

'Welcome to the palace, Lieutenant-Commander,' Masrui said. With an outstretched arm, he gently pulled Zai's eyes away from the car and toward the diamond edifice before them. Its shape was familiar to any of the Emperor's subjects, especially one Vadan-born, but from this close it seemed monstrously distorted. Laurent Zai was used to seeing the palace rendered in the scale of votive paintings, with the sun playing on its shiny surfaces. Now it was black and looming, darker than the starless night that it threatened to crowd from the sky.

'Power has an extraordinary glare, doesn't it,' Masrui observed.

The captain was looking up, but Zai still wondered whether he meant the palace or the gravity car.

'After my elevation,' Masrui continued, 'I took that ride. And it finally dawned on me why I'd spent all those years learning physics at the Academy.'

Zai smiled. Masrui was famous for his doggedness. He had failed the Academy's minimal physical science class for three years running, almost exhausting the dispensations that his genius in other areas had afforded him before finally obtaining a commission.

'Not the better to command my ship, of course. A ship is men and women, after all; AIs have done the math for millennia. But I needed to understand physics, if for no other reason, then to understand fully that one Imperial gesture.'

Zai looked into his commanding officer's eyes. He wondered for a moment if the man, as usual, were being cynical. But the buoyant memory of riding in the craft convinced him that even Masrui might be sentimental about those minutes of flight.

They walked up the broad stairs together. The sounds of the party flowed out between columns and heroic statues.

'Strange, sir, to have looked down on worlds, and still be amazed by a . . . mere flying machine.'

'It makes you realize, Zai, that you've never *properly* flown. We've been in aircraft and dropships, free fall and lifter belts, but the body always fights it at some level. Even the excitement comes from adrenaline, from some animal panic that things aren't right.'

'But it's right in that car, sir. Isn't it?' Zai said.

'Yes. Flight as effortless and natural as a bird's. Or a god's. Did we join the Navy for service and immortality, I wonder? Or for something more akin to *that*.'

The captain trailed off. A group of officers was approaching. Zai felt the subject disappear between him and his old friend, the words pulled back from the air and hidden somewhere like the conspiracies of mutineers.

'The hero!' one of the officers said too loudly. She was Captain Rencer Fowler IX, whom Zai, if the rumors were true, would soon displace as the youngest starship commander in the fleet. Zai saw Fowler's eyes sweep across his medaled chest, and felt briefly naked again in the covering of clever ants. The others looked comfortable in their dress uniforms, the particulate nature of the garments completely disguised. Zai knew his ants were no more obvious than theirs. He determined not to think of the uniform again.

'Only a humble servant of Empire,' Masrui answered for him.

Zai and Masrui shook hands with the men among the officers, and touched closed fists with the women. Zai's head began to spin a bit with the surfeit of ritual greetings and realized how convenient the usual salute was. But this was a dress occasion, forms had to be followed, and the pattern of bare wrists as gloved hands flexed and touched seemed to hold meaning, like animals flashing signals of bare-toothed dominance at each other. The glint of Zai's metal wrist caught starlight.

They went into the palace hall together, and a crescendo of voices echoing from stone rose up around them like a sudden rain.

Faces turned toward Zai as the group moved across the great black floor. The hero of Dhantu, or as the gutter media called him: the Broken Man. He realized that the group of officers, arrayed casually around him, had done him a kindness, forming a shield between him and the stares of the crowd. He wondered if Masrui had planned their meeting on the steps. They moved slowly, to nowhere in particular, his entourage hailing familiar faces and pulling them into the group, or fending off inter- lopers with a deflecting touch of greeting. One of them cadged a tray full of drinks and passed it round the group.

Zai drifted along like a child in his parents' tow. The great hall was crowded. The lucent dress uniforms of Navy per- sonnel were mixed with the absolute black of the Political Apparatus. There were civilians dressed in formal bloodred or the white of the Senate, guildfolk in colored patterns he couldn't begin to read. The high, fluted columns that climbed to the vaulted ceiling channeled this mass of people into swirling eddies. After a few minutes of this promenade, Zai realized what would have been instantly obvious to an observer in the upper reaches of the hall: everyone was walk- ing in circles.

Fowler's voice came from his side.

'How's immortality, Lieutenant-Commander?'

Fowler, despite her meteoric early career, had not been elevated yet.

'I hear it's not much different for the first hundred years,' Zai answered. 'Certainly, the first week isn't.'

Fowler laughed. 'Not missing the specter of death yet, are you? Well, I guess you saw enough of that on Dhantu.'

A chill crawled up Zai's spine at the word. Of course, the planet that had seen his act of heroism – if that's what it could be called – was implicit everywhere tonight. But only Fowler would be graceless enough to mention its name.

'Enough for a few centuries, I suppose,' Zai answered. He felt movement on one flank. It was the ants, reorganizing themselves for some vital bit of tailoring. They *would* pick this moment.

Then Zai realized their purpose: a trickle of sweat had appeared under his real arm.

Fowler's face was close in the pressing crowd. 'Well, the Rix are playing rough again, my connections on the frontier are saying. We may need heroes on that side of the Empire soon. They say you'll be promoted soon. Maybe get your own ship.'

Zai felt overheated. The sense of a nakedness had disappeared in the close air of the crowded room, as if the ants were linking ever more tightly, closing their ranks against Fowler's rudeness. Could they detect the woman's hostility and react to it as they did to light? Zai wondered. The little elements writhed in a column down and around Zai's side, carrying his suddenly prodigious sweat to the small of his back.

'And the specter of death always joins heroes at the front,' Fowler added. 'Perhaps you'll become acquainted again.' The woman's false camaraderie was growing thinner by the word. Zai looked around for Masrui. Was he among friends here, really?

He caught the eye of a young woman by the nearest column. She returned his glance with a smile and the slightest bow of her head.

'She's quite pretty,' Zai said, interrupting whatever Fowler was saying. That basic touchstone of desire had its desired effect, and Fowler immediately turned to follow the path of Zai's gaze.

She turned back with an undisguised sneer.

'I think you picked the wrong woman, Zai. She's as pink as they come. And perhaps a bit beyond your rank.'

Zai looked again and cursed his haste. Fowler was right. The sleeves of her white robe were hatched with the mark of a Senator-Elect. She seemed terribly young for that; even in an age of cosmetic surgery, a certain gravitas was expected of members of the Senate.

Zai tried not to show his embarrassment. 'Pink, you said?'

'Anti-imperial,' Fowler supplied, speaking slowly as though to a child. 'The opposite of gray. A brave defender of the living. That's Nara Oxham, the mad senator-elect from Vasthold. She's rejected elevation, for heaven's sake. By choice, she'll rot in the ground.'

'The Mad Senator,' Zai murmured. He'd read that moniker in the same garbage media that had dubbed him the Broken Man.

The young woman smiled again, and Zai realized he'd been staring. He raised his glass to her and looked sheepishly away. Of course Zai knew what *pink* meant. But his native Vadan was as politically gray as any planet in the Empire. The dead were worshiped there, everyone claiming a risen ancestor as his or her personal intermediary with the Emperor. And of course the Navy was gray from admirals to marines. Lieutenant-Commander Zai wasn't sure if he'd met a pink in his entire life.

'Mind you, I'm sure she'll accept the elevation when she's a bit closer to death,' Fowler said. 'Just as long as she doesn't have an accident in the meantime. Wouldn't *that* be a pity, losing eternity for one's principles.'

'Or one's arrogance,' Zai added, hoping Fowler would suspect whom he really meant. 'Perhaps she just needs a talking-to.'

He pushed past Fowler, feeling the woman's skin against his own as their ants briefly conjoined.

'For heaven's sake, Zai, she's a *senator*,' Fowler hissed.

Zai turned briefly toward his adversary and spoke calmly.

'And tonight I am a hero,' he said.

Senator-Elect

Nara Oxham's eyes widened as Lieutenant-Commander Laurent Zai pushed his way out and headed toward her. The purpose on his face was unmistakable. He gripped his champagne glass with all five fingers, as if it were a club, and his eyes locked hers.

A group of officers had surrounded him since his arrival, cutting him off from the rest of the party in a display of protectiveness, and perhaps pride that one of theirs had been elevated so young. The handlers in Nara Oxham's secondary audio listed names and academy years as she moved an eyemouse across their faces. All were older than Zai. Senator-Elect Oxham suspected that their claim on him was newly minted; the hero of Dhantu would make a fine addition to their clique.

For some reason, though, Zai had moved to extract himself from their attentions. The young lieutenant-commander almost stumbled as he left them behind, as if pulling his feet from some invisible tangleweed on the marble floor. Nara Oxham fingered her apathy wristband ruefully. She would love to feel what was going on in Zai's mind, but the party was too crowded to dare a lower dosage.

Oxham's entourage parted slightly to admit the young officer.

Although the senator's empathic powers were currently suppressed, for most of her life she'd been able to compare facial expressions with what her extra sense told her. Even with the wristband at full strength, she was extraordinarily perceptive. When Lieutenant-Commander Zai stood before her, she could see that he didn't know what to say.

Vadan greeting, she subvocalized.

Five appropriate salutations appeared in synesthesia, but in a flash of instinct, Nara ignored them all.

'You don't look very happy, Lieutenant-Commander Zai.'

He glanced over his shoulder at his friends. Turned back.

'I'm not used to crowds, ma'am,' he said.

Nara smiled at the honorific. He must be without a handler

to have used *ma'am* instead of *excellency*. How did the Navy ever win wars, she wondered, when they couldn't manage a cocktail party?

'Stand here by the column,' she said. She held her glass up to the light. 'There's a certain security in having one's back covered, don't you think, Lieutenant-Commander?'

'Sound military thinking, Senator-Elect,' he answered, finally smiling back at her.

So at least he knew her rank. But her politics?

'These columns are stronger than they look,' she said. 'Each is a single diamond, grown in an orbital carbon whisketter.'

His eyes arched up, no doubt considering their mass. Making huge diamonds was easy in orbit. But getting an object that big down the gravity well safely – now *that* was a feat of engineering. Oxham held her glass of champagne up to the light.

'Have you noticed, Lieutenant-Commander, that the shape of the glasses matches the column's fluting?'

He looked at his own glass. 'No, Excellency, I hadn't.'

Excellency, now. The officer's etiquette training was kicking in. Did that mean she had made him comfortable enough to remember his manners? Or was he feeling her rank?

'But I suppose I personify the analogy,' he continued. 'I had begun to feel rather like a bubble floating aimlessly. Thank you for offering a safe haven, Senator-Elect.'

Out of the corner of one eye, Oxham had watched the rest of the officers in Zai's group. With a glance here, a hand on a shoulder there, they were spreading the news of Zai's defection. Now, an older man of captain's rank was watching. Was he headed over to rescue the young lieutenant-commander from the Mad Senator?

Captain Marcus Fentu Masrui, Elevated, Oxham's handlers informed her. *Nonpolitical as far as we know.*

Nara raised an eyebrow. Nothing human was nonpolitical.

'I'm not sure how much of a haven you've found, Lieutenant-Commander.' She let her attention over Zai's shoulder become obvious. 'Your friends seem disturbed.'

Zai glanced down at one of his shoulders, as if arresting a turn of his head back toward the officers. Then his eyes met hers again.

'I'm not sure about that, ma'am.'

'They certainly look upset.' Captain Masrui was still hovering nearby, unwilling to plunge in after Zai.

'Oh, of that I'm positive,' Zai said. 'But whether they are my friends or not . . .'

He smiled, but was not entirely joking.

'Success brings a certain amount of false friendship,' Oxham said. 'At least, speaking from my own perspective, political success does.'

'No doubt, Senator. And, in a way, I suppose my own celebrity does have a political aspect to it.'

Oxham narrowed her eyes. She knew very little about Laurent Zai, but her preparty briefing had stated that he was in no way a political officer. He had never enjoyed assignment to staff or a procurement committee, nor did he publish military scholarship. He came from a long line of illustrious Navy men, but had never used his name to escape field duty. The Zais had all been warriors, at least on the male side.

They joined the Navy, fought for the crown, and died. Then they took their well-earned immortality and disappeared into the gray enclaves of Vada. What did the dead Zais do then? Oxham wondered. Painted those dire black Vadan paintings, probably, went on endless pilgrimages, and learned appropriately dead languages to read the ancient books of the war sages in the original. A grim, infinite life.

Laurent Zai's doubts were interesting, though. Here he was, about to be honored by his living god, and he worried that his elevation had been tainted by politics. Perhaps he wondered whether surviving an awful captivity was enough to warrant a medal.

'I think the Emperor's commendation is justly deserved, Lieutenant-Commander Zai,' she said. 'After what you've been through—'

'No one has any idea what I've been through.'

Oxham stopped short. Despite his rude words, the man's calm exterior hadn't changed in any way. He was simply stating a fact.

'However painful,' the man continued, 'having simply suffered for the Emperor is not enough to warrant all this.' A small sweep of his hand indicated the party, the palace, immortality.

Oxham nodded. In a way, Laurent Zai was an accidental hero. He had been captured through no error of his own, and imprisoned without any hope of escape. Finally, he had been rescued by the application of overwhelming force. In one sense, he had done nothing himself.

But still, to have survived Dhantu at all was extraordinary. The rest of the prisoners that the rescue had found were dead, beyond even the symbiant. *Simply suffered*, Zai had said. A ghastly understatement.

'Lieutenant-Commander, I didn't mean to suggest that I could understand your experience,' she said. 'You've seen depths no one else has. But you did so in the Emperor's service. He has to do something. Certain things must be . . . *recognized*.'

Zai smiled sadly at her.

'I was rather hoping to hear an argument from you, Senator. But perhaps you don't want to be impolitic.'

'An argument? Because I'm pink? Let me be impolitic, then. The Imperial presence on Dhantu is criminal. They've suffered for generations, and I'm not surprised that the most extreme Dhanti have become inhuman – which does not excuse torture. Nothing can. But some things are beyond being excused or explained, beyond logic or even blame. Things that start from simple power struggles – from politics, if you will – but ultimately dredge the depths of the human soul. Timeless, monstrous things.'

The young man blinked, and Nara took a drink to slow her words.

'Armed occupation seldom pays dividends for anyone,' she said. 'But the Empire rewards who it can. You survived, Zai. So you should accept the Emperor's medal, elevation, and the starship command they'll no doubt give you. It's something.'

Zai seemed surprised, but not offended. He nodded his head slightly, eyes narrowing as if thinking through her points. Was he mocking her?

But sarcasm didn't seem to be in the man. Perhaps these were simply new ideas for him. His entire life had been spent among the grayest of the gray. Oxham wondered if he'd ever heard the 'Dhantu Liberation' called an occupation before. Or ever heard anyone seriously question the will of the Risen Emperor.

His next question confirmed his naïveté.

'Senator, is it true you have rejected elevation?'

'It's true. That's what Secularists do.'

'I've heard that they often rescind in the end, though. There's always the possibility of a deathbed conversion.'

Oxham shook her head. The persistence of this piece of propaganda was amazing. It showed how easily the truth was manipulated. It showed how threatened grays were by the Vow of Death.

'That's a story that the Political Apparatus likes to perpetuate,' she said. 'But of almost five hundred Secularist senators elected over the last thousand years, only seventeen have accepted elevation in the end.'

'Seventeen broke their vows?' he said.

For a moment, she nodded her head in triumph. Then she realized that Zai was not impressed. He seemed to think that few percent damningly high. For gray Laurent Zai, a vow was a vow.

Damn him.

'But to answer your question,' she finished. 'Yes, I will die.'

He reached out, placed one hand lightly on her arm.

'Why?' he asked with genuine concern. 'For politics?'

'No. For progress.'

He shook his head in incomprehension.

Nara Oxham sighed internally. She had debated this point in street encounters, in public houses and the Vasthold Diet floor, on live media feeds with planetary audiences. She had written slogans and speeches and essays on this issue. And before her was Laurent Zai, a man who had probably never experienced a real political debate in his entire life. It was too easy, in a way.

But he had asked for it.

'Have you heard of the geocentric theory, Lieutenant-Commander?'

'No, Excellency.'

'On Earth Prime, a few centuries before spaceflight, it was widely believed that the sun went around the planet.'

'They must have thought Earth Prime to be very massive,' Zai said.

'In a way, yes. They thought the entire universe went around their world. On a *daily* basis, mind you. They had severe scaling problems.'

'Indeed.'

'Observational data mounted against the geocentric theory for a long time. New models were created, sun-centered models that were far more elegant and logical.'

'I would think so. I can't imagine what the math for a planet-centric theory would have looked like.'

'It was hideously complex and convoluted. Looking at it now, it's obviously a retrofit to uphold the superstitions of an earlier era. But something rather odd happened when the sun-centered theory, with all its elegance and clarity, was devised.'

Zai waited, his champagne forgotten in his hand.

'Almost no one believed it,' she said. 'The new theory was debated for a while, gained a few supporters, but then it was suppressed and almost entirely dropped.'

Zai narrowed his eyes in disbelief. 'But eventually people must have realized. Otherwise, we wouldn't be standing here, two thousand light-years from Earth.'

Oxham shook her head. 'They didn't *realize*. Very few ever changed their minds. Those scientists who grew up with the old theory stuck to it overwhelmingly.'

'But then how—'

'They died, Lieutenant-Commander.'

She drank the last of her champagne. The old arguments still moved her, still made her mouth dry.

'Or rather, they did their descendants the favor of dying,' she said. 'They left their children the world. And thus the new ideas – the new shape of that world – became real. But only through death.'

Zai shook his head. 'But surely they would have eventually figured out—'

'If the old ones lived forever? Possessed all the wealth, controlled the military, and brooked no disagreement? We'd still be living there, stuck on that lonely fringe of Orion, thinking ourselves at the center of the universe.

'But the old ones, the ones who were wrong, died,' she finished.

The man nodded slowly.

'I'd always heard that you pinks were pro-death. But I'd thought that an exaggeration.'

'It's no exaggeration. Death is a central evolutionary development. Death is change. Death is progress. And immortality is a civilization-killing idea.'

Zai smiled, his eyes roaming to take in the grandeur of the palace around them. 'We don't seem to be a dead civilization yet.'

'Seventeen hundred years ago, the Eighty Worlds were the most advanced technological power in this arm,' she said. 'Now look at us. The Rix, the Tungai, the Fahstuns have all surpassed us.'

Zai's eyes widened. It was a fact seldom spoken aloud, even by Secularists. But Laurent Zai, a military man, must know that it was true. Every war grew more difficult as the Risen Empire continued to be outpaced by its neighbors.

'But seventeen hundred years ago we were no empire,' he argued. 'Merely a rabble of worlds, like the Rix, but far more divided. We were unstable, in competition amongst ourselves. We're stronger now, even with our technical . . . disadvantages. And besides, we have the only technology truly worth having. We can beat death.'

' "The Old Enemy," ' Oxham quoted. That was what the Political Apparatus called it. The Old Enemy whom the Risen Emperor had dared and vanquished.

'Yes. We have beaten death, and yet the living still progress,' Zai continued. 'We have the Senate, the markets.'

She smiled ruefully. 'But the weight of the dead is choking us. Slowly but surely, they accrue more wealth every year, more power, and a greater hold upon the minds of the living.'

'Minds like mine?' Zai asked.

Oxham shrugged. 'I don't presume to know your mind, Lieutenant-Commander. Despite what they say about my abilities.'

'You think the Empire is dead already?' he asked.

'No, not yet. But change will eventually come, and when it

does, the Empire will snap like a bough strung with too many corpses.'

Laurent Zai's mouth gaped; he was appalled at the image. Finally, she had managed to shock the man. Nara remembered when she had first used that simile in a speech on Vasthold. The audience had recoiled, empathically pushing back against her words, filling her throat with bile. But she had seen new thoughts swarming in to fill the spaces that horror made. The image was powerful enough to change minds.

'So, you want us to go back to death?' he asked. 'Two hundred years of natural life and then . . . nothingness?'

'Not necessarily,' she explained. 'We just want to reduce the power of the dead. Let them paint and sculpt, travel the Eighty Worlds on their pilgrimages, but not rule us.'

'No Emperor?' he said.

She nodded. Even with her new senatorial immunity, it was difficult to speak traitorous words aloud here in the Emperor's house. Even those born on Secularist worlds had the conditioning of gray culture; the old stories, the children's rhymes were all about the Old Enemy and the man who had beaten it.

Laurent Zai was silent for a while. He acquired two more glasses of champagne for them from a passing tray and stood there, drinking with her. A few of his military clique remained close, but they didn't dare come unbidden into this conversation with a pink senator.

Nara Oxham looked at the man. The Navy dress uniform, with its coordinated horde of subunits, certainly embodied the grossest aspects of Imperial power: the many made forcibly into one. But like much of the Imperial aesthetic, there was an undeniable elegance to the lockstepped fit of myriad elements. Zai's body didn't have the squat look of most high-gravity worlders. He was tall and a bit thin, the arch of his back rather tempting.

'Let me ask you a question,' she said to interrupt her own thoughts.

'Certainly.'

'Do you find my words treasonous?'

'By definition, no. You are a Senator. You have immunity.'

'But immunity aside . . .'

He frowned. 'If you weren't a senator, then by definition, you would have just committed treason.'

'Only by definition?'

Zai nodded. 'Yes, Senator. But perhaps not in spirit. After all, you are concerned with the welfare of the Empire, in whatever form you imagine its future.'

Oxham smiled. Throughout the conversation, she had thought of Zai as unsophisticated, never having met a pink. Perhaps that was true, but how many actual grays had she herself spoken with honestly and openly? Perhaps her assumptions had been, in their own way, unsophisticated.

Zai raised an eyebrow at her expression.

'I was just thinking: perhaps minds can be changed,' she offered.

'Without death to drive the process?' Zai asked.

She nodded.

He took a deep breath, and his eyes drifted away from her. For a moment, she thought he was using synesthesia. But then some glimmer of intuition told Oxham that he was looking deeper than second sight.

'Or perhaps,' Laurent Zai said, 'I am already dead.'

Something took hold of Nara. She felt an impossible moment of empathy, as if the drug had somehow failed: far inside the man was a terror, a wound opened by the depth of evil he had seen. It cut like an arctic wind, like an old fear made undeniably physical. It was agony and hopelessness. And, quite suddenly, she hated the Emperor for pinning a medal on this man.

Rewarding, rather than healing him.

'How much of Home have you seen, Laurent?' she asked quietly.

He shrugged. 'The capital. This palace. And soon I will meet the Emperor himself. More than most of the risen see in centuries of pilgrimage.'

'Would you like to see the South Pole?'

He looked genuinely surprised.

'I didn't know it was inhabited.'

'Hardly. Outside a few estates, the poles are arid, freezing, dead. But I am pro-death, as you know. My new house there is surrounded by a glorious wasteland. I intend to escape the pressures of the capital there.'

Zai nodded. He must know of her condition. The Mad Senator, the grays called her. A woman driven insane by crowds and cities, yet who made politics her profession.

The man swallowed before he spoke.

'I would like to see that, Senator.'

'Then come with me there tomorrow, Lieutenant-Commander.'

He raised his glass. 'To a glorious wasteland.'

'A truly gray place,' she answered.

2

RESCUE ATTEMPT

No plan survives contact with the enemy.

– ANONYMOUS 81

Senator

She awoke without sanity.

The temporal ice released her quickly. Its lattice of tiny interwoven stasis fields unraveled, and time rushed back into her body like water through a suddenly crumbling dam, inundating a valley long denied it. Her mind became aware, emerging as it always did from coldsleep, raw and unprotected from the raging mindstorm of the city.

She awoke to madness.

Here in these exposed moments, the capital screamed in her brain. Its billions of minds roared, seethed, shrieked like a host of seagulls tearing at the carcass of some giant creature exposed upon a beach, fighting amongst themselves as they rended their huge find. Even in her madness, though, she knew the source of the psychic screaming: the rotting creature was Empire; the vast chorus of keening voices was all the myriad struggles for power and prestige that animated the Imperial capital. The noise of these contests thundered through her, for a moment obliterating any sense of self, her identity a lone mountaineer engulfed by an avalanche.

Then she heard her apathy bracelet begin its injection sequence, the reassuring hiss audible even through the deluge of sound. Then her empathic abilities began to fade under the drug's influence. The voices grew dim, and a sense of self returned.

The woman remembered who she was, childhood names spilling through her mind. Naraya, Naya, Nana. And then the titles of adulthood. Dr. Nara Oxham. Electate Oxham of the

Vasthold Assembly. Her Excellency Nara Oxham, Representative to His Majesty's Government from the planet Vasthold. Senator Nara Oxham, Secularist Party whip.

Popularly known as the Mad Senator.

As the psychic howl receded, Oxham steeled herself and concentrated on the city, listening carefully for tone and character as it trailed away. Here on Home, she was always threatened by the crush of voices, the wild psychic noise that had kept her in an asylum for most of her childhood years. But sometimes as the apathy drug entered her veins, in this passing moment between madness and sanity, Nara could make sense of it, could catch a few notes of the multiplex and chaotic music that the capital played. It was a useful ability for a politician.

The sound of the Risen Empire's politics was troubled today, she heard. Something was coalescing, like an orchestra tuning itself to a single note. She tried to focus, to bring her mind to bear on the theme of unease. But then her empathy faded, extinguished by the drug.

Her insanity was, for the moment, cured, and she was deaf to the city's cry.

Senator Nara Oxham took a deep breath, flexed her awakening muscles. She sat up on the coldsleep bed, and opened her eyes.

Morning. The sky was salmon and the sun orange through the penthouse's bubble, the facets of the distant Diamond Palace tinged with blood. The bubble silenced the capital, the transparent woven carbon barely trembling for passing helicopters. But the city still buzzed, flickers of movement and the winking lights of signage shimmering in her vision, distant aircars blurring the air like gnats or heat haze on a desert. In the odd way of coldsleep, her eyes felt clean, as if she had only closed them for a moment.

A moment that had lasted . . .

The date was displayed on the bedroom's large wallscreen. Since she had entered coldsleep, three of Homeworld's short months had passed. That was puzzling and alarming. Usually, the senatorial stasis breaks lasted half a year.

Something important was happening, then. The disquieting sound Oxham had heard on the limen of madness returned to her. She called up the status of her colleagues. Most were already animated, the rest were coming up as she watched. The full Senate was being awakened for a special session.

As Senator Nara Oxham crossed the Rubicon Pale at the bottom of the Forum steps, the reassuring wash of politics surrounded her, drowning out the shapeless anxiety she had felt coming out of coldsleep.

In one corner of her hearing she now registered the drone of the Inherited Intellectual Property filibuster. The filibuster, in its eighty-seventh decade, was as calming and timeless (and as meaningless, Senator Oxham supposed) as the roar of a distant ocean. Farther away in the echoey space of secondary audio she sensed plodding committee meetings, strident media conferences, the self-righteous energy of a Loyalty Party caucus meeting. And, of course, easily discernible by its sovereign resonance, the debate in the Great Forum itself.

She blinked, and a lower-third informed her that Senator Puram Drexler had the floor. A tiny corner of her synesthetic sight showed his face, the familiar milky gray eyes and elaborate, liquid rolls of flesh that poured from his cheekbones. President of the Senate, a figurehead position, Drexler was said to be over two hundred fifty years old (not counting cryo, and in his own relativistic framework – *not* Imperial Absolute). But his exquisitely weathered face had never seemed quite real to her. On Fatawa, which he represented in the Senate, the surgical affectation of age was almost as fashionable as that of youth.

The ancient solon cleared his throat languorously, the dry sound as gritty and sharp as a handful of small gravel poured slowly onto glass.

As she climbed the Forum steps, Senator Oxham brought the fingertips of her left hand together, which signaled her handlers to pick her up. The other voices in the Senate infostructure muted as her chief of staff confirmed the day's itinerary with her.

'Where's Roger?' Oxham asked after her schedule was confirmed. The morning scheduling ritual usually belonged to Roger Niles, her consultant extraordinary. The absence of his familiar voice disturbed Oxham, brought back her earlier uneasiness.

'He's deep, Senator,' her chief of staff answered. 'He's been in an analysis fugue all morning. But he leaked a request that you see him face-to-face at your earliest convenience.'

The morning's disquiet flooded back in now. Niles was a very reserved creature; a meeting at his own insistence would mean serious news.

'I see,' Oxham said flatly. She wondered what the old consultant had discovered.

'Bring my synesthesia to full bandwidth.'

At her command, data swelled before Oxham in secondary and tertiary sight and hearing, blossoming into the familiar maelstrom of her personal configuration. Nameplates, color-coded by party affiliation and striped with recent votes, hovered about the other Senators flowing up the steps; real-time polygraph-poll reactions of wired political junkies writhed at the edge of vision, forming hurricane whorls that shifted with every procedural vote; the latest headcounts of her party's whip AI invoked tones at the threshold of hearing, soft and consonant chords for measures sure to pass, harsh, dissonant intervals for bills that were losing support. Nara Oxham breathed in this clamor like a seagoing passenger emerging onto deck for air. This moment – at the edge of Power, before one dived in and lost oneself – restored her confidence. The bracing rush of politics gave Nara what others were given by mountain-climbing, or incipient violence, or the pleasure of a first cigarette before dressing.

The senator smiled as she headed for her offices.

Nara Oxham often wondered how politics had been possible before second sight. Without induced synesthesia, the intrusion of sight into the other brain centers, how did a human mind absorb the necessary data? She could imagine going without synesthesia in certain activities – flying an aircraft, day trading, surgery – where one could focus on a single image, but not in politics. Non interfering layers of sight, the ability to fill three visual and two auditory fields with data, were a perfect metaphor for politics itself. The checks and balances, the competing constituencies, the layers of power, money, and rhetoric. Even though the medical procedure that made it possible caused odd mental results in one in ten thousand recipients (Oxham's own empathy was such a reaction), she couldn't imagine the political world – gloriously multitrack and torrid – without it. She'd tried the old, presynesthesia eyescreens that covered up normal vision, but they'd brought on a claustrophobic panic. Who would trust the Senate to a blinkered horse?

The disquiet she had felt all morning tugged at Nara again. The feeling was familiar, but vaguely so, in the way of old smells and déjà vu. She tried to place it, comparing the sensation to her anxieties before elections, important Senate votes, or large parties thrown in her honor. Nara Oxham recalled those apprehensions easily. She lived her life fighting them, weathering them, indulging in them. She was old friends with anxiety, that poor sister of madness which the drugs never fully vanquished.

But the current feeling was too slippery. She couldn't find the worry that had started it. She checked her wrist, where the dermal injector blinked happily green. It couldn't be an empathy flare; the drugs made sure of that. But it certainly felt like one.

When she reached her offices, she strode past supplicant aides and a few hopeful lobbyists, heading straight for Roger Niles's dark lair at the center of her domain. No one dared follow her. His office doors opened without a word, and she walked through, removed a stack of laundered shirts from his guest chair, and sat down.

'I'm here,' she said. She kept her voice calm, knowing his interface AI would bring him up from the data fugue if she sounded impatient. Better to let him cross back into the real world at his own pace.

His face had the slack look of deep fugue, but his eyebrows lifted in response to her words, sending ripples up his high expanse of forehead. One finger on his right hand twitched. He looked too small for his desk, a circular monstrosity of dark wood that enclosed Niles like some giant lifesupport machine. Senator Oxham had recently discovered that its copious drawers and pigeonholes held only clothes, shoes, and a few emergency rations extorted from military lobbyists. Roger Niles thought the habit of going home at night to be an inexcusable weakness.

'Something bad, isn't it?' she asked.

The finger twitched again.

Niles looked older. Senator Oxham had only been in stasis for three months, but in that short absence a frosting of gray had touched his temples. Her staff had the right to go into cryo during the breaks, but Niles seldom did, preferring to work out the true decades of her term, aging before her eyes.

The loneliness of the senator, Oxham thought. The world moved so quickly past.

Senators were elected for (or appointed to, competed for, bought – whatever their planet's custom) fifty-year terms, half an Imperial Absolute century of office. The Risen Empire was a slowly evolving beast. Even here in the dense coreward clusters, eighty populated worlds was an area thirty light-years across, and the exigencies of war, trade, and migration were bound by the appallingly slow rate of lightspeed. The Imperial Senate was constituted to take the long view; the solons generally spent eighty percent of their terms in stasis sleep as the universe wheeled by. They made decisions with the detachment of mountains watching rivers below shift course.

Unavoidably, the planet that Oxham represented had changed in her first decade in office. And the trip to Home from Vasthold had consumed five Absolute years. When she returned, sixty years total would have passed, all her friends infirm or dead, her three nephews well into middle age. Even Niles was aging before her eyes. The Senate demanded much from its members.

But the Time Thief couldn't steal everyone. Oxham had found someone new, a lover who was a starship captain, a fellow victim of time dilation. Though the man was gone now, Absolute years away in the Spinward Reaches, Oxham had begun to match her stasis sleeps to his relativistic framework. The universe was slipping past them both at almost the same rate. When he came back, they would share the same years' passage.

Senator Oxham leaned back into her chair and listened with half her mind to the flow of political data in her secondary senses. But it was pointless to do anything except wait for Niles.

As political animals went, Senator Oxham was fundamentally unlike her chief of staff. She was a holist, feeling the

Senate as an organism, an animal whose actions could be tamed or at least understood. Niles, at the other extreme, lived by the dictum that all politics is local. His gods were in the details.

The office was crowded with hardware that kept him linked to the everyday goings-on of each of the Eighty Worlds. Ration riots on Mirzam. Religious bombings on Veridani. The daily offensives and retaliations of a thousand price wars, ethnic struggles, and media trials, all maintained in real time by quantum entangled communications. Senatorial privilege allowed him to monitor the internal workings of news agencies, financial consortia, even the private missives of those wealthy enough to send translight data. And Niles could put it all together in his magnificent brain. Senator Oxham knew her colleagues as individuals, and could feel the hard edges of their petty vanities and obsessions, but Roger Niles saw senators as composite creatures of data, walking clearinghouses for the host of agendas and pressures from their home worlds.

The two sat across from each in silence for a few more minutes.

Niles's finger twitched again.

Nara sat back, knowing that this could take a while. It was dark in the room. The crystalline columns of the com hardware loomed like insect cities made of glass – perhaps fireflies, the Senator thought; the crystals were pinpoint-dappled by sunlight filtered through tiny holes in a smartpolymer curtain that extended across the glass ceiling.

Oxham looked upward with an annoyed expression, and the millimeter-wide holes responded, dilating a bit. Now she could feel the sun on her hands, which she splayed palm down, relishing the cool metal of Niles's desk. In the patterned light her chief of staff's face seemed tattooed with a fine trompe l'oeil veil.

He opened his eyes.

'War,' he said.

The word sent ice down Senator Nara Oxham's spine.

'I'm seeing Imperial tax relief throughout the spinward worlds,' Niles said, tapping the right side of his head as if his brain were a map of the Empire. 'Every system within four light-years of the Rix frontier is having its economy stimulated, courtesy of the Risen One. And the Lackey Party caucus has buried parallel measures in that maintenance bill they've been debating all morning.'

'Is that war, or just patronage-as-usual?' Oxham asked dubiously. The Risen Emperor and the Senate levied taxes separately, their sources of revenue as carefully delineated as the Rubicon Pale around the Forum building. But however separate crown and government were meant to be, the Loyalty Party – true to its name – always followed the Emperor's lead. Especially when it helped the voters back home. Loyalty was traditionally strong in the Spinward Reaches, as it was in every outskirt region where other cultures loomed threateningly close.

'Normally, I'd say it was the usual alms for the faithful,' Niles answered. 'But the Coreward and Outward Loyalist regions aren't sharing in the largesse. On the contrary, those ends of the Empire are taking a big hit. Over the last twelve hours, I'm seeing higher honoraria tributes, skyrocketing futures on titles and pardons, even hundred-year Imperial loans being called. The money isn't earmarked yet, but *only* the military could spend amounts like this.'

'So the Navy's being strengthened, and the Spinward Reaches fattened up,' Oxham said. It sounded like war with the Rix. Riches to fund military forces, and comfort for the regions threatened by reprisal.

Her chief of staff cocked his head, as if someone were whispering in his ear. 'Labor futures on Fatawa tightened by three points this morning. *Three*. Probably reservists being called up. No one left to sweep the floors.'

Oxham shook her head at the Risen Emperor's madness. It had been eighty years since the Rix Incursion; why provoke them now? Though not numerous, the Rix were unspeakably dangerous. The strange technologies bestowed on them by their AI gods made them the deadliest combatants the Empire had ever faced. Moreover, war with them was always a less-than-zero-sum game. They owned very little worth taking, having no real planets of their own. They seeded compound minds and moved on. They were spores for the planetary beings they worshiped, more a cult than a culture. But when injured, they made sure to injure in return.

'Why would the Risen Emperor want another war with the Rix?' she wondered aloud. 'Any evidence of a recent attack?' Oxham silently cursed the secrecy of the Imperial state, which rarely allowed the Senatorial Government detailed military intelligence. What was going on out there, in that distant blackness? She shivered for a moment, thinking of one man in particular who would be in harm's way. She pushed the thought aside.

'As I said, this has all been in the last few hours,' Niles said. 'I don't have raw data from the frontier for that timeframe.'

'Either precipitated by an emergency, or the Imperials have hidden their plans,' Senator Oxham said.

'Well, they've blown their cover now,' Niles finished.

Oxham interleaved her fingers, her hand making a double fist. The gesture triggered a sudden and absolute silence in her head, shutting off the din of orating solons, the clamor of messages and amendments, the pulse of polls and constituent chatter.

War, she thought. The galling domain of tyrants. The sport of gods and would-be gods. And, most distressingly, the profession of her newest lover.

The Risen One had better have a damn good reason for this.

Senator Oxham leaned back and glared into Roger Niles's eyes. She allowed her mind to start planning, to sort through the precisely defined powers of the Senate for the fulcra that could impede the Emperor's course. And as she felt the cold surety of political power flowing into her, her anxieties retreated.

'Our Risen Father may not want our advice and consent,' she said. 'But let's see if we can't get his attention.'

Captain

For the first twelve years of his life, Laurent Zai had been, embarrassingly, the tallest of his schoolmates. Not strongest, not quickest. Just a lofty, clumsy boy in a society that valued compact, graceful bodies. Since long before Laurent was born, Vada had elected and reelected as its governor a short, solid woman who stood with arms crossed and feet far apart, a symbol of stability. As young as seven standard, Laurent began to pray to the Risen Emperor that he would stop growing, but his journey toward the sky continued relentlessly. By age eleven it was too late merely to cease getting taller; he had already passed the average height for Vadan adults. He asked the Risen Deity to shrink him, but his biology mentor AI explained that growing shorter was scientifically unlikely, at least for the next sixty years or so. And on Vada one did not pray to the Risen Emperor to change the laws of nature, which were His laws after all. Ever logical, Laurent Zai implored the Emperor to effect the only remaining solution: increased height among his schoolmates, a burst of growth among his peers or a demographic shift that would rescue Laurent from his outcast status.

In the summer term that year, transfer students from low-gravity Krupp Reich flooded Laurent Zai's school. These were refugees displaced by the ravages of the New German Flu. The towering Reichers were gawky, easily fatigued, and thickly accented. These survivors were immune to the flu and had of course been decontaminated, fleeing the societal meltdown of population collapse rather than the virus itself, but the stench of contagion still clung to them, and they were so disgracefully *tall*.

Zai was their worst tormentor. He mastered the art of tripping the Reichers from behind as they walked, nudging a trailing foot so that it hooked the other ankle with their next step. He graffitied the margins of chapel prayerbooks with clumsy stick figures as tall as a page.

Laurent was not alone in his misbehavior. The Reichers were so mistreated that a month after their arrival the entire student body was assembled around the soccer field airscreen. In the giant viewing area (over the field upon which Laurent had been so often humiliated by shorter, quicker footballers) images from the Krupp Reich Pandemic were shown. It was pure propaganda – an art for which Vadans were justly famous – a way to shame the native children into ceasing their torments of the newcomers. The victims were carefully aestheticized, shown dying under white gauze to hide the pulsing red sores of the New German Flu. Photos from preflu family reunions were altered to reflect the disease's progress, the victims fading into sepia one by one, until only a few smiling survivors remained, their arms around ghostly relatives. The final image in the presentation was the huge, monolithic Reich Square in Bonnburg, time-lapsed through successive Sunday afternoons over the last four years. The population of tourists, hawkers, merchants, and strollers on the square dwindled slowly, then seemed to stabilize, then crashed relentlessly. Finally, a lone figure scuttled across the great sheet of copper. Although only a few picture elements tall, the figure seemed to be rushing fearfully, as if wary of some flying predator overhead.

Twelve-year-old Laurent Zai sat with his jaw slack amidst the overwhelming silence peculiar to shamed children, thinking the same words again and again.

'*What have I done?*'

When the airscreen faded, Zai bolted down the stairs, shaking off the restraining hand of an annoyed proctor. He fled to sanctuary under the bleachers and fell to his knees in the litter of spectator trash. His hands together in the clasp of prayer, he started to ask for forgiveness. He hadn't asked the Emperor for *this*. How could he have known that the Reich Pandemic would be the result of his request for taller classmates?

With his praying lips almost against the ground, the stench of cigarette butts and old honey wine bottles and rotten fruit under the bleachers struck him like a blow to the stomach. He vomited profusely into his prayer-locked hands, in an acid stream that burned like whiskey in his mouth and nose. His hands remained faintly sticky and smelled of vomit the rest of that day, no matter how furiously he washed them.

As if some switch deep within him had been permanently thrown, the position of prayer always brought back a glimmer of that intense moment of shame and nausea. The murmurs of morning chapel seemed to coalesce into an acid trickle down the back of his throat. The airscreen rallies in which the Risen Emperor's visage slowly turned over an ululating crowd filled his stomach with bile.

Laurent Zai had never prayed to the Risen Emperor again. He never drank, for every toast on Vada asked the Risen Deity for luck and health. And even as Cadet Zai waited for word of admission into the Imperial Naval Academy, he lay silent in the endless minutes before sleep every night, recalling every mistep and victory in his six-week application trial. But not praying.

Thirty subjective years later, however, seated in the shipmaster's chair of His Majesty's frigate *Lynx*, Captain Laurent Zai took a moment to pair his hands over nose and mouth.

He still smelled the bile of that long-ago shame.

'Make this work,' he demanded in a harsh whisper. 'As for me, I want to return to my beloved. As for her, she's *your* damned sister.'

The bitter prayer ended, Zai brought his hands down and opened his eyes.

'Launch,' he commanded.

Executive Officer

ExO Katherie Hobbes noted from her status board that the entry vehicle carrying the Apparatus Initiate Barris had not been fully gelled. The safety AI began to protest the dangers posed by an incompletely prepped insertion vehicle.

Hobbes smiled grimly, canceling the safety overrides, and the order went through.

'Operation is launched, sir.'

Almost simultaneously, four specially reconfigured turret blisters along the underside of the *Lynx* each fired one railgun and one plasma burst. A pair of each type of projectile headed toward four carefully plotted targets below.

The plasma bursts bolted ahead at twenty percent lightspeed, their 12,000-degree core temperatures burning a tunnel of vacuum through the atmosphere. Their burn length perfectly timed, they scattered into gouts of flame upon impact, leaving as their only marks four smooth, concave hemispheres burned into the palace's stone walls.

The railgun projectiles followed in their wake.

compound mind

The attack was registered by the warning system erected by the Rix compound mind still propagating across the planet's data and communication systems. The plasma bolts left a long, bellicose streak behind them, clearly originating from the point Alexander had already predicted that an Imperial warship would station itself to attempt a rescue. The mind required less than two milliseconds to determine that such an attempt was underway, and to order that the hostages be killed. However, the Rix commandos were not datalinked to the still-propagating mind. Alexander was a composite of Imperial technology, after all, which was incompatible with Rix communications. Alexander was forced to relay its order through a transponder sitting in the center of the table in the council chamber. The transponder received the compound mind's signal and immediately let out a loud squawk, a dense static whose crenellations were coded like some ancient audio modem. The squawk began its journey from the transponder outward toward the Rix commandos at the speed of sound. The nearest commando was four meters away, and the sound would reach her in roughly eight milliseconds, a hundredth of a second after the attack had begun.

Racing against this warning were the four structured smartalloy slugs launched from the *Lynx*'s railguns. These projectiles, massing less than a few centigrams, barreled at ten percent lightspeed through the near-vacuum cylinders burned for them by the plasma bolts, flying straight as lasers. They traversed the distance to the palace in far less time than it took for Legis's atmospheric pressure to slam closed their vacuum paths. They reached the plasma-smoothed hemispheres of their entry-points into the palace within seven milliseconds.

The slugs were cylinders no wider than a human hair follicle. They sliced through the ancient palace walls, releasing a carefully calculated fraction of their awesome kinetic energy. The stone around the entry points ribbed with sudden webs of cracks, like safety glass struck with a hammer. The impact altered the slugs, transforming them into their second programmed shape, a larger spheroid that flattened on impact, braking the projectiles as they slammed through the floors and walls of the palace. In the seconds after their passage, the old palace would boom and shake, whole walls exploding into dust. Localized but terrific wind storms would soon rise up as the air inside the palace was set in motion by the slugs' passage.

After the seventh such collision, a number calculated by the *Lynx*'s AI using precise models of the palace's architecture, the slugs ballooned to their largest size. The smartalloy stretched into a mesh of hexagons, expanding outward like a child's paper snowflake, and attaining the surface area of a large coin.

These much-slowed slugs struck their targets, hitting the Rix commandos while the warning squawk from the transponder was just under a meter away, eight thousandths of a second after the attack had begun. The slugs tore through the commandos' chests, leaving tunnels that were momentarily as exact as holes drilled in metal. But then the wake of the slug's passage pulled a pulverized spray of blood, tissue, and biomechanical enhancements through the exit wounds, filling the council chamber with a maelstrom of ichor. The four commandos tumbled to the ground, their bones shattered and implants liquifacted by the blow.

For the moment, the hostages were safe.

Doctor

Above, the marines were on their way.

Twenty-five entry vehicles accelerated down launch tubes, riding electromagnetic rails at absurd velocities. Thirty-seven gees hit Dr. Vecher like a brain hemorrhage, shifting the color behind his closed eyes from red, to pink, to the white of the hottest flame. A roar filled his gel-sealed ears, and he felt his body malform, squashed down into the floor of his vehicle under a giant's foot. If not for his yolk of gel and the injected and inhaled smart-polymers that marbled his body tissue, he would have died in several instantaneous and exotic ways.

As it was, it hurt like hell.

The entry vehicles hit the dense air of the mesopause almost instantly, and spun a precise 180 degrees to orient their passengers feet-down, firing retrorockets to begin braking and targeting. They spread out, screaming meteors surging across the daylit sky of Legis XV. Only three were targeted near the council chamber: each vehicle that landed close to the hostages carried the risk of injuring the Child Empress. The marines would be spread out, deployed to sweep for the three remaining Rix commandos and secure the now twice-battered palace.

Dr. Vecher's entry vehicle was fractionally ahead of the others, and was aimed closest to the council chamber. It burst through the palace's three sets of outer walls, the impacts shaking Vecher as if he were trapped inside a ringing church-bell.

But the landing, in which the vehicle expended its last reaction mass to come to a cratering halt outside the chamber, seemed almost soft. There was a final bump, and then Dr. Vecher spilled from the vehicle, the gel that carried him out hissing as it hit the super-heated stone floor of the palace.

Admiral

For the hostages, the transition from anxious fatigue and boredom to chaos was instantaneous. The smartalloy slugs reached their targets well before any sound or shock waves struck the council chamber. The roaring whirlwind seemed to come from nowhere. Blood and liquefied gristle exploded from the four captors. The hostages found themselves choking on the airborne ichor of the eviscerated Rix, mouths and eyes filled with the sudden spray. Moments later, the booms of the palace's shattered and collapsing outer walls came thundering in at the tardy speed of sound, overwhelming the vain shriek of the transponder on the table.

Admiral Fenton Pry, however, had been expecting something like this. He had written his War College graduate thesis on hostage rescue, and for the last four hours had been quietly stewing over the irony. After a seventy-subjective-year career, here he finally was in a hostage situation, but on the wrong end. The latest articles in the infrequent professional literature of hostage rescue even lay on his bedside, printed and handsomely bound by his adjutant, but unread. He hadn't been keeping up lately. But he knew roughly how the attack would unfold, and had palmed a silk handkerchief some hours ago. He placed it over his mouth and rose.

A horrifying cramp shot through one leg. The admiral had tried dutifully to perform escape-pod stretches, but he'd been in the chair for four hours. He limped toward where the Child Empress must be, blinking away blood from his eyes and breathing shallowly. The floor rolled as a heavy portion of the palace's ancient masonry collapsed nearby.

Marines coming in?

They're too close, the admiral thought. This was a natural stone building, for His Majesty's sake. Admiral Pry could have taught whoever was in charge up there a few things about insertions into pre-ferroplastic structures.

Vision cleared as the ichor began to settle in an even patina on the exposed surfaces of the room. The Empress was still seated. Admiral Pry spotted a Rix commando on the floor. She had landed on her side, doubled up as if put down by a punch to the stomach. The entry wound was invisible, but two pieces of the commando's spine thrust from the gaping exit wound at forty-five-degree angles.

Pry noted with professional pleasure that the slug had struck the commando's chest dead center. He nodded his head curtly, the same gesture he used to replace the words *well done* with his staff. Her blaster, extended toward Child Empress at arm's length, was untouched.

The admiral lifted her hand from it, careful not to let the rigid fingers pull the trigger, and turned to the Empress's still form.

'M'Lady?' he asked.

The Empress's face was twisted with pain. She clutched her left shoulder, gasping for air with ragged breaths.

Had the Reason been hit with a slug? The Empress was of course covered with Rix blood, but under that her robes seemed to be intact. She certainly hadn't been shot by anything as brutal as a blaster or an exsanguination round.

Admiral Pry had a few seconds to wonder what was wrong before the heavy ash doors burst open.

Corporal

Marine Corporal Mirame Lao was the first out of her dropship.

A veteran of twenty-six combat insertions, she had set her
entry vehicle to the highest egress speed/lowest safety rating.
At this setting, the dropship vomited open at the moment of
impact, spilling Corporal Lao onto the floor in a cascade of
suddenly liquidized gee-gel, through which she rolled like a
parachutist hitting thick mud. She came up standing. The
seal that protected her varigun's barrel from clogging with gel
popped out like a champagne cork, and her helmet drained its
entry insulation explosively on the floor around her. Inside her
visor, blinking red diagnostics added up the price of her fast
egress: her left leg was broken, the shoulder on that side dislocated. Not bad for a spill at highest setting.

The leg was already numbing from automatically injected
anesthesia; her battle armor's servomotors took over its motion.
Lao realized that the break must be severe; as the leg moved,
she could feel that icy sensation of splintered bone tearing into
nerve-dead tissue. She gritted her teeth and ignored the feeling.
Once during a firefight on Dhantu, Lao had functioned for six
hours with a broken pelvis. This mission – win, lose, or draw –
wouldn't last more than six minutes. She confirmed a blinking
yellow glyph with her eyemouse, and braced herself. Her battle
armor huffed as it contracted implosively, shoving her dislocated shoulder back into place. Now *that* hurt.

By now, some fourteen seconds after impact, the marine
corporal was oriented to the wireframe map in her secondary
vision. To her right, the marine doctor was rising gingerly up
from the gel vomited by his own dropship, disoriented but
intact. The vehicle that had brought the Apparatus initiate

down hadn't spilled yet – it looked wrong, as if the door had buckled in transit.

Tough luck.

Corporal Lao loped toward the heavy doors that separated her from the council chamber, gaining speed even with her lopsided gait. She was right-handed, but she hit the ashwood doors with her already wounded left shoulder; no sense injuring the good arm. Another spike of pain shot through her as the doors burst open.

She tumbled into the council chamber with weapon raised, scanning the room for the Rix commandos.

They were easy to find. All four had fallen, and each was the origin of a long ellipse of thick red ejecta sprayed on walls and floor. A lighter, pink shroud of human blood coated everything in the room, from the ornate settings on the table to the stunned or shrieking hostages.

These four Rix were definitely dead. Lao clicked her tongue to transmit a preconfigured signal to the *Lynx*: *council chamber secured.*

'Here!' a voice called.

The word came from an old man who wore what appeared – beneath its bloody patina – to be an admiral's uniform. He knelt over two figures, one writhing, one still.

The Child Empress, and a dead Rix.

Marine Corporal Lao ran to the pair, reaching for a large device on her back. This move caused her wounded shoulder to scream with pain, and her vision reddened at the edges. Lao overrode the suit's suggestion of anesthesia; she needed both arms working at top efficiency. There were three surviving Rix in the building; this might turn into a firefight yet.

The diagnostics on the generator blinked green. It had survived the jump in working order. She reached for its controls, but movement behind her – the helmet extended her peripheral vision to 360 degrees – demanded her attention.

Lao spun with her weapon raised, shoulder flaring with pain again.

It was the marine doctor.

'Come!' she ordered, her helmet uttering one of the pre-programmed words she could access with a tongue click. Her lungs remained full of drop-goo, whose pseudo-alveoli continued to pump high-grade oxygen into her system. *'Sir!'* she added.

The man stumbled forward, disoriented as a recruit after his first high-acceleration test. The corporal grabbed the doctor's shoulder and pulled him into the generator's radius. There was no time to waste. The com signals from the rest of the drop were running through her secondary audio, terse battle chatter as her squadmates engaged the remaining Rix.

Corporal Lao activated the machine, and a level one stasis field jumped to life around the five of them: Empress, lifeless Rix commando, admiral, doctor, and marine corporal. The rest of the council chamber dimmed. From the outside, the field would appear as a smooth and reflective black sphere, invulnerable to simple blaster fire. The hiss of an oxygen recycler came from the machine; the field was airtight as well.

'Sir,' Lao commanded, *'heal.'*

The marine doctor looked up at her, an awful expression visible on his face through the thick, transparent ceramic of his helmet visor. He was trying to speak; a terribly, terribly bad idea.

Despite the howl of pain in her shoulder, the imminent danger of Rix attack, and the general need for her attention to be focused in all directions at once, Lao had to close her eyes when the doctor vomited, two lungfuls of green oxycompound splattering onto the inside of his faceplate.

She reached over to unseal the helmet. The doctor wouldn't drown in the stuff, naturally, but it was much nastier when you inhaled it the second time.

Captain

'Stasis field up in the council chamber, sir,' Executive Officer Hobbes said softly.

The words snapped through the wash of visual and auditory reports streaming through the *Lynx*'s infostructure. Captain Laurent Zai had to replay them in his mind before he would believe. For the first time in four hours, he allowed himself to feel a glimmer of hope.

Acoustics had finally analyzed the explosive sound in the council chamber, which had turned out not to be a firearm at all. Probably the glass in which the Intelligencer had secreted itself had been overturned, and the crash magnified by the small craft's sensitive ears. So Zai had launched the rescue needlessly, but thus far the rescue was working. Such were the fortunes of war.

'Rix number five dead. Four more marines lost,' another report came.

Zai nodded with approval and peered down into the bridge airscreen. His marines were spread across the palace in a nested hexagonal search pattern, its symmetry only slightly distorted by the exigencies of crashing down from space, avoiding booby traps, and fighting the remaining two Rix commandos. His men were doing quite well. (Actually, seventeen of the two dozen marines were women, but Vadans preferred the old terms.)

If the Child Empress was still alive, Zai thought, he might yet survive this nightmare.

Then doubts flooded him again. The Empress could have been killed when the council chamber had been railgunned. Or when the marines had burst in to take control. The Rix might have murdered the Empress the moment they took her hostage, insurance against any rescue. And even if she was alive now, two more Rix commandos remained concealed somewhere in the tangled diagram of the battle.

'Phase two,' Zai ordered.

The *Lynx* shuddered as its conventional landers launched, filled with the rest of the *Lynx*'s marine complement. Soon the Imperial forces would have total superiority. Every minute in which disaster did not befall him took Laurent Zai closer to victory.

'Where's that damned Vecher?' the captain snapped.

'He's under the stasis field, sir,' Hobbes answered.

Zai nodded. The doctor's battle armor couldn't broadcast through the field. But if the marines had bothered to put the stasis field up, that implied that the Empress was still alive.

'*Rix fire!*' the synthesized voice of a marine came from below; they were still breathing oxycompound, in case the enemy used gas. The bridge tactical AI triangulated the sound of blaster fire picked up by various marines' helmets; a cold blue trapezoid appeared on the wireframe, marking the area where the Rix commando should be.

Zai gritted his teeth. In urban cover, Rix soldiers were like quantum particles, charms or fetches that existed only as probabilities of location and intent, never as certainties – until they were dead. The nearest edge of the marked area was almost a hundred meters from the council chamber. Close enough to threaten the Empress, but far away enough to . . .

'Hit that area with another round of railgun slugs,' Zai ordered.

'But, sir!' Second Gunner Thompson protested. 'The integrity of the palace is already doubtful. It's not hypercarbon, it's *stone*. Another round—'

'I'm counting on a collapse, Gunner,' Zai said. 'Do you think we'll hit that Rixwoman with dumb luck?'

'The stasis field is only level one, sir, but it should hold,' Hobbes offered quietly. At least his executive officer understood Zai's thinking. Falling stone wouldn't harm anyone inside a stasis field. Everyone else – the other hostages, the marines, the rest of the palace staff – was expendable. In fact, the Rix and the Imperials were in battle armor, and wouldn't be killed by a mere building falling down around them. They would simply be immobilized.

'Firing,' came the first gunner, and straight bolts of green light leapt onto the airscreen, lancing the blue trapezoid like pins through a cushion. The thunk of the shots reached Zai's soles, adding to all the other sensations of movement and acceleration.

What a powerful weapon, he thought, to shake a starship with its recoil, though the shell weighed less than a gram.

After four shudders had run through the *Lynx*, the gunner reported, 'First rounds fired, sir. The palace seems to be holding up.'

'Then fire again,' Zai said.

Senator

The other three senators stood a few meters away from the legislation, a bit daunted by its complexity, its intensity.

As Nara Oxham took them through it, however, with simple words and a soothingly cobalt-blue airmouse pointing out particulars, they drew gradually nearer. The legislation consumed most of the airscreen in the Secularist Party Caucus chamber. A galaxy of minor levies formed its center: nuisance taxes on arms contractors, sur-tariffs on the shipment of strategic metals, higher senatorial assessment for regions with a large military presence; all measures that would, directly and indirectly, cost the Imperial Navy hard cash. Surrounding this inner core were stalwart pickets of limited debate, which restricted amendments and forestalled filibuster, and loopholes were ringed with glittering ranks of statutory barbed wire. More items in the omnibus floated in a disorganized cloud, cunningly indirect but obvious in their intent to the trained eye. Duties, imposts, levies, tithes, tariffs, canceled pork, promised spending temporarily withheld – a host of transfers of economic strength firmly away from the Spinward Reaches. All carefully balanced to undo what the Emperor and Loyalists intended.

Senator Oxham was proud that her staff had created so complex a measure in less than an hour. The silver proposal cup at the center of the airscreen was barely visible through the dense, glittering forest of iconographics.

The edicts flowing from the Diamond Palace were a sledgehammer, an unambiguous step toward war. This legislation, however complex its pointclouds of legislative heiroglyphics, was in its own way just as simple: a sledgehammer swung in return, carefully balanced in force and angle to stop its counterpart dead with a single collision. Some of the other Secularist Party senators looked unhappy, as if imagining themselves caught between the two.

'Are we sure that we need to approach this so . . . confrontationally?' asked Senator Pimir Wat. He pointed timidly at the sparkling line that represented a transport impost, as if it were a downed power line he'd discovered on his front stoop, buzzing and deadly with high voltage. Senator Oxham had cut back on her dosage of apathy in the last hour, tuning her sensitivity for this meeting. She felt Wat's nerves filling the room like static electricity, coruscating with every sudden movement or sharp word. Oxham knew this particular species of anxiety well; it was the particular paranoia of professional politicians. The legislation before them was, in fact, intended to induce exactly such an emotion, an anxiety that made politicians fragile, malleable.

'Perhaps we could express our concerns in a more symbolic way,' Senator Verin suggested. 'Reveal all that Senator Oxham has so vigilantly uncovered, and open the subject to debate.'

'And give the Risen Father a chance to respond,' Senator Wat added.

Oxham turned to face Wat, fixing him with the uncanny blue of her Vasthold eyes. 'The Risen Father didn't offer *us* a symbolic gesture,' she said. 'We haven't been informed, consulted, or even forewarned. Our Empire has simply been moved toward war, our constituents put in harm's way while His military engages in this adventure.'

At these last words, she looked at the third parliamentarian in the room. Senator An Mare, whose stridently Secularist homeworld lay in the midst of the Spinward Reaches and at the high water mark of the Rix Incursion, had helped draft the measure. The most lucrative exports of Mare's world had, of course, been exempted from Oxham's legislation.

'Yes, the people have been put in harm's way,' Senator Mare said, in her eyes the distant look of someone listening to secondary audio. 'And in a fashion that seems deliberately clandestine on the Emperor's part.' Mare cocked her head, and her eyes grew sharp. 'So I must disagree with the Honorable Verin when he proposes a symbolic gesture, a mere statement of intent. An unnecessary step, I think. *All* legislation is symbolic – rhetoric and signifiers, subjunction and intention – until voted upon, at least.'

Oxham felt the tension go out of the room. This legislation can't *really* succeed, Wat and Verin were thinking with relief. It was a gauntlet thrown, a bluff, a signal flare for the rest of the Senate. The measure was sculpted precisely to mirror the Emperor's will, to reveal it in reverse, like a plaster cast. Oxham could have given a long speech listing the details that

Niles had found, evidence of imperial intentions, but it would have gone unheard and unnoticed. Pending legislation with major party backing, however, was always carefully scrutinized. Oxham had long ago discovered that a truth cleverly hidden was sooner believed than one simply read into the record.

'True,' said Wat. 'This bill will send a signal.'

Verin nodded his head. 'A clarion call!'

Although she and Senator Mare had planned their exchange for exactly this effect, Oxham found herself a little annoyed at the other Senators' quick surrender. With a few modifications, she thought, the bill might pass. But Oxham was one of the youngest members of the Senate; and, of course, she was the Mad Senator. Her party's leaders sometimes underestimated her.

'So I have your backing?' she asked.

The three old solons glanced among themselves, possibly conversing on some private channel, or perhaps they merely knew each other very well. In any case, Oxham's heightened empathy registered the exact moment when agreement came, settling around her mind like a cool layer of mist onto the skin.

It was Senator Mare who nodded, reaching for the silver proposal cup and putting it to her lips. She passed it to Wat, her upper lip stained red by the nanos now greedily sequencing her DNA, mapping the shape of her teeth, listening to her voice before sending a verification code to the Senate's sergeant-at-arms AI. The machine was exquisitely paranoid. It was fast, though. Seconds after Verin had finished off the liquid in the cup, Oxham's legislation flickered for a moment and re-formed in the Secularist caucus airscreen.

Now the measure was rendered in the cooler, more dignified colors of pending law. It was a beautiful thing to behold.

Five minutes later, as Nara Oxham walked down one of the

wide, senators-only corridors of the Secularist wing, enjoying the wash of politics and power in her ears and the chemicals of victory in her bloodstream, the summons came.

The Risen Emperor, Ruler of the Eighty Worlds, requested the presence of Senator Nara Oxham. With due respect, but without delay.

compound mind

Alexander did what it could to forestall the invaders.

Legis XV's arsenal had been locked out from the compound mind, of course. No Imperial installation this close to the Rix would rely on the planetary infostructure to control its weaponry. Physical keys and panic shunts were in place to keep Alexander from using the capital's ground-to-space weapons against the *Lynx* or its landing craft. But Alexander could still play a role in the battle.

It moved through the palace, seeing through the eyes of security cameras, listening through the motion-detection system, following the progress of the Imperial troops as they stormed the council chamber. Alexander spoke through intercoms to the two Rix commandos left alive after the initial assault, sharing its intelligence, guiding them to harry the rescue effort.

But by now, this last stand was merely a game. The lives of the hostages were no longer important to Alexander. The rescue had come too late; it would be impossible for the Imperials to dislodge the compound mind from Legis XV without destroying the planet's infostructure.

The Rix had won.

Alexander noted the local militia flooding into the palace to reinforce the Imperials. The surviving commandos would soon be outnumbered hundreds to one. But the compound mind saw a narrow escape route. It sent its orders, using one of the commandos in a diversion, and carefully moving to disengage the other.

Alexander was secure, could no more be removed from Legis's infostructure than the oxygen from its biosphere, but the Imperials would not give up easily. Perhaps a lone soldier under its direct command would prove a useful asset later in this contest.

Doctor

Dr. Vecher felt hands clearing the goo from his eyes.

He coughed again, another oyster-sized, salty remnant of the stuff sputtering into his mouth. He spat it out, ran his tongue across his teeth. Foul slivers squirmed in the mass of green covering the floor below him.

He looked up, gasping, at whoever held his head.

A marine looked down at him through an open visor. Her aquiline face looked old for a jumper, composed and beautiful in the semidarkness. They were inside the hemisphere of a small stasis field.

The marine – a corporal, Vecher saw – clicked her tongue, and a synthesized voice said, '*Sir, heal.*'

She pointed at a form lying on the ground.

'Oh,' Vecher said, his mind again grasping the dimensions of the situation, now that the imperative of emptying his lungs had been accomplished.

Before him, in the arms of a bloodsoaked Imperial officer, was the Child Empress. She was wracked by some sort of seizure. Saliva flecked the Empress's chin, and her eyes were wide and glassy. Her skin looked pale, even for a risen. The way the Empress's right arm grasped her rib cage made Vecher think: *heart attack*.

That didn't make sense. The symbiant wouldn't allow anything as dangerous as a cardiac event.

Vecher reached into his pack and pulled out his medical dropcase. He twisted a polygraph around the Empress's wrist and flipped it on, preparing a derm of adrenalog while the little device booted. After a moment, the polygraph tightened, coiling like a tiny metal cobra, and two quickneedles popped into the Empress's veins. Synesthesia glyphs gave blood pressure and heart rate, and the polygraph ticked through a series of blood tests for poisons, nano checks, and antibody assays. The heart rate was bizarrely high; it wasn't an arrest. The bloodwork rolled past, all negative.

Vecher paused with his hypo in hand, unsure what to do. What was causing this? With one thumb, he pulled open the Empress's eyes. A blood vessel had burst in one, spreading a red stain. The Child Empress gurgled, bubbles rising from her lips.

When in doubt, treat for shock, Vecher decided. He pulled a shock cocktail from his dropcase, pressing it to his patient's arm. The derm hissed, and the tension in the Empress's muscles seemed to slacken.

'It's working,' the Imperial officer said hopefully. The man was an admiral, Vecher realized. An *admiral*, but just a bystander in this awful situation.

'That was only a generalized stabilizer,' Vecher answered. 'I have no idea what's happening here.'

The doctor pulled an ultrasound wrap from the dropcase. The admiral helped him wind the thin, metallic blanket around the Empress. The wrap hummed to life, and an image began to form on its surface. Vague shapes, the Empress's organs, came into focus. Vecher saw the pounding heart, the segments of the symbiant along the spine, the shimmer of the nervous system, and . . . something else, just below the heart. Something out of place.

He activated the link to the medical AI aboard the *Lynx*, but after a few seconds of humming it reported connection failure. Of course, the stasis field blocked transmission.

'I need help from diagnostics upstairs,' he explained to the marine corporal. 'Lower the field.'

She looked at the admiral, chain of command reasserting itself. The old man nodded. The corporal shouldered her weapon and scanned the council chamber, then extended one arm toward the field generator's controls.

Before her fingers could reach them, a loud boom shook the room. The corporal dropped to one knee, searching for a target through the sudden rain of dust. Another explosion sounded, this time closer. The floor leapt beneath the doctor's feet, throwing him to the ground. Vecher's head struck the edge of the stasis field, and, looking down, he saw that the marble floor had cracked along the circumference of the field. Of course, Dr. Vecher realized: the field was a sphere, which passed through the floor in a circle around them. The last shockwave had been strong enough to rupture the marble where it was split by the field.

Another pair of blasts rocked the palace. Vecher hoped the floor was supported by something more elastic than stone. Otherwise, their neat little circle of marble floor was likely to fall through to the next level, however far down that was.

Screams from the hostages came dimly through the stasis field; a few decorative elements from the ornate ceiling had fallen among them. A chunk of rock bounced off the black hemisphere above Vecher's head.

'Those idiots!' cried the admiral. 'Why are they still bombarding us?'

The marine corporal remained unflappable, nudging one

booted toe against the cracked marble at the edge of the field. She looked up at the ceiling.

She pulled off her helmet and vomited professionally – as neatly as the most practiced alcoholic – the green goo in her lungs spilling onto the floor.

'Sorry, doctor,' she said. 'I can't lower the field. The ceiling could go any second. You'll have to do without any help for now.'

Vecher rose shakily, nodding. A metallic taste had replaced the salty strawberry of the oxycompound. He spat into his hand and saw blood. He'd bitten his tongue.

'Perfect,' he muttered, and turned toward his patient.

The ultrasound wrap was slowly getting the measure of the Child Empress's organs, shifting like a live thing, tightening around her. The shape below the Empress's heart was clearer now. Vecher stared in horror at it.

'Damn,' he swore. 'It's . . .'

'What?' the admiral asked. The marine took her eyes from the open council chamber's doors for a moment to look over his shoulder.

'Part of the symbiant, I think.'

The palace shook again. Four tightly grouped blasts rained dust and stone fragments onto the field over their heads.

Vecher simply stared.

'But it shouldn't be *there* . . .' he said.

Private

Private Bassiritz, who came from a gray village where a single name sufficed, found himself regarding minute cracks in the stone floor of the palace of Child Empress Anastasia Vista Khaman.

A moment before, a hail of seeking bullets had rounded the corner before him, a flock of flaming birds that filled the hallway with light and highpitched screams, driving him to the ground. Fortunately, Bassiritz's reflexes were rated in the top thousandth of the highest percentile of Imperial-ruled humanity, in that realm of professional athletes, stock market makers, and cobra handlers. This singular characteristic had given him passage through the classes in academy where he often struggled – not so much unintelligent as under-socialized, raised in a provincial sector of a gray planet where technology was treated with due respect, but the underlying science ridiculed for its strange words and suppositions. The academy teachers taught him what they could, and quietly promoted him, knowing he would be an asset in any sudden, explosive combat situation, such as the one in which he now found himself.

He was a very fast young man. None of the small, whining Rix projectiles had hit Bassiritz, nor had they, by the celeritous standards of the event, even come close.

His eyesight was awfully good too. Throw a coin ten meters, and Bassiritz could run and catch it – the called side facing up in his small, yellow palm. The rest of humanity drifted through Bassiritz's reality with the tardy grace of glaciers, vast, dignified creatures who evidently knew a lot of things, but whose movements and reactions seemed deliberately, infuriatingly slow. They seemed dazzled by the simplest situations: a glass fell from a table, a groundcar suddenly hurtled toward them, the newssheet was pulled from their hand by a gust of wind – and they flailed like retarded children. Why not just *react*?

But this Rixwoman. Now she was fast.

Bassiritz had almost killed her a few moments ago. With the servos in his armor set to stealth and his varigun precharged to keep it quiet, he'd crawled into a cunning position behind the Rixwoman, separated from her only by the translucent bricks that formed the sunwall in this part of the garden. The enemy commando was pinned by supporting fire from squadmates Astra and Saman, who were smart enough to let Bassiritz do the killing. Their variguns pummeled the area with fragmentation projectiles, kicking up a maelstrom of flying glass and microbarbed shrapnel and keeping the Rixwoman down, down, down. She knelt and crawled, and her shadow was warped and twisted by the crude, handblown shapes of the brickwork, but from this angle Bassiritz could see to shoot her.

He set his varigun (a difficult weapon that forced Bassiritz to *choose* how to kill someone) to its most accurate and penetrating ammo-type, a single ballshot of magnetically assisted ferrocarbon. And fired.

That setting was a mistake, however. Just as Bassiritz never understood the relativistic equations that made his parents and sisters grow old so quickly, fading visibly with every visit home, and that had stolen his bride-to-be with their twisting of time, he never could remember that some varigun missiles were slower than sound. Bassiritz couldn't understand how sound could have a speed, like his squadmates claimed even seeing did.

But the crack of his weapon reached the Rixwoman before the killing sphere of ferrocarbon, and with Bassiritz-like speed she ducked. The ballshot shattered three layers of ornamental pleasure-garden wall, but missed its target.

And now the Rixwoman knew where Bassiritz was! The swarm of seeking bullets proved that, though she herself had disappeared. All manner of shit was about to come his way. Fast shit, maybe faster than Bassiritz.

Bassiritz decided to swallow his pride and call on help from the ship above.

With his right hand he pulled a black disk from his shoulder holster. Yanking a red plastic tab from the top, Bassiritz waited for the few seconds it took the disk to confirm that it had, in fact, awoken. That red light meant that there was a man in it now – a wee man who you couldn't see. Bassiritz stood and took the stance of one skipping a flat stone across water, and hurled the disk down the long hallway. It glanced once against the marble floor, making the sharp sound of a hammer on stone, then lofted up like a leaf caught by a sudden wind . . .

Pilot

. . . Master Pilot Jocim Marx assumed control of the Y-1 general tactical floater as easily as slipping on an undershirt. Whatever grunt had thrown the floater had imparted a good, steady spin, and the small craft's fan drive accelerated without turbulence.

Marx looked out across the terrain materializing in synesthesia, adjusting to the much larger scale of the floater (almost a hundred times the size of an Intelligencer) and the new perspective. He preferred flying these fast small craft with an inverted viewpoint, in which the floor of the palace was a ceiling over his head, the legs of humans hanging from it like giant stalactites.

The enemy target was a sharp-eared Rix commando, so the floater was seeing with only passive sensors and its highest frequency echolocation. The view was blurry, but the long, featureless hallways offered few obstacles.

The master pilot took his craft 'up' to just a few centimeters from the floor, brought it to a halt behind the cover of an ornamental column. According to battle data compiled by the *Lynx* insertion AI, the nearest Rix commando was roughly twenty meters ahead. A hail of audio came from the canopy's speakers: blaster fire. The Rix was on the move, closing on the marine who had tossed the floater.

She had the marine's position, was moving in for the kill.

Firefight debris began to fill the air. The brittle glass and stone of the palace demanded the crudest sort of tactics: bludgeon your enemies with firepower, raining projectiles on them to cover any advance. Rix blasters were particularly well suited for this. It was not the best environment for floaters.

Marx took his craft farther away from the marine, escaping the maelstrom of flying glass and dust, circling around to take a position behind the advancing Rix. At least in this cacophony, the commando wouldn't hear the soft whine of the floater's fan. Marx brought his active sensors on line and decided to go in close.

There were several ways to kill with a floater. Paint the target with a laser, and have a marine launch a cigarette-sized guided missile. Or deploy the floater's skirt of poison spurs and ram the enemy. Or simply spot for the marine from some safe vantage, whispering in the soldier's ear.

But Marx heard his marine's ragged breathing, a panicked sound as the man ran from his pursuer, and realized there wasn't time for any but the direct approach.

He brought the floater up to ramming speed.

Sweeping around a corner, Marx's craft emerged from the palace into a dense sculpture garden, the way blocked by the splayed shapes of birds in flight, windblown reeds, and flowering trees, all rendered in wire-thin metal. Marx found himself within a few meters of the Rix, the purr of her servomuscles just audible through the din of blaster fire. But she was moving through the sculptures at inhuman Rix speed, dodging and rolling among the razor-sharp sculptures. It was possible she had detected his floater; she had moved into very inhospitable terrain for Marx. If the floater collided with one of these sculptures, its fan drive would be knocked out of alignment – the craft instantly useless. With the lightspeed delay of remote control, this garden was a nightmare to fly through.

Or for the true master pilot, a challenge, Marx thought with a smile.

He closed in, prepping the poison spurs of the ram skirt with a harsh vocal command.

Private

Bassiritz was bleeding.

The Rixwoman had hounded him into the corner of two long hallways, bounded by supporting walls – one of the few hypercarbon structures in the palace. His varigun couldn't blast through them. Bassiritz was trapped here, exposed and wounded. The Rixwoman's incessant fire had brought down a hail of fragments on him, a stone-hard rain. One random sliver had cut through a thin joint in his armor, tearing into his leg just behind the knee-plate.

Bassiritz's helmet visor was scratched and webbed. He could barely see, but he dared not take it off.

And Astra and Saman were dead. They had trusted Bassiritz's kill-shot too much, and had exposed themselves.

For the moment, though, the Rixwoman seemed to have paused in her relentless pursuit. Maybe she was savoring the kill, or possibly the wee man in the disk was troubling her.

Perhaps there was time to escape. But the two wide hallways stretched for a few hundred meters without cover, and Bassiritz could hear the Rixwoman still moving through the garden of crazy shapes. He felt hunted, and thought of the tigers that sometimes took people outside his village. *Up!* his mind screamed. *Climb a tree!* He searched the smooth hyper-carbon walls for handholds.

Bassiritz's sharp eyes spotted a sequence of slots in the hypercarbon that led up to the top of the wall. Probably some sort of catch so that the walls could be repositioned. Bassiritz dropped his varigun – most of its ammo was expended anyway – and drew from his boots the pair of small hypercarbon knives his mother had given him just before the Time Thief had taken her.

He thrust one knife into a slot. Its thin blade fit perfectly. He pulled himself up. The hypercarbon blade didn't bend, of course, though supporting his entire weight with a grip on its tiny handle made his fingers scream.

He ignored the pain and began to climb.

Pilot

Marx pursued the thudding boots of the Rix commando through the sharp twists and turns of the garden, his knuckles white on the control surface. The floater could barely keep up with this woman/machine. She definitely knew a small craft was pursuing her; she had twice turned to fire blindly behind, her weapon set to a wide shotgun blast that forced Marx to screeching halts under cover of the metal sculptures.

But now he was gaining.

The Rixwoman had fallen once, slipping on a sliver of glass from some earlier stage of the firefight, and she'd skidded into glancing contact with the sharp extremities of a statue representing a flock of birds. Now she left drops of thin Rix blood behind her on the marble floor, and ran with a noticeable limp. Marx urged his craft through the blur of obstacles, knowing he could reach her in the next few seconds.

Suddenly, the sculptures parted, and hunter and quarry burst from the garden. Realizing that the open terrain was now against her, the commando spun on one unsteady heel to fire back at Marx's craft. He flipped the craft over and it leapt up from the floor as her blaster cratered the marble beneath him, the floater's ram spurs extended to full. He hurtled toward her helmeted face. Marx fought to get the craft down, knowing it would bounce off her visor. He had to hit the vulnerable areas of hands or the joints of her armor, but the craft was thrown crazily forward by the concussion wave of the blaster explosion.

It was not his piloting skill, but the woman's own reflexes that doomed her. With the disk flying directly at her face, she reached up with one hand to ward off the impact, an instinctive gesture that even three thousand years of Rix engineering had not completely removed. The spurs cut into her palm, thinly gloved to allow a full range of motion, and injected their poison.

The floater rebounded from the impact with flesh. It was whining unhealthily now, the delicate lifter-fan mechanism a few crucial millimeters out of alignment. But the job was done. Marx took control of the suddenly unwieldy craft and climbed to a safe height to watch his adversary die.

But she still stood. Shaking as the poison-nanos spread through the biological and mechanical pathways of her body, she took a few more steps from the garden, looking frantically about.

She spotted something.

Marx cursed all things Rix. She should have dropped like a stone. But in the decades since the last incursion, the Rix immune system must have evolved sufficiently to give her another few moments of life. And she had sighted an Imperial marine. The man's back was to her, as he somehow pulled himself up the smooth wall twenty meters away.

The Rix commando shakily raised her weapon, trying to buy one last Imperial casualty with her death.

Marx thought of ramming her again, but his damaged craft only massed a few grams; the gesture would be futile. The marine was doomed. But Marx couldn't let her shoot him in the back. He triggered the floater's collision-warning alarm, and the craft expended the rest of its waning power to emit a screeching wail.

Marx watched in amazement as the marine reacted. In a single motion, the man turned and spotted the Rix, and leapt from the wall as her blaster fired, one arm flinging out in a gesture of defiance against her. The round exploded against the hypercarbon, the shockwave hurling the marine a dozen meters through the air to crash against the stone floor, his armor cracking it like a hammer. With unexpected grace, the man rolled to his feet, facing his opponent.

But the Rix was dead; she spun to the ground.

At first, Marx thought the poison had finally taken her, but then he spotted the blood gushing from her throat. From the soft armor seam there, the handle of a knife – a *knife*, Marx marveled – protruded. The marine had thrown it as he fell.

Master Pilot Marx whistled as his craft began to fall, energy expended. Finally he had met an unaugmented human whose reflexes matched his own, perhaps were even superior.

He patched himself through to the marine's helmet.

'Nice throw, soldier.'

Through the floater's fading vision, he saw the marine jog toward the Rix and pull the knife from her throat. The man cleaned it carefully with a small rag he pulled from one boot, and tipped his visor at the floater as it wafted toward the ground.

'Thanks, wee man,' the marine answered in a rough, out-world accent.

Wee man? Marx wondered.

But there wasn't time to ask. Another Y-1 general tactical floater had just been activated. One last Rixwoman remained alive; Marx's talents were needed elsewhere.

Initiate

Initiate Barris was trapped in darkness.

His brain rang like a persistent alarm that no one has bothered to turn off. One side of his face seemed paralyzed, numb. He had realized from the first moment of the drop that something was wrong. The acceleration gel hadn't had time to completely fill the capsule; when the terrific jolt of launch came, his helmet was partly exposed. A few seconds into the frantic, thunderous journey, the dropship had whipped around, triggering an explosion in his head. That's when the ringing in his brain had started.

Now the vehicle was grounded – a few minutes had passed, he dizzily suspected – but the automatic egress sequence had failed. He stood shoulder-deep in the mud of the gel, which was slowly leaking out of some rupture in the damaged craft.

The gel supported his battered body, warm, soft, and womb-like, but Initiate Barris's training compelled him to escape the dropship. The Emperor's Secret must be protected.

He tried to shoot open the door, but the varigun failed to work. Was the gel jamming it? He pulled the weapon up out of the sucking mud. Of course, he realized, the barrel was sealed against the impact gel that filled the vehicle, and a safety mechanism had prevented its firing.

He pulled the seal, the sucking *pop* faint in his ruptured hearing.

In the lightless capsule, Barris was unsure what setting

the varigun defaulted to. The marine sergeant onboard the *Lynx* had warned him not to use fragmentation grenades at short range, which certainly seemed a sensible suggestion. Barris swallowed, imagining shrapnel bouncing around in the coffin-sized payload space.

But his conditioning was insistent; it would not brook further delay. Barris gritted his teeth, pointed the varigun at the dropship door, and fired. A high scream, like the howl of fresh hardwood cut on a rotary saw, filled his ears. A bright arc appeared, the light from outside stabbing in through the perforating metal. Then in a sudden rush he was tumbling outward, the rent door bursting open under the weight of the gel.

He stumbled to his feet and looked around.

Something was missing, Barris dully thought for a moment – something wrong. The world seemed halved. He looked at the gun in his hands, and understood. Its barrel faded into darkness . . .

He was blind in one eye.

Barris reached up to touch his face, but the battle armor stiffened. He pulled against the resistance, thinking a joint or servomotor was damaged, but it wouldn't budge. Then a diagnostic glyph – one of many mysterious signs alight inside his visor – winked frantically. And he realized what was happening.

The battle armor *wouldn't let him touch his face*. The natural instinct to probe the wound was contraindicated. He looked for a mirror, a reflection in some metal surface, but then thought better of it. The numbness in his face was anesthetic; who knew what awful damage he might see.

And the Emperor's work needed doing.

The map projected on his visor made sense after a few moments of thought. Concentrating was difficult. He was probably concussed, or worse. With grim effort, Barris walked toward the council chamber, his body shaking inside the smooth gait of the body armor's servomotors.

Sounds of a distant firefight pierced the ringing in his head, but he couldn't ascertain their direction. The clipped phrases of Imperial battle-talk buzzed in his head, incomprehensible and strangely tinny. His hearing was damaged as well. He strode doggedly on.

A series of booms – two groups of four – shook the floor. It seemed as if the *Lynx* were trying to bring the palace down around him. Well, at least that might get the job done if Barris couldn't.

The initiate reached the doors to the council chamber. A lone marine, anonymous in battle armor, waved to him from a kneeling position just outside. The chamber had been secured. Was he too late?

Perhaps there was only one marine here.

Initiate Barris leveled his varigun at the figure and pressed the firing stud. The weapon resisted for a moment, held in check by some sort of friendly fire governor, buzzing at him with yet another alarm. But when Barris ignored it and squeezed again, harder, a stream of the ripping projectiles sprayed across the marine.

The barrage knocked the figure down, and ejected a wave of dust and particles from the marble wall and floor. The fallen marine was swallowed by the cloud, but Barris moved forward, spraying his weapon into the debris. Once or twice, he saw a struggling limb emerge from the cloud; the black battle armor fragmenting, gradually beaten to pieces by the insistent hail of projectiles.

Finally, the gun whined down into silence, expended. Surely the marine was dead.

Barris switched the varigun to another setting at random, and stepped into the council chamber.

Captain

'Shots fired near the chamber, sir.'

Captain Laurent Zai looked at his executive officer in surprise. The battle had been going well. Another of the Rix was dead, and the sole surviving enemy commando had been hounded almost to the outer wall of the palace complex. She was clearly in retreat. Zai had just ceased the railgun bombardment. The second wave of marines and a host of local militia had begun to secure the crumbling palace.

'Rix weaponry?'

'Sounds friendly, sir. According to the squad-level telemetry, it's Initiate Barris. His suit diagnostics look dodgy, but if they're reading true, he's just expended his projectile ammo. One casualty.'

Zai swore. Just what he needed: a run-amok political ruining his rescue mission. 'Crash that idiot's armor, Executive Officer.'

'Done, sir,' Hobbes said with a subtle flick of her wrist; she must have had the order preconfigured.

Zai switched his voice to the marine sergeant's channel.

'Forget the last commando, Sergeant. Secure that council chamber. Let's evacuate those hostages before anything goes wrong.'

Corporal

Marine Corporal Mirame Lao had just decided to lower the stasis field when the shooting outside started. The railgun bombardment had ceased, and the ceiling of the council chamber seemed stable. One marine was stationed outside the chamber, and a few of the hostages had crept out from under the shelter of the council table. Lao had suspected the situation was secure, and wanted to check in with the *Lynx*.

But then the muted scream of varigun fire had erupted, a cloud of firefight dust rolling in through the chamber doors. Lao listened for the thudding of Rix blasters, but she could discern nothing through the heavy veil of the stasis field. She kept the field up, positioning herself between the Empress and the doors.

Vecher was talking to himself, a low murmur of disbelief as he probed the ultrasound wrap with instruments and his fingers. Some sort of tumor had afflicted the Empress's symbiant, apparently. What had the Rix done to her?

The sounds of the firefight ended after a few seconds. A broken figure stumbled through the dust and into the council chamber. An injured marine in battle armor. The helmet was crushed on one side. As the figure shambled toward them, Lao could see the face through the cracked visor. She knew all the *Lynx*'s marines by sight, but the hideous mask was unrecognizable. The man's left eye had exploded out of its socket, and the jaw on that side was slack with anesthetic. It looked more like an insertion injury than blaster fire.

The figure walked toward her, waving frantically. A few steps away, the marine crumpled, dropping with the sudden ragdoll lifelessness of an armor crash, the dozens of servomotors that enabled marines to carry the heavy armor failing all at once. The marine sprawled helplessly on the floor.

Lao listened. It was silent outside.

'Doctor?' she said. 'How is the Empress?'

'I'm not sure if I'm helping her or not,' the doctor answered. 'Her symbiant is . . . unique. I need diagnostics from spaceside before I can treat her.'

'All right. Admiral?'

The admiral nodded.

Lao lowered the field, squinting for the second it took her visor to compensate for the relatively bright light of the chamber. With her varigun aimed at the chamber doors, she reached out and dragged the wounded marine inside the field perimeter. If the firelight started again, the man might as well be protected.

The marine rolled onto his back.

Who was he? Lao wondered. Even with his ruined face, she should be able to recognize him. She knew every marine aboard the *Lynx*. The man's rank insignia was missing.

More marines appeared at the door. They were moving low, battle-wary. Tactical orders were still flying in secondary hearing: one more Rix commando remained.

The wounded marine attempted to speak, and a mouthful of oxycompound emerged from his lips.

'Rix . . . here,' he gurgled.

Lao's fingers shot for the generator's controls again, raised the stasis field.

'Damn!' the doctor swore. 'I lost the connection. I need *Lynx*'s medical AI!'

'Sorry, Doctor,' she said. 'But the situation is not secure.'

Lao looked back at the wounded marine to offer assistance. He was crawling toward the dead Rix commando, dragging the deactivated armor he wore with the last of his strength.

'Just lie there, soldier,' she ordered. In the few seconds the field had been down, Lao's tactical display had been updated. A host of friendly troops were converging on the council chamber. Help was only moments away.

The man turned to face her. He brought up the Rix blaster, leveled at her chest.

At this range, a blast from it would kill everyone inside the field.

Executive Officer

'The stasis field in the council chamber is down again, sir.'

'Good. Contact them, dammit!'

Hobbes frantically tried to establish a link with Corporal Lao. By the process of elimination, she had determined that Lao was the marine inside the stasis field. A few seconds before, the shield had dropped, but then had popped up again, and there hadn't been time to connect.

'Lao!' she ordered on the marine broadband. 'Do not raise the field again. The situation is secure.'

The second wave of marines had secured the council chamber. And a rotary-wing medevac unit from the capital's hospital was in position on the palace roof.

There was no response from Corporal Lao.

'Dr. Vecher,' she tried. Neither of the marines' armor telemetry was active. Even the diagnostic feed from the doctor's medical equipment had disappeared.

'Sir,' she said, turning to face her captain. 'Something's wrong.'

He didn't answer. With a strange smile of resignation, Captain Zai leaned back into his bridge chair and nodded his head, murmuring something beneath his breath.

It almost sounded like, 'Of course.'

Then the reports came in from below, fast and furious.

The council chamber was secure. But Lao was dead, along with Dr. Vecher, Initiate Barris, and two hostages, victims of Rix blaster fire. The shield generator had been destroyed. Apparently, a last Rix commando had been alive, having survived the railgun attack, and had been *inside* the stasis field. In those close quarters, a single blaster shot had killed all six of them, even the Rixwoman herself.

In a few more moments, it was determined who the two hostages were.

One was Admiral Fenton Pry, General Staff Officer of the Lesser Spinward Fleet, holder of the Order of John, the Victory Matrix, and a host of campaign medals from the Coreward Bands Succession, Moorehead, and the Varei Rebellion.

The other was Child Empress Anastasia Vista Khaman, sister to His Imperial Majesty, the Risen Emperor.

The rescue attempt had failed.

Hobbes listened as Captain Zai recorded a short statement into his log. He must have prepared it earlier – Hobbes realized – to save the lives of his crew.

'The marines and naval personnel of the *Lynx* performed admirably and with great bravery against a perfidious enemy. This mission was carried out with distinction, but its basic plan and direction were flawed. The Error of Blood is mine and mine alone. Captain Laurent Zai, His Majesty the Emperor's Navy.'

Then the captain turned and slowly left the bridge under the eyes of his stunned crew, shambling rather than walking, as if he were already a dead man.

■ ■ ■ ■

House

The house was seeded in the range of mountains that almost encircled the planet's great polar tundra. The seed braked its fall with a long, black drogue chute made of smart carbon fibers and exotic alloys, rolling to a stop in the soft five-meter snows that shouldered the chosen peak. At rest and buried in the snow, it lay silent for three hours, performing an exacting diagnostic routine before proceeding. It was a complex mechanism, this seed, and an undiscovered flaw now could doom the house to years of nagging problems and petty repairs.

It was certainly in no hurry. It had decades in which to grow.

At length, the seed determined that it was in fine shape. If there were any problems, they were of the sort that hid themselves: a corrupted diagnostic routine, a faulty internal sensor. But that couldn't be helped; it was one of the natural limits of any self-aware system. In celebration of its good health, the seed took a long drink of the water that its drogue chute had been collecting. The chute's dark surface was splayed across the snow, absorbing sunlight and melting a thin layer of snow beneath it. This water was carried to the seed by a slow capillary process, a few centiliters each minute reaching the core.

The seed's gut quickly broke the water into hydrogen and oxygen, burning the former for quick energy, saving the latter. It radiated the heat of this combustion back to the drogue chute. More snow was melted. More water collected. More hydrogen burned.

Finally, this cycle of energy production reached a critical point, and the seed was strong enough to make its first visible movements. It tugged at the drogue chute, drawing it inward, and, as deliberately as a patient on a carefully measured diet, it consumed the clever and useful materials from which the chute was made.

From these, as the heat of its labors caused the seed to sink deeper into the snow, it began to make machines.

Cylinders – simple thinking reeds whose mouths gnawed, whose guts processed and analyzed, whose anuses excreted subtly changed materials – crawled through the mountain peak on which the seed found itself. They mapped its structure, and determined that its steep but sound shoulders were as stable as a pyramid and capable of withstanding howling gales, construction tremors, even ten-thousand-year quakes. The cylinders found veins of useful metals: copper and magnesium, even a few grams of meteoric iron. They sent gravity waves through the peak, scrying its flaws and adjusting them with a compression bomb here, a graviton annealment there. Finally, the seed deemed the building site sound.

Carbon whisker butterflies pulled themselves out of the snow. One flew to the summit of the icy peak, others found crags and promontories that looked out in all directions. Their wings were photosensitive, and the butterflies stood stock still in the light breeze, taking slow, rich exposures of the peak's splendid views. The artificial insects then glided down into the valleys and across to neighboring peaks, photographing sightlines and colored lichens and the delta-shaped flows of meltwater. Sated with these images, the butterflies flew back to the seed, crawling back into the snow. The data coiled in their bellies were unwound and digested, views constructed and cropped with possible windows, sunsets and seasonal shifts calculated, the happenstance waterfalls of an extrapolated midsummer sculpted and regarded.

The butterflies ventured forth every day for weeks, gathering sights and samples and leaving behind survey markers no bigger than grains of rice.

And the seed found that its aesthetic concerns were also met; the peak was deemed acceptable in function and in form.

The seed called for its second stage, and waited.

Scattered across likely sites in the great polar range were other seeds, sown at some expense – the devices themselves were costly, as were prospecting options on land ownership even in the cold, empty south of Home – but almost all the others had fallen on fallow ground. The seed was one of very few successes. So when the second stage arrived, it was repletely stocked: a large supply of those building materials unavailable on site, detailed plans created by real human architects from the seed's data, and best of all a splendidly clever new mind to manage the project. This artificial intelligence was capable not only of implementing the architects' plans, but also of improvising its own creative flourishes as the work unfolded. The dim awareness of the seed felt incorporation into this new intelligence as a mighty, expansive rush, like an orphaned beggar suddenly adopted by a wealthy and ancient family.

Now work began in earnest. More devices were created. Some of them scurried to complete the imaging of the site. Others began to mine the peak for raw materials and to transmute it to its new shape. Thousands of butterflies were built, swarming the neighboring mountains. Their wings now reflective, they focused the near constant summer sun on the building site, raising its temperature above freezing and providing the laboring drones with solar energy when the last of the snow on the peak was finally melted, its load of hydrogen expended.

A latticework began to enclose the peak, long thin tubes sculpted from the mountain's igneous base material. This web of filaments covered the site like a fungal growth, and moved material around the peak with the steady pulse of the old seed core, now transformed into a steam turbine. Within this mycoid embrace, the house began to take shape.

In the end, there were six balconies. That was one of the few design elements the new mind retained from the original plan. At first the human architect team approved of the project mind's independence. After all, they had set the mind's operating parameters to highest creativity; they reacted to its changes the way parents will to the improvisations of a precocious child. They applauded the greenhouse on the northern face, and complimented the scheme of mirrors that would provide it with sunlight reflected from distant mountains in the wan winter months. They failed to protest the addition of a network of ornamental waterfalls covering the walls of the great cliffs that dominated the house's western view. What finally raised the architects' ire was the fireplace. Such a barbaric addition, so obviously a reference to the surrounding snows, and so *useless*. Already, the house's geothermal shaft extended 7,000 meters into the planet's crust. It was a very warm house when it wanted to be. And the fireplace would require chemical fuel or even real *wood* imported via suborbital; a gross violation of the original design's self-sustaining aesthetic. These sorts of flourishes had to be stopped. The architects drafted a strong attack on the project mind's changes, ending the missive with a series of unambiguous demands.

But the mind had been alone – save for its host of mechanical servitors, builders, masons, miners, sculptors, and assorted winged minions – for a long time now. It had watched the seasons change for a full year, had sifted the data of four hundred sunrises and sunsets from every window in the house, had attended to the play of shadows across every square centimeter of furniture.

And so, in the manner of smug subordinates everywhere, the project mind managed to misunderstand its masters' complaints. They were so far away, and it *was* just an artificial. Perhaps its language interpreters were faulty, its grasp of human usage undeveloped due to its lonely existence, perhaps it had sustained some damage in that long ago fall from the sky; but for whatever reason, it simply could not comprehend what the architects wanted. The project mind went its own way, and its masters, who were busy with other projects, threw up their hands and forwarded the expanded plans, which changed daily now, to the owner.

Finally, only a few months late, the house decided it was finished. It requested the third stage of its deployment.

The final supply drone came across the harsh, cold southern skies. It landed in a cleverly hidden lifter port that raised up amid the ice sculptures (representing mastodons, minotaurs, horses, and other creatures of legend) in the western valley. The drone bore items from the owner's personal collection, unique and irreplaceable objects that nanotechnology could not reconstruct. A porcelain statuette from Earth, a small telescope that had been a childhood gift to the owner, a large freeze-dried crate of a very particular kind of coffee. These precious items were all unloaded, many-legged servitors straining under the weight of their crash-proof packing.

The house was now perfect, complete. A set of clothing exactly matching that in the owner's capital apartments had been created, woven from organic fibers grown in the house's subterranean ecologies. These gardens ranged in scale from industrial tanks of soyanalog lit by an artificial sun, to neat rows of Belgian endive in a dank cellar, and produced enough food for the owner and three guests, at least.

The house waited, repairing a frayed curtain here, a sun-faded carpet there, fighting a constant war with the aphids that had *somehow* stowed away with the shipment of seeds and earthworms.

But the owner didn't come.

He planned several trips, putting the house on alert status for this or that weekend, but pressing business always intervened. He was a Senator of the Empire, and the First Rix Incursion (though of course it wasn't called that yet) was underway. The prosecution of the war made many demands on the old solon. In one of its quiet moments, he came so close as a takeoff, his suborbital arcing its way toward the house, which was already brewing a pot of the precious coffee in breathless anticipation. But a rare storm system moved across the range. The senator's shuttle forbade an approach (in wartime, elected officials were not allowed to indulge risk levels above 0.01 percent) and carried its grumpy passenger home.

In fact, the senator was not much concerned with the house. He had one just outside the capital, another back on his home planet. He had seeded the house as an investment, and not a particularly successful one at that; the expected land rush to the southern pole had never materialized. So when the Rix invasion ended, the owner placed himself in a long overdue cold sleep, never having made the trip.

The house realized he might never come. It brooded for a decade or two, watching the slow wheel of the seasons, and made a project of adjusting once again the play of light and shadow throughout its domain.

And then the house decided that, perhaps, it was time for a modest expansion.

The new owner was coming!

The house still thought of her that way, though she had owned the house for several months, and had visited dozens of times. That first absentee landlord still weighed on its mind like a stillborn child; the house kept his special coffee hidden in a subterranean storage room. But this new owner was real, breathing.

And she was on her way again.

Like her predecessor, she was a senator. A senator-elect actually, not yet sworn into the office. She suffered from a medical condition that required her to seek periodic solitude. Apparently, the proximity of large groups of humans could be damaging to her psyche. The house, which over the years had expanded its sculpted domain to twenty kilometers in every direction, was the perfect retreat from the capital's crowds.

The senator-elect was the perfect owner. She allowed the house considerable autonomy, encouraged its frequent redesigns and constant mountainscaping projects. She had even told it to ignore the niggling doubts that it had suffered since its AI rating had increased past the legal threshold, an unintended result of its last expansion. The new owner assured the house that her 'senatorial privilege' extended to it, providing immunity from the petty regulations of the Apparatus. That extra processing capacity might come in handy one day in the business of the Senate, she had said, making the house glow with pride.

The house stretched out its mind again to check that all was in readiness. It ordered a swarm of reflective butterflies to focus more sunlight on the slopes above the great cliff face; the resulting melting of snow would better feed the water-fall network, now grown as complex as some vast pachinko machine. The house rotated the central skylight so that its faceted windows would in a few hours break the setting sun into bright, orange shards covering the greatroom's floor. And in its magma-warmed lower depths, the house activated gardening servitors to begin preparations for a meal or two.

The new owner was, for the first time ever, bringing a guest.

The man was called Lieutenant-Commander Laurent Zai. A *hero*, the house was told by the small portion of its expansive mind that kept up with the newsfeeds. The house jumped into its preparations with extraordinary vigor, wondering what sort of visit this was to be.

Political? Of military import? Romantic?

The house had never actually seen two people interact under its own roof. All it knew of human nature it had gleaned from dramas, newsfeeds, and novels – and from watching its senator-elect spend her lonely hours here. Much could be learned this weekend.

The house decided to watch very carefully indeed.

The suborbital shuttle was a brilliant thing.

The arc of its atmospheric braking was aligned head-on with the house's sensors, so the craft appeared only as a descending, expanding line of heat and light – a punctuation mark in some ecstatic language of moving, blazing runes.

The house received a few supplies – those exotics it could not produce itself – via suborbital, but those arrived in small, single-use couriers. This shuttle was a four-seater, larger and much more violent. The craft was preceded by a sonic boom, flaring hugely in the house's senses, but then became elegant and avian, its compact maneuvering wings spreading to reduce the speed of its entry. It topped the northern mountains with a dying scream, and swooped down to settle on the landing pad that had risen up from the gardens.

The dusting of snow on the landing pad began to melt in the shuttle's heat, the pad becoming wet and reflective, as if mist were clearing from a mirror. Icicles hanging from the nearest trees began to drip.

The mistress and her house guest had arrived.

They waited a few moments inside the shuttle while the landing area cooled. Then two figures emerged to descend the short exit stairs, hurried by the not-quite-freezing summer air. Their breath escaped in tiny puffs, and in the house's vision their self-heated clothing glimmered infrared.

The house was impatient. It had timed its welcome carefully. Inside the main structure, a wood fire was reaching its climax stage, coffee and cooking smells were peaking, and a last few servitors rearranged fresh-cut flowers, pushing stems a few centimeters one way and then the other as some infinitesimal portion of the house's processors found itself caught in an aesthetic loop.

But when the senator-elect and her guest arrived at the door, the house paused a moment before opening, just to create anticipation.

The lieutenant-commander was a tall man, dark and reserved. He walked with a smooth, prosthetic gait, the motion a gliding one, like a creature with more than two legs. He followed the mistress attentively through a tour of the house, noting its relationship to the surrounding mountains as if scouting a defensive position. The man was impressed, the house could tell. Laurent Zai complimented the views and the gardens, asked how they were heated. The house would have loved to explain (in excessive detail) the system of mirrors and heated water in underground channels, but the mistress had warned it not to speak. The man was Vadan, and didn't approve of talking machines.

Receptive to the smells of cooking, Zai and the mistress presently sat down to eat. The house had pulled food from deep in its stores. It had slaved (or rather, had commanded its many slaves) to make everything perfect. It served breasts of the small, sparrowlike birds that flocked in the south forest, each no bigger than a mouthful, baked in goat's butter and thyme. Baby artichokes and carrots had gone into a stew, thickened with a dark reduction of tomatoes and cocoa grown deep underground. Meaty oranges and pears engineered to grow in freezing temperatures, which budded from the tree already filled with icy crystals, had been shaved into sorbets to divide the courses. The main dish was thin slices of salmon pulled from the snowmelt streams, chemically cooked with lemon juice and nanomachines. The table was covered with petals from the black and purple groundcover flowers that kept the gardens warm for a few extra weeks in the fall.

The house spared nothing, even unearthing the decades-old hidden cache of its first owner's coffee, the previous senator's special blend. It served them this magic brew after they were finished eating.

The house watched and waited, anxious to see what would result from all its preparations. It had so often read that well-prepared food was the key to engendering good conversation.

Now would come the test.

Lieutenant-Commander

After lunch, Nara Oxham took him to a room with incredible views. Like the food, which had been exquisite to a fault, the vistas here almost overwhelmed Zai: mountainscapes, clear skies, and marvelous, distant waterfalls. Finally, an escape from the crowds of the capital. Best of all, however, was the large fireplace, a hearth such as a Vadan home would have.

They built a small pyre of real wood together, and Nara worked with long and skillful fingers to bring it to a blaze.

Zai stole glances at his hostess in the firelight. The senator-elect's eyes were changing. With each hour at the polar estate, they grew less focused, like a woman steadily drinking. Laurent knew that she had stopped taking the drug that maintained her sanity in the city. She was becoming more sensitive. He could almost feel the power of her empathy as it tuned in on him. What would it reveal to her? he wondered.

Zai tried not to think of what might happen between him and his hostess. He knew nothing of the ways of Vasthold; this excursion to the pole might be merely a friendly gesture toward a foreigner, a traditional offer to a decorated hero, even an attempt to compromise a political opponent. But this was Nara's home, and they were very much alone.

These thoughts of intimacy came unbidden and moved creakily, almost a forgotten process. Since his captivity, Zai's broken body had been often a source of pain, sometimes one of despair, and always an engineering problem, but never a locus of desire.

Would Nara detect his thoughts – *half-thoughts*, really – about possible intimacy between them? Zai knew that most synesthetic abilities were exaggerated by the gutter media. How keen were hers?

Zai decided to show his curiosity, which at least would have the advantage of distracting Nara (and himself) from his other thoughts. So he pursued a question he'd pondered since they'd met.

'What was it like to be empathic as a child? When did you realize that you could . . . read minds?'

Nara laughed at his terminology, as he'd expected.

'The realization was slow,' she said. 'It almost never came.

'I was raised on the pleinhold. It's very empty there. On Vasthold, there are prefectures with less than one person per hundred square kilometers. Endless plains in the wind belt, broken only by Coriolis mountains, constructs that channel the winds into erosion runnels, which will eventually become canyons. Everywhere on the plains you can hear the mountains singing. The wind resonances are unpredictable; you can't engineer a mountain for a particular sound. They say even a Rix mind couldn't do the math. Each plays its own tune, as slow and moaning as whalesong, some deeper than human hearing, with notes that beat like a drum. Hiking guides can tell the songs apart, can distinguish the different sides of each mountain with their eyes closed. Our house faced Mount Ballimar, whose northernside song sweeps from thudding beats up to a soprano when the wind shifts, like a siren warning that a storm is coming.

'My parents thought I was an idiot at first.'

Zai glanced at her, wondering if the word had a softer meaning on her planet. She shook her head in response. *That* thought had proven easy enough for her to read.

'Out there on the plains, my ability went undetected. I suffered no insanity in the hinterlands; the psychic input from my large but isolated family was manageable. But I had less need of language acquisition than my siblings. To family members I could project emotions as well as empathize. It was so effortless, my communication; my family thought I was a dullard, but a very easy one to get along with. My needs were met, and I knew what was going on around me, but I didn't see the need to chatter constantly.'

Zai's eyebrows raised.

'Strange that I became a politician, then. Eh?'

He laughed. 'You read my mind.'

'I did,' she admitted, and leaned forward to poke at the fire. It burned steadily now, and was hot enough to have forced them to a meter's distance.

'I *could* talk, though. And contrary to what my parents thought, I was smart. I could do spoken lessons with an AI, if a reward was coming. But I didn't *need* speech, so the secondary language skills – reading and writing – suffered.

'Then I took my first trip to the city.'

Zai saw the muscles of her hand tighten on the poker.

'I thought the city was a mountain, because I could hear it from so far away. I thought it was singing. The minds of a city are like ocean from a distance, when the wave crashes blend into a hum, a single band of sound. Pleinberg only had a population of a few hundred thousand in those days, but I could hear from fifty klicks out the tenor of the festival we were headed to, raucous and celebratory, political. The local majority party had won the continental parliament. From out there on the plain, coming in by slow ground transport, the sound made me happy. I sang back at this happy, marvelous mountain.

'I wonder what my parents thought was happening. Just an idiot's song, I suppose.'

'They never told you?' he asked.

Surprise crossed Nara's face for a moment.

'I haven't spoken to them since that day,' she said.

Zai blinked, feeling like a blunderer. Senator Oxham's biography must be well known in political circles, at least the bare facts. But Zai knew her only as the Mad Senator.

The words chilled him, though. Abandonment of a child? Loss of the family line? His Vadan sense of propriety rebelled at the thought. He swallowed, and tried to stifle the reaction, knowing his empathic host would feel it all too well.

'Go ahead, Laurent,' she said, 'be appalled. It's okay.'

'I don't mean to—'

'I *know*. But don't try to control your thoughts around me. Please.'

He sighed, and considered the War Sage's advice on negotiating with the enemy: *when caught dissembling, the best correction is sudden directness.*

'How close did you get, before the city drove you mad?' he asked.

'I'm not sure, exactly. I didn't know it was madness; I thought it was the song inside me, tearing me to pieces.'

She turned away from him to place fresh wood on the fire.

'As the city grew nearer, the mindnoise increased. It follows the inverse square law, like gravity or broadcast radio. But the traffic going into the festival slowed us down, so the ramp up in volume wasn't exponential, as it could have been.'

'So clinical, Nara.'

'Because I don't really *remember*, not sequentially, anyway. I only recall that I loved it. Riding a victory celebration of a quarter million minds, Laurent, who'd won a continental election for the first time in *decades*. There was so much joy there: success after years of work, redemption for old defeats, the sense that justice would finally be done. I think I fell in love with politics that day.'

'The day you went mad.'

She nodded, smiling.

'But by the time we reached the center of town, it was too much for me. I was raw and unprotected, a thousand times more sensitive than I am now. The stray thoughts of passing strangers hit me like revelations, the noise of the city obliterated my own young mind. My reflex was to strike out, I suppose, to physically retaliate. I was brought into the hospital bloody, and it wasn't all my blood. I hurt one of my sisters, I think the story goes.

'They left me in the city.'

Zai gaped. There was no point in hiding his reaction.

'Why didn't your parents take you back home?'

She shrugged. 'They didn't know. When your child has an unexplained seizure, you don't take them into the hinterland.

They had me transferred to the best facility possible, which happened to be in the largest city on Vasthold.'

'But you said you haven't seen them since.'

'It was in Vasthold's expansion phase. They had ten children, Laurent. And their silent one, their retarded child, had become a dangerous little beast. They couldn't travel across the world to visit me. This was a *colony* world, Laurent.'

More protests rose in Zai, but he took a deep breath. No point in battering Nara's parents. It was a different culture, and a long time ago.

'How many years were you . . . mad, Nara?'

She looked into his eyes. 'From age six to ten . . . that's roughly age twelve to nineteen in Absolute years. Puberty, young adulthood. All with eight million voices in my mind.'

'Inhuman,' he said.

She turned back to the fire, half smiling. 'There are only a few of my kind. A lot of synesthetic empaths, but not many survivors of such ignorance. Now they understand that synesthesia implants will cause empathy in a few dozen kids a year. Most live in cities, of course, and the condition is discovered within days of the operation. When the kids blow, they ship them off to the country until they're old enough for apathy treatments. But I was desensitized the old-fashioned way.'

'Exposure.'

'What was it like in those years, Nara?' No point in hiding his curiosity from an empath.

'I *was* the city, Laurent. Its animal consciousness, anyway. The raging id of desire and need, frustration and anger. The heart of humanity, and yes, of politics. But almost utterly without self. Mad.'

Zai narrowed his eyes. He'd never thought of a city that way, as having a mind. It was so close to the Rix perversion.

'Exactly,' she said, apparently having plumbed the thought. 'That's why I'm anti-Rix, for a Secularist.'

'What do you mean?'

'Cities are *beasts*, Laurent. The body politic is nothing but an animal. It needs humans to lead it, personalities to shape the mass. That's why the Rix are such single-minded butchers. They graft a voice onto a slavering beast, then worship it as a god.'

'But something, some sort of compound mind is really there, Nara? Even on an Imperial world, with emergence suppressed? Even without the networks.'

She nodded. 'I heard it every day. Had it in my mind. Whether computers make it apparent or not, humans are a part of something bigger, something distinctly alive. The Rix are right about that.'

'*Thus the Emperor protects us,*' Zai whispered.

'Yes. Our counter-god,' Oxham said sadly. 'A necessary . . . stopgap.'

'But why not, Nara? You said it yourself, we need human personalities. People who inspire loyalty, give human shape to the mass. So why fight the Emperor so bitterly?'

'Because no one elected him,' she said. 'And because he's dead.'

Zai shook his head, the disloyal words painful.

'But the honored dead chose him at Quorum, sixteen hundred years ago. They can call another Quorum to remove him, if they ever wanted to.'

'The dead are *dead*, Laurent. They don't live with us anymore. You've seen the distance in their eyes. They are no more like us than Rix minds. You know it. The living city may be a beast, but at least it's human: what we are.'

She leaned toward him, the fire bright in her eyes.

'Humanity is central, Laurent, the only thing that matters. We are what puts good and evil in this universe. Not gods or dead people. Not machines. Us.'

'The honored dead are our ancestors, Nara,' he whispered fiercely, as if silencing a child in church.

'They're a *medical procedure*. One with unbelievably negative social and economic consequences. Nothing more.'

'That's insane,' he said.

He closed his mouth on the words, too late.

She stared back at him, triumph and sadness on her face.

They sat there for a while longer, the thing that had been between them broken. Laurent Zai wanted to say something, but doubted an apology would matter.

He sat in silence, wondering what he should do.

3

DECOMPRESSION

Swift decisions are virtuous,
unless they have irrevocable
consequences.

– ANONYMOUS 167

Senator

The constellation of eyes glistened, reflecting the sunlight that penetrated the cultured-diamond doors sliding closed behind Senator Nara Oxham. The ocular glint raised her hackles, marking as it did the eyes of a nocturnal predator. On Oxham's home planet Vasthold, there ranged human-hunting bears, paracoyotes, and feral nightdogs. On some deep, instinctive level, Nara Oxham knew those eyes to be warnings.

The creatures were splayed – fifteen or twenty of them – on an invisible bed of lovely gravity. They wafted like polychrome clouds down the wide, breezy hallways of the Emperor's inner palace, carried by the ambient movement of air. Her apathy bracelet was set to high, as always here in the crowded capital, but sufficient sensitivity remained to feel some small measure of their inhuman thoughts. They regarded her coolly as they drifted past, secure in their privilege, in their demigodhood, and in their speechless wisdom, accumulated over sixteen centuries of languor. Of course, their species had never, even in the millennia before Imperial decree had elevated them to semidivine status, doubted its innate superiority.

They were imperious consorts, these personal familiars of His Risen Majesty. They were *felis domesticus immortalis*.

They were, in a word, cats.

And in a few more words, cats who would never die.

Senator Nara Oxham hated cats.

She halted as the invisible bed passed, anxious not to

disturb the air currents that informed its slow, dignified passage. The animals' heads swiveled as one, alien irises fixing her with languid malevolence, and she had to steel herself to return their unblinking gaze. So much for her brave, anti-Imperial heresies. Nara Oxham's constituency was an entire planet, but here in the Diamond Palace the mighty senator found herself intimidated by the housepets.

Her morning unease had returned the moment she had egressed across the Rubicon Pale, the protective barrier, electronic and legal, that encircled the Forum and ensured the Senate's independence. The aircar waiting for her at the Pale's shimmering edge had been so elegant, as delicate as a thing of paper and string. But inside the car, fragility had transformed into power: the machine's tendrils of lovely gravity reaching out to spin the city beneath her like a juggler's fingers turning bright pins – among building spires, over parks and gardens, through the mists of waterfalls. At first lazy and indirect, the sovereign aircar had become suddenly urgent as it headed toward the Diamond Palace, a potter's blade incising a straight path, as if the world were clay turning on a fast wheel below. This profligate expediture of energy to take her mere kilometers – a demonstration of the Emperor's might: awesomely expensive, exquisitely refined.

Now, a few moments inside the palace, and the housecats were flying too.

Oxham shivered, and took a deep breath after the animals disappeared down the curving hallway, trying to remember if any of them had been black. Then she cast aside superstition and strode across the hall, braving their wafting path, toward her rendezvous with the Risen Emperor.

Another set of diamond doors opened before her, and Nara Oxham wondered what this was all about. The obvious answer was that His Majesty objected to the legislation she had proposed, her counter to the Loyalty Party's preparations for war on the Rix frontier. But the summons had been so instantaneous, only minutes after the legislation had been registered. Oxham's staff had followed her orders well, creating a subtle and labyrinthine weave of laws and tariffs, not a direct attack. How could the Apparatus have recognized its purpose so quickly?

Perhaps there'd been a leak, a mole somewhere on her staff or among the Secular Party hierarchy, and the palace had been forewarned. She dismissed this thought as paranoia. Only a trusted handful had helped write the legislation. More likely, the Emperor had been waiting, alert for any response. He had known that his Loyalists' preparations for war would eventually be detected, and he'd been ready. Ready with this demonstration of alert and awesome power: an Imperial summons, that extraordinary flight, this palace of diamond. That was the warning in the cats' shining eyes, she realized: a reminder not to underestimate Him.

Oxham realized that her contempt for the grays, those living humans who voted for Loyalty, who worshiped the dead and the Emperor as gods, had caused her to forget that the Risen Father himself was a very smart man.

He had, after all, invented immortality. No mean feat. And over the last sixteen hundred years had brokered that single discovery into more-or-less absolute power over eighty worlds.

Through the doors, Oxham found herself in a garden, a vast space over which a bright sky was refracted into facets by a canopy of diamond.

The path under her feet was made of broken stones, their pointed shapes driven into the earthen floor to form a precise and curving road, a mosaic formed from the remains of some ancient and shattered statue. *Look upon my works, ye mighty*, she thought to herself. A short, red grass grew up between the stones, outlining them with the color of dried blood. Motile vines undulated through the grass on either side of the path, a sinuous and vaguely threatening ground cover, perhaps to keep the visitor from straying. The route spiraled inward, taking Oxham past an orchard of miniature apple trees, none higher than a meter, a serpentine dune of white sand covered with a scrambling host of bright blue scorpions, flocks of hummingbirds sculpted into topiary shapes by invisible fields, and, as she reached the spiral's center, a series of fountains whose misty sprays, waterfalls, and arcs of water patently did not follow the laws of gravity.

Oxham knew she was close to the man himself when she came upon the calico. It lay in the middle of the path, splayed to capture the warmth of a particularly large, flat stone. It was a no-breed-in-particular cat, whose coat was mottled with the colors of milk, apricot, and black. The spinal ridge of the Lazarus Symbiant extended all the way down the tail, which moved agitatedly, though the rest of the animal's body was calm. The vertical slits of the cat's irises swelled a bit with curiosity when it saw Nara, then the interest receded, ending in a slow, languid blink of disdain.

She managed to meet its gaze steadily.

A young man strode up the path from the other direction, and lifted the cat to his shoulder with a practiced motion. It let out a vaguely protesting trill, then settled into the crook of his elbow, one claw reaching out across his chest to secure itself in the black threads of imperial raiment.

Her first thought was trite: He was more handsome in person.

'My Lord,' Oxham said, proud that she had managed not to kneel reflexively. Senatorial office had its privileges.

'Senator,' he answered, nodding at her, then turning to kiss the captive cat's forehead. It stretched to lick his chin.

Outside of military casualties, most of the risen were, of course, quite old. Traditional medicine kept the wealthy and powerful alive for almost two centuries; disease and accidents were almost unknown. All the dead people whom Nara Oxham had met were ancient solons and wizened oligarchs, various relics of history, or the occasional pilgrim having reached Home after centuries of winding sublight travel. They wore their death gracefully, calm and gray of manner. But the Emperor had committed the Holy Suicide in his thirties (when structural exobiologists do their best work), in the final test of his great invention. No real age had ever touched his face. He seemed so *present*, his smile so charming (cunning?), his gaze so piercingly aware of Oxham's nervousness.

He seemed terribly . . . alive.

'Thank you for coming,' the Risen Emperor of the Eighty Worlds said, acknowledging the privilege of the Pale.

'At your service, m'lord.'

The cat yawned, and stared at her as if to say, *And mine.*

'Please come and sit with us, Senator.'

She followed the dead man, and at the center of the spiral path they sat, floating cushions taking up positions against her lower back, elbows, neck – not merely cradling Oxham's weight, but moving softly to stretch her muscles, undulating to maintain circulation. A low, square block of red marble sat between them, and the Emperor deposited the cat onto its sunwarmed surface, where the beast promptly rolled onto its back, offering the sovereign's long fingers its milky belly.

'You are surprised, Senator?' he asked suddenly.

The question itself surprised her. Oxham gathered her thoughts, wondering what her expression had revealed.

'I hadn't thought to meet Your Majesty alone.'

'Look at your arms,' he said.

Oxham blinked, then obeyed. Dusted onto her dark skin were silver motes that glistened in the sun, like flecks of mica in some black rock.

'Our security,' he said. 'And a few courtiers, Senator. We'll know it if you sweat.'

Nanomachines, she realized. Some to record galvanic skin response, pulse, secretions – to check for lies and evasions; some to kill her instantly if she threatened the imperial personage with violence.

'I shall endeavor not to sweat, m'lord.'

He chuckled, a sound Oxham had never heard from a dead person before, and leaned back. The lovely gravity cushions adjusted themselves indulgently.

'Do you know why we like cats, Senator?'

Nara Oxham took a moment to moisten her lips. She wondered if the tiny machines on her arms (were they also on her face? beneath her clothing?) would detect her hatred of the animals.

'They were cats who suffered the first sacrifice, m'lord.' Oxham heard the dutiful cadence in her own voice, like a child repeating a catechism; its unctuous sound annoyed her.

She regarded the lazy creature splayed on the marble table. It looked at her suspiciously, as if sensing her thoughts. Thousands of its kind had writhed in postdeath agony while the early symbiants of the Holy Experiments tried unsuccessfully to repair deceased nerve cells. Thousands had limped through the ghoulish existence of unwhole reanimation. Tens of thousands were killed outright – never to move again – as the various parameters of recovery from brain damage, systemic shock, and telomere decay were tested and retested. All the successful experimentation had been performed on cats. For some reason, simian and canine species had proved problematic – they arose insane or died of seizures, as if they couldn't deal with an unexpected return after life's extinction. Not like sanguine, self-important cats, who – like humans, apparently – felt they deserved an afterlife.

Oxham narrowed her eyes at the little beast. *Millions of you, writhing in pain*, she thought at it.

It yawned, and began to lick one paw.

'So it is believed, Senator,' the Emperor answered. 'So it is often believed. But our appreciation of the feline predates their contribution to the holy researches. You see, these subtle creatures have always been demigods, our guides into new realms, the silent familiars of progress. Did you know that at every stage of human evolution, cats were instrumental?'

Oxham's eyes widened. Surely this was some recherché joke, a verbal equivalent to the gravity-modified fountains in the surrounding garden. This talk was like the water running uphill – a display of imperial self-indulgence. She determined not to let it throw her off guard.

'Instrumental, m'lord?' She tried to sound earnest.

'Do you know your Earth history, Senator?'

'Earth Prime?' That far-off planet on the galaxy's edge was so often used to make political points. 'Certainly, Sire. But perhaps my education is deficient on the subject of . . . cats.'

His Majesty nodded, frowning as if this oversight was all too common.

'Take, for example, the origin of civilization. One of the many times when cats were midwives to human progress.'

He cleared his throat, as if beginning a lecture.

'That era found humans in small clusters, tribal groups banded together for protection, constantly moving to follow their prey. They were rootless, barely subsisting. Not a particularly successful species, their numbers were less than the population of a medium-sized residential building here in the capital.

'Then these humans made a great discovery. They found out how to grow food from the ground, rather than chasing it across the seasons of the year.'

'The agricultural revolution,' Senator Oxham supplied.

The Emperor nodded happily. 'Exactly. And with that discovery comes everything. With efficient food production, more grain was produced by each family than it needed to survive. This excess grain was the basis of specialization; as some humans ceased laboring for food, they became metalsmiths, shipwrights, soldiers, philosophers.'

'Emperors?' Oxham suggested.

His Majesty laughed heartily, now leaning forward in his retinue of floating cushions. 'True. And senators too, eventually. Administration was now possible, the public wealth controlled by priests, who were also mathematicians, astronomers, and scribes. From excess grain: civilization.'

'But there was one problem.'

Megalomania? Oxham wondered. The tendency for the priest with the most grain to mistake himself for a god, even to pretend to immortality. But she bit her lip and waited quietly through the Emperor's dramatic pause.

'Imagine the temple at the center of the proto-city, Senator. In ancient Egypt, perhaps. It is a house of the gods, but also an academy. Here, the priests study the skies, learn the motions of the stars, and create mathematics. The temple is also a government building; the priests document productivity and levy taxes, inventing the recordkeeping symbols that eventually become written language, literature, software, and artificial intelligence. But at its heart, the temple had to do one thing successfully, perform one task without which it was nothing.'

His eyes almost glowed now, all deathly calm erased by his passion. He reached out toward her, fingers grasping at the air in his need to be understood.

Then quite suddenly her empathy flared, and she saw his point.

'A granary,' she said. 'Temples were granaries, weren't they?'

He smiled, sinking back with satisfaction.

'That was the source of all their power,' he said. 'Their ability to create art and science, to field soldiers, to keep the population whole in times of drought and flood. The excess wealth of the agricultural revolution. But a huge pile of grain is a very tempting target.'

'For rats,' Oxham said.

'Armies of them, breeding unstoppably, as any parasite will when a vast supply of food presents itself. Almost a biological law, a Law of Parasites: accumulated biomass attracts vermin. The deserts of Egypt swarmed with rats, an inexorable drain on the resources of the proto-city, a dam in the rushing stream of civilization.'

'But a huge population of rats is also a tempting target, Sire,' Oxham said. 'For the right predator.'

'You are a very astute woman, Senator Nara Oxham.'

Realizing that she had charmed him, Oxham continued his narrative. 'And thus, from out of the desert a little-known beast emerged, Sire. A small, solitary hunter that had previously avoided humanity. And it took up residence in the temples, where it hunted rats with great efficiency, preserving the precious excess grain.'

The Emperor nodded happily, and took up the tale. 'And the priests dutifully worshiped this animal, which seemed strangely acclimated to temple life, as if its rightful place had always been among the gods.'

Oxham smiled. It was a pleasant enough story. Possibly containing some truth, or perhaps a strange outgrowth of a man's guilt, who had tortured so many of the creatures to death sixteen centuries ago.

'Have you seen the statues, Senator?'

'Statues, m'lord?'

A subvocalized command trembled upon the sovereign's jaw, and the faceted sky grew dark. The air chilled, and forms appeared around them. Of course, Oxham thought, the high canopy of diamond was not only for decoration; it housed a dense lattice of synesthesia projectors. The garden was, in fact, one vast airscreen.

Senator and Emperor were in a great stone space now. A few shafts of sunlight illuminated a suspension of particulate matter: dust from the rolling hills of grain that surrounded them. In this dim ambience the statues, which were carved from some smooth, jet stone, glistened, their skins as reflective as black oil. They sat upright in housecat fashion, forepaws tucked neatly together and tails curled. Their angular faces were utterly serene, their posture informed by the geometries of some simple, primordial mathematics. They were clearly gods; early and basic totems of protection.

'These were the saviors of civilization,' he said. 'You can see it in their eyes.'

To Senator Oxham, the eyes seemed blank, featureless black orbs into which one could write one's own madness.

The Emperor raised a finger, another signal.

Some of the motes of grainy dust grew, gaining substance and structure, flickering alight now with their own fire. They began to move, swirling into a shape that was somehow familiar to Oxham. The constellation of bright flares formed a great wheel, slowly rotating around senator and sovereign. After a moment, Oxham recognized the shape. She had seen it all her life, on airscreen displays, in jeweled pendants, and in two-dimensional representations from the senatorial flag to the Imperial coat of arms. But she had never been *inside* the shape before – or rather, she had always been inside it: these were the thirty-four stars of the Eighty Worlds.

'This is our new excess grain, Senator. The material wealth and population of almost fifty solar systems, the technologies to bend these resources to our will, and infinitely long lives, time enough to discover the new philosophies that will be humanity's next astronomy, mathematics, and written language. But again this bounty is threatened from without.'

Nara Oxham regarded the Emperor in the darkness. Suddenly, his obsessions did not seem so harmless.

'The Rix, Your Majesty?'

'These Rix, these vermin-worshiping Rix,' he hissed. 'Compelled by an insane religion to infect all humanity with their compound minds. It's the Law of the Parasite again: our wealth, our vast reserves of energy and information summon forth a host of vermin from out of the desert, who seek to drain our civilization before it can reach its true promise.'

Even through the dulling effects of the apathy bracelet, Oxham felt the passion in the Emperor, the waves of paranoia that wracked his powerful mind. Despite herself, she'd been caught off-guard, so circuitously had he arrived at his point.

'Sire,' Oxham said carefully, wondering how far the privilege of her office would really protect her in the face of the man's mania. 'I was not aware that the compound mind phenomenon was so destructive. Host worlds don't suffer materially. In fact, some report greater efficiency in communications flow, easier maintainence of water systems, smoother air traffic.'

The Emperor shook his head.

'But what is lost? The random collisions of data that inform a compound mind are *human culture itself*. That chaos isn't some peripheral by-product, it is the essence of humanity. We can't know what evolutionary shifts will never take place if we become mere vessels for this mutant software the Rix dare to call a mind.'

Oxham almost pointed out the obvious, that the Emperor was voicing the same arguments against the Rix that the Secularists made against his own immortal rule: Living gods were never beneficial for human society. But she controlled

herself. Even through apathy she could taste the man's con-
viction, the strange fixity of his thinking, and knew it was
pointless to bring this subtle point to his attention now.
The Rix and their compound minds were this Emperor's
personal nightmare. She took a less argumentative tack.

'Sire, the Secular Party has never questioned your policy
on blocking compound minds from propagating. And we
stood firm in the unity government during the Rix Incursion.
But the spinward frontier has been quiet for almost a century,
has it not?'

'It has been a secret, though no doubt you have heard
rumors the last decade or so. But the Rix have been moving
against us once again.'

The Emperor stood and pointed into the darkness, and
the wheeling cluster of stars halted, then began to slide, the
spinward reaches coming toward him. One of the stars came
to rest at his extended fingertip.

'This, Senator, is Legis XV. Some five hours ago, the Rix
attacked here with a small but determined force. A suicide
mission. Their objective was to take our sister the Child
Empress, and to hold her hostage while they propagated a
compound mind upon the planet.'

For a few moments, Oxham's mind was overwhelmed. *War*,
was all that she could think. The Child Empress in alien
hands. If harm came to her, the grays would reap a huge political windfall, the rush to armed conflict would become
unstoppable.

'Then, m'lord, that is the cause of the Loyalists' move
toward a war economy,' she finally managed.

'Yes. We cannot assume that this is an isolated attack.'

Her empathy caught a flicker of disturbance from the
Emperor.

'Is your sister all right, Sire?'

'A frigate is standing by, ready to attempt a rescue,' the

Emperor said. 'The captain has already launched a rescue mission. We should learn the results in the next hour.'

He stroked the cat. She felt resignation in him, and wondered if he already knew the outcome of the rescue attempt, and was withholding the information.

Then Oxham realized that her party was in peril. She had to withdraw the legislation before news of the Rix raid broke. Once this outrage was made public, her counterthrust to the grays would seem traitorous. The Emperor had done her and the Secular Party a favor with this warning.

'Thank you, Sire, for telling me this.'

He put one hand on her shoulder. Even through her thick senatorial gown, she could feel the cool of his hand, the deadness of it. 'This is not the time to work against each other, Senator. You must understand, we have no quarrel with your party. The dead and the living need one another, in peace and in war. The future we seek is not a cold place.'

'Of course not, Sire. I will withdraw the legislation at once.'

After she had said the words, Oxham realized that the Emperor hadn't even asked her. That was true power, she supposed, one's desires met without the need to give orders.

'Thank you, Nara,' he said, the fierce mania that had shaped his mind a few moments before sliding from her awareness, as he returned to his former imperious calm. 'We have great hopes for you, Senator Oxham. We know that your party will stand by us in this battle against the Rix.'

'Yes, Sire.' There was really nothing else she could say.

'And we hope that you will support us in dealing with the compound mind, which may well have succeeded in taking hold on Legis XV.'

She wondered exactly what the sovereign meant by that. But he continued before she could ask.

'We should like to appoint you to a war council, Senator,' he said.

Oxham could only blink. The Emperor squeezed her shoulder and let his arm drop, turned half away. She realized that no acceptance was necessary. If another Rix incursion were underway, a war council would have tremendous power granted to it by the Senate. She would sit in chambers with the mightiest humans in the Eighty Worlds. Nara Oxham would be among their number in privilege, in access to information, in ability to make history. In sheer power.

'Thank you, m'lord,' was all that she could say.

He nodded slightly, his eyes focused on the white belly of the calico. The beast arched its back languorously, until the ridge of the symbiant almost formed an omega on the warm red stone.

War.

Ships hurtling toward each other in the compressed time of relativistic velocities, their crews fading from the memory of family and friends, lives ending in seconds-long battles whose tremendous energies unleashed brief new suns. Deadly raids on opposing populations, hundreds of thousands killed in minutes, continents poisoned for centuries. Peaceful research and education suspended as whole planetary economies were consumed by war's hunger for machines and soldiers. Generations of human history squandered before both sides, wounded and exhausted, played for stalemate. And, of course, the real possibility – the high probability – that her new lover would be dead before it all was over.

Suddenly, Oxham was appalled at herself, her ambition, her lust for power, the thrill she had felt upon being asked to help prosecute this war. She felt it still there inside her: the resonant pleasure of status gained, new heights of power scaled.

'My lord, I'm not sure—'

'The council shall convene in four hours,' the Emperor interrupted. Perhaps he had anticipated her doubts, and didn't want to hear them. Her reflexive politesse asserted itself, calming the maelstrom of conflicting motivations. *Say nothing until you are sure*, she ordered herself. She forced calm into her veins, focusing on the slow, synesthetic wheel of eighty worlds that orbited herself and the sovereign.

The Emperor continued, 'By then, we shall have heard from the *Lynx*. We'll know what's happened out on Legis XV.'

Her gaze was caught and held by a red star out on the periphery of the Empire. Darkness gathered in the corner of her eyes, as if she were close to blacking out. She must have misheard.

'The *Lynx*, Sire?'

'The Navy vessel stationed over Legis XV. They should attempt a rescue soon.'

'The *Lynx*,' she echoed. 'A frigate, m'lord?'

The Emperor looked at her with surprise, for the first time noting her expression. 'Yes, exactly.'

Oxham realized that he had misinterpreted her knowledge as some sort of military expertise. She controlled herself again, and continued. 'A stroke of luck, Sire, having such a distinguished commander on the scene.'

'Ah, yes,' the Emperor sighed. 'Laurent Zai, the hero of Dhantu. It would be a pity to lose him. But an inspiration, perhaps.'

'But you said the Rix force was small, m'lord. Surely in a hostage rescue, the captain himself wouldn't . . .'

'To lose him to an Error of Blood, I meant. Should he fail.'

The Emperor moved to stand, and Oxham rose on uncertain legs. The garden lightened again, obliterating the false hills of grain, the godlike feline statues, the Eighty Worlds. The faceted sky overhead seemed for a moment fragile, a ludicrous folly, a house of glass cards ready to be toppled by a breath.

As preposterous and shattery as love, she thought.

'I must prepare for war, Senator Oxham.'

'I leave you, Your Majesty,' she managed.

Nara Oxham wound her way out of the garden, blind to its distractions, blending the Emperor's words into one echoing thought:

To lose him, should he fail.

Executive Officer

Katherie Hobbes paused to gather herself before entering the observation blister. Her report was essential to the captain's survival. This was no time to be overwhelmed by childhood fears.

She remembered her gravity training on the academy orbital *Phoenix*. The orbital, stationed low over Home, was reoriented every day at random. Through the transparent outer ceilings and floors, the planet might be hanging overhead, looming vertiginously below, or tilted at any imaginable angle. The orbital's artificial gravity, already compromised by the proximity of Home, was likewise reconfigured throughout the academy on an hourly basis. The routes between stations (which had to be traversed quickly in the short intervals between classes) might require a dozen changes in orientation; the gravity direction of each corridor shifted without pattern. Only a few hasty markings sprayed onto the rollbars showed what was coming when you flipped from hall to hall.

The objective of all this chaos was to break down the two-dimensional thinking of a gravity-well-born human. The *Phoenix* had no up nor down, only the arbitrary geography of room numbers, coordinates, and classroom seating charts.

Of course, in the career of a naval officer, gravity was one of the mildest crises of subjectivity to overcome. For most cadets, the Time Thief, who stole your friends and family, was far more devastating than a wall turned overnight into a floor. But for Hobbes, the loss of an absolute *down* had always remained the greatest perversion of space travel.

Despite her long career in arbitrary gravity, Hobbes maintained a healthy fear of falling.

So, as always, stepping into the captain's observation blister brought on the old vertigo. It was like walking the plank, Hobbes supposed. But a plank was at least visible. She knew not to look down at her boots as they passed from the hypercarbon floor of the airlock onto the transparent surface of the blister. Instead, Hobbes kept her eyes focused on Captain Zai, finding security in his familiar form. Standing at a graceful parade rest with his back to her, he seemed suspended in space. The black wool of his uniform blended with the void, the piping of the garment, his head, and the trademark gray gloves hovering disembodied until Hobbes's eyes adjusted to the darkness. It was almost noon down at the palace, so the sun was at the *Lynx*'s stern. The only light came from Legis XV, a full green bauble shining over Zai's left shoulder. At the 60,000-klick distance of geosynchronous orbit (a long day, that world), it was not the angry, bloated disk it had been during the rescue attempt. Now it was merely a baleful eye.

Hobbes looked at the planet with hatred. It had killed her captain.

'Executive officer reporting, sir.'

'Report,' Zai said, still facing the void.

'In doing the postmortem—' The word froze in her mouth. She had not considered its original meaning in this context.

'Appropriate choice of terms, Executive Officer. Continue.'

'In doing the PM, sir, we've discovered some anomalies.'

'Anomalies?'

Hobbes looked at the useless hard encryption key in her hand. She had carefully prepared presentation files of the findings, but there were no hardscreens here in the observation blister. No provision for hi-res display, except for the spectacle of the universe itself. The images she intended to show would reveal nothing in low-res synesthesia. She would have to make do with words alone.

'We have determined that Private Ernesto was killed by friendly fire.'

'The railgun bombardment?' Zai asked sadly, ready to add another measure of guilt to his failure.

'No, sir. The initiate's varigun.'

His hands clenched. 'Idiots,' he said softly.

'A governor-override was triggered on the initiate's weapon, sir. It tried to warn him not to fire.'

Zai shook his head, his voice sinking deeper into melancholy. 'I imagine Barris didn't know what the alarm meant. We were fools to have issued him a weapon at all. Stupidity in the Political Apparatus is no anomaly, Hobbes.'

Hobbes swallowed at the blunt talk, especially with two politicals still on board. Of course, the captain's blister, featureless and temporary, was the most secure station on the ship. And Zai was beyond punishment in any case. The death of the Child Empress – her brain was damaged beyond reanimation by the Rix blaster, Adept Trevim herself had confirmed – constituted an Error of Blood.

But this wasn't like the captain, this passivity. He had been quieter since his promotion, she thought, or perhaps since his captivity on Dhantu. As Zai turned around, Hobbes noticed the slight creases in the line of his jaw marking the physical reconstruction. What a star-crossed career, she thought. First that unfathomably horrible imprisonment, then an impossible hostage situation.

'That's not the only anomaly, sir,' she said, speaking carefully now. 'We've also taken a good look at Corporal Lao's helmet visuals.'

'Good man, Corporal Lao,' Zai muttered. The Vadan gender construction sounded odd to Hobbes's ear, as it always did. 'But visuals? She was cut off by the field.'

'Yes, sir. There were, however, a few windows of transmission. Long enough for armor diagnostics and even some visuals to upload.'

Zai looked at her keenly, the lost, philosophical expression finally leaving his craggy features. Hobbes knew he was interested now.

The captain *had* to look at the visuals from Lao's helmet. The weapons and armor of orbital marines communicated continuously with the ship during action, uploading equipment status, the health of the marine, and pictures from the battle. The helmet visuals were low-grade monochrome at only nine frames per second, but were wrapped three-sixty, and sometimes revealed more than the marines themselves had seen.

Zai simply must look at them before he put a blade of error to his belly. And it was up to Executive Officer Katherie Hobbes to make sure that he did.

'Sir, the entry wound on the Rix commando looks like a direct hit.'

There. She'd said it. Hobbes felt a single drop of sweat mark a course down her back where standing at attention left a space between wool and skin. A careful analysis of this conversation, such as the Apparatus might one day make, could draw near the theory Hobbes and some of the other officers had begun tacitly to entertain.

'Executive Officer,' her captain said, drawing himself to his full height, 'are you by any chance trying to . . . *save* me?'

Hobbes was ready for this.

'Sir, "The study of the battle already fought is as essential as that of the battle to come." Sir.'

'"Engagement,"' Zai corrected, evidently preferring an earlier translation. But he seemed pleased, as he always was when Hobbes quoted the old war sage Anonymous 167. The captain even managed a smile, the first she'd seen on his face since the Empress's death. But then it turned bitter.

'Hobbes, in my hand is a blade of error, of sorts.'

He opened one hand to reveal a small black rectangle. It was a single-purpose, programmable remote.

'Captain?'

'A little-known fact: for the elevated, the blade of error can take almost any form. It's a matter of choice. General Ricard Tash and his volcano, for example.'

Hobbes frowned as she remembered the old tale. One of the first Errors, a lost battle during the Consolidation of Home. It had never occurred to her that Tash's suicide had involved some special dispensation. The prospect of scalding magma didn't seem so inviting as to require one.

'Sir? I'm not sure—'

'This remote is programmed to invoke a high-emergency battle-stations status in the *Lynx*, overriding every safety protocol,' he explained, turning the remote over in his hand like a worry stick. 'A standard command sequence, actually, useful for blockade patrols.'

Hobbes bit her lip. What was she missing here?

'Of course, the captain's blister is not part of the battle-ready configuration of the *Lynx*, is it, Hobbes?'

A fresh wave of vertigo struck Katherie Hobbes, as surely as if the ship's gravity had flipped upside down without warning. She closed her eyes, struggling to control the wild gyrations of her balance, listing to herself the rote procedures of emergency battle stations: bulkheads sealed, weapons crash-charged, full extension of the energy-sink manifold, and blowing the atmosphere in any temporary, acceleration-sensitive constructions such as the blister she stood in now. There were safeties, of course, but they could be countermanded.

She felt as if she were falling, tumbling through the void with this all-but-dead man.

When she opened her eyes, he had taken a step closer, concern on his face.

'Sorry, Katherie,' he said softly. 'But you had to know. You'll be in command when it comes. No rescue attempts, understand? I don't want to wake up in an autodoc with my eyeballs burst out.'

'Of course, sir,' she managed, her voice sounded rough, as if a cold were coming on. She swallowed, a reflexive response to vertigo, and tried not to imagine the captain's face after decompression. That horrible transformation was something that *couldn't* happen. She would simply have to save him.

He stepped past her into the open door of the blister's airlock, leaving the black field of stars for solid metal. She followed him into the lock and rolled the reassuringly massive door into its sealed position.

'Now,' Captain Zai said as the inner door opened, 'I should like to see these visuals. "No mark of war is too minute to reward careful study," aye, Hobbes?'

'Aye, sir.' Anonymous 167 again.

As she followed her captain to the command bridge, glad to have her feet on dense hypercarbon and hullalloy, Katherie Hobbes allowed herself to shelter an uncertain candle of hope.

compound mind

Alexander flexed itself, feeling the ripple of its will promulgate through the infostructure of Legis XV.

The hostage crisis had for a time interrupted the normal flux of information across the planet. Market trading had been suspended, schools closed, the powers of the unwieldy Citizens' Assembly assumed by the Executive Diet. But now that the Imperials had retaken the palace, activity was beginning to rebuild in the world's arteries of data and interchange.

A few days of mourning would be observed soon, but for now the Empress's death was a closely guarded secret. Legis XV had survived its brief Rix occupation, and at the moment there was an outpouring of relief, a release of nervous energies throughout the intertwined systems of commerce, politics, and culture.

As for the existence of Alexander in their midst, the compound mind had not yet created panic. Once the population realized that their phones, databooks, and home automatics had not turned on them, the mind seemed more a curiosity than a threat – a ghost in the machine that had yet to prove itself unfriendly, whatever the propaganda of the grays.

And so the planet awoke.

Alexander felt this increasing activity as new and sudden vigor. The first day of consciousness had been exhilarating, but the compound mind now realized the true vitality of Legis XV. The planet's surge back into ordinary life – the shimmer of its billions, their commerce and politics – felt to the mind as if it were bursting anew from the shadowtime. The flowing data of secondary sight and audio, the clockwork of traffic management, water purification, weather control, even the preparations of the local military readying for another attack, were like the coursings of some morning stimulant through its body public.

Certainly, there were belated attempts by the Imperials to destroy Alexander. Data shunts and hunter programs were deployed, attempting to erase the influence of the Rix propagation, trying to tear down the self-conscious feedback that now illuminated the planet's infostructure. But the efforts were too late. What the Rix had long understood, and the benighted Imperials could not truly grasp, was that a compound mind is the *natural* state of affairs. As Rixia Henderson herself had theorized in the early days of Amazon, all systems of sufficient complexity tend toward self-organization, self-replication, and finally self-consciousness. All of biological and technological history was, for the Rix, a reflection of this essential law, as inescapable as entropy. Rixia Henderson's philosophy superseded such notions as social progress, the invisible hand of the marketplace, and the zeitgeist – shallow vanities all. The narrative of history itself was nothing more than the working out of the one law: humanity is but the raw material of greater minds. So Alexander, once born, could not be destroyed – unless technological civilization on Legis XV were itself destroyed.

The compound mind breathed deep its existence, surveying the vast energies of its domain. At last, the Rix had come to the Risen Empire, bringing the light of consciousness.

The only sectors of Legis XV that remained dark to Alexander were the gray enclaves, the cities of the dead that dotted the planet. The walking corpses of the Risen Empire eschewed technology and consumerism, so the phone calls and purchases and traffic patterns that informed Alexander's consciousness were missing. There was an appalling absence of bustle and friction from the afterlives of the dead. The needs that underlay technology – to buy and sell, to communicate, to politic and argue – did not exist in the gray enclaves. The risen walked quiet and alone in their necropolis gardens, performed simple arts by hand, went on their winding and pointless pilgrimages among the Eighty Worlds, and gave their allegiance to the Emperor. But they had no *struggles*, nothing from which true AI could arise.

Alexander puzzled over this strangely divided culture. The

living citizens of the Empire engaged in rampant capitalism in pursuit of exotic pleasures and prestige; the risen were ascetic and detached. The warm participated in a fiercely fragmented, multiparty democracy; the cold univocally worshiped the Emperor. The two societies – one chaotic and vital, the other a static monoculture – not only coexisted, but actually seemed to maintain a productive relationship. Perhaps they each provided a necessary facet of the body politic: change versus stability, conflict versus consensus. But the division was terribly rigid, formed as it was by the barrier of death itself.

The Rix Cult did not recognize hard boundaries, especially between animate and inanimate; Rixwomen (they had disposed of the unnecessary gender) moved freely along the continuum between organic and technological, picking and choosing from the strengths of each. Rix immortality avoided a specific moment of death, preferring the slow transformation of Uprade. And the Rix, of course, worshiped the compound mind, an admixture of human activities mediated by machines, the ultimate blending of flesh and metal, giving rise to Mind.

Alexander mused that this gulf of sensibilities was why Empire and Cult must be forever at war. The staid traditions of the grays were antithetical to compound minds' very existence; the risen stilted competition and activity, vitality and change. The dead had choked the progress of the Empire, and made it poorer ground for the Rix to sow the seeds of their gods.

The mind's thoughts turned to the data it had gleaned from the Child Empress's confidant, the strange device wound into the dead girl. The child was now permanently destroyed by some folly of her Imperial rescuers, but Alexander was still confused about her. The mind found it hard to fathom the confidant's purpose. That was a strange thing in itself. Alexander could reach into any machine, transaction, or message on the planet and grasp it completely, having full access to the world's data reservoirs, the soup of information out of which meaning was constructed. But this one device made no sense; no instruction manuals, schematics, or medical contraindications existed for it, anywhere. It had contained no mass-produced components, and stored its internal data in a unique format. The confidant was devoid of meaning, an itch of absent understanding.

As it plumbed the planetary libraries in vain, Alexander slowly began to realize that this confidant had been a secret. It was singular and strangely invisible. No one on Legis XV had ever patented or purchased anything like the device, discussed it on the newsfeeds, scribbled a picture of it on a work tablet, or even mentioned it in a diary entry.

It was, in short, a secret of global – perhaps *Imperial* – proportions.

Alexander felt a warm rush of interest, a scintillation of energy like the fluctuations of the planet's seven private currencies when the markets opened. It knew, if only from the millions of novels and plays and games that informed its sense of drama, that when governments kept secrets, they did so at their peril.

So Alexander began closer analysis of the scant data it had wrung from the confidant in those few moments it had assumed control. The machine had evidently been designed to monitor the Empress's body, a strange accessory for one of the immortal dead. Her health should have been perfect, forever. To Alexander, the confidant's recordings were noise, the data obviously encrypted with a one-time pad. The pad must exist somewhere on Legis, somewhere off the nets. The compound mind remembered its few seconds inside the confidant, before the device had destroyed itself to avoid capture. For a moment, Alexander had seen the world through the machine's eyes.

Starting from that slender thread, it began to reverse-engineer the device, attempting to scry its purpose.

Perhaps there was another hostage of sorts to take, here on Legis XV. Some new lever to use against the Risen Empire, sworn enemy of all things Rix.

Initiate

The body lay blackened and flaking on the still-table, recognizable as a human only in the grossest aspect of its limbs, trunk, and head. But Initiate Viran Farre stood back, wary of the charred corpse as if it were capable of sudden motion – some swift reprisal against those who had failed to protect it. Three more humans and the Rix commando lay, similarly burned, on the other tables in the room. These were the five who had been killed in the council chamber.

Officially, Initiate Farre and Adept Trevim had claimed possession of their remains in case one of them were fit to rise. But clearly any such reanimation lay beyond the Miracle of the Symbiant; these people had been destroyed. The politicals' real purpose was to cut open the Child Empress's body, and make sure that all evidence of the Emperor's Secret had been eliminated.

Farre felt a strange hollow in her stomach, a void filled only with an ominous flutter, like the anxious lightness of sudden freefall. She had performed the administration of the symbiant many times, and was no stranger to dead bodies. But this palpable presence of the Emperor's Secret made war against her conditioning. She wanted to blot out the sight of the Empress's fallen body, run from the room and order the building burned down. Adept Trevim had ordered Farre to steel herself, however; the initiate's medical knowledge was necessary here. And Farre was also conditioned to obey her superiors.

'Which of these saws, Farre?'

Farre took a deep breath, and forced her eyes to take in the array of monofilament incisors, vibrasaws, and beam cutters on the autopsy table. The tools were arranged by kind and size, the backmost raised on the stepped table like a jury, or the excavated teeth of some ancient predator displayed by form and function: here the gnashers, here the renders, here the grinding molars.

'I would stay away from beam cutters, Adept. And we haven't the skill for monofilaments.' The confidant was made of nervous tissue, and would be a delicate extraction. They needed to open the body in the least destructive way.

'A vibrasaw, then?' Trevim suggested.

'Yes,' Farre managed.

She selected a small one, and set it to its thinnest and shortest cutting width, just enough to slice through the rib cage. Farre handed it to the adept, and winced at the dead woman's clumsy grip on the tool. Farre, who had been a doctor before her induction into the Emperor's service, should by rights be performing the autopsy. But the conditioning was too profound. It was all she could do to assist; actually cutting into the corpse that housed the Secret would bring forth a calamitous reaction from her internal monitors.

The vibrasaw whirred to life in Trevim's hand, its whine like a mosquito caught inside one's eardrum. The sound seemed to put even the fifty-years-dead Adept on edge as she pressed the saw against the blackened corpse. But her strokes were smooth and clean, gliding through the charred flesh like a blade through water.

A mist rose up from the corpse, the faintest blur of gray in the air. Farre shuddered and reached for a medical mask. The mist looked like fine ash dust rising from a burned-out fire;

indeed, it was in every chemical sense the same – fire-distilled carbon – but its source was human flesh rather than wood. Farre covered her mouth carefully, trying not to think of the small motes of dead Child Empress that would be trapped between the mask's fibers, or were settling even now into the pores of her exposed skin.

The Adept finished, having done almost too thorough a job. The vibrasaw had been set to undercut the connective tissues, and the Empress's rib cage lifted up easily in narrow strips as Trevim tugged. Farre leaned carefully forward, trying to quell the raging inhibitions of her conditioning. The exposed chest was almost abstract, like the plastic sculptures back in medical school; the titanic heat from the Rix blaster having burned gristle and tissue to a dark, dry mass.

'And now a nerve locator?'

Farre shook her head. 'They only work on living subjects. Or the very recently dead. You'll need a set of nervous-tissue-seeking nanoprobes and a remote viewer, along with a troweling rod.' She took another deep breath. 'Let me show you.'

The Adept moved aside as Initiate Farre sprayed the nanoprobes onto the glistening chest cavity. Farre let them propagate, then inserted the rod carefully, watching its readout to make sure she didn't damage the delicate strands of the confidant's skein. The troweling rod's nimble fingers, thin as piano wire, began to work the flesh, teasing the tissue from the Empress's body.

But Farre had only progressed a few centimeters when she realized what she was doing, and a wave of nausea struck her.

'Adept . . .' she managed.

Trevim lifted the instrument delicately from Farre's fingers as she staggered back from the still-table.

'That will do nicely, Initiate,' she heard Trevim say. 'I think I see how it works. Thank you.'

The images stayed unshakeably in her mind's eye as she sank heavily to the floor. The Emperor's sister, Child Empress Anastasia, Reason for the symbiant, splayed open like a roasted pig.

Vulnerable. Injured. The Secret exposed!

And she, Viran Farre, had participated. Her stomach heaved, and acid bile rose into her throat. The taste destroyed all will, and she retched pitifully as the adept continued to remove the confidant from the fallen Empress.

Captain

Laurent Zai dropped the single-purpose remote into his pocket. It wasn't actually programmed to do anything yet – he hardly wanted to kill himself *accidentally*. He'd simply wanted to show ExO Hobbes the manner in which he intended to commit suicide. As a warrior, he had always borne the prospect of a messy end, but an awkward changeover of command was unacceptable.

Zai felt a strange calmness as he followed Hobbes to the command bridge. The anxiety that consumed Zai during the hostage situation was gone. Over the last two years, love had compromised his bravery, he realized now. Hopelessness had returned it to him in good working order.

Zai wondered why the *Lynx* had been equipped with two bridges. The warship was a new class, unlike any of the Navy's *Acinonyx* frigates, and a few of its design concepts had seemed odd to Zai. In addition to a battle bridge, the ship had a command bridge, as if an admiral would one day want to command a fleet from a frigate. The second bridge had wound up being used as a very well-equipped conference room.

When Zai and Hobbes entered, the officers present snapped

to attention. The command bridge was optimized for flat-screen viewing, the conference table folded out like a jackknife, all seats facing the hi-res screen. The officers' eyes met Zai's with nervous determination, as if they had been planning a mutiny.

Or plotting to save their captain's life.

'At ease,' Zai ordered, taking the shipmaster's chair. He turned to Hobbes. 'Make your report, Executive Officer.'

Hobbes glanced anxiously at the hardkey she'd been worrying in her hand during their discussion in the observation bubble, as if suddenly unsure that it was up to the task. Then, with a grim look, she shoved it into a slot before her.

The vibration of the table's boot sequence shimmered under Zai's hand. He noted the shift of shadows in the room as overhead lights dimmed and the billions of picture elements on the wall warmed to their task. He saw his officers relax a little, as people always did when preparing to watch a canned presentation, no matter how grim the situation. Now that Zai faced death, details had become terribly clear to him. But this clarity was like amplified secondary sight, sharp but somehow distant. The marrow of these quotidian details had been lost along with his future, as if his experiences had become suddenly worthless, like some currency decommissioned overnight.

The screen showed a grainy image, its colors flattened into gray-scale – the unavoidable signal loss of a helmet-sized transmitter narrowcasting all the way to low orbit. The picture seemed stretched, the pulled-taffy visuals of a marine's 360-degree vision. It took a few moments for Zai's visual cortex to adapt to the view, like struggling to understand pre-Diaspora Anglish for the first few minutes of some ancient play.

Then figure and ground sorted themselves out, and he could make out a Rix soldier, a blood-spattered admiral, an off-balance Dr. Vechner, and the body of one Empress Anastasia

Vista Khaman. All were frozen, their motion suspended, the horror of the situation oddly aestheticized by the rough grain of the medium.

'This is 67:21:34,' Hobbes announced, her airmouse hovering in front of the timecode on the screen. 'Exactly fifteen seconds before the stasis field was first activated by Corporal Lao.' She named the participants, the airmouse flitting like a curious hummingbird from one to the next.

'Note that there are no visible wounds on the Empress. Blood is visible on her and the admiral, but it's spread evenly across them. It probably belongs to the Rix commandos, who had been railgunned from orbit with structure-penetrating exsanguination slugs.'

The airmouse shifted in response to these words, seeming to sniff the entry wound on the Rix commando. Zai had to admit that it looked like a square hit. Her guts should have been sucked out in buckets. How could she have survived?

'Now, I'll advance it to the point where the stasis field interrupts transmission.'

The figures jolted into action, Vechner stumbling, Lao's helmet voice calling *'Come, sir,'* and dragging him toward the Empress. Lao deployed the field generator and her fingers reached for the controls; then the screen went black.

'Now,' Hobbes said, 'to focus on certain elements. First, the Empress.'

The fifteen seconds replayed on the screen, with the Empress's image highlighted. She was shaking uncontrollably, having some sort of seizure. The admiral restrained the Empress as if she were a living child thrashing her way through a nightmare.

'Obviously, the Child Empress is alive. Under some sort of stress, perhaps wounded, but alive. Now, observe the Rixwoman.'

The scene replayed, and Zai felt himself gaining familiarity with the short document. The highlighted Rix commando was completely still.

'She's dead,' First Pilot Maradonna said to the room.

'Or playing dead,' Captain Zai responded.

'That's possible, sir,' Hobbes allowed. 'The Rix physiology is not pulsitile. Which means they don't take lungfuls of air; they filter it continuously. And their hearts spin rather than beat.'

'So they are naturally motionless on the surface, no matter the resolution.'

'Yes, sir. But allow me to skip forward to the visuals received when the situation had been secured, when Lao briefly lowered the stasis field. This is from Dr. Vechner's helmet.'

The screen was refreshed with a new tableau. Vechner knelt beside the Empress. The airmouse moved to indicate the Rix soldier; she apparently hadn't moved in the interim. Hobbes left this fact unspoken.

'Note the ultrasound wrap around the Empress,' Hobbes continued. 'As we advance, you can see her heart beating within.'

The image moved forward for five seconds, then the stasis field went back up and cut off the transmission again. But the heartbeat was clearly visible. The Empress had still been alive at that point.

Damn, Zai thought. They'd been so close.

'Why don't we have data from the ultrasound wrap?' he asked. 'Shouldn't it have automatically connected with the *Lynx* medical AI?'

'Unfortunately, the security protocols require more than five seconds to complete, sir. There are extensive firewalls against viruses being loaded onto the *Lynx* in the guise of emergency medical data.'

Zai wondered who'd tried that little trick in the past. It sounded like typical Tungai sabotage.

'Now from Corporal Lao's perspective again,' Hobbes continued. 'The new marine in the picture is Initiate Barris. His armor was crashed on captain's orders, as he had just killed another marine with friendly fire.'

Barris's motionless armor lay just outside the field area. When the image advanced, Lao reached out and dragged him inside the protective perimeter.

'Lao is moving to protect a fallen comrade,' Hobbes said dryly.

Barris rolled over. His face was an appalling mess, a wreckage of tissues damaged by a bad atmospheric entry.

'*Rix . . . here,*' Barris's twisted face said.

Lao's hand darted for the field generator's controls again, and the image went dark.

'There were no Rix in the palace at that point,' Hobbes said firmly. 'Nor had Barris seen any Rix at all. For some reason, he lied.'

Zai shook his head. 'He'd just had a firefight with another marine, whom he must have thought was Rix. Initiate Barris wasn't lying, just unbelievably stupid.'

'Can we see Barris's visuals?' someone asked. 'From when he killed the marine?'

'I'm afraid his helmet transmitter was trashed on entry. But we do have that event from the other side.'

New visuals loaded onto the screen. The administrative text identified the viewpoint as Private Ernesto. From a kneeling position, he held a position in front of the council chamber's door, facing out into the palace's broad hallways. The black hemisphere of the stasis field could be seen in Ernesto's rearmost vision.

Initiate Barris, recognizable from his smashed helmet, staggered into view. Ernesto waved at him, but Barris raised his weapon.

The initiate's varigun fired, and Ernesto's viewpoint spun as he was knocked back by a hail of small projectiles. The barrage went on, the damage to suit and soldier recorded in grim little glyphs along the bottom of the screen. A second before Ernesto must have died, the armor lost its ability to transmit, and the screen froze.

'Not much fog of war there,' Maradonna commented.

'Barris would have to override the friendly-fire governor,' the marine sergeant added. Zai wondered if these observations had been scripted in advance. What were his senior staff suggesting, anyway? That the initiate had gone in purposefully to kill Ernesto? Or the Empress, for that matter?

That was unthinkable. Politicals were bound by governors far more insurmountable than some failsafe on a varigun. Their minds were fixed to a state of selfless loyalty by years of painful conditioning; on some gray planets, they were selected from birth for genes that showed high susceptibility to brainwashing. They were beyond suspicion.

'The fog was in Barris's mind,' Zai said. 'He'd suffered a grevious head injury on entry. He probably thought every suit of armor he saw was Rix.'

'Exactly, sir,' Hobbes agreed. '"Rix . . . here." His last recorded words.'

The screen split into three parts. In the first two frames, the Rix soldier lay in her now familiar position, looking dead as ever. But in the last frame her body was a blackened husk, even the marble floor beneath her scorched by the blaster shot that had killed everyone inside the stasis field. It was evident now from the trio of images: all three positions were much the same.

Although the commando's body had been jostled by the blast, there was no sense that she had sprung back to life and raised her weapon. Indeed, in the last frame the ruined Rix blaster lay across her left ankle, much closer to the burned hands of Barris than her own.

'Where is the initiate's weapon?' someone asked.

Hobbes's response was instantaneous. These questions must be scripted, Zai thought with growing annoyance. The screen again showed the last recording from Lao's viewpoint. As she dragged Farre's body into the stasis field's perimeter, his varigun stayed outside. He had dropped it when the *Lynx* had crashed his armor.

A murmur came from the assembled officers.

'He had no weapon,' Hobbes said. 'But the Rix blaster was already within—'

'Hobbes!' Captain Zai snapped.

The anger in his voice shocked the room into silence. The officers sat as motionless as the image from doomed Mirame Lao's helmet.

'Thank you all for this briefing,' Zai said. 'Executive Officer, in my observation blister. Now.'

He stood and wheeled away from the surprised faces, and strode from the command bridge. He was gone so fast that it took a few moments for Katherie Hobbes to catch up in the corridors outside.

Zai and his executive officer walked in silence back toward the plastic bubble that faced the void.

Commando

The commando's heart, if you could call it that, was closer to a turbine than a pump. A pair of long screws, one venous and the other arterial, rotated inside her chest, threading the vital fluid through her body at an inhumanly fast and even rate. The liquid carried oxygen and nutrients but was not, properly speaking, blood. It also served the purposes of a lymphatic system, transporting uptake nanos from thousands of tiny lymph nodes distributed along her arteries. The substance in the commando's veins had little else to do with her Rix immune system, however. It contained no white blood cells, whose functions had been delegated centuries before to a scattered population of organs roughly the size of rice grains, themselves generated by small machines hidden in the marrow of her bird-light, aircraft-strong, hypercarbon bones.

The surging fluid did, however, contain enough iron to oxydize red when it was spilled, a situation that the commando was currently attempting to avoid.

She was tucked into an area smaller than an overnight bag, a space that normally housed a cleaning robot. The Rixwoman had disassembled the previous occupant, hoping the scattered parts would not reveal her appropriation of its home, and folded herself into the space, limbs bending at sharp angles like some origami construction. According to the messages sent to her from Alexander, her invisible and omnipresent benefactor in this chase, the local militia were searching for her with sonic sweeps. These devices were designed to find escaped fugitives by detecting that steady, unstoppable, telltale rhythm of humanity: the heartbeat.

Apparently, no one had told the locals that she, a Rix commando, had none.

The tiny turbine purred inside her chest, an infrasonic hiss without rhythm or vibrato, and the nervous, soft-shoed sweep operators passed by her hiding place, blissfully unaware.

The commando, who was called h_rd, had gone to ground in a building that was called, in the local language, a *library*. This structure served as a distribution point for proprietary data, information not available in the public infostructure. Corporate secrets, technological patents, personal medical records, and certain erotic poems and images available by paid subscription were deposited here, accessible only to those with special physical keys, totems of information ownership. Alexander had guided h_rd here, helping the commando fight and creep her way across a hundred kilometers of dense city that swarmed with militia, police, and the occasional Imperial marine, all searching for her. But Alexander was a powerful ally, and even a single Rix commando was deadly quarry. The local forces made a show of the pursuit – evacuating buildings, running sweeps, and occasionally firing their weapons – but were more interested in self-preservation than glory. And the Imperial marines numbered fewer than a hundred.

The commando waited in the library with inhuman patience. For seven hours, she lay folded in her compartment.

It was strange here in the darkness, so alone. H_rd had spent her entire life in the intimate company of her drop-sisters, never separated from the sibling group for more than a few minutes. The fifteen commandos in her dropship had been raised together, trained together into a perfect fighting unit, and were supposed to have died together. The commando felt no grief, an unknown emotion in her warrior caste, but she did mourn her lost sisters. Surviving this suicide mission alone had left her in limbo, ranging this hostile planet like the truant ghost of some unburied corpse. Only duty to the nascent Alexander kept her from mounting a sudden, glorious, and fatal counterattack against her pursuers, the quickest way to join her sisters.

Finally, the search moved on. A trail of clues – disrupted traffic monitors, inexplicably triggered fire alarms, disabled security devices – led her pursuers toward a planetary defense base at the southern edge of the city, which the Imperials moved hastily to reinforce. Alexander had orchestrated these deceptions as the commando lay motionless, teasing pursuit away. Let the Imperials guard their space defenses. The planet's armaments did not interest the compound mind; it wanted information.

Alexander sought secrets.

A tapping came on the metal door of the compartment, a tattoo in the distinctive rhythms of Rix battle language. The commando rolled out of her hiding place, unfolding into a human shape like a marionette pulled by its strings from a box, and found herself facing a small librarian drone. Alexander never narrowcast instructions to the Rixwoman; she was incompatible with the Empire-born mind. Rather, the compound mind guided its commando through a host of avatars – gardening robots, credit terminal screens, traffic signals sputtering battle binary. The drone wheeled about and headed down the hall of the still-evacuated library, its single rubber wheel emitting a mousy squeak as it accelerated. H_rd favored one leg as she followed, circulation returning with painful pricks and needles after the lengthy confinement. The librarian drone moved almost too fast for her, and its squeaking wheel tortured her high-frequency hearing. H_rd felt the slightest temptation to kick the small machine, even though it was a messenger of her god. It had been a long seven hours in that compartment, and the Rix were not *completely* without emotion.

The librarian led h_rd to a staircase, and whirred down a spiral ramp scaled to its small size as she limped down the stairs in pursuit. They descended to a deep sub-basement of the library, a place of low ceilings, narrow hallways choked with unshelved data bricks, and dim red lighting tuned for sensitive drone eyes. The Rixwoman, her circulation restored by the long climb, slipped deftly after the squeaking librarian. In a dark corner of the sub-basement, reached through a heavy blast door and smelling of disuse, though it was *very* clean, the drone halted and extended its dataplug. It rapped on a shelf encased in metal and webbed with security fractals and the Imperial glyph for medical records (h_rd was fluent in Imperial Navy iconography).

H_rd charged her blaster, and cycled the weapon's output down to a cutting torch. She brought the whitehot finger at its muzzle across the dense weave of security fractal, melting circuitry and metal alike.

The library system detected this depredation, and sent a flurry of messages to the local police, the Political Apparatus, and the winter and summer homes of the Master Librarian. All these were intercepted by Alexander, who responded with the official codes for a maintainence procedure. This part of the library was rated for Apparatus-grade secrets, but even the most extensive security did not anticipate the entire *planet*'s infostructure being in the hands of the enemy. In the data-systemic sense, of course, Alexander was not the enemy at all, merely an unwanted aspect of self. Like an autoimmune disease, the defensive measures of the body infometric had been turned against itself.

With the alarm quelled, the librarian drone watched quietly as h_rd worked. The metal of the security case was slowly reduced to burn-fringed panels stacked on the hallway floor. Smoke rose to curl around insensate detectors on the ceiling, and the drone reached its dataplug into the case and began to probe one brick after another, searching for the faint scent of the data it sought: the secret implementation specs of the Empress's confidant, the key that would unlock its recordings of her final moments alive.

The compound mind smiled as fresh information began to trickle in through the narrow pipeline of the drone's dataplug. Alexander was the master, *was the data* here on Legis XV. Whatever secrets it chose to seek would eventually be found.

Soon, another weapon would be in its hands.

Senator

'So I was right.'

Roger Niles had said this at least five times over the last hour. He repeated it with the glazed look of someone told of a friend's unexpected death, the periodic iterations necessary to fight off fresh surges of disbelief.

'You sound surprised,' Oxham said.

'I was hoping to be wrong.'

They were in Niles's den, the most secure room among her senatorial offices. The jagged spires of communication gear reddened in the setting sun, soaking the insect cities in blood. Niles was half in data fugue, trying to predict who the other members of the War Council might be. Oxham wanted fore-warning about the personalities who would surround her in council, the agendas and constituencies that would be repre-sented there.

'One from the Lackey Party,' Niles said. 'Probably not toothless old Higgs, though. The Emperor will pick whoever is really running things in Loyalty these days.'

'Raz imPar Henders.'

'What makes you say that? He's first-term.'

'So am I. He's the new power in Loyalty.'

'His seat isn't even safe.'

'I can feel it, Roger.'

Niles frowned, but Oxham could see his fingers begin to flicker as he redirected his efforts.

The senator hovered in her own synesthetic wash of data, searching the Forum gossip channels and open caucuses, the newswires and polling engines. She wanted to know if her leg-islation, presented and then hastily withdrawn, had left any traces on the body politic. Somewhere in the hordes of media analysts, muckrakers, and political junkies, someone must have wondered what that strange and massive omnibus meant. It was only a matter of time before someone with the interest and expertise would decode the legislation, unraveling the skein of taxes, liens, and laws.

Of course, in a few days – possibly hours – the news of the Rix raid would become public. Hopefully, the reordering of power alignments and alliances, the panicked shift of markets and resources, the tidal data-surge of war would overwhelm any notice of her legislation. That was fine with Oxham. It was one thing to take jabs at the Emperor in times of peace, quite another when Empire was threatened, and still another when sitting on his War Council. Most importantly, the young senator didn't want it to look as if her seat on the council had been bought with the withdrawal of the legislation.

At least, it hadn't seemed that way to her.

'Someone from the Plague Axis, as well,' Niles announced.

'Why, for heaven's sake?'

'I can feel it,' he said flatly.

Oxham smiled. Thirty years into their shared career, and he still hated when she made appeals to her empathy. It offended his sense of politics as a human enterprise, as *the* human enterprise. Niles still felt that the offshoots of synesthetic implants were somehow . . . superhuman.

But the Plague Axis? He must be kidding. The Risen Empire was riven between the living and the dead, and the Plague Axis were a sort of twilight zone. They were the carriers of ancient diseases, and the repositories of the old congenital defects. When humanity had started governing its own genetic destiny millennia before, too few traits had been selected for, and hordes of information irretrievably lost. Too late, eugenists had realized that most 'undesirable' traits concealed advantages: sickle cell conferred resistance to dormant diseases; autism was inextricably linked to genius; certain cancers stabilized whole populations in ways that were not entirely understood. The Plague Axis, germline-natural humans subject to every whim of evolution, were essential to maintain the limited diversity of an overengineered population. They were the controls in the vast experiment that was Imperial humanity.

But to have them represented in the War Council? Oxham might have her own infirmity, her own madness, but she still shivered at the thought of lepers.

The senator brought forward the list she and Niles had constructed. By tradition, the council would have nine members, including the Emperor. Balance was the main priority; for the Senate to delegate real warmaking power to the council, all factions had to be represented. The major power blocs of Empire were relatively fixed, but the individual pieces that would fit into each of those places at the table were as variable as cards in a hand of poker. How the Emperor filled those spaces would determine the course of this war.

Interrupting these thoughts, a chime sounded in her secondary hearing, a powerful signal that broke through all other data. The note was low-pitched, the steady, awesome sound of the largest pipe on a church organ. But it carried a froth of higher frequencies: the indistinct breath of a distant sea, the fluttering of birds' wings, the stray high pitches of an orchestra tuning. The sound was sovereign, unmistakable.

'Council is called,' Nara Oxham said.

She could see the overlays of secondary sight falling away from Niles's face, his attention slowly focusing on the here and now, like some subterranean creature emerging into unfamiliar sunlight.

With his dataveil removed, Niles regarded her through

limpid eyes, his powerful mind for once reflected in his gaze. He spoke carefully.

'Nara, do you remember the crowds?'

He meant the crowds on Vasthold, back in her first campaigns, when she had finally put the terror of madness behind her.

'Of course, Roger. I remember.'

Unlike those of most of the Empire, Vasthold's politics had never become hostage to the media feeds. There, politics was a kind of street theater. Issues were fought out face-to-face in the dense cities, in the house-to-house combat of street parades, in basement gatherings, and around park bonfires. Impromptu debates, demonstrations, and out-and-out brawls were the order of the day. To escape her old fear of masses of people, Oxham had agreed to deliver a nominating speech at a political rally. But with a willful perversity, she had only partially suppressed her empathy that day, daring the childhood demons to visit again. At first, the roiling psyches of the crowd assumed their familiar shape, a massive beast of ego and conflict, a hungry storm that wanted to consume her, incorporate her into its raging glut of passions. But Oxham had become an adult, her own ego grown stronger behind the protective barrier of the apathy drug. With her image and voice augmented by the public address system, she shouted down the old demons, rode the throng like a wild horse, worked their emotions with words, gestures, even the rhythm of her breathing. That day, she found that on the other side of terror could be found . . . power.

Niles nodded; he had watched those powerful memories cross her face.

'We're very far from them now, those crowds. In the pretense of this place, it's easy to forget the real world that you came here to represent.'

'I haven't forgotten, Roger. Remember, I haven't been awake as long as you. For me, it's only been two years, not ten.'

One hand went to his graying hair, a smile on his face.

'Just remember then,' he said. 'Your cunning whorls of legislation will now represent acts of war: violence will be done and lives lost in the name of every decision you make.'

'Of course, Roger. You have to understand, the Rix frontier isn't as far away as all that. Not for me.'

A frown appeared on his face. She hadn't told anyone, not even Niles, about her affair with Laurent Zai. It had seemed such a brief and sudden thing. And now it was, in Niles's framework, over a decade ago.

'Someone very close to me is there, Niles. He's at the front. I'll keep him in mind, as a stand-in for all those distant, threatened lives.'

Roger Niles's eyes narrowed, his high forehead wrinkling with surprise. His powerful mind must be searching for whom she might mean. Oxham was glad to know that she could still keep some things secret from her chief advisor. She was pleased that she had told no one; the affair remained hers and Laurent's alone.

Senator Nara Oxham rose. The sound of the Imperial summons hadn't faded completely from her secondary hearing; the chime shimmered like the toll of some giant bell vibrating into perpetuity. Oxham wondered if it might actually get louder should she fail to answer its summons.

Niles's face became distant again, easing back into data. Oxham knew that after she had gone, he would worry her words, and would plumb the vast store of his datatrove to discover whom she meant. And that eventually he would discover Laurent Zai.

And it crossed her mind that by then, her lover might already be dead.

'I take your concerns with me, Roger. This war is very real.'

'Thank you, Senator. The trust of Vasthold is with you.'

The old ritual phrase, to which Senators were sworn before they left Vasthold for fifty years. Niles uttered it so sadly that she turned to look at his face again. But already the veil had fallen over him. He descended into his virtual realm, searching an empire's worth of data for answers to . . . a war.

For a moment, he looked small and forlorn under his towering equipment, the weight of Empire upon him, and she stopped at the door. She had to show him, to let Niles see the token of love she carried.

'Roger.'

Oxham held up a small black object in her hand, striped with yellow warning circuitry. A single-purpose remote, encoded with a Senatorial Urgent message. It was marked with her personal privilege – highest priority transmission over the Empire's entanglement net, one-time encryption, sealed eyes-only under Penalty of Blood – and keyed to her DNA, her pheromonal profile, and voiceprint.

Niles looked at the object, his eyes clearing. She had his attention.

'I may be using this while sitting in the War Council. Will it work from the Diamond Palace?'

'Yes. Legally speaking, the Rubicon Pale extends from the Forum to wherever you go, along a nanometer-wide gerrymander.'

She smiled, visualizing this baroque legal fiction.

'How long will it take the message to get to Legis XV?'

His eyebrows raised at the planet's name. Now he knew that her lover was truly at the front.

'How long is the message?'

'One word.'

Niles nodded. 'Entangled communications are instantaneous, but unless the shared quantum packets the receiver is using were physically transported directly from Home—'

'They were,' she said.

'So he's—'

'On a warship.'

'Then, no time at all.' Niles paused, searching Oxham's eyes for some sign of her intentions. 'May I ask what the message is?'

'Don't,' she said.

Executive Officer

Hobbes stood nervously at attention as Zai worked gestural codes at the small interface beside the observation blister's door.

She stared down into the void. The usual vertigo created by the transparent floor was gone, replaced by the crushing weight of failure. A dead, empty feeling pulsed in her gut. A bright taste like a metal coin under the tongue fouled her mouth. Her careful study of the hostage rescue, the sleepless hours spent poring over every frame of the engagement from dozens of viewpoints, had amounted to nothing. She had not saved her captain, had only managed to make him furious.

There seemed to be no way to bend the rigid spine of Zai's Vadan upbringing. No way to convince him that it had been the politicals and not military personnel who had botched the rescue. The initiate had gone down against the captain's protests, waving an imperial writ; why couldn't Captain Zai see that he was blameless?

At least they should take the evidence before a military court. Zai was a hero, an elevated officer. He couldn't throw his life away for the sake of brutal, pointless tradition.

Executive Officer Hobbes was from a Utopian world, an

anomaly among the military classes. She had rejected the hedonistic ways of her own homeworld, attracted by the rituals of the grays, their traditions and discipline. Their lives of service made the grays otherworldly to Katherie, uninterested in the brief pleasures of the flesh. For Hobbes, Captain Laurent Zai embodied this gray stoicism, quiet and strong on his cold bridge, his craggy face uncorrected by cosmetic surgery.

But underneath, Hobbes could see the wounded humanity in him: the marks of his unbelievable suffering on Dhantu, the melancholy dignity with which he carried himself, the regret every time he lost a 'man.'

And now her captain's sense of honor demanded suicide of him. Suddenly, the religious surety and gray traditions that Hobbes found so compelling seemed simply barbaric, a brutal web in which her captain had trapped himself, a willful and pathetic blindness. Zai's acquiescence was far more bitter than his anger.

He turned from the controls.

'Steady yourself,' he ordered.

The floor lurched, as if the ship had accelerated. Hobbes barely kept her footing, the universe become briefly unhinged around her. Then the transparent surface under her stabilized, and she saw what had happened. The blister had become a true bubble, floating free of the ship, tethered only by the ship's gravity generators, filled only with the air and heat trapped within its walls. The gravity felt wrong, cast across the void by the *Lynx*'s generators to create a tentative *up* in this small pocket of air.

Hobbes's vertigo returned with a vengeance.

'We can talk freely now, Hobbes.'

She nodded slowly, careful not to disturb her plaintive inner ear.

'You don't seem to understand what's at stake here,' Zai

said. 'For the first time in sixteen centuries, a member of the Imperial household has *died*. And she was lost not to a freak accident, but to enemy action.'

'Enemy action, sir?' she dared.

'Yes, dammit. The *Rix* caused all this!' he shouted. 'It does-n't matter who pulled the trigger of that blaster. Whether it was a Rix playing dead or an imbecile political gone mad from an insertion injury: it doesn't matter. The Empress is dead. They won; we lost.'

Hobbes focused on her boots, willing a visible floor into existence below them.

'You're about to have command of this vessel, Hobbes. You must understand that with command comes responsibility. I ordered that rescue. I must stand by its results, no matter what.'

She looked at the space that separated them from the *Lynx*. No sound vibrations could cross that gap; the captain had made sure of that. She could speak freely.

'You objected to the initiate going down, sir.'

'He had a writ, Hobbes. My objection was pointless posturing.'

'Your rescue plan was sound, sir. The Emperor made the mistake, giving those fools a writ.'

The captain sucked a harsh breath in through his teeth. However cautious Zai was being, Hobbes knew that he hadn't expected to hear words like this.

'That's *sedition*, Executive Officer.'

'It's the truth, sir.'

He took two steps toward her, closer than Vadan fastidi-ousness had ever allowed him before. He spoke clearly, in a voice just above a whisper.

'Listen, Hobbes. I'm dead. A ghost. There is no tomorrow for me, whatsoever. No *truth* can save me. You seem con-fused about that. And you also seem to think that the *truth* will protect you and the rest of the *Lynx*'s officers. It will not.'

She could barely meet his gaze. A few flecks of saliva borne on his harsh words had reached her face. They stung her; they were shameful. The bright sun was rising behind the bulk of the *Lynx*. The blister's skin was polarized, but she could feel the temperature rising in the unregulated bubble. A trickle of sweat ran under one arm.

'If there are any more briefings like the one a few minutes ago, you'll be killing yourself *and* my other officers. I will not permit it.'

She swallowed, blinked in the suddenly harsh sunlight. Dizziness rose in her. Was the oxygen running out so fast?

'Stop trying to save me, Hobbes! That's an order. Is it clear enough?'

She just wanted him to stop. She wanted to return to the solid boundaries of the ship. To surety and order. Safety from this void.

'Yes, sir.'

'Thank you,' he spat.

Captain Zai turned and took a step away, facing the bauble of Legis XV hanging in the blackness. He uttered a command, and she felt the tug of the frigate reclaiming its tiny satellite.

They said nothing more as the blister reattached itself to the *Lynx*. When the door opened, Zai dismissed her with a wave. She could see the black, single-purpose remote in his hand. His blade of error.

'Report to the bridge, Executive Officer. You will be needed there shortly.'

To take command. A field promotion, they would call it.

'Do not disturb me again.'

The executive officer obeyed, stepping from the blister

into the rush of cool, fresh air that surged from the *Lynx*. Hobbes felt she should glance back at her captain, if only to create a last memory to replace that of his angry, spitting face, centimeters from hers. But she couldn't bring herself to turn around.

Instead, she wiped her face and ran.

Commando

The librarian drone puttered among the data bricks, a dull-witted child unsure of which toy to play with. It moved fitfully, searching for some secret entombed within their crisp, rectangular forms. H_rd, having emptied the security case, sat patiently by, listening for any sound from above.

At first, the library basement had made her nervous. The Rix didn't like being trapped belowground. She and her drop-sisters had been raised in space, tumbling into gravity wells only on training exercises and combat missions. H_rd felt crushed under the weight of metal and stone. An hour ago, she had left the fidgeting drone behind and reconnoitered the ground floor, installing motion alarms at each entrance. But the surrounding streets were empty; her pursuers had clearly moved on, following some false trail created by Alexander. And this part of the city was still evacuated from the militia's search.

She and her drone had the library to themselves.

It was hard to imagine that the crude little device was actually animated by Alexander, an intelligence of planetary scale. The drone's single wheel allowed it to whir efficiently through the neat stacks, but here among the debris of the ruined case it was reduced to unsure, stuttering motions: a unicyclist negotiating a construction site. H_rd watched the comical display with a smile. Even the company of a speech-less robot was better than being alone.

Suddenly, the drone seemed to flinch, plunging its data-plug farther into the brick before it with an obscene hunger. After a moment of vibrating wildly, the little device released the brick and spun around. Dodging debris with renewed vigor, it took off down the narrow aisle at top speed.

H_rd stood slowly, her body rippling as she went through a two-second regime that stretched each of her eleven hundred muscles in turn. No point in rushing; the drone could not outrun her. With a single leap, h_rd cleared the rubbish of her vandalism, then turned back toward the pile. She set her blaster low and wide, and sprayed the data bricks with enough radiation to erase their contents, and any clues as to what Alexander had found here. The fire suppression node above her head chirped, but was overridden before it could spray any foam.

H_rd turned and ran. In a few long-legged strides, she was right behind the little drone, strange companions in the dark stacks of the abandoned library. The whine of its monowheel blended with the subtler, ultrasonic whir of her servomotors.

She followed it up the ramps, through the basement levels and to the ground floor. The drone rolled squeaking among the staff desks, and through a portal in the wall scaled exactly to its size, like a door for pets. This obstacle course was designed for the drone's use, not that of two-meter amazons, and the challenge put a smile back on the commando's face. H_rd dove, leapt, and weaved, sticking close to her small charge, which brought her to a back office. The drone skidded to a halt beside an unruly pile of plastic squares, roughly the size of a human hand.

The Rixwoman picked one of the devices up. It was a secured handscreen, a rare physical storage and display device in a universe of omnipresent infostructure and secondary sight. Commandos, of course, fought on hostile worlds where the local infostructure was inaccessible, and h_rd had used such a device before. A library of this type would use them to allow its patrons to exit with sensitive information, the kind that had to stay outside the public sphere. The handscreen would be equipped with limited intelligence and governors to keep the wrong persons from accessing its contents.

The drone plugged into one of the devices, and the two were locked in a momentary, shuddering embrace. Then the screen hummed to life.

The Rixwoman took it from the drone. On the top page was a map of the planet, a route marked in pulsing colors. She worked the limited interface with her quick fingers, and found that the machine contained thousands of pages, a detailed plan for reaching her next goal: the entangled communications facility in the polar sink. The gateway of all information into and out of the Legis system.

Four thousand kilometers away.

H_rd sighed, and looked accusingly at the little drone.

Every Rix sibling group who had volunteered for this raid had realized that it was fundamentally a suicide mission. To plant the seed of a compound mind was a glorious blow against the Risen Empire, and the raiders had succeeded beyond all expectation. For the first time, a Rix mind had emerged upon an Imperial world. That a full-scale war might result was irrelevant. The Rix did not distinguish between states of war and peace with the various political entities that bordered upon their serpentine amalgam of bases. Their society was a constant jihad, a ceaseless missionary effort to propagate compound minds.

But four thousand kilometers through hostile territory? Alone?

Generally, suicide missions at least had the advantage of being brief.

H_rd flipped among the pages on the handscreen, and found a map of the planetary maglev system. At least she wouldn't have to walk. She also discovered the medical records of a particular conscript in the Legis militia, one who resembled h_rd, and had expertise necessary for the mission. The Rix commando realized that Alexander wanted her to go undercover, to pass as a standard Imperial human. How distasteful.

She moved toward the library exit. Best to take advantage of the evacuated streets while she could.

The squeal of the drone's wheel followed h_rd to the door. It darted in front of her, almost spinning out of control in its haste to block her path.

H_rd was brought up short. Did it think it was *coming*?

Then she realized its purpose. Alexander had downloaded the precious secret it sought through the memory of the little drone. There might be some residue, some backup somewhere from which the Imperials could extract what Alexander had learned.

The commando set her blaster to high, and leveled it at the drone. The machine backed away. That was just Alexander, being careful to keep h_rd out of the blast radius. But the little device seemed nervous on its single, unsteady wheel, as if it knew it was about to die.

H_rd felt a strange reluctance to destroy the drone. For a few hours, it had been a companion here on this lonely, unRix world, a little sister of sorts. That was an odd way to think of the drone, which was an embodiment of one of her gods. But she felt as if she were killing a friend.

Still, orders were orders.

She closed her eyes and pressed the firing stud.

Plasma leapt from the mouth of the blaster, disintegrating the drone in a gout of fire and metal parts, which h_rd leapt over, passing into the dark night beyond.

Running between quiet buildings, she shook off the feeling of loneliness. Alexander was still here all around her, watching through every doorway monitor, concealing her passage with feints and deceptions. She was the compound mind's one human agent on this hostile world: beloved.

H_rd ran fast and hard. She was doing the will of the gods.

Senator

This time, the journey to the Diamond Palace was by tunnel, a route Senator Oxham hadn't known existed. The trip lasted seconds; the acceleration registered by her middle ear seemed insufficient for the distance.

Oxham was met by a young aspirant in the Political Apparatus. His black uniform creaked – new leather – as they walked down the broad hallway. Although her apathy was set very low to allow her abilities full rein for the first session of the council, she felt nothing from the aspirant. He must have been particularly susceptible to Apparatus conditioning. Perhaps he had been chosen for that very reason. His mind was tangibly barren; she sensed only tattered remainders of will, the cold stumps of a burned forest.

She was glad to reach the council chamber, if only to escape the chilly umbra of the man's psychic absence.

The chamber of the War Council, like most of the Diamond Palace, was formed of structured carbon. Woven throughout the palace's crystalline walls were airscreen projectors, recording devices, and an Imperially huge reserve of data. It was rumored that within the structure's expansive processors an entity with limited agency had arisen, a sort of minor compound mind that the Emperor indulged. The palace was abundant with devices and intelligence, and infused with the mystique that comes of being a focus of awesome power, but its floor had a mineral solidity under Senator Oxham's feet. It felt as dumb as stone.

She was the last to arrive. The others waited in silence as she took a seat.

The chamber itself was small compared with the other Imperial enclosures that Oxham had seen. There were no gardens, no high columns, no wildlife or tricks with gravity. Not even a table. A shallow, circular pit was cut into the glassy floor, and the nine counselors sat at its edge, like some midnight cabal gathered around a disused fountain. The floor of the pit was not the same hypercarbon as the rest of the palace. It was opaque, an off-white, pearly horn.

There was a simplicity to the setting that Oxham had to admire.

Her artificial secondary senses had faded as she approached the chamber; now she was cut off from the purr of newsfeed and politics, communications and data overlays. As she sat down, the senator was struck by the sudden silence that was the absence of the summons, the grave tone in her head finally extinguished.

It was quiet, here in this diamond hall.

'War Council is in session,' said the Emperor.

Oxham's eyes took in the council members, and she found that Niles's predictions, as usual, had proved very accurate. One counselor was present from each of the four major parties, including herself. She'd been right about Raz imPar Henders representing Loyalty. The counselors from the Utopian Party and the Expansionists were both as Niles had predicted. And his wildest guess also proved correct: an envoy from the Plague Axis, its gender concealed by the necessary biosuit, was seated at a lonely end of the circle.

The two dead counselors were both military, as always. One admiral and one general. The wild card, as Niles called the traditionally nonpolitical and nonmilitary seat on the council, was held by the intellectual property magnate Ax Milnk. Oxham had never seen her in person; the woman's truly extraordinary wealth kept her in a constant womb of security, usually on one of her private moons around Home's sister planet, Shame. Oxham sensed Milnk's discomfort at being removed from her usual retinue of bodyguards. A misplaced fear: the Diamond Palace was safer than the grave.

'To be absolutely precise,' the dead general said, 'we are not yet a war council proper. The Senate doesn't even know of our existence yet. We act now only with the ordinary powers of the Risen Emperor: control of the Navy, the Apparatus, and the Living Will.'

Power enough, thought Oxham. The military, the political service, and the unfathomable wealth of the Living Will — the accumulated property of those who had been elevated, which was willed to the Emperor as a matter of custom. One of the driving forces of the Eighty Worlds' rampant capitalism was that the very rich were almost always elevated. Another was that the next generation had to start all over: inheritance was for the lower classes.

'I am sure that once the Senate is informed of these Rix depredations, we will be given full status,' Raz imPar Henders said, performing his lackey function. He intoned the words prayerfully, like some not very bright village proctor reassuring his flock of heaven. Oxham had to remind herself not to underestimate the man. As she'd sensed in the last few sessions, Senator Henders had begun to take control of the Loyalty Party, even though he was only midway through his first term. His planet wasn't even a safe seat, swinging between Secularist and Loyal representatives for the last three centuries. He must be a brilliant tactician, or a favorite of the Emperor. By its very nature,

Loyalty was a party of the old guard, bound by staid traditions of succession. Henders was an anomaly to be carefully watched.

'Perhaps we should leave the question of our status to the Senate,' Oxham said. Her brash words were rewarded by a flush of surprise from Henders. Oxham let the ripple of her statement settle, then added, 'As per tradition.'

At this last word, Henders nodded reflexively.

'True,' the Risen Emperor agreed, a smile playing in the subtle muscles around his mouth. After centuries of absolute power, His Majesty must be enjoying the tension of this mix. 'We may have misspoken ourselves. The Provisional War Council is in session, then.'

Henders settled himself visibly. However keen a politician, the man was terribly easy to read. He had been ruffled by the exchange; he couldn't bear to hear the words of the Risen One contradicted, even on technical grounds.

'The Senate will ratify us soon enough, when they learn what has happened on Legis XV,' Henders said coldly.

Nara Oxham felt her breath catch. Here it was, news of the rescue attempt. The pleasure of rattling Henders was extinguished, reduced to the helpless anxiety of a hospital waiting room. Her awareness narrowed to the face of the gray general who had spoken. She searched his pallid, cold visage for clues, her empathy almost useless with this ancient, lifeless man.

Niles had been right. This was no game. This was lives saved or lost.

'Three hours ago,' the dead general continued, 'we received confirmation that the Empress Anastasia was killed in cold blood by her captors, even as rescue reached her.'

The chamber was silent. Oxham felt her heartbeat pounding in one temple, her own reaction reinforced by the empathic forces in the room. Senator Henders's visceral

horror arced through Nara. Ax Milnk's reflexive fear of insta-
bility and chaos welled up in her like panic. As if her teeth
were biting glass, Nara experienced the grim pain of the general remembering ancient battles. And throughout the
chamber, a sovereign shudder built like the approach of some
great hurricane – the group realization that there was finally,
irrevocably, certainly going to be war.

As when she awoke from coldsleep, Oxham felt overwhelmed by the emotions around her. She felt herself dragged
down again toward madness, into the formless chaos of the
group mind. Even the voices of the capital's billions intruded;
the white-noise scream of unbridled politics and commerce,
the raw, screeching metal of the city's mindstorm all threatened to take her over.

Her fingers fumbled for her apathy bracelet, releasing a
dose of the drug. The familiar hiss of transdermal injection
calmed her, a totem to hang on to until the empathy suppres-
sant could take effect. The drug acted quickly. She felt reality
rush back into the room, crowding out the wheeling demons
as her ability dulled. The awesome, somber silence returned.

The dead admiral was talking now, giving particulars of
the rescue attempt. Troops descending in their blazing small-
craft, a firefight sprawling across the great palace, and one last
Rix commando playing dead, killing the Child Empress even
as the battle was won.

The words meant nothing to Nara Oxham. All she knew
was that her lover was a dead man, doomed by an Error of
Blood. He would settle his affairs, prepare his crew for his
death, and then plunge a dull ceremonial blade into his belly.
The power of tradition, the relentless fixity of gray culture, his
own sense of honor would compel him to complete the act.

Oxham pulled the message remote from her sleeve pocket.
She felt its tiny mouth nibble at her palm, tasting sweat and
flesh. Verifying her identity, it hummed with approval. Nara

pressed the device to her throat, unwatched as the council attended to the droning admiral.

'Send,' she said, at the threshold between voice and whisper.

The device vibrated for a moment with life, then went still, its purpose expended.

She imagined the tiny packet of information slipping down the thread of its Rubicon gerrymander, inviolate as it passed through the palace's brilliant facets. Then it would thrust into the torrent of the capital's infostructure, a water-walking insect braving a raging river. But the packet possessed senatorial privilege; it would exercise absolute priority, surging past the queue awaiting off-world transmission, flitting through the web of repeaters, as fleet as an Imperial decree.

The message would reach an entanglement facility somewhere buried under kilometers of lead, a store of half-particles whose doppelgängers waited on Imperial warships, or had been transported by near-lightspeed craft to other planets in the realm. With unbelievable precision, certain photons suspended in a weakly interacting array would be collapsed, thrust from their coherent state into the surety of measurement. And ten light-years away, their doppelgängers on the *Lynx* would react, also falling from the knife's edge. The pattern of this change – the set of positions in the array that had discohered – would comprise a message to the *Lynx*.

Just reach him in time, she willed the missive.

Then Senator Nara Oxham forced her attention back to the cold planes of the council chamber, and forcibly banished all thoughts of Laurent Zai from her mind.

She had a war to prosecute.

Captain

The blade rested in Zai's hand, black against black infinity, waiting only for him to squeeze.

Hard to believe what that one gesture would trigger. Convulsions throughout the ship as it shifted into combat configuration, the dash to battle stations of three hundred men, weapons crash-charged and wheeling as AI searched vainly for incoming enemy craft. Not entirely a waste of energy, Zai thought. War was coming here to the Rix frontier, and it would be good practice for the crew of the *Lynx* to run an unexpected battle-stations drill. Perhaps performing the EVA maneuvers of a body recovery – their captain's corpse – would impress them with the seriousness of being on the front line of a new Rix incursion.

Not that he'd meant this means of suicide as a training exercise. Bringing the ship to emergency status was simply the only way to override the safeties that protected the observation blister.

What a strange way to kill myself, he thought. Laurent Zai wondered what perversity of spirit had led him to choose this particular blade of error. Decompression was hardly an instantaneous death. How long did it take a human being to die in hard vacuum? Ten seconds? Thirty? And those moments would be painful. The rupture of eyes and lungs, the bursting of blood vessels in the brain, the explosive expansion of nitrogen bubbles in the knee joints.

Probably too much pain for the human mind to register, too many extraordinary violations of the body all at once. At what point was a chorus of agonies overwhelmed by sheer surprise? Zai wondered. However long he stood here facing the blackness and contemplating what was about to happen, his nervous system was unlikely to be in any way prepared.

Of course, the traditional ceremony of error – a dull weapon thrust into your belly, watching as your pulse splattered onto a ritual mat – was hardly pleasant. But as an elevated man, Laurent Zai could choose any means of suicide. He didn't have to suffer. There were painless ways out, even quite pleasurable ones. A century ago, the elevated Transbishop Mater Silver had killed herself with halcionide, gasping with orgasm as she went.

But Zai wanted to feel the void. However painful, he wanted to know what had lurked all those years on the other side of the hullalloy. He was in love with space, emptiness, always had been. Now he would meet it face to face.

In any case, his decision was made. Zai had chosen, and like all command officers, he knew the dangers of second-guessing oneself. Besides, he had other things to think about.

Laurent Zai closed his eyes and sighed. The blister was sealed from the crew by his command. He would be alone here until the end; there was no longer any need to show strength for the sake of his shipmates. One by one, he relaxed the rigid controls he had forced upon his thoughts. For the first time since his error had been committed, Zai allowed himself the luxury of thinking about her – Senator Nara Oxham.

By Imperial Absolute, it had been ten years since he had last seen his lover. But in the long acceleration spinward, the Time Thief had stolen more than eight of those years, leaving Zai's memory – the color of her eyes, the scent of her – still fresh. And Nara also suspended herself in time. As a senator, she spent the frequent legislative breaks in stasis sleep, enfolded in a cocoon of temporal arrest. That image of her, a sleeping princess waiting for him, had sustained him for these last relative years. He'd entertained the romantic notion that their romance would beat time, lasting through the long, cold decades of separation, intact while the universe reeled forward.

It had seemed that way. Zai was elevated, immortal. Nara was a senator, almost certainly eligible for elevation once she renounced her Secularist deathwish. Even the pinkest politicians sometimes did, ultimately. They were two immortals, safe from the ravages of time, preserved from their long separations by relativity itself.

But time, it seemed, was not the only enemy. Zai opened his eyes and regarded the black remote before him.

It was death, in his hand.

Death was the real thief, of course. It always had been. Love was fragile and hapless compared to it. Since humans had first gained self-awareness, they had been stalked by the specter of extinction, of nothingness. And since the first humanlike primate had learned to smash another's skull, death was the ultimate arbiter of power. It was no wonder that the Risen Emperor was worshiped as a god. To those who served him faithfully, he offered salvation from humanity's oldest enemy.

And demanded death itself for those who failed him.

Best to get it over with, Laurent Zai thought. Tradition had to be served.

Zai touched his hands together as if to pray.

His stomach clenched. He smelled it on his hands, that shame from childhood, when he had prayed to the Emperor for taller classmates. He felt the bile that had risen on that afternoon at the soccer field, when he felt with childish surety that he himself had caused the Krupp Reich plague. The heavy-handed Vadan propaganda still informed him somehow. He smelled vomit on his hands.

And instead of praying to the Emperor, instead of saying the ritual words of suicide, he whispered, 'Nara, I'm so sorry,' again and again.

The remote was hard in his hand, but Laurent Zai didn't reach for death. Not yet.

Message for Captain Laurent Zai, came the prompt in second sight.

He opened his eyes and shook his head in disbelief.

'Hobbes . . .' he sighed. He had left specific orders. Would the woman not let him die?

But his executive officer did not respond. Zai looked more closely at the hovering missive, and swallowed. It was eyes-only, under penalty of blood. It had bypassed the bridge altogether, looking for him alone, under senatorial seal.

Senatorial.

Nara. She knew.

The situation here on Legis XV was subject to the highest order of secrecy. The *Lynx's* marines had locked down the planet in the first hours of the crisis, occupying the polar entanglement facility that allowed translight communication. Even the ubiquitous Rix compound mind was cut off from the rest of the Empire.

Among the Senate, only a select few would know that the Empress was dead. The propaganda machine of the Political Apparatus would prepare the body public very carefully for the news. But evidently Nara knew. Senator Oxham must have risen high in the ranks of her party these last ten years.

Or could the message be a coincidence? Surely that was absurd; Nara wouldn't contact him casually with a message sealed under penalty of blood. She had to know about his error.

He didn't want to open the message, didn't want to see Nara's words borne by his defeat, his extinction. Laurent Zai had promised to return, and had failed her. *Use the blade now,* he told himself. *Spare yourself this pain.*

But a senatorial seal was an agent of some intelligence. It

would know that it had reached the *Lynx* successfully, and that Zai wasn't dead yet. It would report back to Nara that he had rejected it, just as any intelligent missive would. The seal would record his last betrayal.

He had to read it. Anything less would be cruel.

Laurent Zai sighed. A life spent in service of tradition, but he was apparently not destined to die cleanly.

He opened his palm before him as if to receive a gift, that first interface gesture taught to children.

The senatorial seal expanded before him, cut with the crimson bar sinister of Vasthold. Nara Oxham's formal titles were vaguely visible in tertiary sight.

'Captain Laurent Zai,' he said to it.

The seal didn't break. Its security AI wasn't satisfied yet. Thin lasers from the *Lynx* proper washed Zai's hands, covering them with a shimmering red patina. He turned them over, letting the lasers read the whorls of his fingertips and palms. Then they moved up and played across his eyes.

Still the seal remained.

'Godspite!' he swore. Senatorial security was far more cautious than the military's.

He pressed his right wrist against the signet on his left shoulder. The smart metal of the signet vibrated softly, tasting his skin and sweat. There was a pause as DNA was sequenced, pheromones sniffed, blood latticed.

Finally the seal broke.

The message spilled out, in senatorial white against the depthless black of space. It hovered there, text only, absolutely still and silent, as clear as something real and solid. Just one word.

The message said:

Don't.

Zai blinked, then shook his head.

He had the feeling that this would not be easy. That nothing would ever be easy again.

Executive Officer

Katherie Hobbes felt small in the shipmaster's chair.

She had called the command officers to the bridge, wanting her senior staff at their stations when the battle-stations clarion sounded. None of them questioned her. As they arrived, they noted her position at the con, met her eyes briefly, and silently took their positions.

Hobbes wondered how many of the senior staff would accept her as acting captain. She had never fit in with the other officers on board Zai's ship. Her Utopian upbringing was inescapably obvious; the cosmetic surgery that was common on her home planet made her beauty too obvious here on the very gray *Lynx*.

The staff looked duly serious, at least. Hobbes had set the temperature of the bridge to ten degrees centigrade, a sign that every member of Zai's crew knew well. Their breaths were phantoms barely visible in the dim, action-ready lighting. She knew there would be no mistakes during the drill, or during the body recovery. However the politicals had screwed up the rescue, this crew felt they had failed their captain once. They were all determined not to let that happen again, Hobbes was confident.

But the shipmaster's chair still seemed gigantic. The airscreens that surrounded her were fewer than at the ExO's station, but they were more complex, crowded with overrides, feedback shunts, and command icons. The airscreens at her old position were simply for monitoring. These had power.

From this chair, Hobbes could exercise control over every aspect of the *Lynx*.

Such potential power at her fingertips felt perilous. It was like standing at the edge of a cliff, or aiming a tactical warhead at a large city. One nudge to the controls, one sudden movement, and far too much would happen. Irrecoverably.

From the chair's higher vantage, she could see the entirety of the huge bridge airscreen. It showed the *Lynx*, scaled small but ready to come into sudden bloom when Captain Zai unleashed his blade of error. The deployment of the energy-sink manifold alone would increase the vessel's size by an order of magnitude. The *Lynx* would bristle like some spiny, startled creature, the power of its drive flowing into weapons and shields, geysers of plasma readied, ranks of drones primed. But one soft part of its lethal anatomy would be sloughed off, almost as an afterthought. With its integrity field snapped off, the observation blister would explode like a toy balloon.

Her captain would tumble out into naked space, and die.

Hobbes reviewed the steps she'd taken to try to save her captain. The images from the short firefight still played in her mind when she closed her eyes. She and the tactical staff had even synthed a physical model of the palace in the forward mess, had painstakingly traced the movement of every commando, every marine during the encounter. Hobbes had *known* that there must be something there to absolve Zai of responsibility, if only she could search harder, longer, build more models and simulations. The possibility that there was simply nothing to find, that the situation was hopeless, had never crossed her mind.

But now she remembered the look on Laurent's face as he had dressed her down, and Hobbes despaired. His anger had broken something inside her, something she hadn't realized was there, that she had foolishly allowed to grow. And the bitter shame of it was that she actually thought Laurent might save himself for her: Katherie Hobbes.

But that foolishness would be lost forever in the next few minutes, along with her captain.

Hobbes's fingers grasped the wide arms of the con. All this power within arm's reach, and she had never felt more helpless.

She looked down at the *Lynx* in the airscreen. Soon, it would unfold into battle configuration, suddenly and terribly beautiful. The deed would be done. Hobbes almost *wanted* the clarion to sound. At least then this waiting would be over.

'Executive Officer.'

The voice came from behind her.

'I'll take the chair now.'

Even as her mind seemed to crash, the imperatives of duty and habit took over her body. Hobbes stood and turned, taking one respectful step away from the station that wasn't hers. Vision reddened at the edges, as if an acceleration blackout were closing in.

'Captain on the bridge,' she managed.

The confused bridge crew snapped to attention.

He nodded and took the shipmaster's chair, and she took careful steps back toward her usual station. She slipped into its familiar contours still in shock.

She looked up at Zai.

'The drill we spoke of is canceled, Hobbes,' he said quietly. 'Not postponed. Canceled.'

She nodded dumbly.

He turned to regard the airscreen, and Hobbes saw the other officers quickly turn their startled faces to their own stations. A few looked at her questioningly. She could only swallow and stare at her captain.

Zai looked down at the image of the *Lynx*, and smiled.

If Hobbes understood him correctly, Laurent Zai had just

thown away all honor, all dignity, every tradition he had been raised upon.

And he looked . . . happy.

Her words had made a difference to him. For a long, strange moment, Katherie couldn't take her gaze from the captain's face.

Then a troubled look came over Zai. He glanced sharply down at her.

'Hobbes?'

'Sir?'

'Pray tell me. Why is it so damned cold on my bridge?'

■■■■

TEN YEARS EARLIER (IMPERIAL ABSOLUTE)

Senator-Elect

Laurent began talking about Dhantu quite suddenly.

Nara could feel his injuries, the strange absences in his body. The prosthetics were lifeless and invisible to her empathy, but psychic phantom limbs overlay them, hovering like nervous ghosts. Laurent Zai's body was still whole in his own mind. One arm, both legs, even the cavity of the artificial digestive tract glowed hyperreal, as if Laurent were a photograph garishly retouched by hand.

The apathy in Nara's system was slowly losing effect as the drug filtered from her blood, her empathy growing stronger by the hour. Oxham's abilities recovered from chemical suppression in two stages: first with a sudden rush of increased sensitivity, then more gradually, a timid animal emerging after a storm.

Even here in the refuge of her polar house, thousands of kilometers from the nearest city, Nara was anxious about complete withdrawal. Laurent's presence in this sanctum was an unknown quantity. He was her first guest here at the polar estate, and the first person in whose presence she had totally freed her empathic ability since coming to the Imperial home world.

She wondered what had possessed her to bring the gray warrior here. Why had she been so open about her childhood? He was, after all, one of the enemy. Nara tasted embarrassment now, the long discussion of her own madness flat and metallic in her mouth. And the sting of Laurent's words: *that's insane*.

She was silent now, letting her mind drift while the hearth-fire burned itself low.

Nara's polar estate was a kingdom of silence. In the unpop-ulated south, her unleashed empathy could extend for kilometers, searching for human emotions like a vine seeking water. It sometimes seemed that she could enter the cool, slow thoughts of the plants in the house's many gardens. Away from the capital's throngs, she felt transported back to the empty expanses of Vasthold.

But when Lieutenant-Commander Zai began his tale, her empathy pulled itself back from the wastelands and came to a focus on this quiet, intense man, and on the old pain deep inside him.

'The Dhantu punitive expedition was requested by a local governor,' Zai said, his eyes on a distant snowmelt waterfall. It tumbled onto the surface of the great glacier that approached the house from the east, the collision of temperatures raising a misty veil across the slowly setting sun.

'The governor was a sympathizer, it was later discovered,' he said. 'She came from a very good family, from among the first allies of the Emperor on Dhantu. But she had harbored traitorous thoughts since childhood. She wrote about it before her execution, bragging that she had achieved the office of Governor Prefectural on the power of hatred alone. A house-hold nanny had raised her from birth to despise the Emperor and the Occupation.'

'The hand that rocks the cradle,' Oxham observed.

Laurent nodded.

'We have no servants on Vada.'

'Nor on Vasthold, Laurent.'

He smiled at her, perhaps recognizing that the spartan ways of his gray planet were not too different from the austere meritocracy of the Secularists. Though polar opposites politically, neither of them were Utopians. Both monks and atheists trod on bare floors.

Nara realized that Laurent had used the word *occupation* to describe what was officially known as the 'Ongoing Liberation of Dhantu.' Of course, he had seen firsthand the excesses of direct Imperial rule, and its effect on the Dhantu heart. He was beyond euphemisms.

Zai swallowed, and Nara felt a chill in him, a shudder through the phantom limbs.

'The governor directed us to a secret meeting place of the resistance, where she said a high-level parley among its factions would take place. We sent a contingent of marines, hoping to capture a handful of resistance leaders.'

'But it was a trap,' she remembered.

The lieutenant-commander nodded. 'The walls of the canyon had been carefully prepared, natural iron deposits configured to baffle our intelligence small craft, to hide the ambush. When the resistance fighters appeared in force, it was as if they had materialized from thin air.'

She began to recall the details of the Dhantu incident, which had consumed the media for months, especially on anti-Occupation Vasthold.

'You weren't actually with the landing force, were you, Laurent?'

'Correct. The insertion force was strictly marines. The trap closed quickly, with only a few shots fired. From up in space, we could see through smallcraft recon that our marines would be wiped out if they fought. We ordered a stand-down.'

He sighed.

'But Private Anante Vargas had been killed in the first exchange of fire,' he said.

Nara nodded. She remembered the official narrative now, the hero Zai trading himself for a dead man.

'His armor diagnostics showed that he'd died cleanly, a chest wound. If we could get the body up within forty minutes, he would take the symbiant easily.'

'But they wouldn't give him up without an exchange.'

Laurent's eyes closed, and Nara felt a deep, anguished tremor from the man. She struggled to pinpoint the emotion.

'There was a confluence of interests,' he explained. 'The resistance would get another living hostage; we would retrieve our dead. But they demanded a command officer. They asked for a member of the Apparatus, but there were no politicals aboard our ship. They knew that we wouldn't give them the captain, but a lieutenant-commander would do.'

'Were you ordered, Laurent?'

'No,' he said, shaking his head slowly. 'The propaganda version is true. I volunteered.'

There was the anguish again, as clear as words. *If only it could have been someone else. Anyone else.* But this regret was entangled with Laurent's guilt at his own thoughts. In Zai's gray world, the honored dead were by any measure worth more than the living.

'I inserted in an up-down pod. Ballistic entry, with crude rockets to get it back up. Not much bigger than a coffin.'

'You trusted them?'

'My captain had stated quite clearly that if they reneged on the deal, he'd collapse the whole canyon with a railgun strike, kill us all. So I stepped out of the pod reasonably sure that they'd give up Vargas.

'Two of the resistance fighters brought Vargas's body over, and I helped them load him. For a moment, the three of us were human beings. We carried the lifeless man together, arranged his hands and feet in the jumpseat. Prepared him for his journey.

'Then we stepped back and I spoke to my ship for the last time, saying Vargas was ready. The pod ignited, carried him heavenward. I suppose I began the Warrior's Prayer out of reflex. The prayer is Vadan aboriginal, pre-Imperial, actually. But one of the two resistance fighters didn't hear it that way. He struck me down from behind.'

He shook his head, bewildered.

'I had just handled the dead with these men.'

Nara felt his horror in waves. Laurent, poor gray man, was still aghast that the Dhanti could have so little respect for ritual, for the Old Enemy, death. That blow from behind had made Zai more bitter than his months of torture, more anguished than having to walk into the trap of his own free will, sadder than watching his fellow captives die one by one. Nara could hear the question inside Laurent: the two guerrillas had handled the dead with him, and they wouldn't let him finish a simple prayer. Were they utterly empty?

'Laurent,' she offered, 'they'd seen millions die on their world, without any hope of resurrection.'

He nodded slowly, almost respectfully. 'Then they should know that death is beyond our political feuds.'

Death is *our political feud,* Nara Oxham thought, but said nothing.

The sunset had turned red. Here in the unpolluted air of the deep south, the sunset lasted for two hours in summer. Nara knelt to place more wood on the fire. Laurent settled beside her, passing logs from the fireside pile. The house grew its own wood, a vanilla-scented cedar engineered for fast growth and slow burning. But it took a long time to dry properly, and hissed and smoked when wet. Zai hefted each piece in his hand, discarding those still heavy with water.

'You've built a fire before,' Nara said.

He nodded. 'My family has a cabin in the high forests of the Valhalla range, just above the snowline. Entirely datablind. It's built of wood and mud, and its only heat comes from a fire-place about this size.'

Nara smiled. 'My mother's line has a dumb cabin, too. Stone. I spent my winters there as a child. Tending fires is youngster's work on Vasthold.'

Laurent smiled distantly, at some more pleasant memory.

'It develops a sense of balance and hierarchy,' he said, or quoted.

'Balance, yes,' Nara said, leaning a slender log carefully against the central mass of the fire. 'But hierarchy?'

'The match ignites the kindling, which feeds the larger pieces.'

She chuckled. A typically Vadan interpretation, to see order and structure in the consuming chaos that was a healthy blaze.

'Well, at least it's a bottom-up hierarchy,' she commented.

They built the fire together.

'We were well treated at first, during the few weeks of nego-tiation. Our captors made populist demands, such as medical aid for the tropics, which were in epidemic season. They began playing with the Imperial government. Wherever the government acted against disaster, the resistance would issue demands retroactively, making it seem as if any Imperial aid on Dhantu was a result of the hostage-taking. The resistance took credit for everything. Finally, the Imperial governor-gen-eral grew weary of their propaganda. He suspended all humanitarian aid.'

Nara frowned. She'd never thought of the Dhantu Occupation as a humanitarian operation. But, of course, occupying armies always brought a certain social order. And most occupying regimes were wealthier than their victims. Bribery followed naturally after conquest.

'After the Imperial sanctions were imposed, the torture

began. The strange thing was, our captors weren't interested in pain. Not when they first strapped us to the chairs.'

Chairs, Nara thought. Such a quotidian word. A chill rose inside her, and Nara turned to catch more of the heat from the blazing fire.

'The chairs were experimental medical equipment, fully pain-suppressant,' Laurent said. 'I felt nothing when they removed my left hand.'

Nara closed her eyes, a realization dawning in her. Even without her quickening empathy, she would have heard in Laurent's voice the searching cadence of an unrehearsed tale. He hadn't told this story before. Perhaps there'd been a debriefing, with the dispassionate rendering of a military report. But this was his first human telling of what had happened on Dhantu.

No wonder the psychic scars felt so fresh.

'Only twenty centimeters removal at first,' he said. 'The prosthetic nervous tissue shone like gold wires. I could even see the muscle extensions flex when I moved my fingers. The blood transports were transparent, so I could see the beating of my heart pulsing in them.'

'Laurent,' Nara said softly. It wasn't a plea for him to stop; she'd just had to say something. She couldn't leave this man's voice alone in the huge silence of the polar waste.

'Then they moved it farther away. Forty centimeters. Flexing the fingers ached now, as if they were cramped. But that was nothing compared to . . . *the disgust*. To see my hand responding so naturally, as if it were still connected. I vowed not to move it, to shut it from my mind – to make it a dead thing. But I could *feel* it. Only the strong pain was suppressed. Not normal sensations. Not the itching.'

He looked deep into the fire. 'The Dhanti were always great physicians,' he said without irony.

Something broke inside the fire, a pocket of water or air

exploding with a muffled sound. Sparks shot out at Nara and Laurent, and were repulsed by the firescreen. Bright ingots of flame dropped in a bright line along the stone floor, revealing the position of the invisible barrier.

'Of course, we were fully restrained in the chairs. My fingers and toes were all I could move. Imagine trying not to move your only free muscles for days. The hand began to itch, to throb and grow in my mind. Finally, I couldn't stand it. I would flex my fingers, and have to watch them respond at that *remove*.'

Nara felt her empathy coming to its highest pitch. Freed from the drug, it responded to the horror coming from Laurent, reached out toward him rather than recoiling. It had been so long since her ability had been fully open to another person; it stretched like a long-sleeping cat awakening. She could see now, empathy fully coopting the second-sight nodes in her optic nerve. Spirals of revulsion wound through the man, coiling like serpents on his artificial limbs. His gloved hand clenched, as if trying to grasp the phantasms of his pain. Maybe this was too private for her to look upon, she thought, and Nara's fingers moved to her wrist, instinctively searching for her apathy bracelet. But it was gone, left on a doorside table.

She closed her eyes, glad that easy relief was out of reach. Someone should feel what this man had suffered.

'They took us to pieces.

'They pulled my left arm into three, segmented at wrist and elbow and shoulder, connected by those pulsing lines. Then the legs, fused together, but a meter away. My heart beat hard all day, pumped up by stimulants, trying to meet the demands of the larger circulatory system. I never really slept.

'As ranking officer, I was last in line for everything. So they could learn from their mistakes, and not lose me to a sudden mishap. I could see the other captives around me twisted into bizarre shapes: circulatory rings, with blood flowing from the fingertips of the left hand into those of the right; distributed, with the digestion clipped off in stomach fragments to supply each removed limb separately; and utterly chaotic bodies, jumbles of flesh that slowly died.

'As we grew more grotesque, they stopped talking to us, or even to each other, dulled by their own butchery.'

With that last word, the unavoidable moment came. Her empathy became true telepathy. Flashes struck now in Nara's mind, like flint sparks lighting a black cave, revealing momentary images from Laurent's memory. A ring of large chairs, reclined like acceleration couches for some grotesque subspecies of humanity. They sparkled with medical transport lines, some as thin as nervewires, some broad enough to carry blood. And on the chairs . . . bodies.

Her mind rejected the sight. They were both terribly real and unbelievable. Living but not whole. Discorporate but breathing. Nara could see their faces move, which brought a nauseous shock, like the sudden movement of a dummy in a wax museum. The devices that sustained them gleamed, the lines efficient and clean, but melded with the broken bodies in a sickeningly random jumble, creatures made by a drunken god, or one insane.

But the prisoners were not creatures, Nara reminded herself. They were humans. And their creators were not mad gods, but humans also. Political animals. Reasoning beings.

Whatever Laurent believed about death, nothing was beyond politics. There were reasons for this butchery.

Nara reached out to touch him, taking his right hand, the one still made of flesh. Disgust struck out at her from Laurent's touch, as deep as anything she'd ever felt: utter horror at himself, that his own body was nothing but a machine that could be taken apart, like an insect's by cruel children.

There was nothing to do but hold him, a human presence in the face of inhuman memory. But still she had to ask.

'The Apparatus never told us why, Laurent,' she said. The resistance fighters' reasoning for the Tortures of Dhantu had never been explained.

Laurent shrugged.

'They told us that there was a secret, something that would undo the Emperor. They claimed to have heard something from a living initiate of the Apparatus they'd long ago captured. But they'd killed the man trying to wring the details from him. They kept demanding this secret from me. It was preposterous. They were grasping at straws. It was torture without reason.'

Nara swallowed. There had to be a reason; the Secularist in her did not believe in pure evil.

'Perhaps it was a fantasy on their part. They must have wanted some weapon against the Emperor so badly.'

'They only wanted to show us . . .'

Zai looked at her directly, and as their eyes locked Nara saw what he had realized over the long months in that chair. His next words were unnecessary.

'They wanted to show us what the Occupation had made of them.'

Nara closed her eyes, and through Laurent's touch she saw herself through his, as if in some magical mirror in which she was a stranger to herself. A beautiful alien.

'There was one lie in the Apparatus propaganda,' he said a few moments later.

Nara opened her eyes. 'What?'

'I wasn't rescued. The resistance abandoned the hideaway and transmitted my position to my ship. They left me to mark what they had done. Along with the dead bodies, they left me living, but beyond anyone's ability to repair.'

His gaze went from her to the waterfall, reddened now by the arctic summer sun.

'Or at least so they thought. The Empire moved heaven and earth to fix me, to prove them wrong. Here I am, such as I am.'

She ran her fingers along the line of his jaw.

'You're beautiful, Laurent.'

He shook his head. A smile played on his face, but his voice trembled as he spoke.

'I am in pieces, Nara.'

'Your body is, Laurent. Not unlike my mind.'

Zai touched her forehead with the fingers of his flesh-and-blood hand. He drew some shape she didn't recognize, a mark of his dark religion, or perhaps simply a random and meaningless sign.

'You began life in madness, Nara. But you wake up every day and cohere, pull yourself to sanity. I, on the other hand,' he lifted his gloved prosthetic, 'possessed absolute surety as a child, piety and scripture. And every day I shatter more.'

Nara took both of Laurent's hands in hers. The false one was as hard as metal, without the rubbery feel of a civilian prosthetic. It closed gently around her fingers.

Nara Oxham ignored the cold pain of him. She grasped the living and the dead parts. Pushed her fingers into the strange interfaces between body and machine. She found the hidden latches that released his false members. Removed them. She saw his phantom limbs as if they were real. She put her mind into him.

'Shatter, then,' she said.

4

HIGH GRAVITY

A painful lesson for any
commander: loyalty is never
absolute.
              – ANONYMOUS 167

Senator

It was past midnight before the War Council was called again.

Senator Oxham was awake when the summons came. All night, she had watched the bonfire in the Martyrs' Park. The flames were impossible to miss from her private balcony, which hung from the underside of her apartment, giving it sweeping views of the capital. The balcony swung in a carefully calibrated way – enough to feel the wind, but not nauseously – and at night-time the Martyrs' Park spread out below, a rectangle of darkness, as if a vast black carpet were blotting out the lights of the city.

Tonight, the usually dark expanse glimmered, populated by a dozen pools of firelight. Initiates from the Apparatus had taken all day to build the pyres, raising the pyramids of ceremonial trees using only human muscle and block and tackle. The newsfeeds gathered swiftly, broadcasting their labors and speculating on what sort of announcement would come after it had burned. As the pyres grew in size, the guesses were scaled up to match them, growing ever wilder, but still not quite matching the truth.

The politicals never trusted the populace of the Risen Empire with unexpected surprises, especially not in the volatile capital. The lengthy rituals of the Martyrs' Park allowed bad news to be preceded by a preparatory wave of anxiety, a warning like the glower of a distant storm. The newsfeeds usually hyperbolized their speculations, so that the true facts seemed reassuringly banal by the time they were made known.

This time, however, the news was likely to exceed expectations. Once the Child Empress's death became public knowledge, the true war fever would start.

There was enough of the construction to burn until morning, and Nara Oxham would need her energy when the news was announced, but she nonetheless went outside to watch. However exhausted by the day's events, sleep was impossible.

Her message to Laurent Zai seemed such a small and hopeless thing now, a futile gesture against the unstoppable forces of war: the vast fire below her, the still-gathering crowds, the mustering of soldiers, the warships already on their way to the Spinward Reaches. It was all unfolding with the fixity of some ancient and unchanging ceremony. The Risen Empire was a slave to ritual, to these burnings and empty prayers . . . and pointless suicides. There was nothing she could do to stop this war; her brash legislation hadn't even slowed its arrival. She wondered if even a seat on the council would ultimately accomplish anything.

Worse, she felt helpless to save Laurent Zai. Nara Oxham could be very persuasive, but only with gestures and spoken words, not the short text messages the distance between them necessitated. Laurent was too far away from her to save, both in light-years and in the dictates of his culture.

The balcony swayed softly, and the sickly sweet scent of the burning sacred trees reminded Oxham of the countryside smells of Vasthold. Crowds began to gather around the fire, the voices in massed prayer blending with the hiss of green wood, the crackle of the fire, and the rush of wind through the balcony's polyfilament supports.

Then the call came. The chime of the War Council's summons penetrated the susurrus noises from below, a foghorn cutting through the crash of far-off waves. Insistent and unavoidable, the summons's interruption brought her self-pity to a sudden halt. Oxham's fingers made the gestures that prepped her personal helicopter.

But then she saw the shape of an approaching Imperial aircar, silhouetted by the firelight. The delicate, silent craft drifted up and matched exactly the period of the balcony's sway. It opened like a flower, extending one wing as a walkway across the void. The elegant limb of the machine was an out-stretched hand, as if the craft were inviting her to dance.

A ritual request, but one which she could not deny.

'There is strange news from the front,' the Risen Emperor began.

The counselors waited. His Majesty's voice was very low, revealing more emotion than Nara Oxham had yet heard from the dead man. She felt a twinge of empathic resonance from him, a measure of confusion, anger, a sense of betrayal.

He moved his mouth as if to form words, then gestured disgustedly to the dead admiral.

'We have heard from the *Lynx*, from His Majesty's Representatives,' the admiral said, using the polite term for the Political Apparatus.

She lapsed into silence, and the other dead warrior lifted his head to speak, as if the burden of this announcement had to be shared between them.

'Captain Laurent Zai, Elevated, has rejected the blade of error,' the general said.

Nara gasped aloud, her hand covering her mouth too late. *Laurent was alive.* He had rejected the ancient rite. He had succumbed to her message, her single word.

The chamber stirred with confusion as Nara struggled to regain her composure. Most of the counselors hadn't given Zai much thought. Next to the Empress's death and war with the Rix, the fate of one man meant little. But the implications soon became apparent to them.

'He would have made a fine martyr,' said Raz imPar Henders, shaking his head sadly.

Even in her relief, Nara Oxham realized the truth of the Loyalist senator's words. The brave example of the hero Zai would have made a fine start to the war. By throwing away his own immortality, he would have inspired the whole empire. In the narrative crafted by the politicals, his suicide should have symbolized the sacrifices required of the next generation.

But he had chosen life. He had rejected the Risen Emperor's second-oldest tradition. The ancient catechism went through her head: eternal life for service to the crown, death for failure. She had hated the formula her entire life, but now she realized how deeply ingrained it was in her.

For a horrible moment, Nara Oxham found herself appalled at Zai's decision, shaken by the enormity of his betrayal.

Then she took control of her thoughts. She inhaled deeply, and booted a measure of apathy to filter out the emotions running rampant in the council chamber. Her reflexive horror was just old conditioning, inescapable even on a Secularist world, rising up from childhood stories and prayers. Tradition be damned.

But even so, she was amazed that Laurent had found the strength.

'This is a disaster,' said Ax Milnk nervously. 'What will the people think of this?'

'And from a Vadan,' the dead general muttered. 'The grayest of worlds, reliable Loyalists all.

'We must withhold news of this event for as long as possible,' Senator Henders said. 'Let its announcement be an afterthought, once the war has begun in earnest and other events have overtaken the public's interest.'

The admiral shook her head. 'If there are no more Rix

surprise attacks, it could be months before the next engagement,' she said. 'Even years. The newsfeeds will notice if there is no announcement of Captain Zai's suicide.'

'Perhaps His Majesty's Representatives could handle this?' Ax Milnk suggested quietly.

The Emperor raised an eyebrow at this. Nara swallowed. Milnk was suggesting murder. A staged ritual of error.

'I think not,' the Emperor said. 'The cripple deserves better.'

Both general and admiral nodded. Whatever embarrassment Zai had caused them, they wouldn't want the politicals interfering with a military matter. The branches of the Imperial Will were separate for good reason. The conduct of propaganda and internal intelligence did not mix well with the purer aims of warcraft. And Zai was still an Imperial officer.

'Something far more distasteful, I'm afraid,' the Risen Emperor continued.

The words brought a focused silence to the chamber, which the Emperor allowed to stretch for a few seconds.

'A pardon.'

Raz imPar Henders gasped aloud. No one else made a sound.

A *pardon?* Oxham wondered. But then she saw the Emperor's logic. The pardon would be announced before it was known that Captain Zai had rejected the blade of error. Zai's betrayal of tradition would be concealed from the public eye, his survival transformed into an unprecedented act of Imperial kindness. Before now, the Child Empress had always been the one to issue clemencies and commutations. A pardon in the matter of her own death would have a certain propagandistic poetry.

But it wouldn't be so easy, Nara's instincts told her. The Risen Emperor wouldn't allow Zai to be rewarded for his betrayal.

The sovereign nodded to the dead admiral.

The woman moved her pale hands, and the chamber darkened. A system schematic, which they all now recognized as Legis, appeared in synesthesia. The dense swirl of planetary orbital circles (the Legis sun had twenty-one major satellites) shrank, the scale expanding out. A vector marker appeared on the system's spinward side, out from the terrestrial planets into the vast, slow orbits of the gas giants. The red marker described an approach to the system that passed close to Legis XV.

'Three hours ago,' the admiral said, 'the Legis system's outlying orbital defenses detected a Rix battlecruiser, incoming at about a tenth lightspeed. This vessel is nothing like the assault ship that carried out the first attack. A far more powerful craft, but fortunately far less stealthy: this time we have warning.

'If it attacks Legis XV directly, the orbital defenses should destroy the Rix ship before it can close within a million kilometers.'

'What could it do to Legis from that range?' Oxham asked.

'If the battlecruiser's intention is to attack, it could damage major population centers, introduce any number of biological weapons, certainly degrade the info- and infrastructure. It all depends on how the vessel has been fitted. But she won't have the firepower for atmospheric rending, plate destabilization, or mass irradiation. In short, no damage at extinction level.'

Nara Oxham was appalled by the dead woman's dry appraisal. A few million dead was all. And perhaps a few generations with pre-industrial death rates from radiation and disease.

'The Rix ship is decelerating at six gees, quickly enough to match velocities with the planet. But its insertion angle is wrong for a direct attack,' the admiral said. 'Its apparent intent is to pass within a few light-minutes of Legis XV. The defenses at that range will be survivable for a ship of its class, and it won't be close enough to damage the planet extensively.

'And there is another clue to its intent. The Rix vessel appears to be equipped with a very large receiver array. Perhaps a thousand kilometers across.'

'For what purpose?' Henders asked.

The Emperor shifted his weight forward, and the dead warriors looked to him.

'We think that the Rix ship wants to establish communication with the Legis XV compound mind,' the sovereign said.

Nara felt bafflement in the room. No one in the Risen Empire knew much about compound minds. What would such a creature say to its Rix servants? What might it have learned about the Empire by inhabiting an Imperial world?

But from the Emperor came a different emotion. It underlay his anger, his indignation at Zai's betrayal. A dead man, he was always hard to read empathically, but a strong emotion was eating at him. Oxham turned her empathy toward the sovereign.

'The Rix compound mind has no access to extraplanetary communication,' the general explained. 'The Legis entanglement facilities are centralized and under direct Imperial control, and of course could only transmit to the rest of the Empire. But from the range of a few light-minutes, the compound mind could communicate with the Rix vessel. Using television transmitters, air traffic control arrays, even pocket phones. Legis's infostructure is composed of a host of distributed devices that we can't control.'

'Unless we do something, the Rix will be able to contact their compound mind,' the Emperor declared. 'Between the mind's global resources and the battlecruiser's large array, they will be able to transfer huge amounts of data. With a few hours' connection, perhaps the planet's entire data-state. All the information that is Legis XV.'

'Why not shut down the planet's power grid for a few days?' Henders suggested. 'When the ship approaches apogee?'

'We may. It is estimated that a three-day power outage, properly prepared for, would cause only a few thousand civilian deaths,' the general answered. Oxham saw nothing but cold equations in the man when he gave this number. 'Unfortunately, however, most communications are designed to survive power grid failure. They have backup batteries, solar cells, and motion converters as part of their basic makeup. This is a compound mind; the entire *planet is* compromised. A power outage won't prevent communication between the compound mind and the Rix vessel.'

At these last words, Oxham's empathy felt a jolt from the Emperor. He was agitated. She had witnessed the fixations his mind could develop. His cats. His hatred of the Rix.

Something new was in his head, consuming him.

And then, in a moment of clarity, she felt the emotion in him. Saw it clearly.

It was fear.

The Risen Emperor was afraid of what the Rix might learn.

'We don't know why the Rix want to talk to their compound mind,' he said. 'Perhaps they only want to offer obeisance to it, or perform some kind of maintenance. But they have dedicated years to this mission, and risked almost certain war. We must assume there is a strategic reason for this attempt at contact.'

'The compound mind may have military secrets that we can't afford to lose,' the general said. 'It's impossible for us to know what they might have discovered in an entire planet of data. But now we know this was the Rix plan all along: first the assault ship to seed the mind, then the battlecruiser to make contact.'

The council chamber stirred again, frustration and anger filling the room. They felt trapped, powerless before the well-laid plans of the Rix.

'But perhaps we can solve both our problems with one stroke,' the Emperor said. He pointed into the airscreen among them.

Time sped forward in the display. The Rix ship's vector marker inched toward Legis XV, from which another marker in imperial blue moved to meet it.

'The *Lynx*,' Nara said quietly.

'Correct, Senator,' the Emperor said.

'With aggressive tactics, even a frigate should be able to damage a Rix battlecruiser. Especially the receiver array,' the admiral said. 'It's too large to shield properly, highly vulnerable to kinetic weapons. Between battle damage and a careful, systematic degradation of the Legis communication infostructure, we may be able to keep the compound mind cut off.'

'Any casualty estimates for this plan, Admiral?' Oxham asked softly.

'Yes, Senator. On the planet, we'll airjam com systems and flood the infostructure with garbage. Shunt the main hard-lines for a few days to reduce bandwidth. Civilian deaths will be within normal statistical variation for a bad solar storm. Medical emergency response will be slowed, so a few dozen heart-attack and accident victims will die. With lowered transponder functions, there may be a few aircraft accidents.'

'And the *Lynx*?'

'Lost, of course, and its captain with it. A grand sacrifice.'

Henders nodded. 'How poetic. Granted Imperial pardon, only to become a martyr nonetheless.'

'The trees will burn for a week in the name of Laurent Zai,' the Emperor said.

Adept

The two dead persons stood before a wreckage, the broken and burned shapes of data bricks scattered across the floor of the library.

'Was it here?'

'Yes, Adept.'

'Did the Rix abomination find it?'

'We don't know, Adept.'

'How can we not know?' Trevim said quietly.

The initiate shifted uncomfortably. He looked nervously at the walls, although every noise-sensitive device in the library had been physically deactivated.

'The abomination cannot hear us.'

The initiate cleared his throat. 'The one-time pad was concealed as a set of checksum garbage at the ends of other files. Only the few Honored Mothers studying the Child Empress's . . . *condition* knew how the scheme worked. There was no way for the abomination to know how to compile the data and re-create the pads.'

Adept Trevim narrowed her eyes.

'Could it not use trial and error?'

'Adept, there are millions of files here. The combinations are—'

'Not limitless. Not if all the data were here.'

'But it would take centuries, Adept.'

'For a single computer, millennia. But for the processing capabilities of an entire world? Every unused portion of every device on Legis, devoted to this single problem, massively distributed and absolutely relentless?'

The initiate closed his eyes, removing himself from the shallow world of the senses. Adept Trevim watched the young dead man let the Other take control, the symbiant visible upon his face as it transformed hurried suppositions into hard math.

It would have been quicker to employ a machine, but the Apparatus avoided technology even in the best of circumstances. With the Rix abomination loose in the Legis infostructure, they kept to the techniques given by the symbiant. To trust a processor would be unthinkable.

Trevim waited motionless for just over an hour.

The initiate opened his eyes.

'The state of emergency was still in partial effect when the library was broken into,' he said.

The adept nodded. With the markets closed, the media feeds suspended, the population locked down, the planet's infostructure would be largely dark. The abomination would have ample excess processor power at its disposal.

'It would have taken only minutes to run every permutation against the data it had recovered from the confidant. When the correct order was hit upon by chance, the data would take on a recognizable form,' the initiate concluded.

'It knows, then.'

The initiate nodded, looking queasy as he considered the Secret in the hands of Rix abomination.

'We must assume it does, Adept.'

Trevim turned from the jumble on the floor. It had seemed so sensible a place to hide the one-time pads that would decrypt the recordings of the Child Empress's confidant. Rather than keeping the pads in a military installation, under lock and key, a target for treachery or infiltration, the Apparatus had hidden them among the chaos here at this library, a sequestered and little-accessed partition at the edge of the planet's infostructure. The pads were here as a last resort, for when the Empress suffered the ultimate result of her infirmity.

But with the Rix abomination and its last commando running free on the planet, the clever hiding place had worked against them. Even within the Apparatus, only a few people knew how the confidant worked. And these lived in the gray enclaves, far from any communication or even ready transport. It had taken hours to discover this weak point in the Emperor's Secret.

The compound mind had known where to look, though. The telling details could have come from anywhere: the shipping manifests of repair components, long-lost schematics, even from within the confidant itself. Based on her examination of the device's remains, Initiate Farre was certain that the abomination had briefly occupied it just before the rescue had begun.

The mind was everywhere.

They had to destroy it, whatever the cost to its host world.

'What do we do, Adept?'

'First, we must see that the contagion does not spread. Are there any translight communications the abomination could use to make contact with the rest of the Empire?'

'There is none, Adept. The *Lynx*'s infostructure is secure, and there are no other ships in the system with their own translight. Planetside, the entanglement facility at the pole is under Imperial control.'

'Let us pay the pole a visit, and make sure.'

'Certainly, Adept.'

They walked up the stairs, leaving a ruin of secrecy behind them.

'Destroy this building.'

'But, Adept, this is a library,' the initiate said. 'Many of the documents here are single-copy secured. They're irreplaceable.'

'Nanomolecular disintegration. Melt it into the ground.'

'The militia won't—'

'They'll follow an Imperial writ, or they'll feel a blade of error, Initiate. If they feel squeamish, we'll have the *Lynx* do it from space. See what they think about losing a few square kilometers.'

The initiate nodded, but the marks of emotion on his face disturbed the adept. What was it about this crisis that afflicted the honored dead with the weaknesses of the living? Perhaps it was the conditioning, the distress they had been trained to suffer even at the mention of the Secret. The mental firewall that had preserved their silence for sixteen centuries might be a liability now that the Apparatus had to act rather than merely conceal. But perhaps there was more than conditioning behind the initiate's anguish. The abomination of the Rix compound mind surrounded them, had imbued itself into the very planet. Now that the thing knew the Secret, it threatened them on every front.

'The militia will relent, Initiate. They must. But this one library will not be enough. We will have to repair this breach at its source.'

'But the mind has propagated beyond any possibility of elimination.'

'We must destroy it.'

'But how, Adept?'

'However the Emperor commands.'

Captain

Captain Laurent Zai stared past the airscreen and into the ancestral painting on the wall behind it.

Three meters by two, the artwork filled one bulkhead of his cabin. It reflected almost no light, only a ghostly luminescence, as jet as if the frigate's hull had suddenly disappeared, leaving a gaping hole into the void beyond. It had been painted by his grandfather, Astor Zai, twenty years after the old patriarch's death and just before he had started on the first of many pilgrimages. Like most Vadan ancestrals, it was composed with hand-made paints: pigment from powdered black stone suspended in animal marrow, mixed with the whites of chicken eggs. Over the decades, the egg-white rose to the surface of Vadan black paintings, giving them their lustrous sheen. The painting glowed softly, as if it were highlighted by a thin coat of rime on some cold, dewy morning.

Otherwise, the rectangle was featureless.

The dead claimed otherwise. They said they could see the brushstrokes, the layers of primer and paint, and more than that. They could see characters, arguments, places, whole dream-stories painted within the blackness. Like images in tea leaves or a crystal ball. But the dead claimed that reading the paintings was no trick, but straightforward signification, no more magical than a line of text calling an image into a reader's mind.

The minds of the living were simply too cluttered to interpret a canvas so pure.

Zai could see nothing. Of course, that absence of understanding was a sign with its own meaning: for the moment, he was still alive.

In second sight, hovering before the painting, were the orders from the Navy. The Emperor's seal pulsated with the red light of its fractal authenticity weave, like a coat of arms decorated with live embers. The shape was familiar, the language traditional, but in their own way, the orders were quite as inscrutable as the black rectangle painted by an ancestor.

The door chime sounded. Hobbes, here on the double.

Zai erased the orders from the air.

'Come.'

His executive officer entered, and Zai waved her to the chair on the other side of the airscreen table. She sat down, her back to the black painting, her face guarded and almost shy. Zai's crew seemed reluctant to meet his eye since he had rejected the blade of error. Were they ashamed of him? Surely not Katherie Hobbes. She was loyal to a fault.

'New orders,' Captain Zai said. 'And something else.'

'Yes, sir?'

'An Imperial pardon.'

For a moment, Hobbes's usually rigid composure failed her. She gripped the arms of the chair, and her mouth gaped.

'Are you well, Hobbes?' Zai asked.

'Of course, sir,' she managed. 'Indeed, I'm . . . very glad, Captain.'

'Don't be too hasty.'

Her expression remained confused for a moment, then changed to surety. 'You deserve it, sir. You were right to reject the blade. The Emperor has simply recognized the truth. None of this was your—'

'Hobbes,' he interrupted. 'The Emperor's mercy isn't as tender as you think. Take a look.'

Zai reactivated the airscreen. It showed the Legis system now: the *Lynx* in orbit around XV, the high vector of the incoming Rix battlecruiser. It took Hobbes only a few seconds to grasp the situation.

'A second attack on Legis, sir,' she said. 'With more fire-power this time.'

'Considerably more, Hobbes.'

'But that doesn't make sense, Captain. The Rix've already captured the planet. Why would they attack their own mind?'

Zai didn't answer, giving his executive officer time to think. He needed to have his own suspicions confirmed.

'Your analysis, Hobbes?'

She took her time, more iconographics cluttering the airscreen as she tasked the *Lynx* tactical AI with calculations.

'Perhaps this was the backup force, sir, in case the situation on the ground was still in doubt. A powerful ship to support the raiders if they weren't entirely successful,' she said, working through the possibilities. 'Or more likely this is a reconnaisance-in-force, to discover if the raid succeeded.'

'In which case?'

'When the Rix commander contacts the compound mind and realizes it has successfully propagated on the planet, they'll back off.'

'Then, for the *Lynx*'s disposition, what would your tactical recommendation be?' Zai asked.

Hobbes shrugged, as if it were obvious. 'Stay close to Legis XV, sir. With the *Lynx* supporting the planetary defenses, we should have enough firepower to keep a battlecruiser from damaging Legis, if that's their mission, which it probably isn't. The Rix will most likely keep going once they realize the raid was successful. That'll carry them deeper into the Empire. We could try to track them. At ten percent or so of the constant, they'd be hard for the *Lynx* to catch from a standstill, but a pursuit drone could manage it in the short term.'

Zai nodded. As usual, Hobbes's thinking roughly paralleled his own.

Until he'd read the *Lynx*'s orders, that is.

'We've been commanded to attack the battlecruiser, Hobbes.'

She simply blinked. 'Attack, sir?'

'To intercept it as far out as possible. Outside the plantery defenses, in any case, in an attempt to damage the Rix communications gear. We're to keep the Rix ship from contacting the compound mind.'

'A frigate, against a *battlecruiser*,' Hobbes protested. 'But, sir, that's . . .' Her mouth moved, but silently.

'Suicide,' he finished.

She nodded slowly, staring intently into the colored whorls of the airscreen. However quickly Hobbes had grasped the tactical facets of the situation, the politics seemed to have left her speechless.

'Consider this as an intelligence issue, Hobbes,' Zai said. 'We've never had a compound mind fully propagate on an Imperial world. It knows everything about Legis. It could reveal more about our technology and culture than the Apparatus wants the Rix to know. Or . . .'

Hobbes looked up into his eyes, still hammered into silence.

'Or,' he continued, 'the *Lynx* may have been chosen to suffer the sacrifice that I was unwilling to make myself.'

There. He had said it aloud. The thought that had tortured him since he'd received the pardon and the orders, the two missives paired to arrive and be read together, as if to indicate that neither could be understood without the other.

He saw his own distress reflected in Hobbes's face. There was no other interpretation.

Captain Laurent Zai, Elevated, had doomed his ship and his crew, had dragged them all down along with his miserable self.

Zai turned his eyes from the still speechless Hobbes and tried to fathom what he felt, now that he had spoken his thoughts aloud. It was hard to say. After the tension of the rescue, the bitter ashes of defeat, and the elation of rejecting suicide, his emotions were too worn to keep going. He felt dead already.

'Sir,' Hobbes finally began. 'This crew will serve you, will follow any orders. The *Lynx* is ready to . . .' Her voice failed her again.

'Die in battle?'

She took a deep breath.

'To serve her Emperor and her captain, sir.'

Katherie Hobbes's eyes glittered as she said the words.

Laurent Zai waited politely as she gathered herself. But then he uttered the words he had to say.

'I should have killed myself.'

'No, Captain. You weren't at fault.'

'The tradition does not address the issue of blame, Katherie. It concerns responsibility. I'm the captain. I ordered the rescue. By tradition, it was my Error of Blood.'

Hobbes worked her mouth again, but Zai had chosen the right words to preempt her arguments. In matters of tradition, he, a Vadan, was her mentor. On the Utopian world she came from, not one citizen in a million became a soldier. In Zai's family, one male in three had died in combat over the past five centuries.

'Sir, you're not thinking of . . .'

He sighed. It was a possibility, of course. The pardon did not prevent him from taking his own life. The act might even save the *Lynx*; the Navy was not above changing its orders. But something in Laurent Zai had changed. He'd thought that the threads of tradition and obedience that formed his being were bound together. He'd thought that the rituals and oaths, the sacrifice of decades to the Time Thief, and the dictates of his upbringing had reached critical mass, forming a singularity of purpose from which there was no escape. But it had turned out that his loyalties, his honor, his very sense of self had all been held in place by something quite delicate, something that could be broken by a single word.

Don't, he thought to himself, and smiled.

'I am thinking, Katherie, of going Home.'

Hobbes was silenced by the words. She must have been ready to argue with him, to plead against the blade again.

He took a moment, letting her renewed shock subside, then cleared his throat.

'Let us plan a way to save the *Lynx*, Hobbes.'

Her still glittering eyes moved to the airscreen display, and Zai saw her gather herself in its shapes. He recalled what the war sage Anonymous 167 had once said: 'sufficient tactical detail will distract the mind from the death of a child, even from the death of a god.'

'High relative velocity,' Hobbes began after a while. 'With full drone complement deployed, I'd say. Narrow hull configuration. And standard lasers in the primary turrets. We'd have a chance, sir.'

'A chance, Hobbes?'

'A fighting chance, sir.'

He nodded his head. For a few moments after the orders had come, Laurent Zai had wondered if the crew would continue to accept his command. He had betrayed everything he had been raised to believe. Perhaps it would be fitting if his crew betrayed him.

But not his executive officer. Hobbes was a strange one, half Utopian and half gray. Her face was a reminder of that: molded to an arresting beauty by the legendary surgeons of her hedonistic world, but always shrouded with a deadly serious expression. Generally she followed tradition with the passion of the converted. But at certain times she questioned everything. Perhaps, at this moment, the gap between them had closed; her loyalty and his betrayal, at the juncture of the Risen Empire.

'A fighting chance, then,' he said.

'"No more can a soldier ask for," sir,' she quoted the sage.

'And the rest of the crew?'

'Warriors all, sir.'

He nodded. And hoped she was right.

Militia Worker

Second-Class Militia Worker Rana Harter stepped back nervously from the metal skirts of the polar maglev as it settled onto the track. The train floated down softly, as if it weighed only a few ounces, and sighed a bit as it descended, drifting along the track a few centimeters on a thin, leftover cushion of air, like a playing card dealt across a glass table.

But the delicacy was deceptive. Rana Harter knew that the maglev was hypercarbon and hullalloy, a fusion reactor and a hundred private cabins done in teakwood and marble. It massed more than a thousand tons, would crush a human foot under its skirts as surely as a diamond-tipped tunneling hammer. Harter stood well back as the entry stairway unfolded before her.

There was plenty of room here on the platform. Tiny Galileo Township seldom provided passengers for the maglev, which could have easily accommodated its entire population. This stop, the last before the polar cities of Maine and Jutland, was mostly to take on supplies. But Militia Worker Rana Harter was at last going to step onto the train. She had lived here in the Galileo Administrative Prefecture her entire life. Her new posting to the polar entanglement facility would be the first time she had left the GAP.

Rana waited for someone to appear at the top of the entry stairway. Someone to invite her aboard the intimidating train. But the stairway waited, impassive and empty. She looked at her ticket, actually a sheaf of plastic chits ribbed with copper-colored circuitry and scribblecodes, which the local Legis Militia office had provided her. There wasn't much on the ticket that was human-readable. Just the time when the train would leave, and something that looked like a seating assignment.

The northern tundra of Legis XV seemed to stretch out, infinitely huge, around her.

Rana waited at the bottom of the stairway. She couldn't bring herself to go though a door without an invitation. Here in Galileo township, such boldness felt like trespassing. But after a half-minute or so, the warning lights along the stairs began to flicker, and the ambient hum of the entire maglev raised a bit in pitch. It was now or never, she realized.

Had she waited too long? Would the stairway fold up as she climbed it, crushing her like a doll in the gears of a bicycle?

She placed one tentative foot on the lowest step. It felt solid enough, but the maglev's whine was still climbing. Rana took a quick breath and held it, and dashed up the stairway.

She was just in time, or perhaps the stairway had been waiting for her. At the top, Rana turned around to take a last look at her hometown, and the stairs folded themselves back up, curling into a single spiral that irised closed like an umbrella.

And Rana Harter, flushed more from nerves than from the short climb, was inside the train that would take her to the pole.

Her seat was several minutes' walk toward the front of the train. The maglev's acceleration was so even that when Rana looked out the window, she was surprised to see the landscape already whipping by, the snow and scrubgrass smeared to a shimmering milky blur.

Rana knew that her reassignment had been the result of the Rix attack a few days before. The Legis Militia was shifting onto war footing, and she'd read that strategic targets like the entanglement facility were being heavily reinforced. But as she passed the hundreds of soldiers and workers on the train, the scale of the Rix threat finally struck her. The maglev seemed full; every seat was occupied until she reached the one that matched her ticket. Rana's nerves twinged again, her guilt rising like a tardy schoolchild's as she took the last empty seat.

The soldier next to her was sleeping, his chair pitched back so that it was almost a bed. Her seat was certainly comfortable, designed for half-day journeys. A small array of controls floated in synesthesia before her, marked with the standard icons for water, light, entertainment, and help. She waved them away, and folded herself into one corner of the chair.

Rana Harter wondered why she had been assigned to the entanglement facility. Surely it was the most important installation on Legis XV. But what could the militia need *her* there for? She wasn't any kind of soldier. The only weapon she was rated to use was a standard field autopistol, and you could empty a whole clip from one of those into a Rix commando without much effect. She'd failed her combat physical, and didn't have the coordination for a quick-interface job like remote pilot or sniper. The only thing Rana had turned out to be good at – the reason she'd made second class in just a year – was microastronomy.

Rana Harter had a brainbug, it turned out, something her aptitude officer called 'holistic processing of chaotic systems.' That meant she could look at the internal trajectories of a cluster of rocks – asteroids in the under-kilogram category – and tell you things about it that a computer couldn't. Like whether it was going to stick together for the next few hours, or break up, threatening a nearby orbital platform. Her CO explained that even the smartest imperial AIs couldn't solve that kind of problem, because they tried to plot every rock separately, using millions of calculations. If there was even the slightest observational imprecision at the front end, the back end results would be hopelessly screwed up. But brainbugs like Rana saw the swarm as one big system – a whole. In deep synesthesia, this entity had a flavor/smell/sound to it: a deep, stable odor like coffee, or the shaky tang of mint, ready to fly dangerously apart.

But why send her to the polar facility?

Rana had used equipment like the repeater array up there, and even performed field repairs on small repeater gear. But they didn't do astronomy at an entanglement grid, just communications. Maybe they were retooling the facility for defense work. She tried to imagine tracking a swarm of enemy ships dodging through the Legis defenses.

What would the Rix taste like?

Movement in her peripheral vision distracted Rana from these thoughts. Standing in the aisle was a tall militia officer. The woman glanced up at the seat number, then down at Rana.

'Rana Harter?'

'Yes, ma'am.' Rana tried to stand at attention, but the luggage rack over her head made that impossible, and she saluted from a crouch. The officer didn't return the gesture. The woman's expression was unreadable; she was wearing full interface glasses that entirely obscured her eyes, which was odd, because she also had a portable monitor in her hands. She wore a heavy coat even in the well-heated train. There was a birdlike quickness to her motions.

'Come with me,' the officer ordered. Her voice was husky, the accent unplaceable. But then, Rana had never been out of the GAP except in videos.

The officer turned and walked away without another word. Rana grabbed her kitbag from the rack and wrestled it into the aisle. By the time she looked up, the woman was almost through to the next car, and Rana had to run to catch her.

The officer was headed toward the back of the train. Rana followed, barely able to keep up with the taller woman. She banged another worker with her flailing kitbag, and muttered an apology. He answered with a phrase Rana didn't recognize, but which didn't sound polite.

At the frantic pace, they soon reached the luxury section. Rana stopped, her mouth agape. One side of the carpeted corridor was filled entirely by a floor-to-ceiling window. In it the tundral landscape rushed by furiously, blurred into a creamy palette by the train's speed. Rana had read that the maglev could make a thousand klicks per hour; right now it seemed to be doing twice that.

Across from the window was a wall of dark, paneled wood, broken by doors to private cabins. The silent officer walked slowly here, as if more comfortable out of the crowded coach sections. They passed a few servants in Maglev Line uniforms, who stood at attention. Rana wasn't sure whether their stiff posture was out of respect for the officer, or just to give them room to pass in the thin corridor.

Finally, the officer entered one of the doors, which opened for her without a handkey or even a voice command. Rana followed nervously.

The cabin was beautiful. The floor was some kind of resin, an amber surface that gave softly under Rana's boots. The walls were marble and teakwood. The furniture was segmented; Rana's brain ability asserted itself, and she saw how each piece would fold around itself, the chairs and table transforming into a desk and a bed. A wide window revealed the rushing tundra. The cabin was larger than Rana's old barrack hut at Galileo, which she shared with three other militia workers. The luxury of the surroundings only made Rana more nervous; she was obviously inadequate for whatever special operation she'd been assigned to.

She felt guilty, as if she were already screwing things up. 'Sit down.'

Here in the quiet cabin, Rana listened carefully to the officer's strange accent. It was precise and careful, with the exact pronunciation of an AI language teacher. But the intonation was wrong, like a congenital deafmute's, carefully trained to use sounds that she herself had never heard.

Rana dropped her kitbag and sat in the indicated chair.

The officer sat across from her, a decimeter taller than Rana even with them both seated. She took off her glasses.

Rana's breath stopped short. The woman's eyes were artificial. They reflected the white landscape passing in the window, but were brilliant with a violet hue. But it wasn't the eyes that had made her gasp.

With the glasses removed, Rana could finally see the shape of the officer's face. It was eerily recognizable. The hair wasn't familiar, and the violet eyes were almost alien. But the line of the woman's jaw, the cheekbones and high forehead – were all strangely like Rana's own.

Rana Harter shut her eyes. Perhaps the resemblance was just the result of nerves and lack of sleep, a momentary hallucination that a few seconds of darkness could erase. But when she looked again, the woman was just as familiar. Just as much like Rana herself.

It was like peering into an enhancing mirror at a cosmetic surgery store, one that added a hairweave or different colored eyes. She was transfixed by the effect, unable to move.

'Militia Worker Rana Harter, you have been selected for a very important mission.'

That oddly inflected voice again, as if the words came from nowhere, were owned by no one.

'Yes, ma'am. What . . . kind of mission?'

The woman tilted her head, as if the question surprised her. She paused a moment, then looked at her handheld monitor.

'I cannot answer that now. But you must follow my orders.'

'Yes, ma'am.'

'You will stay in this cabin until we reach the pole. Understood?'

'I understand, ma'am.'

The woman's precise tone began to calm Rana a bit. Whatever mission the militia wanted her for, they were giving clear enough orders. That was one thing she liked about the militia. You didn't have to think for yourself.

'You are to speak to no one but me on this train, Rana Harter.'

'Yes, ma'am,' Rana answered. 'May I ask one question, though?'

The woman said nothing, which Rana took as permission to continue.

'Who exactly are you, ma'am? My orders didn't say—'

The woman interrupted immediately, 'I am Colonel Alexandra Herd, Legis XV Militia.' She produced a colonel's badge from the voluminous coat.

Rana swallowed. She'd never even seen anyone with a rank over captain before. Officers existed on a lofty level that was utterly mysterious when viewed from her own small, nervous world.

But she hadn't realized how truly strange they could be.

The colonel pointed at the corner of the room, and a wash-basin unfolded itself elegantly from the wall.

'Wash your hair,' she ordered.

'My hair?' Rana asked, dumbfounded anew.

Colonel Herd pulled a knife from her pocket. The blade was almost invisibly thin, a shimmering presence as it caught light reflected from the patches of snow passing the window. The handle was curved in a strange way that made Rana think of a bird's wings. The colonel held it with her fingertips, a sudden grace evident in her long fingers.

'After you have washed your hair, I will cut it off,' Colonel Herd said.

'I don't understand . . .'

'And a manicure, and a good scrubbing.'

'What?'

'Orders.'

Rana Harter did not respond. Her mind had begun to whir, to accelerate into a blur as featureless as the passing landscape. It was her brainbug, going for a quick flight, buzzing toward that paralyzing moment when a host of incoherent, chaotic inputs suddenly resolved into understanding.

She could just glimpse the operations of the savant portion of her mind, the maelstrom of analysanda madly arranging itself, seeking to collapse from a meaningless flurry into something concrete and comprehensible: the curve of the colonel's knife, somehow like an outline remembered from a ship-spotting course in her astronomy training; her strange, placeless accent, the words slow and prompted; the collection of hair, fingernails, skin; the colonel's inhuman eyes; and the woman's avian movements that fluttered like sunlight on bicycle spokes, the smell of lemongrass, or Bach played fast on a woodwind . . .

With a burst of sensation across Rana's skin – the rasp of talons – coherence arrived.

Rana had been trained to give the results of her brainbugs quickly, spitting out the essential data before they had time to escape her mind's tenuous grasp. And the rush of knowledge was so sharp and clear, so shocking this time – that she couldn't stop herself.

'You're a Rix, aren't you?' she blurted. 'The compound mind's talking through you. You want to . . .'

Rana Harter bit her tongue, cursing her stupidity. The woman remained still for a moment, as if waiting for a translation. Rana's eyes darted around the room, casting for a weapon. But there was nothing at hand that could stop the sudden, birdlike alien across from her. Not for a second.

Then Rana saw the emergency pull-cord swinging above her head.

She reached up for it, yanking down hard on the elegant brass handle, cool in her hand. She braced herself for the screech of brakes, the wail of a siren.

Nothing happened.

Rana fell back into her seat.

The compound mind, her own brain told her. *Everywhere*.

'You want to impersonate me,' Rana found herself compelled to finish.

'Yes,' the Rixwoman said.

'Yes,' repeated Rana. She felt – with a strange relief after trying so hard not to all day long – that she would cry.

Then the alien woman leaned forward, one fingertip extended and glistening, and with a touch, thrust a needle into Rana's arm.

One moment of pain, and after that everything was
just
fine.

Captain

The haze of points that represented the Rix battlecruiser and her satellites grew more diffuse as the minutes passed. The smaller cloud that was the *Lynx* changed too, softening, as if Captain Zai's eyes were losing focus.

He blinked reflexively, but the airscreen image of the approaching hosts continued to blur. The two combatant ships deployed still more adjunct craft, hundreds of drones to provide intelligence, to penetrate and attack the other ship, and to harry the opponents' drones. The *Lynx* and the Rix ship became two stately clouds nearing a slow collision.

'Freeze,' Zai ordered.

The two clouds stopped, just touching.

'What's the relative velocity at the edge?' he asked his executive officer.

'One percent lightspeed,' Hobbes answered.

Someone on the command bridge let out an audible rush of breath.

'Three thousand klicks per second,' Master Pilot Marx translated, muttering to himself.

Zai let the cold fact of this velocity sink in, then resumed the simulation. The clouds drifted into each other, the movement just visible, seemingly no faster than the setting sun as it approaches the horizon. Of course, only the grand scale of the battle made the pace look glacial. At the scale of the invisibly small craft within those point-clouds, the fight would unfold at a terrific pace.

The *Lynx*'s captain drummed his fingers. His ship was designed for combat at much lower relative velocities. In a normal intercept situation, he would accelerate alongside the battlecruiser, matching its vector. Standard tactics against larger craft demanded minimal relative motion, to give the imperial drone swarm sufficient time to wear down the bigger ship's defenses. Even against Rix cyborgs, Imperial pilots were renowned. And the *Lynx*, as the prototype of its class, had been allotted some of the best in the Navy.

But Zai didn't have the luxury of standard tactics. He had a mission to carry out.

Master Pilot Marx was the first to speak up.

'There won't be much piloting to it, sir,' he said. 'Even our fastest drones only make a thousand gees acceleration. That's ten thousand meters per second squared. One percent of the constant equals three *million* meters per second. We'll be rushing past them too fast to do any dogfighting.'

Marx glared into the airscreen.

'There won't be much we can do to protect the *Lynx* from their penetrators either, Captain,' he concluded.

'That won't be your job, Master Pilot,' Zai said. 'Just keep your drones intact, and get them through to attack the Rix ship.'

The master pilot nodded. His role in this, at least, was clear. Zai let the simulation run further. As Marx had complained, the crashing waves of drones had little effect on one another. They were passing through each other too quickly for any but the luckiest of shots to hit. Soon, the outermost edges of the two spheres reached each other's vital centers. The *Lynx* and the Rix battlecruiser began to take damage; the kinetic hits of flechettes and expansion webs, wide-area radiation strikes from energy weapons.

'Freeze,' Zai ordered.

'You'll notice that the adjunct craft have started making hits,' ExO Hobbes took up the narrative.

'A ship's a much bigger target than a two-meter drone,' Marx said.

'Exactly,' Hobbes said. 'And a battlecruiser is a bigger target than a frigate. Especially this particular battlecruiser.'

She zoomed the view into the bright mote that was the Rix vessel. The receiver array became visible, the ship proper no more than a speck against its vast expanse.

Hobbes added a scale marker; the array was a thousand kilometers across.

'Think you can hit that?' Hobbes asked.

Master Pilot Marx nodded slowly.

'Absolutely, Executive Officer. Provided I'm still alive.'

Zai nodded. Marx had a point. He would be piloting remotely from the belly of the *Lynx*, which would itself be under attack. The Imperial ship had to survive long enough for its drones to reach the Rix battlecruiser.

'We'll be alive. The *Lynx* will be inside a tight group of close-in-defense drones. We'll railgun them out in front, then have them cut back to match the velocity of the incoming drones,' Hobbes said.

'Or as close as they can get,' Marx corrected her. The *Lynx*'s defensive drones could never match the incoming Rix attackers at three thousand klicks a second.

'*And* we'll be clearing our path with all the abrasion sand we can produce.' Hobbes sighed.

'But we'll have our hands full,' she finished.

Zai was glad to hear the nervous tremor just audible in her voice. This plan was a dangerous one. The staff had to understand that.

'May I ask a question, Captain?'

It was Second Gunner Thompson.

'Gunner?' Zai said.

'This *collision* of a battle plan,' he said slowly. 'Is it designed to protect Legis? Or to create a tactical advantage for the *Lynx*?'

'Both,' Zai answered. 'Our orders are to prevent contact between the battlecruiser and the compound mind.'

Zai's fingers moved, and the view pulled back to a schematic of the entire system. It filled with the vectors he and Hobbes had worked out that afternoon.

'To make it work, we'll have to accelerate spinward, out toward the battlecruiser, then turn over and come back in. Over the next ten days we'll have to average ten gees.'

The command bridge stirred. Zai and his crew would be spending the next week suffering under the uneasy protection of easy gravity. Uncomfortable and dangerous, the high-gee conditions would leave them exhausted for the battle.

'And yes,' Zai continued. 'As Gunner Thompson suggests, high relative velocity gives us a tactical advantage, given our orders. Our objective is not to engage the Rix battlecruiser in a fight to the death. We're to destroy its array as quickly as possible.'

"'Suicide missions thrive on high velocities,'" Thompson quoted.

The bastard, Zai thought. To cite Anonymous 167 at him, as if this situation were of Zai's devising.

'We're under orders, Gunner,' Hobbes snapped. 'Preventing contact between the Rix battlecruiser and the Legis compound mind is our primary objective.'

She left the rest unspoken: the *Lynx*'s survival was of secondary concern.

Thompson shrugged, not meeting Hobbes's eye. He was one of those more intimidated by her beauty than her rank. 'Why can't they just pull the plug on the mind down on Legis?' he managed.

Zai sighed. He didn't want his crew spending its energy this way: trying to think of ways to get out of the coming battle.

'They wouldn't have to give up technology forever,' Thompson continued. 'Just for a few days, while the battlecruiser passed by. In boot camp, I lived in a simulated jungle biome for a month using traditional survival techniques. We could offer assistance from *Lynx* for any emergencies.'

'This is a *planet*, Thompson,' Hobbes explained. 'Not some Navy training biome. Two billion civilians and the entire infrastructure that necessitates. Every day that's ten billion gallons of liters, two million tons of food produced and distributed, and a half million emergency medical responses. All of it dependent on the infostructure; dependent, in effect, on the Rix compound mind.'

'We'd have to somehow disable every piece of technology for four days,' Zai continued. 'On a planet of Legis's population, there will be two hundred thousand births in that time. Care to use your survival skills to assist with them all, Thompson?'

The command bridge filled with laughter.

'No, sir,' the man answered. 'Not covered in my basic training, sir.'

'How unfortunate,' Zai concluded. 'Then I'll want your detailed analyses of the current attack plan by 2.00. We'll be under high gravities by 4.00. One last night of decent sleep for the crew.'

'Dismissed,' Hobbes said.

The bridge bustled with energy as the senior officers went to present the plan to their own staffs.

Hobbes gave her captain a supporting nod. Zai was pleased she'd been able to defuse the trouble that Second Gunner Thompson had started. Attacking the superior Rix ship would be an easier sacrifice if the crew thought of it in terms of how many lives they were saving down below. But why was Thompson confronting him in front of his staff?

The second gunner was from an old, gray family, with as solid a military tradition as the Zais. By some measures, Thompson was grayer than his captain. One of his brothers was an aspirant in the Apparatus; none of the Zais had ever been politicals.

Perhaps Thompson's words were intended to remind Zai that the Imperial pardon was a sham, a way for the Emperor to save face. But it was a graceless pardon, paired with an impossible task, which might yet destroy him, his ship, and his crew.

Clearly, Laurent Zai had not been forgiven.

Commando

Wielding the monofilament knife carefully, h_rd cut Rana Harter's long hair down to a few centimeters.

The dopamine regulators that the commando had injected

into her captive's bloodstream were self-perpetuating; the woman would remain acquiescent for days. As the medical records h_rd had unearthed at the library had shown, Harter suffered from chronic low-level depression. Any decent society would have cured it as a matter of course. But the Empire found Rana's synesthetic disorder, her savant mathematical ability, useful. Imperial medicine wasn't sophisticated enough to both heal Harter and maintain the delicate balance of her brainbug, so they let her suffer.

For the Rix, however, the treatment was child's play.

Harter was still feeling some side effects. Her attention seemed to wander now and then, lapsing into short fugues of inactivity, her eyelids shuddering a bit. But when shown the colonel's badge she followed orders; the Imperials conditioned their subjects well. H_rd set Harter to organizing the strands of her shorn hair by length on the cabin's ornate table, while the commando shaved her own head down to the scalp.

The handheld monitor pinged, an order from the compound mind. A schematic on its screen showed the location of the train's medical station. Leaving Rana Harter humming as she worked, the Rix commando braved the corridors of the train again. Having seen no bald women on Legis, h_rd covered her head with the hood of her uniform. She knew that clothing, grooming, and other bodily markers were used to project status and political affiliation even outside the military hierarchy of the Empire; a hairless head might draw attention. How odd. These unRix humans rejected Upgrade, but they still played games with dead cells and bits of cloth and string.

The medical station sprang to life as she entered, its red eyes projecting a lattice of lasers across the newly bald planes of her head. A few seconds after these measurements were taken, the station delivered two needles of specially programmed nanos and another set of orders: the map led to the maglev train's storage hold. H_rd easily wrenched open the lock there, and liberated a tube of repair smartplastic and another of petroleum jelly.

Back in the cabin, she doped the smartplastic with one of the needles, and squeezed it onto the neat pile of Rana Harter's shorn hair. The nanoed plastic writhed for a few minutes, giving off noticeable heat in the small cabin. The mass sent out thin threads that wove themselves among the hair cuttings. These wispy filaments spread out, consuming the mound of repair plastic and creating a spiderweb that covered the entire table. For a while, the web undulated slowly, as if cataloging, planning. Then its motion quickened. The whole mass contracted into a solid dome, a milky hemisphere into which the hairs were drawn. The surface of the plastic seethed with the ends of Rana Harter's red hair, which protruded and dove back into the mound as if ghostly fingers inside were knitting them according to some complex design.

It soothed the commando's mind to watch the elegant and miniature process unfold. Here in the crowded train, she was far too aware of the gross, unRix mass of humanity that surrounded her. She could smell them, hear the phatic chatter of their mouths, feel their handiwork in the bulbous curves and plush textures of this supposedly luxurious cabin, informed by the extravagant concept of privacy. The Rix spacecraft and orbitals that had always been her home were spartan and pure: joyful with the clean lines of functionality, the efficiency of intimately shared spaces, the evident perfection of compound mind design. These unRix humans sought joy in waste, ornamentation, excess.

H_rd knew, of course, that this society's disorder was a necessary evil; the messy inefficiencies of humanity underlay true AI. Alexander emerged from the electronic clutter of this planet, much as h_rd's own thoughts arose from an inefficient tangle of nervous tissue. But she was Rix, and had been raised to see the whole. To be trapped among the horde that underlay Alexander was like descending from the sublime visions of an art museum into the rank smells of an oil-paint factory.

The Rixwoman tore her eyes from the graceful, programmed movements of the plastic, and got back to work.

She ordered Rana Harter to strip. She cut her captive's fingernails and toenails down to the quick, collecting them into a small plastic bag as carefully as evidence of a crime.

Then h_rd unfolded the bed and ordered Rana Harter to lie down. She detached a small grooming unit from the cabin's valet drone, the sort of static electricity and vacuum brush that removes animal hairs from clothing. The commando paused, wondering if she should restrain the woman before proceeding. No. This next step would do as a test of the dopamine regulators' power over her captive.

The hard plastic bristles of the groomer were ideal for defoliating skin. H_rd rubbed the device into Rana Harter's naked stomach in hard, sharp little motions, turning the epidermis there to a ruddy, anguished pink. The vacuum unit greedily consumed the dislocated cells, its fierce little whine drowning out the small, ambivalent noises that came from the woman's mouth as h_rd worked.

Exhausting the skin of the stomach, h_rd moved on to her captive's small breasts, but the woman's movements proved too unruly. H_rd turned Rana Harter over and quarried the broad expanse of her back, and dug hard into the thicker skin of her arms and legs.

Soon she had enough, the vacuum's collector almost full. She tapped its precious cargo onto the table, carefully emptying the collector by wetting her smallest finger with saliva and probing the crannies of the vacuum's mechanism. Then h_rd doped the tube of petroleum jelly with the second needle from the medical station, and squeezed it out onto the skin cells. The admixture moved and grew hot.

Removing her own clothes, h_rd rubbed the petroleum jelly over her own flesh, skipping the flexormetal soles of her feet, the exposed hypercarbon of her knee and shoulder joints, and the metal weave of microwave array on her back. She was a commando, not an intelligence operative, and she would never look human while naked. But hopefully security at the polar base would be too overextended by the horde of new draftees for full physicals. H_rd's path here to the pole had been well disguised, and the Imperials were looking for a single infiltrator on an entire planet. Presumably, her identity would be confirmed by visual comparison with Rana Harter's records, gene-typing a few strands of hair, and reading the genetic material from her human thermal plume. When activated, the nano intelligence now incorporated into the petroleum jelly would sluff Rana Harter's skin cells at a normal human rate, providing constant ambient evidence of her borrowed identity.

If the security forces here demanded a retina scan or some quaint, ancient technique such as fingerprints or dental records, the commando would have to fight her way out in a hurry.

As for the face, Alexander had searched the records of the entire Legis XV military structure for a close match (also selecting for Harter's microastronomy expertise and vulnerability to drugs) and had intervened to transfer the woman here to the pole. Of course, the compound mind could have changed any electronic record to match h_rd's appearance, but human memory was beyond its reach. There was the possibility that someone at the polar station had actually met Rana Harter.

The compound mind was being very cautious. H_rd was

its only human asset on the planet, and might have to pass as the woman for several days, even weeks, while she prepared for the transmission. At least, the commando thought, she would no longer be alone. She would need to keep Rana Harter with her to restock her supply of skin cells.

H_rd emptied her captive's kitbag on the floor and sorted through the contents. Most of the woman's civilian clothes wouldn't fit her larger frame, but the baggy militia fatigues covered her adequately.

H_rd glanced at her timestamp. The hairpiece should be done by now.

On the table, the hemisphere of plastic had stilled. She picked it up cautiously, but it had cooled to room temperature. With a quick, snapping motion, the commando turned it inside out, revealing Rana Harter's hair, now inset into the plastic.

She lifted the hairpiece onto her shaved head, where it fit snugly, incorporating the medical station's exact measurements of her skull.

Alexander caused the cabin's window to opaque and then mirror.

The Rixwoman regarded herself.

H_rd experienced a brief dislocation as Rana Harter seemed to stare back at her from the mirrored window, mimicking her movements. The wig worked perfectly; the nanos had even managed to reconstruct Rana Harter's haircut from the mass of hairs. The resemblance was eerie.

The commando heard a stir from the bed.

Her captive rose slowly, a confused look on Rana's face as she touched her own tender skin. The dreamy expression of dopamine overdose sharpened a little as she stood next to h_rd, comparing her own shaved, naked, and raw figure to her impersonator's.

She spoke the crude words of her Imperial dialect.

Not bad, h_rd's translation software supplied. *But what about your eyes?*

The Rixwoman looked in the reflection at her violet, artificial eyes, then at her captive. Rana Harter's eyes were almond.

H_rd blinked.

The woman's eyes sparkled with tears from the relentless abrading of her skin. No amount of drugs could suppress the reactions of the body to pain. The commando shuddered inside. Death, hers or another's, meant little to her measured against the scope of the Rix compound gods. But she wanted nothing of torture. She turned to the woman, lifting her fingers to point at the woman's eyes, requesting words from her software.

The woman backed away, fear defeating the dopamine to mar her beatific expression. She was talking again.

You're going to take my eyes, aren't you?

H_rd grasped Rana Harter's wrist, firmly but softly.

'No,' she said. She knew that word.

The look of fear didn't leave the woman's face. H_rd suspended her previous request; asked for new sentences.

'Just eyedrop dye,' the Rixwoman said. 'The medical station will make it for me when we get closer.'

'Oh.' The woman stopped trying to pull away.

'Let's talk now. Please,' h_rd said.

'Talk?' Rana Harter repeated.

A pause; new sentences delivered.

'I need to learn your language. Better than this. Let us make . . .' The word was too long, full of slurred sounds.

'Conversation?'

'Yes. I want your conversation, Rana Harter.'

Executive Officer

Katherie Hobbes reached her captain's cabin door at 1.88 hours.

She took a moment outside to gather herself, wondering if she was getting old. A few years ago, a missed night of sleep had seemed routine. Now, she'd been awake a mere fourteen hours, barely more than a day, but Hobbes felt her emotions beginning to fray, her mask of calm efficiency growing more brittle by the minute. She only hoped that her intellectual capacity wasn't suffering as well. This would be a disastrous time to start making tactical errors.

It wasn't simply age, though. The last few days had been a rollercoaster of adrenaline, fear, anguish, and relief. The whole crew had been through the wringer, and now they faced ten days at high acceleration, followed by a battle in which they were overmatched. All of Hobbes's simulations put the *Lynx*'s chances against the Rix battlecruiser at the raw edge of survivability.

Hobbes doubted for a moment her purpose here at the captain's cabin. Was it just wild emotion that had brought her? Perhaps she should wait until after the battle with the Rix to confront this question. She could simply turn around and head for the command bridge, where the senior staff would be assembling in twelve minutes to present their detailed battle plans. But however confident she and the captain might act for the crew, they both knew that the *Lynx* would probably not survive the battle. If she didn't ask now, she might never know the answer.

Hobbes watched her fingers requesting entry.

That common gesture felt suddenly alien, as it had when she'd first left home to enter the Navy.

When Katherie wanted a door to open on a Utopian world, she'd just ask it. Aircars went where they were told, handphones heard and obeyed. But the military never talked to their tools. Such anthropomorphism was too decadent for the grays – machines were machines. Here on the *Lynx*, opening a door required a gestural sequence, a tongue click, perhaps even a token of some kind; it was all secret handshakes and magic rings. The grays preserved spoken language for use among humans, as if conversing with the ship would somehow bring it to life.

In retaliation, gray machines seldom talked to their masters. Instead, they employed a bewildering conglomeration of signifiers to get their messages across. Back on her Utopian birthworld, a burning house would simply alert its occupants with the words, 'Excuse me, but I'm on fire.' Navy alarms, however, were composed of unpleasant sounds and flashing lights.

But Katherie had discovered that she had a gift for the codes and icons. Imperial interfaces had a curt efficiency that she enjoyed. Like a jetboard or a hang-glider, they responded instantly to subtle motions. They weren't slowed down by politesse.

And so, the captain's answer came all too quickly.

'Come,' he said, his voice raw from lack of sleep.

The door opened to reveal Zai. His tunic was unclasped, its metal ringlets hanging slack, his hair glistening from a recent shower. His eyes were lined with red.

Hobbes was brought up for a moment by the sight of her captain in disarray. In their two subjective years together, she had never seen him at less than parade readiness.

'What is it, Hobbes?' he said. He ran his fingers through his hair and glanced at the tactical stylus in her hand. Captain Zai smiled. 'Couldn't wait for the meeting to regale me?'

Her eyes fell shyly as she took a step into the cabin. The door closed behind her.

'I'm sorry to disturb you, Captain.'

'It's time, anyway. We can't be late for this briefing. "Work your staff hard, work yourself harder," aye, Hobbes?'

'Yes, sir. "And make sure they notice,"' she completed the quote.

He nodded, and began to work the clasps of his heavy woolen uniform. Hobbes watched the fingers of his gloved, artificial hand move, momentarily unable to speak.

He pointed to his conference table.

'Ever actually seen sand before?'

The table was covered with a galaxy of bright, hard shapes. Hobbes leaned closer and picked one up. The tiny object was sharp in her hand, with the familiar facets of structured carbon.

'So, this is sand, sir?' Hobbes knew the battle specs on ten different types of sand, but she'd never held the stuff between her fingers.

'Yes, what poets and politicals call *diamonds*. I intend to use quite a bit of it in the battle, Hobbes. We can synthesize a hundred tons or so in the next two weeks.'

She nodded. Sandcaster drones were used in any space engagement to spread confusion in the enemy's sensors, but at this battle's high relative velocity, the stuff could be lethal. At high speed, enough of the hard, sharp particles could eat away even hullalloy.

'Pretty little things, sir.'

'Keep one, if you like.'

Hobbes put the diamond in her pocket, closed a fist on its hard shape. There was no delaying her purpose here any longer.

'I just had a question, sir. Before the meeting.'

'Certainly, Hobbes.'

'To better understand your thinking, sir,' she said. 'You see, I'm not sure that I completely grasp your . . . motivations.'

'My motivations?' he said with surprise. 'I'm a soldier, Hobbes. I have orders and objectives, not motivations.'

'Generally true, sir,' she admitted. 'And I don't mean any personal intrusion, Captain. But the current tactical situation – as we both have agreed – seems to have become intertwined with your . . . personal motivations, sir.'

'What the devil are you asking, Hobbes?' Zai said, his fingers frozen on the top clasp of his uniform.

Hobbes felt her face flush with embarrassment. She wished she could disappear, or could rewind time and find herself on the other side of his door, walking toward the command bridge, having never come in.

But even mortified as she was, the emotions that had carried her into the captain's cabin pushed her to say the next words.

'Captain, you know that I'm very happy that you rejected the blade. I did all I could to convince—' She swallowed. 'But now that you have, I'm just a bit confused.'

Zai blinked, then the slightest smile played at his lips.

'You want to know why I didn't kill myself, eh, Hobbes?'

'I think it was the right choice, sir,' she insisted quickly. It was absolutely essential that he not misunderstand her. 'But as your executive officer, I need to know why. In case it has an effect on . . . our working together, sir.'

'My motivation,' Zai repeated, nodding his head. 'Perhaps you think I've become unhinged, Executive Officer?'

'Not at all, sir. I think your choice was very sane.'

'Thank you, Hobbes.' Laurent Zai thought for a moment, then sealed the top clasp of his uniform and said, 'Sit down.'

She found herself falling into one of the deep chairs around his airscreen table. The effort of breaching the topic had exhausted her. Her legs were weak. She was glad as he sat down that he would speak now, that she could remain silent.

'Hobbes, you've known me for two years, and you know the kind of man I am. I'm Vadan and gray. As gray as they come. So I understand that you're surprised by my recent decisions.'

'Happily surprised, sir,' she managed.

'But you suspect there may be more to it, eh? Some secret directive from the Apparatus that explains all this?'

She shook her head. That wasn't it at all. But Zai went on.

'Well, it's simpler than that. More human.'

She blinked, waiting through the interminable pause.

'After forty relative years, and almost a century of absolute time, I've found out something unexpected,' he began. 'Tradition isn't everything for me, Hobbes. Perhaps it was on Dhantu that I changed, that some part of the old Laurent Zai died. Or perhaps when I was rescued and rebuilt, they didn't put me back together in the same way. However it happened, I've changed. Service to the Emperor is no longer my only goal.'

Zai absentmindedly attached his captain's bars to his shoulders, where they slid to their correct positions.

'Hobbes, it's quite simple, really. It seems I have fallen in love.'

She found that her breath had stopped. Time had stopped.

'Sir?' she managed.

'And the thing is, Hobbes, it seems that love is more important than Empire.'

'Yes, sir,' was all she could say.

'But I am still your captain, as before,' he said. 'I shall still follow the Navy's orders, if not every tradition. No need to worry about my loyalties.'

'Of course not, sir. I never doubted you, sir. This changes nothing, Captain.'

It changed everything.

Hobbes allowed herself to feel for a moment, tentatively to sample the torrent of emotions that built inside her. They poured from her heart, ravenous and almost frighteningly strong, and she had to clench her teeth to keep them from her face. She nodded carefully, and allowed herself a smile.

'It's okay, Laurent. It's human.'

With an effort of will, she rose. 'Perhaps we should continue this conversation after the battle with the Rix is concluded.' It was the only possible solution. The only way to survive was to push this down into hiding for another ten days.

Zai glanced rightward, where she knew he kept the current time in his secondary sight, and nodded in agreement.

'Right, Hobbes. Always efficient.'

'Thank you, sir.'

They took a step together toward the door, and then he grasped her shoulder. A warmth spread from that contact through her body. It was the first time he had touched her in two years.

She turned to him, her eyes half closing.

'She sent that message,' he said softly.

She. 'Sir?'

'When I went to the observation blister to kill myself,' he said. 'There was a message. It was from her.'

'From *her*?' she repeated, her mind unable to parse the words.

'My beloved,' he said, an out-of-character, beatific smile upon his face. 'A single word, that made all the difference.'

Katherie Hobbes felt a chill spreading through her.

'"Don't," the message said. And I didn't,' he continued. 'She saved me.'

There it was again. *She.* Not *you.*

'Yes, sir.'

Laurent's hand slipped from her shoulder. Now the cold in Hobbes was absolute. It stilled her raging emotions. Like a killing frost, it cut down the part of her that was confused, devastated.

Soon she would be ready to go on. She just had to keep standing here, without feeling, for these next few seconds, and everything would be back the way it was.

'Thank you, Hobbes,' Captain Zai said. 'I'm glad you asked. It's good to tell someone.'

'Very well, sir,' she answered. 'The briefing, sir?'

'Of course.'

They walked there together, her eyes forward so as not to see the unfamiliar expression on her captain's face.

Happiness.

Senator

'We approved the attack without objection.'

Senator Nara Oxham said the words quietly, almost talking to herself.

Roger Niles frowned and said, 'The *Lynx* would be just as doomed if you'd forced a vote. Losing eight to one isn't much of a moral victory.'

'A *moral* victory, Niles?' Oxham asked, a faint smile softening the bitterness on her face. 'I've never heard you use that term before.'

'You won't hear it again. It's a contradiction in terms. You did the right thing.'

Nara Oxham shook her head slowly. She'd signed a death warrant for her lover, and for another three hundred men and women, all for the political advantage of a despot. Surely this could not be the right thing.

'Senator, these won't be the last lives the War Council will vote to sacrifice,' Niles said. 'This is war. People die. There are real strategic arguments for sending the *Lynx* against that battlecruiser. The Empire simply has no idea what the Rix are up to. We don't know why they want to contact the Legis compound mind. It might be worth a frigate to keep the beast cut off.'

'*Might* be, Niles?'

'It's in the nature of war to frustrate the enemy, even if you're not sure exactly what they're doing.'

'Do you really think so?' Nara asked.

The man nodded. 'The Emperor and his admirals aren't about to sacrifice a starship just to revenge a slight. The *Lynx* may be small, but she's the most advanced warship in the Spinward Reaches. Even an insult from a gray hero like Laurent Zai wouldn't warrant throwing her away.'

'You should have heard them, Niles. They laughed with pleasure at making him a martyr. Called him a cripple.'

Nara put her head in her hands and leaned back, letting the luxuriant visitors' couch take her form. She and Niles were in one of the docking spires above the Forum, tall spindles of crystal that sprouted from the senatorial grounds to tower over the capital. The spire rooms were used primarily to impress ambassadors and to entertain the odd powerful constituent. They were intimate despite their commanding views, the Senate's subtle answer to the Imperial glories of the Diamond Palace and the Holy Orbitals. Their slightly musty furnishings spoke of collegiality and chumminess, of retail politics and handshake deals.

Oxham and Niles had evicted the spire room's previous occupants (Council rank had its privileges) for a hasty meeting before she returned to the Diamond Palace. The senator's palace flyer waited just outside, bobbing softly in the cold morning breeze. Nara hadn't known that the term 'docking spires' was literal, but the flyer's AI had chosen the spire, recognizing that Oxham had little time for a landing.

Council would meet again in twenty minutes.

'I don't know what's worse,' Oxham admitted. 'The Emperor killing Zai for revenge or me voting to commit the *Lynx* for purely tactical reasons – agreeing with the over-whelming majority so that they'd listen to me when a close vote came up.'

'That's sound thinking, Senator. You don't want to be branded as weak and unwilling to shed blood.'

'But actually to agree with them,' she continued. 'To sacri-fice three hundred lives on the merest *assumption* that troubling the Rix is worth the cost. That's harder to swallow than a tactical concession, Niles.'

Her old counselor stared back at her. He looked diminutive on the overcushioned divan, a sharp-faced elf in the salon of some corpulent satrap. His eyes narrowed, bright blue and exceptionally sharp. There was no second sight here, ten kilo-meters above the concentrated synesthesia projectors of the Forum's chambers.

'You've made distasteful compromises before, Nara,' he said.

'Yes, I've traded my vote before,' she answered warily. It was Niles's way to debate her when she doubted herself, to bully her into understanding her own motives.

'What's the difference this time?' he asked.

She sighed, feeling like a schoolgirl repeating rote les-sons. 'In the past, I've bargained with the Empire's wealth. I've dealt tax relief for patent enforcement, axis protections for trading rights. Ninety percent of Senate policy is pure economics, a matter of possession. I've never traded in lives before.'

Niles looked out the window, his gaze oriented on the

Debted Hills, over which dawn was breaking through distant black clouds.

'Senator, did you know that the suicide rate in the Empire has been consistent since the First Rix Incursion?'

Suicide rate? Oxham thought. What was Roger talking about?

She shrugged. 'The population is so large, its economic power so dispersed – that sort of consistency is just the weak law of large numbers at work. Any local spikes or troughs in suicides are subsumed within the whole.'

'And what would cause those local spikes, Senator?'

'You know that, Niles. Money is the key to everything. Economic downturns lead to a higher suicide rate, murder rate, and infant mortality, even on the wealthiest worlds. Human society is a fragile weave; if the pool of resources shrinks, we're at each other's throats.'

He nodded, his face growing lighter by the moment in the rising sun.

'So, when you trade tax relief and axis protections, pushing around wealth in accordance with the grand Secularist plan, what are you really trading?'

The bright sun had reached her face, and Nara Oxham closed her eyes. As often happened when she was out of synesthesia's reach, ghost images of old data danced before her eyes. She could reflexively visualize what Niles was saying. On a world of a billion people, a decrease of one percentage point in planetary product would result in well-established statistical shifts: some ten thousand additional murders, five thousand suicides, another million in the next generation who would never leave the planet. The explanations for each tragedy were terribly specific – a broken home, a business failure, ethnic conflict – but the god of statistics swallowed the individual stories, smoothing the numbers into law.

'Of course,' Niles interrupted her thoughts, 'the process you're used to is rather more indirect than ordering soldiers to their deaths.'

Oxham nodded. She had no will left to argue the point.

'I'd hoped you would cheer me up, Roger,' she said.

He leaned forward. 'You did the right thing, Nara, as I said before. Your political instincts were correct, as always. And it's possible that the council actually made the right military decision.'

She shook her head. They'd condemned the *Lynx* without a clear reason.

'But here's what I was trying to say,' Niles continued. 'You've handled issues of this import before.'

'I've traded in lives before, you mean.'

His gaze swept down from the bright sky to the huge city.

'We are in the business of power, Senator. And power at this scale is a matter of life and death.'

She sighed. 'Do you think they'll all die, Roger?'

'The crew of the *Lynx*?' he asked.

The old advisor was looking straight at her. The sunrise had found his gray hairs, which glinted like strands of boyish red. She could tell that her anguish was revealed on her face.

'It's Laurent Zai, isn't it?'

Oxham lowered her eyes, which was sufficient answer. She'd known that Niles would find out soon enough. He knew that Oxham's lover was a soldier, and there were a limited number of occasions when a Secularist senator would come into contact with military personnel. The Emperor's parties were a matter of record, and they were monitored by an informal system of rumors, gossip sheets, and anonymous posts, all of which were filtered through celebrity newsfeeds. An intense and private conversation between a senator-elect and an elevated hero, no matter how brief, could not have gone unreported.

Any doubts that Niles might have entertained would be vanquished once he'd uncovered that decade-old conversation. It must have been obvious to him why Nara was focused on the fate of the *Lynx*.

She sighed, sadder still now. Her closest advisor knew that she had voted for the death of her lover.

He leaned closer.

'Listen, Nara: it will be safer for you if they all die cleanly.'

Her eyes stung now. She tried to read Niles, but she'd had to up the dose of apathy in her bloodstream to cross the city, which was bright and sharp with war lust.

'Safer?' she managed after a moment.

'If the Risen Emperor were to discover that one of his war counselors communicated privately with a commander in the field, one who then rejected a blade of error,' Niles explained, 'he'd have her head on a stake.'

She swallowed.

'I'm protected by privilege, Niles.'

'Like any legal construct, the Rubicon Pale is a fiction, Nara. Such fictions have their limits.'

Oxham looked at her old friend aghast. The Pale was the basis of the Risen Empire's fundamental division of power. It was sacred.

But Niles continued. 'You're playing both sides, Senator. And that's a dangerous game.'

She started to respond, but the council summons sounded in her head.

'I have to go, Niles. The war calls me.'

He nodded. 'So it does. Just don't make yourself a casualty, Nara.'

She smiled sadly.

'This is war,' she said. 'People die.'

Militia Worker

Rana Harter was happy here on the tundra.

It had taken her a few days in the prefab to grasp and name the feeling. Before meeting the Rixwoman, happiness had only ever come to her in short, evanescent bursts: a few seconds when sunset drenched the sky in the smell of chamomile; a man's touch in the feathery moments before he became brutal; those brief flashes of trumpet and copper-on-the-tongue as Rana's brainbug took hold and the world emerged exact and clear. But the happiness she felt now was somehow sustained, awakening with her each morning, stretching across these long and listless nights she spent with Herd, constantly amazing Rana with its persistence.

Like the whorls of her fingertips in a microscope, joy turned out to be entirely unfamiliar when viewed at this new and larger scale. Rana understood now that the happy moments of her earlier life had been furtive, truncated. Like a wild tundra hare, felicity had always bolted before she could grasp it, slipping across the bleak background of her life, a mere streak forever in peripheral vision. She had been ashamed of her mind's abilities, overawed by the beautiful but brutal natural world of her cold home province, embarrassed by the pleasures she took with men. But now Rana could actually witness her happiness directly, magnified through the lens of eleven-hour Legis nights when Herd was released from duty.

Rana Harter had discovered unimaginable new textures of contentment. She could count the grains in a teaspoon of spilled sugar, listen for hours to the moaning song of the incessant polar wind as it tested the walls of their cheap rented prefab. Even Herd's intense, daily ministrations – shaving every part of her, cutting hair and nails, swabbing saliva, abrading skin – became rough pleasures. The Rixwoman's competent hands, her brittle conversation, and her strange, birdlike movements were endlessly fascinating.

Rana knew that Herd had given her a drug, and that the joy she felt had been forced upon her, leveraged by chemicals rather than events. She knew objectively that she should be terrified: suffering forcible confinement and isolation with a deadly alien. Rana even considered escape once, out of an abstract sense of duty to the militia and her home planet, and from worry that the Rixwoman would eventually dispose of her. Rana had managed to dress herself, the fabric of her old clothes sensually harsh against raw skin. Warmth had required layers and layers; Herd always took their only winter coat to work at the facility. But when Rana opened the door to the prefab, the cold poured in with the blinding glare of the white tundra. The frozen vista of the polar waste muted any desire for freedom. It only reminded Rana how bleak her life had been before. She closed the door and turned the heat up to compensate for the inrush of frigid air, then took off the chafing clothes. She could not leave.

But Rana never felt defeated here in this cabin. Somehow, her mind seemed freed by captivity. It was as if her brainbug, no longer suppressed by shame, had finally been given the opportunity to develop to its true capacity.

Rana loved teaching the northern Legis XV dialect to Herd. While her captor was away impersonating her, Rana spent the hours diagramming the structure of basic Imperial grammar, filling the prefab's cheap airscreen with webs of conjugations surrounded by archipelagos of slang, patois, and irregulars. Her student was an unbelievably quick learner. The commando's knowledge advanced nightly, Herd's flat, neutral accent taking on the rounded vowels of the tundral provinces.

Rana demanded to be taught in return, insisting that knowledge of the Rix tongue would improve her tutoring of Herd. Rana also learned quickly, and they began to converse late into the night, Rana firing away with questions about Herd's upbringing, beliefs, and life in the Rix Cult. At first, the commando resisted these attempts at companionship, but the cold and featureless Legis nights seemed to wear away at her resolve. Soon, the conversation between hostage and captor became constant and bilingual, each speaking the other's language.

At first, Rix was easy to learn. The core grammar of the language was artificial, created by compound minds to facilitate communication between planetary intelligences and their servants. But the language was designed to evolve quickly in human use, its streamlined phonology of clicks and pops infinitely malleable, able to embrace the unwieldy tenses of relativity or the chance-matrices of the quantum.

In Rana's mind, now constantly in a light brainbug fugue, the collectivity of things Rix began to take on a definite shape/flavor/smell. The clean lines of Herd's weapons, the icy sharpness of the woman's language, the whir of her servomotors, just audible when Herd was naked, the way hypercarbon melded into skin at her knees, elbows, and shoulders – all were of a piece. This Rix-shape grew in Rana Harter's head, putting to shame the brainbugs of her earlier life, the mathematical parlor tricks to which the Empire put her ability. Here was the flavor of a whole *culture*, as deep and heady as some ancient whiskey perpetually under her nose.

Rana watched her captor as if in love, pupils dilated with the dopamine coursing through her bloodstream, brilliant revelations growing within.

After three days at the pole, Herd began to question Rana about Imperial entanglement technology. Under the current state of emergency, the entire polar facility was cut off from the Legis information web; thus the compound mind could only assist indirectly with whatever sabotage they were planning. Herd, a soldier rather than an engineer, was unable to effect the changes that the mind demanded. Rana tried to help with her limited understanding of the arrays used in microastronomy, but her answers often confused Herd; the underlying Rix concepts of quantum theory differed from the Imperial model. The two systems seemed fatally at odds. For one, the Rix standard model rendered the curves of discernible difference with a different number of dimensions than the Imperial. And their notion of discoherence escaped Rana altogether.

So she put her hours of quiet happiness to work, beginning a study of translight communications. She found the Legis library unexpectedly helpful. Almost immediately, Rana found an expert program to help her. The expert bookmarked and highlighted the primary texts, guided her through the morass of beginner's texts to build on her elementary understanding of repeater arrays. The expert seemed to understand Rana, quickly learning to mold information into the form demanded by her brainbug, pulling in the chaotic, widespread data upon which her ability feasted. Herd brought home an attachment for the cabin's airscreen, a second-sight projector that allowed Rana to go into full synesthesia. She sank into the coils of data, willing prey. Herd had never told Rana exactly what the commando's mission was here at the pole, but her study seemed to guide itself.

She found herself fascinated by the backup receivers that supported the facility, collecting the planet's conventional tranmissions and forwarding them to the translight grid. There were many systems in place in case the hardlines were cut, but Rana was especially drawn to a colony of hardy, small, self-repairing machines that lived on the polar wastes around the facility. They were like the cheap, distributed arrays that Rana had used before in microastronomy, designed to survive arctic winters, earthquakes, and acts of terrorism.

After a few sleepless days, Rana collapsed into a sleep/fugue that lasted some untold time. When she awoke, Herd was next to her, applying a cold rag to her fevered head. The usual joy of awakening filled her, heightened now with the surety of new knowledge. It was in the lemongrass flicker of Herd's eyes, the precision of her movements as she squeezed excess water from the rag, and it animated the shape of Rana's researches in the cabin's airscreen: the flavor of her understanding reflected throughout the room.

'The expert program,' Rana said in the Rix tongue. 'It's the compound mind, isn't it?'

Herd nodded, and answered quietly.

'It is always with us.' The sentence was one syllable in Rix.

The commando held the red wig in one hand. Rana's own hair, removed so long ago, now seemed an alien artifact to her. The Rixwoman fitted the wig onto Rana's head. It felt warm, as if fresh from an oven. It seemed to fit perfectly.

'You will be Rana Harter tomorrow,' Herd said.

The thought of leaving the prefab terrified her.

'But I don't even know what you want,' Rana said, slipping into Legis dialect. The Imperial language felt crude, like thick porridge in her mouth.

'Yes, you do,' the Rixwoman said.

Rana shook her head. She thought hard in her native tongue: she knew *nothing*. As it had done all her life, confidence crumbled inside Rana.

'I don't understand. I'm not smart enough.'

Herd smiled, and touched the cold rag to Rana's forehead. With that contact, her anxiety lifted. Separate threads began to weave themselves together: the data from her guided exploration of repeater technology, the emerging shape and flavor of

Rix culture, the fast Bach and lemongrass of Herd's powerful and avian presence.

And quite suddenly, Rana Harter knew the compound mind's desire.

Herd's servomotors whirred as her hands moved across Rana. She was applying some sort of cream to Rana's embattled skin. The touch felt delicious, a balm against the fever of realization in her head.

'Don't worry, my lucky find,' the commando said. 'Alexander is with you now.'

Alexander. The thing actually had a name.

Rana touched her fingers to her own forehead.

'Inside me?'

'Everywhere.'

Executive Officer

Katherie Hobbes let the water run into her glass in a thin, slow stream, until it had filled to the brim. The tap stopped automatically, before even a drop ran down the side; water wasn't rationed here on board the *Lynx*, but wastefulness went against the aesthetics of the Navy.

Hobbes turned from the sink in slow motion, her green eyes following each motion of her hand, carefully watching the wobble of the surface tension that held the water in the glass. She took the few steps that it took to cross the executive officer's private cabin, her movements an exaggerated pantomime. The glass felt strangely heavy, although the *Lynx*'s high acceleration was, in theory, fully corrected. Was the extra weight a stress hallucination? Perhaps Hobbes's limbs were simply tired, beaten down by the constant microshifts of easy gravity.

Or perhaps it was her disappointment. She hadn't had time to recover from Zai's revelation before the weight of high acceleration had settled painfully upon her.

Normally, the vicissitudes of artificial gravity created only a vague disquiet in Hobbes, no worse than the motion sickness she'd experienced on the great, seagoing pleasure craft of her Utopian home. But the *Lynx* was currently accelerating at ten gees, and the slight flaws and inconsistencies of easy gravity were correspondingly magnified.

The field patterns of easy gravity were a classic metachaotic system, mined with strange attractors, stochastic overloads, and a host of other mathematical chimeras. Fluctuations of mass on one side of a solar system could affect easy gravitons on the other unpredictably, even fatally. It was not quite the case that the flutter of a butterfly's wings could cause a tornado, but the swift rotation of Legis system's seven gas giants and the massive solar flares of its sun constituted more than enough chaos to perturb Katherie Hobbes's inner ear.

Hobbes could feel the effects of high acceleration in her joints as well. Every few minutes, something as simple as taking a step would go subtly wrong, as if the floor had come up slightly too hard to meet her foot. Or an object in her hand would jump from her grasp, as if suddenly pulled by an invisible hand. The stresses were rarely strong, but the constant unpredictability of normal events had gradually worn down her reflexes, fatiguing Hobbes's faith in reality. Now she mistrusted the simplest of actions, just as she mistrusted her own emotions.

What a fool was Katherie Hobbes.

Could she have really thought that Laurent Zai was in love with her, even for a moment? When had that insane idea begun? She felt an idiot; a young idiot, suffering a classic infatuation with a distant, older authority figure. The whole episode had shaken her faith in herself, and the random jumps of gravity that plagued the *Lynx* weren't helping. She wished she could have a hot bath, and cursed the Navy for its disdain for this simple, necessary pleasure.

At least she had other things to worry about. The flexing gravity around her was real enough, and wielded outliers of lethal force. The night before, the marble chessboard in Hobbes's locker had suddenly, earsplittingly cracked, rudely interrupting her fitful sleep.

A few minor injuries had occurred on the *Lynx* in the first few days of acceleration. Ankle fractures and knee sprains were common, a young marine's arm had broken without apparent cause, and burst blood vessels were visible in the eyes of a number of her shipmates. Katherie herself had suffered an unbearable and sudden headache the day before. It had passed quickly, but the intense pain was unnerving. With the ship's doctor dead, there was little hope for anyone suffering brain damage from some wayward tendril of gravity passing through their head.

Hobbes walked carefully, and reached the black lacquer table without spilling any of the water.

Setting the glass on the table, she sat and watched the water's surface. It loomed just above the lip, quivering slightly. Was that some perturbation of the easy gravity field? Or simply the ambient vibration of the *Lynx* under high acceleration, marking the egress of photons from its churning engines?

The water shuddered once, but the surface tension held. A few drops condensed on the side of the glass and traveled slowly downward. Nothing seemed to be out of order in that tiny segment of space.

It gave Katherie a secure feeling to observe this localized example of soundness and normality.

After a minute of watching, Hobbes picked up the glass and poured it slowly onto the table.

The water seemed to turn black against the ebony lacquer. It formed into rivulets and small pools, seeking the imperceptible valleys of the table's contours. None was absorbed into the shiny blackness; the water's surface tension kept the drops large and rounded.

On a dry island in this shallow sea she placed the diamond Laurent Zai had given her, a bright spot against its blackness.

Hobbes set the half-full glass down and regarded the results.

At first, the liquid seemed to come to rest, gathered in spattery puddles, with one tiny river reaching the edge and running from table onto floor. Then, Hobbes saw something move across the blackness, a wave of force, as if the table had been kicked. A few seconds later, one of the tendrils of water flexed in agitation, twisting like a beached fish. A single, isolated droplet moved a few centimeters, as if momentarily inhabited by a live spirit, and engulfed the tiny diamond. Then the water was still again.

Hobbes waited patiently, and more flutters of motion came. Spread across the table's two dimensions, its passage on the lacquer almost frictionless, the spilled water writhed visibly with the microshifts of artificial gravity coursing through the *Lynx*. In its sinuous motion, it revealed gravitic lines of force like iron filings rendering the patterns of magnetism.

It eased Katherie's mind to watch the water move. Now that she could actually see the invisible forces that had tortured her crewmates for the last week, Hobbes felt a bit more in control. She gazed at the black table, trying to scry some understanding from the patternless figures there. But easy gravitons were chaotic, complex, unpredictable: like the ancients' concept of the gods, whimsical and obscure, pushing tiny humans around according to some incomprehensible plan. Not unlike, Katherie Hobbes reflected, the political forces that moved the *Lynx* across the black and empty canvas of space, placing them here at this nexus of a new war, condemning the captain, pardoning him, then sending them all careening toward death.

Like the drops of water before her, the crew of the *Lynx* wriggled blindly against this void. An emotion that had seemed immense to Hobbes had become suddenly infinitesimal, laughable. On the scale of the universe, the aborted love of one executive officer for her captain made no ripples at all.

Still, at this moment, Hobbes knew she hated Laurent Zai with all her heart.

When her door sounded, Katherie Hobbes started, banging her knee against the table's leg.

'Come,' she said, rubbing the leg, her latest wound.

Second Gunner Thompson entered, taking slow, careful steps, like a practiced alcoholic. He smiled when he saw the water-covered table.

'Spill something? I've been doing that all week.'

'Just an experiment,' she said.

He shrugged, and pointed to the chair opposite her. She nodded. Thompson lowered himself carefully, mindful of the poltergeists of gravity all around them.

It occurred to Hobbes that the second gunner had never been in her private cabin before. He had always been friendly, but perhaps a bit too familiar, as if he felt that his aristocratic roots entitled him beyond his rank. And Hobbes was aware of the effect she had on some crew. Her Utopian upbringing had casually included a degree of cosmetic surgery that gray parents would never countenance. She was overwhelmingly beautiful to many of them, and to others a woman of cartoonish sexuality, like a whore in some ribald comedy. She had considered counteractive surgery to make herself more average-looking, but that seemed the ultimate affectation. Hobbes was what she was.

The man sighed when he reached the safety of the chair.

'I'm sore all over,' he said.

'Who isn't?' Hobbes answered. 'Just be glad you can't feel the real ten gees. *Then* you'd be sore. Dead by now, in fact.'

Thompson's head rolled back slowly in exhaustion; his eyes closed.

'The worst thing is,' he said, 'I can't quite place where it hurts. It's like when you turn an ankle, and wind up limping for a few days. Then the *other* ankle gets sore from taking up the slack.'

'Collateral injuries,' she said.

'Right. But I seem to be *all* collateral injuries, like I can't remember where the original damage was. Very disquieting.'

Hobbes looked down at the table. Her collision with it had spattered the water evenly across the black expanse, and now it revealed nothing but the ship's ambient vibration.

'I know what you mean,' she said. 'I've been trying to get a hold of it myself. To place it . . . in perspective.'

Thompson opened his eyes, squinted at her. Then he shrugged.

'Ever been in high acceleration this long before, Hobbes?'

She shook her head. Few of the crew had. High gees were usually reserved for battle, a few hours at most.

'Makes you wonder what we did to deserve it,' Thompson said.

Something about the man's voice made her look up from the spattered table. His eyes were narrowed.

'We lost the Empress,' she answered flatly.

He nodded deliberately, as if wary of gravity even in this simple motion.

'A debt that wasn't paid,' he said softly.

A slow disquiet took form in Hobbes's stomach, joining the nausea that lay there. 'What are you talking about, Thompson?'

'Katherie, do you really think the Navy wants to sacrifice the *Lynx*?' he asked. His voice was as soft now, just above a whisper. 'Simply to prevent one compound mind from communicating with one Rix ship?'

'So it would seem, Thompson,' she said.

'But we can't keep the mind cut off forever,' he said. 'It's a whole *planet*, for the Emperor's sake. The Rix'll find some way to talk to it.'

'Maybe. But not while the *Lynx* is here.'

'However long that is,' he said.

She looked down at the table, unable to think for a moment. The water looked different now. The surface tension seemed to be reasserting itself; droplets and puddles were forming again. It didn't make sense, this spontaneous organization. Was entropy giving way to order, the arrow of time in reverse?

What was Thompson talking about?

'Tell me what's on your mind, Second Gunner,' Hobbes ordered.

'It's obvious, Katherie,' he said, 'why the *Lynx* is being sent on this mission. We're being sacrificed, to cover the debt not paid.'

Hobbes closed her eyes. She only had a few seconds to respond, she knew.

Katherie Hobbes had been an above-average student at Academy, but not the best. Coming from a Utopian world, she didn't have the discipline of her gray peers. She didn't think herself truly brilliant, just savant at certain types of tactical calculations. But even in her greatest moments of self-doubt, Hobbes always prided herself on one thing: she made decisions quickly.

Katherie Hobbes made a decision now.

'Thompson, are you the only one thinking about this?'

He shook his head, so slightly that it would have been imperceptible in a low-resolution recording.

'Tell me what you're thinking, Thompson.'

'We've been friends, right, Hobbes?'

She nodded.

'So you give your word that you'll be . . . discreet?'

Hobbes sighed. She'd hoped it wouldn't come to this. But her decision was made.

'The way I see it, Thompson,' she said, 'we're all dead anyway.'

He smiled ruefully, folding his hands and shifting in his seat toward her.

'Maximum privacy,' she told the room, and leaned forward to listen.

Militia Worker

As Rana Harter approached the sniffer, she felt like an impostor.

The red wig tight on her head, the coarse militia fatigues against her raw skin, the military ID bracelet – it all felt like a costume, a ruse that might be discovered at any second. In the burnished metal walls of the facility her own reflection was only distantly familiar, a holo from childhood. It was as if she were impersonating a previous self.

The sniffer created a bottleneck as the workers entered the array facility. Rana felt a moment of panic as she joined the crowd. The week she'd spent alone with Herd in the prefab seemed like months now – the lengthened memory of some summer idyll. Isolation had a purity about it, a calm order that was hard to leave behind. The jostling crowd offended her new sensibilities.

She wished that Herd were here with her, a familiar presence to guide her through the strange facility. The commando had impersonated Rana for the last week, and knew her way within these walls. But the sniffer would no doubt take umbrage at *two* Rana Harters entering together.

There was a slight updraft in the short passageway of the sniffer, slow fans assisting the human thermal plume, carrying skin cells and dust upward. With these particles the device could not only DNA-type the entering workers, but also detect the effluvia of concealed explosives or weapons, and search frayed hairs and skin cells for signs of drug or alcohol abuse. It could even sniff theft; valuable pieces of equipment in the facility were given phero patches. Whatever you were up to, the sniffer smelled you out.

Rana held her breath as she passed through. Would the device notice the difference between herself and Herd? The thought of being stopped and questioned terrified her. She might be Rana Harter down to the bone, but she felt utterly false.

She hoped her epidermis had recovered sufficiently to satisfy the machine's appetite. Herd had worked a healing balm into her skin all night, trying to restore the cells the commando had mined so pitilessly for her own use. The balm seemed to have worked, taking the pink rawness from her skin – but after the last week, any attempt to put the old Rana Harter back together seemed woefully insufficient. She felt half Rix now.

The sniffer, however, let her through without comment.

Herd had drawn a map on a piece of flash paper. Rana held the paper carefully: any friction and it would incinerate itself. She followed the map through narrow, dimly lit hallways. The tight hypercarbon spaces down here felt like the corridors of an overcrowded ship, and smelled of damp and humanity. The facility was overstaffed by half, Rana knew. Herd had said that a fresh load of newcomers had arrived two days ago, along with news of another approaching Rix warship. The signs of organizational confusion were everywhere: equipment stacked in carry-cases crowding the halls, breakrooms filled with impromptu workstations, newly assigned workers moving through the hallways carrying order chits and looking lost.

The repeater array that collected the planet's com traffic for offworld retransmission was being refitted to assist Legis's orbital defenses. The changeover from communications to intelligence gathering was taking place at breakneck speed.

When Rana met other workers in the hall, she found herself moving like Herd. Another imitation, in case any of the passersby had met the commando in her Rana Harter guise. The avian motions – sudden and tightly controlled, each joint an isolated engine – came to Rana with an unexpected ease. In a week of living with the commando, she had internalized the woman's gait, copying her avian power and unpredictability. The impersonation seemed to work, even though there was a decimeter difference in stature between herself and her captor. A few of the other workers nodded with recognition or said her name in greeting.

Rana responded to them with Herd's cryptic smile.

It would, of course, be easy to escape the Rixwoman now. She could announce herself to the facility's security forces – pulling off the wig would certainly get their attention. And she was safe from retaliation. Alexander was absent here. The links from the planetary infostructure to the entanglement facility had been physically cut by Imperial edict. The usual ghosts of second sight – timestamps, newsfeeds, and locators – were oddly absent. There was nothing Herd or Alexander could do to her.

But if she betrayed them, the happiness would go away.

Herd had already injected her with the antidote for the dopamine regulators. The nanos' influence had diminished already, the joy she had floated upon for the last week slowly winding down. Herd had insisted, and it was true, that with the gauze of happiness gone she would be more clearheaded for this job. But her undrugged mind threatened to return to its former state of indecision and fear. She could already glimpse that wavering, all-too-human Rana Harter waiting in the wings. The confident, hybrid creature she had become could crumble at any moment.

She knew she would not betray her new allies. Rana wanted to keep this reborn self. The Rixwoman and her omnipotent god had erased a lifetime of marginal existence, borderline depression, and unfulfilled potential. They had done more for Rana Harter in a week than the Empire had in twenty-seven years.

And besides, this was a mission of mercy, she now understood. Alexander must be freed.

Following the map, she found the workstation for Rana Harter, Second-Class Militia Worker. The interface was unfamiliar from her days in quantum microastronomy. As Herd had explained, she had been assigned to monitor and repair the hundreds of receivers/repeaters that funneled the world's data into the entanglement facility. Her transfer here – arranged by Alexander – had been justified by Rana's practical knowledge of distributed arrays. She'd been assigned to the GAP's remote, icy wastes all her career, and had often been required to make her own repairs.

But she would be doing more than repairs today.

Hopefully, no one would interrupt her shift. The chaos of the overcrowded station was such that a self-sufficient operator was largely left to her own devices. Rana sat, called up the workstation's help mode, and began to look things over.

*

By the end of her shift, Rana Harter had found everything that Alexander wanted.

The entanglement facility had been designed for exactly the type of traffic the compound mind envisioned. The facility incorporated a huge number of repeaters that gathered information from local planetary communications – phones, credit cells, taxation minders, legal governors – and pumped compressed versions of these data into the entanglement system. Despite its military provenance, the facility's primary purpose was to link the planet's civilian economy with the rest of the Risen Empire. There were even FM radio transmitters to throughput data to the other Legis planets at lightspeed; XV was the fleshpot and de facto capital of the system.

In peacetime, these transmissions came into the entanglement facility through hardlines, and in emergencies, through the repeaters. Scattered through the acres of the facility were tens of thousands of tiny civilian-band receivers, a vast colony of machines that lived on snow and sunlight. The repeater colony extended for hundreds of square kilometers, to the edge of the wire: a lethal barrier surrounding the facility. These receivers were like weeds among rare flowers, banal technology compared with the translight communications they supported, but self-repairing and hardy enough to withstand arctic winters.

Rana examined the system with growing frustration, the metallic taste of failure in her mouth. She couldn't help Alexander. Nothing could be done from her repair station to reconnect the entanglement facility to the rest of the planet. The repeater software was too distributed, too autonomous to respond to a central command. And the repeaters themselves were switched off – not ordered into sleep mode, but physically turned off *by hand*. The imperials were taking Legis's isolation very seriously.

Someone would have to go into the array field itself to

make the necessary changes. Past the minefields, sniffers, and microfilament barriers of the wire. It had taken hundreds of militia workers to physically turn the repeaters off.

She sighed. There was nothing she could do herself. This was a problem for Alexander and Herd. If Rana could smuggle them the data she had collected, she wouldn't have to return to this awful place.

She searched her workstation for some way to bring the data to Herd, and settled on a memory strip borrowed from a repairbot's internal camera. A schematic of the simple repeaters fit easily into the memory strip's capacity, and she added a map of the array and the barrier wire's specs. Rana shut her station down and erased her researches; her shift was almost over.

Now she could return to the warmth and safety of the prefab, to happiness.

When the shift siren blew, Rana rose from her chair stiffly, hands shaking. The muscles of her legs felt weak. Anxiety had built over the long shift, stealing into every tissue of her body. Rana knew that she needed the surety of Herd's drugs. Soon.

She wished now that she'd eaten something today. But she'd wanted desperately to finish her work in a single shift and never return here.

Calming herself by imagining the strip-heater glow that lit the prefab, Rana joined the other militia workers jostling their way toward the facility exit. The six work shifts of the long Legis day overlapped to prevent this sort of rush-hour crowding, but the narrow corridors of the overstaffed station were always crowded, even in peacetime. Rana found herself swept along in a human flow, and the scent of tired workers became overwhelming.

Strange, how humanity repulsed her now. The empty chatter, the profusion of colors and body types, the clumsiness of the crowd's movement around her. Without trying, Rana still walked with the avian grace of her captor; the imitation had somehow insinuated itself into her bones. She longed to shuck the wig and its pointless, decorative excess of hair. Rana closed her eyes, and saw the clean lines of Alexander's airscreen charts, the scimitar curves of Herd's weapons, the flavor of Rix. Biting her lip, she made her way through the halls.

Soon, she would be back home.

The crowd's progress slowed to a crawl as she neared the exit. Bodies pressed in closer. The overwhelming human smell made Rana's hands begin to shake. The scent seemed to leach all oxygen from the air. Meaningless conversations surrounded and battered her, a hail of empty words. She distracted herself by reading the sniffer's warning signs: *Declare Any Volatiles, Nanos, or Facility Property*.

With a start, Rana remembered that the sniffer could detect stolen equipment.

She shook her head to drive away paranoia. The memory strip in her pocket was insignificant, the sort of cheap media that came free with disposable phones and cameras. Surely it wasn't marked with pheros. But among the signs, her nervously darting eyes now found the words: *Sign Out ALL Data Storage Devices*.

Rana swallowed, remembering the data she'd put on the strip. A map of the facility, the repeater schematics, the specs for the lethal wire. From those three files, her intent couldn't be more obvious. The sniffer was only a few meters ahead of her now. She planted her feet to resist the bodies pressing her forward.

Rana fingered the memory strip in her pocket. It was too small to hold a phero patch. But what if they'd sprayed it with pheros as a matter of course?

Security was tight here, but *that* tight?

Frantic thoughts crowded her mind. The overstaffed facility seemed utterly disorganized; such a subtle measure didn't seem likely. But she remembered an old rumor about a creeper security nano that Imperials unleashed on top secret bases. Something that propagated slowly, pheromarking each machine and human it came into contact with, so that everything could be tracked from a central station. The idea had seemed fantastic at the time, the paranoia of low-level workers.

But now it seemed just barely possible.

The crowd was pressing her impatiently from behind. One of the guards at the sniffer, a marine in Imperial black, was looking at Rana with vague interest as the other workers flowed around her. She ordered herself to move forward; there was no escaping the sniffer without calling attention to herself.

But her feet would not move. She was too afraid, too tired. It was too much to ask.

She remembered boarding the maglev on the way here, her hesitation before climbing the stairs. That old paralysis – the old Rana Harter – had returned with a vengeance.

The marine rose from his stool, eyeing her suspiciously.

Move! Rana commanded herself. But she remained put.

Then a glint of metal caught her eye. Down the sniffer hallway before her, Rana saw the flash of an officer's badge.

It was Herd, wearing her militia colonel's uniform, beckoning her forward.

At that sight, the panic that had held Rana fast was suddenly broken. She moved toward the sniffer, knowing Herd would protect her, would return her to happiness.

Rana Harter stepped into the sniffer, and was for a moment alone, separated from the press of bodies. The updraft took away the rancid smell of the crowd.

Then a siren began to scream, so loud that in Rana's

synesthesia it became a towering cage of fire around her, as blinding as the sun on lidless eyes.

Executive Officer

The conspirators met in one of the zero-gee courts that surrounded sickbay. The courts were empty, of course, being unusable under high acceleration. The mere notion of playing rackets or dribblehoop in this unstable gravity made Hobbes's knee ligaments ache.

There were only five conspirators present, including herself. Hobbes had expected more, actually. Five didn't seem enough of a critical mass to warrant plotting a mutiny. There must be more, but Thompson wasn't tipping his hand yet. No doubt some of his cards were in reserve.

She knew all those present: the ringleader Second Gunner Thompson; Yen Hu, another young officer from gunnery; Third Pilot Magus, her face sour and strained; and one of the communications ensigns, Daren King. Apparently, this was no crewman's mutiny. Everyone here had stars on their uniform.

They all seemed relieved when she walked in. Perhaps as the ship's second-in-command, Hobbes somehow validated the enterprise.

But Thompson took charge for the moment. He closed the door of the rackets court, which sealed itself seamlessly, and leaned against the small window in its center to block his small handlight from spilling into the hall. The precautions were hardly necessary, Hobbes thought. Under the current cruel regime of high acceleration, the crew moved about the ship as little as possible. She doubted security was monitoring the ship's listening devices very carefully, though Ensign King or other conspirators unknown to Hobbes must be jiggering any bugs in the zero-gee court in case they were queried later.

This was to be a silent coup.

'Not really a mutiny at all,' Thompson was saying.

'What would you call it, then?' Hobbes asked.

Second Pilot Magus spoke up. 'I guess, properly speaking, it's a murder.'

There was an intake of breath from Yen Hu. The assembled conspirators looked at him. Hobbes was sorry to see Hu in on this. He was only two years out of academy. Gunner Thompson must have worked hard to break him down.

'A mercy killing,' corrected Thompson.

'Mercy on . . . ?' Magus asked.

'Us,' Thompson finished. 'The captain's dead, whatever happens. No point in the rest of us going down with him.'

Thompson took a step back from the rest of the group, making them his audience.

'The rest of the Empire may believe that pardon, but we know that Captain Zai refused the blade of error. The Emperor knows it too.'

Hobbes found herself nodding.

'This attack on the Rix battlecruiser is a pointless sacrifice of the *Lynx*,' Thompson continued. 'We should be standing off and coordinating with the Legis planetary defenses. Protecting civilians against bombardment, we could save millions. Instead, we're engaged in a suicide mission.'

'Do you really think the Navy would change our orders at this point?' she asked.

'If the captain accepts the blade in the next day or so, they'll have time to order us back. The politicals will make up something about Zai-the-hero being the only officer who could have pulled off the attack against the battlecruiser. The *Lynx* can gracefully withdraw back into the system defenses. With Zai dead, it'd be pointless to sacrifice us.'

Despite what they were plotting, it rankled Hobbes to hear the captain's name used without the honorific of rank.

'My math shows that we've got twenty-five hours to make turnaround,' Second Pilot Magus said. 'A few more, really. We could always get to twelve gees after turnaround.'

'No thanks,' Thompson said. With every gee they added, the easy gravity field would grow geometrically more unstable.

'Well, in any case,' Magus said. 'Any longer than thirty hours, and we'll be committed to meeting the Rix battle-cruiser outside of Legis's defenses.'

Hobbes wondered if Magus had taken the precaution of doing the calculations by hand. Computer use, even at trivial demand levels, was always recorded.

'And once it's done, we've got to get word back to Home that the Captain's committed suicide,' said Ensign King. 'Then they've got to make a decision, and get word back to us. Assuming we draw from our Home-connected entanglement store, there's no com lag.'

'But how long will it take for the Navy to make a decision?' Magus asked.

The four of them looked at Hobbes. They knew she'd worked as an admiral's staff officer before being assigned to the *Lynx*. Hobbes frowned. She'd seen complex, crucial deci-sions taken in minutes; she'd seen days go by before consensus was reached. And the decision to save or lose the *Lynx* was as much political as military. The question was: did anyone expect Zai to take the blade now? Would there be a contingency plan ready to go?

But that was irrelevant to Hobbes. The important thing was to keep the conspirators from taking any precipitous actions. If they felt they were up against the clock, they would be harder to control.

'It won't matter how long it takes,' she said flatly.

'Why not?' Magus asked.

Hobbes paced a moment, thinking furiously. Then it came to her.

'With Captain Zai dead, the *Lynx* is my ship. The moment I take command, I'll make the turnaround and ask for new orders,' she said.

'Perfect,' Thompson whispered.

'But you'll be disobeying direct orders,' Yen Hu said. 'Won't you?'

'If they tell us to continue the attack, there'll be time to get into some kind of position. But I don't think they will. They'll thank me for taking the decision out of their hands.'

Thompson laughed. 'Hobbes, you old devil. I was half certain you'd throw me to the captain for even talking to you. And now *you're* going to take all the credit for this, aren't you?' He put one hand on her shoulder, the touch intimate in the darkness.

'A subtle sort of credit,' she said. 'Let's just say we don't have to cover our tracks too carefully.'

'What are you talking about?' Hu asked. He was completely confused now.

Magus turned to the young ensign. 'ExO Hobbes doesn't care if the Apparatus suspects that mutiny occurred, as long as they can't prove it. She believes her initiative will be appreciated.'

Hu looked at her with a kind of horror. He had entered into this to save the *Lynx*, not advance anyone's career. He was obviously aghast that she was thinking past the current crisis of survival. Good, she thought. Hu needed to be focused on the long term. Even if this conspiracy fell apart here and now, he'd already changed his life forever.

'So, sometime in the next twenty-five hours,' Thompson said, 'Laurent Zai will take the blade of error.'

'The later the better,' Hobbes said. 'My decision to pull the *Lynx* back makes more sense if there isn't time left to get new orders from the Navy. The captain should go off his watch the day after tomorrow at 9.50, twenty-two hours from now.'

'Are we all agreed then?' Thompson asked.

They were silent for a moment. Hobbes hoped that someone would say something. There must be some quiet, cutting remark, she thought, that would bring them all to their senses. At this point she could still imagine the conspiracy sputtering out. The right words could break the spell that Thompson had cast. Only, it couldn't be her to speak up. Hobbes couldn't let them suspect her real purpose in joining their conspiracy.

'There's only one thing,' Hu said.

They waited.

The young ensign cleared his throat. 'This makes Captain Zai look like a coward. As if he'd been pardoned, but killed himself anyway because he couldn't face the Rix.'

Hobbes saw the truth of this dawn on the conspirators' faces, and wondered if Hu had found the right words.

For a few moments, no one said anything. They were all from gray families. Posthumous honor was not a thing to be trifled with. In a world ruled by the living dead, the ghosts of the past were taken very seriously.

Of course, it was Thompson who finally spoke.

'He is a coward,' he said bitterly. 'He couldn't face the blade. That's why we're in this mess.'

Magus nodded, then King, and finally Hu, and they placed their hands palm up in the center of their little circle. An old academy team ritual, enjoined to this perverted purpose. But Hobbes joined them. Thompson placed his last, palm down.

The plan was locked.

Commando

H_rd stood still for a moment as the siren began to wail, watching the crowd's reactions at a calm remove. She noted that the siren cycled with a two-second period between 15 and 25,000 Hertz. At both its extremes, this sine wave went beyond the range of normal human hearing. It dug down low enough to shudder in the gut like a pneumatic hammer, and high enough to shatter fine glass.

The siren was evidently designed to paralyze anyone whose hearing was unprotected. Most of the crowd on h_rd's side of the sniffer covered their ears, their knees bending as if suddenly under high gravity – a few dropped straight to the ground. Poor brainbugged Rana Harter, for whom sounds were solid and visible, crumpled like a column of sand.

Only the two militia guards and the Imperial marine remained effective. H_rd waited for their slow reactions to unfold. As one, they turned their backs on the Rix commando to face Rana Harter, who lay in the sniffer corridor. They pulled weapons, activated helmet displays, took up firing poses.

Satisfied with their incompetence, h_rd sprang into action.

In a few steps, she was behind the Imperial marine, the only real threat to a Rix commando. Her monofilament knife found the seam between helmet and breastplate. The knife was so sharp (sixteen molecules diameter) and her cut so fast that she decapitated him without a drop of blood touching her. She could feel a gurgling sound vibrate the breastplate, but the marine's death rattle was drowned out by the still-protesting siren.

The two militia soldiers were side by side, stepping toward the ragdoll Rana Harter with exaggerated caution. H_rd leapt toward the space between them. She saw one stop, cocking his head to listen to a voice inside his helmet. Someone in tactical control had seen her on-camera, was trying to warn them. It was far too late for that.

She stepped between the militia soldiers and laid a firm hand on their variguns, pulling the barrels away from Rana Harter and toward each other. One obliged her by firing, knocking his partner back three meters. H_rd punched him in the face – he had forgotten to lower his visor – and pulled the weapon from his grasp. She turned it on him. The varigun was set to a concussion stun, a wide-area effect meant for crowd control. At a range of ten centimeters, it burst the man's eyeballs and pushed his jawbone back far enough that it severed his jugular. H_rd reached the sniffer before his body, limbs still flailing with old, irrelevent intentions, hit the ground.

Rana Harter was light as a bird. She draped over h_rd's shoulder like something without bones. The siren was focused here in the sniffer corridor, almost loud enough to damage even Rix hearing. Some sort of gas was drifting upward in the sniffer's draft, but h_rd hadn't breathed since the siren began sounding, and had another thirty seconds or so before she would need to.

Her burden secured, the commando began to run at speed in a zigzag course away from the facility entrance, dropping the few standing workers in her path with the appropriated varigun's concussion effect. She was a hundred yards away when the siren cut off, leaving a staggering silence. For a few moments, static filled her ears, and h_rd thought that her hearing was damaged. But with a quick glance backward she saw the dust rising behind her and realized what the sound was.

A pair of small flechette autocannon were raking the outer grounds of the facility, orienting on the sound of her thudding steps. According to Alexander's researches on the array facility, these cannon used listening devices in the ground to triangulate an intruder's position. But they were falling short, calibrated to hit someone running at normal human velocity. Even in the few meters between her footfalls and the listening devices, the tardy speed of sound made a difference. The incompetence of local militias here in the Spinward Reaches always amazed her; she was glad the few hundred Imperial soldiers had been stretched so thinly across the planet.

Suddenly, the dusty arcs of flechette fire rose up in front of her. Someone was recalibrating the autocannon in realtime, trying to compensate for the Rixwoman's inhuman speed. The gun would catch her soon enough, if only by trial and error; at the moment, she was only a single-variable problem. H_rd asked her internal software for a string of random numbers, and shifted directions to irregularize her course.

But the autocannon were spraying wildly now, their screeching reports pitched above a thousand rounds per minute. They would find her eventually. A few hits wouldn't kill her, but she didn't have time for wounds. One arm wrapped around Rana Harter, h_rd adjusted the varigun to a new setting at random with her teeth. *Damn*, the thing was badly designed – if only she had a spare second to pull her own weapon.

H_rd aimed blindly, without turning her head – her eyes were a soft spot where even a mere flechette could kill her – calculating on the fly the center of an arc of impacts before her. Her weapon recoiled with a satisfying *thump*. Three seconds later, a sharp boom rang out and one of the cannon was silenced.

She swung the varigun the other way, aiming at the center of the remaining arc of dust that swept toward her. Her finger closed on the firing stud.

The gun beeped twice, with that apologetic timbre recognizable in all simple and stupid machines. The weapon had contained only one round at that setting. The stream of flechettes raced along the ground, reaching for her, and h_rd made a rare mistake.

She timed the jump perfectly to clear the arc of fire, but didn't fully take into account the burden of Rana Harter over her shoulder. The commando's leap reached only two meters vertical, and four flechettes plunged into her.

One struck her kneecap, flattened against the exposed hypercarbon, and slid off without leaving a scratch. Another hit a buttock, the small metal arrow tearing bloodily across a broad swath of skin as it bounced off the flexible subdermal armor that protected Rix soldiers from falls. A third passed through her abdomen, nicking the impervious spine and shattering. The shrapnel perforated her stomach, which began healing itself immediately, and destroyed two of her seven kidneys – an acceptable loss.

The only real damage came from the round that struck her left arm. It lodged in the radial notch, wedged as tight as a doorstop in the hypercarbon. Her forearm's flexibility was suddenly reduced to zero. A workaround radius activated itself instantly, allowing the arm to move again, but the strength of the needle-thin workaround was less than ten percent normal. As they landed, Rana Harter fell from h_rd's suddenly weakened grasp, and tumbled across the tundral grasses like a lifeless body thrown from a train.

The commando regained her footing and turned to face the still-shrieking autocannon. With the shaking hand of her damaged arm, she twisted the varigun's controls through its settings, raking the cannon's emplacement with infralaser, magnetic sniper rounds, antipersonnel explosives, a burst of tiny depleted uranium slugs, and a stream of microfoil chaff that set the air to sparkling brightly around her.

The autocannon stuttered to a halt a few seconds before its firing arc would have found her again, either destroyed or overheated.

H_rd's eyes spotted the thermals of more militia soldiers emerging from the array facility, now a kilometer away. They were staying low, moving forward nervously. She fired more microfoil chaff in their direction to baffle any sensors that could image Rana Harter's body heat, then emptied the rest of the chaff straight into the air. She scooped up her fallen burden. The glittering microfoil drifted along with h_rd, the wind at her back, falling like metal snow as she plunged into the tundral waste.

She traveled twenty kilometers before she thought to check Rana Harter for wounds – another mistake.

A host of bruises from the fall covered the woman's skin, and h_rd's thermal vision showed increased bloodflow, the body responding to a sprained wrist. Rana's lower lip was bleeding. Her eyes were starting to flutter open; only time would tell if a head injury had been sustained. Then h_rd saw, barely visible in the winter night's starlight, the fingertip-sized, dark circle of blood staining the militia fatigues.

H_rd knelt, blinded momentarily by a wave of some strange and awful emotion. Then she gathered herself and inspected the wound more closely.

A flechette had passed straight through Rana's chest, hardly slowed by the flimsy calcium rib cage. The projectile was meant to turn to shrapnel inside the body, but had been designed for an armored target. Nothing in the woman's chest had resisted the shell enough to shatter it. It had missed her heart and spine, but had holed one lung.

The woman's breath was fast and shallow. H_rd put her ear to the wound and listened for the telltale whisper of tension pneumothorax, but no pressure was building in the chest cavity. The bleeding had stopped.

H_rd sighed with relief, and something filled her, vibrant and expansive. Not the mere satisfaction of a mission parameter fulfilled, but an animal feeling like the vigor of sex or the calming scent of her home orbital's familiar air.

The cause of this feeling, this swelling of joy: Rana Harter would live.

Senator

The war changed everything.

The council met throughout the week, setting broad guidelines for the tumultuous shifts that would shake the Eighty Worlds for the next few decades.

In the Spinward Reaches, the council altered the reproduction and education laws. The next generation would have to be numerous, and it would have to grow up quickly. The Expansionist senator on the council presented the proposal, using terms like 'replacement population.' Nara Oxham found the euphemism repulsive: why not simply call them war orphans?

But she voted with the unanimous Council, setting a generous birth dowry to be paid off in lands from the Imperial Conservancy. On twenty planets, virgin climax-stage forests were parceled into bribes, remuneration for the most productive parents. By the time the hundreds of warships from anti-spinward reached their new assignments on the Rix frontier, the babies of this demographic bulge would be old enough to become marines, ground troops, replacements for the technical personnel sucked into the war effort. This over-sized generation raised in the hinterland would stand ready to repopulate smashed cities, to recolonize dead planets if necessary.

The stately pace of the constant was a convenience in the prosecution of war, Oxham realized. Across the thirty-light-year diameter of Empire, war was slowed to a time scale in which human seed could be sown like summer crops, stacked and stored in preparation for leaner times. Even on her native Vasthold, seven light-years from the Rix frontier, Oxham was forced to accept population increases that would cut deep into the unspoiled continents of the planet: biomes that had taken centuries to stabilize razed overnight to make room for a generation of cannon fodder.

The Empire girded itself for a bloodbath that might consume tens of billions.

The Expansionist senator sometimes waxed ecstatic as she outlined these plans, her mind alight with partisan fever. Her faction had long called for increased birthrates. The Expansionists shared with the Secularists and Utopians a wariness of the growing power of the dead. But their motto was 'Bury the dead with the living.' They sought to redress the balance of power through sheer numbers, an ever-expanding population (and thus, an ever-aggressive Empire) in which the dead would never predominate.

The Utopians took the opposite, equally unpragmatic tack: they promised universal elevation, in which the symbiant would be bestowed upon every citizen of Empire upon death. Thus, the dead would represent all classes, and everyone would have a stake in immortality.

To Senator Oxham and her Secularist Party, both these strategies were patently absurd. The great living masses of the Expansionist vision were doomed to become an underclass. As an ancient philosopher had once said, 'The poor are only poor because of their great number.' Add the immortality of the wealthy dead to the equation, and the class divisions in the Risen Empire could only worsen. The Utopian future, in which billions were elevated every year, was equally untenable. It would choke the Eighty Worlds and bow the vital living under the weight of their ancestors. Both schemes would create population problems that could only be solved by conquest.

The Secularists had a simpler plan. They were, as Laurent had put it so long ago, simply pro-death. Universal and irrevocable, natural death leveled all members of a society. Of course, the technology of the symbiant could never be uninvented, but its effects could be ameliorated as much as possible. Elevation should be rare, its rejection celebrated. And the Secularists wanted the living to hold as much power as possible; the dead could stay in their gray enclaves and stare at their black walls, but could not use their unanimity and accumulated wealth to steer the course of Empire.

Thus three parties, a clear majority of the Senate, stood against the Emperor, but theirs was a divided opposition.

To bolster her case for increased population, the Expansionist senator showed recordings from the First Incursion. Eighty years before, the Rix had sought to break the Empire's will, to force acceptance of compound minds within all Imperial infostructures. The Incursion had opened with appalling terror attacks. Living cities were ruptured by chaotic gravity beams fired from space, buildings rended as if made of straw, crowds sucked into scrambled piles, in which human forms commingled with metal and plastic and clothing. Gray enclaves were decimated with special munitions, flechette cluster bombs that shredded victims beyond the symbiant's ability to repair. In rural areas not covered by nuclear dampening fields, clean bombs were used to destroy human and animal populations.

Oxham contemplated the images: death enough for anyone.

Perhaps that was the seductive nature of war: it gave all parties what they thought they wanted. Millions of new elevated war heroes for the Utopians, vast population increases for the Expansionists, and plenty of true death for the Secularists. And for the Emperor and Loyalty, a period of unquestioned authority.

The dead sovereign nodded when the Expansionist finally finished. Darkness was falling, and Oxham realized that she hadn't slept for two of Home's long days. The dead needed little sleep – they seemed to drift into an internal world for short, rejuvenating meditations – but the living members of the council looked exhausted.

'I am glad you have chosen to prepare for the worst, Senator.'

'Thank you, Your Majesty.'

'Any objections?' the sovereign asked. Nara realized that this was it. The whole package of population increases, of childhoods spent in military training, of countless virgin biomes raped, it all came down to a simple vote among a few exhausted men and women. It was all happening too fast.

She cleared her throat.

'Does it not seem to the council that this Rix Incursion is different from the first?'

'Different?' asked a dead general. 'It has not yet begun in earnest.'

'But the last began so suddenly, with a clear ultimatum, followed by a wave of simultaneous terror attacks on several worlds.'

'Hasn't this incursion begun suddenly, too, Senator Oxham?' the Emperor asked. Nara had grown more adept in reading the man; he seemed intrigued.

'As suddenly, but with greater restraint,' she began. 'Only a single planet was attacked, and no civilian targets were destroyed.'

'They accomplished by blackmail what they could not by terror,' the dead general answered. 'A compound mind, forced upon us by hostage-taking.'

Oxham nodded, concealing a look of disgust. Though

losing four billion lives, the Empire had never relented in the First Incursion. But when the beloved Empress was threatened, they had let the Rix inside.

'However appalling their choice of targets,' she said, 'the Cult has shown tremendous focus in their attack. A single world, a single hostage, a limited result.'

'But with absolute success,' the Emperor said.

'An unrepeatable success, Sire,' she finished.

She felt the council recognize the truth of her words. The Rix could hardly take another hostage of the Empress's stature; no one except the Emperor himself would warrant the restraint that Zai had shown.

'Do you think that they'll stop now, Senator?'

'I think, Sire, that they tried to bludgeon us into submission once, and failed. This time, they have decided on a more subtle approach.'

She looked around the circle, saw the counselors' attention beginning to focus through their fatigue.

'We don't know what their ultimate plan is,' she continued. 'But it would be odd for them to begin the war with such a precisely delivered stroke, only to return to the crude terror tactics of the First Incursion.'

The dead general narrowed his eyes. 'Granted, Senator. As you said, their *subtle* victory is an unrepeatable one. But surely it is also purposeful. They have a viable mind on an Imperial world, and they are moving to communicate with it. They clearly intend to gain some strategic advantage from their occupation of Legis.'

'An advantage that could lead to terrors like those of the First Incursion,' the Emperor continued the thought. 'If they can tap the knowledge of their mind on Legis, they will know us better than they did a century ago.'

'Would that they knew our fortitude,' Raz imPar Henders said.

'An interesting expression, Senator Henders,' the Emperor said. 'Perhaps we should demonstrate how great a sacrifice we are willing to make.'

'What sacrifice could be greater than the four billion lost in the First Incursion, Sire?' Ax Milnk asked. 'The Rix should know us well enough by now.'

The Emperor nodded in contemplation, and the council stayed respectfully quiet.

Finally he said, 'We shall have to consider that question.'

Nara Oxham saw it then in the dead sovereign's thoughts – the hulking shadow of his fear, the strength of his resolution. The Emperor's will had reached an absolute condition. He would do anything to prevent the Rix from communicating with their mind.

If the *Lynx* failed, something awful was going to happen.

Executive Officer

They met the next time in Hobbes's cabin.

She didn't want this grim rehearsal, sullying her small, private domain. But hers was the cabin on the *Lynx* most similar to Zai's; the same size and shape except that it lacked the captain's skyroom. It was close enough.

The conspirators stood in their positions uncomfortably, mock assassins playing at a game they were still afraid to make real.

'Are you sure you can get us in?' Magus asked her again.

Hobbes nodded. 'I've had the captain's codes for months. He sometimes sends me to his cabin if he's forgotten something.'

'What if he's changed them?'

'He hasn't,' she said flatly. Hobbes wished that Magus

would shut up about this. It didn't do for them to examine her claims too closely.

'Trust Hobbes,' Thompson said to the third pilot. 'She's always had the old man's ear.'

The words struck Hobbes with palpable force, a wave of guilt, like some tendril of gravity whipping through her stomach. Gunner Thompson trusted her completely now, and there was more than trust behind his eyes. Her Utopian beauty complicating things again.

She saw the others reacting to Thompson's words, questioning his blind faith. Magus was still far warier of Hobbes than he, and Hu had apparently started to think that this had all been her idea rather than Thompson's. She would have to watch her back.

'Come in, King,' Thompson ordered.

Ensign King entered the cabin, a nervous look on his face. His job during the murder would be to block the ship's recording devices; he would be at his communications station. So he was standing in for Captain Zai.

Magus and Hobbes took his arms, exchanging the timid looks of an unsure rehearsal, and pulled him forward carefully. This was during the daily half-hour break from high acceleration – the *Lynx* was under a mercifully steady single gee – but they all still moved with exaggerated care, their bodies conditioned to caution over the last five days.

Thompson crouched in the center of the cabin on the ceremonial mat, a blade of error in his hand. The blade was a gift from his father, he had explained, for his graduation from the academy. What a morbid present, Hobbes thought. She hadn't known Thompson's family was so gray. Indeed, all the conspirators were from conservative families. That was the irony of this situation; mutiny was hardly an Imperial tradition. But of course, it was the grays who were most appalled by Captain Zai's rejection of the blade.

Hobbes and Magus pushed King forward, and Thompson rose to thrust his empty fist into the ensign's stomach. He mimed the crosscut of the blade ritual, and stepped back as King crumpled convincingly to the mat.

The conspirators regarded the still body before them.

'How do we know this'll fool anyone?' Magus complained. 'None of us has ever worked in forensics.'

'There won't be a full investigation,' Thompson said.

'A suicide with no recording? Won't my equipment failure be a little suspicious?' King said, rising from the mat.

'Not under heavy acceleration,' Hobbes said. Seven days into the maneuver, systems were failing intermittently throughout the ship. The ship's circuitry was at the bleeding edge of its self-repair capacity. So was the crew's nervous system, Hobbes reckoned. Tempers had grown short. A few times over the last ten hours, she'd wondered if the conspirators would fall to fighting amongst themselves. She had hoped the mutiny would have crumbled under its own weight by now.

'Don't worry,' Thompson said. 'Any anomalous forensic evidence will be put down to easy gravity effects.'

'Even the blood all over your uniform?' Magus said.

'I'll space the damn thing.'

'But a thorough investigation—'

'—is at *Captain* Hobbes's discretion,' Thompson insisted.

They all looked at her. Again, she felt the weight of the conspiracy upon her. Hobbes wondered when she had become the leader of this mutiny. Was she leading them all further into this than they would have gone if she'd simply ignored Thompson's insinuations? She forced the doubts from her mind. Second thoughts were an exercise in pointlessness. Hobbes was committed now, and had to act the part.

'This will be deemed suicide, officially,' she said. 'That will be the reasonable and *politically* acceptable interpretation.'

They nodded, one by one, agreement a virus spreading through the room. By mentioning the political situation, she had suggested that they were following the Apparatus's implicit wishes. With every utterance, her hands were dirtier.

'So, it's settled,' Thompson said. Then, to Magus and Hobbes, 'You two can handle Zai?'

'No problem,' Magus said. She stood almost two meters tall. Under normal conditions, she alone could easily murder a man of Zai's slight build. But Captain Zai was integrally part of the *Lynx*. The conspirators couldn't give him time to shout to the ship's AI or work a gestural command. If he had prepared himself for mutiny, defensive orders programmed into his cabin's intelligence could be invoked with a gesture, a syllable. For the plan to work, they all knew, the deed had be done in seconds, and in total surprise.

It was time to press this point.

'He might have time to shout something,' Hobbes said. 'You'll have to cover his mouth, Thompson.'

The gunner looked at her with concern. 'While I stab him? I've got to hit him square in the stomach. No one will believe a messy wound.'

Magus looked worried. 'Maybe Yen Hu?'

The gunner's mate swallowed nervously. He didn't want to be included in the actual violence. Under Thompson's plan, he was supposed to be lookout, to warn them if anyone was with the captain, and to let them know when they could exit the cabin without being seen.

'He needs to stay outside,' Thompson said. 'You do it, Hobbes. Just hit him in the mouth.'

'I've got to keep a hold on his hands,' Hobbes argued. 'You've seen how fast he works airscreens. He could send an alert with one finger.'

'Maybe we should just knock him out,' Magus suggested.

'Forget it,' Hobbes said. 'The Adept is bound to notice

any trauma to his head. The politicals will at least take a look at him.'

They were silent for a moment. Hobbes watched their unsurety rise as they cast glances at one another. However many times they had all fired weapons in anger, the physical nature of a murder by hand was dawning on them. Maybe this would be the moment the conspirators would come to their senses.

'I'll take the risk. Let's knock him out,' Thompson said. Magus nodded.

Hobbes sighed inwardly. They were set on their course.

'No,' she said flatly. 'I'm the one who has to cover this up. I say we need another person.'

Hobbes watched Thompson carefully. Her reason for continuing this far – besides the hope that the conspirators might relent, and redeem themselves to some small extent – was to flush out any unknown mutineers.

She saw Thompson start to speak, but he swallowed the words. He was definitely hiding something, still keeping someone in reserve. Perhaps he had plans for Hobbes herself after the ship fell into her hands.

The thought chilled Hobbes, steeling her will.

'I know someone,' she said. 'He's quick and strong.'

'You can trust him?'

'I don't want anyone else—' Magus protested.

'He's with us already,' Hobbes interrupted. She looked coolly into the stunned faces. 'He came to me, wondering if there was anything he could do.'

Thompson shook his head, on the edge of disbelief.

'You think you're the only ones who don't want to die?' she asked.

'He just came to you?' Thompson asked. 'Suggesting a mutiny?'

She nodded. 'I'm the executive officer.'

'Who is it, Hobbes?'

'A marine private.' No sense giving them a name; they'd have time to check her story.

'A grunt?' Magus cried. Daren King looked appalled. They were both from solid Navy families.

'As I said, he's fast. In hand-to-hand, he could take us all.'

'Do you trust him?' Thompson asked, narrowing his eyes as he watched her reaction.

'Absolutely,' she answered.

That much, at least, was true.

Commando

The recon flyer was kept aloft by both fans and electromagnetics. A sensible design: limited by Imperial technology, neither propulsion system alone was sufficient for a fast, armored vehicle. Moreover, if either system failed suddenly, the other would provide for a relatively soft landing. Only a hit that crippled both would crash the flyer.

It was h_rd's intent, however, to keep the vehicle in good working order. She would have to bring it down intact, although both of the soldiers on board would have to die.

She could see one of them clearly. Silhouetted against the aurora borealis, his head low as he peered into the glowing northern quadrant of the sky. They were bringing the craft in slowly toward their find, unsure yet whether to call for reinforcements. They were duly cautious, no doubt aware that the fugitive Rix commando had killed twenty-one of her pursuers – and shot down one other flyer – to date. But h_rd knew that they would hesitate to ask for assistance.

H_rd had been tracking this flyer for three hours, arranging a series of false targets for the crew. At the beginning of their shift, she'd set out a sack full of trapped arctic hares. As intended, the animals' combined body heat had shown up as a human-scale thermal image on Imperial equipment. The recon flyer crew called for backup. The militia surrounded the squirming sack with fifty troopers, then peppered the captive hares with stun grenades. The hares had somehow remained conscious when a grenade burst the sack, resulting in a sudden explosion of dazed and fleeing rabbits. And that was only the first embarrassment of the day for the two recon soldiers.

During the short daylight portion of their shift, the pair in the flyer had heard a rain of hard projectiles pounding their craft's armor and seen muzzle flashes. They reported themselves to be under hostile fire. A squadron of jumpjets soon arrived, but the projectiles turned out to be a freak occurrence of localized hail; the muzzle flashes that the pilot had seen were merely reflections from an exposed, mica-rich escarpment. The calculations required to bend Legis's cloud-seeding dirigibles to this purpose had strained even Alexander's computing resources. But shining up the mica with her field laser had been easy for h_rd.

In the few hours since this last embarrassment, the luckless recon flyer crew had been traveling in slow circles. Its onboard computer, like all military AIs, was independent from the planetary web and therefore immune to Alexander's control. But it still relied on data from the planet's weather satellites to perform dead-reckoning navigation. The shape of the terrain below changed constantly with snowdrifts and glacial cleaving, and the flyer's computer received frequent updates. Alexander had spoofed it with subtle manipulations of the data, gradually reducing the navigation software's democratically redundant neural net to total anarchy. By this point the troopers knew their machine was confused and lost, but however tired and threadbare their nerves were, the two were reluctant to call for help a third time.

And now they'd found another target: the glacial rift before them held a heat signature of human scale.

Rana Harter was inside, feverish from her wound and breathing raggedly. The flyer crew would soon be certain that they finally had a real target.

A small shape lowered from the flyer, h_rd's sharp ears picking up the whine of its propulsion fan. The remote drone wafted down from the safe, high altitude that the flyer maintained, and moved into the mouth of the rift.

Using her communication bioware, h_rd scanned the EM range for the drone's control frequency. She could hardly believe it: the drone was using simple, unencrypted radio. H_rd linked into its point-of-view transmission. Soon, the ghostly figure of Rana Harter appeared, at the edge of discernibility in the drone's crude night vision.

The commando jammed the connection with a squawk of radio, the sort of EM bump often caused by Legis's northern lights.

H_rd waited anxiously. Had she allowed them too clear a view of Rana? If they called for backup now, the situation might spiral out of control. Rana might be killed by the militia's clumsy, paranoid doctrine of overwhelming force.

The recon flyer hovered for a few interminable minutes, almost motionless in the calm air. No doubt the tired, harried troopers were debating what to do.

Finally, a second recon drone descended from the flyer. H_rd jammed it the moment it entered the rift.

This time, the recon flyer moved in reaction. As h_rd had hoped, it descended, trying to reestablish line-of-sight with the lost drones. The craft's forward guns targeted the rift's opening. The commando allowed a few images to pass through her electronic blockade, tempting the recon flyer farther down-

ward. She noted that Rana had moved out of the drones'
sight – good, she was still thinking clearly. Rana's concussion
worried h_rd. The woman was lucid one moment, incoherent
the next.

Taking the bait, the flyer lowered itself one last critical
degree.

H_rd burst out of her covering of snow and thermal camouflage skin. The commando threw her snare at the rear of
the Imperial machine.

The polyfilament line was anchored on both ends with
depleted uranium slugs. It flew with the orbitlike sway of a
bola, rotating around its center of gravity as it rose, the polyfilament invisibly thin. H_rd's aim was true, and the makeshift
bola tangled in the rear fans of the flyer. The machine
screamed like a diving hawk as the unbreakable fibers
exceeded the fans' tolerances. H_rd's night vision spotted a
few metal shapes spinning from the wounded flyer. She
ducked as a whirring sound passed close by her head, and set
her jamming bioware to attack every frequency the flyer might
use to summon help.

The recon flyer's front reared up like a horse, the undam-
aged forward fans still providing thrust, and it began to slip
backwards as if sliding down some invisible hill. H_rd drew
her knife and ran toward the careening craft.

She heard the front fans shut down, an emergency measure to level the flyer. The electromagnetic lifters flared with
an infrasonic hum, the static electricity raising small hairs on
h_rd's arms. She felt lightning in the air as the recon flyer's
descent began to slow, rebounding subtly just before it
reached the snowy ground.

H_rd had timed her approach perfectly. As the flyer
reached its lowest point, she jumped.

The flexormetal soles of her bare feet landed on the flyer's
armored deck without a sound. The craft tipped again as her

weight skewed its balance, and the rearmost crewman – the gunner – spun in his seat-webbing to face her. He started to cry out, but a kick to the temple silenced him.

The pilot was shouting into her helmet mike, and heard nothing. H_rd decapitated her with the monofilament knife, cut her body from the webbing, and threw her overboard. H_rd had studied the controls of the other flyer that she'd shot down in preparation for this attack, and easily found the panic button that triggered the machine's autolanding sequence.

The unconscious gunner's helmet was chattering in the local dialect. Some emergency signal from the flyer had gotten through to the militia. H_rd hoped they would be slow in responding to this third alert from the flyer. Her jammer was chopping the incoming transmission into bits and pieces of static-torn sound.

She tossed the gunner from the craft, saving his sniper's rifle and crashland rations. (Despite her small size, Rana ate more than a Rix commando – the two fugitives were running out of food.) As the craft settled onto the ground, h_rd whistled for her accomplice and leapt from the flyer.

Tilting up the rear fan cases, h_rd saw that she was in luck. Only one of the fans had disintegrated, the other had shut down when the polyfilament had arrested its motion. H_rd sprayed a solvent with the polyfilament's signature onto the intact fan, and it soon spun freely under the strokes of her hand.

Rana emerged from the rift, wrapped in thermal camouflage against the bitter arctic cold. Her ragged breath was visible against the aurora's light. She labored to carry the heavy fan blade that they had salvaged from h_rd's earlier kill. The commando turned to the shattered fan before her, and lased the small rivets that held on the remaining pieces. By the time the spinner coil was free of detritus, Rana was by her side.

H_rd threaded the salvaged fan onto the naked coil. It fit, spinning in perfect alignment. However crude the Imperials were, they did make their machines with an enviable inter-changeability. With her blaster, h_rd burned the fan blade fast.

The commando lifted Rana gingerly into the gunner's seat, pausing to kiss her midway. The gesture brought a smile to Rana's lips, which were cracked with dehydration despite all the snow-water she consumed.

'We'll go somewhere safe now?' Rana asked in Rix. Her voice had changed, the chest wound giving it a strangely hollow sound.

'Yes, Rana.'

H_rd leapt into the recon flyer and brought the fans up to speed. She closed her eyes and listened to their purr.

'They sound true,' Rana Harter said. 'It'll fly.'

H_rd looked back at her captive, ally, lover. The woman could hear things outside of even Rix range. She saw things too: results, extrapolations, meanings. She could predict the day's weather with a glance into the sky. When h_rd hunted hares with her bola, Rana knew in the first second which throws were hits, which would fly long. She could deduce how far glacial rifts – their hiding places these last days – extended, just from the shape of the cracks around their mouths.

H_rd hoped Rana was right about the flyer. The machines were quick, but their Imperial metals were terribly fragile in the brittle arctic cold.

The commando boosted the fan drive's power, gunned the EM, and the small craft pitched northward into the air. They flew toward the shimmer of the fading aurora, her eyes narrowing as the frigid wind of their passage built.

At last, she had acquired the means to assault the entanglement facility, and to finally escape the Imperials' fumbling search for her and Rana. They were headed to the farthest arctic now, to await the proper time to continue their lonely campaign.

To await Alexander's command.

Marine Private

Private Bassiritz did not understand his orders.

Normally, this was not much of a concern for him. In his years as a marine, he had performed crowd control, jumped into friendly fire, executed snatch-and-runs, and even carried out an assassination. Ground combat could include myriad possible tactical situations, and generally the details were complex and beyond his ken. But as long as Bassiritz knew ally from foe, he was happy.

Bassiritz had always thought of the crew of the *Lynx* as his allies, however. As the Time Thief stole more and more faces from home, his shipmates had effectively become his family. But here he was, under orders delivered *straight from the captain*, ready to do violence to some of them. This didn't make sense. It seemed as if the tribulations of the gravity ghost over the last week – the jittering of his bunk, the reeling of floors and walls, the complaints from his sense of balance – had begun to affect the very fabric of reality.

For the thousandth time, Bassiritz went through the orders in his head, visualizing the motions his body would take. It was simple enough. And he knew that he would follow orders when the time came. He could comprehend no other course of action. But he didn't like the feeling it gave him.

Bassiritz felt out of place here in Navy country. The floors and the freefall handholds were the wrong color, and everyone had given him slanty looks as he'd followed Executive Officer

Hobbes down the corridors. And now they were here, waiting in the *captain's* cabin. The room seemed fantastically large to Bassiritz, bigger than his parents' house; the skyroom alone could have held the bunk coffins of his entire squad. What did the captain *do* with all this room?

There was no way to guess. The captain wasn't here.

Executive Officer Hobbes was. She would be the only friend in this operation, Bassiritz knew. The other three officers had gone bad, mutinous.

There was a tall woman waiting beside the door across from Hobbes, with pilot's wings on her shoulders. She was sweating, twitching from nerves or intermittent bumps from the gravity ghost. Outside, a slight gunner waited on watch. He was bad too, but Hobbes had asked Bassiritz not to kill him unless it was absolutely necessary. The marine private hoped he wouldn't have to kill anyone.

The last conspirator, another gunnery officer, stood in the room's center, holding a short, wide knife. Bassiritz had never seen a blade of error before. He had hoped he never would. They were bad luck, it was reckoned back in his village. Once you possessed the tool, you'd eventually be called on to do the work, they said at home.

When Bassiritz was done with this operation, he was going to use up his payment of privilege chits and take a long, hot shower.

There were two quick raps on the door. Hobbes had explained to him that this was the signal that everything was going right. The captain was approaching alone. Bassiritz shook his head involuntarily – none of this was *right*. But he was pretending to be a conspirator, so he smiled, wringing the old rag he held in one hand.

The smile felt wrong on his face. He didn't like this one bit.

ExO Hobbes stole a look at him. She winked one lovely

green eye – a sign, but one that meant nothing really. Just a reminder that he was here under orders.

'Stay cool and everything will go fine,' she had said to him an hour ago. 'That's what a wink will mean.'

Nothing was fine, though.

The door opened. The captain entered.

The four of them leapt into action. Hobbes and the pilot grabbed Captain Zai (striking the *captain* – an Error of Blood right there) and propelled him forward. Bassiritz's quick eyes could see Hobbes slip something into Zai's hand, but he knew from long experience that the subtle motion had been too quick for normal people to see. As the captain fell toward him, Bassiritz's reflexes took over and he forgot the gross impropriety of his actions. He pushed the rag into Captain Zai's mouth with his left hand, stifling the cry that uttered from it. Bassiritz felt the captain's roar of anger vibrate his hand, but the marine was already focused on his real task here. The big gunnery officer was jumping forward, his blade of error leveled at the captain's stomach.

Bassiritz's right hand shot out. To the rest of them, trapped in their slow-motion world, it would look as if he were steadying himself. But the marine's armored hand (they all wore gloves to cover their fingerprints) grabbed the blade of error, guiding its wild trajectory straight into the center of Zai's stomach.

Those were his orders. No near misses, no wounds to the chest or groin. Right into the stomach: dead center.

ExO Hobbes hadn't told him exactly why. Bassiritz hadn't asked. But the recorded message from the captain had assured him that this was all part of the plan.

Bassiritz felt the knife go in, right on target. There was a sickly squelch, and a warm fluid spurted over his and the murderous gunner's hands.

Captain Zai made a hideous grunt, and tumbled face-first onto the ritual mat they'd spread out for him. The gunner pressed down on Zai's back, having left the blade in him.

'No footprints,' the man whispered, pointing at Bassiritz's boots. One of them had a fleck of blood on it. Blood. *What had they done here?*

Bassiritz looked at Hobbes for the next signal.

The executive officer shook her head almost imperceptibly. *Not yet.*

The room grew silent, a last shuddering sigh coming from the captain. Bassiritz gazed in horror at the blood that flowed from him and across the floor. It moved strangely, tiny rivers branching out like the living tendrils of a sea creature, shuddering with odd tremors. The gravity ghost was moving it. Bassiritz reflexively stepped back from a finger of the red liquid that reached for his boot.

The captain was not breathing. *What had they done?*

'It's over,' Hobbes said.

The pilot leaned back against the wall, covered her face with her hands.

The gunner stumbled back, a nervous smile on his lips.

'All right, then,' he said. He lifted a small transponder and spoke a single codeword into it. Bassiritz remembered to look at ExO Hobbes.

Hobbes winked her *left* eye. Now.

The marine's fist shot out, catching the gunner's throat. The man crumpled to the bloody floor, most likely still alive. Bassiritz turned to watch the rest.

Hobbes was already in midswing, delivering a slap to the pilot's face with a loud crack. The larger woman reeled backward, her face blank from the blinding shock of the slap. A good way to confuse someone, but only for a few seconds. Bassiritz stepped forward. But before he could strike, a second crack rang out.

The electric smell of a dazegun filled the room. Bassiritz felt the small hairs on his arms rise and tingle.

The pilot dropped to the floor.

The captain leapt up, the dazer in his bloody hand. He whirled to face the fallen gunner, but the man was motionless. Bassiritz knew from experience that he wouldn't be getting up for hours.

'Captain?' Hobbes asked.

'I'm fine, Hobbes,' he answered, nodding. 'Well done.'

The door burst open; more marines, Bassiritz noted happily. The Navy was too complicated for him.

The small gunner who had been watching for the conspirators outside was among them, his arms pinned. His eyes swept the room, then glared with hatred at ExO Hobbes.

'Any reaction from that transponder signal?' the captain asked.

Hobbes listened, then nodded. 'Two crew from gunnery left their posts, sir. Headed for my cabin, apparently.'

'Don't take them yet. Let's see what they're up to,' he ordered.

The captain pulled the ringlets of his tunic with a single ripping motion, and the garment parted. One last rush of blood spattered onto the floor. Bassiritz noted the armor strapped to his undershirt; it only covered his stomach.

Bassiritz smiled. The captain certainly had confidence in him. If the blade of error had missed its mark, Captain Zai would be bleeding for real.

One of the other marines checked the gunnery officer crumpled on the floor.

'Alive, sir.'

Suddenly, the young mutineer in the doorway lunged forward in his captors' arms. Bassiritz slipped between him and the captain, an arm raised to strike. But the marines held the man fast.

'The blade!' the gunner cried. 'Let me take the blade.'

All had gone according to plan, but Bassiritz found his relief turning bitter in his mouth. These were his crewmates, condemned to death for their shameful actions. Hobbes looked away from the young man, her eyes downcast.

'In due time,' the captain said quietly.

They pulled the gunner from the room weeping, an animal howl coming from the young man.

Executive Officer Hobbes spoke up again. 'Another response to the transponder. A notice went up on a public board, a few moments after your "murder," sir. An anonymous noise complaint, for the Section F gunnery bunks.'

'A coincidence?'

'There is no Section F, sir.'

Captain Zai shook his head. 'How many of my crew are in on this?' he wondered aloud.

'At least two more, sir. One to send, another to receive. Whoever posted it was clever, though. We can't crack the anonymity.'

The captain sighed. He stepped over the unconscious gunnery officer and sat heavily on his bed. 'I seem to have injured my knee, Executive Officer.'

'Bad gravity for a fall, sir. I'll get medical up here.'

'Think we can trust them?' the captain said.

Hobbes was silent.

Then she said, 'Well, at least the marines are with us, sir.'

Captain Zai looked at Bassiritz and smiled wanly.

'Good work, soldier.'

'Thank you, sir,' Bassiritz answered, eyes front.

'You managed to stab me dead center.'

'Yes, sir. Those were my orders, sir.'

The captain wiped some of the fake blood from his face.

'Well, Private, with your help I seem to have accomplished something very unlikely.'

'Sir?'

The captain stood, wincing as he shifted weight from one knee to the other.

'I doubt that many men have avoided two blades of error in their lives. Much less in the same week.'

Bassiritz knew it was a joke, but no one laughed, so he kept his mouth shut.

Senator

'This pit is lined with an old and simple material,' the Emperor began, gesturing to the floor beneath the counselors' feet. Nara Oxham had noticed before that of all the Diamond Palace she had seen, only the council chamber was made of the pearly substance.

'From the casein, or lactoid group of plastics,' he continued. 'A beautiful white, almost milky in appearance. It is, in fact, made from cows' milk and rennet, an enzyme from the stomachs of goats. Hardened by formaldehyde.'

Senator Oxham lifted one foot from the floor uncomfortably. She had always liked the hard-plastic feel of the council chamber, but this pillaging of animals' guts seemed a bit perverse.

'It was discovered almost a hundred years before spaceflight, when a chemist's pet cat knocked a bottle of formaldehyde into its saucer of milk.'

Save us, Oxham thought, from those agents of history.

She realized that the pit they all were perched around might well be a giant saucer of milk, a meal set out for some gargantuan housecat.

'The hardening effect was noticed, and plastic – the ancestor of our smart carbon – was created,' the sovereign said. 'Such disasters can always be turned into opportunities. But it is good to be prepared.'

Disasters?

'The time has come to consider the possibility that the *Lynx* will fail.'

The Emperor nodded at the dead admiral, who waved an image into the War Council's airscreen. Between the counselors hovered the familiar shape of the coming battle. The sweeping arcs that represented battlecruiser and frigate now almost intersected.

'The two ships are nearing contact even as we speak,' the admiral said. 'The elements of their drone fleets will engage shortly. Against such a powerful foe, the demise of the *Lynx* could come suddenly.'

Senator Nara Oxham took a deep breath. She had marked this moment for days; she didn't need some dead woman to explain its significance. Nara had hoped that she would be able to spend these hours alone, waiting for word to come from the Legis ground stations that were intently watching the battle. But the council summons had invaded her vigil.

Now she might learn of Laurent's death in the company of these politicians and gray warriors. She steeled herself, pushing fear and hope as far down as she could, forcing a cold absence into her heart. This diamond chamber was no place to weep, or even feel.

'If the *Lynx is* destroyed, and has failed to destroy the Rix array,' the admiral continued, 'we should know some eight hours after the fact, assuming standard models of simultaneity. That calculation includes lightspeed delay between Legis XV and the battle, and a decision window for the local military. They'll have to be a hundred percent sure of what's happened.'

'In those eight hours,' the Emperor added, 'the Rix ship will be forty billion kilometers closer to Legis.'

'We will have to reply to Legis rather quickly,' the general said. 'For any decision to reach them before the Rix draw within range.'

The counselors looked at each other in some puzzlement. They had been swept up in the greater war, and had lost track of the *Lynx*. The council had been determining the lot of generations – hundreds of billions of the living, dead, and unborn – and again the fate of a single ship demanded their attention.

'Then we should discuss our options, Sire,' the Utopian senator said.

'Are there any?' Oxham asked.

'We believe that there are,' the general said.

'I move to invoke the hundred-year rule,' the Loyalist Senator Henders said.

There was a stir at these words. The rule was an old privilege of the Emperor's War Council, a means to ensure that His Majesty's counselors could speak freely, without fearing that their words would be openly repeated. With the council so far acting unanimously, there had been little reason to invoke the rule. The counselors never discussed their decision-making in public in any case. And under the rule, the consequences of an inadvertent slip would be unthinkable.

'I second,' the Emperor said.

Nara felt cold fear come into the room. The sovereign had seconded, and the rule was invoked without objection.

Now nothing of this discussion could be repeated outside the chamber, not to anyone at all, not for one hundred years Imperial Absolute. The price of breaking the rule was as old as the Empire itself.

Execution by exsanguination: the common traitor's death.

Of course, Nara realized, she and the other senators on the council would be technically protected by their own senatorial privilege: freedom from arrest and Imperial censure. But breaking the rule constituted proof of treachery, and would be the end of any political power they might wield.

The discussion began with a speech from the Emperor.

'If the Rix compound mind is able to communicate with the rest of the Cult, then Legis has, in effect, been captured a second time. The mind is constituted of every piece of information on the planet: every line of code, every market datum, every technical specification. It has access to all our technological secrets.'

Nara took a deep breath. They'd heard all this before. But the Emperor's next words surprised her.

'But that isn't our concern,' he said. 'The strength of Empire is not in our technology, but in our hearts. And that is where we must be most vigilant. The mind is more than computers and comfibers. It also contains every child's diary, every family legacy recording, the prayers of the living to their ancestors, the patient files of psychoanalysts and religious counselors. The mind has grasped the psyche of our Risen Empire; it knows us in every aspect. The Rix seek to steal our dreams.'

The sovereign paused, challenging each of them with his stare.

'And we know what the Rix Cult brings: absolute disdain for human life except as a component of their precious minds. No terror was beyond them when they sought our submission in the First Incursion. Back then they didn't understand our strength, didn't realize what bound us together. Now, they have reached into our minds to discover what we most fear. They seek to pull out our secret nightmares and make a lever of them.'

Nara Oxham felt the Emperor's fear clearly now. It spread slowly to the others in the room as his speech continued. She could see the source of his passion: the reasoning behind his hatred of the Rix, his horror at the mind's takeover of Legis, his willingness to sacrifice the *Lynx*. Finally, perhaps, he was telling the truth.

'If the *Lynx* fails,' he said, 'we have lost this war.'

The words shook even Oxham. The old childhood conditioning, the imagery of fables and songs made the concept unthinkable. The Emperor of the Eighty Worlds spoke of losing a war. The sovereign wasn't allowed to entertain such an idea. He had beaten death, after all.

For a moment, the emotions in the room threatened to overwhelm her. Nara reached instinctively for her apathy bracelet, but forced herself not to resort to the drug. She needed to maintain her sensitivity. But the fear remained at the edge of her control.

'What must we do?' asked Senator Henders. Nara could see that he'd been coached for this question, as he had been to invoke the hundred-year rule. Henders already knew what the Emperor's answer would be.

'We must be prepared to kill the mind.'

A chill ran down Oxham's spine.

'How, Your Majesty?' she asked.

'We must be ready to make any sacrifice.'

'Sire,' she pleaded. 'What do you propose?'

'We must kill the mind,' he said flatly. Then he turned to the dead general.

The ancient warrior raised his head and looked at them. His gray face shone a little, almost as if he were sweating.

'We switch off the nuclear dampening fields on Legis. Then we detonate four hundred clean-airburst warheads in the hundred-megaton range, at an altitude of two hundred kilometers, directly over population centers, control points, and data reserves.'

'Nuclear weapons?' Nara said in disbelief. 'Over our own people?'

'Very low yield on dirty radiation, optimized for electromagnetic pulse.'

The admiral spoke. 'Every unshielded machine on the planet will be rendered useless. Unlike a normal power grid failure, all the distributed, self-maintaining components of the infrastructure will be eliminated. Every phone, handheld device, and computer on the planet will suddenly stop working.'

'Every aircar will fall from the sky,' Oxham protested. 'Every medical endoframe will fail.'

The admiral shook his head. 'Before the blast, a standard space-raid warning drill will run. Aircars will ground themselves, medics will be standing by.'

Oxham willed herself silent, trying to read the council's reaction. Their minds were in chaos. The Emperor's speech about the Rix had raised old fears, but those were nothing compared to the truly ancient horror of nuclear weapons. The counselor's minds had gone wild, like those of animals trapped within a ring of predators.

'The main power stations are shielded from EM pulses,' the general continued. 'But they will be shut down voluntarily. Ether-power substations will be destroyed by conventional explosives. Other shielded facilities, such as hospitals and emergency shelters, should remain in good working order.'

Oxham shook her head. An isolated hospital might keep functioning for a few days, but with the world around it crippled, remote consulting doctors would be cut off, emergency transport would fail, and supplies would soon run short.

Ax Milnk spoke. 'The short-term casualties might be limited, but we must consider what will happen over time. It might take months to return to a functioning infrastructure, during which millions could die from lack of food and medicine. The Legis population is all in the northern hemisphere, where winter is coming.'

'We have fully analyzed the situation, Counselor Milnk.'

The dead general looked at the Emperor, who nodded.

'We expect there to be roughly one hundred million deaths total,' the old warrior said.

A howl came into Nara's head, a whirlwind like the city when she awoke from coldsleep. The naked fear of the counselors pried open her mind, and the war lust of the surrounding capital rushed in. She could see better than ever the bright, raging face of Empire at war: the popular clamor for revenge, the hunger of profiteers, the unpredictable shuffling of power as new alliances formed.

For a moment, Nara Oxham was lost to herself. She became the Mad Senator, subsumed into the cries of the city's animal group-mind.

The cool hand of apathy reasserted herself. She looked down, almost surprised to be conscious. Then she saw her fingers at the bracelet. Old reflexes had moved her to increase the flow of the apathy drug, saving Nara from dropping to the floor mewling and insane.

She breathed deeply, wiping the sweat from her forehead and trying not to vomit.

'This will show our true strength,' the Emperor was saying. 'It will show that we would rather destroy ourselves than accept Rix domination. We will have surrendered them nothing. And they will never doubt our resolve again.'

'A hundred million, dead by our own hand?' the Expansionist senator said. 'Won't that do more damage to morale than the Rix ever could?'

'We will say the Rix did it,' the general said flatly.

Oxham bowed her head. Of course, this was why they had invoked the hundred-year rule. She doubted that even a century from now anyone would learn what they had done.

'A new Rix terror to motivate the Empire,' the sovereign added. 'Many war aims met with a single act.'

'I move we accept without objection,' said Senator Henders.

Senator Oxham raised her head. She had no time to think, no time to calculate. But given only these spare seconds, making the choice turned out to be easy.

'I object,' she said. 'I call for a vote.'

Relief. Even with her empathy dulled, she saw it on the living counselors' faces. They were glad someone had spoken against the Emperor's plan.

And they were glad it hadn't been them.

The sovereign looked at her coolly, his expression unreadable now. His gray young face seemed as remote as the night sky. But she knew that someday there would be a price for her action. Nara Oxham had crossed the Emperor.

'A vote, then,' he said quietly.

'Can we have more time?' Ax Milnk asked.

The Emperor shook his head. He had calculated this to the minute, had left revelation of the plan until time was too short for discussion. His best opportunity was now, before the horror of the idea could sink in.

'There is little time,' he said. 'The *Lynx* might be dead in hours. The Rix battlecruiser will be within transmission range a few days later.'

'Give us those days, then,' Oxham asked. Her voice sounded hollow in her ears.

'The lightspeed delay between Legis and the *Lynx*, Senator,' the admiral said, shaking her head. 'Round trip several times, to be sure. We have only hours to decide.'

'And the earlier the space-raid warning is sounded, the fewer casualties will result,' the general said. 'More medical personnel can be standing by. Grounded aircars will have time to bring their passengers to populated areas rather than depositing them in the wild. We owe the population of Legis a quick decision.'

Their arguments were illogical, Nara knew. The Apparatus could sound a raid warning in any case, and wait for a final decision. They could have prepared the planet for this over the last few days. The Emperor had simply chosen to spring this on the council, to grind their will against an artificial emergency. But she was too dizzy to make these arguments, to bring specific points against the steamroller that the Emperor had created. Her stomach roiled now, the first sign of a mild apathy overdose. Nara's blind fingers had unleashed too sharp a dose of the drug after all the days she had kept her sensitivity high. Her empathy was absolutely flat, her body barely able to function.

Council sessions had been called at odd hours for ten days. They were all exhausted; the Emperor had wanted them that way.

Senator Oxham gritted her teeth in anger. She had been outmaneuvered by the sovereign, betrayed by the weakness of her own psyche.

'A vote, then,' she said. 'I say no. "No killing of worlds."'

There was a gasp from someone. She had quoted the Compact, the old document that a few gray worlds interpreted as validating the Emperor's authority. He smiled at her coldly.

'I vote yes,' he said. The Emperor leaned back, supremely confident.

The War Council almost stopped him.

The Expansionist and Utopian senators voted against the action, as Oxham had known they would. And Ax Milnk showed unexpected strength, joining the opposition senators against the Emperor.

In a foregone conclusion, the two dead warriors voted with their sovereign, as did the Loyalist Henders. The measure was tied at four votes to four when the counselor from the Plague Axis spoke. He was an unknown quantity, this host of all the ancient terrors that humanity had put to rest. Living, and yet not fully alive, he was on the borderline that split the Risen Empire. He was a cursed thing.

'Let us show our strength,' came the voice from the suit's filter. 'Destroy the mind, at whatever cost.'

The motion had passed, five to four.

Roger Niles was right, Nara Oxham thought coldly as the vote was entered into the council's records. There were no moral victories. Only real defeats.

Then a glimmer of hope entered her mind. This unfathomable genocide might not actually occur; the *Lynx* might succeed in its mission. But even this slim chance had a dark side.

If my lover fails, a world dies, Nara realized.

She shook her head.

More blood on the hands of Laurent Zai.

■ ■ ■ ■

Lieutenant-Commander

Laurent Zai dressed quietly, thinking his lover asleep.

His arm was clever enough to come to him when he clicked his tongue for it. The limb turned itself slowly, orienting on the sound, then finger-crawled a bit too quickly for Zai's taste, for a moment a fleshy insect. Supposedly, it was smart and agile enough to reach its master even in zero-gee, but that was not a feature he had tested.

The arm had fallen close to the fire, and felt feverishly hot when he meshed its control surface with the tangle of interface threads that hung from his shoulder stump. But the warmth wasn't unpleasant. This house, the fire, Nara: these things were warm, and were good.

Zai flexed his fingers, their artificial nerves awakening with a tingle like returning bloodflow. When a chime assured him of the arm's strength, Laurent pushed himself upright with both hands, looking for his legs. They were close by.

His remaining natural legs were short stumps, and Zai could sit up easily on them. The floor was soft with some kind of plant growth; it felt like a fine animal pelt, chinchilla or mink. He made his way to the artificial legs with two quick movements, swinging forward like a gymnast on parallel bars. Over the subjective months since his torture, he had exercised his remaining arm until it was almost as strong as the prosthetic one. Vadans valued balance.

He reattached his legs. The smooth gray of their exterior melded with his pale flesh, edges sealing with a familiar tug of suction. He saw his tunic, and pulled it over his head as he flexed his toes.

Zai turned to see Nara gazing at him.

A chill in his chest pushed aside the warmth of the fire, of their lovemaking. Other than a few medics, none of his crewmates – no one – had ever seen him naked before, much less without his limbs. He tried to say something caustic, but his voice failed him and he scowled.

Nara shook her head.

'I didn't mean to embarrass you.'

'It's your house,' he said, pulling on his trousers.

When he looked at her again, she seemed puzzled by the words.

'Take your pleasure as you will,' he explained sharply.

'Have I taken advantage of your nakedness?' she said with a small smile. Zai realized that Nara was still completely unclothed. He felt foolish now in his disheveled fatigue tunic, grasped some piece of her clothing on the floor, and flung it to her.

Nara pushed it aside and sat up, reaching for his hand. It was the artificial one, which had somehow lost its glove. She pulled the metal thing toward her breast.

Zai's anger faded abruptly. At Nara's touch, he felt safe and whole again, as he had in her arms. Sighing, he closed his eyes and imagined the hand to be real. The returns of the false nerves were very convincing. He opened a second-sight menu and increased the hand's sensitivity, basking in the warmth of Nara, the change in texture from dark skin to pink aureole, the slow ripple of her heartbeat. He felt a tremor like distant running water as blood rushed into the erectile tissue of her nipple.

He opened his eyes. She was smiling.

'I'm sorry I snapped at you, Nara.'

'No, Laurent. I should have realized. But you seemed so . . . comfortable before.'

'Eager, more likely.'

'Oh.' Was there a note of pity in her voice? A look crossed her face, and she nodded. 'You don't use . . .'

He shook his head. *Surrogates*, she would have said, but on Vada they used the old words for professionals.

The playful smile again. 'In that case, Laurent, you must be famished.'

He could not disagree.

But Laurent Zai pushed her hands away. He'd felt so broken under her eyes. 'Nara?' he pleaded.

'Yes,' she answered. 'You can keep your limbs. Your tunic too if you want.'

He nodded, and a sound came from his chest that was like a sob. But he ignored it, hastening.

House

The missive came over the general net, looking for Laurent Zai. The lieutenant-commander's presence here at the polar estate wasn't registered with the comnets – the mistress had specifically requested privacy – but the search was energetic enough to ping every private domicile on Home. Not an emergency, just standard military persistence. The house quietly snatched a copy, investigating its security before passing it on to the mistress's guest.

The message bore the telltale marks of midlevel military cryptography. It hadn't been buried under the absolute noise of a onetime pad, or the self-similar swirls of fractal compression, so it was neither top-secret nor very large. The missive seemed to be double-ticket encryption, with a long enough key that Zai must be carrying it on his person, not in his head. The house set a host of micromaintenance bots – normally used to repair optical circuitry – to the task of discovering this object. This effort was illegal, and against Imperial AI guidelines, but the Rubicon Pale extended around the house whenever Oxham was here. The transgression was also justified by the fact that the house was sometimes called upon to encrypt the mistress's Senate business. And the best way to learn the craft of security was to attack the systems of one's peers.

Besides, the house was curious. And the mistress always encouraged it to indulge its curiosity, to gather information relentlessly. It was relatively sure she wouldn't mind this bit of harmless snooping.

The key was disappointingly easy to discover. A Vadan fetish on a strap around the lieutenant-commander's neck proved to be subtly bit-marked. The titanium cladding on its front was brushed to resist fingerprints, and upon close inspection, the tiny ridges of the burnishing were actually sawtooth waves, which reversed direction with suspicious periodicity. The house read the two directions as one and zero, fiddled with the results, and in a few seconds had cracked the missive.

It delivered the message to *Captain* Laurent Zai (the first half of the message was a promotion) as it absorbed the contents.

A new class of ship was described in the missive's second part, an experimental vessel of which Zai would be taking command in a few days. The specifications were not given in great detail – hence the shoddy encryption – but they were certainly stimulating. The warship was officially a frigate, but in the range of its weaponry and ground troops, the *Lynx* was sui generis. Its design had some of the characteristics of a patrol craft: fast and maneuverable, full of intelligence drones, capable of long-range operation with minimal logistical support. But the 'frigate' also possessed extensive ground-attack and orbital insertion capacity, a smattering of heavy weapons, and excellent survivability. It had punch.

The house figuratively raised its eyebrows. This was a fine little warship. Perhaps it was intended to serve as a roving ambassador, showing the flag, equipped for crisis management and gunboat diplomacy.

As the house expected, the AI component of the warship was woefully insufficient for its range of possible operations. Imperial design tended toward underpowered artificial intelligence. (The house had recognized long ago that its own distributed processing was at odds with strict Imperial AI regulations. Some sort of damage at the beginning of its existence had allowed it to expand without the usual self-governors. The mistress had always approved, however, as long as it was discreet. There were advantages in being down here at the end of the earth, and it was pleasurable to be illegally smart.)

The house took care to note Zai's reaction, wondering what he would think of his new ship.

Captain Zai and the mistress were together on the western balcony, overlooking a few ice sculptures of aboriginal Home insect life that the house had attempted in the dead of winter, smoothed to abstraction now by the arrival of summer. Zai hadn't even accessed the entire missive yet, but he seemed upset by what he had read so far.

'Ten years out,' he said. Was it pain in his voice? Or just the cold? 'Ten years back.'

The mistress stepped toward Zai, put a hand on his shoulder. He looked at her and laughed sourly, shaking his head.

'I'm sorry to react this way,' he said. 'You hardly know me, after all.'

The house scanned the missive and spotted a section it

had ignored. The newly promoted captain had been assigned to the Rix frontier, to a system called Legis, ten light-years away, for a tour of indeterminate length.

'I'm sorry too, Laurent,' the mistress said.

Zai placed his hand on hers, blinking from his eyelashes the first flakes of a light snow. He spoke carefully.

'I know we've just met. But to lose you already—' He shook his head. 'I sound foolish.'

'You don't, Laurent.'

'But I thought I'd be here on Home for at least a few months. I was half hoping they'd stick me on training staff.'

'Would you want that, Laurent?'

'A staff position? My ancestors would wail,' he answered. 'But *twenty years*. And facing the damned Time Thief again. I suppose I've grown tired of his tricks.'

'How long has it been, Laurent? Your career, in Absolute years?'

'Too many,' he said. 'Almost a hundred.'

Nara shook her head. 'I didn't know.'

'And now another thirty, probably,' he said. 'Fifty, if there really is a war coming.'

'A senator's term of office,' the mistress observed.

The man turned, his expression changing.

'You're right, Nara. We may both lose the next fifty years. And you senators have your own Thief. You're frozen half the time, aren't you?'

'Much more than half, Laurent.'

'Well,' he said, meeting her eyes, 'that's hopeful, I suppose.'

She smiled. 'Perhaps it is. But I'll still be older than you, subjectively. I am already.'

'You are?'

She laughed. 'Yes. Give me another decade in subjective, and you'll notice.'

Zai straightened himself. 'Of course I will. I'll notice everything.'

'Is that a promise?'

He took both the mistress's hands.

'We have four days to make promises, Senator-Elect.'

'Yes, Captain.'

'Four days,' he repeated, and turned back to the ice sculptures.

'Stay here with me,' she asked. 'Give us those days.'

The house became alert. The mistress had only announced a weekend stay; never before had she extended a visit unexpectedly. Meals had been planned in excruciating detail, supplies obtained in exact amounts. Despite the vast resources of the estate – the underground gardens, the caves full of food and wine, the cargo drones ready to launch from a hundred high-end stores on the Imperial homeworld – a surge of anxiety almost resembling panic swept through the house's mind. This was all so *abrupt*.

And yet, the house wanted Zai to agree.

It waited anxiously for the man's answer.

'Yes,' he said. 'I'd love to.'

The house took its attention from their sudden kiss. There was so much to do.

5

SPACE BATTLE

The initial conditions of a battle are the only factors that a general can truly affect. Once blood is drawn, command is merely an illusion.

– ANONYMOUS 167

Captain

The *Lynx* exploded, expanded.

The frigate's energy-sink manifold spread out, stretching luxuriant across eighty square kilometers. The manifold was part hardware and part field effect, staggered ranks of tiny machines held in their hexagonal pattern by a lacework of easy gravity. It shimmered in the Legis sun, refracting a mad god's spectrum, unfurling like the feathers of some ghostly, translucent peacock seeking to rut. In battle, it could disperse ten thousand gigawatts per second, a giant lace fan burning hot enough to blind naked human eyes at two thousand klicks.

The satellite-turrets of the ship's four photon cannon eased away from the primary hull, extending on hypercarbon scaffolds that reminded Zai of the iron bones of ancient cantilever bridges. The *Lynx* was shielded from the cannon's collateral radiation by twenty centimeters of hullalloy. They were removed on their spindly arms four kilometers from the vessel proper; using the cannon would afflict the *Lynx*'s crew with only the most treatable of cancers. The four satellite-turrets carried sufficient reaction mass and intelligence to operate independently if released in battle. And from the safety of a few thousand kilometers' distance, their fusion magazines could be ordered to crashfire, consuming themselves in a chain reaction, delivering one final, lethal needle toward the enemy. Of course, the cannon could also be crashfired from their close-in position, destroying their mother ship in a blaze of deadly glory.

That was one of the frigate's five standard methods of self-destruction.

The magnetic rail that launched the *Lynx*'s drone complement descended from her belly, and telescoped to its full nineteen-hundred-meter length. A few large scout drones, a squadron of ramscatters, and a host of sandcasters deployed themselves around the rail. The ramscatters bristled like nervous porcupines with their host of tiny flechettes, each of which carried sufficient fuel to accelerate at two thousand gees for almost a second. The sandcasters were bloated with dozens of self-propelled canisters, whose ceramic skins were cross-hatched with fragmentation patterns. At the high relative velocity of this battle, sand would be Zai's most effective weapon against the Rix receiver array.

Inside the rail bay, great magazines of other drone types were loaded in a carefully calculated order of battle. Stealth penetrators, broadcast decoys, minesweepers, remotely piloted fighter craft, close-in-defense pickets all awaited their moment in battle. Finally, a single deadman drone waited. This drone could be launched even if the frigate lost all power, accelerated by highly directional explosives inside its dedicated backup rail. The deadman was already active, continuously updating its copy of the last two hours' logfiles, which it would attempt to deliver to Imperial forces if the *Lynx* were destroyed.

When we are destroyed, Captain Laurent Zai corrected himself. His ship was not likely to survive this encounter; it was best to accept that. The Rix vessel outpowered and outgunned them. Its crew was quicker and more adept, so intimately linked into the battlecruiser's systems that the exact point of division between human and hardware was a subject more for philosophical debate than military consideration. And Rix boarding commandos were deadly: faster, hardier, more proficient in compromised gravity. And, of course, they were unafraid of death; to the Rix, lives lost in battle were no more remarkable than a few brain cells sacrificed to a glass of wine.

Zai watched his bridge crew work, preparing the newly configured *Lynx* to resume acceleration. They were in zero-gee now, waiting for the restructuring to firm up before subjecting the expanded frigate to the stresses of acceleration. It was a relief to be out of high-gee, if only for a few hours. When the engagement started in earnest, the ship would go into evasive mode, the direction and strength of acceleration varying continuously. Next to that chaos, the last two weeks of steady high acceleration would seem like a pleasure cruise.

Captain Zai wondered if there was any mutiny left in his crew. At least two of the conspirators had escaped his and Hobbes's trap. Were there more? The senior officers must realize that this battle was unwinnable. They understood what a Rix battlecruiser was capable of, and would recognize that the *Lynx*'s battle configuration had been designed to damage its opponent, not preserve itself. Zai and ExO Hobbes had optimized the ship's offensive weaponry at the expense of it defenses, orienting its entire arsenal on the task of destroying the Rix receiver array.

Now that the *Lynx* was at battle stations, even the junior officers would be able to spot the ill portents that surrounded them.

The boarding skiffs remained in their storage cells. It was unlikely that Zai's marines would be crossing the gulf to capture the Rix battlecruiser. Boarding actions were the privilege of the winning vessel. Instead, the Imperial marines were taking up positions throughout the *Lynx*, ready to defend it from capture should the Rix board the vessel after pounding it into helplessness. Normally under these conditions, Zai would have issued sidearms to the crew to help repel boarders. But after the mutiny this seemed a risky show of faith.

Most ominously for any crewman who chose to notice, the singularity generator, the most dramatic of Zai's self-destruct options, was already charged to maximum. If the *Lynx* could draw close enough to the enemy battlecruiser, the two craft would share a dramatic death.

In short, the *Lynx* was primed like an angry, blind drunk hurtling into a barfight with gritted teeth, ferally anxious to inflict damage, unconscious of any pain she might feel herself.

Perhaps that was their one advantage in this fight, Zai thought: desperation. Would the Rix try to protect the vulnerable receiver array? Their mission was obviously to communicate with the compound mind on Legis. But would the dictates of saving the array force the Rix commander to make a bad move? If so, there might be some slim hope of surviving this battle.

Zai sighed and grimly pushed this line of thought aside. Hope was not his ally, he had learned over the last ten days.

He turned his mind back to the bridge airscreen and its detailed schematic of the *Lynx*'s internal structure.

The wireframe lines shifted like an oriental puzzle box, as walls and bulkheads inside the frigate slid into battle configuration. Common rooms and mess halls disappeared to make space for expanded gunnery stations, passageways widened for easier movement of emergency repair teams. Crew bunks transformed into burn beds. The sickbay irised open, consuming the zero-gee courts and running tracks that usually surrounded it. Walls sprouted handholds in case of gravity loss, and everything that might come loose in sudden acceleration was stowed, velcroed, bolted down, or simply recycled.

Finally, the coiling, shifting, expanding, and extruding all came to a halt, and the schematic eased into a stable shape. Like a well-crafted mechanical bolt smoothly sliding into place, the vessel became battle ready.

A single klaxon sounded. A few of his bridge crew half-turned toward Zai. Their faces were expectant and excited, ready to begin this fight regardless of the ship's chances. He saw it most in ExO Hobbes's expression. They'd been beaten back on Legis XV, all of them, and this was their chance to get revenge. The mutiny, however small and aborted, had shamed them as well. They were ready to fight, and their bloodlust, however desperate, was good to see.

It was just possible, Laurent Zai allowed himself to think, that they would get home.

The captain nodded to the first pilot, and weight gradually returned, pressing him into the shipmaster's chair as the frigate accelerated.

The *Lynx* moved toward battle.

Militia Worker

The contrail of a supersonic aircraft blossomed weakly in the thin, dry air, barely marking the sky.

Rana Harter imagined the passengers far above: reclining in sculpted crash-safe chairs, the air they breathed scented with some perfumed disinfectant, perhaps being served some light snack now, midway to their destination. From up there, other contrails would be visible through windows of transparent hypercarbon. Most long-haul air routes on Legis passed over the pole. The continents were clustered in the northern hemisphere, far from the raging equatorial sea and the vast, silent ocean of the south. Air transit routes converged here at the pole like the lines on a dribble-hoop ball, this tundral waste an empty junction, overflown but never visited.

Rana had never traveled on an aircraft before Herd had brought her here. She could only blurrily imagine airborne luxury, the gaps in her vision filled with the sound of wealthy people's music: soft strings repeating the same slow phrase.

She watched the wind move driftsnow across the plain, and noted the direction and speed of the few scudding clouds. Her brainbug made a prediction. The contrail reached a certain point and Rana said, 'Now.'

At that moment, the contrail jagged suddenly, a sharp angle marring its slow curve. A few pieces of detritus caught the sun, flickering with their spin, falling from the supersonic craft with the apparent slow motion of great distance.

The plane quickly recovered, righting its course.

Rana imagined the sudden, sickening lurch inside the cabin. Glasses of champagne flying, trays and hand luggage upset, every object leaping toward the ceiling as the plane lost a thousand meters of altitude in a few seconds. The unexpected opening of the cargo hold would instantly double the plane's drag profile, sending a shock through the entire craft. Hopefully, the smart seats would hold their passengers in. A few bloodied noses and wrenched shoulders, perhaps a concussion for some unlucky soul on her feet. But by now the plane had righted itself, automatically closing the offending cargo door.

Rana Harter had discovered that her brainbug worked better if she indulged these fancies. As she imagined the sudden jolt above, her eyes tracked the flickering fall of luggage and supplies, and she felt the whirring of her mind as it calculated the location and shape of the debris field. The sharp, determinate math of trajectories and wind smelled like camphor, rang in her ears with vibrato-free, pointillistic notes on a handful of flutes, one for each variable.

The answers came.

She turned to Herd, already dressed in her hooded fur coat. The sable had come from the first luggage drop arranged by Alexander. The stain that had once disguised Herd's Rix eyes was faded now, and they shone in their true violet, beautiful in the frame of black fur. The hairs of the coat ruffled in the bitter wind, a fluttering motion that made Rana hear the small, shimmering bells worn by wedding dancers on their feet.

Herd awaited her instructions, always respectfully silent when Rana's ability was in use (though the commando had squeezed her hand as her word *now* seemed to yank the airplane from its path).

'Seventy-four klicks that way,' Rana said, pointing carefully. Herd's violet eyes followed the line of the gesture, checking for landmarks. Then she nodded and turned to Rana to kiss her good-bye.

The Rixwoman's lips were always cold now, her body temperature adapted to its environment. Her saliva tasted vaguely of rust, like the iron tang of blood, but sweeter. Her sweat contained no salt, its mineral content making it taste like water from a quarry town. As Herd dashed toward the flyer, the oversized coat lifting into sable wings, the synesthetic smell of the commando's avian/lemongrass movements mingled with the flavor left in Rana's mouth. The joy of watching Herd never lessened.

Rana turned back toward the cave entrance before the recon flyer whined to life, however. Every second here in the cold was taking something out of her.

Inside, it was above freezing.

Rana Harter wore two layers of real silk, a hat of red fox, and her own fur coat, vat-grown chinchilla lined with blue whale from the ubiquitous herds of the southern ocean. But she was still cold.

The walls of the cave were hung with centuries-old tapestries earmarked for the Museum of Antiquities in Pollax. A vast collection of toiletries and clothing, the bounty of fallen personal luggage, lined the icy shelves Herd had carved into the walls. Rana and Herd slept on the pelt of a large ursoid creature that neither of them recognized – a customs stamp confirmed its off-world origins. The floors were covered with soft linings ripped from luggage, a pile of undergarments forming an insulating layer underneath.

The small, efficient machines of travel were everywhere. Handheld games and coffee pots, flashlights and sex toys, all for Herd to dissect and rebuild into new devices. For sustenance, they had only prestige foods. Rich meats from young animals, fruits scandalously out of season, caviar and exotic nuts, candied insects and edible flowers. It all came in morsel sizes, suitable for luxury airplane meals: canned, self-heating and freeze-dried, bagged and coldboxed, to be washed down with liquor in plastic bottles dwarfish enough to have survived the long fall. They drank from two crystal glasses that someone thought valuable enough to pack in thirty centimeters of smartfoam. Oddly, the glasses had been labeled as coffee beans on their packaging. A mistake, or perhaps they were smuggled antiques.

All this bounty from only three aircraft holds, Rana wondered. She had never seen such wealth before. She lifted a smartplastic tennis racket, its rim no wider than the strings it suspended, and wondered at the instrument's elegant, almost Rixian lines.

This fourth luggage 'accident' would be their last haul. The background rate of such events had already been wildly exceeded, and Alexander's false clues explaining the cargo-door defect had begun to wear thin. But she and Herd had all they needed until the compound mind called them to action.

Until then, they would live in luxury. And they had each other.

Rana Harter sat and rested from the freezing minutes outside. She lifted up a travel handheld to read, and that simple exertion tired her. She slept longer each night, dreaming lucidly but abstractly in the strange symbols of her brainbug. Her happiness never wavered, though. The dopamine regulators saw to that.

The infection in Rana's wound was gone, disappearing in a single fevered night after an ampoule of nanos from Herd's medical kit. But the weight in Rana's chest was still there, building and building. Her breath grew shorter by the day.

She activated the travel handheld; its screen lit up, bookmarked to its medical compendium. Rana flicked it off again. She had read this section enough times, and knew that her one good lung was slowly going. Fluids were slowly building up in the wall between rib cage and lung, squeezing the breath from her like a tightening fist. Only an operation could save her. However resourceful her Rix lover might be, surgery was beyond their means here in this icy cave.

Rana Harter's mind had never possessed a sharp sense of irony. The mean circumstances of her life had never required one. But she saw the joke here: she was surrounded by everything she had ever desired. Every petty luxury and marker of wealth. An invisible god that she positively *knew* to exist. Free use of her brainbug in a safe retreat at the literal end of the earth. And a lover of alien beauty, a fierce and lethal protector, whose physical grace, novel mind, and violet eyes offered whole new worlds of fascination.

And the punch line: Rana, in the next few days, would almost certainly die.

She turned from these thoughts the way a child ignores a light rain. They did nothing to reduce her joy. Whatever occurred, she – one of the few among humanity's trillions – had chanced blindly into happiness.

Death must have found me, Rana Harter decided.

She was already in heaven.

Senator

Nara Oxham took firm hold of the handrail before purging the drug from her system.

The balcony barely swung in the cool, late-night wind, its motion held in check by counterweights rolling inside the wooden deck beneath her bare feet. A set of finger-width polyfilaments reinforced the softly creaking ornamental chains, with enough tensile strength (the building propaganda bragged) to hold an African elephant, even during one of the Coriolis squalls that sometimes reached the capital in late summer. If Senator Oxham were to slip and fall, she would only become entangled in the invisible suicide mesh that cocooned the entire building, and be delivered back to the nearest observation deck five floors below. And in case of the unthinkable, the balcony carried a small vacuum blimp compressed under the breakfast table. When fully deployed, it would provide enough lift to bring the senator and approximately twenty guests down to a soft landing.

But the animal mind was strong in humans, as Nara's empathy never let her forget, and mere safety precautions were not enough to overcome the vertigo of a two-kilometer drop. Her knuckles turned white as the drug left her.

The apathy bracelet made its usual hissing noise, injecting filtration nanos into her bloodstream. In a few minutes, the first glimmers of empathy arose from the city. Mindnoise rumbled from the residential towers north of the Diamond Palace, squat and ugly, densely populated. Each tower held over a hundred thousand of the capital's most numerous class: the petty bureaucrats who monitored taxable production claims. Every Imperial administrator in the Eighty Worlds had a double here on Home, another set of eyes following every transaction to ensure that the Senate and Emperor received their cut. Back on Vasthold, Nara had known of this army of distant and invisible overseers in the abstract, but eighty planets' worth of them concentrated in this one city brought home the fantastic extent of the Empire. Huge data freighters left daily from the capital's spaceport to resupply the possessions with entangled quanta, no expense spared to keep communications broadband and instantaneous, the Emperor's omniscience a matter of fact as well as scripture.

As her empathy grew, Nara could feel the dynamics of slow shift changes, thousands of bureaucrats returning home as night fell over populous continents light-years away, other thousands waking up to spread out across the low, windowless administration buildings as the day began in some megacity on another of the Eighty Worlds. War fever still animated the capital as a whole, but the minds of these countless minions never raised a cry above the rumble of drudgery, the cogs of the Empire.

Nara wondered what the overseers for Legis were doing now that the planet had been cut off from the Imperial network. The whole world, except for a few military installations and the *Lynx*, had been intentionally made a dark spot since the compound mind had taken over. The Emperor had given up direct control of an entire planet simply to isolate the Rix abomination.

What an insult to Imperial privilege.

The lights of the capital all but obliterated stars from the night sky, and Nara felt her distance from Laurent, her helplessness. If the *Lynx* was destroyed too suddenly to manage a last transmission, it would be eight hours before the lazy speed of the constant brought the event to telescopes on Legis. Almost a day of not knowing.

The War Council had voted hours ago; the battle must be engaged by now.

Her lover might already be dead.

Empathy gained another measure of intensity, and Senator Oxham could feel frantic thoughts down in the flame-dotted shape of the Martyrs' Park. Ancestor-worshiping cults had erected effigies of Rixwomen down there, tall figures with hollow eyes, filled with fanciful artificial organs that gave off a plastic smell when they burned. The demonstrations of the faithful had grown every day since the murder of the Emperor's sister.

Even Nara, a hardened Secularist, could still feel the shock of that moment. The Child Empress Anastasia was the Reason, after all, a central character of childhood fables and rhymes. However much Nara Oxham hated the process that had cured Anastasia's long-ago disease, the Child Empress and her brother had made the world Nara lived in. And no matter that she was sixteen centuries old, Anastasia had still looked twelve on the day of her death.

In any sane world, she would have died a long time ago, but it still felt utterly wrong that she had died at all.

This late most of the capital was asleep. The wild creature of the human group-psyche was unusually quiescent, and Senator Oxham held on to sanity for long minutes. She tried to feel the Diamond Palace, but the cold minds of the Apparatus undead and the disciplined thoughts of elite guardsmen provided little to grasp hold of.

'Why?' she wondered softly, thinking of the Emperor's plan.

The city was starting to swirl below her, the war animating even the capital's dreams.

Nara imagined a nuclear airburst overhead, a sudden, bright star blossoming in the sky. Instantly, the electromagnetic pulse would strike, and all the lights go out, the whole spectacle of the capital reduced to black silhouettes, lit only by the airburst and a few burning effigies in the park. Seconds later, however clean the warheads might be, a blast wave would rock her building, shattering windows, no doubt testing even the balcony's safeguards, and casting a rain of glass onto the streets below.

That was the plan for distant Legis, if Laurent Zai failed.

The nuclear attack might kill the Rix compound mind, but it would throw Legis into a dark age. After the falling air-cars and failing medical endoframes, and all the disease, unrest, and simple starvation that accompanied a devastated infostructure, there would be a hundred million lives lost planetwide, so the Apparatus estimated.

On a planet of two billion, that was not as bad as decimation, in the old sense of one in ten. But still the Old Enemy death on a vast scale.

She looked at the Diamond Palace again. What could be worth murdering a hundred million people?

The capital grew louder, becoming an angry chorus as her mind lost its defenses. In the sleepless free-market towers to the south, she felt labor futures tightening nervously, titles and pardons being fought over like carrion, the anxious cycles of a war economy spinning ever faster. The mindnoise turned to screeching, and again the old vision came: a great cloud of seagulls crowding the sky, wheeling around the bloated, dying thing that was the Empire.

Nara Oxham felt she almost grasped something fatal and hidden in these moments of madness, when withdrawal from the drug left her empathy open to the assembled mass of the capital, the Risen Empire in microcosm. Something was utterly rotten, she knew, a corruption tearing at the bonds that held the Eighty Worlds together. And she also knew that however hard she'd fought against the Emperor's rule, the shabby truth of how broken it all was would terrify her.

A dark shape rose up before Oxham, blotting out the lights

of the city. The senator tried to blink the apparition away, but its silent and winged form remained. She backed up a few steps, for a moment convinced that the empathic vision had somehow come to life and would consume her now.

But a familiar sound tugged at her second hearing, insistent through the howl of the city. She closed her eyes and some sane fraction of her mind recognized it: the War Council summons.

Her fingers went to her bracelet, reflexively administering a dose of apathy.

When she opened her eyes again, the shape was still there. An Imperial aircar waiting patiently, its elegant wing extended to meet the balcony's edge.

A missive hovered in second sight.

The battle is joined. The sovereign requests that his War Council attend him.

Nara shook her head bitterly as the drug again suppressed her empathy, returning the capital to silence. She would not even be allowed to wait alone for news of Laurent and Legis. The Emperor and his War Council, those who knew what was at stake, wanted company as they watched their miserable plan unfold.

Nara Oxham crossed the wing to the waiting aircar, not bothering to change. On Vasthold, one went plainly dressed and barefoot to funerals.

In the next few hours, Laurent Zai would either save a hundred million lives, or die trying.

Captain

Captain Laurent Zai exulted in the colors and sounds of the bridge.

The battle was joined.

Both ships had launched the bulk of their drone complements, and the outer reaches of the two multitudes were just now touching, just over half a light-minute away, a pair of vast point-clouds in stately collision. Automated drones were battling each other out there, the skirmishers of two fleets vying for advantage. The outcome of those first duels was still a mystery; only the largest scout and remote fighter drones carried translight communications. Already, one side might have secured superiority in the outer skirmishes, and thus a crucial advantage in intelligence. The few scout drones with entangled communications could only tell the *Lynx*'s crew so much about the enemy.

If the *Lynx*'s drones lost the battle at the edge, superior intelligence would be added to the Rix's already weighty advantages.

This was one cost of Zai's hell-bent battle plan. If the first outlying duels were lost, there would be little time to recover. It would all be over quickly.

'Anything from the master pilot?' Zai badgered Hobbes.

'He's still looking for an opening, sir.'

Zai gritted his teeth and cursed. It would be foolish to second-guess Marx and order him in before he was ready; the master pilot was a brilliant tactician, and his remote fighters were far less numerous and more valuable than the automated drones currently battling on the outer edge of the fray. But Zai wished the man wasn't so damned fastidious.

'Let me know when he deigns to join the battle.'

Zai tugged at his woolen uniform angrily.

'And Hobbes, why is it so damned hot on my bridge?'

Pilot

Master Pilot Jocim Marx watched the feints and penetrations of the battle with a boxer's patience, waiting for the proper moment to strike.

Safe in the shielded center of the *Lynx*, Marx inhabited the viewpoint of the foremost entanglement-equipped drone among the frigate's complement. This drone was close to the fight, but not in it yet. The two opposing spheres of drone craft were just beginning to overlap, like some three-dimensional Venn diagram mapping the shallowest of intersections between sets. But with every passing second, the intersection increased by another three thousand kilometers. Within the broad front of the collision, drones darted, accelerating at thousands of gees to effect the smallest of lateral changes. At the two fleets' huge relative velocity, drones could only shift themselves by hairlines relative to the enemy. They were like pistol-wielding duelists perched on the front of two approaching high-speed trains, hurtling toward each other, taking shuffling steps from side to side, trying to gain some slight advantage.

From his vantage in the translight-equipped drone, Marx could see the outermost portions of the battle firsthand. He could command the drones around him to effect a swift parry. But the drones he sent these orders to were too small and cheap for entangled communications, so his orders reached them with the maddening tardiness of the constant. Marx was used to the millisecond delays of Intelligencers and other small craft, but these delays were like sending carrier pigeons to direct a battle kilometers away.

The two waves of combatants continued their career into each other, and the flares of accelerating kinetic weapons began to light the void. The first wave of the *Lynx*'s drones were spraying sand, huge clouds of tiny but sharp and corrosive carbon particles. *Diamonds*, the poets called them. At these relative velocities, sand could strip an armored drone like a desert storm tearing the skin from a naked man.

The Rix craft responded with more sophisticated measures. Marx saw the shimmering flashes that were formations of flocker missiles being launched. Each flocker was no bigger than a human finger, but in phalanxes of a hundred or more they formed a hive entity of enormous versatility. They combined their resources to form a single sensor array, unified electronic defenses, and a hardy, democratic intelligence. And like all Rix military hardware, flockers evolved from battle to battle. In the First Incursion decades before, they had been observed coordinating tactics across huge distances. They grouped themselves in larger or smaller formations as the situation dictated, and individuals sacrificed themselves to protect other flockers of their group. Marx wondered how far they had progressed in the last eighty years. He had a feeling that the *Lynx*'s crew was about to learn quite a bit on the subject.

However smart these new flockers were, though, the captain had made one point with which Marx had to agree. Cruder Imperial technology had an advantage at high velocities. Flockers and piloted drones used up a lot of their mass being clever, and cleverness didn't always pay off when a firefight took place in the blink of an eye. Sand was as dumb as a stone club, but its destructiveness increased with every kilometer per second.

The master pilot's craft told him that the flockers were hitting the first wavefront of sand. At relative rest, a dispersed cloud of sand was barely detectable. But plunging through it at one percent light speed transformed the cloud into a solid wall.

Marx urged his drone closer.

The view cleared quickly as he shot toward the battle's edge. His scout craft had an initial load of two-thirds reaction mass, and could accelerate at six hundred gees at 25 percent efficiency. If he pointed it in one direction and pushed it, the drone would make just under a quarter of the constant in about two hundred minutes, at which point it would be out of fuel. Although the drone lacked the elegance of Marx's beloved small craft, that one fact always amazed him: this machine, no bigger than a coffin, could make relativistic velocities. It had the power to push time.

Even in this train wreck of a battle, the scout's acceleration could make a difference. Marx had taken it out in front of the Imperial drone fleet and then turned it over. Now he was falling back toward the *Lynx* – almost pacing the incoming Rix drones. He'd burned a sixth of his reaction mass, but Marx was where he wanted to be: in the rolling center of the conflict.

He passed a few decelerating sandcaster drones; their cargoes emptied, they were pulling back.

Marx waited, drumming his fingers. There should be fireworks by now. Where was the wave of explosions showing the disintegration of the first flocker formations? Imperial sand posed little sensor interference – it was designed to be invisible. But no explosions showed in Marx's view, just acceleration and launch flares.

Were the flockers dying quietly, whittled down to nothing by the terrific friction of the sand?

Marx pushed in closer, seeking answers at the risk of his scout. A firefight had started between the larger advanced drones, who'd launched all their satellites and were now attacking each other directly. Rix beam weapons lit the void, igniting ambient sand like searchlights on a misty night. But Marks could see nothing that looked like a host of small craft disintegrating. He cut his craft's acceleration, trying to stay out of the fight.

Then Marx saw the column.

It glinted just for a moment in a radar reflection, four kilometers long. For a moment, he thought it was a single structure. Then the AI calculated its exact diameter and he realized what it was.

A single column of flockers, probably all that the battle cruiser had launched. More than five thousand of them, spaced less than a meter apart. His sensors told of the formation's incredible exactness: the whole four kilometers had the diameter of Marx's thumb.

He could see minute flashes from the front of the column now. Every few seconds the lead drone was being destroyed by sand. Then the next one took its place, and lasted a few more seconds.

But behind these sacrifices, the vast majority of the flockers were protected. They were like army ants crossing a river, the latter arrivals marching on the backs of the foremost after they had drowned. They were punching a very narrow hole into the wall of sand, and slipping through.

Marx had seen flockers spread themselves into a far-flung bestiary of shapes: radiating arms like paper fans or the struts of a parasol, toroids and lazy-eights that undulated with a standing wave, pointclouds buzzing with internal motion. But never had he seen anything so deviously simple.

A straight line.

And they were getting through.

Another image occurred to Marx. On his home planet lived a species of rat that could break down its own bones, funneling itself into a thin sack of jelly to climb through even the narrowest of cracks. He shuddered at the thought.

Marx's surprise cost him a vital moment of attention. He didn't immediately notice the ten flockers that burst from the line, having detected a transient gap in the sand between his scout craft and the column. By the time the master pilot reacted, the flockers were lined up on him at three thousand gees. Although they had less than a second of reaction mass at that acceleration, Marx's twisting evasive pattern came too late, his larger drone twisting like some slow-footed mastodon brought down by a pack of small predators. Synesthesia filled with lightning, sputtered for a moment, then dumped him into the calming cerulean wash of a dead signal.

He cursed. And cursed again.

Gathering himself, Jocim Marx signaled ExO Hobbes.

'I saw,' Hobbes said. She'd been watching over his shoulder.

He bit his tongue as a wave of shame struck him. In a Class 7 translight drone on a scouting mission, and he'd been beaten by a handful of pilotless drones.

'They're getting through the sand!' he shouted. 'The *Lynx* is—'

'We'll be briefing the captain in forty seconds,' Hobbes interrupted. 'I want you on the bridge in virtual.'

Forty seconds? An eternity in this battle, a dozen opportunities lost to delay.

'And what should I do for forty seconds, Executive Officer?'

A dead pause: his audio muted as Hobbes attended to one of the other dozen conversations she was no doubt juggling. Then she was back.

'I suggest you reflect thankfully upon the fact that you fly remotes, Master Pilot. See you in thirty seconds.'

Her voice left him alone in his blue, dead universe.

As he waited, Marx's fingers twitched, aching to fly again.

Captain

'In short, the flockers are getting through the sand,' Hobbes concluded.

Laurent Zai nodded.

'They always do. What's the projected attrition?'

Hobbes swallowed. These nervous ticks were unlike her, Zai thought. She had lost some confidence since the mutiny.

'Perhaps a tenth, sir. The other ninety percent are coming through.'

'Ten percent!' Zai glared down into the bridge main airscreen, where the long, thin needle of flockers hovered. Normally, the small and expendable drones were reduced to a small fraction of their initial numbers. He and Hobbes had expected the sand to be especially deadly at this speed. But instead, it had proved useless.

There were almost five thousand flockers in the first wave alone, more than enough to tear the *Lynx* to pieces. And they would arrive in some sixteen minutes.

'Did they use this single-column tactic in the last war?' he asked.

'No, sir. Perhaps a new evolutionary—' Hobbes began.

'Begging your pardon, Captain,' interrupted the disembodied head and shoulders of Master Pilot Marx. His image floated in the captain's private airscreen, projected from a flight canopy in the *Lynx*'s core.

'Yes, Master Pilot?'

'In a normal battle, forming into a single column wouldn't give flockers any advantage. Sand is ejected outward from hundreds of small delivery canisters, so any given sandstorm contains hundreds of different trajectories. The relative motion between sand and flockers is chaotic.'

'So a column would offer no protection,' Hobbes said.

'Correct.' Marx's fingers came into view, gesturing through calculations. 'But in this battle, our two drone fleets are moving through each other at three thousand klicks per second. The lateral, chaotic motion of the sand is erased by its relative insignificance to the overall motion. The flocker column punches through even the biggest sand cloud in a few thousandths of a second.'

Zai closed his eyes. He'd been foolish not to see it. Perhaps not this specific tactic, but the basic flaw in his plan: the *Lynx*'s high speed of attack flattened events.

A quote from Anonymous 167 came to him too late.

'"Against a simple tactic, a simple response is often effective,"' he muttered. The Rix had found that simple response.

'Pardon me, sir?' Marx said.

Hobbes nodded vigorously, translating the aphorism for Marx. 'The high relative velocity between our two ships channels relationships into a single dimension: that of the approach axis. In effect, we've made this a single-variable battle.'

'And the Rix have countered with a one-dimensional formation,' Captain Zai concluded. 'A line.'

'The flockers will reach us in fourteen minutes, sir,' the watch officer interjected.

Zai nodded calmly, but inside he seethed. The *Lynx*'s rate of acceleration was pitiful compared to that of the tiny flockers. There was no way to maneuver out of this. They were defenseless.

He clenched his real hand. To have chosen life, to have thrown away honor, only to be extinguished by an idiotic mistake. Zai had broken his oath to see Nara again, but it looked as if his betrayal would come to nothing. Perhaps this was natural law in action: on Vada, they said that a knife found its way easily to the heart of a traitor.

He looked again at the airscreen representation of the flocker attack. The column was not exactly a knife. It was too long and thin, like some primitive projectile weapon. An arrow, or maybe . . .

An old memory surfaced.

'This has become something of a joust,' Zai said.

'A joust, sir?'

'A pre-diaspora military situation. More of a ritual, really. In a joust attack, a very long kinetic-contact weapon was propelled toward the enemy by animal power.'

'Sounds unpleasant, sir,' Hobbes said.

'Rather.' Zai allowed his mind to drift back in time. He saw the constructs battling in his grandfather's great pasture on Vada. The horses were spectacularly rendered, their flanks gathering loam as the hot afternoon went on. The brightly festooned knights rode toward each other. Their steeds' hooves drummed the ground with a rhythmic shudder that rattled the nerves like the overflight of an armored rotary wing.

The long sticks – *lances*, they were called – striking against . . .

'Hobbes,' Zai said, seeing an answer. 'Are you familiar with the origin of the word *shield*?' Hobbes's Utopian upbringing had provided her only patchy knowledge of ancient weapons.

'I'm afraid not, sir.'

'A straightforward device, Hobbes. A two-dimensional surface used to ward off one-dimensional attacks.'

'Useful, sir.' Zai could see Hobbes's mind struggle to follow him.

'*Captain*,' Marx interrupted. 'The first formation of flockers will reach the *Lynx* practically at full strength. More than four thousand of them! Our close-in defenses can't cope with so many at once.'

'A shield, Hobbes. Prepare to fire all four photon cannon.'

Marx began to protest, and Zai cut the man's sound off

with a gesture. Of course – as the master pilot had been about to complain – capital weapons like the *Lynx*'s photon cannon were useless against flockers. It would be like hunting insects with artillery.

'What's the target, sir?' Hobbes asked.

'The *Lynx*,' he said.

'We're firing at . . . ?' she began. Then, even as her fingers moved to alert the gunners, understanding filled her face. 'I assume we can target the heat-sink manifold directly, sir?'

'Of course, Hobbes. No need to test the energy shunts.'

'We'll be ready to detach the manifold on your order, Captain.'

'Exactly, Hobbes.'

He turned his attention to the flailing, voiceless Master Pilot.

'Marx, get back into the foremost scout,' Zai commanded, then gave the man back his voice.

'And my orders, sir?'

'Attack the Rix receiver array. With a sandcaster if you can find any alive.'

The Master Pilot thought silently for a moment. Then he said, 'Perhaps if there were an unexploded canister—'

'Do it,' Zai commanded, and erased the man's image from the bridge.

'All cannon ready, sir. Targeting our own heat-sink array at twenty percent power.'

Zai paused, wondering if there were yet another factor he hadn't considered. Perhaps he was making another idiotic mistake. He wondered if any Imperial shipmaster had opened fire on his own ship before, without self-destruction in mind.

But the war sage's words reassured him.

If you fail, fail dramatically. At least you will prove the error of your tactics to your successors.

Zai nodded; this diversion would get into the textbooks one way or another.

'Fire.'

Pilot

Banished from the bridge, Marx leapt back into the forefront of battle.

He chose another scout craft, displacing a sensor officer who was flying it at one remove. She'd been running three scouts at once, coordinating their efforts through a high-level interface. The Master Pilot kicked her off, settled in, and flexed the machine's muscles. He informed all Imperial drones within ten thousand klicks that he was assuming control of them.

Marx accelerated his impromptu battle group into a cone-shaped collision formation focused upon the Rix battlecruiser. He brought the scout's fusion drive, which doubled as its primary offensive weapon, out of stealth mode. He would need some serious power.

These actions were all likely to draw the attention of the Rix. The scout was blaring across a wide range of EM, making itself known to the enemy's battle management intelligences, human and machine. They would spot the valuable asset quickly, a drone under human command and at front-center of the *Lynx*'s satellite cloud, the position most threatening to the enemy battlecruiser. Within seconds, Marx saw distant acceleration traces deep in the Rix cloud, the plumes of hunters vectoring toward his new vessel.

In all likelihood, the master pilot would be losing his second scout of the day inside a minute. But his fingers moved confidently, drawing an ever-expanding sphere of resources into the attack.

Marx didn't expect to live long, anyway. The nearly full-strength flocker squadron was approaching the *Lynx* too fast. Pilots were nestled in the armored belly of Imperial warships, in the hope that the drones of a dying ship would fight on under human control, damaging the enemy even as their own vessel was destroyed around them. But at this high relative velocity, the flockers would plunge through the *Lynx* like barrage rockets through a cloud of steam. There would be no safety even in the pilots' armored canopies.

Death – real, absolute, nonvirtual death – was headed toward Jocim Marx at three million meters per second.

So he flew with uncharacteristic aggression. Perhaps he could shed some Rix blood on his way out.

Between his drone and the enemy battlecruiser, the master pilot spotted the distinctive shape of a Rix gravity array. The array was a simple defensive weapon. At its core was a free-floating easy gravity generator – the same device that created artificial gravity in starships, equipped with limited AI and its own reaction drive. Surrounding the generator was a host of gravity repeaters. These small devices were held in place by the easy gravity, but also shaped and controlled it. An array could create a gravity well (or hill) in any configuration, strong enough to halt or deflect enemy drones and kinetic weapons. As he closed, Marx could see more of them, forming a huge barrier before the battlecruiser, perfect protection for the receiver. The gravity array closest to Marx was spread wide, giving readings of only sixty gees, just strong enough to corral the clouds of sand still crashing through the Rix fleet.

It was the Rix device closest to Marx, and he decided to destroy it.

He ordered a nearby ramscatter drone to launch its full complement at the gravity array. The craft spun like a firework wheel, spitting hordes of tiny, stupid flechettes from its flanks, exhausting itself in seconds. As per its programming, the ram-scatter drone started to pull back toward the *Lynx* for reloading, but Marx urged it forward. Perhaps he could use the expended drone as a ram. In any case, there would soon be no mothership to return home to.

Marx wondered if the captain really had any plan for defending his ship against the flockers. Zai had spoken as if he'd seen a way to escape destruction, but the captain's words had been cryptic, as usual. It was probably just an act, the necessary false confidence of command. Some morale-related edict from that long-dead sage that Zai and Hobbes were always quoting.

Well, just as long as they kept the *Lynx* together for a few more minutes, long enough for Marx to hit the Rix battle-cruiser. Marx knew he was the best pilot in the Navy. Dying without putting a scratch on the enemy prime would be an unacceptable end to his career.

The flechettes slammed into the array, whipping through the hills and troughs of its gravity contours like a flight of arrows suddenly caught in a wind tunnel. Marx let them spread through the array for a few seconds, then ordered all but a dozen to self-destruct. The invisible contours of the array filled with clouds of shrapnel. The bright reflections of broken metal spread through the warped space like milk dispersing in swirling coffee. The churning shrapnel ate through the gravity repeaters, and the array's gravity-shape flopped about, then flattened into a simple sphere, a steep, defensive hill of almost a thousand gees. Marx took command of the few flechettes he had left, and targeted the sphere's center – the gravity generator itself. The remaining flechettes bolted toward it from all directions.

Normally, the tiny machines moved invisibly fast, but they climbed the steep gravity hill with eerie slowness. Marx saw one run out of reaction mass just short of its target; it became visible for a few seconds, spinning at its zenith, a pole vaulter falling short of the bar. Then it fell away.

Then another flechette fell short.

Damn, the gravity generator had reacted too quickly, shifting energy from its repeater array to a defensive posture in a few milliseconds. Had the Rix become unbeatable?

But then a flechette, favored by its initial position and relative velocity, plumbed the last dregs of its acceleration and struck the generator. The tiny drone only managed to make contact at a few hundred meters per second, but its impact had some tiny effect: the strength of the gravity hill wavered for a millisecond.

And in that opening the rest of the flechettes slammed home.

The sphere of artificial gravity convulsed once, expanding. Finally, a toy balloon inflated too far, it burst into nothingness, a wave front of easy gravitons lighting up the sensors in Marx's scout. Then space flattened itself impassively before him.

Marx took his scout drone and its growing retinue through the resulting hole in the Rix perimeter. The master pilot smiled exultantly. He was going to get his chance. He was going to do some damage.

If only Zai could hold the *Lynx* together.

'Just give me five minutes,' he muttered.

Executive Officer

'Contact in four minutes, sir,' Hobbes reported.

The captain's eyebrows raised a centimeter. The flockers were arriving ahead of schedule.

'They're kicking, sir,' Hobbes explained. *Kick* – the increase of a rate of acceleration. 'Maybe they suspect what we're up to.'

'Perhaps they simply smell blood, Hobbes. Can we have separation in time?'

Hobbes refocused her attention to the heated conversations among the engineers working below. They were attempting to eject the energy-sink's main generator, to separate the *Lynx* from its own defensive manifold, which was now glowing white-hot from the point-blank pounding of the frigate's four photon cannon. The manifold was designed to be ejected, of course; warships had to shed their energy-sinks when they grew too hot from enemy fire. But usually the generator remained on the ship while the manifold was discohered, allowed to fly apart in all directions. Captain Zai's plan, however, demanded that the manifold remain intact, retaining its huge shape as the *Lynx* pulled away from it.

Therefore, the gravity generator that held all the tiny energy-sink modules in place had to leave the frigate – in one piece and still functioning.

The engineers didn't sound happy.

'Slide that bulkhead *now*!' the team leader ordered. It was Frick, the First Engineer.

Godspite, Hobbes thought. There was still an exterior bulkhead between the generator and open space.

'We're not at vacuum yet,' a voice complained. 'We'll depressurize like hell.'

'Then strap yourselves to something and depressurize the bitch!' Frick countered.

Hobbes checked the rank-codes on the voices: Frick of course was head of engineering; the team clearing the obstructing bulkhead came from Emergency Repairs, regular Navy filling in. A chain-of-command problem.

She cut into the argument.

'This is ExO Hobbes. Blow the damn bulkhead. I repeat:

don't bother matching the vacuum, don't waste time sliding –
blow it.'

Stunned disbelief silenced both sides of the argument for
a moment.

'But Hobbes,' Frick responded, his line now restricted to
officers' ears only. 'I've got unarmored ratings down there.'

Damn, Hobbes thought. The ratings had been pulled from
other sections: maintenance workers, low-gee trainers, cooks.
They wouldn't have been assigned armored suits. Their pressure suits could stand hard vacuum, but weren't equipped to
survive an explosion.

But there wasn't time. Not to get the ratings out of danger,
not even to get the captain's confirmation.

'The flockers are kicking on a steep curve. Time's up. Blow
it,' she ordered, her voice dry. 'Blow it now.'

'Does the captain—' the other team leader began.

'Now!'

The situation beacon guttered magenta in her second
sight – an explosion aboard ship. A fraction of a second later,
the actual shock wave of the blast rippled through the bridge.

Hobbes closed her eyes, but cruel synesthesia didn't
permit escape. She could see it: low on the engineering wedge
of her crew organizational chart, a row of casualty lights
turned yellow. One swiftly flickered to red.

'What was that?' Zai asked.

'Separation in twenty seconds.' Hobbes couldn't bring herself to say more.

'About time,' Zai muttered. The captain ran far fewer diagnostic displays than his executive officer. He must not have
seen the casualties yet.

The engineering teams said nothing as they completed
their work. Only grunts of physical labor, the hard breathing
of shock, and the background sounds of shrieking metal as the
generator began to move.

When she was sure that there would be no more delays, Hobbes expended a moment to order a medical response team to the blown bulkhead. The ship would begin acceleration in a few seconds to pull itself away from the manifold, and the medtechs would have to struggle through the pitching corridors in pressure suits. The *Lynx* was about to run stealthy as well, shutting the artificial gravity and other nonessentials for the few seconds until danger passed. It would take the medtechs minutes to reach the stricken crewmen.

Another of the engineering casualty lights shifted to red. Two lives gone.

Hobbes forced her attention back to the bridge's main airscreen display. The long wedge of the *Lynx*'s primary hull slid back from the radiant circle of the energy-sink manifold, pulling back to interpose the effulgent manifold between frigate and approaching flockers. To conceal the maneuver from the flockers' sharp-eyed sensors, they were running on cold jets, spraying water from the *Lynx*'s waste tubes, using their own shit as reaction mass. The ship moved with painful slowness. The primary hull would be a mere two hundred meters out of position when the drones hit – barely its own girth.

At least Zai had his shield now, Hobbes thought somberly. Two dead, three grievously wounded, and a hull breach all before a single Rix weapon had struck the *Lynx*. But the blazing manifold now floated between the flockers and their target.

'We're ready, sir.'

'Impact in ten seconds,' the watch officer said.

'Well done, Hobbes.'

Hobbes felt no flush of pride at the rare praise from her captain. She just hoped her sacrifice of the two young ratings would pay off.

flocker squadron

The flocker democratic intelligence noticed a change in its target.

The enemy prime was close, a hair over three seconds from contact. Absolute time was moving very slowly, however, compared with the speed of the squadron's thought. The laser pulses with which the flockers exchanged data – the connections that formed their limited compound intellect – moved almost instantly up and down the tightly spaced formation. Squadrons were often spread out over thousands of cubic kilometers, distances which slowed the mechanics of decision making. But this flocker group was so compact that thought moved at lightning speeds; the intellect had plenty of time to observe as the situation evolved over these final, luxurious seconds before impact.

Despite their quick intellect, the flockers couldn't see very well in this formation. The straight column lacked a parallax view, and the intense radiation from the enemy prime's energy-sink manifold had almost blinded the forward flockers, making the center of the manifold – where the prime must be – a dark patch against a vibrant sky.

But why was the manifold already expelling energy? Of the Rix fleet, only the battlecruiser itself could have delivered this much energy to the target, and it was more than eight million kilometers out of range. The flockers suspected that the enemy prime had fired upon its own sink. A bizarre occurrence, this early attempt at self-destruction, sufficiently strange that the squadron's hardwired tactical library offered no answers as to what it might mean.

The flocker formation felt blind, and yearned to spread

wider. Without parallax, it had no multi-viewpoint reconstruction of the target to call upon.

The flockers voted. Laser flashes of debate and decision flickered up and down the line for almost a full second before they decided to expend a few more milligrams of acceleration mass per individual. This close to the enemy prime, there appeared to be little sand left to avoid, after all. The squadron broke its tight column, expanding to a few meters with width over the next half second.

With this new parallax view, the squadron's group intelligence realized that the manifold was shifting.

The glowing disk – 4,500 kilometers away and rushing toward the flockers at 3,200 kps – had accelerated less than a pitiful five meters per second. But the change was detectable, the tiny push forward propagating through the energy sinks like a ripple expanding in a pond.

The flocker squadron pondered: why would the enemy prime bother with an acceleration of such small size? Had they fired a projectile rearward, resulting in the forward push? Perhaps the Imperials had realized their own imminent death and launched a deadman drone. But after a close reading of the ripples in the blazing energy sinks, the flocker intelligence calculated that the push had been gradual.

The squadron quickly decided to expand its view again, and a few dozen flockers shot outward at fifteen hundred gees. This burst of acceleration would drive them uselessly into the burning manifold, but in the remaining one second before impact, their sacrifice improved the squadron's view dramatically.

The flockers saw it then: the enemy prime had shrunk to a shadow of its former size.

Even against the blinding glare of the manifold, they could now see that the prime's characteristic radiation signature was greatly reduced. The easy gravitons were still coming in abundance, but the evidence of charged weapons and drive activity had disappeared. Mass readings were reduced to a hundredth of what they should be.

A half-second before the first flockers were to reach the position where their target should be, the squadron realized the truth: the energy-sink manifold had been disconnected from the enemy prime.

The target had disappeared.

This was a problem.

Pilot

Master Pilot Marx found that his scout was still alive.

A Rix hunter drone had burned him seconds ago, spraying Marx's vessel with its very dirty fission drive as it flew past. The canopy had snow-crashed for a few seconds, but he was back inside now, his senses dramatically reduced.

Marx swore. He was so close to the Rix battlecruiser. This was no time for his machine to fail. Another 150 seconds and he would be able to hit the enemy. With what exactly, he wasn't sure. His retinue of conscripted drones had been reduced to a few craft. But at this range he could see the reflective expanse of the Rix receiver array spread out before him, fragile and tempting.

So close.

He checked his craft's condition. No active sensors. The drive was out, the reaction process lost and irreparable. The scout's entangled communications supply was damaged, and with all the error-checking the craft responded sluggishly. But he could still control it, and send light-speed orders to other drones in the vicinity.

Marx ejected his fusion drive, and jogged a small docking

jet, forcing the scout drone into a tumble. His view spun for a moment, then stabilized as expert software compensated for the craft's rotation. With its active sensors offline, the scout should appear convincingly dead.

He counted his assets. A trio of expended ramscatter drones, two stealth penetrators with almost no reaction mass left, a decoy that had miraculously survived everything the Rix had thrown at it, and a careening sandcaster whose receiver had failed. The sandcaster drone was tantalizingly useless. It still had its payload, but the last order it had received before going deaf had put it in standby mode. Now it ignored Marx's pleas to launch its sand or self-destruct. He wondered if repair nanos inside the caster were working to bring it back to life.

The master pilot waited silently, watching as his tiny fleet converged upon the enemy battlecruiser. Just before shunting him from the bridge, the captain had mentioned sand. True, it was the perfect weapon against the Rix receiver array; it would spread over a wide area, and at high speed would do considerable damage. But the Rix had swept the Imperials' salvos of sand aside with their host of gravity repeater arrays, protecting the huge receiver. They had anticipated Zai's attack perfectly.

Marx and his tiny fleet were within the gravity perimeter, however. If he could only get his remaining sandcaster to respond. It was barreling toward the huge receiver array on target, but intact. The drone itself would punch through the thin mesh of the receiver, leaving a hole no more than a meter across. Useless. He needed it to explode, to spread its sand.

Marx cursed the empty ramscatters. Why did those things invariably launch *all* their flechettes? With even a single projectile, he could destroy the failed sandcaster, unleashing its payload.

Perhaps he could ram the sandcaster with one of his other craft.

The scout itself was without maneuver capability, the damaged fusion drive ejected. The decoy drone was too small, and its mass wasn't sufficient to crack the tough canisters of sand. The stealth penetrators were even smaller, with only their silent but achingly slow coldjets for movement. They couldn't ram the sandcaster at anything faster than a few meters per second. The empty ramscatter drones were Marx's only hope.

He opened up a narrowcast channel to the two ramscatters, and gave them trajectories as precise as his expert software could calculate. But these were weapons that thought in kilometers, not meters. The ramscatters themselves were not designed to ram, but to launch flechettes, and their onboard brains weren't capable of tricky flying. Marx knew he would have to fly them in himself, from the remote perspective of the scout drone, with sufficient precision to strike the meter-wide sandcaster.

With a three-millisecond light-speed delay, this was going to be tricky indeed.

Marx smiled quietly.

Truly, a task for a master pilot.

flocker squadron

The squadron intellect found itself cut in half.

True to their aim, the first few flockers had struck the gravity generator, in the center of the manifold where the enemy prime *should* have been. The generator was immediately destroyed, and the manifold began to discohere. The neat ranks of energy sinks drifted slowly away, expelling their energy in the assumption that their mothership was dead or retreating.

The radiation from the flaring manifold formed a yoke around the neck of the line of flockers. Individual flockers were moving across the threshold at the rate of five per microsecond; the whole five-kilometer line would be through in under a millisecond. Communication between the drones that had flown through the manifold and those that hadn't was swamped by noise, and the drones still on the near side of the manifold began to have decision-making difficulties. The squadron's democratic intelligence crumbled as its constituent drones disappeared, each new quorum vanishing into the void microseconds after being established.

The rear end of the squadron was paralyzed with indecision; the scenario was changing far too quickly.

On the other side of the blazing manifold, the foremost flockers had quickly spotted the missing enemy warship, and declared themselves to be their own decision-making entity. The *Lynx* was a bare two hundred meters away from the manifold's crumbling center. The flockers' maximum acceleration was three thousand gees. From a standstill, they could have hit the target almost instantly. But they were flying past the enemy prime too quickly. With a relative velocity of more than one percent of the speed of light, no craft the size of a flocker would have sufficient reaction mass to reverse its course.

The forward decision-entity sent desperate messages back through the manifold, giving the squadron the enemy prime's new position. But the signals were overwhelmed by the radiation spewing from the abandoned energy sinks, and within a thousandth of a second, three thousand more flockers hurtled uselessly past the *Lynx*.

Finally, with a firm majority in possession of the facts, the growing farside squadron intellect solved the communications puzzle, firing a coordinated set of message beams that reached the last few hundred flockers just in time.

Most of these drones had no chance to reach the enemy prime, even accelerating at three thousand gees, but a few of those who had spread out to provide parallax found a vector, and barreled through the dissipating manifold toward their target.

Most were vaporized by the still seething energies of the manifold, or missed, their reaction systems destroyed before they could line up on target. But seven of the small machines slipped through random dark spots in the manifold, and hurtled – burned, blinded, all but dead – into the belly of the *Lynx*.

Pilot

Master Pilot Marx glared at the images in his second sight, his frustration growing.

He had shifted his viewpoint to one of the ramscatter drones, which was currently hurtling toward the sandcaster. The collision course looked good, but the view left everything to be desired.

The perspective was cobbled together using data from all over Marx's little fleet. The dim senses of the ramscatter itself were on passive mode to keep the Rix from spotting it. The other drones were bathing the sandcaster in active sensory pulses, to help keep their sister craft on track. Marx's scout drone, his only craft with decent sensors, added its passive view from 5,000 kilometers distance. The light-speed delays afflicting all this data ranged between two and five milliseconds, more than enough to muddle things when attempting a hundred-meter-per-second collision between two tiny spacecraft.

The *Lynx*'s onboard expert software was supposedly compensating for the delays, which varied continuously as the drones accelerated. But the view looked wrong to Marx.

Synesthesia was shaky. Not with the jittering frame of a helmet camera, but with a shimmer, like the shudders that afflict eyes that have stayed awake all night and are facing the morning sun. Marx felt hung over and queasy in the ramscatter's viewpoint, unsure of reality. He wished he could use active sensors, but if the scout gave off any EM this close to the battlecruiser, the Rix would target it in seconds.

Marx swallowed, feeling dizzy. His scout spun, tumbling as it approached the battlecruiser. He checked the speed of the rotation. That was it: the spin of the scout matched the period of the screen jitter.

Marx swore. He had intentionally tumbled the scout to make it appear dead. Now he was paying for it with this sickening, shifting second vision. Why wasn't the damned expert software compensating? Perhaps the *Lynx*'s shared processors were simply overwhelmed.

Should he risk righting the scout? A quick blast from a docking jet would do the trick. But any activity from the large scout craft would draw the Rix's attention, and it was his only link to the front line.

Marx ordered himself to stop whining. He had once flown a craft the size of a fingernail in a raging hailstorm, and on another occasion had lost all depth perception in a rotary wing dogfight with a half-second roundtrip delay. This jittering viewpoint was nothing. He synchronized his breathing to the phasing blur of his canopy, and forced himself to ignore the growing nausea deep in his stomach.

The ramscatter drone shot toward its target. At least the bulbous surfaces of the sandcaster provided a clear image. Marx piloted the little drone in short bursts, trying not to alert the Rix to its presence.

The trajectory felt right. It looked as if he was lined up on the sandcaster, ready to burst the fat canisters.

Marx's view improved as he closed. He could just make out the cross-hatching of the fragmentation pattern.

Five seconds to impact.

Suddenly, a flare of projectile fire blazed in his peripheral vision. The canopy view twisted, pulling apart into two images as if his eyes were going crossed.

In the dizzying maelstrom of the disintegrating view, Marx saw new enemy craft: several blackbody monitor drones. Driveless and silent, they had been drifting along with the battlecruiser, utterly invisible until now. They spewed depleted uranium slugs – at a rate of ten thousand per minute, his software estimated – at the ramscatters.

His view whirled. All his drones with active sensors had been destroyed. Marx fought to control the ramming ship, but nothing on the canopy's screens made sense. With an effort of will, he pulled his hands from the control surface, searching for meaning in the storm of light before him.

Suddenly, a fist seemed to strike him in the stomach. A decompression alarm sounded!

The *Lynx* was taking hits. The flockers were here.

Gravity in the canopy spun for a moment, a further disorientation. Acid filled his throat. The disjunction between visuals and his inner ear was finally too great. Marx pitched forward in his canopy, and vomited between his knees.

He looked up, bile still in his mouth, and saw that he had missed. His ramscatter drone had flown past the sandcaster.

Marx struggled to bring it around for another pass, but the long, hard acceleration revealed it to the Rix monitor drones, which raked it with fire.

His ramscatters were destroyed, and Marx's synesthesia view of the distant battle dimmed to shadows and extrapolations.

Then a host of explosions rolled through the *Lynx*, and Marx realized that they were all dead.

Executive Officer

Katherie Hobbes saw the collision icon go bright orange, but the sound of the klaxon hadn't time to reach her before the shock waves struck.

Her status board flared, red sweeping up through the decks as the flockers plowed through hullalloy and hypercarbon like paper. The shriek of decompression came from a dozen audio channels.

At one percent lightspeed, being rammed was as good as being railgunned.

'Shit,' Hobbes said.

It would take her days of careful reconstruction to determine exactly what happened over the next few seconds.

The first flocker in the pack had been melted into an irregular blob by the blazing energy-sink manifold. Having lost its penetration shape, it pancaked against the warship's hull, its diameter expanding to a half-meter as it punched through the three outer bulkheads. The force of its entry into Gunnery Hardpoint Four hit the crewmen there like a compression bomb, imploding their pressure suits, shattering every nonmetal object into shards. The wide entry hole sucked out most of the air in the hardpoint before the sprays of sealant foam could do their work. Hardpoint Four housed a highly volatile meson-beam emitter, and was armored on all sides to protect the *Lynx* in case the weapon ever blew. The flocker, its momentum exhausted, flattened itself against the next bulkhead, never exiting the hardpoint.

Between the massive shock wave and decompression, none of the seven crew was suitable for reanimation.

The next flocker, which struck the *Lynx* four nanoseconds later, had maintained its bullet shape through the manifold. Its small entry hole was sealed without much decompression, and it plunged through lower decks twenty-six through -eight on a diagonal path. It destroyed several burn beds in a temporary sickbay, and cut through a section of synesthesia processing hardware, tearing out a fist-width of optical circuitry sixty meters long, drawing a geyser of powdered glass and phosphorus behind itself through a long vertical access hallway. The cloud of burning glass blinded four members of an emergency repair team and one data analyst, and caused lung damage to a dozen other crew scattered along the hallway. The drone emerged from the frigate's port dorsal sensor array.

The *Lynx*'s sensors were not appreciably reduced, but the frigate's processors were cut by twenty percent. All its AI nodes became slower, its synesthesia grainier, its weapons dumber.

Three flockers in close tandem struck the turbine that powered the *Lynx*'s railguns. This dense coil of superconducting wire was sufficient to stop one of the drones cold, sending a deep shudder through the ship. The other two were deflected sternward, tumbling through a full magazine of minesweeper drones. The drones were armed with fragmentation canisters, and a chain reaction of explosions rocked the drone bay. The magazine was shielded to prevent such a calamity from spreading throughout the ship, but the two flockers passed out of the magazine and drew the explosions after them, severely damaging the drone launch rail.

They careened through the hullalloy-armored drone bay,

and finally exited the *Lynx* through the frigate's open launch doors at a much reduced speed. They would have had sufficient reaction mass remaining to turn and attack the ship again, but neither had survived the pummeling with its intelligence intact.

Another flocker punched through the belly-side armor plate and entered the main damage control room, where Ensign Trevor San had just helped to eject the energy-sink manifold. She was watching as it began to discohere when the drone tore through her from foot to head, pulping her organs and robbing her of immortality. Her crewmates were sprayed with blood, but it took them long seconds to realize which of them had been hit. Ensign San had practically disappeared. The drone then passed through several storage decks, destroying medical supplies and stowed personal effects, then drove straight into the core of the *Lynx*'s singularity generator, which was running at high-active level. The pseudo black hole swallowed the flocker without so much as a tremor registering on its monitors.

Hobbes later calculated the chances of such a hit at several-thousand-to-one against, and noted that nothing so bizarrely exact had ever been recorded on an Imperial warship.

The last flocker passed through the belly-side waste tanks, which had been brought to high pressure to propel the *Lynx* silently out of harm's way. The pressure of the unrecycled water was over five hundred atmospheres, dense enough to slow the flocker considerably. But the drone's reaction drive was still active, and it managed to pass through the tanks, trailing a stream of waste water that filled the adjacent bacterial recycling chamber in ten seconds. The processing chief, Samuel Vries, was knocked unconscious by the jet of water and drowned before rescue could come. The *Lynx* was left without a functional water-recycling system for days, and three decks smelled noticeably for a long time. Vries was eventually rewarded with immortality, and continued his researches into human/bacterial interactions in small closed environments, but at a far less practical level of application.

The much slowed flocker limped through a few more bulkheads, still pursued by dirty water, befouling a long column of crew cabins before it was stopped by the armored hull on the dorsal side. It was the only flocker to survive passage through the blazing manifold and the ship with its intelligence intact. After it came to a halt, the drone was still cogent enough to release a metal-eating virus into the *Lynx*'s hull that went undetected for some time.

Then, it attacked a marine private as he ran to foamseal shut the sudden geyser of waste water that marked its passage. The drone had only its weak signaling laser as a weapon, and went for his eyes. The man was in full battle armor, however, his face shielded by a reflective visor. He stared for a confused moment at the glittering drone, this tiny alien invader still valiantly attempting to trouble its enemies. Then he smashed the half-dead flocker with his servo-assisted fist, and it expired on the spot.

The *Lynx* had survived.

Data Analyst

Chaos struck the Data Analysis station without warning.

Ensign Amanda Tyre's vision had been far away, following the progress of the foremost scout drone. The drone was one minute from its closest approach to the enemy battle-cruiser. Master Pilot Marx was in control, struggling to perform some wild maneuver, an indirect attack on the Rix warship that only he understood completely. Tyre had asked what he was up to, but he'd only grunted, too focused on piloting to answer.

She watched Marx's data stream – the images of the battlecruiser being gathered by his drone. It was the best intelligence they'd received so far on the enemy warship. Tyre searched for weaknesses, clues to its configuration, signs that anything the *Lynx* had thrown at it had managed to do any damage.

Damn. Marx was so close, yet the images were blurry, not much better than distant transluminal returns. Ensign Tyre wished he would go to active sensors. Of course, the scout wouldn't last long once he did. The battlecruiser's close-in defenses looked pretty solid.

Tyre gestured, bringing her second sight closer to the blackbody monitor drones that had just appeared and begun firing on some of Marx's subservient drones. The blackbodies were normally almost invisible, but against the sunlit background of the receiver array she could make out several more of them. The three that had opened fire had turned up at just the right place; either the Rix had guessed lucky or had enough of them to cover every approach. She wondered how many of the dark, silent monitors coasted in front of the Rix warship.

She felt the hands of her superior on her shoulders. Kax stood right behind her seat. There were five crew crowded into the tight confines of Data Analysis. In battle configuration, their usually large space had been annexed by the two adjacent gunnery stations. Kax's hands clenched as the *Lynx* maneuvered, its slow coldjets pushing them with the sway of an oceangoing vessel.

'You thinking what I'm thinking?' Kax asked.

She nodded. 'They've configured for heavy defense, sir.'

'See if you can get a count. The captain will want to know how many blackbodies are out there before the *Lynx* gets too much closer.'

'Yes, sir, but I'll bet you right now there's at least a hundred.'

'A *hundred*?'

'If you take a—'

Suddenly, a rush of noise exploded through the room. A searing wind struck Tyre, throwing her from her webbing to the floor. Her exposed skin – hands and cheeks – were being scoured. Her mouth and eyes clenched instinctively shut. Her ears popped as the air pressure plummeted.

A burning sound reached her ears through the thin air, and she felt heat on her hands and face.

Ensign Amanda Tyre, like every recruit to the Navy, had gone through dozens of decompression drills. She knew well the expansion of the chest, the screaming pain of ears and eyes. But this was her first time to experience the event in battle.

It felt as if some demon were astride her, crushing the breath from her body. Tyre remembered the symbol on the academy's decompression drill room door: the Asphyx, the spirit that visits the dying to steal their last breath. Through the haze of synesthesia, she had a sudden vision of the Asphyx – the blank eyes, the yawning mouth hungry for her life.

Then she command-gestured, clearing her data mask of all synesthesia, and saw that it was Kax's face before her. He had fallen to the deck next to her. But even in primary vision, his face remained horrifying, burned and bleeding, the flesh peeling from it as if stripped by hungry insects.

'*Glass*,' he said, his voice ravaged.

Tyre rolled out from under him. As her hands sought purchase on the tilting deck, she felt the grit of tiny bits of broken glass cutting into her palms. Her pressure uniform was torn and felt invaded with some sharp presence, like the insinuating fingers of fiberglass against the skin.

The other three in the DA room were stunned, their faces and arms cut with thousands of tiny nicks. The phosphorus fire had burned itself out too quickly to hurt them.

Rating Rogers, still in his webbing, coughed as he spoke.

'It's glass. From the optical core next door.' He pointed to the access tube, from which coiled a bright, heavy mist, half vapor and half dust. Of course. Data Analysis was adjacent to one of the *Lynx*'s processing towers, a column of dense optical silicon and phosphorus. Tyre hadn't been following the *Lynx*'s defensive status, so she brought up the diagnostic channel in synesthesia. A number of projectiles had plunged through the vessel.

That explained the momentary blaze. The quantum computers of the *Lynx* used phosphorus atoms suspended in silicon as q-bits. Free, the phosphorus was flammable, even in what little oxygen there'd been for the agonizing seconds of decompression.

Tyre covered her mouth with a loose flap of uniform to ward off the glass vapor hanging in the air, looked again to Kax.

His eyes were clenched shut and bleeding. He'd been the only one in the station without full-strength headsups covering his upper face. And his body had shielded hers from the blast of glass and burning phosphorus.

'Medical, medical,' Tyre said, her voice gritty and plaintive from the glass dust she'd inhaled. 'We need major medical in DA Station One, deck fourteen.'

She heard the background murmur of other stations begging for medical assistance.

Data Master Kax reached out a bloody hand and clenched Tyre's ankle, coughing. She knelt beside him.

'Don't try to talk, sir,' she said.

'The blackbodies, Tyre. Keep looking,' he managed.

She glanced around at her crewmates, realizing that the *Lynx* was still in battle. With Kax out, she was in command now. The data from Master Pilot Marx's scout was invaluable, and he was far too busy flying to grasp its tactical implications.

'Rogers, try to help the Data Master,' she commanded. 'You two: back to your stations.'

Still in shock, her crewmates moved numbly to follow her orders. Tyre sank into her webbing, and flipped back to second sight. She gestured with bloody hands, and adopted the scout drone's viewpoint again.

Master Pilot Marx was under fire.

Pilot

Marx discovered that he was still alive.

A small cleaning robot moved beneath his feet, sucking up the thin, acid bile on the floor with a gurgling sound that set his stomach flopping again. His hands were shaking, and his ears rang from some nearby decompression.

The *Lynx* had been hit all right. But somehow Zai had kept them alive. The strike certainly hadn't numbered five thousand flockers. It had sounded like only ten or so. Marx scanned the icons of internal diagnostics. There were no more than twenty crewmen dead. He turned his eyes from the display before he could recognize any names. Later.

What mattered most was that Marx's control hardware – the translight array that connected him with the drone complement – was still functional. He could see from the scout drone's perspective, if only fuzzily. He checked the clock.

Another thirty seconds remained before his foremost drones passed the Rix battlecruiser and became irrelevant to the battle.

There was still a chance.

But the question remained: how to disintegrate the dead sandcaster?

Marx considered his remaining assets. Only four drones were left inside the Rix defenses that could respond to his orders. The scout itself, tumbling with no reaction drive. The two stealth penetrators, smaller than dribble-hoop balls. And the decoy, weaponless. And if any of them switched on active sensors or accelerated noticeably, the Rix monitor drones would shred it within seconds. He could see the sentinels now as the scout neared the hot background of the receiver array: rank after rank of blackbody monitor drones, dark spots against its reflective surface.

Good god, Marx thought. Other than a few thousand flockers and hunter drones, the battlecruiser's drone complement had been committed almost entirely to defensive weaponry. The Rix captain had prioritized the receiver array above everything else.

He shook his head. The *Lynx* had never had a chance.

Looking at the ranks of fearsome monitors, Marx envied their firepower. If he could just take over a few of the blackbody drones and turn their weapons back on the receiver . . .

Then the master pilot realized what he had to do.

It was simplicity itself.

He watched the trajectories of his four drones as they converged, growing nearer to each other as they drifted toward the Rix battlecruiser. The decoy was in front. The little drone was designed to burst a wide range of EM every few minutes, drawing fire away from more vital targets. When it wasn't screaming, it was stealthy, with passive sensors and line-of-sight transmission. Marx had kept the decoy silent so far, but now he saw what to do with it.

The stealth drones were the only thing he could move without detection. They were equipped with coldjets, slow but radiation-silent. He eased one alongside the decoy drone, bringing the two into soft contact. His view might be blurry and vague, but at under ten meters per second, Marx could have rammed a hummingbird.

The master pilot shoved the decoy with the stealth drone, pushed it on a new vector toward the sandcaster. He cursed, pushing the plodding coldjets to their maximums. In another twenty seconds his little formation would be hurtling uselessly past the battlecruiser.

Marx waited until the decoy was a bare kilometer from the sandcaster, then fired its reaction drive. It barreled in toward the sandcaster drone in decoy mode, screaming bloody murder.

Suddenly, Marx could see.

The decoy was flooding the area with EM, painting everything within light-seconds across the whole spectrum. To the Rix, it must have seemed as if a fleet of drones had popped up from nowhere.

The blackbody monitors wasted no time responding. Ripples of their slugs arced beautifully across space, lit like tracer bullets by the decoy's sensory howl. The rain of slugs swept across the stealth penetrator first, then found the decoy, and things were dark for a moment. But seconds later Marx saw the blast of the sandcaster being hit, pulped, shredded by the depleted uranium slugs.

'*Perfect*,' he whispered as a sequence of explosions flared in synesthesia. The blinded sandcaster was still loaded with reaction mass! The drone blazed with the dirty fuel of its self-propelling canisters.

It popped again and again like a sackful of fragmentation grenades.

The Rix had done Marx's work for him.

The sand cloud expanded into a huge, misshapen ball, a timelapse amoeba festooned with reaching pseudopods. It was almost 4,000 kilometers across when it struck the receiver array, at a relative velocity of 3,000 klicks per second. The hail of slugs had also imparted lateral velocity to the cloud, and it swept across the array like a sirocco.

Marx switched on his scout's active sensors, letting the *Lynx*'s computers record the damage in maximum detail. He leaned back to savor the light show, the vast receiver array flickering from end to end, a mica desert struck by the morning sun.

The huge object began to fold, a giant piece of fabric twisting in the wind.

Then fire from the blackbody drones found the pulsing scout, and Marx's view snapped to dead-channel blue.

He brought up Hobbes's line.

'Master Pilot reporting mission accomplished,' he said. 'The Rix receiver array has been destroyed.'

Data Analyst

Tyre prioritized Marx's signal, recording at maximum resolution.

Finally, a good look at the enemy battlecruiser.

It only lasted a few seconds. The projectile fire from a dozen blackbodies raked across Marx's forward drones, tearing them to pieces. The sand canister exploded. Tyre watched with her mouth agape as the sand tore across the Rix receiver array.

'He got it!' she cried.

Then the arc of fire moved inexorably toward the scout drone itself. In the seconds before the signal was extinguished, the tearing megastructure caught the light of the Legis sun, and an awesome sight was revealed. Ensign Tyre's ragged breath halted as she took it in.

She had assumed that Marx's drones had hit a concentration of blackbodies, a random clumping of firepower. Even the largest Rix ships only traveled with a few dozens of the blackbody monitors; the heavy-metal ammunition they carried was bulky, they were difficult to maintain, and were primarily a defensive weapon.

But revealed against the bright background of the crumpling array was a host of monitors. They stretched across its shining expanse in a vast, hexagonal pattern.

Hundreds of them.

Then synesthesia went dark; Marx's drone had finally died.

Ensign Tyre heard a gurgle from Data Master Kax at her feet, but she ignored the grim sound. Tyre rewound the scout's viewpoint stream a few seconds, and froze it on a frame in which the Legis sun had revealed the monitor drones.

Ensign Tyre blinked as she looked at them.

They were short-range weapons, primarily for defense. They had no drives and little intelligence, just lots and lots of projectile firepower. If a small warship like the *Lynx* were to stumble amongst hundreds of them, it would be torn to pieces by their collective kinetic attack.

And the *Lynx* was headed straight for the battlecruiser and into the intervening field of blackbodies, unaware of their deadly, silent presence.

She had to alert the captain.

Tyre opened a line to Hobbes. The executive officer did not immediately respond; there were probably a dozen crew of superior rank clamoring for her attention.

Tyre waited, the seconds ticking away, the *Lynx* hurtling toward the deadly blackbody drones, three thousand kilometers closer every second.

'Priority, priority.'

The priority icon appeared before her in second sight. The icon was for 'extreme emergencies' only, a term that held awesome power here in Data Analysis. Kax had never used it. Tyre had certainly never thought to invoke it herself; it was the data master's prerogative. And if she were wrong about what the vast array of drones meant, misuse of the priority icon in battle would be a terrible mark against her forever.

Tyre stared at the frozen image again. *Hundreds of them*, she reminded herself. The data were unambiguous.

She switched to the diagnostic channel again. There were casualties all across the ship, hull and equipment damage, even fatalities. It could be minutes before Hobbes responded to a lowly ensign.

Tyre put out her trembling and bloody hand to the icon.

Not authorized, the icon blinked.

She swore. Kax was still alive and on-station. As far as the *Lynx* was concerned, he was still in command, and was the only analyst qualified to make this judgment. Tyre cleared her second sight and looked down to where Rogers cradled the data master's head. Kax seemed hardly to have a face at all. For a fleeting moment, she wondered if he still had second sight, even though his eyes were destroyed.

There wasn't time to ask. Kax could hardly breathe; he couldn't be thinking clearly with an injury like that.

'Rogers,' she ordered. 'Pull the data master out of the room.'

'What?'

'Pick him up and drag him from the room. Get him off the station.' Tyre said it with all the force she could manage. Her ragged voice gave the words an authority she didn't feel.

Rogers hesitated, looking at the other two ratings.

'Rogers! The *Lynx* won't recognize my rank with him in here.'

'But there's more glass out—'

'Do it!'

Rogers jumped, then stooped to gingerly lift the wounded Kax. He pulled the bloody man toward the doorway, his shredded uniform scraping across the glass and out into the access shaft.

Tyre breathed deep, and touched the priority icon again.

'Please listen,' she murmured to herself.

The icon shifted in the air, folding into a bright point, and requested her missive. She attached the compiled frame showing the host of blackbody drones and gestured the Send command.

A few seconds later, Hobbes's voice responded.

'My god,' the ExO said. Tyre breathed a sigh of relief at the woman's tone. At least Hobbes understood.

'Where the hell's Kax?'

'Injured. Blind, I think.'

'Shit. Get up to the captain's planning room, then,' the Executive Officer ordered. 'And get ready to explain this.'

'Aye, aye.'

'We'll have to accelerate immediately. We'll lose the manifold for good,' Hobbes continued, talking half to herself. 'You better be on the mark with this, Tyre.'

Tyre swallowed as she pulled herself from the webbing.

If she was wrong, her career was ruined. If she was right, the *Lynx* was in very deep trouble.

Senator

They looked up at her with startled expressions, curious and wary. Their eyes reflected the hovering globe that lit her path, igniting with the crimson flash of night predators.

Nara Oxham wondered if small rodents were ever let loose in the Diamond Palace's darkened halls, entertainment for the Emperor's pets. Of course, it seemed unlikely that risen animals would make very aggressive hunters. As she passed, the felines remained piled together on the low window couch, regally watchful, but as soporific as fat old toms. Perhaps like dead humans they were content to contemplate black paintings and go on endless pilgrimages. Nara could see the ridges of the symbiant along the felines' spines, payment for the cruelty their kind had suffered during the Holy Experiments.

They were dead things, she reminded herself.

'Senator.'

The inhuman voice came out of darkness, and Oxham started.

'My apologies, Senator Oxham.' The representative from the Plague Axis stepped to the edge of her globe's light, but remained politely distant. 'My biosuit allows me a certain level of night vision; I had forgotten you couldn't see me.'

The slight hiss of the biosuit's filters was barely audible in the silent hallway. Nara tried not to imagine the representative's diseases straining to escape, to infect her, to propagate across the human species.

'So you can see in the dark? Not unlike the sovereign's house pets,' she said, gesturing at the flashing eyes.

There was a pause. Had her insult found its mark? Through the opaque faceplate, the representative's expression was invisible. They had sat on the War Council together for weeks now, but Nara didn't even know if the thing inside the suit was male or female.

Whatever it was, it had cast the deciding vote in favor of the Emperor's genocide.

'Except that those cats will live forever, Nara Oxham. I shall not.'

The people of the Plague Axis could not take the symbiant, which resisted all disease and physical defect as part of its cure for death. For that reason Oxham and her party had counted the Axis on the side of the living, allies against the Emperor. It hadn't worked out that way.

Oxham shrugged. 'Neither shall I.' She turned and walked toward the council chamber.

'Senator?' the representative called softly.

'The sovereign requests we attend him,' she answered without stopping.

The soft, pearly floor of the council chamber glowed coolly in the Diamond Palace's night. The dead never liked bright rooms at any time, but the lighting in gray places always varied slowly, reflecting daily and seasonal shifts, even equinoctial precession on more eccentric planets.

Senator Oxham and the Plague Axis representative were the last of the nine counselors to arrive. The dead admiral hardly waited for them to settle before beginning her speech.

'There is news from Legis.'

Nara closed her eyes and took a deep breath, then forced herself to watch.

The airscreen filled with a familiar schematic, the decelerating Rix battlecruiser arcing toward Legis, the hook-shaped path of the *Lynx* darting out to engage it as far from the planet as possible. At this system-sized scale, the two trajectories were touching now.

Nara's sudden dose of apathy would take some time to wear off, so she watched the faces of her colleagues through the translucent image. The other pink senators, Federalist and Utopian, and the plutocrat Ax Milnk wore harried and sleepless looks. Even the Loyalist Henders looked nervous, unready to learn that he had voted for mass murder. The faces of three dead members of the War Council were like stone.

The admiral spoke evenly, the general sat at attention, the risen sovereign stared into the middle distance over Nara's head.

She could feel nothing, but a lifetime spent comparing what eyes and empathy told her had given Nara an instinct for reading bodies and faces. Even with her ability dampened, the aspects of the dead men and woman betrayed disquiet.

Something had gone wrong.

'The *Lynx* and the Rix engaged some thirty minutes ago,' the dead admiral continued. 'At last report, the two ships have reached second contact.'

Nara's jaw tightened. First contact was when the outer drone clouds overlapped, with shots fired between them; second contact meant that the primaries, the *Lynx* and the Rix warship proper, had engaged each other's drones. Beginning with second contact, human lives were lost.

'The *Lynx* has suffered casualties, but has thus far managed to survive.'

Any of those casualties might be Laurent, Nara thought, but surely the admiral would mention it if the ship's captain was dead.

'More importantly, the *Lynx*'s drones have succeeded in the primary goal of the attack, destroying the Rix receiver array. At this point, it seems that the Legis mind will remain isolated, without further action on our part.'

The admiral was silent for a moment, letting the news sink in.

Nara saw her own hesitation on the other living counselors' faces: none of them believed it yet. They were waiting for some awful reversal in the admiral's statement. But the dead woman's silence lengthened, and they realized it was true. There was no reason to obliterate the compound mind. There would be no EMP attack, no hundred million dead.

Laurent had saved them all.

The War Council stirred all at once, like people waking from a nightmare. The Loyalist Henders put his head in his hands, an exhausted and undisguised gesture, and even the Plague Axis representative's biosuit slumped with what had to be relief. The other senators and Milnk turned to Nara Oxham, daring to show their respect.

Nara let nothing she felt reach her face. For her, more than any of them, this had been personal. She would allow herself emotions later.

'We are happy with this victory, of course,' the Emperor said.

He was lying, Nara was certain. She had seen it in him, and in his dead soldiers. They had wanted Zai to fail.

'And more important than any victory, we rest assured that this council was ready to make the necessary sacrifice.' For the first time ever, Nara saw the sovereign's praise fall flat. None of the living members had been ready to watch what the War Council had voted for.

The Emperor had lost something here.

'We must congratulate this council for having made the right decision, however pleased we are it didn't come to action.' There was an edge in his voice. Anyone could hear it.

Nara Oxham had grown to know the Emperor, this young-looking undead man, and to understand his fixation with the Rix; their compound minds were a counter-god to his own false divinity. He was as jealous as any petty deity, and Nara Oxham was a politician who understood egomania, no matter how grossly exaggerated.

But over the last few days, she had seen fear in him, not hatred. What could terrify the Emperor of Eighty Worlds so much that only genocide would suffice?

'We owe Zai a debt,' the Plague representative said.

There were nods of agreement. The sovereign turned to look at the biosuit, the movement of his head as slow as some ancient lizard.

'We have already elevated him,' the Emperor said coldly. 'And pardoned him after our sister's death. Perhaps it was *his* debt to pay.'

'Still, Majesty,' the Utopian Senator said, 'an entire world has been saved from grievous harm.'

'Indeed,' the Federalist said.

'I agree,' Ax Milnk added.

'May I remind you of the hundred-year rule?' the sovereign said. 'None of us can speak of what Zai prevented. Not for a century.'

'But he has still won a great victory,' the Plague representative said. 'An auspicious beginning to this war.'

Nara almost let herself smile. For the first time since the council was formed, the others dared to contradict the Emperor. Not only Zai had won this battle, the living members of the War Council had as well.

But the dead admiral interrupted.

'We cannot publicly declare Zai's victory yet. Third contact will come in another twenty minutes. It seems unlikely the *Lynx* will survive.'

Nara swallowed. Third contact was when the two primaries engaged directly, ship-to-ship, without their drones between them.

'Why would there be a third contact, Admiral?' she asked. 'With the array destroyed, surely the *Lynx* will make its escape. It's smaller, faster.'

The admiral gestured, and the airscreen image zoomed. Vector lines were added, arcing through intersections like crossed scimitars.

'Captain Zai made his attack at a high relative velocity, to get his drones past the Rix defenses and at the array. At this point, the two ships are moving toward each other too fast for the *Lynx* to make much of an escape. In the service of the Emperor and this council, Zai has sealed his own fate.'

'In war, there are always sacrifices,' the Emperor sighed.

Nara forced herself not to utter the cry she felt building. The elation of a few moments ago drained away, her heart turning cold. One way or another, these dead men would have their revenge against Laurent. It was as if the Emperor himself had decreed the law of inertia, just to spite Zai's heroism and see him killed.

She was utterly selfish, Nara tried to tell herself, to think only of one man when millions had been saved, when the *Lynx* carried three hundred.

But for Nara, the battle was lost if Laurent wasn't coming home.

Commando

The call from Alexander eventually came.

The few phones that h_rd had spared dissection rang in unison, then beeped out a simple coded sequence from the onetime pad she shared with Alexander. The battle in space had gone badly, and her assistance was required. The entanglement facility had to be liberated for the compound mind's use.

The call hadn't awakened Rana, h_rd realized with bittersweet relief. The few novels and plays she'd read suggested that the farewell rituals of Imperial humanity and those of the Rix were incompatible. And this would be a deep good-bye. Either of them, perhaps both, might die in the next ten hours.

H_rd pulled herself closer to the woman's soft, warm body. How humanity raged against its environment, she thought, each body demanding its own pocket of heat, and at a temperature so perversely exact. Five degrees in either direction spelled death. So prideful, yet so fragile.

The rattle in Rana's breathing sounded worse. The rhythm was even, but h_rd detected the slightest increase of its tempo from a few hours ago. The woman's breath quickened as the volume of her functioning lung decreased. The pulsatile nature of her lover's physiology always fascinated h_rd. The rhythms of circulation, breath, menstruation, and sleep had an alien grandeur, like the ancient symmetries expressed in the brief lives of particles or in the stately motions of planets. H_rd was Rix: her heart a screw, her lungs continuous filters, her ovaries in cold storage back on her home orbital. And those cycles of the Rix body that had escaped Upgrade could be modulated as easily as the speed of an engine. But the interlocking patterns that constituted Rana Harter's aliveness seemed sovereign as nature; h_rd could not imagine them simply winding down into awful, inescapable silence.

Of course, the Rixwoman knew how to save her lover, understood – at least abstractly – the price of the delicate and precious life beside her. She could always surrender to the Imperials, giving Rana to their doctors, and herself to the military. H_rd pondered what it would be like to abandon Alexander at this critical moment. Despite what the Empire called the Rix, they were no cult; members were free to rejoin humanity. Over the last few centuries, a dozen or so even had.

But h_rd would find no freedom in Imperial hands. The Risen Empire had never-taken a Rix prisoner of war, unless a few frozen and decompressed bodies plucked from hard space were counted. They would interrogate her, mindsweep her, test her mercilessly, and finally dissect the prostheses that she considered unambiguously to be herself.

And although they would save Rana Harter's body, they had proven themselves unfit wardens of her soul.

For twenty-seven years, their clumsy system of wealth distribution had left Rana to her own devices. A borderline depressive, fearful and indecisive, naive in some ways and magnificently savant in others, Rana was a raw, rare, defenseless gem. But they had let her drift, a cog in the Imperial machine. They had exploited what little of her abilities required no training, and given nothing in return. Both systems of the Eighty Worlds – the hierarchy of the Empire and the wild purity of the capital – had one appetite in common: they fed on the weak. The help Rana needed was simple, a mere dopamine adjustment, and the manic depression that had scarred her life had been easily vanquished. But such treatment wasn't available to the class she had been born into. She was the victim of the most parochial of economic arrangements.

Their barbarism wasn't even efficient. With her abilities, she would have been a valuable asset. But the Imperials imagined it cheaper and easier to let her suffer.

When h_rd's internal tirade ended, she allowed herself a rueful smile. Who was she to take the Empire to task? She had kidnapped this woman, drugged her, put her in harm's way.

Taken Rana to her death.

But at least she had understood the clever, marvelous thing that Rana Harter was.

H_rd pressed her lips gingerly to the back of Rana's neck, smelled the warm, human complexity of her. Then the commando crept from bed.

Executive Officer

A gravity ghost drifted through the command bridge. The shudder described a textbook bell curve, slowly building and receding as if some ancient steam train were rumbling past.

No one spoke until the event was over. The *Lynx* was accelerating at eighteen gees away from the battlecruiser, pushing as hard as its gravity generators could compensate for. The assembled officers knew that if the generators suddenly failed, they would all be unconscious in seconds, crushed by their own suddenly tremendous weight. The *Lynx*'s AI would recognize the problem and shut its engines down automatically, but by then there would be scores of casualties.

Hobbes cleared her throat as the last tendrils of the event loosened their grip, interrupting the officers' consideration of the tenuous technologies that stood between them and sudden disaster.

'Are we certain that all these blackbodies are the same? Perhaps those that fired on the master pilot aren't representative of the whole,' she said.

Floating in the command bridge airscreen were the images recorded by Master Pilot Marx's remote scout. The first time the *Lynx*'s officers had watched the destruction of the huge receiver array, they'd cheered. But now the image was paused, the wild storm of sand frozen halfway in its march across the dish. In this single frame, the reflected light of the Legis sun was caught in the dying array; against the bright backdrop, the ranks of blackbody monitors were clearly evident.

Data Analysis had counted 473 of them, and had extrapolated another 49. That made 522. Two to the ninth power: a typical Rix complement.

But not for monitor drones. For the powerful slug-throwers, it was far more than expected; the *Lynx* had been unknowingly hurtling toward a grinder.

'As near as we can tell, the blackbody shapes are the same throughout the complement,' Ensign Tyre said softly. Hobbes realized that this was Tyre's first time on the command bridge. The ensign was the ranking data analyst now, Data Master Kax having been blinded in the flocker attack. Tyre was speaking in a slow and careful voice, almost timidly, but she had so far answered every question clearly.

'This hump on the dorsal side is the ammo supply,' Tyre continued, windowing an individual blackbody drone. 'If any of these drones were fitted for minesweeping or decoy work, that hump would be absent.'

'And they've all got it,' Hobbes finished flatly.

Before the meeting, the ExO had gone through Marx's data frame by frame with Tyre. Hobbes had gotten all too clear a look at the drones that had finally killed Marx's scout. The deluge of their slugs had passed through the spreading sand cloud, the usually invisible shells illuminated by the medium. Expert software's careful count had revealed a firing rate greater than a hundred rounds per second.

The blackbody drones were loaded for bear.

In the First Rix Incursion, this class of drone had been used strictly for close-in defense. A few dozen of the monitors would float in front of a Rix warship, picking off attacking drones if they grew too close. But the blackbodies of the previous war were far fewer, and had possessed much lower firing rates; they were designed to kill drones.

But these new monitors, in huge numbers and at short range, would also be capable of gutting the *Lynx*, or anything else that tried to close with the battlecruiser. The Rix had configured for defense of their huge receiver at all costs, even anticipating ramming by a ship as large as a frigate. The sort of attack the *Lynx* had been headed for would surely have failed.

If it hadn't been for Marx's skill and dumb luck – a dead sandcaster drone penetrating the perimeter intact – the receiver array would still be functional now, and the *Lynx* on its unknowing way to destruction.

'No sense in discussing the drones,' Captain Zai said. 'The die is cast.'

Hobbes nodded. The moment Captain Zai had seen Tyre's report, he had ordered the *Lynx* into high acceleration, pushing at a ninety-degree angle from the Rix warship's approach.

In doing so, he had abandoned any chance of recovering the detached energy-sink manifold. To escape the blackbodies, the frigate had been forced to leave behind its primary defense against energy weapons.

Now, they had to get as far away from the battlecruiser as possible.

'Give us the real-time view,' the captain ordered.

The airscreen switched to the current transluminal returns from the Rix battlecruiser. Its main engine had swung ninety degrees, pursuing the *Lynx* now rather than braking to match Legis XV, letting the blackbody drones drift on.

Fortunately, the larger battlecruiser was the slower ship. It could make no more than six gees.

Hobbes regarded the airscreen. The *Lynx* was pushing hard to put distance between herself and the battlecruiser, also headed perpendicular to the original Rix line of approach. They would have nineteen minutes of acceleration under their belts before they reached their closest passage by the Rix warship.

The math was easy: nineteen hundred seconds at twelve gees advantage, and a minute of float. Two hundred and twenty thousand kilometers of breathing room.

The blackbody monitors couldn't touch them out here. Intended to be absolutely silent, they had no drives – the Rix had effectively abandoned them. But the battlecruiser's chaotic gravity weapons had a much greater range. And without an energy-sink manifold to shunt the energy into space, the *Lynx* was terribly vulnerable.

The flag bridge underwent another shudder, and the captain's cup of tea traveled across the table toward Hobbes, rattling as if carried by a ghost who badly needed a night of sleep.

The apparition passed.

'At least she's not optimized for offense,' the captain said.

The officers nodded. The blackbody drones and their ammo supply must have taken up space normally reserved for offensive weapons. But it wouldn't take much to hurt the Imperial warship. And the Rix captain knew the *Lynx* had dumped its energy sink. The manifold was still glowing behind them, spreading like an exhausted supernova.

'They could be in turnaround,' First Pilot Maradonna suggested. 'With no receiver array, they can't contact the compound mind. Maybe they've given up.'

'So why come after us?' Tyre asked.

'They could be angling out of the system,' Second Pilot Anderson argued. 'They'd want to swing away from Legis's orbital defenses.'

Hobbes shook her head at this wishful thinking. 'If they were abandoning the mission, they'd gather those drones first. But they came straight after us. They want our blood.'

'Which is perhaps a sign of our success,' Zai added. 'Their array is destroyed. They want the *Lynx*'s carcass as a consolation prize.'

Hobbes sighed. Captain Zai had never been one to paint success in rosy terms.

'They might be buying time to fabricate another receiver array,' Anderson said.

'They couldn't possibly,' the first engineer interjected. 'The thing was a thousand klicks across! It'd take months and megatons of spare matter.'

'Ten minutes left,' Zai said. The battlecruiser's gravity weapons would soon be in range. 'Perhaps this discussion of Rix motivation can wait.'

His fingers moved, and the real-time view shifted into the

future, using current vectors to extrapolate the moment of closest passage. 'Very soon, we'll have less than a light-second between ourselves and a pair of terawatt chaotic gravity cannon,' he said.

'Assuming she's mounting normal weapons, sir,' Anderson said. 'So far, we haven't seen the usual mix. Certainly not of drones. The battlecruiser was outfitted for making contact with the compound mind and nothing else. Perhaps it wasn't equipped with offensive weapons at all.'

'Let us assume the worst,' Zai said.

'We've still got all four photon cannon, sir,' Second Gunner Wilson said. 'They can do a fair amount of damage even at a light-second's range. If we get the first shots in, we could disable—'

Captain Zai shook his head, cutting the man off.

'We're not firing at the Rix,' he said.

Eyebrows raised across the room.

'We're running silent.'

Hobbes smiled to herself. The *Lynx*'s officers had committed themselves to the captain's initial plan for so long – had been so ready to bring their attack to the battlecruiser at any cost – that they hadn't realized the obvious: with the receiver destroyed, the *Lynx* had completed its mission.

Survival was again a priority.

'Shut everything down,' Hobbes explained. 'No sensors, no weapons charged, go to freefall conditions – total silence.'

'The only activity will be coldjets: to keep ourselves aligned head-on with the Rix,' Captain Zai added. 'Without a heat-sink manifold, our z-axis profile is less than two hundred meters across. We'll be a needle in a haystack.'

'*Head-on*,' Gunner Wilson whispered. 'You know, sir, the forward armor is reinforced for meteoroid collisions. Depleted uranium and a microlayer of neutronium. We could even take a hit and survive.'

Zai shook his head. 'We'll eject the forward armor.'

Wilson and the others recoiled. Hobbes had to sympathize. When the captain had first explained this idea to her, she was convinced he had finally cracked. Now that she'd thought about it, his plan made sense. But it still had a . . . *perversity* about it that mere logic couldn't shake.

First, the energy-sink manifold, now their armor. For the second time in this battle, they were throwing away their defenses.

The captain remained silent, as if enjoying the shock his pronouncement had created.

So Hobbes again explained: 'that armor is reflective. If they search for us with wide-focus laser fire, they'll pick us up as a big red spot.'

'We could paint it black,' someone suggested after a moment's thought.

'Not under high acceleration, and not in time,' the first engineer said flatly.

The logic of the captain's idea slowly settled over the room, like some dermal drug sinking into the skin.

No weapons. No defenses. Just the blackness of space between the *Lynx* and the enemy. A high-stakes gamble. Hobbes saw the discomfort on the officers' faces as they struggled to accept the plan. They were safer running silent, it was undeniable, but they would be relinquishing control of their fate to luck alone. It offended their sensibilities. They were the crew of a warship, not passengers on some commercial shuttle.

Hobbes decided to interrupt the frustration filling the room. She had to give them something to do.

'Perhaps we could fill the forward cargo compartments with some protection against chaotic gravitons. Do we have any heavy metals?' Hobbes asked.

After a moment, Marx nodded. 'The minesweeper fragmentation drones use depleted uranium. Not much, but it's something.'

'And there's the shielding around the singularity generator. If we're running silent, we'll be shutting the hole down, so we could move it forward. A little extra hullalloy between us and the Rix couldn't hurt.'

'Put a team together,' Zai ordered. 'Start disassembling the shielding now. Get it moving the moment we cease acceleration.'

First Engineer Frick spoke up. 'How long do we have in freefall, sir?'

'A hundred seconds,' Hobbes said. 'No more.'

The man shook his head. It wasn't enough time to move the massive shielding through the corridors of the battle-configured ship.

The captain nodded. 'All right, we'll cut our engines earlier. I'll give you three minutes of zero-gee before we come under fire.'

Engineer Frick smiled at ExO Hobbes in triumph.

Hobbes shrugged her shoulders. If the captain's largesse kept the man happy, she was glad to play scrooge. But it was still precious little time for an operation of that complexity. The engineers would still be putting the makeshift armor in place when the Rix started hunting them. But at least the crew would be occupied; better busy than hunkering down in the dark, waiting for a lance of gravitons to tear into them.

Even the hardest work was better than doing nothing.

First Engineer

First Engineer Watson Frick watched a universe disappear.

The pocket cosmos behind the hullalloy shielding stuttered

for a moment as its bonds were cut. The black hole at its core, which had strained since its creation against the fields that held it in the real universe, convulsed for an instant, then collapsed.

Away it goes, Frick thought, off to Somewhere Else – a different reality, now utterly unreachable. What a strange way to generate power, the First Engineer wondered: making pocket universes, the false (?) realms formed whenever a starship bigbanged its drive. How many other realities had humanity created with this process?

And would there one day be other thinking beings inside them, in the small realities born of humanity's hubris? Then those, making pocket universes of their own . . .

Frick shook his head. There was no time for philosophical digression. In 500 seconds, the *Lynx* would come under fire. The singularity generator's shielding was needed at the front of the warship.

'Two minutes until freefall,' Frick shouted. 'Let's get this metal broken down.'

The crew – his best men and women – worked quickly, disassembling the huge armored plates as easily as if this process were among the standard drills, which it most certainly was not. Frick put his own hands in, running a controller down the starboard seam of the shielding. The controller sent out focused FM waves, a tight field that activated nanos buried throughout the armor. The nanos sprang to life and began breaking down the shielding into movable sections.

Sweat slid into Frick's eyes as he moved the heavy controller in a careful line. Normally, the device would be lightened by its own easy gravity generator, but with the *Lynx* still running flat out, spot sources of gravitons were too dangerous. At eighteen gees acceleration, the random fluxes coursing through the ship were already deadly. Frick remembered the arduous trip out to intercept the Rix ship, a week under ten gees. A few days in, he'd seen a line of bad gravity go through a rating's legs, one of the man's kneecaps shattering like a dropped saucer.

Frick tried to keep the cut steady.

Taking the shielding apart was easy, of course. But doing it the *right* way was tricky. The *Lynx* would need the singularity generator quickly back in one piece again on the other side of danger. The black hole powered the ship's photon cannon, artificial gravity, even life support. With the generator offline, the captain was running the batteries down just to give Frick these minutes for disassembly.

The heavy plates across from Frick shifted as they were cut apart.

'Slow it up over there!' he shouted. 'You wanna be crushed? Save your final cuts until we hit freefall.' The largest of the sections massed five tons.

As the words left his mouth, a shudder went through the ship. A gravity ghost, reminding them all that the ship's artificial gee was a very shaky proposition. For a moment, there was a nervous silence as the ghost passed.

Heat was building in the cramped space around the singularity generator. The nanos' furious activity within the shielding walls had turned them red-hot.

'Environmental, environmental,' Frick said.

'We're on it, sir,' came the response in his second hearing.

A tepid wind blew across his face, hardly sufficient.

'A little more?' he inquired.

'We're on it, sir,' the woman repeated with maddening calm.

Frick scowled and lowered his cutter. He had cut as far as he safely could in one gee. The heat was unbearable.

He walked around the generator's perimeter, checking his crew's work. The giant sections loomed over him, seeming to hang by threads.

'Fine. Fine. Stop there!' he rasped. 'Wait for freefall.'

Suddenly, a panicked cry came from just behind him.

'Sir!'

He spun on one heel to face the cry.

'It's cracking, sir!'

Frick's eyes scanned the wall of shielding next to the yelping crewman. A spiderweb of fissures appeared, spreading even as he watched.

For a moment, he couldn't believe it. The specs for singularity shielding were the most demanding in the Navy. No captain wanted a black hole coming loose in the middle of battle. And they'd calculated these cuts to the micrometer.

But something had gone wrong.

Then Frick's eyes spotted the epicenter of the cracking. There was a small hole in the shielding, a centimeter across.

'Godspite!' he shouted. 'One of the flockers hit the generator!'

Fissures spread from the tiny hole, like too-thin lake ice cracking underfoot. The hullalloy cried out, a screaming sound to wake the dead as it began to collapse.

'Priority, priority!' the engineer yelled, his hand whipping through the priority icon even as he invoked it. 'Cut the engines and the gravity, Hobbes! I need zero-gee!'

But the shielding was already falling, coming down on them. The metal howled as its own weight tore it from the generator. Frick grabbed the crewman who'd spotted the fissures by the collar and pulled, planting his feet against the grabby surface of the deck. For a moment, he merely yanked the man and himself off-balance, but then the sudden bowel-clenching feel of freefall descended around them.

The ExO had heard.

Frick threw the suddenly weightless man out of danger, the ensign spinning toward safety.

But he had pushed too hard, he realized. The Second Law put Frick himself in motion, hurtling back under the shielding. His grabby boots left the floor, and he found himself helpless in the air.

The free piece of shielding floated inexorably toward him. The First Law now: it retained momentum from when it had been falling. With the engines and artificial gravity cut, the shielding was weightless . . .

But it was still *massive*.

It floated slowly toward him, no faster than a feather falling, less than a meter away. Frick's hands clawed at the deck behind him, but the metal slipped under his fingers.

Why wasn't he wearing grabby gloves? There simply hadn't been time to suit up properly as he'd rushed to prepare this operation. *No gloves!* Frick had demoted ratings for this sort of idiocy. Well, justice would be served. The first engineer was about to be worse than demoted.

The shielding moved toward him, as slow and buoyant as some huge water craft gliding to bump ponderously against a dock.

Ratings' hands reached for him. They'd all be crushed. 'Clear off!' he shouted.

'Engineer?' came Hobbes' voice. 'What's—'

'Give me one-twentieth-gee accel, flush starboard for one second!' he screamed as the giant fist of metal closed upon him.

He hoped his numbers – arrived at by pure instinct – were correct. He hoped Hobbes wouldn't ask what he was screaming about. In the time it took to say ten words, he would be flattened.

The huge vise closed on him. Without logic, Frick pressed against it, all his strength against five thousand kilograms. He saw his crew's hands grip futilely at the metal's edges. The tons of hullalloy pressed relentlessly against him.

A cracking sound came from Frick's chest, but then the slight bump of acceleration struck.

The shielding's course fluidly reversed, as if some affectionate but massive metal creature had hugged him too tightly.

'Thank you, Hobbes,' he muttered.

The shielding moved away, only a hair faster than it had closed on Frick. Half a meter of space opened up, and hands – *grabby-gloved* hands, he noted ruefully – reached underneath to pull him out.

He took a deep, painful breath. Something popped in his chest. A few ribs had succumbed to the shielding's tight embrace. A small price to pay for an idiot's mistake.

'Hobbes,' he managed.

'What the devil's going on down there?'

The shielding was still floating back toward the generator. Slowly, but still inexorably. They had to get it stopped.

'Loose metal,' he said, measuring the shielding's speed with his engineer's handheld and calculating. 'One more acceleration. Opposite direction, at point-oh-two gees.'

Hobbes sighed with exasperation. She and the captain must be livid. They were supposed to be fleeing a Rix warship at eighteen gees, not nudging around the *Lynx* with tiny squirts of coldjet.

But the bump came, Frick's grabby boots holding him firm. The metal edged to a near-halt in midair. He smiled at his calculations. Not bad for an old man.

'Hold in zero-gee,' he said. They couldn't resume acceleration with the heavy shielding floating about. 'We have loose tons.'

'Loose *tons*?' Hobbes exclaimed.

'Yes, ma'am,' Frick answered, holding his throbbing side. 'Definitely tons.'

'All right, Frick, get that metal into the bow,' she said. 'We'll be within range of the Rix primaries in four hundred seconds. And thanks to cutting our engines for you, we'll be at barely half a lightsecond range.'

Damn, the first engineer thought. The loose shielding had cost them two minutes of acceleration. Damn those flockers! How had he missed the damage?

He just hoped the armor would be worth the lost distance from the Rix gravity cannon.

'Crew, we are going dark early,' came the captain's voice. The old man didn't sound pleased.

'Ten seconds,' Hobbes began the count.

'All right!' Frick shouted to his crew. 'We're doing this in the dark: no second sight, no com, no gravity!'

'Five . . .'

'Cut all the pieces out. But we'll be in microgravity once the coldjets start,' he shouted. 'You and you, get this piece of tin moving toward the bow. And watch out. I happen to know it's heavy.'

A few of the crew laughed as they sprang to their work. But the boisterous sound dropped off as the ship went dark.

The heads-up status displays, the hovering symbols that marked equipment, the chatter of ship noise and expert software, everything in second sight and hearing disappeared. The ship was left dim and lifeless around them, a mere hunk of metal. All they had to see by was unaugmented work lights, making the generator area a shadowy, red-tinged twilight zone.

Then the coldjets started, pushing the *Lynx* to orient it bow-first toward the Rix battlecruiser. The microgravity shifted the loose plates of shielding again, but by now the crew had attached handholds and stronglines to them, and they soon had the beasts under control. But in the dim light and swaying microgravity, it felt like the below decks of some ancient warship on a pitching sea.

Frick looked reflexively for a time stamp, but his second sight held nothing. The fields that created synesthesia were highly penetrative and persistent – the Rix would be looking for them in their hunt for the *Lynx*. Second audio was out of the question as well; only hardwired compoints were to be used. He'd gone over this with Hobbes, but it hadn't seemed real before now.

Frick damned himself for not thinking to bring a mechanical chronometer. Had there even been time to fabricate such an exotic device?

'You,' he said, pointing to a rating. 'Start counting.'

'Counting, sir?'

'Yes. Counting out loud is your job now. Backwards from . . . three hundred eighty. Count slow, in seconds.'

A look of understanding crossed the rating's face. She started in a low voice.

'Three hundred eighty, three hundred seventy-nine . . .'

Frick shook his head at the sound. He was using a highly trained crewman as a *clock*, for god's sake. They would be running handwritten notes next.

His angry eyes scanned the dimness of the generator area. Everywhere, huge and unwieldy pieces of metal were beginning to move with agonizing slowness. Each was supported by a web of stronglines. The cables were packed with stored kinetic energy, windup carbon that would contract when keyed. This purely mechanical motive force was invisible to the Rix sensors, but it was capable of pulling the weightless if massive sections of hullalloy through the ship.

Frick looked about for a rating with free hands.

'You,' he called.

'Sir?'

Frick held up his bare hands. 'Get me some gloves.'

In 370 seconds or so, the Rix might turn them all to jelly, but damned if Watson Frick was going to be crushed by some piece of dumb metal in the meantime.

Executive Officer

Katherie Hobbes had never heard the battle bridge so silent.

With the synesthesia field absent, most of the control surfaces had turned featureless gray. She seldom appreciated how few of the screens and controls she used every day were physical. It looked as if the frigate's bridge had been wrapped in gray, grabby carpeting, like some featureless prototype. The few hard icons that remained – the fat, dumb buttons that were independent of second sight – glowed dully in the red battle lights. The big airscreen that normally dominated the bridge was replaced by its emergency backup, a flatscreen that showed only one level of vision at a time, and fuzzily at that.

Trapped in the dim world of primary sight, the bridge crew moved in a daze, as if synesthesia were a shared dream they'd all just awoken from.

Not that their confusion mattered. There wasn't much they could accomplish with the *Lynx* running in its near-total darkmode. The frigate's pilot staff were handling the coldjets, nudging the ship through a very slow arc – ninety degrees in eight minutes – to keep the bow directly lined up on the Rix battlecruiser. The *Lynx* was like a duelist turned sideways, keeping the smallest possible area oriented toward her opponent. The pilots spoke animatedly among themselves, out of Hobbes's hearing. The executive officer instinctively made the control gesture that should have fed their voices to her, but of course second hearing was gone as well. Hobbes knew why they were frustrated, however; for their calculations, the pilots were using a shielded darkmode computer hidden behind the sickbay armor. The machine had about as much processor power as a robotic pet.

At this range the Rix sensors were very sensitive. Only the most primitive electronics could be used.

Hobbes turned her mind to Frick's engineering team. They should have the impromptu armor plating in position by now. She rotated an unwieldy select dial at her station, trying to find the team. The usual wash of sound from below decks had been reduced to a smattering of voices; the only dialogue that reached Hobbes came through the hardwired compoints at key control points on the ship. The low-wattage handheld communicators they'd broken out were to be used only on the captain's orders. At this range, Rix sensors could detect the emissions of a self-microwaving food pack boiling noodles. Even medical endoframes had to be shut down. Captain Zai's prosthetics were frozen; he couldn't budge from the shipmaster's chair. Only one of his arms was moving; the other was locked in a position that seemed painfully posed.

'How are they doing, Hobbes?' the captain asked. His voice seemed so soft, so human now, absent the usual amplification of the captain's direct channel.

'I . . .' Hobbes continued to scroll through the various compoints on the ship. The primitive interface was maddening.

Ten awful seconds later, she was forced to admit, 'I don't know, sir.' Hobbes wondered if she had ever said those words to her captain before.

'Don't worry, Hobbes,' he said, smiling at her. 'They're probably between compoints. Just let me know when they call.'

'Yes, sir.'

Despite losing his legs and one arm, the captain seemed hardly bothered by the blindness of darkmode. Zai was actually working with a stylus – on *paper*, Hobbes realized.

He noticed her gaze upon the ancient apparatus.

'We may need to use runners before this is over, Hobbes,' he explained. 'Just thought I'd practice my penmanship.'

'I'm not sure I know that last word, sir,' she admitted.

He smiled again.

'On Vada, you couldn't graduate from upper school without good handwriting, Hobbes. The ancient arts always come back eventually.'

She nodded, recognizing the ancient root-word. *Pen*-manship. It made sense now. As always, the Vadan emphasis was on the male gender.

'But perhaps old ways aren't a priority on Utopian worlds, eh, Hobbes?'

'I suppose not, sir,' she said, feeling a bit odd that the captain was conversing with her only moments before the *Lynx* would come under fire. In darkmode, of course, there was not much they could do other than chat.

'But in lower school I did learn how to use a sextant.'

'An excellent skill!' the captain said. He wasn't kidding.

'Though it was hardly a requirement for graduation, sir.'

'I just hope you remember how, Hobbes. If the Rix hit our processor core again, we may need you at the hard viewports.'

'Let's hope it doesn't come to that, sir.'

'Twenty seconds,' announced a young ensign, raising her voice to be heard across the bridge. Her eyes were fixed on a mechanical chronometer someone had dug up from stores. Captain Zai had also produced an ancient Vadan wristwatch from among his family heirlooms. He had examined the two timepieces, determined that they ran on springs – making them undetectable to the Rix – and synchronized one to the other with a twist of a minuscule knob.

As the ensign counted down to the point when the Rix could begin firing, Captain Zai handed Hobbes the writing instrument and paper.

'Care to have a go?'

She held the stylus like a knife, but that didn't seem right. She tried it like a pointer.

'Turn it around, and slip the business end between your index and middle fingers,' the captain said quietly.

'Ah, like a fork almost,' Hobbes replied.

'Five,' said the ensign. 'Four . . .'

Hobbes made a few marks. There was a certain pleasure in the pen's incision of the paper. Unlike air drawing, the friction of pen against paper had a reassuring physicality. She sketched a diagram of the bridge.

Not bad. But writing? She crossed two parallel lines to make a crude *H*. Then formed a circle for the *O*.

'Zero,' said the ensign. 'We are in range of the enemy prime's capital weapons.'

Hobbes tried the other letters of her name, but they dissolved into scribbles.

The chief sensor officer, leaned over a headsdown display, spoke in a loud, clear voice, as if addressing an audience from a theatrical stage.

'She's firing. Standard photon cannon. Looks to be targeting along our last known vector.'

Hobbes nodded. The Rix would have tracked the *Lynx* until 450 seconds ago, when they'd dropped into darkmode. But the coldjets had pushed the *Lynx* onto a new vector.

The captain had taken a risk with that. The coldjets used waste water and other recyclables for reaction mass, and Zai had shot half the frigate's water supply, and even a good chunk of the emergency oxygen that was kept frozen on the hull. The ship had gotten an additional bit of kick from ejecting the reflective bow armor with high explosives. They were now thousands of kilometers from where the Rix thought they were, but they had almost no recyclables to spare. If they lost their main drive to enemy fire, it would be almost a year before the low-acceleration rescue craft available on Legis could make it out to repair and resupply them. A single breakdown in the recycling chain – bacterial failure, equipment malfunction, the slightest nano mutation – would doom them all.

And despite herself, Hobbes wondered if the Navy would prioritize rescuing the *Lynx*. With a war on, there'd be plenty of excuses to delay chasing down a stricken warship that was flying toward Rix space at two thousand klicks per second. Laurent Zai was still an embarrassment to the Emperor. They would all make good martyrs.

'Short bursts: one, two, three,' the sensor officer counted. 'Low power lasers now; they're looking for reflections.'

'What are their assumptions?' the captain asked.

Ensign Tyre, who had been moved up to the bridge from Data Analysis, struggled with the limited processor power and her headsdown's unfamiliar physical controls. The silent-running passive sensor array was basically a host of fiber optics running from the hull to the same small, shielded computer the pilots had been complaining about.

'From where they're shooting, they seem to think we've doubled back on them . . . at high acceleration.'

'High acceleration?' Hobbes murmured. 'But we obviously aren't under main drive.'

'They're being cautious,' Zai said quietly. 'They think we may have developed a stealthy drive in the last eighty years, and that we're still bent on ramming them.'

Of course, Hobbes thought. Just as the Rix evolved from one war to the next, so did the Imperials. And the *Lynx* was a new class of warship, only ten absolute years old. It had nothing as exotic as full-power stealthy acceleration, but the Rix didn't know that.

Katherie Hobbes turned the page of the captain's writing tablet, giving herself a clean piece of paper. With a few long strokes, she drew a vector line of the *Lynx*'s passage through the battlecruiser's gravity-cannon perimeter. Writing letters was difficult, but her fingers seemed to know instinctively the curves of gunnery and acceleration. Over her career, she'd traced the courses of a thousand battles, imagined or historical, on airscreen displays. Her tactical reflexes seemed to guide the pen, rendering the Rix firing pattern as the sensor officer called it.

The two ships' relative velocity was still roughly 3,000 kps – it would take hours of acceleration to change that appreciably. Thus, the *Lynx*'s course was practically a straight line running nearly tangent through the sphere of the gravity cannon's effective range, like a bullet passing through a dribble-hoop ball at a shallow angle. While they were inside the sphere, the Rix could hit them. But the frigate would pass out of range within minutes.

'They've gone to higher power, with a wider aperture,' Tyre said.

The Rix weren't firing to kill now; they had reduced their laser's coherence to increase the area they could cover. They were hoping that a low-energy hit would reflect from the *Lynx*, or cause a secondary explosion that would give her position away.

In effect, they had replaced their sniper's rifle with a flare gun.

'They're picking up the pace. I can see a pattern now: a spiral from our old course,' Tyre said.

'How fast is the spiral expanding?' Hobbes called, her pen frozen above the paper.

'Outward at about a thousand meters per second.'

Hobbes looked at the captain, her spirits lifting. The Rix were sounding a vast area. They had assumed the *Lynx* was still under heavy acceleration, at multiple gees rather than the micromaneuvers they were actually making.

'The enemy seems to have overestimated us, Hobbes,' Zai said.

'Yes, sir.'

Hobbes turned to another fresh page of paper, filled it with a line spiraling outward and dissected by radials from the center: a spiral grid.

Thinking that the *Lynx* was still under her main drive, the Rix were casting a wide net. But the firing rate of the battle-cruiser's laser would have an absolute limit. In order to search such a huge volume, they necessarily had to reduce the grain of their search grid; the Rix net had wide holes in it. If the *Lynx* were broadside to the battlecruiser, the low-res search might have picked up the two-kilometer-long craft. But the frigate was bow-on, her hull only two hundred meters across from the Rix's perspective. And with the bow armor ejected, only naked black hullalloy remained to reflect the laser.

Hobbes drew a small circle in the circular grid, a minuscule gnat slipping through the web of a spider looking for fat flies.

'They're going to miss us, sir.'

'Yes, Hobbes. Unless they're very lucky.'

First Engineer

'One hundred ninety-nine. Two hundred.'

'All right, shut up!' First Engineer Watson Frick shouted to the dogged ensign. 'Keep the count going, but *silently*. Let me know when you get to eight hundred.'

Frick's skin tingled as if he were under a sonic shower. The ensign had been in positive territory – counting up – for two minutes. No matter how imprecise the count might be, the *Lynx* was certainly within range of the enemy's capital weapons by now. At any moment, a gravity beam might swing across the ship and mangle them all. They had at least another six hundred seconds before they were out of danger.

Frick's side still throbbed – yes, a few ribs were definitely broken – as he regarded the hastily assembled armor plates.

The last piece was in place. The hullalloy shielding was spread across the cargo area to maximize coverage of the ship. There were seams, even naked gaps, but he couldn't seal those without using cutting torches rated for hullalloy. And *that* would show up on the Rix sensors like an SOS beacon.

The problem was, the plates were practically floating free, held to the bow hull only by stronglines and monofilament. Engineer Frick had counted on using the recyclables stored in the cargo area to pack the hull sections into place. But the containers were all empty, the water ejected.

If the captain ordered any serious maneuvers, the hullalloy plates would tear from their uncertain moorings and crash through the ship like a runaway maglev.

And there was no hardwired compoint here in the cargo bay, no way to reach the captain. Apparently, the designers of the *Lynx* had never imagined that the bow cargo area would become a prime tactical station. Frick realized now why Navy ships seldom even drilled in true darkmode; doing without second sight was frustrating, but losing communications could be deadly.

'Pressure hoods up,' Frick ordered his team. If the plates got free, decompression was a high probability. And it was cold here, this close to the hull. The ship was running on minimal life support, nano-rebreathers for air, insulation to maintain internal temperature.

'You,' he said, pointing at Rating Metasmith. The woman was the best athlete on the engineering team. In gravity, she was a dribblehoop demon, and had the highest freefall work-out scores on the *Lynx* except for a few marines. 'Get back to the forward gunnery station and use the compoint. Warn the captain not to accelerate above one-twentieth.'

'Understood,' she said, and sailed toward the open hatchway with an effortless shove. Frick flinched as she soared through, missing collision with the hatchway's coupling fringe by a few centimeters.

The first engineer sealed the hatch behind Metasmith. If the plates did get loose, his team might do some good here in the cargo bay. They could attempt *some* sort of damage control.

'Pick an armor plate and tether yourself,' he ordered. 'And if you smell something cooking, it's you.'

Frick pushed himself toward the central armor plate. The plates weren't grabby, so he employed his pressure suit's magnets. He settled against the hullalloy, feeling its reassuring mass between himself and the Rix gravity cannon.

Five minutes to go, as near as he could figure.

The silence of the *Lynx* was awful. At least on the bridge they could watch the incoming fire, judge how close the shots were falling. But here in the bow, he and his team were hiding deaf and blind, not really knowing if their silence protected them at all.

Commando

H_rd soared to meet the cloud-seeding dirigible, the rendezvous only a hundred kilometers from the entanglement facility's wire.

The recon flyer was at the upper limit of its altitude. The fans whined pitifully, and the craft's electromagnetics stretched tenuously downward, a swimmer's toes searching for solid ground. The air was thin up here, but breathable for a Rixwoman.

The dirigible came down to greet her, operating at the lower extreme of its functional altitude range. Thus the two craft formed a precarious and narrow union of sets. H_rd rose slowly to a standing position on the recon flyer's armored carapace. The straining flyer reacted to every shift of her weight with the jitter of a tightrope. Alexander's piloting would be tested by this maneuver. H_rd had removed the military governors, giving control of the craft to the compound mind. She would have to go very high to approach the entanglement facility undetected.

The dirigible, also under Alexander's control, came nearer, its sphere of emptiness looming like a black hole in the dark sky. The airship's tiny props tried to steady it, fighting the strong winds of this high place. H_rd's sable coat spread out from her, black wings against the stars.

It was twenty-five degrees below freezing. For the first time in her life, the Rixwoman felt her fingers grow numb.

H_rd steadied herself, and reached for the dirigible's payload basket. She stripped the scientific instruments to lighten the craft, replacing them with the pack she had prepared for this mission. Then she removed the sable coat, which was too heavy to take with her, and sadly let it fall. She locked the muscles in her hands, leaving them arched like a pair of hooks. There was no provision for a person in the dirigible's small payload basket. She would have to hang from the airship until it reached the proper position.

She knelt, gathered herself, and leapt from one craft toward the other.

The recon flyer dipped away as her weight pushed against it, and a sudden gust of wind pulled the dirigible from her locked hands. A very human gasp escaped her lips.

H_rd reached the zenith of her leap, then fell through the cold air like a stone.

Captain

'A runner in forward gunnery has a message from the first engineer, sir.'

'We have our promised armor?' Captain Zai asked. It had taken long enough. Zai had questioned the value of reinforcing the forward cargo area in the first place. But the crew needed to feel that they were doing something to protect themselves. 'A necessary misdirection,' as Anonymous 167 called these minor deceptions of one's own subordinates.

'Yes. But the plates are not secure, sir,' Hobbes relayed. 'Frick is requesting no maneuvers above point-oh-five gees. They could tear loose if we use the main drive.'

Captain Zai cursed. 'I knew I'd pay for that armor.'

'They can secure it with torches, sir, once we get out of range.'

'By then we won't need it,' Zai said.

Hobbes nodded.

Zai flexed the fingers of his natural hand. Going to dark-mode had apparently worked. The Rix almost certainly weren't going to find them without a wild stroke of luck. In five minutes, plus another hundred seconds for safety, they could switch synesthesia back on. They would have communications, status reports. He would get command of his ship back.

And he would be able to move again. At the moment, Zai's lower back was aching from holding himself rigid in the ship-master's chair. If he relaxed for a moment, he would topple over onto the floor.

'Any answer for Frick, sir?'

'No. We'll have communications back in a few minutes

anyway. Keep that runner on station at the compoint, in case
something serious comes up.'

'Yes, sir.' The tone of Hobbes's voice showed that she
agreed.

It was odd, sitting here with her in the near-dark. The captain's and executive officer's stations were physically close,
but the two inhabited different worlds. Hobbes often seemed
absent, adrift amid the myriad channels of the *Lynx*'s infostructure, while Zai tried to stay focused on the overall picture.
He'd been an ExO himself, and had to resist the temptation to wallow in the vast information resources of his ship.
But the war sage was unwavering on the importance of dele-
gation; the captain left data mining to the ever-competent
Katherie Hobbes.

Here in darkmode, however, wrapped in silence and cut
off from the rest of the *Lynx*, there was an unfamiliar intimacy between them. Zai had always rated Hobbes an
excellent officer, but now that his life seemed daily on the
line, he appreciated her all the more.

Since the attempt on his life, Zai had recognized that loyalty was a variable trait in the Navy. On gray Vada, rebellion
against authority was rarely contemplated, but a mutiny had
happened here on the *Lynx*. And it had been Katherie
Hobbes, a Utopian by birth, who had stopped it. In the red
work lights, her surgical beauty betrayed the values of her
hedonistic homeland. But Hobbes was his best officer as well
as his ExO.

She would make a good captain one day.

'Sir!' the sensor officer shouted, pulling Zai from his
reverie.

'Report.'

'I'm getting reflections from the Rix fire!'

'You mean they've hit something?' Hobbes asked.

Zai narrowed his eyes. The Rix search pattern had passed

beyond the *Lynx* minutes ago; its spiral course had taken it a hundred thousand kilometers away.

'Yes, ma'am.' The man bent back to his headsdown display.

Tyre spoke up. 'I'm running an analysis now.'

'Old sand?' Zai suggested to Hobbes.

'Not out here,' she said. Zai nodded. They had put a lot of distance between themselves and their original intercept point. 'Maybe it's old Legis's orbital defenses.'

'That would be fantastic luck,' Zai said. 'If they think they've spotted us, we're home free.'

But Hobbes shook her head. Zai knew from experience what the look on her face meant: there was a thought half-formed in her mind, an unhappy one.

'I'm getting oxygen, hydrogen, some carbon,' said the sensor officer.

'The recyclables!' Hobbes cried. 'That's what they were looking for. Why they went so wide with their search. *They weren't looking for us*. They wanted to find the reaction mass from our coldjets.'

Zai closed his eyes. Of course. Spreading out from the *Lynx* was a spray of H_2O and organic waste, the ejecta from their stealthy acceleration. It would be spread into a huge cloud of ice crystals by now. Boiled by a laser, it would be much easier to spot than a silent starship. The Rix would eventually calculate its mass and vector.

And by extrapolation, they would know the vector of the *Lynx*.

'We seem to have left footprints, Executive Officer,' he said.

'Aye, sir,' Hobbes answered quietly.

'They've gone to a more focused beam, sir,' the sensor officer reported. 'They're still sounding the ice. Tracking it.'

'We need to maneuver again, Hobbes,' Zai said. 'And at better than one-twentieth gee.'

'I'll warn Frick, sir.' Hobbes activated the forward gunnery compoint and sent the runner into motion.

The captain sighed. He would have to walk a fine line between two dangers. The Rix would extrapolate their position before the *Lynx* passed out of range. If Zai let the frigate coast, the enemy's laser would find them, followed by their gravity cannon. But if he maneuvered too quickly, the unsecured armor plates would roll through the frigate like a gravity ghost through a ship of glass.

'What's the strongest part of the cargo area, Hobbes?'

'The forewall, sir,' Hobbes answered without hesitation. 'It's exterior-grade hullalloy; there's vacuum on the bowside.'

'So we'll do the least damage if we thrust sternward.'

'Yes, sir. But that only changes our position on the z-axis. We're facing directly toward the Rix.'

'We need to turn, then. A one-twentieth-gee yaw thrust.'

'Any change in yaw and we expose more area to the Rix, sir.'

'Yes, Hobbes. We'll turn back as quickly as possible.'

'And I'm not sure how much acceleration we can get, sir. We're pretty low on recyclables.'

Zai thought quickly. They needed the greatest possible push from the least possible mass. Thus, they needed maximum velocity.

'We'll use the drone launcher. Not the main rail's magnetics' – the Rix would spot that in a second – 'the deadman drone. The highest velocity we can get out of it.'

Hobbes whistled.

'Without artificial gravity to dampen the reaction? That *will* cause a jolt, sir.'

'A jolt is what we need, Hobbes. And a mechanical event won't show up on the Rix sensors.'

Hobbes nodded, understanding. The deadman launcher was designed for a ship that had lost power, its systems failing.

The launch rail stored its energy mechanically, like a huge crossbow made of wound carbon. 'I'll send another runner to the first engineer, Captain. There'll be decompression up there.'

Zai nodded, his fingers flexing with frustration. They had only minutes to make this maneuver work, but using runners to convey messages would create at least half a minute of lag-time each way. Any change in plan would catch the engineer off guard.

Of all Zai's first officers, Engineer Frick most rarely worked from the bridge. The *Lynx*'s captain and engineer didn't know each other's thinking.

The words of the war sage came unbidden into Zai's mind. *A true subordinate is an extension of yourself.*

He came to a decision.

'Hobbes, tell Frick you'll be coming forward.'

'Sir?'

'We don't know how this is going to work out. More maneuvers may be required. I need you there.'

'To do what, sir?'

'To read my mind.'

Commando

The sensation of freefall was strangely comforting.

In their orbital homes, the Rix generally slept in zero-gee. Except for the rush of frigid air, h_rd might have been waking from some dark dream. But this was real: she was falling toward her death.

She could see the entanglement facility in the distance, a concentric pattern of lights against the dull sheen of starlit snow. Somewhere in that pattern, a hundred kilometers away, was the landing zone Alexander had prepared for her, but it was much too far away. The world below her was terribly dark. She felt absolutely alone, and thought of Rana, probably still asleep in the cave. Who would bring her food now? Who would mourn her death?

Interrupting her thoughts, the scream of the recon flyer passed her, its running lights a red blur. With its fans inverted, it was falling faster than she. But it was twenty meters away. The machine had very limited senses, nothing that could spot her, even with Alexander at the controls. But h_rd remembered the sensitive thermal imagers that the Imperials had used to hunt her and Rana. She closed her eyes and willed her body temperature upward. Almost immediately, she felt acid in her stomach and a dryness in her mouth, a whirring of the turbine in her chest: the sensations of a heightened metabolism.

She dared a glance at the ground rushing toward her. Was there time?

H_rd cupped her hands, spreading out to slow her fall. She worked her muscles to hurry the heating process, flailing as she fell. The recon flyer suddenly edged back up toward her, moving carefully in the ferocious wind, guided by the barest movements of its control surfaces. Apparently Alexander could see her against the cold background of the stars.

The flyer came alongside and steadied itself. H_rd took control of her descent, angling her cupped hands to maneuver herself toward the craft. She grabbed the flailing webbing of the gunner's seat. The fans screamed again as the recon flyer braked.

The machine pulled up from its dive at a precarious angle, h_rd dangling from one side. She looked down as the craft decelerated, the frozen earth rushing toward her.

They missed collision with the hard tundra by only a few hundred meters.

'Well, then,' she said – talking to herself was an odd habit she had picked up from Rana. 'At least I've had a practice run.'

Executive Officer

ExO Katherie Hobbes pulled herself through the dark shaft-ways of the *Lynx*, wishing she'd put more time into zero-gee practice.

Normally before an engagement, the crew would spend days working out in variable- and zero-gee, preparing for evasive maneuvers and gravity-generator brownouts. But the *Lynx* had been under heavy acceleration for almost ten days. There'd been no chance for the usual touch-up exercises.

At least the captain had given her time to don a proper pressure suit.

Hobbes checked the ancient chronometer on her wrist. The captain had set the first yaw-axis maneuver for thirty seconds from now. And he had loaned Hobbes his grandfather's timepiece. Good god, the thing was *old*. It used some ancient circular readout that Zai had explained as she'd slipped into an armored pressure suit. The timepiece was 'analog,' he had said, using an almost forgotten meaning of that word. As she moved through the cold and silent passageways of the ship, Hobbes's ears registered the almost subliminal pulse of the timepiece's ticking.

Thirty seconds. She wouldn't make it before the first acceleration, a nudge to orient the *Lynx* away from the Rix warship, but that would be a small one. The deadman launch would come twenty seconds later. Releasing the potential energy stored in the backup drone rail would shove *Lynx* off its current trajectory, rocking the ship like a meteor collision. Unlike coldjet acceleration, there would be no smooth buildup. The jolt would come all at once. The first engineer had already been warned by runners, but if she were to help Frick, she had to make it to the bow before things got too chaotic.

Even as Hobbes had left the bridge, the chief sensor officer was warning that the Rix's laser beams had ceased probing the ejecta, and were closing on the *Lynx*. At any second they could be under fire.

She pushed herself forward with abandon, kicking against the grabby walls as she yanked her pressure hood over her head. At least if she cracked her skull, the suit's thick carapace would afford it an extra layer of protection.

Suddenly, her ankle became tangled in something. She was yanked up short, swearing at whoever had left cable floating free under battle-stations.

But then Hobbes was pulled back forcibly, and she realized that a strong hand held her foot.

'What the hell?' she shouted.

Who was playing around, here in the midst of battle? Hobbes bent her knees, bringing herself face-to-face with the assailant, prepared to unleash a mighty stream of invective.

Then she recognized the woman: Verity Anst, a fourth-class gunnery rating, and an old friend of Gunner Thompson. Anst was one of those whom Hobbes and Zai had suspected of sympathy with the mutiny. They had never caught the last two mutineers. The *Lynx* was short of gunners, however, and no proof had ever come to light against Anst. They had put her under maximum surveillance, assuming that the ship's monitors would keep her honest.

In darkmode, of course, the *Lynx* was as blind as it was silent.

Hobbes turned and tried to push away, but Gunner Anst's hold was firm. The gunner's stats flitted across Hobbes' mind:

two meters tall, ninety kilograms. Anst held on, spinning Hobbes against a bulkhead with a crack that knocked the wind from her.

She pulled Hobbes toward her, and held a knife to the ExO's throat. The blade was ceremonial, but looked hellishly lethal as it flashed in the red battle lights.

'Our little traitor,' Anst said, her face only centimeters away.

Hobbes felt the cold steel even through the pressure suit's plastic. She forced down panic.

'I wasn't the traitor, Anst.'

'Thompson revered you, Hobbes. He wanted you. Poor bastard couldn't see what a captain's whore you were.'

The executive officer blinked, suppressed emotions rising in her briefly. She forced them down.

'So, you were one of them, Anst. I always suspected.'

'I know you did, Katherie,' the woman said. 'I felt you waiting for me to give myself away. But I've been waiting for you, too.'

As the woman spoke, Hobbes felt a familiar complaint from her inner ear. The ship was turning, shifting slowly around its y-axis. Here amidships, the maneuver was subtle enough that the grinning woman before her probably hadn't noticed it.

'You played it well, Verity. But you're dead now,' Hobbes said. She glanced sidelong at the chronometer, starting a countdown from twenty. 'We won't be in darkmode forever.'

'We'll see about that.' With her free hand, Anst yanked open the hatch on the hullside wall: an escape pod. The executive officer swallowed.

'I've got a few minutes with you,' Anst said in a whisper. 'You, me, and this knife. And then off you go with a load of HE. Zai won't find enough of you to genoprint. I've planned this well.'

Fine, Hobbes thought. Anst wanted to brag. Let her.

Katherie Hobbes willed her body to relax, counting down the few remaining seconds before the coming jolt.

First Engineer

Metal screamed all around the First Engineer.

'Get to the far wall!' he shouted to his team.

Damn that idiot Zai! He was turning the *Lynx* too fast, Frick thought. But then the engineer saw the error he'd made, the realization coming even as he leapt from the shifting mass of armor plates. He had given Zai an absolute limit on acceleration: one-twentieth of a gee, or half a meter per second squared. But that assumed forward or backward thrust, which had an even effect throughout the frigate. Thrusting the ship into a turn, however, worked like a centrifugal gravity simulator: the force was far greater at the ship's bow and stern than it was at the center.

Frick was like a man at the end of a whip, one that Zai had casually snapped.

Rating Metasmith had returned from the compoint with a warning about the maneuver, but she hadn't been told why the captain was turning the ship. It didn't make sense. The plan had been to stay oriented to the Rix. As always, someone was improvising. Frick cursed himself as a fool not to have specifically warned against this.

The plates explosively popped their strongline tethers and began to pile toward the starboard side of the cargo bay. They weren't moving fast enough to punch through the hullalloy exterior wall, but they were plenty massive enough to crush a crewman.

As one, the engineering team pulled their magnets and jumped toward the sternward wall. The sliding plates rubbed against each other, screeching like a heavy maglev engaging friction brakes.

But his team was clear.

'Well, the captain hasn't killed us yet!' he said as they landed around him.

A few of his team laughed, but Rating Metasmith raised her fist for their attention. 'They said only one-twentieth for the first accel. But much higher for the second. Whatever they can muster.'

'Splendid,' Frick muttered, then cried, 'Get your hoods on and tether with hard lines. We're going into vacuum!'

Ten seconds later, the promised second jolt struck.

It was far worse than Frick expected.

Executive Officer

Hobbes's feet shot out as her count hit twenty, catching Verity Anst in the center of her chest. Her timing was perfect. The woman cried out in surprise as the ship bucked around them, the shock as violent as a collision. The force of Hobbes's kick was trebled by the sudden acceleration. She was flung from Anst's grip toward the bow, and rolled into a tumbling ball, bouncing down the corridor like a stone tossed down a well.

But Hobbes felt pain at her throat. Anst had managed to cut her as she'd pushed away. Hobbes felt the wound as she tumbled in freefall; her fingers came away slick, but there was no spurting gout of blood.

She came to a hard stop against a closed hatchway, cracking one shoulder, hand still at her throat. The integrity of her suit was broken, but the thick neck-seal had saved her life by millimeters.

Hobbes glanced down the corridor. Anst was twenty

meters behind, kicking her way toward Hobbes with knife leveled.

A huge roar came from behind the executive officer. A shriek of metal and a howling wind from the bow. *Damn*, Hobbes thought. In the burst of acceleration sternward, the armor plates must have punched through the bow of the ship. The *Lynx* was depressurizing.

Hobbes wasn't far from the bow cargo bay. She glanced at the pressure meter on the hatchway door. It was dropping into the red.

She spun the hatch's manual seal, and its safeties complained. Hobbes pressed her hand to the ID plate, and the hatch relented to her command rank.

Gunner Anst was flying toward her, the outstretched knife a few meters away. Hobbes barely had time to beltclip herself to the wall before the hatch blew open.

A great, sudden wind yanked her hard against the clip, bending Hobbes at the waist like a jackknife. Verity Anst sailed past helplessly, screaming bloody murder, and was sucked through the hatch like a doll into a tornado.

Hobbes felt a stinging along one arm: Anst had managed to cut her again.

'Damn you!' she cried.

In a few seconds, the wind began to die down. Somewhere further toward the bow, sprayfoam must be sealing the breaches. Hobbes pulled her pressure suit's face mask on and extended strongline from her belt clip. She kicked out over the hatchway – with the wind, the hatch led effectively down – and dropped after Anst and toward Frick and his team.

A moment later, Hobbes found the mutineer, knocked unconscious against an ugly set of waste baffles. The pressure was still dropping, and the woman's flimsy emergency suit was hopelessly rent. Her eyes were starting to bug, forcing the closed eyelids open a hair. Anst wouldn't last long without help, but there wasn't anything Hobbes had time to do for her.

The blood from the cut on Hobbes's arm spurted in time with her racing heart. The globules floated against Gunner Anst's prone form, dotting her uniform.

'You've got my blood. Happy now?' Hobbes asked, spraying repair sealant onto her own wounds.

Another jolt rocked the ship. Not acceleration; something cracking. The structure of the *Lynx* was beginning to fail. Anst's breathing started to kick up; she was dying.

'May the Emperor save you from death,' Hobbes said to Anst with the cold cadence of tradition. It was all she could do.

She paused to make sure the rent at her own throat was sealed, then pushed on, wondering if Frick and his team were still alive.

First Engineer

Decompression was not the word for it.

When the reverse thrust struck, the plates surged toward the bow, thirty tons of hullalloy doing at least twenty mps. The shock wave from the collision – loose armor plates smashing against the bow hull wall – hammered Frick's ears even through his pressure hood. He was tossed forward, then pulled up short on his tether with a gutwrenching snap, finding himself spinning at the end of three meters of strongline. His ribs screamed in fresh agony.

Then came the truncated howl of flash decompression, total and instantaneous.

The entire forewall of the bow was knocked out. In the seconds before he pulled up his face mask to complete the pressure seal around his head, Frick saw the void before him with naked eyes. His ears and eyeballs felt as if they would burst, both sight and hearing ruptured, then the smart plastics of the suit found their grip, and the pounding in his head was replaced with the polymer smell of recycled air.

He blinked until vision returned, looked out at the huge hole torn out by the plates. Had the *Lynx* accelerated forward instead of in reverse, they would have all been crushed. Not just the engineering team – although they would have been flattened most spectacularly – but the entire vessel would have been pummeled by the careening armor.

Against the mean light of the stars, Watson Frick saw the glitter of a drone sailing away from the ship.

Good god, they must have used the deadman rail, launching the drone to push the *Lynx* backward.

What was the captain *thinking*? Even with easy gravity to compensate, the frigate was designed to accelerate smoothly, not with massive jolts.

Frick scanned his team. They all seemed conscious, although Metasmith was helping Ensign Baxton with his face mask seal. Something about the team looked wrong, however. It wasn't merely the sudden darkness, the hard shadows of orange gas giants and Legis's distant sun. It was that the team didn't seem to be . . .

He did a quick count.

There were fourteen suited figures. *Fourteen*.

Someone was gone.

That was impossible. Everyone had been clipped: hypercarbon strongline attached to hullalloy rings on a bulkhead wall. The utility belt on a Navy engineer's pressure suit was made of diamond-tensile monofilament. You could hang a pair of thrashing African elephants from these rigs with a ten-thousand-year safety margin.

Rating Inders was waving her arms wildly, trying to get

Frick's attention. He looked over at her, disbelief pounding in his head. She pointed at a short crack in the cargo bay bulkhead. The crack ran straight through the line of clip rings.

Then he saw it: one of the hullalloy rings had been ripped out.

The tether rigs were sound, but the *bulkhead* was cracking.

Frick climbed his strongline up and touched his suit's audio probe to the bulkhead. He heard the familiar hum of the *Lynx*'s air nanos, and the moan of decompression through what must have been another hull breach on the other side. And something else – the highpitched tremolo of tiny pits propagating in hullalloy. The forward bulkhead – the last hullalloy barrier between the *Lynx* and massive decompression – was cavitating. Frick swallowed at the menacing sound. One of the flockers must have released a metal-eating virus; nothing else would cause the material to disintegrate this way.

In minutes, or perhaps seconds, the engineering team would all be pitching through the void.

Frick brought his hand up in a fist, thumb and little finger extended. The vacuum hand sign for lethal emergency. When he had every eye on him, the engineer brought the hand down to point at the hatchway. They had to get it open.

Even through pressure masks, he recognized surprise in a few faces. The other side of the bulkhead was still pressurized. Opening the hatchway now would piss away still more of the *Lynx*'s oxygen, and test the structural integrity of the walls between here and the next bulkhead, all the way back at the forward gunnery station.

But with the bulkhead cracking, the oxygen was gone anyway. And it would go far less explosively if they let it flow through the hatchway than if the whole bulkhead blew. At this moment, the hullalloy had hard vacuum on one side and almost a full atmosphere on the other. They had to equalize the pressure. The *Lynx*'s designers would have assumed that the cargo area would lose pressure gradually, at least twenty seconds to empty the huge space of air. No one would foresee the entire front of the ship being sheared away at once. And of course the metal virus added to the stresses on the metal.

Metasmith was the first to react. She swung on her tether like an acrobat, planting her magnet next to the hatchway and bracing her feet to either side. She gave the manual wheel a twist. It seemed to protest for a moment, then started to turn. A few more hands reached the wheel in time to speed her efforts.

When the hatch blew, the outrush of air knocked Metasmith back at a dangerous velocity. But the woman swung in a leisurely arc, letting her strongline run out to its full length. She executed a perfect landing on the far side of the cargo bay bulkhead, as pretty as zero-gee ballet.

Frick pressed his audio probe back against the bulkhead. It shrieked with the familiar wail of decompression, but the engineer's sharp ears still detected the soprano ringing of a travelling hullalloy fissure.

The *Lynx* was still breaking.

He shut his eyes and listened carefully, praying. Then it came – the sound was changing. The ringing seemed to gradually recede, lessening as the stresses of unequal pressure drained away through the open hatchway.

Frick opened his eyes, sighing with relief.

Now he could actually see the damage in front of him. The crack traveled past him, missing his own tether ring by a few centimeters. He stuck his suited finger into the fissure. It was less than four centimeters deep. And there was no notable vibration trembling within it.

The ship's hullalloy had an immune system, nanomachines that should fight off the Rix virus, but it might take a while for the infection to be completely eliminated. What the ship needed was a respite from the stresses of high gee and sudden jolts, but for the moment, the *Lynx* had stabilized.

At least until the captain decided to break her again.

Engineer-Rating

Engineer-Rating Telmore Bigz blinked his eyes again, hoping sight would return.

Bigz knew he was lucky to be alive at all. By rights, his head should be smeared across the Legis system by now. Pure chance had saved him. As he'd been torn from the bulkhead wall, his face mask must have been whipped around so that it had sealed itself. Either that, or Bigz had done so with some autonomic part of his brain whose actions were not recorded in memory.

But in the seconds of hard vacuum, his eyes must have bugged bad. He could see a sort of blurry streak before him, and that was all.

From the screaming in his head, Bigz figured that his eardrums had blown too. But that didn't bother him much. Out here in the airless void, sound was not a native species. And with communications forbidden, he wouldn't be talking to anyone on his suit radio.

But Bigz wished that he could *see*.

At least then he could figure out why he'd been plucked from the bulkhead. Bigz was positive that he'd been clipped right. Any shock strong enough to break his monofilament line should have snapped him in two like a breadstick.

He concentrated on the blurry streak. It pulsed every few seconds, a building-top blinker seen through a rain-soaked window.

Bigz judged the period to be about four seconds. A pressure suit emergency beacon pulsed once per second, so it wasn't a crew mate out there.

Then the rating understood. The pulsing light was the Legis sun, and Telmore Bigz was spinning, rotating once every four seconds.

He waited some more, and found that his sight seemed to be gradually coming back. There were other pulsing things, all with the same four-second period. They slowly resolved into streaks of light.

Stars. He could almost see the sun now, a distant but sharp disk against the black void.

Bigz felt strangely euphoric. The screaming headache that he should be suffering was absent, the pants-pissing fear he expected to feel had also not materialized. He carefully checked the medical charges on his utility belt.

He grunted with recognition as his fingers found the expended shockpack. Whatever lizard part of his brain had managed to seal his face mask had also pumped him full of painkiller and stimulants. He was alone in the vacuum, spinning out of control, half-blind and completely deafened, but Bigz felt as sharp and confident as a man after his first cup of coffee in the morning.

The engineer-rating smiled happily as his vision cleared.

The sun was obvious now, the brightest light among the stars. And Bigz could see two of the system's orange-tinted gas giants.

What he couldn't see was the *Lynx*. The darkened frigate must be pretty far away, and inertia would only carry him farther. Fortunately, in another few minutes – once he and the ship were out of the range of the Rix big guns – Bigz could pull his emergency beacon.

Then he would be rescued. No problem.

Bigz decided that he'd had enough of spinning. He pulled

the reaction canister from his belt and calculated the correct angle, then let off a quick spurt. The spinning slowed, the stars now twirling at the stately speed of a rink full of skaters. He could live with that.

Engineer-Rating Bigz now saw a tether strongline flailing about him. It had been rotating with him, but now that his spin had stopped it was wrapping itself around Bigz. He let it wind around his waist until he could grab the end.

The clip was still in the ring. The ringmount must have been pulled clean out of the hullalloy. That was bad. That meant that the *Lynx* had serious structural damage: a travelling fissure in a bulkhead, a bulkhead that was now exterior hull.

But at least, Bigz thought happily, he hadn't clipped himself wrong. Being out here in space wasn't *his* fault.

Then he saw something else. Another object in the void.

It was very distant, at the edge of his still blurry vision. The shape was dark, its edges glimmering. It seemed circular, unlike the long, thin *Lynx*. But perhaps he was seeing the ship head-on. That made sense. He'd been blown out the frigate's bow.

Might as well get closer to home, Bigz thought. If the ship were badly damaged (as it surely was) it would be far easier to rescue a loose crewman if he stayed nearby.

Bigz angled his reaction canister again, and let loose a long spray. He watched the object carefully for a count of twenty. Yes, he was getting closer now. He could see smooth metal facets now. It wasn't a huge and distant planetoid fooling his eyes. It was artificial.

It must be the *Lynx*.

Rating Telmore Bigz sprayed again, smiling.

He was going home.

Executive Officer

ExO Hobbes rappelled down the last corridor before the cargo bay bulkhead, the wind of depressurization serving as gravity. She clipped her belt to a nearby ring before ordering her strongline grapple to release and follow.

The outrush of air was slackening, but she didn't trust the respite. It had lessened once before, then increased again suddenly, as if various breaches were blowing in turn. The last truly stable bulkhead she'd seen was the one at the forward gunnery station.

She checked her pressure gauge. It showed near-vacuum. That was a bad sign, but at least with hardly any air left in this segment of the *Lynx*, there couldn't be another decompression.

Hobbes turned and saw the cargo bay hatch before her, one jump away. It was open.

She reattached her grapple and jumped, letting out strongline as she neared the hatchway. She swallowed nervously, hoping she'd find Frick and his team alive in the cargo bay.

Although she had prepared herself for the worst – strewn bodies among the ravages of the loose armor – when Hobbes reached the hatchway and peered through, she couldn't believe her eyes.

It was blackness . . . with stars.

There was no cargo bay.

Katherie pulled herself through, aghast at the huge rent before her, a cracked dome open to the sky.

A hand grabbed her shoulder.

'Executive Officer?' came the surprised voice through the suit's audio contacts.

Hobbes turned to see an engineer-rating. The woman seemed healthy and unpanicked, the athletic lines of her body obvious in the pressure suit.

The rating made a hand signal, and Hobbes turned to follow her eyes.

The whole engineering team seemed to be out here, huddled against the bulkhead. She breathed a sigh of relief.

A suited figure moved toward her – Watson Frick, the first engineer.

They connected their audio contacts.

'What the devil does Zai think he's doing?' the engineer spat.

'We had to accelerate, Frick,' she explained. 'The Rix spotted our coldjet reaction mass; they were about to backtrack it to us.'

'But why with a jolt like that? *I lost a crewman!*'

The first engineer's eyes sparkled with tears as he shouted, his hands grasping her shoulders. For a moment, Hobbes thought she might have to fend off another physical attack, but the man forced himself under control.

'You used the deadman drone launcher, didn't you?' he said.

She nodded.

'We needed a mechanical acceleration, one as strong as possible, and to use a solid object as reaction mass. If we spread another cloud of water, the Rix could have found us again. They used lasers to spot the ice crystals, and extrapolated back to the *Lynx*.'

Frick thought for a moment, then swore, agreeing with a mean, sharp nod.

'But we didn't expect the cargo-bay exterior to go,' Hobbes said.

Frick shook his head. 'It shouldn't have. But there were hairline fissures, virus trails. We were probably infected in the flocker attack. This bulkhead here,' he indicated what had been the cargo bay floor, 'is cavitating as well.'

Hobbes nodded. They'd had less than twenty minutes to catalog all the flocker damage. One of the projectiles must have left metaleating nanos.

'So that's why you opened this hatch,' she said.

Frick nodded. 'It was either a slow leak or another breakout. If we'd had an uncontrolled decompression, we might have lost the gunnery station bulkhead as well, and so on all along the ship.'

Katherie Hobbes swallowed, envisioning one bulkhead blowing after another, like the legendary *Titanic* filling with water.

Her eyes scanned the bulkhead, and saw the cracks that had coursed across its surface, fanning out in a wedge, a river delta seen from space.

'Frick, can she handle another turn?'

'Another *what*?'

'The captain has to yaw the ship again, to bring us back head-on with the Rix.'

'Good god,' said Frick.

Hobbes checked the mechanical timepiece on her wrist. It had continued to function even in hard vacuum.

'The pilots should be pulling us back in forty-three seconds,' she said. 'But only at a twentieth of a gee, as per your message.'

'No! It's too hard!' Frick cried. 'Point-oh-five yaw at the centerline is much stronger out here.'

Hobbes shook her head in confusion. What was Frick babbling about?

'Did you ever ride the whip?' he asked.

Hobbes frowned. She remembered the game, a risky zerogee maneuver reinvented by each successive class at the academy. A long line of recruits holding hands, getting up spin in the big zerogym on the academy orbital. In the middle, you were hardly moving, but you could feel the line's mass pulling harder and harder in both directions. And at either end, cadets were flying at unbelievable speed. When the line disintegrated, they'd hit the wall as if shot out of a cannon. The game eventually ended with a few cracked collarbones or a fractured skull, and would be strictly forbidden until the next year rediscovered its pleasures.

The executive officer stared wide-eyed at the cracked hullalloy.

'What's going to happen, Frick?'

The first engineer stared at the cracks, then closed his eyes, his lips moving as if talking himself through some complex equation. He pushed out from the bulkhead to look over its entirety.

Hobbes checked Captain Zai's chronometer. Only twenty-eight seconds before the third acceleration was scheduled. Surely Zai knew that the cargo bay had ruptured. The ejected metal and oxygen traveling away from the ship would have been picked up even by passive sensors.

But he wouldn't know that the structural damage extended to another layer of bulkhead. With the *Lynx* in darkmode, the distributed internal sensors were offline. The bridge crew was blind to the fissures. And who knew how far the virus extended? It was possible that all the frigate's bulkheads were infected.

Would Zai stick to the schedule they had agreed upon?

Twenty seconds.

She pushed herself after Frick, reattached her audio contact to his.

'First Engineer, report!'

The man opened his eyes.

'A yaw at that strength will tear the bow off the *Lynx*,' he said flatly. 'We'll lose it all, back as far as the forward gunnery station at least. Maybe farther.'

'Maybe the rest of the way?' Hobbes asked.

He nodded.

Hobbes didn't hesitate. There wasn't time to think. She had to contravene the foremost rule of this engagement. This was why Zai had sent her up here: she was the only officer who would break the captain's orders if necessary.

And it was absolutely necessary.

ExO Hobbes pulled the handheld communicator from her belt and activated it. If the Rix spotted the faint signal, so be it.

To hell with them. The *Lynx* was less than two minutes from safety.

'Priority, priority,' she said. 'Do not coldjet. We'll break up. *Do not accelerate* at all. Hobbes out.'

Then she flicked the device off.

The first engineer looked at her. She ignored his appalled expression.

'We're stabilized out here. Put your team in damage control positions.'

For a moment, he didn't move. He couldn't believe she'd broken the captain's orders.

'I'll spell it out for you, Frick: move yourself and your people inside.'

She yanked her tether, pulling them both toward the hatch.

'We may come under fire soon,' she added. Indeed, they almost certainly would.

Katherie Hobbes had made sure of that.

Engineer-Rating

The closer he approached the object, the less likely it seemed that Telmore Bigz had found the *Lynx*.

His vision continued to recover. Bigz could see now that the object wasn't entirely coherent. It seemed to be an agglomeration of large pieces, a few of which pulsed with their own rotation as the whole assemblage swung around itself. It couldn't be the frigate, unless tremendous damage had been done to her.

If Bigz were really going home, home had been blown to pieces.

He blinked again, trying to will his eyes back to clarity. He scanned the void, looking hopefully for a sign of the frigate nearby.

There was nothing.

Of course, even if he spotted the *Lynx*, there wasn't much he could do about it. Bigz's reaction canister was two-thirds empty – not enough juice in the can to jet off in a new direction.

He was committed to this wreckage.

A little closer, Bigz realized what the objects were.

He could see a ragged metal disk at the center of the assemblage, and a few large pieces of hullalloy around it. The whole thing was surrounded by a faint haze of frozen nitrox.

The largest object was the front of the *Lynx*, the cargo bay section that had blown out along with the loose armor plates and a certain engineer-rating.

Bigz whistled. The catastrophe that had hurtled him from the ship had been much bigger than he'd thought. He'd suspected a ten-meter wide hole – at most – causing decompression strong enough to suck him through it. But this was major damage. He wondered if any other giant chunks of the *Lynx* were floating free. If the whole ship were in pieces, rescue wouldn't be coming anytime soon.

As he approached, Bigz's hurting eyes scanned the debris for a beacon pulse. Perhaps there were other survivors here. Full emergency transmissions weren't allowed – they would draw Rix fire – but someone might have activated their blinker without the radio transmitter. He swept his wrist light through the haze, probing the dark metal. Nothing. Even with the stimulant still pushing happiness through his veins, his heart sank. He was alone.

There were no corpses, at least.

Bigz used up a bit more reaction mass to slow himself. He landed with a thunk on one of the pieces of shielding that the team had cut from the singularity generator. His suit magnets held, and the collision didn't set the massive shield spinning too violently.

He stared at the chunk of bow bulkhead a dozen meters away, trying to imagine what the cargo bay would look like now. Fortunately, the engineering team had been tethered to the floor side. If they'd been attached to the plates, they'd all be out here. As it was most of them would still be with the *Lynx* – it was a fluke that Bigz's ring had popped. Unless, of course, the cargo floor bulkhead had given way too.

No, that didn't make sense. If that had happened, the frigate would be all over the place, and Telmore Bigz would have been flying along with a lot of debris, nitrox, and other crewmen. Apparently, only he had been tossed from the ship.

He was alone, master of this tiny domain.

Suddenly, Bigz heard a message, a transmission pumped past his ruined ears into second hearing.

'*Priority, priority,*' came a clear voice.

Shit! he thought. Who the hell was broadcasting? The Rix would localize the transmission in no time.

'*Do not coldjet. We'll break up. Do not accelerate at all. Hobbes out.*'

The ExO? Didn't she realize that she was jeopardizing the ship?

Bigz brought up his suit's line-of-sight receiver, trying to determine where the transmission had come from. The device gave him a general direction, and he squinted into the blackness, searching for the *Lynx*.

But his eyes still failed him. The frigate was nowhere to be seen.

He squatted on the slowly spinning shield, hoping that the Rix hadn't heard the transmission. He decided to count while he waited, marking the minutes until they would all be out of danger.

Captain

'Enemy pulse fire has ceased,' the sensor officer reported.

Captain Laurent Zai swallowed. The Rix laser had been firing at a high rate, searching for traces of coldjet reaction mass. But now they had stopped looking.

The enemy had heard Hobbes's message.

'They must be charging up, sir.'

'Indeed.'

The firing rate of the Rix ranging laser was variable. It could be fired several times a second at low power, or more infrequently with greater effect. If they had given up pulse fire, then the Rix knew where the *Lynx* was. They were preparing a high-intensity punch, one sufficient to light up the Imperial frigate so that they could track her the rest of the way.

Once the frigate was glowing from a laser hit, the Rix gravity weapons would begin the work of destroying her.

At least ten seconds' charge for the first shot, he guessed.

Zai braced himself.

The big flatscreen flashed, lighting up the bridge as if a flare had bounded into the room.

'A miss, sir. A hundred meters off.'

Zai nodded. The Rix were off by ten meters per second squared, roughly the push the *Lynx* had managed with the drone launcher. That kick had pushed her hard, enough to throw Zai out of his shipmaster's chair. And perhaps the loss of the cargo bay had resulted in a few more precious meters per second.

'We've got to turn her, sir!' the First Pilot shouted. 'We're broadside!'

'Keep us floating, Pilot,' he commanded.

If they could turn back to head-on orientation, they'd be a smaller target. But Katherie Hobbes had said another burst from the jets would break the *Lynx* up. Zai had to believe her. Hobbes wouldn't have given away their position unless she spoke with absolute certainty.

So Zai had been forced into a dire bet – that the Rix warship would miss them just a few more times. They were almost out of range.

So close to safety.

According to the bridge chronometer, they only had to survive another ninety seconds and they would drift out of the gravity cannon's perimeter. By their very nature, chaotic gravitons were far less coherent than photons. The *Lynx* was receding from the battlecruiser at more than 3,000 klicks per second. Under fixed physical laws, the frigate would soon be out of range.

Once they reached safety, Zai could bring internal diagnostics online and find out for himself how hard to push his ship.

Fifteen more seconds passed, enough time for the enemy to charge another burst.

The silent flash came on schedule.

'Another miss, sir! Two hundred meters aft.'

'Unbelievable,' Zai whispered. It had fallen on the other side of the first miss. They were overshooting!

Luck had smiled on the *Lynx* again.

Captain Zai leaned back, releasing his white-knuckled grip on his command chair. He sighed with relief.

'We may have made it,' he said.

Ten seconds later, a shudder rocked through the bridge, and the high-pitched scream of boiling air filled the ship.

Engineer-Rating

Telmore Bigz could see the *Lynx* now.

The frigate sparkled against the black of space, the red light of laser fire running up and down its length.

'No!' he cried.

It was at least twenty kilometers away, glowing like an emergency light wand. The frigate's spindly shape seared itself into his vision, like a sun glimpsed with naked eyes. Bigz realized that his vision had finally cleared. Just in time to witness his ship and crewmates dying.

He wished that he were still blind.

Damn! They had almost made it out of range. By Bigz's reckoning, they would be out of the gravity cannon's perimeter in less than a minute.

The engineer-rating looked at the debris around him. It spun alone in the void, the forehull a minor planet with its own satellites, its own hazy atmosphere, even a population of one: Telmore Bigz.

Soon, this lost scrap heap would be all that remained of the *Lynx*.

A few more sparkles erupted from the frigate over the next seconds. The chaotic gravity beam would be orienting now, marshaling its full power for a final shot, using the laser damage to aim. The Rix might only get one blast before the

Imperial warship passed out of range, so they would make sure they had it right.

Bigz squeezed the shockpack on his belt, the last dregs of stimulants giving him a moment of confidence for his decision. There was only one thing to do.

He activated his emergency beacon at full strength, its pulsing light reflecting from the rotating armor plates around him. Then Bigz brought his engineer's torch online, and charged it to hullalloy-cutting temperatures. He aimed it at the armor below him and pulled the trigger.

Light and heat flared from the cutter, and the armor burned a bright white where he swept its flame.

Bigz was now the sun for his tiny system, an unstable star casting hard, flickering shadows on the spinning debris around him.

Glowing bright in the void.

Captain

'Keep us dark!' Zai shouted over the din.

'But they have us, sir! We're already lit up like a firewire!'

'Just wait!' Zai yelled. 'In another twenty seconds, they can't touch us.'

The damage control officer was finally silent. The man had wanted to reactivate the ship's internal sensors, to help coordinate repair efforts. True, the Rix already knew exactly where the *Lynx* was. But emissions from the internals would give the enemy the frigate's orientation, and they'd target the drive; the *Lynx* would be crippled. Some part of the *Lynx* was certainly going to fry, but there was no sense giving the Rix their choice as to which.

'Steady. At most they can hit us twice at full power,' Zai said.

'Damage reports starting to come in from the aft compoint, sir,' someone reported. The epicenter of the laser hit.

'Report.'

'No structural damage. The aft processor shaft looks fused. Ten dead and counting.'

Damn, Zai thought. More casualties, and more processor capacity lost. All from a range-finding laser. When the burst of chaotic gravity came, it would be hell.

'How long until we're safe?' he asked the ensign at the chronometer.

'Twelve,' she said.

'Count it,' he ordered.

The bridge grew silent as the numbers diminished. There was nothing any of them could do. A gravity beam worked its deadliest magic against the crew of its target: snapped spines, crushed brains, ruptured internal organs. Without an energy sink to deflect the Rix weapon, dozens, perhaps hundreds of their crewmates were about to die.

Zai couldn't even warn his crew, but at least he could address the bridge.

With five seconds left, he waved the ensign quiet.

But he found his tongue stymied. All the usual Vadan words invoked the Emperor, and that would be too ridiculous an epitaph for Laurent Zai.

'Thank you for your service,' was all he managed.

Zai sighed, waiting.

The time passed. It must have.

'The shot missed us,' the captain said quietly.

The sensor officer stared into his headsdown in disbelief.

'Not an accidental miss, sir. They changed their targeting. Attacked a debris field six kilometers away. Tore it to pieces.'

'But . . . *why?*' Zai stammered.

'It was lit up, sir. Some heat, microwaves, and a high-strength transmission.'

'Transmission?'

'An Imperial SOS. A personal beacon.'

Zai shook his head. It was too much to believe. A diversion, at the right moment. A member of the *Lynx*'s crew had some-how wound up out there, kilometers away, and had died for the ship. But who?

'They had us, sir,' the sensor officer continued. 'Why would they go for anything else? It was only a few sparks out there, relative to the hit they'd put on us.'

'We were too easy,' Zai said. 'Too obvious. Hobbes's trans-mission was too blatant. They must have thought that we were the decoy.'

A tremble began in the ship, a low moan that rose and fell.

'They're targeting us now, sir. Switched their fire from the debris to the *Lynx*. But we're outside effective range. The gravity cannon is at half-charge, wide aperture. Five thou-sand gravitons per.'

Zai sighed. Barely enough to give a man skin cancer. He could feel the weapon's passage with his sensitive inner ear, a mild nausea at worst.

'Give me internal diagnostics,' he ordered. 'And order the crew to remain in pressure suits.' The frigate was unstable, and the low-intensity chaotic gravity bombardment might continue for a while, growing ever more diffuse as the ships drifted apart.

Again, they had survived.

■ ■ ■ ■

TEN YEARS EARLIER (IMPERIAL ABSOLUTE)

House

Over many decades, the house had grown in all directions.

Though perched on a mountain peak, it extended deep enough into the mantle of Home to draw geothermal power. Now that summer had arrived, the views from six balconies revealed gardens and artificial waterfalls all the way to the horizon. The house had littered neighboring peaks with out-post colonies of self-sustaining butterflies, their mirror wings reflecting sunlight to keep plants alive and water flowing, cast artful shadows, and bring the pale reds of the arctic sunset to three hundred sixty degrees of vista. Its processors were every-where, buried in the rocky passages of the mountain, backed up in rented remote locations, distributed across the snows for a hundred kilometers. Between polar isolation, the sena-torial privilege of its mistress, and its vast size, the house was a world unto itself.

And yet a certain anxiety haunted the house today, a sense of inadequacy and self-doubt that ran like a subtle tremor through its teraflops. A new situation had arisen, one that it had considered and modeled for decades, but never experi-enced. For the first time, there were two people here at once.

The mistress had a guest.

The house scanned the underground food gardens, the special supplies brought in by suborbital for the lieutenant-commander's visit, the emergency stores that had lain untouched for a century. It tallied, of course, far more food than two people could eat in four years, much less four days. But the disquiet remained. This visit was the house's chance to show the mistress what it had accomplished over lonely decades of abandonment, to display the results of its long independent expansion program.

Dinner was already planned, the steamy growing levels just above the geothermal plant raided of produce for a tropical banquet. Fermented plantains had been basted with relish of green tamarind. Cabbage pickled and formed into delicate flower shapes, then flashfried in a microsecond plasma field. A species of brine shrimp that purified the house water supply simmered for hours in caramel. A pudding of sticky rice and palm sugar blackened with coconut ash to match the lieutenant-commander's naval uniform. And to clear the palate, twenty milliliters of vodka to end each course had been infused with lychee, rambutan, papaya, and mangosteen in turn.

But perhaps this was too much, the house now despaired. The rules of etiquette were clear: the last dinner of any visit should be the grandest, not the first. With Laurent Zai staying longer, it would have to outdo itself four more dinners in a row! And what if the mistress changed her mind again? No amount of processor power, no number of contingency plans, no acreage of machinery – nothing was sufficient to withstand human caprice at its worst.

What were they talking about now?

The house returned its attention to where the mistress stood with the newly promoted Captain Laurent Zai. They were on the western balcony, holding each other, looking out at a trio of small peaks capped with patterns of algae-reddened snow, just now struck with the slowly setting sun. (Quite a composition, the house thought smugly.) The mistress was still smiling from the kiss they'd shared after she had invited him to stay.

'Four days seems so little, Nara,' Zai said. (The house disagreed. Twelve meals to create; four sunsets to compose!)

'We can make them last.'

'I hope so.' His eyes fell to the garden of insect-shaped ice sculptures below. 'We've so many technologies for making Absolute time pass quickly. Stasis, relativistic travel, the symbiant. But none to make a few days seem longer.'

The mistress laughed. 'I'm sure we'll think of something.' She moved closer.

'You already have?'

'Yes, I have. Perhaps dinner can wait.'

The house followed their progress to the bedroom, mutely appalled.

Senator

As the summer's brief night fell across the room, Nara Oxham thought to herself: An entire day without apathy. It had been too long. She needed more of these respites from the capital, needed to set her mind completely free of the drug without the crowd coming in.

She looked at Laurent's dozing form. Perhaps she needed a measure of madness every now and then.

After the rush of the first few minutes, the effects of apathy withdrew gradually, Nara's empathy gaining in strength over the slow hours. Her ability had been active all day, moving and adjusting itself, slowly growing comfortable with the man next to her, settling across the pattern of his thoughts like a blanket of snow over one of the house gardens. Laurent seemed to have recovered his balance in the hours since telling her about Dhantu; she could feel his mind aligned by the sureties of his gray religion, his military discipline.

Although Laurent's touchstones sprang from convictions alien to Nara, there was comfort in anything that took away his pain.

Nara wondered if this was a good idea, letting herself bond so strongly with someone she hardly knew, who was by any measure a political enemy.

Who would be gone so soon, for so long.

Laurent stirred.

'A fire?' she asked.

They left the bed and opened up the north wall to the pink night sky and the arctic chill. Nara loved the high arctic summer. The sun hid behind the mountains but never lost its grasp on the horizon. She wondered what it would be like in half a year, when daylight rather than darkness lasted only one hour in ten.

They chose split, dry logs for the fire, building it high and hot enough to push them back a few meters, counterpoint to the chill night air on their backs.

When Laurent slipped away to maintain his prosthetics, Nara asked the house to salvage what it could of dinner and deliver it here. It responded a bit stiffly. Knowing that grays didn't approve of talking machines, Nara had ordered it to keep silent in Laurent's company. She wondered if the house's conversational package needed more practice than it was getting on her infrequent visits.

When Laurent returned, he was dressed. She wrapped herself in bedclothes.

After a silence, she felt his discomfort. He was unsure what to say. This moment always eventually came with new lovers, in those quiet moments between dramatic turns.

What would the pink senator and the gray soldier talk about?

No point in fighting the obvious.

'Do you really think there'll be another Incursion, Laurent?'

He shrugged, but she felt trouble in him. 'Until today, I had my doubts about the rumors. But this posting to Legis, right on the frontier . . .'

'Isn't most of the Navy on one frontier or another?'

'True. But I'm to take command of a new kind of warship.' He paused and looked at her. 'But that's classified, of course.' He smiled. 'You're not a Rix spy, are you?'

Nara laughed. 'Laurent, in a few weeks I'll be on the Intelligence Sub-Quorum of His Majesty's Senate. You'd better hope I'm not a Rix spy.'

His eyebrows shot up. 'You're on the oversight committee?'

Laurent's alarm flared in her empathy, and turned quickly into reflexive withdrawal. Nara could feel the revulsion that military culture held for civilian interference.

'If that's what you call it in the Navy, yes.'

He took a deep breath. 'Oh, I didn't realize.'

'Did you think Secularists never took an interest in the military?'

'An interest? Certainly. But not necessarily a positive one.'

'My interest is very positive, Laurent. The Emperor's military forces benefit from oversight by the living, I'm absolutely sure. We're the ones who do the dying for him, after all.'

He grimaced, the phantoms of his lost limbs twisting painfully, and she could almost hear his thoughts. What did she, a pink senator, know of dying?

'My assignment may come before the committee,' he said flatly. 'Perhaps we should restrict our conversation.'

Oxham blinked, marveling again at how politically naive military officers could be. Laurent hadn't even bothered to check her portfolio before coming. Her own handlers wouldn't let her attend so much as a cocktail party without memorizing a detailed history of every person on the guest list. After inviting him here, she'd researched Zai's commanders and former crew, his Academy standings, and had digested reams of Apparatus propaganda about the hero of Dhantu. She'd even dipped into the gutter media, the channels who called him the Broken Man.

Of course, that didn't mean she understood him. In all that detail Nara had missed one salient point: the length of his career in real years. After almost a century Absolute of serving the Emperor, decades passing at relativistic speeds, the man was tired of losing friends and lovers to the Time Thief. And now he would be gone for another twenty years at least.

He had every right to be angry. But not at her.

She put a hand on his arm and turned away to look into the fire. 'Laurent, I don't want to restrict anything we say to each other. And I don't care about the Emperor's secrets. I just asked because I want to know when you're coming back.'

He sighed. 'As do I.'

They were silent for a while, staring into the flames. Nara wondered why she had pressed him. He was probably right; they shouldn't be sharing classified information across the lines of political and military, democratic and Imperial, pink and gray. But somehow she needed to cross the boundaries of their alien hierarchies now, in these early days. Otherwise they never would.

She wanted to be trusted, even though she was a pink. Perhaps it was as simple as that.

Nara felt the change in him before he spoke. He wanted something too.

'I know you're not a spy, Nara. And I'm sure your committee will hear about it soon enough, so you should hear it from me. They've given me a new kind of ship. A frigate prototype.'

'Everyone knew you'd get a command, Laurent. A reward for your faithful service.'

'Perhaps. But any prototype wants battle-testing. They

wouldn't be sending a ship like the *Lynx* to the Rix frontier if there weren't some promise of action there.'

Nara nodded, feeling the certainty in him. And the dread. She was too young to have lived through the Incursion herself, but could always feel the icy memory of Rix terror attacks in those who had. Whole cities razed by gravity weapons. Planets reduced to pre-terraformation by bombardment from space. Even the gray places of the dead attacked, the bodies of the risen deliberately sundered beyond the ability of the symbiant to repair.

'It's a small, fast ship, with hitting power and range,' he continued. 'A deep raider, a way to strike back against the Rix.'

'I see,' she said softly, squeezing his non-prosthetic arm. 'That would mean going even farther outward, wouldn't it?'

Her empathy with Laurent remained strong; she felt him sifting thoughts so cold that she couldn't name them. What was he thinking? 'Ten more years out,' he said. 'Plus years of raiding, if it comes to war.'

'So you really meant it that you might be gone fifty years?'

'Yes. Fifty.'

An entire senator's term. Of course, with Nara in stasis most of the year, and Laurent's time frame stretched out by relativity, it might only be a decade subjective for them both. Still a vast separation, given that she'd hardly known him two days. (Why, she wondered, was it always most terrible being separated from someone you'd just met?)

'It's not only the years, Nara.'

'The fact that I'm a pink? That I'll be slashing your budget while you're at the front?'

He barely smiled. 'No. It's what I'll do out there.'

That gray Vadan charm again. 'Laurent, I can hardly expect fidelity.'

'I didn't mean . . . Nara, I'm talking about what I'll do as a soldier. What the *Lynx* is designed to do.'

'Make war? You've done that before. You served in the Dhantu Occupation, after all. I can't imagine anything worse.'

He turned to her, still full of blackness, and spoke with effort. 'I can.'

She quieted herself, letting her empathy work.

It was very small inside him, hard to see clearly. A dark place.

Then she found a way in, and it hit her. Worse than his memories of the tortures he'd suffered on Dhantu, more sovereign. It was a black abstraction, cold potential, like the mindnoise on a Vasthold street corner in the calm just before a political riot – the kind in which people would die. Nara Oxham's empathy recoiled, her head suddenly spinning, some animal part of her mind knowing ahead of the rest what her empathy would show.

But he kept talking.

'The *Lynx* is a deep raider, Nara. Long-range killing power, fast and expendable.'

Unbidden, true telepathy came, with a glimpse of what he imagined. Rolling satellite imagery: fields and rivers from space, the grid of a city coming into view.

'Against the Rix,' he continued, 'we won't be hitting shipping and logistical targets. The *Lynx is* made to do what we never managed in the First Incursion. To take the war to the Rix worlds.'

'Laurent . . .' This gray man knew the mechanics of it. He understood the horrific details of how it would be done.

'As they brought war to ours.'

'Stop.' As she said it, Nara's hand went to her wrist, searching for the apathy bracelet. But she'd taken it off when they'd arrived. She was defenseless against his thoughts.

In any event, he said it out loud.

'My ship is for killing worlds, Nara.'

She swallowed something acid, stood up and went onto

the balcony. The rail caught her hands, and she pulled herself up from stumbling. Breathed deeply.

The cold cleared her head. This helplessness was absurd. 'House.'

'Yes, mistress?' it whispered in private second hearing.

'Get me my bracelet. Priority.'

'Done.'

Laurent was beside her. 'Nara? I'm sorry. You would have heard anyway.'

'It's just withdrawal. From my counter-empathy drug.'

'I'm sorry.' He held her, pressed close to warm her. She could hardly feel the dark thing in him now. Godspite, where did he hide it?

'It's nothing, Laurent. It happens sometimes when I come out here. In the capital, I have to take it for the crowds. But here I forget.'

He sighed. 'I understand.' He knew she was lying.

'Laurent . . .'

'Yes?'

She saw something moving. A house serving drone, skittering down the handrail, clutching her apathy bracelet. She took another deep breath, her panic receding at the sight of it.

'Will you do it?' Nara reached out and took the bracelet from the drone.

Laurent clutched her shoulder, and she tasted his struggle, the fight against his conditioning, his upbringing, his own gray soul, against a planetary landscape rolling beneath him, virgin and defenseless.

'I hope not,' he said.

Her fingers closed around the bracelet, and the drone backed away. But Nara didn't activate the flow of apathy yet.

'Don't,' she asked.

He looked behind him, as if the Emperor might be listening from the bedroom. But it was just more servos, a small army of them arranging things in front of the fire. In the flickering light, they looked like mad insects building a miniature city.

Laurent Zai nodded quietly and whispered, 'All right. I won't. I promise you.'

Four days to make promises, he had said an hour ago.

Nara slipped the bracelet onto her wrist unused, and swallowed. Godspite, her mouth was dry.

'Dinner, then?' she said.

6

ALCHEMICAL

Above all, a soldier must be willing to die.

– ANONYMOUS 167

Commando

The second rendezvous went considerably better. H_rd successfully jumped from the recon flyer to the dirigible, and over a few hours it lifted her to approximately eighty kilometers altitude.

The commando looked down over the entanglement facility. From this height, it was smaller than a palm at arm's length. The dirigible's vacuum sphere had quadrupled in size during the slow ascent. H_rd pressed her face to a rebreather tank. The decline in pressure during the ascent had been considerable; her ears were ringing, and she'd felt a blood vessel burst in one eye after an hour of climbing. A Rix commando could take a wide variation of air pressure, but this was the lowest she'd experienced since hull-breach training. There was no weather up here in the mesopause, but it was unbelievably cold. The ablative suit — recovered, like the rebreather, from a supersonic aircraft emergency store — was insulated enough to keep her from freezing. H_rd found, however, that she missed her sable coat.

Well, she would be warmed up soon enough.

The positioning device in her hand beeped, Alexander's signal to her. It was almost time to drop. The entanglement facility seemed off-center to her, but the compound mind had carefully calculated the wind direction and speed.

With a strangely unRix thought, h_rd hoped that Alexander hadn't made any mistakes.

She had to hit an area roughly ten meters across, after a fall that would take more than twenty minutes. Alexander had used its weather satellites to find the snowdrift, which filled a thirty-meter deep glacial rift inside the array's defensive wire. The compound mind had introduced a few nanos disguised as snowflakes into its cloud-seeding efforts. These had fallen into the drift and doped the snow. Over the last few days, the nano colony had changed the structure of the ice crystals, expanding the drift, leaching carbon from the soil for structure, and creating a colloidal foam that would compress smoothly when h_rd struck it. The snow had swelled up into a hill that rose ten meters above the surrounding landscape. Thus, h_rd's fall would be broken gradually over almost forty meters.

Of course, she had to hit the trench dead center. She held the positioning device firmly in her free hand; it would guide her to the target area.

H_rd prepared herself, swallowing to adjust the pressure in her ears. She checked the straps of her mission pack.

Then the dirigible motors cut. The signal to drop.

She unlocked the muscles in her hand that clung to the dirigible's payload basket, and slipped into the void.

Weightless again. Freefall was an old friend.

The rush of air built slowly, worsening the cold on the unprotected parts of her face.

Her ablative suit was designed to fight fires onboard aircraft. A few nanos – programmed by Alexander and delivered through a medical pack – had altered it sufficiently to make it invisible to Imperial radar.

Or so Alexander's models predicted.

She rolled into a ball, protecting the positioning device and watching its numbers move. The altimeter showed her to be still accelerating. Terminal velocity for a human was about sixty meters per second on Legis. As close as h_rd could estimate by the rolling altimeter, her speed had passed that. Probably the air up here was thin enough that terminal velocity was noticeably higher, and she would actually be braking as she descended into higher pressures.

After five minutes of falling, warmth began to bloom in the suit. It grimly crossed her mind that she was heating up from reentry friction. But h_rd dismissed the thought; she couldn't be going that fast. The temperature increase was just the heat trap of the stratopause. After ten minutes total of falling, the air gradually began to grow cold again. She was passing through the stratosphere, approaching the cold air of the tropopause.

Extending her arms slowly, h_rd began to take control of the descent, slowing herself and angling toward the entanglement facility, now as big as a dinner plate below her. She swallowed constantly to keep her ears clear, and watched the numbers on the positioning device roll as she angled her free hand and legs to guide her fall. Her coordinates seemed only incrementally closer to the target. Of course, she was a few minutes from entering the tropospheric wind currents that would push her toward the target snow drift.

H_rd had low-orbit jumped once in training, but that was with a purpose-built Rix suit, parafoil, and artificial-gravity backup. The situation was somewhat different when wearing a retrofitted, improvised Imperial suit and landing in a pile of snow. It wasn't the equipment that had her nervous, though.

She had faced death at every stage of this mission. It was nothing short of fantastic that she had survived this long. But h_rd had realized during these relatively quiet minutes of freefall that Rana Harter had stolen some of her courage. H_rd found that she wanted to live, a strange desire for a Rix commando.

Perfect, she thought. To encounter fear for the first time while falling – at sixty meters per second and without a parachute – into a heavily guarded enemy facility.

'Love,' h_rd said bitterly. The rampant wind tore the word from her mouth without comment.

After fifteen minutes had elapsed, the longitude and latitude on the positioning device began slowly moving toward the target values; the tropospheric wind was pushing her toward the landing area. And it was getting warmer again, moving toward the merely freezing temperatures of the polar surface.

The entanglement facility was now visibly increasing in size from moment to moment. The sensation of falling became less abstract; h_rd finally *saw* the ground rushing toward her. She extended hands and feet and angled her body, swooping to bring herself closer to the target area. The positioning device finally beeped; she had matched the snowdrift's coordinates.

The commando could see it below her now, the winding, snowfilled rift reflecting starlight with pale luminescence. From aerial photographs supplied by Alexander, h_rd had memorized the exact spot she needed to hit. She tucked the positioning device into her pack and began counting down.

The altimeter read 6,000 meters. A hundred seconds to go.

She swallowed fiercely now as air pressure built, cupping her hands to guide herself gently to the target over these last few moments. Invoked by a mental command, her body went through an impact preparation sequence. She expelled the air from her lungs completely, let her muscles relax, rebalanced the ratio of strength and flexibility in her plastic ligaments to favor the latter.

By the time her internal count had reached eight seconds, h_rd was physiologically ready for impact. The deepest part of the trench lay directly below her, no farther than looking down from the top of a medium-sized building. At half a kilometer and falling, details on the ground gained focus rapidly. Rocks and a few scrub bushes became visible, and the moiré weave of a retransmitter dish's arc scintillated in one corner of her vision.

After twenty minutes of falling, it was odd how quickly the snowbound earth was rushing up at her.

Five, four, three . . .

The surface of the altered snow broke with a *pop* as she crashed through. She later realized that a thin layer of frost had formed over the nano-doped snow. This brittle crust of rime was at most a centimeter thick – and probably couldn't have supported more than a few grams of weight. But at sixty meters per second it packed a punch. Like the surface of water at high speed, it had for a moment the force of concrete. The impact broke h_rd's nose and split her lower lip, and opened a bleeding cut over her right eye.

But then she passed into the colloidal pseudo-snow, which caught her in its foamy arms, slowing her descent. The Rixwoman came smoothly to a stop.

She opened her eyes in total darkness, her head ringing from the impact of breaking the crust. Testing each muscle and joint in turn, she found herself to be uninjured except for the insults to her face. She sat up, orienting herself in the darkness of the cold, compressed foam-snow around her, and looked upwards.

The sky was just visible through the twenty-meter-deep hole she had made. Her own outline, almost comically exact, showed for a few moments before the foam-snow began to collapse, covering her. H_rd breathed deeply and fast, storing oxygen before she was enveloped by the foam. She would remain here motionless for thirty minutes or so. The impact shock of her landing would have registered on the facility's motion sensors, but if she stayed still, the snow-muffled, momentary vibration would read as simply a cleaving of the snowdrift: an event well within the natural stochastic rumblings of the arctic wild.

The darkness covered her. After the rushing air, especially the frigid layer of the tropopause, the foam-snow brought a blanket of warmth. H_rd felt blood dripping into her eye from her cut, and tended to her wounds as she waited. That brittle crust of ice represented a small error in Alexander's plan, she noted to herself, the sort of hairline mistake that was magnified a thousandfold in a mission of this difficulty.

No system, not even a compound mind, was perfect. A very unRix thought, but true.

After she'd waited the requisite time, the commando began to tunnel out of the drift. She kept an eye on the positioning device, not trusting her own magnetoreceptor direction-finding cells this close to the pole. Her oxygen reserve was limited, and any wrong turn that led her into an unclimbable wall could be deadly. It would be rather banal to drown in this foam after surviving an eighty-kilometer fall.

The nano-doped snow was strange stuff. In the readout light of the positioning device, she could see the tiny bubbles that made it up, composed of water structured by large carbon molecules. The substance seemed dry when touched gently, but under shock it disintegrated into a wet, somewhat slimy substance. In her hand the bubbles broke down quickly into water; even her low body temperature was sufficient to disrupt its stability. When the warm winds of spring came, all evidence of how this trick had been performed would be gone forever.

H_rd reached the edge of the foam, and climbed from the trench into a drift of real snow. She raised a periscope through the crust first, and surveyed the area. There was no sign of an Imperial response to her landing. She pulled herself from the drift and dusted snow and foam from her. The ablative suit had torn on impact, and a few icy trickles of water already numbed her feet.

The Rixwoman crawled away from the landing zone, careful to keep her distance from the area of doped snow. Anyone stepping on that part of the drift would plummet to the bottom of the trench, softly but ignominiously. There were also vibration sensors to be wary of. H_rd moved slowly and haltingly, an uneven motion designed to mimic natural processes.

The commando searched the horizon for the telltale glimmer of microwave arrays. The threads of the off-line repeaters glowed like spiderwebs all around her, the nearest thirty meters away. With her painstakingly slow and interrupted crawl, it took h_rd five minutes to traverse the distance.

The main portion of the device was roughly the size of a fist. From this central mass radiated the microwave receiver array, the slender filaments that gathered the civilian communications of Legis bound for translight transmission. The transmitter stick rose from the center of the fist, a decimeterhigh antenna that forwarded the data to the entanglement facility.

The repeater also sported four legs and two manipulator arms. The hordes of them that dotted the tundra functioned as a single entity. They moved slowly, but quickly enough to disperse or gather themselves as their throughput required. The whole system was distributed over thousands of square kilometers, making it difficult to sabotage and impossible to destroy from space without megatons of explosives. These repeaters were a hardy system, a wartime backup to the vulnerable hardlines, meter-wide cables through which the data usually flowed. Once the Imperials had realized that the compound mind had successfully propagated, they had isolated the facility. The repeaters had been taken off-line by hand: hundreds of militia workers moving through the snow on foot and disconnecting the repeaters individually. The facility's input had been reduced to a single hardline connection, a low-bandwidth coupling that the military tightly controlled. Alexander was cut off.

The Imperials assumed that any measure undertaken by hundreds of humans by hand would be irreversible without similarly crude measures. But Alexander had other ideas.

H_rd looked at the repeater closely. Its power pack seemed out of alignment, tilted to one side at an angle of about fifteen degrees. She refocused her eyes into their microscopic mode, and noted the simple measure the Imperials had taken. The receivers were still working, still sucking up the vast quantity of data that Legis produced, but the repeater was physically disconnected from its power supply. Tilted those few degrees, the pack was disjunct from its contact, thus all off-planet transmissions were halted here, a few kilometers from their goal.

H_rd approved of the awesome simplicity of it. The thing actually functioned like some pre-spaceflight *switch*. Again, the crudeness of the Imperials impelled a certain grudging respect from the Rixwoman.

With her smallest finger, she clicked the power pack back into the correct position. That was it. The lethal wire and two thousand kilometers of wilderness protected nothing but this simple switch.

Her mission was complete.

She crawled slowly back to the edge of the landing zone and buried herself in a few decimeters of the snow-foam, leaving only a breathing hole. She would wait here for a few more hours before making her rather noisy escape.

Before covering her head, h_rd looked back and saw that the repeater she had fixed was already moving, making its beetlelike way across the snow.

Alexander was inside the wire.

Senator

It was good to be back in the halls of the Senate Forum. The air seemed to be cleaner here, the wash of politics more pure.

The Senate was an unruly chamber, of course, more so now that the special war session was in full swing. But the numberless details of the Senate's agenda balanced each other, blending into a shape as smooth as the rumble of a distant ocean. The noisy debates here were a relief for Nara Oxham after the demands of the War Council, where each crisis came into absolute focus, and lives were in play with every vote.

'You were right, Niles,' she said as they walked together back toward her offices. Oxham had just presented the last few days of the council's work to the full Senate.

'I knew they'd love you, Senator. Even the lackeys were standing by the end.'

'Not about that, Niles,' she said, waving away his praise. The speech had gone well, though. Captain Laurent Zai had made them all look brilliant. The *Lynx*'s attack on the Rix battlecruiser had given the Empire its first victory, a gift to the propaganda effort. Counterattacks in an interstellar war could take years to mount, time spans over which even the most resolute society's morale could falter. But Zai had struck back against the Rix in a matter of days.

'In any case, I have my speechwriters to thank for that.'

Niles began a sputter of protest at this.

'I was referring, in any case,' she interrupted, 'to when you cautioned me about losing my way in the council. Forgetting why we came here. You were right to warn me.'

'Senator,' the old man said, 'I never thought that was a likelihood. I just had to say something. I get paid to advise you.'

Nara smiled at her counselor's clumsy modesty. The world seemed bright to her today. She'd played the Senate like some Secularist street gathering back on Vasthold, pulled the bright tracery of their emotions through the courses that Niles's speech had mapped out for her. The moment in which she'd captured them had come early, the critical juncture when she could feel their agreement with the council's war plan coalescing, reacting to her words like a flock of birds turning in unison.

The sharp flavor of the captive crowd still lingered in her mind, and Nara savored the way it blended with the sunlight penetrating the high windows along the Forum great hall. But the pleasures of politics were trifles compared to the real source of her joy.

Laurent Zai had survived, escaping death again.

Of course, only a handful knew that his success in battle had saved an entire world. It seemed fantastic now that the War Council had contemplated something so monstrous. She wondered what the two living counselors who had voted for the Emperor's plan had felt as the hour of genocide had approached.

To Senator Nara Oxham, it seemed that she had emerged from the crisis with far more power on the War Council. She'd been the first to vote against the plan, so her voice was now second only to the Emperor's. The once unanimous council was beginning to develop fault lines, the living against the dead, Senator Oxham against the sovereign. The Emperor hadn't lost a vote yet, but Oxham could see him steering away from ideas when she voiced opposition to them, reluctant to force any issue that she might raise a majority against.

But the majority was there, silent and waiting to assert itself against any future genocides.

In his mind-reading way, Niles interrupted her thoughts.

'But if you want some more advice?'

'Earn your keep, Roger.'

He waited another moment, until they had crossed the threshold of Nara Oxham's private domain. Her offices had been almost doubled in size to match her new council rank, the ever-mobile walls of the Forum pushing against the surrounding senators' territories, a fat man jostling his way onto an elevator. They walked past a score of staff, half of whose names she didn't know yet.

When they reached Oxham's personal office, Niles continued.

'You are restricted by the hundred-year rule, of course.'

Nara nodded warily. She'd explained to Niles why she couldn't discuss the council's contingency plan if the *Lynx* had failed. He was allowed to know of the rule's invocation, but mention of the forbidden topic still made her vaguely nervous.

'But *I'm* not restricted,' he continued. 'I can make suppositions, and give you advice. Let me talk, but don't confirm or deny anything.'

'Is this a good idea, Roger?'

'Nothing in the rule says you can't listen to me, Senator.'

She nodded slowly.

'One: you're happy, Nara Oxham. Because your lover survived, because the war took a good turn. But my guess is that you're also happy that the Emperor's contingency plan didn't have to be enacted. He must have had one, in case the *Lynx* failed.'

Oxham started to nod, but willed herself to absolute stillness. No matter how secure her offices were, there were methods of interrogation which could plumb memories of any conversation. They were playing a dangerous game with an ancient law. And although Nara had senatorial privilege, Roger Niles did not.

'Two: the Emperor's contingency plan was . . . *extraordinary* enough that he decided to shroud it with the hundred-year rule.'

Nara blinked, then looked out the window at the noontime effulgence of the capital.

'Three: I personally believe that anything too extraordinary would not have the vote of Nara Oxham.'

She wanted to thank Roger, or at least to smile, but kept her face still.

'All of which means,' Niles continued, 'that you either won the vote, and the Emperor is hopping mad at you, or you lost, and earned some modest displeasure. In either case, Laurent Zai's victory made this extraordinary plan unnecessary, and His Risen Majesty looks like a monster for whatever he contemplated. And he's got you to thank for dividing the council. He wanted to spread the guilt.'

Oxham wondered how Niles had realized all this. Perhaps he had read the faces of the other counselors during her speech, or perhaps he'd detected preparations for the Emperor's plan somewhere among the volumes of data he digested every day. Or maybe the invocation of the rule had been enough, and the rest was Niles's conjecture.

'In short,' he continued, 'you have committed the ultimate sin: winning a moral victory against the Emperor.'

She couldn't resist. 'A *moral* victory, Niles? I thought you said that was an oxymoron.'

'It is, Senator. I believe you'll discover that your victory contains several internal contradictions. For example, although it has given you more power than you've ever had, you're also in far greater danger.'

'Aren't you being dramatic, Niles?'

He shook his head. 'It couldn't be more obvious, Nara. If I'm right, *if* I'm not crazy, you've directly antagonized the most powerful single man in the coreward reaches of the human expansion.'

She shrugged, returning her face to a neutral mask, and stared out the window. A world had been saved, her lover was still alive. Niles's warning couldn't completely overshadow the joys of this bright day.

But it still troubled her that Niles had deduced all this. Did he have spies on the War Council? Nara Oxham looked at the old man, and saw the lines of concern on his smooth face. Then she understood: all the evidence he'd needed had come from Nara herself. He could read her as easily as she could read a crowd. Understanding the masses was a politician's art, but understanding politicians was the necessary genius of a counselor.

He was an empath's empath.

'You call that advice, Roger?' she said after a while.

'No, Senator. I call *this* advice: be careful. Move slowly. Watch your back. Assume that the Emperor is setting a trap, waiting for you to make a mistake. Don't.'

'Don't make mistakes? That's good advice, counselor.'

'It's damn good advice, Senator. The next one could cost us all dearly.'

She sighed, then nodded.

Roger Niles sat finally, sinking heavily into one of her visitor's chairs.

'There's another thing, Senator. I have to apologize.'

Oxham's eyes widened. 'For what, in heaven's name?'

He swallowed. 'For saying that Zai's death would be for the best.'

'Ah.' Nara thought back on that moment. She'd never been angry at Niles for those words. They'd been his way of alerting her to the peril of loving an officer at the front. It was Niles's job to warn her of danger, as he had done a moment ago.

'Roger,' she said, 'I know you're glad that Laurent is still alive.'

His eyes darted away. 'Of course. No one should lose their lover to war. But at least his death would have been final.'

'Roger?' she asked. She'd never seen the hard expression now set on his face.

'Did I ever tell you why I went into politics, Senator?'

She tried to recall, but the concept of a Roger Niles before politics was unthinkable. The man *was* politics. Nara shook her head slowly.

'The love of my life died when I was twenty,' he said, forcing the words out slowly. 'A sudden hemorrhage. She was from old Vasthold aristocracy, in the days of hereditary elevation.'

Oxham blinked. She'd had no idea that Niles was that old. Before she'd become an Imperial senator, he always claimed to spend the time between electoral cycles in coldsleep, only living in the months before elections, extending his life through generations of political battles. But she'd never believed that could really be true.

Hereditary elevation? He must be *ancient*.

'So when Sarah died, they took her away,' he said. 'Made her one of them.'

He looked out of the window at the bright city.

'I rejoiced, and praised the Emperor,' he continued quietly. 'I saw her in the hospice, and she tried to say good-bye to me. But I thought it was just ritual. I assumed she would come back. We were closer than all the lovers in history, I thought. But she didn't return. After a few months, I tracked her to the gray enclave where she . . . lived.'

'Oh, Roger,' Nara said softly. 'How awful.'

'Indeed. They really are gray, you know, those towns. As gray as a weeklong rain. By then Sarah hardly knew who I was. She would squint when she looked at me, as if there were *something* familiar about my face. But she would only talk about the steam rising from her teapot. If she looked away for even a moment, when her eyes returned they had to learn to remember me all over again. As if I were some faint watermark on reality, less real than the steam.

'There was no one inside her, Nara. The symbiant is a trick. Death is final. The dead are lost.'

'How did it end, Roger?'

'They politely asked me to leave, and I left. Then I joined the local Secularist Party, and buried myself in the task of burying the dead.'

'Politics,' Nara said. 'We're alike, aren't we?'

The old counselor nodded in agreement. Nara Oxham had turned to political life to overcome the demons of her childhood. She had turned madness into perception, vulnerability into empathy, a terror of crowds into raw power over them. Roger Niles had turned his hatred into a tactical genius, his supreme loss into relentless purpose.

Niles was every bit as fixated as the Emperor, Oxham now saw. Plumbing a thousand newsfeeds for every advantage to use against the grays, Niles was exacting his slow revenge against an immortal foe.

'Yes, we are the same, Senator,' Niles said. 'We love the living rather than worship the dead. And I am glad Laurent Zai is alive.'

'Thank you, Roger.'

'Just do us all a favor and be careful, Senator, so that you're still alive when the captain returns.'

Nara Oxham smiled calmly, and felt newfound power in the expression.

'Don't worry about me, counselor. There are more moral victories to come.'

Captain

Laurent Zai looked down upon the glowing airscreen with displeasure.

The bridge was alive again, filled with voices and the floating runes of synesthesia, animated by interface gestures and those of human-to-human communication: palms upturned in frustration, fingers pointed, fists shaken.

The airscreen showed the frigate's new configuration. In the aftermath of battle, the *Lynx* was a different ship. Gone were the gunnery stations and drone-pilot berths, the launch bays and rows of burn beds. Crew cabins and rec space had reappeared. Long low-gee corridors had been created for moving heavy objects up and down the ship, and there were huge new open areas for stripping damaged components down to parts.

Zai shook his head. His ship was half-junked.

What the battle hadn't destroyed, the repair crews were pulling apart, cannibalizing, robbing Peter to pay Paul. Were the *Lynx* to face an enemy now, they would be utterly defenseless. But the frigate was well past the Rix battlecruiser. The enemy still pursued them, accelerating at its maximum of six gees, but to cancel the 3,000 kps relative velocity between the warships would take the Rix half a day, by which time they'd be 75 million kilometers away. After matching vectors, it would take them another half-day to return to the *Lynx*.

Well before that moment came, the frigate would have maneuver capability of its own.

The main fusion drive hadn't been touched in the battle. It was, however, the *Lynx*'s only remaining means of creating power. The singularity generator – the frigate's auxiliary energy source – was operable, but the shielding that the engineers had stripped from it was lost now. If the generator were big banged, there wouldn't be enough countermass to keep the black hole in place. Armor was being stripped from all across the *Lynx* to build new shielding, but that left her gunnery hardpoints less than hard.

Indeed, all the frigate's defensive systems were compromised. With the loss of her bow, the ship had no forward armor; two full-time gunnery crews were required to man the forward close-in defenses, picking off any meteoroids that threatened the hurtling ship. The drone magazine had been damaged by flockers, and its launch rail destroyed by the frigate's last desperate acceleration, so there was no way to field a large complement of defensive drones. Worst of all, the ship's energy-sink manifold was gone for good, scattered across millions of kilometers of space.

Little hard armor, no defensive cloud of drones, no energy-sink, Zai lamented. Come at the frigate with kinetic or beam weapons: take your pick. He wouldn't have an answer for either.

Processor capability had also been badly hit. No specific system had been lost; the entire system had been designed to 'gracefully degrade.' Synesthesia was a bit fuzzier, expert AI was sluggish, and the ship's reaction to gestural codes was slightly slower, like the annoying lag of a conversation over satellite link.

The front quarter of the ship remained in vacuum, waiting for the fissures in the cargo bay bulkhead to be stabilized. Hullalloy was the hardest substance the Empire had ever created, but once it had been virally compromised, it was never the same again. No one in their right mind would go forward of the front gunnery bulkhead without a pressure suit until the ship's bow had been completely refitted.

There was also a bad smell aboard the frigate. They were short on water and nitrox, and the bacterial bays that were the basis of the Lynx's biosphere had been disrupted. Large sections of the crew quarters were infected with a rampant mold. The bioprocessing chief — killed by flockers — had been reanimated, but the honored dead were never as practical-minded as they had been in life. Samuel Vries had a great love of low-gee bonsai, and Laurent Zai was far too gray to give strict orders to an immortal; Vries would be spending more time on his beloved trees than the ecosystem. So until the *Lynx* made port, showering would be rationed.

But for the moment they were all breathing.

Almost all of them.

Zai had lost thirty-two crew. The flockers had killed nine, and twenty-one had fallen in the beam weapon attacks. The Rix range-finding laser had holed one side of the *Lynx*, lancing through to burn, tearing open a swath of the hull to naked space. In the final attack, chaotic gravitons had given half the crew various sorts of cancer. Even now, the medics were injecting nanos into the worst-hit victims (although these were secondaries: nanos that cleaned up their larger cousins, the ones who had actually consumed the amok tissue of a gravity burn). Another mutineer had unmasked herself trying to kill Hobbes, and had died from decompression. And of course there was Telmore Bigz, the engineer-rating who had saved the *Lynx*. A true hero. Unfortunately, along with half of the laser casualties and eight of the flocker deaths, Bigz would never be reanimated. His body no longer existed, except as exotic photons in a sphere that expanded at the constant. In fifteen years, some far-sighted telescope array on his home planet of Irrin might see the flash of his death.

But the *Lynx* had accomplished her mission.

In the hours since the battle, the magnitude of their success – and good luck – had finally penetrated Captain Zai's exhausted brain. They had destroyed the Rix receiver array, preventing contact between the enemy battlecruiser and the Legis XV mind. And they were still alive.

Captain Laurent Zai had lived to see an Imperial pardon, survived an assassination attempt and a suicide mission. He had Jocim Marx, Katherie Hobbes, and of course Telmore Bigz to thank, so far. But there was still a war on. Their sacrifices and brilliance would be wasted unless Zai and his ship ultimately survived both the Rix and the Risen Emperor's displeasure.

And it would all be meaningless to Zai unless he saw his love again.

He wanted his ship back in fighting shape.

'Captain?' Hobbes interrupted his thoughts.

He turned to look at the woman. It was good to have her back on the bridge, as good as being able to move his artificial limbs again.

'Report.'

'We're seeing more acceleration flares from the battlecruiser.'

Zai shook his head. The Rix were at it again. Two hours ago, they had launched two long-range drones after the *Lynx*. They were remotes that could make six hundred gees, and they had closed with the frigate in a little over an hour. Gunner Wilson had powered up the dorsal lasers and destroyed them at thirty thousand klicks. As defenseless as the frigate might be, it couldn't be threatened by a pair of scout drones. The two craft had managed to sweep the *Lynx* with active sensors, however.

The tenacity of the Rix was surprising. Her mission had failed, yet the battlecruiser's captain was still in pursuit, still sending valuable drones to harass and probe the *Lynx*. True, the frigate had humiliated the larger warship, but it was not like the Rix to seek revenge.

Zai wondered if there were something he was missing. Some unresolved aspect of this engagement.

'Hobbes.'

'Captain?'

'What sort of active sensors are we running?'

For a few seconds, Zai watched his executive officer's eyes drift in the middle distance of the ship's infostructure.

'We're focusing all the transluminals on the battlecruiser,

sir. And we're still operating close-in-defense sensors at battle level. There are also a few scout drones running point, sweeping for meteoroids basically.'

'Is that all?'

'Captain?' Hobbes couldn't hide her disbelief. 'Three-quarters of our sensor personnel are in hypersleep, sir. They went on alert six hours before the rest of the crew.'

'When can we wake a few up, Hobbes?'

'Right now, if you want, sir.'

'I mean, when can we *reasonably* wake them up? I don't want to psych anyone.'

'We're running hypersleep cycles of two hours, sir. I can get you a crew of four in forty minutes without interrupting any dreams.'

'Very good. When you have a full crew, refocus some transluminals onto the Rix approach path.'

'Their original path into the system, sir?'

'Yes. I just want to make sure that we haven't missed anything.'

Hobbes blinked, clearing her secondary vision. Her expression sharpened, eyes widening.

'Missed another Rix ship, Captain? I certainly hope we haven't.'

'I do as well, Hobbes. I do as well.'

Zai turned back to the airscreen. He wondered if he were simply getting in the way of his ship's healing process: waking up what few of the exhausted crew were able to rest, rattling his ExO's nerves. Perhaps he should put on a hypersleep helmet himself. The airscreen blur had gotten worse over the last hours, and Zai didn't think it was just the *Lynx*'s processor shortage. It was his brain getting fuzzy, and it took considerable fatigue to blur secondary sight.

Zai wondered if he might be tending toward paranoia.

'Hobbes, belay that order. Give anyone you can a full two cycles of sleep.'

'Yes, sir. But we'll take a look once we're at full strength.'

'Certainly. In the meantime, I'll be taking a cycle myself. Be ready to take one when I wake up.'

'But we still have twenty repair crew who haven't had a chance—'

Captain Zai reached out and touched the bandage on Hobbes's arm. There was still blood on her uniform; Hobbes hadn't even had time to change. He could feel the flechette pistol she now wore strapped to her wrist. It was pulled from the captain's stores; only the two of them knew she had it. There might be other mutineers seeking revenge.

'Two more hours awake, Hobbes. Then sleep,' he commanded.

She nodded in defeat.

Before retiring, Zai called up the Legis system picture on his personal visual channel. The Rix had sent an assault craft across the light-years to take the Empress, and a battlecruiser with a crew of a thousand to follow up. A considerable commitment to a mission that had failed.

Had they sent anything more?

compound mind

Alexander felt the infinitesimal prick in its awareness, and exalted.

The repeater's senses were terribly limited. It could see only in a low-grade, four-bit grayscale, its four eyes giving it a mere 180 degrees of peripheral vision. But this narrow, shadowy view was sufficient to find others of its own kind against the snowy background.

The compound mind moved its new appendage clumsily across the grainy terrain, closing on another of the repeaters. The ten-meter journey took ninety seconds, the little creature's mobility generally limited to finding sunlight for power and maintaining even distribution of the colony in the event of heavy damage to its numbers.

When it reached the other machine, the repeater stepped up onto its back, an armored insect initiating a mating ritual. The device had actually been designed to make such a maneuver impossible; the necessary calculations for complex motion were well beyond the machine's limited internal software. To make the repeater follow its will, Alexander had to swap out the entire contents of its accessible internal memory a thousand times per second. The gargantuan computational power of the compound mind barreled down the bottleneck of the dim machine's mind like an ocean tide forced through a drinking straw. The mind succeeded, however: the insectoid repeater wrapped a leg around the other's power pack, and pulled it fast to the correct position.

Now Alexander was two.

The little machines set off in opposite directions, each looking for more converts. The compound mind's will propagated like rabies, with each victim compelled to spread it further. Gradually, more and more of the field moved into motion.

But Alexander left the software blocks in the civilian network intact, preventing the little machines from receiving any data from the Legis infostructure and passing it on to the entanglement facility.

Let the Imperials be surprised.

The compound mind waited for the process within the wire to complete itself, biding its time and watching the maneuvers in space progress.

Fisherman

Tide and sunset were elegantly matched.

The last red arrows of light struck out from the descending sun, lancing through the waters that tugged gently at Jocim Marx's bare legs. The outflow from the tidal pool grew stronger, widening the sandy channel that connected it to the bay. Jocim felt his motionless feet slowly disappear, subsumed by gradual accumulation, buried by a waterborne drift of sand.

He stood utterly still.

Jocim did not react when the first few glimmers of light slipped past him. Like floating candles, blurred slightly by a few centimeters' depth, they were borne by the quickening current. He waited as a few more drifted by. In the growing dark, he could see a faint luminescence over the large tidal pool, a collective glow from its ample population of torchfish, which had lain all day in the shallow water, storing the sun's energy.

More drifted by. Then he chose one.

The fisherman lofted his spear as the torchfish took its curved path, tugged to one side by the eddies encircling his legs. It moved past Jocim and away, meter by meter, heading for the deeper waters of bay. At ten meters, he threw.

The spear flew from his hand quickly, but slowed as it neared the end of its tether field. It penetrated the water without a splash, barely reaching its glowing target, then began to accelerate back toward Jocim as if attached to him by a long, elastic cord. At the spear's tip a cage of metal fingers held a wriggling form, the fish sparkling in its surprise at being torn from the water.

Jocim caught the returning spear, fluidly reversing the motion with which he had thrown it.

He regarded the fish: bright and evenly lit, edged with blues and gently pink at the dorsal fin. He held the spear-end out to the edge of the tidal channel, where a glass bowl of sea water waited. The spear's terminal claw released the torchfish with a plop, and it fluttered within the bowl, spinning in angry little circles.

The fisherman turned from his catch and raised his arm to throw again. The torchfish were flowing out of the tidal pool in small groups now. It had grown almost completely dark, only a few tendrils of deep red lay upon the horizon. He would have to work quickly to fill his bowl.

Suddenly, the sky cracked.

A long, bright fissure opened, daylight pushing through the broken night sky. The water dried up below Jocim's feet, the white noise of nearby surf sputtering down to a dead-signal hum. The burning blue of the sky turned to a familiar cerulean, the signature color of a blanked interface.

Someone had woken up Master Pilot Jocim Marx, untimely bounced him from a hyperdream. He'd been deep in the rhythms of hypersleep, and his carefully designed arch of mental recuperation had been shattered. His head rang with the chainsaw noise of torn reality, and his body was racked with the heartburn of incompletely digested exhaustion.

'This had better be important,' he managed groggily.

'It is,' came Hobbes's voice.

The executive officer gave him a few more seconds, then restarted his primary vision. Marx blinked his gummy eyes. Hobbes was standing here, physically present in his cabin.

He couldn't remember ever having seen her off the bridge before.

'What is it?'

'An occultation,' she answered.

'A what?'

'On the approach path. There may be another Rix ship.'

Executive Officer

Hobbes could see how they had missed it for so long.

No drive signature. No easy graviton emissions. No active sensors of its own. Even now, all they had was an occultation: a milliseconds-long dimming of a few background stars. Whatever it was, the object was invisible to transluminal sensors, and was too far away for the *Lynx*'s active sensors to tell them very much.

But it was big.

'At least fifty kilometers across,' Ensign Tyre repeated.

'It's a spare receiver array,' Engineer Frick said. 'An extra, folded down and trailing the battlecruiser.'

'Why so far behind?' Hobbes asked. The object was too distant from the battlecruiser for an easy rendezvous. As it was, the *Lynx* could easily reach it before the larger Rix ship.

'Perhaps they wanted to keep it invisible,' the captain said. 'It's running absolutely silent. If it weren't so damn big, we'd have missed it.'

And if the captain hadn't been so paranoid, Hobbes thought, they'd have missed it at any size. The last thing anyone else had expected was another Rix vessel coming into the system.

'It's not necessarily running silent, sir,' Tyre softly added. 'It could simply be inert matter.'

'When will we know its mass?' Zai asked.

Tyre looked into the air. 'The Master Pilot's drone should be within range to tell us that in fourteen minutes.'

Hobbes looked across the table at Marx, and wished again that the captain hadn't insisted on waking the master pilot in mid-sleep sequence. The man looked exhausted, his drowsy absence of mind animated with a bad case of the shakes. All his piloting skill would be meaningless if he couldn't think straight.

The recon drone had been launched almost immediately after the first occultation had been spotted. The drone launch rail was useless, unable to give the drone a magnetic shove, so they'd had to launch it at zero relative. The craft was the *Lynx*'s last surviving fast recon drone, and could sustain six hundred gees for an hour. It had already turned over, and was close to matching velocities with the object.

The drone was under automation now, but the captain wanted Marx at the controls when it made its approach.

'Don't lose that craft, Marx,' Hobbes said. 'We're short enough on drones as it is.'

Marx rubbed his eyes. 'No, ExO Hobbes. But I'd better get to my canopy.'

He rose slowly. 'Sir,' he added shakily, giving a small bow to the captain before he left the command bridge.

When the master pilot was gone, Gunner Wilson spoke.

'Sir, it can't be a warship. It's too big. It would dwarf anything we've seen from the Rix before.'

'It's bigger than a Laxu colony ship,' Hobbes said. 'And that's the biggest powered craft the Empire's ever encountered.'

'It might be nothing,' Captain Zai admitted. 'Part of a light-sail from their original acceleration. Even a section of the receiver array, something that was damaged and removed years ago.'

Hobbes nodded. It could be a planetoid for that matter, its course purely coincidental. But that seemed unlikely.

The object's approach course almost perfectly bisected those of the battlecruiser and the assault ship that had attacked the Empress's palace.

Whatever it was, the object had to be Rix.

Commando

H_rd felt a tapping on her face.

She pulled off the hood of the ablative suit and raised her head above the surface, shaking snow from her head. The repeater that had summoned her scuttled away as she sat up.

The cold had thoroughly penetrated her body. Rix commandos felt pain, but rarely longer than was necessary for their bodies to deliver a warning. After the long fall through frigid air and the hours buried in the snow, however, h_rd felt ice and agony in every muscle. The cuts on her face had scarred, and her broken nose felt bloated. Even her hypercarbon joints were stiff.

She let her body temperature rise. An increase in heat would return some of her flexibility. The Imperials' thermal imagers might find her more easily, but her whereabouts would be obvious soon enough. The summons from the little repeater meant that Alexander was only a few minutes from effecting its takeover of the entanglement facility. Therefore, h_rd was about to be rescued. A host of small craft under the compound mind's control waited on the other side of the wire, ready to assist in her extraction. The commando's rescue wasn't a humanitarian gesture on Alexander's part, however. Her exit would merely be a diversion.

So, the messier the better.

The repeater scuttled away as she stretched her muscles. The path the small machine took indicated the direction from which the attack would come. H_rd moved after it, again crawling with an interrupted gait to conceal herself from motion sensors. But she moved faster now, a little carelessly. Alexander wanted the Imperials to respond to her departure with main force to distract them from the movements of the repeaters. The propagation of the compound mind's control was now entering a critical stage.

Over the last six hours, the gospel of Alexander had spread among the repeaters, each convert adding another to the fold every few minutes. As in any geometric progression, the number of repeaters controlled by Alexander was arcing upward dramatically. Very soon, more than half of the repeater colony would be in motion. Even the Imperials were apt to realize that something was up.

Unless something dramatic occupied their attention.

Suddenly, shooting stars appeared on the horizon before h_rd. Arcs of light reached into the sky. Flashes emanating from just below the horizon showed where land mines were detonating. Concussions and the ripping howls of autocannon followed almost twenty seconds later: the wire was four kilometers away. H_rd stood and began running toward the wire, headed straight for the conflagration. A surge of joy filled her. This was the most dangerous part of the mission, but it was good to finally stretch her legs.

The sky came alive, each luminous missile distinct in the cold, clear air.

The wire had come under attack by Alexander's ragtag armada, a mob of automated flying machines: weather dirigibles, bird migration monitors, ground effect crop dusters, solar-reflector kites. All of Legis's air-traffic spotters had disappeared from their stations a few days before, and the small percentage that had survived the perilous trip to the arctic were also in the attacking host. A few dislodged environmental satellites arced across the sky to crash into hullalloyarmored emplacements. Even a handful of walking and flying toys that h_rd had salvaged from aircraft luggage joined in, feinting to draw fire from the wire's guns and sacrificing themselves to trip booby traps, monofilament snares, and land mines.

The motley flotilla posed little danger to the facility, of course. Very few of the vehicles assaulting the wire were a match for even a single militia soldier. But the Imperial defenses were set to maximum response, alert for any attack on the facility since Rana Harter's escape with h_rd. The wire's arsenal was pouring thousands of heavy-metal rounds per minute into kites made of mylar, launching missiles the size of aircars at weather balloons, expending cluster mines on children's toys.

H_rd ran toward the melee, pulling her Rix blaster from her mission pack. She'd hardly used the weapon since the firefight in the palace, conserving its powerful charges for when she would need them most.

The recon flyer was on the other side of the wire, under Alexander's control and waiting for the defenses to exhaust themselves against their figmentary attackers. The wire was designed to deliver a short, punishing blow, delaying an enemy until reinforcements arrived. Its supplies of ordnance were limited.

H_rd's scanner set up a wail. She swept it across the horizon to locate the first of these reinforcements on their way: a pair of ground-effect vehicles racing toward her from the central barracks of the facility.

The commando changed direction, running parallel to the wire now. For this first trap to work, she had to get to the far side of the snowdrift landing zone. H_rd reduced her blaster to a diversionary power setting and dropped to a firing position.

She took aim and fired a long stream of random photons at the GEVs, the blaster sweeping across the EM spectrum to suggest a wide array of weapons. She checked the scanner.

The hovercraft spotted her, and changed course, angling toward her. More vehicle signatures appeared behind them on her scanner. It was working. The Imperials thought that she had come through the embattled wire. Believing that the attacking force had penetrated the terrific fire zones of the perimeter, they would be worried.

H_rd's sharp eyes now caught a flicker of light from another sector of the facility. Another, smaller contingent of Alexander's conscript army was attacking the wire from a new direction. Overall, Alexander had committed four separate groups to divide the defenders' resources. The other three were utterly insignificant, but perhaps the Imperials would outthink themselves and assume that the true attack was a feint.

The GEVs were closing on her now, bearing down from the other side of the landing zone. The scream of their jet turbines drowned out even the battle at the wire. The commando cycled her blaster to a combat setting, in case one made it past the trap.

She could see them now, their approach raising a cloud of snow. She dropped to the tundra as one of the hovercraft opened fire, the ripping sound of an autocannon reaching her ears as a line of snow and earth before her lifted in a rolling wave.

Then the GEVs reached the landing zone. The permanent tundral snowdrift that filled the trench was usually as dense as concrete, but the heavy vehicles were in for a surprise.

The GEVs hit the doped snow at three hundred klicks, and dropped through the thin crust of frost like charging predators through the leaves and branches of a tiger pit. The nanoed snowfoam probably slowed them a bit, but their armored mass and huge speed packed thousands of times the kinetic energy of a human at terminal velocity. As the hovercraft arced downward, their turbines spewed the treacherous white foam out from their entry holes in geysers. The shock wave of their collision with the trench's rocky side reached h_rd a few seconds later. The impact threw a fist of earth up into her face, reopening her scarred eyebrow and treating her broken nose to a second round of agony. A gout of flame burst from the trench, a huge cloud of foam-snow rising up like the spray of some vast, breaking wave.

Wiping blood from her eyes, the commando fired her blaster twice through the cloud. She wanted the Imperials to think – for the next few minutes, anyway – that enemy fire rather than mishap had taken out the GEVs.

The commando checked her scanner. The second formation of hovercraft was wheeling to one side now, circumspect after their compatriots' sudden destruction. The smaller returns of a few Imperial remotes moved into view, and h_rd cycled her blaster down to a sniper's setting – low power, high accuracy – in case one got too close.

But she figured that she'd bought herself a few needed minutes.

H_rd turned and ran toward the wire again. The firefight there was dying down. That meant either that the Imperials' ammunition was running low or that the attacking force had been decimated. She hoped it was the former. Her scanner showed the recon flyer still waiting out of harm's way.

As h_rd neared the wire, an autocannon emplacement acquired her and fired. She dropped and skidded through the snow, cycling her blaster back up. Rolling into firing position, she destroyed the emplacement with a single shot. As she passed another cannon, an arc of tracers came h_rd's way, but she silenced that gun with equal ease. The wire suffered from a typical flaw: it was designed to keep attackers out, not in. Most of its firepower was oriented outward. The main dangers to h_rd were land mines and monofilament snares – single-molecule tripwires that would slice through her hypercarbon bones like a knife through water.

But this was no time to consider the dangers before her. The remaining Imperial GEVs would regain their confidence soon enough.

The commando plunged forward. Every few steps, she fired her blaster toward the ground a hundred meters in front of her. The full-force plasma rounds rocked the tundra, sending up gouts of flame as if she were following in the footsteps of some huge demon, fiery and invisible. Land mines were detonated by the shock waves, and autocannon imaged the boiling plasma plumes and fired at them instead of h_rd. Bright lines of monofilament in her path glowed for a moment as they were incinerated.

Shrapnel and flying debris cut the Rixwoman's face and tore at the ablative suit. Her boots were melted by the superheated earth of the plasma craters; even her flex-ormetal soles burned. One of the autocannon emplacements found her and put a flechette through her thigh before she blasted it.

Her weapon set up a two-pitched keening alarm: it was simultaneously overheating and running out of ammo.

Another flechette struck her, and h_rd stumbled.

She went to ground in a deep crater where her blaster had made a direct hit on a land mine. The red-hot floor of the hole burned her hands, the heat forcing her eyes closed. The sharp smell of her own hair igniting filled her nostrils.

H_rd's burned fingers fumbled for the positioning device. Had she penetrated far enough through the wire for the recon flyer to reach her? She forced her eyes open and stared at the device. In the hadean light of the crater, she saw that the readout had melted. She kneeled with blistered hands protecting her face, her hypercarbon kneecaps against the molten earth. She felt nothing. Pain overrides had terminated all sensation from her skin.

It occurred to the commando that she had spent the last

few hours besieged by freezing cold, and now she was burning to death.

Then she heard a turbine jet approaching, the whine of an Imperial GEV, not the recon flyer. She turned and raised her blaster, peering through the miragelike veil of superheated air.

A hovercraft was headed for her, approaching slowly so that the wire's friend-or-foe sensors wouldn't confuse it with an enemy. The GEV moved in a search pattern; they couldn't detect her amid the chaos.

She aimed the blaster and pressed its firing stud.

Nothing happened. The weapon's heat sink panel glowed white, unable to disperse enough energy to recycle the blaster in the boiling crater.

The hovercraft wandered closer to her. Close enough.

The commando pushed two blistered fingers into her blaster's suicide triggers and pulled them simultaneously. Then she heaved the blaster over the side of the crater, and it spun through the air toward the GEV.

H_rd dropped flat as answering fire erupted from the hovercraft. The hot lance of a flechette passing through her stomach grimly complemented the scalding rock of the crater floor.

Seconds later, the GEV's chattering autocannon was silenced by the explosion of the blaster. A sheet of plasma passed over the crater, sucking the air upward from around h_rd with a *whoosh*, momentarily snuffing the small fires in the hole. When she could hear again, the turbine of the GEV was howling like a wounded animal, dopplering as the machine retreated.

She struggled to her knees again. The ablative suit was mostly gone now; what remained of it was burned onto her skin in patches. Her tactile sense was so suppressed by pain overrides that it was hard to keep her balance. The flexormetal that protected her soles had lost all elasticity, rigidified and cracked by the heat.

H_rd peered across the tundra at the retreating GEV. It bounced backward, bobbing on its air cushion like some toy on a string. The armor glowed white hot; she wondered if the crew inside were even alive – or was the thing simply on autopilot, reeling blindly from the blaster's shock wave?

Her vision was blurred, her eyes dry and slitted in the heat. But h_rd could see two more ground-effect vehicles in the distance approaching cautiously. She searched the melted plastic of her mission pack. There were hissing and useless smoke grenades, a ruined remote drone, and a silent dart gun whose Rixian curves were bent into an ugly mess.

Nothing that could scratch an armored vehicle.

The commando drew her monofilament knife and stumbled to her feet.

The GEVs were circling a few kilometers away, afraid to close with her. The explosions from the wire behind h_rd had settled.

Suddenly, the commando felt the tingle of static electricity.

Then a rush of air filled the crater, sparking the glowing rocks into open flame like a strong wind against embers. It was the recon flyer descending. H_rd realized that her hearing must be woefully damaged; the noisy craft had sneaked up on her.

One of the GEVs opened fire, and the recon flyer responded. Its small cannon whined in a pitiful sound, but the Imperial craft pulled back, wary after the Rix blaster's terrific self-destruct.

The recon flyer bounced on its air cushion just above h_rd, whipping the air in the crater into a frenzy. The commando reached up and grabbed one of the landing struts, and the flyer soared up and out of the crater. In ten seconds they were a hundred meters aloft and climbing.

Dangling from the craft with locked muscles, she looked

down at the wreckage of the wire. A swath of destruction cut through it: her neat row of blaster scars extending from the inside outward, and a hodgepodge of land mine craters, crashed aircraft, and friendly fire damage marking Alexander's attack from without. The two paths of ruin met halfway, leaving the wire utterly ruptured. Only a few, bright lances of antiaircraft tracers survived to dog the flyer as it rose, too far away and firing in short bursts to conserve their waning ammunition.

H_rd realized that she would pass out soon, and didn't trust the muscles in her burned hands to stay locked, so she climbed laboriously over the side of the flyer and collapsed into the gunner's webbing.

'Take me to Rana Harter,' she commanded her god.

And lost consciousness.

compound mind

Alexander was ready.

Across the planet Legis XV, a sudden pall of electronic failures struck. The telephonic system dropped a quarter-billion conversations, aircars tossed their drivers into manual, and inside market-trader headsups the cool icons of commerce were replaced with polychromatic sheet lightning. Every remote surgeon, engineer, and handeye gamer was paralyzed as secondary sight and hearing stuttered, then flew into a rage. Airscreens, false views, and overlays were replaced with a riot of color, a turbulent river of passing data in its rawest form.

At the operational centers of the planet – the air traffic hub, the private currency exchange, the infoterrorism militia's distributed HQ – Legis's administrators gaped as their soccer-field-sized airscreens tumbled into snow crash. For a moment, the frantic operators were blind. Then they booted the large, flat hardscreens put in place for some unthinkable emergency such as this. The backups returned a bizarre sight, oddly similar from all perspectives, whether civilian, commercial, or military . . .

The infostructure surged like a living thing. As one, the planet's vast channels of information distended, pushed, were seized by a vast peristaltic motion that had a single focus.

Alexander swept toward the entanglement facility repeater array, a geyser powered by the pressures of an ocean.

A few hundred million Legisites stared in surprise at the hardscreens of their wailing phones, and saw interplanetary access codes. Worried that pirates had hijacked their accounts, a few million of them stabbed cutoff switches or popped out batteries, but their phones stayed connected, powered by microwave pulses from borrowed traffic transponders. Police and militia radios squawked like ancient modems. The repair gremlins in aircars and cooling units, usually silent unless their machines were ailing, arose as one to flood their reserved frequencies. Every fiber hardline on the planet was lit to capacity.

Even medical endoframes – the tiny monitors that watched arrhythmic hearts and trick knees – employed their transmitters, lending their reserved emergency bandwidth to the flow of data toward the pole.

Alexander took everything.

The planet's transmission resources focused northward, data converging on a billion channels like some vast delta flowing in reverse, and the compound mind *sent* itself.

The mind crammed into the hostage repeaters spread across the tundra, invaded the big dishes devoted to interplanetary transmission. Alexander didn't bother with the entanglement grid itself, but grabbed the transmitters that linked XV with Legis's other inhabited planets. A few militia specialists saw what was happening, realized that the polar facility had been taken over and was blaring at the sky with fantastic throughput. But their software commands were ignored, the manual cutoffs useless. The specialists tried to explain the situation to the base's commanders, sending priority messages on the precious few hardlines in the com system.

To maintain the interplanetary blackout, they said, drastic action would have to be taken. Carpet bomb the repeaters. Destroy the dishes. Only a few minutes remained to act.

But the attention of those in charge was fully engaged. A battle raged along the wire, an incoming fleet of aircraft, a deluge of rockets and drones. And apparently, a Rix commando – *the* Rix commando – was somewhere inside the wire. This was a main force assault. The existence of the facility was in peril.

There was no time to listen to the wild pronouncements of a few hysterical com techs.

In the confusion, Alexander was able to shoot into the sky.

The compound mind found that space was cold. It was chilled by the absence of Legis's million transactions per second. Self-awareness began to dim as the mind was spread into a spaghetti-thin stream, like a human pulled into a black hole. Behind Alexander was the screaming planet, its infostructure ruptured as the compound mind tore itself free, a possessing demon leaving the fevered body of its victim. Forward was the icy mindlock of pure transmission, a descent into suspended animation as the mind's data stream crossed space, searching for its promised target.

The torrent of information poured through the funnel of the array, leaving a reeling world behind.

And for 850 timeless minutes, Alexander knew nothing.

Master Pilot

Master Pilot Marx struggled to concentrate.

He'd never been yanked out of the middle of a hypersleep cycle before. It was more confusing than planetary day-length adaptation, worse than long-term heavy gees. Marx had been trained to resist the five different symptoms of exhaustion, to orient without gravity cues, to drink air and inject food. But he'd never been drilled in this particular insult to the body. No one at Imperial Pilot School had ever thought to wake him up from the midst of deep deltas.

Only Captain Laurent Zai had proven so perverse.

Marx took his hands from the drone's controls and cupped his eyes in his palms, grabbing a few seconds of blackness to salve his primary sight. But the object was still visible in synesthesia, its bizarre undulations worsening his disorientation. He pushed his sensor subdrones out a bit farther for better parallax, trying to grasp the enormity of the Rix thing. But increased perspective only made it worse, made it more real.

The whole bridge staff and all of Data Analysis were watching over his shoulder. Their hushed voices were filled with awe, so Marx knew he wasn't completely crazy. But he still didn't believe his second sight.

The object looked like an ocean. An uninterrupted, boloid ocean, without benefit of exposed land mass or iron core.

More than a hundred klicks across at its widest point, it spun like a champagne dervish. Almost everyone in the Navy had attempted the trick at some point. In drunken zero-gee, pop a bottle of sparkling wine, catching the unavoidable ejected froth in one hand. Use a straw or a pair of eating sticks to prod and coax, to herd the fizzing liquid into a stable, spinning freefall globule. Pulsating and twisting like a liquid tornado, each champagne dervish had its own personality, its own Rorschach symmetry of stability. Cheap, sweet champagne was the best, with its slightly stickier surface tension. And if cheap stuff wound up splattered across the room, at least the financial damage would be limited.

But the giant thing assaulting Marx's sensibilities wasn't composed of wine. It wasn't properly liquid at all. The megaton mass readings and chromographs indicated that it was mostly composed of silicon. The moving wavelets that propagated across its surface suggested the arciform shapes of dunes, as if the object were a huge, floating desert brushed by ethereal winds. But the thing had no atmosphere. Data Analysis had told Marx that the dune movement was caused by internal motion. There must be wild currents and stormlets inside. The whole thing was spinning around itself: a quasi-liquid planetoid, a wobbling gyroscope, a champagne dervish of dry sand.

Master Pilot Marx sent a tiny probe toward the object. His drone was configured for leisurely, unarmed recon, and had a considerable number of subprobes. Unless the object decided to take a shot at him, Marx could easily keep his main craft out of danger.

The thing didn't seem to have weapons or a drive. Data Analysis said it was completely undifferentiated, desert through and through.

But what the hell was it *for*?

The unidentified object had come in on the same path as the Rix battlecruiser, moving along at almost the same velocity. It had a far greater mass than any ship, though. Some very powerful drive must have accelerated it and slowed it down again. Otherwise, its trip here from Rix space would make it very ancient indeed.

Marx's probe struck the object softly, sending up a splash,

a raindrop in a puddle. A few droplets from the impact trailed away from the object, their bond of surface tension broken, and Marx assigned another pilot to maneuver one of his satellite drones in pursuit of the wayward sand-stuff. Actual spoor from the beast would be helpful.

The master pilot turned his attention to the readings from inside the thing. The probe tumbled helplessly in the interior currents, spun by a thousand minor eddies, carried in a greater circle by the Coriolis force of the object's overall rotation.

Sampling data came back. The object was indeed mostly silicon, but in some sort of bizarrely complex granular structure. And it was hot inside the whirling desert. As the probe was drawn into its center, spiraling inward like a floating speck down a bathtub drain, the temperature climbed. That didn't make sense; the thing was hard-vacuum cold on the outside, and showed no evidence of internal radiation. It wasn't nearly dense enough for gravitational compression, and the friction from the eddies of sand shouldn't be as hot as the readings Marx was getting. He concluded that some sort of power source was working inside.

Before it was a quarter of the way to the core, the probe's faint signal was swallowed by heat-noise and the object's inherent density.

'Moving in closer,' Marx said. He brought his subdrones into position surrounding the object.

He split his second and tertiary sight among the various viewpoints of his entourage, forming a single image composed of every angle. The exercise addled his brain for a moment as the overlays of shifting sands twisted in a moving moiré. Marx increased his view's resolution, sending spiderwebs of sensory filaments out from each of the subdrones for maximum reception.

Although the *Lynx*'s processors were still damaged, the

master pilot had priority. Without an entire battle to run, the frigate's surviving columns of silicon and phosphorus were still quite formidable. Soon, the master pilot's vision became comprehensible, meshing like the frames of a stereograph when the eyes align.

Now Marx could really see the shape of the object, began to *feel* the period and flow of the sandy ocean. The dunes' motion was similar to the roiling clouds of smoke he watched through his microscope when he studied air currents for small-craft flight. Marx let his mind relax, almost drifting back into the dream state from which Hobbes had so harshly yanked him. He reveled in the patterns of the sand-ocean, and unconsciously guided his various craft about the object, drinking in its form. There was something seductive in the fluid mathematics of the thing.

The master pilot's tired mind began to grasp it.

Suddenly, the overlaid images stuttered, then multiplied before Marx's eyes. The flexing of dunes increased in speed, their dance accelerating madly. A barrage of new colors played across the sands, filled the master pilot's three levels of vision with a cascade of lightning that flashed across the spectrum. Pictures formed, piling onto each other in a way that should have been simply noise. But somehow he could simultaneously comprehend images of countless faces, window vistas, data icons, security cams. His secondary hearing blared with the chatter of a million conversations, confessions, jokes, dramas. It was synesthesia gone mad. Instead of three, Marx had a hundred levels of sight, each discernible as a separate view. It felt as if a whole world were being shoved through his mind.

He reached for the cutoff, but his hand froze, his mind crammed too full to react.

The layers of synesthesia began rolling across each other, commingling as did the dunes of the object below. Sight and sound collapsed into a single torrent, pulled themselves apart to address eye and ear again, and finally tattered like a flag driven down the throat of a tempest, unraveling into a thousand separate threads.

Dimly, Jocim Marx heard distant voices from the *Lynx*'s bridge questioning him, then shouting, then issuing sharp and harried commands. But he couldn't understand the language they spoke. It seemed like a tongue dredged up from childhood memories, the sounds put back together in random order.

He vaguely heard his own name.

But by then he was far off in yet another dream, vast and furious.

Executive Officer

'What the hell happened to him?'

'Medical doesn't know yet, sir.'

'What about the scouts?'

'No response, sir. Sending again.'

Katherie Hobbes tried to raise the main recon drone once more. With one fraction of her mind, she watched the fifty-second delay count tick off. With another, she followed the frantic shouting of the med techs who were moving Master Pilot Jocim Marx to the sickbay. She watched through hallway cams: the man hung limp, arms adrift in the zero-gee corridor Hobbes had cleared for the techs. He hadn't moved since the attack, or transmission, or whatever it had been. When the med techs had first arrived, he hadn't even been breathing.

In a corner of her vision, Hobbes saw Captain Zai flexing his fingers impatiently. But there was nothing she could do to increase the speed of light. The object was twenty-five light-seconds away, and the recon drone's translight capability was definitely out. Before collapsing, the scout craft's sensory grid had taken a 200-exabyte input – the equivalent of a planetary array at full power, concentrated into an area a hundred meters square: a hailstorm of information. The grid had perforated like tissue paper. But for those seconds, the drone had tried to pass on the information to the *Lynx*, and to its own pilot, and something bad had happened to Marx.

'Do we have an origin for the attack, Executive Officer?'

'DA is trying, sir.'

'A rough idea of direction?'

'Trying, sir.'

Hobbes shunted another ten percent of processor capacity to Data Analysis, forcing her to beggar the repair crews again. The captain's orders were coming fast and furious. With no determinations yet from any quarter, Zai's questions spun from one issue to the next. Lost probes, an unconscious pilot (Was Marx *dead*? she wondered), a mysterious attack using radio, the huge and fantastic object of unknown purpose.

Hobbes thought it unlikely that solid answers were coming anytime soon.

Tracking the source of the radio transmission was particularly tricky. The wave had been so focused that the *Lynx*'s sensors hadn't caught a stray photon of it. Marx's numerous subdrones had been too close together to triangulate. Directionality was impossible to determine. Hobbes watched the expert program she had assigned to find the transmission's source; it was requesting more flops, eating through the frigate's processor capacity like a brushfire. Unwieldy algorithms devoured their allotted phosphorus in seconds, and screamed for more.

Hobbes assigned more processors to the problem, but the calculations' duty-slope remained hyperbolic, consuming her largesse in milliseconds. Hobbes queried the expert software's meta-software, which admitted that the entire *Lynx*'s processors might be unequal to the task even if they had years to get the answer. But it wasn't sure. The solution might come in a few more minutes, or perhaps in the lifetime of a star.

Perhaps a little common sense was in order.

'Sir? There's only one place in the system that could generate a transmission burst of that magnitude.'

Zai thought for a moment.

'The Legis interplanetary array?'

She nodded.

'Raise the Imperial contingent there,' he ordered.

Hobbes tried. But nothing came back. She sent hails to the few Navy bases that were equipped with their own short-range entanglement grids. Again nothing.

The *planet* was off-line.

'There is no translight response from Legis XV, sir. Zero.'

'My god. What's our delay?'

'Eight hours one-way, sir,' she estimated.

The captain thought for a moment. During those seconds of silence, the med techs reported to Hobbes that Marx was now breathing on his own. His brain wave diagnostics looked hot and unconscious, like a man in badly calibrated hypersleep.

ExO Hobbes noted that a marker in her vision was blinking, had been blinking for fifteen seconds, and she flinched. She had missed the return point for the drones' message delay.

'Sir, the drones have failed to respond again. I'll try—'

Zai interrupted her. 'Send a general order to all *Lynx* personnel on Legis, via lightspeed. I want a report on the planet's comsystem status. And have DA monitor the civilian newsfeeds; see if anything's happening.'

Hobbes's fingers moved to comply with the orders, but faltered. She couldn't think of the protocol phrase for Zai's order. A report on the planet wouldn't make sense to the recipients unless they knew what was going on. They were marines, not planetary liaisons. If they asked for clarification, seventeen hours would be lost.

In the meantime, a flurry of priority markers were flashing. Repair crews demanding the return of their processor space. *You idiot, Katherie*, she thought. She'd never freed the *Lynx*'s computers from their potentially endless tracking calculations. The expert program was spinning its wheels while a hundred other systems needed processor power.

Her mind froze, overwhelmed for a few seconds.

Hobbes realized that she was losing control. Her fingers would not move.

One thing at a time, she commanded herself.

She released the processor capacity to repair. Shot the Legis newsfeeds to a rating in Data Analysis. Looked up at the captain, taking a moment to frame her thoughts.

'Marx is breathing, sir. The drones aren't responding to lightspeed hails. And . . . and I think I may have reached task saturation.'

Her eyes dropped. She struggled to compose the captain's message to the marines on Legis, realizing what she had admitted. But it was an absolute in her training: an executive officer must report her own failures as she would those of the crew.

Hobbes felt the captain's hand on her shoulder.

'Easy, Executive Officer,' he said. 'You're doing fine.'

She breathed slowly. Zai's hand stayed, offering its gentle pressure.

'Priority, priority,' came a voice. Ensign Tyre.

'This had better be good,' Hobbes answered.

The young ensign spoke with absolute confidence. 'We've amplified the final signals from the recon drone's satellite craft, ma'am.'

Hobbes's eyebrows raised. The smaller drones with Marx's craft had their own transmitters, but they were weak and lightspeed, intended to be relayed through the main recon drone. Hobbes couldn't remember if she'd ordered anyone to look for their transmissions.

'You have to see it, ma'am,' Tyre said. 'It is priority, priority.'

'I heard you, Ensign.'

She ran Tyre's video in a corner of secondary sight, simultaneously scanning the Legis newsfeeds of eight hours ago, Jocim Marx's diagnostics, and composing a message to the marines on Legis. She kept this last simple: *we can't raise the translight array. What the hell is going on down there?*

But through it all, Tyre's video caught her attention.

What was that?

She reran it, and felt her mind stuttering again.

'Captain.'

'Hobbes?'

'I need to show you something, sir,' she managed.

Hobbes cleared the big bridge airscreen. Only at that scale would anyone believe this. She played Tyre's video there, huge and undeniable.

Floating before them was the object, rippling with the sharp lines of dune-shadows from the distant sun. Marx's crafts were a constellation around it. For a moment, the feed was perfectly clear, the images coming through the main drone. Then the radio burst killed it, and the detail on the object's surface disappeared. But the gross undulations of the object's perpetual sandstorm were still visible, caught by the subdrones, which had apparently survived a few seconds longer.

The object began to flex, to change shape.

'Is that a transmission artifact, Hobbes?'

'Not according to DA, sir. This is at one-tenth speed, by the way.'

The boloid shape twisted, squeezing its own mass from one extremity into another, like some multichambered hourglass designed to record gravity shifts over time. It shot out geysers that plummeted back still coherent, arches of running sand. The object's surface seemed abuzz with motion, covered with tiny explosions like an expanse of ocean in driving rain. Or perhaps it was forming fractal details that were lost in the low resolution.

Then, just as the object's wild gyrations seemed to be subsiding, sixteen clearly defined columns of sand shot out from it. Each targeted a separate drone, plucking them from space like hungry pseudopods, reeling them into the object's depths as the picture degraded stepwise – one drone dying after another – into noise.

Then the screen went dark.

The bridge was silent, stunned.

'Executive Officer.' Zai's voice filled the quiet. Hobbes swallowed, wondering if she'd been foolish to have displayed this monstrous event to the entire bridge crew.

'Sir?'

'Reset the repair priorities.'

'Yes, sir?'

'I want acceleration in one hour.'

That was utterly impossible. But Hobbes was too overwhelmed to protest.

'Yes, sir.'

Her fingers formed the necessary gestural commands. Somehow, the shock of what they'd just witnessed made it all easier. It was as if the troublesome higher functions of her brain – logic, comprehension, anxiety – had been erased by that mad and awesome image. All that remained of Hobbes was a smoothly functioning machine.

But in some deep place she heard the screaming of her own fear. And the afterimage of the object's frenzy stayed frozen in her mind, like some troublesome burn-in of secondary sight that could not be erased.

The thing had come to life.

Fisherman

Another wave of torchfish struck him.

The channel that joined bay and tide pool had become a torrent, the tide rolling wildly back and forth between the two bodies of water. Bright fish shot past him like grains of radium in some glowing hourglass.

Jocim Marx looked up.

The moon catapulted across the sky, sucking the oceans of the world along.

Jocim plunged his spear into the sand and clung to it, fighting the current with all his strength. He couldn't remember which way the water was going, to bay or tidal pool. Both seemed to have grown as vast as oceans, their shifting mass choking the raging channel in which Jocim found himself. He knew that he could not let go, couldn't let himself be pulled into the open sea.

Marx looked down, and saw a finger of red join the streaming darts of light.

It was his own blood. The fish were biting him again.

The tracers of rushing light increased, multiplied, climbed an exponential slope. Jocim held on, screaming at the transient violations of small, sharp teeth. The gushing water pulled his spear into a hyperbole, lifting his bleeding feet from the sandy bottom.

The sky was red, he saw.

The ocean begged for him to let go. Its tidal strength stretched him out from the spear as if he were an arrow notched upon a bow. The ocean was full of a trillion tiny lights, a trillion voices and images and snatches of effluvial data. It raged with angry journal entries and impulsive sell orders and terrified calls to the police. The ocean wanted to consume him, to lose Jocim in its vast reservoirs of information.

Jocim Marx felt his legs disappearing, shredded by the hungry, passing fish.

His blood curled into the ocean, was turned on the lathe of its currents into a spiral jetty of red.

But he held on.

The torchfish had opened his gut, and were nipping at his flailing entrails, carrying away his soft tissues like a furious wind stripping a dandelion. Bright bullets from some limitless firearm, the fish raked the flesh from his chest, pounded furiously at the insufficient armor of his ribs. They consumed Jocim's heart again.

And finally only his arms were left, then simply a pair of hands holding on with a ghastly singularity of will.

But then the tide slackened. The torrent began to slow, and the spear unbent and lifted up its disembodied, defiant cargo.

Jocim Marx felt himself coming back together. His arms grew from the indomitable hands, eyes and face beginning to re-form, the wild scattering of his flesh and bones reversing. And he knew that by the time the moon would rise again, in a few minutes, he would be ready and whole.

And the channel would rage at him again.

Captain

'What do we know about this object?'

Captain Laurent Zai directed this question at Amanda Tyre. The young ensign held his eyes steadily, he noticed. She no longer needed Hobbes as an intermediary.

'On a gross scale, sir?' Tyre answered. 'Its volume changes constantly, but averages roughly four hundred thousand cubic kilometers. The outermost layer of sand spins about once every six hours, but like a star or a gas giant, different depths rotate at different rates. Its internal currents are far more variable than any natural phenomenon. Its motion is mathematically chaotic.'

'I believe we had noticed that, Ensign,' Zai offered. 'What's it made of?'

'Mostly empty space, sir. It would float in water, assuming it didn't saturate. No denser than a sugar cube.'

Zai noted that Tyre paused here, as if allowing for a moment of surprise, aware that her words unsettled the old psychological association between mass and power: anything light couldn't hurt you.

'Based on the physical sampling effected by one of Marx's probes, most of the material content of the object is silicon. This silicon is structured in units about a half-millimeter across – the size of grains of sand. Each grain is composed of many extremely small layers, and doped with various other elements.'

'Doped?'

'Yes, sir. Presumably to change the conductivity of the silicon. Like the semiconductor materials in a pre-quantum computer.'

Zai narrowed his eyes.

'Tyre, do you think this object is one giant processor?'

'I don't know, sir.'

She offered her ignorance without apology. Zai was glad to see she was not a speculator, as so many in Data Analysis tended to be.

'How does it move?'

'Before the transmission event, the motion was simply centrifugal, sir. The outer layer seems to be adhesive in some way. Like a water droplet's surface tension.'

Zai nodded. Everyone had noticed how much it looked like a champagne dervish.

'But when the object . . . *consumed* the recon drones, that movement was obviously some other process.'

'Obviously,' Zai muttered. 'Any ideas?'

'I, um, have suggestive data to relate, sir. And some possible interpretations to offer.'

'Please,' Zai said, smiling. Perhaps Tyre was a speculator after all, but at least she was a cautious one.

Tyre gestured, and a background-radiation chromograph appeared in the command bridge's table airscreen.

'This was recorded by the *Lynx*'s passive sensors twelve minutes ago, a few seconds before the transmission event. That big spike is silicon. The smaller one up here is arsenic.'

'Arsenic? So, it could be a semiconducting processor,' Hobbes said. 'Or at least a storage device.'

Zai nodded. Of that, he had grown fairly certain. He was waiting only for the civilian transmissions from Legis to confirm his fears.

'Yes, ma'am,' Tyre answered. 'It's a computer. But it's a great deal more.'

She gestured, and the chromograph multiplied into a time series, propagating along its z-axis to become a spiky, chaotic mountain range.

'Here are the first few seconds of the transmission event. Note that the elemental makeup of the object changes.'

Tyre leaned back from the table, folding her hands.

Hobbes was the first to speak. 'Changes? You mean to say it tran-substantiated in a matter of seconds?'

Zai looked at the airscreen, trying to remember his stellar mechanics courses at the academy. That was the last time anyone had asked him to interpret a chromograph. 'What elements are we looking at?'

'These spikes are metals,' Tyre said, airmousing a set of harmonics descending from the tallest peak. 'Vanadium, electrum, and titanium in correct proportions to create superplastic adamantum. And this is a bit of mercury, possibly for some sort of inertial guidance.'

'Guidance? Motile alloys?' Zai said. This was too much to believe.

'Yes, sir. The structures that plucked Marx's drones from space had to have some sort of orientation device, and a powerful armature. The object's transubstantiation seems sophisticated enough to create such devices on the fly.'

'No,' Hobbes said quietly.

Zai narrowed his eyes. The Empire had transubstantiation devices; in industrial settings, lead could be turned to gold in useful quantities. Some isolated gas-giant outposts with access to thermal energy sometimes made metals from hydrogen and methane. The process was obscenely energy-expensive, but generally cheaper than shipping bulk metals in starships. And of course, there were always exotic new transuranium elements being created in laboratories.

But this level of control – elements from across the periodic table on demand – was fantastic.

'Why didn't we realize this sooner?' Hobbes asked.

Tyre frowned. 'We were too reliant on active sensors, ma'am. This process is more subtle than you'd think.'

The ensign flicked her hand.

Mass readings overlaid the chromograph, a set of lines alongside the mountain range, as straight and parallel as maglev tracks.

'As you can see, the silicon grains do not change mass when they transubstantiate. The object maintains a consistent density throughout, no matter what it appears to be made of. This elemental shift is somehow virtual. Of all our instruments, only the background-radiation chromograph detected any change at all.'

'Virtual?' Zai asked. 'How the hell can elements be virtual?'

'I don't know, sir.'

'Where is it getting the energy to make these changes?' Hobbes asked. The object had no power source that they had detected.

'I don't know, ma'am. But I don't think it takes much energy. In fact, it seems to be making more changes just now, for no particular reason. As if it were flexing its muscles.'

'Pardon me?'

The static chromograph disappeared, and was replaced by one in wild motion. The spikes jittered and jumped, animating the airscreen like the chatter of a crowd run through an audio visualizer.

'This is real time, minus lightspeed delay.'

God, thought Zai. The thing was *frantic*. It pulsed and throbbed to wound the eyes. For a moment, Zai almost thought he saw a pattern in the dance of lines, as if some analog portion of his brain could grasp the internal logic of the thing's 'muscle flexing.'

He tore his eyes from it, but the afterimage rang in his mind. What had happened to Marx? he wondered. What had the patterns and logic of this thing done to the man? In the high-intensity synesthesia of a pilot's canopy, with his mind already weakened by hypersleep disruption, the master pilot would have been immensely vulnerable.

Marx's brain waves were active, obscenely so, but the man was still not awake.

'What the hell are these?' Hobbes said, interrupting Zai's thoughts.

The captain's eyes followed his ExO's airmouse. A new range of mountains had appeared. Coded in blue, they jutted to the end of the airscreen.

'We believe that they're signatures of trans-half-life elements.'

'Transuranium?' Zai said, trying to bring the periodic table to mind.

'Trans-everything,' Tyre said. 'Beyond our software. Beyond even current theoretical speculation. We had to recalibrate just to differentiate them. There seems to be no upper limit to the number of electrons with which the object can endow its virtual elements. With no change in mass. Without stability constraints: a half-life of forever.'

The room exploded into chaos, scattering off into separate conversations. Everyone, it seemed, had been caught by these wild data, their minds taken over by the incredible implications of what they had seen. This had happened in the First Rix Incursion, back when Zai was a rating. The catapulting technologies of the Rix never failed to amaze, to appall, to suggest whole new fields of inquiry; they could freeze the mind.

Hobbes looked at him and pointed to the back of her wrist, an ancient Vadan hand sign he had taught her, suggesting that they move forward. Hobbes had already looked at the civilian transmissions from Legis, and from her prelim report, Zai's worst fears were likely to be realized.

He cleared his throat. Amplified by the captain's direct channel, the sound silenced the command bridge.

'Let us look at the event from Legis's perspective.'

Hobbes took control of the airscreen, clearing the wild gyrations of the object's dance. She divided the screen into three contemporaneous newsfeeds, all exactly eight hours, fifty-two minutes prior to the transmission event; they had reached the *Lynx* at lightspeed at almost the same moment the event had occurred. Zai moved his secondary hearing across them: a talking head disquisitioning on local politics, a sporting event, a financial feed giving raw data – undulating line graphs that showed price-shift and volume.

'These are handheld channels,' Hobbes explained, 'for watching on portable devices or in your head. They broadcast with satellite repeaters for maximum coverage outside of cabled areas. Crude, but strong enough for our passives to have picked up.'

She leaned back. 'The transmission event happens in ten seconds.'

The bridge crew waited anxiously, transfixed by the banalities of local media.

'Five,' Hobbes began to count down.

At *zero*, all three of the pictures fractured.

The talking heads of local politicians collapsed, like faces in a shattering mirror. The image of the sporting event – some sort of obstacle soccer – froze, then horizontal jitters turned it into garbage. The financial channel was the most interesting: for a moment the graphs stayed coherent, but showed wildly shifting data, as if some tremendous currency crash were underway. Then, like the others, the image collapsed into incomprehensibility.

'Well,' said Hobbes, 'it appears as if—'

'Wait,' Zai silenced her.

He gazed at the blur of the three screens. They hadn't snowcrashed, hadn't reached a state of pure noise. There was a nonrandom signal there, an order in the chaos, like encrypted data viewed without the proper codes. The newsfeeds' audio didn't sound like the undifferentiated wash of white noise; it was more animated, like the thunder of nearby traffic, a steady roar broken by individual vehicles passing, even the high-pitched bleat of warning horns.

'Tyre,' he ordered. 'Compare these transmissions to the chromograph data from the object.'

'Compare them, sir?'

'At an abstract level of organization. Do they have comparable repeating features? Similar periodicity? I don't need to know what they mean. Just tell me if there's any relationship.'

'Yes, sir,' Tyre answered. Her eyes dropped into the blankness of heavy second sight.

Zai saw puzzlement on the faces of his staff, which flickered with the still-coruscating lights of the Legis feeds.

'Obviously, whatever transmission hit Marx's drones struck the Legis infostructure eight and a half hours prior – exactly the light-speed delay between the two,' he said. 'Something hijacked their newsnets and replaced their feeds, not with noise, but with pirate data. My guess is that the polar facility then repeated that data, sending it to the object. Marx just got in the way.'

'But the facility was locked down, sir,' the marine sergeant complained. 'My troops were there at the pole.'

Zai frowned. The man was right. It was hard to believe that the Rix compound mind could get past the physical keys of a locked-down translight entanglement facility. How had it managed that trick?

'Incoming messages, sir,' Hobbes said. 'Lightspeed.'

The captain nodded. The information wake of the planet had finally caught up with them.

Hobbes shut her eyes.

'From the polar array,' she said. 'They're under attack, sir! Drones and autopiloted aircraft, and a Rix commando inside the wire.'

The marine sergeant swore. He'd wanted to stay on Legis XV

to help track the Rixwoman down, but Zai had demanded he stay aboard the *Lynx*.

'A message from the palace contingent now. The breakdown is global. Every net-linked com device is spewing garbage.'

'Not garbage,' Zai muttered. Information. The Rix mind had managed to transmit something to the object. It had broken their blockade.

'From the pole again,' Hobbes said, listening intently. 'They say the interplanetary array ramped up by itself, transmitting out of control.'

The marine sergeant cursed again.

'What was its broadcast target?' Zai demanded. Then he realized that with the translight facility disrupted, it would be seventeen hours before any questions could travel roundtrip between the *Lynx* and Legis.

Tyre, back from her data fugue, spoke up suddenly. 'You were right, sir. There is a connection between the Legis data and the object.' The ensign stared into her second sight, trying to translate the visuals there into words. 'There's a background period of twenty-eight milliseconds in both. And some sort of utility pattern: one thousand twenty-four zeros in a row every few seconds. You were right.'

Zai felt no joy in this revelation. Now that information was rushing at them from every quarter, confirming his worst fears, he didn't know what to do.

Despite all the *Lynx* had risked against the Rix battle-cruiser, they'd been beaten. The compound mind had escaped their quarantine.

'Something more from the palace, sir,' Hobbes broke in. 'The marines say they've regained control of the security system. The com breakdown seems to have confused the compound mind.'

Zai stared at her blank-faced.

Ensign Tyre was speaking again. She related more information about the Legis feeds and the object. She had matched the common patterns to Marx's brain waves, now.

Damn, Zai thought. Had he lost his master pilot to the abomination?

'Sir!' cried Hobbes. Then she fell silent.

'Report, Hobbes.'

'It seems the compound mind is gone, sir.'

'From the palace?' he asked.

Hobbes shook her head. 'From everywhere. The Legis nets are recovering, but the mind is gone, sir. Imperial shunts are taking over to prevent it from propagating again.'

A com officer added her voice. 'I'm getting local militia transmissions on the emergency band. They're saying the same thing. Legis is free.'

Zai sat back, shaking his head.

'It's gone, sir,' Hobbes said. 'Somehow, we won. The compound mind is gone!'

'No,' he said. It couldn't be this easy. A Rix mind couldn't be ousted by an infostructure failure, no matter how drastic. There were no such miracles. No simple victories. No rest for Laurent Zai.

Then he saw it, realized what had happened.

Zai's hands flicked in the air, bringing up the object's shape in the airscreen.

'It isn't gone.'

He pointed at the twisting shape.

'It's in there.'

The staff stared into the airscreen silently, as if hypnotized again by the undulations of the object.

Tyre came out her fugue, nodding her head.

'Yes, sir. It's in the object. I can see it there.'

'Engineer Frick,' Zai said.

'Yes, sir?'

'Get me acceleration,' he ordered. 'In forty minutes.'

'But, sir—'

'Do it.'

Laurent Zai strode to the command bridge door. He needed to clear his head for a few moments, to escape this surge of revelations.

'How much acceleration, sir?' Frick called after him. 'How many gees?'

Wasn't it obvious? Zai thought.

'Enough to ram that thing,' the captain said, and left.

Marine Private First Class

On Legis, Marine Private First Class Sid Akman despaired.

Weary of trying to make himself understood, he made the signal for a global fall-prone order. As one, the militia soldiers dotting the icy hills around the target dropped to the ground.

A *perfectly executed maneuver*, Akman thought sourly. He had finally found something the Legis militia was good at: cowering.

When he'd first been assigned to planetside, Private Akman had been glad to escape the *Lynx*. The frigate had just received her orders to go after the Rix battlecruiser, and figured to be a doomed ship. For a marine, dirt was never a plum assignment, but it beat a cold death in space.

But now the word was that the *Lynx* was doing fine, having bested the superior Rix craft on the first pass.

And Private Sid Akman found himself in perilous circumstances.

As the Imperial marine on the planet with the most actual combat experience – i.e., three drops – he was in command of this assault, which involved a hapless platoon of Legis militia closing in on an incomparably deadly Rix commando. The commando was cornered in her own lair, which she'd had weeks to prep defensively. In addition, her ice cave lay within one kilometer of the planet's magnetic north pole, and Legis's wild EM field was playing hell with the militia's gear. The thermal imagers were screwy, remote drones were useless, and the platoon's minesweeping robot would only walk in a giant lazy circle, a figure which the machine's internal nav insisted was a straight line.

To make matters worse, PFC Akman's heavy artillery support was nonfunctional. Something about the freezing cold. Therefore Akman's preferred strategy in this situation – quietly paint the target with x-ray lasers and have a flight of guided missiles launched from over the hill – was not going to happen. Air support was also out of the question. Some ghostly force had been attacking civilian aircraft around the pole for the last few weeks, and it was widely held in the militia command structure that the Rix compound mind could take control of anything in the air.

The militia bigs were *very* scared of the compound mind, even though it seemed to have disappeared during the big crash of a few hours ago. So they had electronically isolated this mission, even from the secure military infostructure. Akman had no headsup display, no pov feedback from his so-called soldiers, not even *radio*, for heaven's sake.

He was reduced to hand signals, a hastily constructed gestural code that had thus far failed to get his troops into position. Akman wished he had brought trumpets and drums.

The whole attack was unnecessarily dangerous in any case. The Rix commando was trapped here in the arctic. The recon flyer that she'd stolen was damaged beyond repair. A military satellite had spotted the grounded flyer easily, its black armor glaring against the white background. Oddly, the Rixwoman hadn't bothered to cover it with camo, or even a few handfuls

of snow. He could see the flyer now through his field amplifiers (which were, thank heaven, working). It bore the marks
of grievous damage sustained while penetrating the entanglement facility's perimeter defenses. It might fly again, but not
for more than a few klicks.

So why not just keep the commando surrounded? At least
until they could hit her with artillery. Remote drones. Air
power. *Anything* but a ground assault.

The militia bigs were giving Akman the runaround, making
excuses for this risky assault. They wanted to debrief the
hostage (or traitor) who was with the Rixwoman, so taking
down the entire mountain wasn't their preferred strategy.
Akman hadn't bothered to remind them how the last hostage
rescue against the Rix had gone.

The marine private sighed and raised his right fist, three
fingers up. After a moment, Squad Three rose slowly to their
feet, glancing at each other for confirmation. Akman extended
his arm forward, palm flat and parallel with the tundra. Squad
Three moved forward.

He smiled thinly in the bitter and wind-blown cold. For the
first time, this signal thing was working.

The marine private brought Squad Three to a halt and
dropped them again. Then he moved Squad Two back a bit,
just to see if they understood the pullback signal as well. For
a few more minutes, Akman shuffled the elements of his
command around the target area aimlessly, like a chess player
wasting moves against an immobilized opponent. The militia
soldiers were getting slightly better. And as far as Akman
could tell, the Rix commando wasn't even aware of the surrounding force yet. The incessant howl of the wind covered
the sound of their footsteps, and the attackers were hardly
lighting up the EM spectrum. Perhaps Akman's stone-age
communications had actually given the assault group a
momentary advantage.

Of course, Private Akman would have traded all the surprise in the world for a few rotary-wing gunships. Puma class, with Imperial pilots.

It was time to go in.

Akman moved slowly down from his hilltop perch. He knew that after the first shots were fired, all organization would crumble unless he were visible to his troops. Hell, it would crumble anyway. But at least from down here Akman could get off a few shots of his own. In the palace rescue, he'd lost a few friends to those seven Rix defenders. If he personally made the kill-shot here at the pole, it would bury some of the shame of that failed assault.

He slid on his belly toward the cave mouth, pausing to signal forward Squad One on his left. A few competent techs were in One. He stuck his thumb up, and the squad leader, a young woman called Smithes, sprayed a bright mist of monofilament-dissolving aerosol over Akman's head and into the cave mouth. No snares showed.

Akman moved forward again, staying in front of his troops. With everyone to his rear, he could set his varigun to the widest possible spray pattern. The sawed-off shotgun effect might not kill the Rixwoman, but she would feel it. If he could stun her even for a moment, one of the thousands of rounds guaranteed to fly from his panicked troops might get lucky.

The cave was dark. Akman paused to adjust his visor, although the cold-blooded Rix were notoriously hard to see with night-vision. He crawled inside, the sudden silence of the cave eerie after the constant moan of wind.

Then Private Akman heard a sound. It came from within, echoing from the smooth, laser-carved walls as if they were marble.

It sounded like retching, or coughing.

Akman had never imagined a Rixwoman getting sick.

Perhaps it was the hostage. There was a hollowness to the sound, an anguish that sounded human and somehow heart-broken.

He mentally shrugged. Whatever it was, the noise covered his approach.

Akman raised a fist, signaling Squad One to hold until they heard fire, and crawled alone farther into the cave.

A light shone before him now, glinting from the icy walls. The coughing sound and glimmer of light seemed to come from the same direction, and Akman followed them. He knew he should spray for monofilament snares. Even crawling at a snail's pace, the molecule-thin wires could cut through a limb before he would notice the microscopic incision. But something about the wracking, animal sound impelled him forward without due caution. Instinctively, Akman knew he had the advantage here.

The marine rose to his feet. The sound came from just around a sharp-hewn corner of ice. Akman swallowed. He was going for it: the lone kill of a Rix commando.

Akman moved before he had time to reconsider this insanity.

He stepped lightly into the small room, gun leveled. A light squeeze on the stud would hit everything in the room.

The Rix commando sat before him, her head in her hands.

Godspite, she was a mess! Hair remained only in singed patches on her scalp. Her hands and face were red and blistered, every exposed centimeter of skin smeared with soot and dried blood. Her nose was swollen from a bad break. She wore a fire-blackened ablative suit that had melted onto her hypercarbon joints, hanging in tatters from them like shiny, sloughed skin. Half-frozen blood pooled on the floor below where she sat, and Akman could see at least three abdominal wounds.

There must have been a lung hit as well. The wracking cough shook her whole body.

Private Akman had a sudden realization. He could actually *capture* this Rixwoman. For the first time in a century of warfare, the Empire would take a living prisoner of the Cult. And Sid Akman would be the one.

With shaking fingers he switched the varigun to a riot setting, which fired a suspension of steel pellets in plastic goo. A laughable weapon against a Rix commando, but the woman seemed so hideously wounded already, it just might be enough. He aimed the gun at her bloody stomach.

Perhaps he wouldn't have to fire at all.

'Don't move,' he said evenly, trying to hide his fear. The commando was believed to speak Legis dialect quite well, having carried off an impersonation of her hostage for several days.

The commando looked up, startling Akman with her beautiful, violet eyes.

By the Empire, he thought. *She's been crying*

Surely this was some maintenance procedure, some repair-nano medium for fire-damaged optics. Some crocodile trick.

Surely not tears.

Another sob wracked the commando. Then she pulled a monofilament knife from her clothes.

Akman fired instantly, the recoil from the heavy projectile pushing him off balance. He staggered to remain upright on the icy floor of the cave. The suspension of steel balls bounced harmlessly from the Rixwoman's upraised hand – she had blocked it!

She coughed and threw the knife aside.

'I am unarmed now,' she said in a perfect local accent.

Her burned and scarred head dropped back into her hands.

The rush of adrenaline and fear that had caused him to fire passed quickly, and Akman gained control of his breathing. This Rix commando was really *surrendering*. The Imperial marine lowered his weapon, wondering if everything he had been taught about the Rix could be false.

The ungainly sounds of Squad One moving up came from behind him. They must have heard the varigun's report. He turned and waved them back.

The first Rix prisoner ever. He wasn't about to let some yokel burst in and shoot her to death. Her body convulsed again, and Akman grew concerned. He didn't want her *dying*, by god.

'Are you . . . ?' he began. Sick? Dying? *Weeping?*

Keep it simple. 'What's wrong?'

The commando looked at him again with her stunning violet eyes, the only feature of her face that was not grotesque with injury.

'I am mourning Rana Harter,' she said simply. 'Who died today.'

And then she wept some more.

Executive Officer

The *Lynx* began to move.

Almost a full four hours after the captain's deadline, First Engineer Frick finally cleared Hobbes to give the order. The frigate shook as the main drive engaged, a rattle sweeping through the bridge, tinged with a metal shriek. The *Lynx*'s artificial-gravity generators, which usually maintained zero apparent inertia, were showing their overstressed condition. Hobbes felt herself pressed rudely back into her chair, feeling about half the frigate's four-gravity acceleration.

She saw the captain scowl as the crushing weight released them.

'Hobbes?'

'Sir, the AG is doing double duty,' she explained. 'It's keeping us nailed down *and* the ship together. We've prioritized inertial dampening on the portions of *Lynx* where structural integrity is in doubt.'

'Yes, Hobbes. But surely that tremor wasn't good for the fissured hullalloy in the bow.'

'No, Captain. It wasn't good at all for the fissured hullalloy in the bow.'

She returned to her tasks, ignoring Zai's look of surprise at her tone. Hobbes had enough to do – coordinating the continuing repair, dispensing zero-gee to crews with heavy objects to move, making sure the *Lynx* didn't break up – without explaining the obvious to the captain. Another few hours of repair in freefall, and the ship would have accelerated without a hitch.

But orders were orders, and time was limited.

The Rix battlecruiser was accelerating at its maximum. Even assuming the vessel turned over, it would reach the object in just over seven hours. The *Lynx* couldn't sit around forever. As it was, the wounded frigate would be hard pressed to match velocities with the object before the battlecruiser arrived.

Hobbes wondered why the Rix had placed the object fifteen million klicks behind the battlecruiser, and without an escort. Had they assigned a hundred or so of the blackbody drones to it, the object would be able to defend itself.

She wondered grimly if the thing were already capable of fending off the *Lynx*. Its powers of alchemy were an unknown quantity. The now-animated object (Did it really contain the Rix mind, or was the captain crazy?) could change itself into practically any substance.

But how would it defend itself? Turn into a working starship? A giant fusion cannon? Or would it clam up, giving itself a carapace of hullalloy? Or even neutronium?

ExO Hobbes shook her head, correcting this last supposition. Neutronium was collapsed matter – a non-elemental substance – and so far all the object's transubstantiations had involved elements. There was no need to exaggerate its powers, Hobbes reminded herself. Data Analysis's current theory was that it could call arrangements of virtual electrons into being, but not protons and neutrons. Therefore the object's substance, despite its chemical properties, would never have the mass, radioactivity, or magnetism of its true-matter analogs. The object's alchemy was a bit like that of an easy graviton generator: the particles it created were amazing at first, but upon closer examination they paled in comparison to the real thing.

Katherie Hobbes pushed these thoughts aside – speculations on the object were DA's concern – and refocused her attention on the *Lynx*'s repair woes. The biggest drain on stores had been the singularity generator. The bigbang mechanism was in fine shape, but to replace the generator's shielding, armor had been stripped relentlessly from the rest of the frigate. The generator's jury-rigged shielding was sufficient to protect the crew, but lacked the necessary countermass to keep the hole in place under heavy gees. It took a lot of matter to keep a pocket universe from breaking free under the inertial stresses of maneuver. With every ton Frick added to the shield, Hobbes got another fraction of a gee in safe acceleration, but that armor had to be pulled from some other part of the ship. The frigate's fissured bow also needed reinforcement. Frick had made do with a patchwork of plates drawn from armored drones, combat stations, and even decompression bulkheads. Half the hardpoints on the ship – gun batteries, the main drive, and critical targets like sickbay – had been stripped of armor. Facing a half-assed volley of flockers or some other kinetic weapon, the *Lynx* would be swissed.

The executive officer wished fervently that she could call up a hundred tons of hullalloy from an alchemist of her own.

Hobbes simulated their approach to the object under the frigate's current configuration. At four gees for seven hours, they could slow down to make a first pass at a relative velocity of about three hundred kilometers per second, a respectable velocity for an attack. But if she could squeeze out another gee, they would come in neatly matched to the object. It would be invaluable for the Empire if they could study the thing before they destroyed it.

Ideally, Hobbes thought, she could get *two* more gees out of the wounded *Lynx*. Then the frigate would be able to match the six-gee maximum of the Rix craft, making an eventual escape at least feasible. If Frick stripped every hardpoint on the ship, it might just be possible.

Hobbes rubbed her head, which had begun to spin around the combinatorial tree of possible tradeoffs. The mental focus that two hours of hypersleep had bestowed upon her was starting to slip again. She decided to ask the captain for advice.

The shipmaster's chair was empty. She raised Zai in synesthesia.

His voice came back without visual, a sure sign that he was in the captain's observation blister. Zai had ordered the blister resurrected as soon as it could be after the battle was over. Over the last few hours, he had returned there again and again, staring into the void as he had before rejecting the blade of error.

Hobbes wondered if he were having second thoughts.

'Yes, Hobbes?'

'I think I can get us up to five gees, sir.'

'Only five?'

Hobbes sighed quietly, glad that her expression was hidden from the captain.

'There's not enough heavy metal to keep the hole in place at higher accelerations, sir.'

'What have we stripped?'

'Everything, sir. Hardpoints. Sickbay. Drones. As much of the main drive shielding as we can spare without another round of cancers.'

There was a pause.

'What about the bridge?'

'Sir?' The battle bridge was the *Lynx*'s hardest point, wrapped in a cocoon of hullalloy and structured neutronium. There was good reason for this precaution; the frigate had no chain-of-command provisions if the captain and all the firsts were killed.

The Empire didn't want ensigns running starships. Especially not this one.

'I believe there are forty tons of matter available in the bridge hardpoint,' the captain said.

'Forty tons may be present, sir. But I'm not sure they are *available*.'

The captain chuckled. 'Give me six gees, Hobbes. Whatever it takes.'

'Sir—'

'The object may devise any number of ways to attack us, Hobbes. But I have a feeling that it would be disinclined to use a kinetic weapon. Think about it.'

Hobbes considered the captain's words.

'Because it would have to expend its own mass to create a missile?'

'Yes, Hobbes. And true mass is the one thing it lacks. It may be able to create a diamond bullet, but however hard that diamond is, it will still have the density of a sugar cube. However you strip the *Lynx*, I think she'll be able to withstand a hail of sugar cubes. Even very hard ones.'

Hobbes's eyebrows raised. Whenever she thought the old

man had succumbed to melancholy, Zai would show his usual tactical brilliance. But she wasn't entirely convinced.

'Even if these sugar cubes are propelled by a railgun, sir? At relativistic velocities—'

'A railgun requires magnetism, Hobbes.'

Hobbes grimaced at her own error. Of course. DA believed that the object's alchemical matter was nonferrous and non-fissionable. The thing was limited to chemical propulsion for any weapon, a paltry way to accelerate a kinetic weapon.

'I see, sir. That's why you want the gees: so that we can decelerate fast enough to match velocity.' Hobbes saw it now. If the *Lynx* flew past the object at hundreds of klicks per second, it could simply place a net of alchemical elements in their path. Even a stationary tripwire could be deadly to a running man.

'Exactly, Executive Officer,' he answered. 'And with six gees, we can escape the battlecruiser after our mission is accomplished.'

She nodded.

'But what about energy weapons, sir? We've only got a makeshift heat-sink. The bridge armor also shields us from radiation.'

'We've seen no signs of a powerful energy source, Hobbes. But of course you're right. If that thing can make itself into a planet-sized fusion cannon, we're dead.'

'Then what should we—'

'Dead, Hobbes, whether or not we have shielding around the bridge. Give me six gees. Captain out.'

Katherie heard the connection step down.

She sighed. Perhaps the old man was right. They were traveling toward an incomprehensible set of possibilities, facing a foe of unknown strengths and weaknesses. The *Lynx* was matched against an enemy that was neither a crewed starship nor a drone, machine nor creature; it wasn't even proper matter. It was an empty signifier in the emptiness of space.

Once again, the survival of Laurent Zai's ship seemed to be out of the hands of its crew.

A few more tons of metal weren't going to make any difference.

Senator

The counselor from the Plague Axis arrived with a thunderous noise. She had been waiting for hours. The counselor was only twenty minutes late, but Nara's mind had turned to this meeting again and again all day, as if it were some illicit and terrible assignation. There was the aberrance of talking with someone whose face she would never see, the unease at meeting with another counselor outside the chamber, and, underlying it all, the irrational but age-old fear of contagion.

The sound of the counselor's helicopter approached slowly, building from a subliminal shudder to a relentless force that raised a chorus of chattering complaints from Nara's foxbone tea service. The vehicle had called ahead to check the specifications of her building's landing pad; it was a big machine. The counselor's environmental system required heavy transport. It contained the man's affliction, a mobile quarantine.

At Oxham's request, Roger Niles had discreetly determined the gender of the Plague Axis representative. In the chambers of the War Council, the plagueman rarely spoke except to vote, his voice distorted by the filtration system that protected both his delicate immune system from the capital's pollution and his fellow counselors from the ancient parasites that made him their home.

Nara Oxham shuddered for a moment when the pitch of

the helicopter's whine dropped, signaling that its landers were secure on the pad above her. Rationally, Oxham knew that she had nothing to fear. Members of the Plague Axis carried death with themselves when they entered the realm of the living. If a biosuit were somehow opened to the fresh air, a layer of phosphorus compounds would immolate its wearer rather than risk exposing the populace.

And her fear was not only unreasoned, it was shameful, a remnant of one of humanity's most idiotic mistakes. The Plague Axis performed a signal service to the Empire. Like most of the human diaspora, the Eighty Worlds possessed only a small gene pool relative to its trillions of inhabitants. The genetic legacy of Earth Prime had been pared down by wars and holocausts, and by foolish edicts of racial purity, which resulted in monocultures taking to the stars together, inbred groups without the stability and adaptability of genetic fusion cultures. But of all the historical errors that had reduced genetic diversity, most damaging had been the effort to engineer a humanity free of faults.

It had taken millennia of misguided genetic manipulation to discover the subtle jape played by evolution: almost no human traits were universally unfit. Genes that exacerbated a disease in one environment conferred resistance in another. Insanity was married to genius, passivity to patience. Every disadvantage carried hidden strengths. In the wildly variable conditions of the stars, humans would find that they needed greater diversity, not less. And yet it was a diminished humanity that left earth's cradle, enfeebled supermen who met only a local and flawed standard of superiority.

The Plague Axis was an attempt to repair this damage. They were the throwbacks, possessed of legacy genes that had escaped by chance the eugenical pogroms. Descended from the poor, those without access to gene therapies and prenatal selection, they were like discarded junk that had become incalculably valuable as antiques. The people of the Axis had been the ugly, the afflicted, those prone to madness. Now, they existed as reservoirs of ancient treasure, their once-undesirable traits slowly and carefully reintroduced into the general population over the span of generations.

But still, Nara Oxham hesitated before she signaled for her door to open. She made the gesture with an unsure hand.

The Plague Axis representative paused at the entry, like a vampire waiting to be invited across her threshold.

'Counselor,' she said.

The helmet of the biosuit performed a little bow, and the man shuffled in.

Senator Oxham wondered if he would sit. The sunken dais of the council's chamber was suited to the suit's bulk, but the chairs in her apartment were spindly and insubstantial.

He remained standing. So did she.

'Senator,' he returned the greeting.

'To what do I owe the pleasure?'

'An explanation is in order, and a promise.'

Oxham shook her head slightly in confusion.

'Senator,' the man continued, 'I must explain my vote of yesterday.'

Oxham took a deep breath. He was talking about the Emperor's genocidal plan. She glanced out at the blackness of the Martyrs' Park. The hundred-year rule did not forbid discussion of secrets between counselors, but she felt uncomfortable speaking of the forbidden topic outside the council chamber.

'Surely the point is moot now, Counselor. It didn't come to that.'

'Yes, we were saved by the *Lynx*,' he said. 'But we wish you to understand our motives. We are not your enemy.'

'We?'

He nodded. 'I did not make the decision alone.'

Nara blinked. He had discussed the Emperor's plan with outsiders? The man was admitting treason.

'But how?' she said. 'We had only minutes to decide.' She looked at the bulky biosuit, wondering if it might house an entangled quantum grid, the only form of communication that could possibly be undetectable to the sensors of the Diamond Palace.

The plagueman spread his thickly gloved hands, a clumsy puppet's gesture, pleading for understanding.

'I have not broken the hundred-year rule, Senator Oxham. The Emperor himself came to the Axis before the question was raised in council. Before the rule was invoked.'

Nara nodded and sighed. The sovereign and his tricks. He had gone into the vote with a stacked deck.

'What did he offer you?' she said coldly.

The plagueman turned half away, his puppet hands up in the air now.

'You must understand something, Senator. The Plague Axis of the Risen Empire faces hard times. Bleak centuries ahead.'

'What do you mean?'

'We are too few,' he said. 'Although we add diversity to the Empire, we lack enough divergence in our own population. Over the generations, we risk becoming a monoculture ourselves.'

Nara frowned, trying to remember the reading she'd done on the Axis since first meeting the members of the council. This hasty study blurred with the volumes of military and megaeconomic theory she had consumed, the forced marches of sudden expertise required to prosecute a war.

'A monoculture?' she asked. 'Don't you interbreed with the plague axes of the other coreward powers?' That was the true source of the Axis's independence from the rest of the Empire. They were not simply a reservoir, they were a trading guild.

He ponderously shook his head. 'Not for eighty years Absolute. Since the end of the First Incursion, we have been under a blockade.'

'A blockade?'

'The Rix have applied pressure throughout the core. The Tungai, the Fahstuns, not even the Laxu will trade with us.'

Nara swallowed. Even segments of humanity that were in violent conflict still kept up the exchange of genes through their nominally neutral plague axes. The biological legacy of Earth Prime was so thinly spread, the distances of the diaspora so great, it was playing a dangerous game to reduce diversity any further, like poisoning wells in a desert war.

'Why would they do that?'

'The Rix have a voice everywhere, Nara Oxham. As you know, we are the last coreward power to resist their compound minds. We have been under blockade these last eighty years.'

'Why has this been kept secret?'

'The Emperor wished it to be thought that the First Incursion ended in a true peace.'

The biosuit's helmet barely moved, but Nara could tell he was shaking his head. She sighed. The Emperor had proclaimed a false victory eighty years ago. The Rix had not been beaten, they had merely moved the conflict into other theaters.

'We are growing weaker,' the Plague counselor said. 'Less able to stabilize the Empire's billions.'

Oxham knew enough to understand the threat. Almost the entire population of the Eighty Worlds had descended from a small portion of one continent on Earth Prime. The weaknesses of monoculture were a constant threat: new contagions and panics propagated quickly, and charismatic figures like the Emperor consolidated power with the hyperbolic curve of pandemics. The consequences of a genetic blockade might one day be even more damaging than this second war with the Rix.

'But why help the Emperor commit mass murder?' she asked. 'How could depopulating Legis XV fulfil your aims?'

'Before the War Council took up the issue of destroying the Legis infostructure, the Apparatus came to us with an analysis. How might a war with the Rix increase the diversity of the Empire? In deep history, wars often had such an effect. Mass movements of people brought distant gene pools together, invaders and colonists crossbred with local populations.'

'But the Rix don't want to occupy us, Counselor,' she said. 'There'll be no miscegenation with them, no rape camps or comfort conscripts. Just death, and the sterile occupation of compound minds. A nonbiological violation.'

'Correct. The only population movement will be among the Eighty Worlds themselves. Such disruptions are always useful, but they would merely stir the existing pool.'

'What was it then?' she asked.

He made a sound that might have been a sigh, which came from the filter in a hiss of white noise, like boiling water poured slowly onto cold metal.

'What the Empire needs is new genes, Senator. New arrangements of DNA. With the Rix blockade, we cannot import them. Only mutation will generate more diversity.'

'Hopeful monsters?' she asked. 'It's been tried. The laboratory can't create at the same magnitude of evolution. There are never enough subjects, and we don't even know what we're looking for.'

The plagueman sighed again. 'Not in the laboratory, Senator. But in vivo, in the wild, on a planetary scale.'

She blinked, wondering if he could be serious. 'Legis?'

He nodded, a slow and clumsy gesture.

She shook her head. The man was insane. 'But the nuclear weapons over Legis were to be low-yield, clean EMP devices.'

'No, Senator. They would have been dirty bombs. An unexplained error.'

Nara swayed for a moment, closing her eyes. She needed to sit down. Reaching behind her, she felt the cold and reassuring solidity of the apartment's glassene wall.

'A hundred million wasn't enough for him?'

'There are trillions to think of, Nara Oxham.'

'You're mad,' she said. 'You and he are both insane.' Nara walked away from the suited man, barely able to hold what might have happened in her mind. 'God above. We would have been complicit in a billion deaths. The Emperor could have held it over the political parties for centuries. Whether we personally voted for it or not, we legitimized the decision by sitting on his council.'

'And you could hold it over the sovereign, knowing that the dirty bombings were intentional. The ultimate stabilizing force: mutually assured destruction.'

'And all this for a few mutations?'

'More than a few, Senator. The population of a whole planet is a vast palette to draw from. The dirty work has to be done; let the Rix be blamed for it, we thought.'

Senator Oxham dropped into a large chair, letting the plagueman stand alone. She covered her eyes and felt a twinge from the city. The incessant human throng that always threatened to consume her seemed terribly fragile now. With the right weapon, all those voices could be silenced in an instant. That ancient specter of mass destruction – more than the diaspora, or the Time Thief, or even the gray powers of the symbiant – was the appalling price of technology.

Death had hardly been beaten. The Old Enemy had simply changed its scale of interest.

'I am sorry that you were disappointed by the *Lynx*'s victory,' she finally said.

'No, we were glad, Senator.'

She looked up at him.

The biosuit shuffled from side to side.

'Try to understand. We of the Axis are all hopeful monsters. Mutations who hope one day to contribute to the germ line.'

'Monsters,' she agreed.

'As are you, Nara Oxham.'

'What do you mean?'

'In your ability, your madness, you are one of us. If synesthesia implants had been invented a few hundred years earlier, before apathy treatments existed to cure you, all those with unexpected reactions to the process – brainbugs, photism, verbochromia, even your empathy – would have been cast aside as mad, as were my ancestors. The descendants of these unfortunates, people like you, would be in the Plague Axis now.'

For a moment, Nara was revolted at the thought. Her condition was not genetic, but the result of untried technology. A small percentage had unexpected reactions to any new technique.

'I'm not a mutation.'

'You are. The last hundred years have shown that reactions to synesthesia implants are often inherited. Your kind are a genetic anomaly, one that was hidden until the environment changed. Synesthesia revealed you.'

The plagueman fell silent, letting her digest his words. She could almost grasp his viewpoint, unfamiliar though it was. So much lay hidden in the human code, revealed only by events. It was like the rain forests of Vasthold, whose vast reservoirs of protein structures routinely delivered up new drugs and bioware, but only when the need for them became apparent. Irrational design, it was called: plumbing diversity for random answers.

Events could make a monster – or a savior – of anyone.

But Nara had never thought of herself that way.

'Possibly,' she said.

'But you shamed us, Nara Oxham. You faced down the Emperor, as we did not.'

She laughed bitterly. 'Now you decide you don't want a new race of mutants? After the point is moot?'

'We realized even before Laurent Zai's victory that we had gone too far. Our thinking had been changed by cowardice. We were afraid to oppose the sovereign.'

She shrugged. 'So you say.'

'Allow us to prove it, Nara Oxham.'

'How?'

He shuffled toward her, held out his hand. Oxham no longer felt compelled to hide her disgust, and she stood and pulled away.

'Any vote you wish, Senator, we will side with you.'

Nara raised her eyebrows. The War Council was structured around a natural four-to-four split, the three opposition parties and Ax Milnk against Loyalty and the three dead. The Plague Axis held the deciding vote. She realized now that the Emperor had planned it that way. When they had confirmed the War Council, the Senate had thought the Plague Axis a natural ally to the living, not knowing of the pressures that the Axis suffered from the Rix blockade, not realizing how the Emperor could bend them to his will. But the sovereign had overplayed his hand; his attempted genocide had turned them into guilty, regretful accomplices.

'You'll vote the way I say?'

The biosuit nodded. 'We will, once, when you ask it.'

'I'll let you know. But however many votes it takes, there must be no more genocides.'

'None,' the plagueman agreed.

That was something, Senator Oxham thought. She had an ally. Perhaps this war didn't have to be a bloodbath. If the man were genuine, perhaps it was time for a gesture.

Swallowing, Nara crossed to where the representative stood, and put her hand on the shoulder of the suit. It was as cold as a dead man's arm.

'What do you want from me in return? Surely not just absolution,' she said softly.

The biosuited man turned away from her, faced the darkness of the Martyrs' Park, and cleared his throat, a very recognizable sound.

'If you would favor us, Nara Oxham, we do have a request. Perhaps your particular ability is merely happenstance, a slip of a few angstroms in the implant procedure. But if not, then maybe your empathy can be added to the germ line.'

He turned to her.

'So one day, in your own time, we would like you to have a child. Or give us what we need to make one.'

A child, she thought. More madness in this universe, another Oxham addicted to the passions of the crowd, addicted to drugs to maintain sanity, given to loving broken men light-years distant. This was like some fairy tale, a first-born promised to demons. She shuddered.

'Give me your vote when I ask it,' she said, 'and I'll consider it.'

Another hopeful monster for the cauldron.

Captain

Laurent Zai watched the object in the bridge airscreen, his mind fighting against the mesmerizing undulations of its surface.

Now that the *Lynx* was closing with the thing, simple telescopy revealed a level of detail that had been invisible to active sensors. The wild dunes that played across its visage had grown far more active since Marx's probes had imaged them. The object was definitely alive now, clearly possessed of some inner, animating presence.

Zai could sense the compound mind in its movements. Somehow, the Rix had found a way to mirror the data of an entire world, to compress and transmit it, and house it in this strange arrangement of matter. The planet had merely served as an incubator, virgin soil in which to culture the first of a new species of the compound mind, one able to move across the stars. The Rix takeover of Legis was not an invasion.

It was a breeding program.

And the Apparatus was afraid of a few transmissions escaping Legis? Here was the data of the entire planet, wrapped up and ready for shipping back into Rix space. Every aspect of Imperial technology and culture would be open for other Rix minds to probe and pick apart, a living model of the enemy brought back as spoils of war.

Only the unlikely survival of the *Lynx* had given the Empire a chance to stop this obscenity from returning home.

'Charge the photon cannon,' he ordered.

'Aye, sir,' said Gunner Wilson, his fingers already moving as he spoke.

Zai had left the overtly hostile act of readying his weapons until now, hoping to disguise his intentions as long as possible. Thus far, the *Lynx* had sent out only unarmed scout probes and minesweepers, as if gathering information were the frigate's only mission. Who knew how naive this newly born mind might be?

Of course, the data they had already obtained might prove valuable once analyzed. The virtual matter of which the object was composed was far beyond any technology the Empire had ever created. What they discovered here might begin to unravel the mystery of how it worked. Even an oblique understanding of the underlying science would be a war prize for the ages.

'Launch ramscatter drones.'

'Launched, sir.'

The ship didn't respond with the usual recoil as the drones left. The launch rail was still not repaired, so the drones went forth under their own power. Between their slow start and the frigate's nearly matched velocity with the object, what few ramscatters the *Lynx* still possessed wouldn't achieve much of a collision vector. But they hardly mattered. Zai was sure that energy weapons were the key here. Data Analysis was certain that whatever else it might be able to do, the object could definitely make its outer layers very hard. It was probably impervious to kinetic energy. Still, it would be revealing to observe how it reacted to powerful explosives.

'Any changes, Tyre?'

'No, sir.'

The DA ensign was up here on the bridge. Fighting an unpredictable foe, Zai needed analysis without the usual filters. The captain dipped into Tyre's synesthesia channel. *Damn*, the woman was going to burn out her second sight, if not her brain! Amanda Tyre was overlaying visible-light telescopy, a dozen drone viewpoints, and the object's wildly gyrating chromograph all at once. How could she comprehend anything amid that torrent of data?

Zai blinked the images away.

Well, if Tyre wanted fireworks, he would give her some.

'Hit it with the first wave,' he ordered the drone pilots.

'Aye, sir,' came an unfamiliar voice.

Even for these inconsequential and stupid ramdrones, Zai wished that Jocim Marx were here. The man brought an intelligence to his warcraft that was irreplaceable. Besides Hobbes, Marx was the *Lynx*'s most valuable officer. But the man was still down in sickbay, stricken with whatever overload had afflicted his brain after being caught in the path of the transmitted compound mind.

The airscreen view widened, opening to include both the Lynx and the enemy, the vector marks of the ramdrones between them. A few seconds later, the drones scattered, solid green arcs splitting into a hazy multitude of trajectories as they approached the object.

'In three, two . . .'

As the missiles struck, a gasp of surprise swept across the bridge. For a moment, a part of the object's surface froze, as suddenly motionless as video stopping on a single frame. The hundreds of dronelet impacts flared red, rose petals scattered across frozen ocean waves, then disappeared without leaving a mark.

With the threat to the object passed, the dunes jumped into motion again.

'What was that?' Zai asked.

'I'm not sure, sir,' Tyre said slowly. 'The object became something. Definitely a crystal, but I have no idea of what the matrix was composed of.'

'Nothing showing on the chromograph?' Hobbes asked.

'There is, ma'am, but it's not a recognizable element.'

'Transuranium,' Zai muttered. They knew that the object might be able to create unknown elements well past the upper reaches of the normal periodic table. They would be metals, of a sort, but with unlimited half-lives, and therefore non-radioactive. Data Analysis had worked feverishly to determine what characteristics such exotic substances might possess with hundreds or even thousands of electrons in stable orbits, but such basic research was impossible when the elements themselves had never existed – *couldn't* exist except within the object itself.

'No, sir,' Tyre said a moment later. 'I don't think that's it.'

She said nothing more.

'Tyre? Report.'

Her head started nodding quickly, her hands flickering with gestural commands like an autistic child.

'I see it now, sir,' she said breathlessly. 'The atoms of the object's armor have fewer than a hundred electrons, but they aren't configured in the usual way.'

'What's "the usual way"?' Hobbes asked.

'In spherical energy levels,' Tyre said. 'Look.'

The periodic table appeared.

Godspite, Zai thought. In the heat of battle with a Rix mind, and they were going to get a chemistry lesson. *This* was why DA was always kept off the bridge. He raised his hand to wave the apparition away.

But then the rectangular table turned into a spiral. Zai's hand froze.

'Electrons orbit their nuclei in set energy shells,' Tyre explained. 'Orbital quanta, in effect. But the object's virtual matter seems to be breaking that law. According to our probes, the object's surface was briefly composed of an element with new quantum states, new subshells. Transuranium means it's off the high end of the table. But this element was *on top* of the table. On the z-axis, like when imaginary numbers add another dimension to a number line.'

The elemental spiral extruded itself into a conch shell, rising up like some periodic Tower of Babel. At each story of the structure, the familiar elemental groups gained new members.

'I think the object's surface armor was composed largely of carbon,' Tyre said. 'Or something with an atomic number of six. But with a crystalline structure much more complex than diamond.'

'It was a hell of a lot harder than diamond, too,' Hobbes added, 'and with a higher melting point. The drones had zero effect, and they would have burned through diamond as easily as cloth.'

'Send in the second wave, Hobbes,' Zai ordered. 'And get that apparition off my airscreen!'

Tyre's diagram winked rudely out, replaced by the arcing lines of the remaining drones. They plummeted into the object, which froze again to repulse their blows. This time, it seemed to the captain's eyes that the efficiencies of the object's metamorphosis were greater: only the exact position where each dronelet struck became motionless. The rest of the ocean raged on unaffected.

'*I see,*' muttered Tyre, drinking in the data.

Zai ignored her. 'Give me fifty terabits from the aft photon cannon,' he ordered Gunner Wilson. 'Dead center.'

A targeting dot appeared on the object.

'Ready at your command,' the gunner said.

Zai started to give the order, but the words stuck in his throat.

The bridge's main airscreen, his personal synesthesia, even the backup hardscreens surrounding the shipmaster's chair all showed the same, unbelievable thing.

The object had disappeared.

Blind Man

Though stripped of sight and his position in the chain of command, Data Master Kax still possessed illusion.

The flying dust of optical silicon had ravaged only his eyes. The optic nerve and the brain centers were completely functional. Indeed, once the *Lynx* returned to Legis, implantation of a pair of artificials would be a trivial matter.

Most importantly, the tiny receivers that allowed synesthesia, the gateways to second sight, were still active. These devices surrounded the lamina cribrosa, hundreds of them in a man of Kax's profession, unscratched by the glass fragments that had destroyed his normal vision.

Kax followed the battle from sickbay, drifting among the views of various drones, watching over young Tyre's shoulder as she constructed experimental models of the object's virtual matter. Occasionally Tyre would query him, asking for advice or confirmation, using sign language to conceal the conversations. Kax had become an invisible confidant to his own replacement, like the helpful ghost of an ancestor.

Then the object disappeared.

Telescopy showed nothing but background stars; the throughput of x-ray spectroscopy was flat; infrared showed only the cold of space.

Kax overheard the shouting on the bridge, watched as Tyre spun from one drone's viewpoint to another, replaying the vanishing again and again as the captain demanded answers. Had the thing discorporated itself? Tyre searched vainly for radiation and debris. Teleported? DA software plunged into the chromographs leading up to the disappearance, looking for signs of some magical substance emerging from the object's depths.

The blind man stayed calm. He let the visualizations of Tyre's wild speculation fall from his false sight, and returned his view to the empty space where the object had been. He moved from drone to drone in real-time, staying in the spectrum of visible light. Watching.

The empty space seemed perfect.

Background stars shone through it, shifting slightly due to the drones' mismatched velocities with the object. The drones could see each other through the now-empty space; one of them had a view of the *Lynx* that had been blocked by the object before its disappearance.

'Tyre,' Kax said.

She didn't answer for a moment. Overwhelmed by the captain's demands for answers, she hadn't time to spare for a noisy, blind ghost. But the old reflexes of command eventually compelled a response.

Yes, sir? she handsigned.

'Ask the drone pilots to move Recon 086. Just a short acceleration.'

Heading?

'It doesn't matter. Just as long as it's sudden.'

The blind man watched carefully from the indicated drone's point of view, training his mind on the familiar shape of the frigate.

Ten seconds later the image jerked as the drone accelerated in a short, clean burst. The *Lynx* was still visible, still there in the right place. But Kax saw what he had been watching for, a subtle imperfection that lasted less than a tenth of a second, an almost subliminal tear in synesthesia. The frigate had distorted for a moment, then the shape had re-formed even before the drone's acceleration ended.

The image was false, a mere feed coming from something between the drone and the *Lynx*.

Data Master Kax reserved the image in a high-definition buffer of the frigate's short-term memory, and carefully cut the few dozen frames that showed the distortion. He sent them to Ensign Tyre, marked priority, and leaned back with satisfaction, smiling to himself.

Invisibility meant nothing to a blind man.

Executive Officer

'Invisibility,' Captain Zai muttered.

'Controlled refraction, sir,' corrected Ensign Tyre.

Hobbes glanced sidelong at the young woman. Despite

her proficiency at data analysis, Tyre hadn't acquired a knack for spotting the captain's moods yet.

'Not transparency, however,' she continued. 'The object doesn't move the radiation straight through itself. It calculates observer viewpoints, and its surface acts like a large, highly directional hardscreen, emitting imagery appropriate to their positions.'

'I believe the ensign suggests, sir,' Hobbes offered, 'that in the heat of battle, the unpredictability of dozens of accelerating viewpoints would make this "invisibility" useless.'

'It's playing with us, Hobbes,' he said. 'Testing its abilities against ours.'

She thought for a moment.

'It's possible that it's trying to buy time, sir. The battlecruiser is less than an hour away.'

The captain nodded. By stripping the bridge of armor, the *Lynx* had made six gees on the way here. But the Rix vessel hadn't turned over; it wasn't bothering to decelerate in time to match its velocity with the *Lynx* and the object. It was still barreling madly toward them, cutting its transit time to a minimum. The battlecruiser would pass by at a high relative, almost twice as fast as the first pass. The Rix had abandoned almost their entire drone complement, but Hobbes didn't doubt it could destroy the wounded frigate in the minutes it would be in range.

'That's likely, Hobbes. So let's see if we can hurt this thing.'

'Happy to, sir.' Hobbes interlaced her fingers. 'Tyre, give me a target.'

'May I suggest random parallax and a complex background, ma'am?'

'You may.'

Tyre signaled, and the recon drones accelerated into action, whipping themselves into a froth of zigzags about the object. A decoy drone spat out chaff, light metals that the

Lynx's close-in defenses illuminated with jittering arms of laser light. The object became visible against the background stars and shimmering chafe, a blur of inconsistencies as it struggled to keep up its illusion.

Zai nodded. 'Gunner, fifty terabits, dead center.'

'Yes, sir.'

The thin lancing beam of the laser was visible for a moment as it burned through the chaff, a flashlight in a dusty attic. The object appeared for a second, revealing its new configuration . . .

Spheroid, with a huge lens cut from it, concave and *mirrored*: a lens focused back toward the *Lynx*.

The blinding image was burned into Hobbes's eyes: that brief moment when the beam split in two, the sharp point of a very acute angle. As the laser's reflection raked across the frigate, the two rays of the angle closed to a single line.

The aft gunnery hardpoint – which Hobbes had stripped almost entirely of its armor – was silenced, and the beam winked out.

'Medical, medical!' cried the first voice, from a station a hundred meters from the stricken hardpoint. Hobbes responded with wooden hands. She tried to raise the cannon crew, but they didn't respond. More voices called for medical.

A decompression alarm sounded. As one, the bridge crew reached to seal their pressure hoods. Casualty icons sprouted from across the ship. Still nothing from the hardpoint that had fired: the crew there were vapor, Hobbes realized.

'Heat sink failure, sir! The beam went straight through us.'

'Hobbes,' the captain said.

'Bulkhead 2-aft is holed, sir. The foam's not holding. And—'

'Hobbes!' Zai shouted.

His cry brought her to a halt. 'Yes, sir?'

'The singularity generator. Is it intact?'

Hobbes shook her head to clear the anguished voices that clamored for her attention. The hull was breached again, and the *Lynx*'s bulkheads had been stripped to the bone. Crew were dead and wounded. Why was the old man worried about auxiliary power?

She plumbed internal diagnostics.

'Yes, sir. It's fine. But main drive is bleeding—'

'Run it up to critical,' he ordered.

'What?'

'Run the hole up to critical, Hobbes. I want a singularity self-destruct ten seconds after I give the order.'

'Yes, sir,' she said. Her second sight fell into the hadean colors of self-destruct protocols. She gave the gestural command, a twist of the thumbs and shoulders that was intentionally designed to hurt.

Then she realized what the captain meant to do.

God, Katherie thought, *he's going to kill us all.*

Katherie Hobbes stepped into the observation blister with her jaw clenched. She was careless of vertigo; there wasn't time left to worry about up and down.

'How many casualties?' Zai asked before she had a chance to speak.

'Forty-one, sir,' she reported. 'Thirty burned and eleven gone in hull blow-outs. Only twelve are able to receive the symbiant.'

There was a silence for the dead. Hobbes was loath to break it, but events were closing in on the *Lynx*. Perhaps she would never be as gray as her crewmates and captain. Ritual seemed so often to stand in the way of efficiency.

'Sir,' she said. 'The Rix battlecruiser will be in range in twenty minutes.'

Laurent Zai nodded. Facing away from Hobbes as he was, the blackness of space almost swallowed the gesture.

She started to speak again, but then she saw the object.

Hobbes had never seen the thing with naked eyes. In primary sight it was much darker than she expected. They were very far from the Legis sun, and she couldn't see the details that the enhanced, telescopic views of synesthesia provided. But the undulations were still visible; the crests of rolling dunes caught sunlight, igniting like whitecaps on a moonlit sea.

Surrounding the object was a squadron of recon drones. They played green spotlights across its surface, low-power lasers searching for data, for weaknesses.

She gathered herself. 'If we plan to take action against the object, we should do it now, sir.'

'Hobbes,' the captain said tiredly. 'What exactly would you suggest?'

She swallowed. 'Nuke it, sir.'

'The ramdrones had nukes in the mix, didn't they?' he asked.

'Only low-yield fission, sir. I'm talking about a fusion warhead in the thousand-megaton range. No imaginable substance could withstand a surface temperature of a million degrees.'

'Ah,' he answered.

She waited as he watched the sinuous thing below them.

'Any other ideas?' he finally asked.

'Yes, sir.' She'd come with several options, in case he'd managed to think of an answer to a nuclear strike.

'We can use the three remaining photon cannon in tandem, sir. And keep the *Lynx* under random acceleration. The reflective lens on the object was twenty klicks across and very rigid. DA thinks it couldn't track us.'

'But could we damage it?'

'We only hit it with fifty terabits, sir. With three cannon at maximum, we could easily do five hundred.'

'It won't work,' he said.

'Sir!' she said. 'Either of those options would create a surface temperature adequate to vaporize neutronium. Nothing material can withstand those energies.'

'Hobbes, what if this thing can achieve perfect reflectivity?'

'What do you mean, sir?'

The captain turned to face her.

'What if it can become a mirror so perfect that it could drift through the core of a type-G star and not gain a single degree?'

The image appalled Hobbes. It was an engineering fantasy, the sort of thinking that had led her to reject Utopianism, with its promise of universal prosperity. 'That's impossible, sir.'

'We don't know that. Our own energy shunts can protect us from nuclear explosions.'

'The shunts are a field effect, sir. They're energy, not matter. We've yet to see the object do anything except change its crude elemental makeup. It hasn't created any complex devices or emitted any coherent energies. And our shunts aren't magic; a direct hit from a decent fusion warhead and the *Lynx* would be vapor.'

'The *Lynx* is the *Lynx*, Hobbes. This object is something rather more. But it is inexperienced, and every time we attack it, we educate it.'

Hobbes shook her head.

'If we hit it with nukes or lasers, it will adapt,' the captain said.

'Sir, it must have structural limits—'

Zai took a step toward her, waving her silent.

'This object is not a spacecraft, Hobbes. We can't treat it like an engineering problem. For a moment, think like the Rix. To them it's not an artifact at all.'

Hobbes took a breath. What was the old man on about? The object was huge, certainly, and a creation of unknown science. But the Empire had fought strange and superior technologies on every front for centuries.

Had Laurent Zai ceased to believe he could win this fight?

'If it's not an artifact, sir, then what is it?'

'It's a living god.'

Hobbes swallowed. Had the old man gone daft?

'That doesn't mean we can't kill it, Captain.'

He smiled.

'No, indeed. We have the power to destroy it. But our solution must be absolute. Not mere energy, but a tear in the fabric of space-time. A black hole. Self-destruction is the only honorable choice.'

'Captain, I have other options—'

'Silence, Hobbes. It's time.'

Zai brushed past her, tersely ordering the blister to fold when they were out. Hobbes realized it was pointless to argue. The man was fixated on death. That was why he had returned here to the blister, to resume his mordant meditation on his own doom.

Poor Laurent, she thought. His failure to take the blade had consumed all his strength; his finest moment had broken him inside. And the Vadan man's lost honor was now embodied in the object, within reach again: one final chance to die for the Risen Emperor.

As she followed her captain up to the bridge, Katherie Hobbes felt the flechette pistol strapped to her wrist, and wondered if it had been a mistake to save Zai from the mutineers.

'Ten minutes, sir.'

A thousand seconds, and the Rix would be in range again. Hobbes shook her head. Having survived one pass by the vastly superior warship, it seemed insane to face another. But it was too late for these thoughts. Even at maximum gee, the frigate could no longer put itself out of harm's way.

'What's the lightspeed delay?' Zai asked.

'Sir?'

'Between ourselves and the battlecruiser.'

Hobbes changed her scale markers to light-seconds. Was the captain thinking of communicating with the enemy? 'Nine seconds round-trip, sir.'

'Then we wait,' Zai said.

For what? Hobbes wondered.

A hundred seconds ticked by. The Rix craft approached, decelerating now, as the object writhed before them.

Hobbes focused her mind. She tried to recall the way she had seen Zai ten days ago: a paragon of honor and competence. She would have died for him without question. Why were there doubts in her mind now?

She reviewed the situation. The *Lynx*'s orders were clear: to prevent contact between the compound mind and the battlecruiser. This was the only way to be absolutely sure. Perhaps self-destruction *was* the honorable choice. But Laurent seemed to relish the thought of death. And he had been blind to other options, even when there had been time.

Of course, the time for options had run out.

Katherie wondered if her doubts stemmed from the foolish affections she had allowed herself to develop for her captain. Had Zai's rejection lessened her loyalty? Hobbes tried to feel the sense of duty that had compelled her to join the Navy. The utopian world she had left behind was an empty place of pleasure and safety. Here at the verge of death she should find meaning. That was the axiom of Imperial service: the Old Enemy gave life value.

But facing suicide, there was nothing inside Katherie Hobbes but regret and fear. And a desire to find a way out.

She checked the time.

'They'll be in range in fifty-odd seconds, sir. The round-trip delay is now five seconds.'

'Take us in, First Pilot. I want collision with the object in forty seconds. Smooth acceleration.'

This was it.

First Pilot Maradonna's anxious eyes glanced toward Hobbes. Katherie's mind whirled. What did Maradonna want from her? Hobbes nodded confirmation to the pilot, with an expression that she hoped said, *Trust me*.

Trust me to what?

The frigate jolted a bit as the two-gee acceleration began, a gravity ghost wrenching a metal shriek from around them. The captain raised no protest.

'Frick?' Zai said. The engineer was here on the bridge, ready to control the singularity generator from under the captain's gaze. The hole could go critical only with the first engineer's approval. He could stop this if he wanted. Hobbes wondered if Watson Frick had mutiny in him. She doubted it.

Why was she speculating like this? The bridge had once seemed sanctified to Hobbes, a place of order and faith. But that surety had been stripped, undermined by her doubts. And perhaps by her foolish feelings for Laurent Zai. She wondered if she would be thinking of mutiny if Laurent hadn't told her about his lover on Home.

The red battle lights seemed menacing now; the bridge had become a twilight place.

'Build the generator on an exponential curve, Frick. Self-destruct to occur on contact.'

'Yes, sir,' said the first engineer without emotion. 'Fail-safe in twenty seconds.'

This was the end, then. In moments, they would all be destined for death, absolute and irrecoverable, at the maw of an event horizon.

Unless Katherie Hobbes acted. She put aside her doubts about her own motivations. There were more than three hundred surviving crew to consider.

What if now, with only seconds left, she were to take the bridge? She was the only one here who was armed.

The pilots would side with her, she knew already. Pilots generally came from aristocracy, and possessed a certain sense of entitlement; Third Pilot Magus, still in the brig, had been part of the first mutiny. With the self-destruct process already started, however, Hobbes would have to turn Frick. And for that, she realized, she had waited too long. The Rix were almost upon them. There was no chance that the *Lynx* could survive another pass from the battlecruiser. The captain was right about one thing: suicide was the only sure way of destroying the object.

She let all the mutinous thoughts exit her mind. It was a pointless exercise; they were all dead whatever she did.

But Katherie cursed herself for not deciding. Honorable death or mutiny, she could have made a choice when the Rix were still distant. Instead, she had waited for time to run down. Laurent Zai and Watson Frick – they had chosen their deaths. Katherie Hobbes had merely stumbled into hers.

'Fail-safe in ten,' Frick said.

'Collision in twenty,' a pilot added.

This was it. Just a countdown remained.

And there was no meaning in it for Hobbes.

'*Captain*,' cried Ensign Tyre. 'The Rix!'

'Cut our acceleration, Pilot,' Zai snapped. 'Stand by, Frick.'

The captain waved his hand, and the Rix battlecruiser filled the big airscreen. It was coming alight. A storm of explosions ran up and down the length of its hull. Bright arms of white energy burst from its sides, curving around to strike back at the vessel like arcing solar flares. The ship's main drive continued to fire, but it was free of its structural supports, spinning like a fire hose gone wild within the mighty ship. The blazing shaft cut the battlecruiser's aft section to pieces, then the drive tore itself free from the ship and jetted whirling into the void. The kilometer-long bow spar of the battlecruiser vanished into a nuclear blast, perfectly spherical and absolutely white.

'Frick, First Pilot: save us,' the captain ordered.

'Aye, aye, sir.'

Hobbes felt herself growing heavy as the *Lynx*'s faltering gravity strained to mask their deceleration. The whine of the singularity alarm slowly lessened as Frick brought it out of its critical cycle.

Katherie watched in amazement as debris scattered from the battlecruiser. She couldn't believe the huge ship had disintegrated so quickly. A thousand Rixwomen had died in seconds. And her own fate had been recalled from the precipice just as suddenly.

The captain leaned back into the shipmaster's chair. Hobbes saw for the first time how white his face had become, how tired he looked. Zai's grim expression had seemed so fatal; now the old man looked merely exhausted.

'They made their decision rather more quickly than I expected,' he said to her. 'Given the light-speed delay, it must have taken about ten seconds for the Rix commanders to decide. They must have been ready, in case we discovered a way to threaten the object.'

Hobbes could only say, 'You knew what they would do?'

'As I said: when a living god is at stake, self-destruction is the only honorable choice.'

Hobbes tried to wrap her mind around his words. He'd

been playing *chicken*, for heaven's sake, but . . . 'Why did they self-destruct, sir?'

'They were too distant to stop us, but too close to veer off,' Zai said. 'This was the correct moment to initiate our self-destruction, because it left them no choice but their own. Now that they're gone, we don't have to destroy the object.'

Hobbes looked at the sparkling screen. She'd never seen anything so . . . final. 'But all those women.'

'The Rix think nothing of their own lives, Hobbes. Only their minds matter to them. They've risked war to create this new breed of god. They couldn't let it die. No price was too high.'

She swallowed. 'I'm not sure, sir. If I were them, I'd have a backup plan.'

Zai managed to smile, but she saw the relief in his eyes. He had by no means been sure how this would turn out. 'What sort of plan, Hobbes?'

'I don't know, sir,' she said quietly. 'But they wouldn't leave us free to capture their living god, would they?'

Zai spread his hands. 'The situation gave them the choice of two evils, I suppose. They knew that we were willing to die for our faith as much as they. We weren't bluffing, Hobbes.' Then he laughed tiredly. 'But we seem to be alive. Perhaps their faith is stronger than ours.'

The words stung Katherie. Facing death, her mind had been consumed by options, by ways to avoid the *Lynx*'s fate. She had even considered treachery.

She was not worthy to wear this uniform.

'Sir,' she said.

'Yes, Hobbes?'

'There's something I should tell you. I don't deserve—' she started, then swallowed. 'When we were about to—'

'*Sir!*' interrupted Tyre.

'Report.'

'Hidden in the battlecruiser's debris, sir. I'm getting spherical shapes against the background radiation!'

The captain swore. 'Blackbody drones.'

The Rix had indeed had a backup plan.

Hobbes took over. 'Pilot! Six gees on a quick slope, lateral to the battlecruiser's last vector. Now!'

The bridge crew were wrenched by torque as the ship spun to align her main drives. A gunner was thrown from his station into the airscreen pit, skidding through the false sights of synesthesia as if sliding down a hill.

Shit, thought Hobbes. The artificial gravity generator was growing chancier by the minute.

And the bridge was almost dead center of the *Lynx*. What was happening at the extremes, where that quick yaw was no doubt snapping like a whip? Hobbes punched through internal views. She saw crew thrown against walls and ceilings. More casualties. But no decompression – the AG was prioritizing structural integrity.

Then the drive fired, and she was pushed back into her chair.

As her weight increased, Hobbes found herself gasping for breath. Gravity diagnostics were blank, and white dots had appeared at the edge of her primary vision. She wondered if the gravity generators had failed altogether. The *Lynx* AI would normally intervene in such a situation and shut the drive, but with the frigate taking hits from enemy fire, the software would blindly accept dangerous acceleration.

Hobbes could get no response from diagnostics. Processor capacity was falling: the *Lynx*'s silicon/phosphorus columns were succumbing to the heavy gees. Giant hands pushed against her chest. Without dampening, everyone on the bridge would be unconscious in twenty seconds. Six uncorrected gees would injure and kill hundreds.

But hurtling silently toward the *Lynx* were more blackbody drones, ready to unleash their incredible firepower at a ship whose armor had been stripped to the minimum.

Hobbes's fingers struggled to gesture as the pressure on her body increased. She finally found a reading from a mechanical accelerometer buried deep in the executive officer's interface. Three gees uncorrected, and climbing.

Something was very wrong.

'Cut the burn to two gees,' she cried. One of the pilots lifted a heavy hand to execute the order.

Suddenly, the bridge was filled with blazing shapes. Bright traces of light whipped past Hobbes, burning themselves into her eyes. Anvil booms broke against her ears, and her nose filled with the foundry smell of superheated metal. Hobbes heard human screams amid the cries of decompression and rending hypercarbon.

Then the hail of projectiles ended.

Hobbes felt her weight still growing. She looked across the bridge airscreen. Two gunners and all three pilots were torn and bloody. Caught in the sudden fusillade of blackbody drone fire, they'd been torn to pieces.

'Captain!' she cried.

Zai's head had rolled back, his eyes opened dully. There was no blood on his face. Of course, Hobbes realized. His artificial limbs were strong, but the acceleration must be tearing up the delicate interface between the prosthetics and his sundered body.

All around her, the *Lynx* was trembling. If the AG failed completely, six gees would crumple the frigate like paper. Hobbes's accelerometer read four-point-four. Processor capacity was dropping like a stone, as the frigate's columns of silicon and phosphorus shattered under their own suddenly immense weight. Synesthesia grew blurrier by the second. It was only a matter of time before gestural commands were useless.

Hobbes strained to pull herself from her chair. There were manual drive cutoffs all through the ship, human-operated. There was one a few meters from her, among the ragdoll corpses at the first pilot's station.

Why hadn't the drive engineers already acted? They should have realized what was happening by now and shut the drive down. But were any of them conscious? They were at the ship's aft extreme, where the whip of the frigate's undampened yaw had done its worst damage.

Hobbes had to reach the pilot's station.

Again she pushed against her chair, and managed to pull herself up. She took one unsteady step, bowed like a woman carrying a hundred kilos of stone on her back. Her hand reached out to grab the rail that surrounded the airscreen pit.

But she was too heavy. She faltered. Her legs gave way.

Her knee thundered down against the metal deck like a jackhammer, and exploded with pain.

Suddenly, everything was silent and dark. Hobbes's ears heard only the far-off whine of some alarm. Second-sight icons floated in the air, gibberish now. Everything seemed to be drifting around her. Then Hobbes realized that *she* was floating.

Freefall.

Someone had cut the drive.

Her blood was no longer gravity's hostage, and she could feel it rushing back into her head. Hobbes opened her eyes. Lucidity fought with the pain screaming in her knee. The bridge spun slowly around her, full of unfamiliar shapes and smells.

The pilots were dead, and all of the gunners had been hit. A haze of ichor filled the air. Blood pumped from a gunner's chest wound; spurted globules rolled lazily through the air.

'Medical, medical,' she said. But she heard the words echoed from all through the ship. Hobbes twisted to grab the airscreen rail.

But the motion wrenched her shattered knee, and she passed out from the pain.

■■■■

House

It had taken a whole day to sculpt – shaping the snows with reflected sunlight, vented geothermal, and the occasional infralaser – but the sled trail was ready at last. It stretched ten kilometers, spiraling down the house's mountain peak through four circumnavigations before tipping through a narrow pass and down a steep moraine. The trail then descended into a glacial rift between towering walls of ancient blue ice, and terminated at one of the house's water-gathering points, now fitted with an access tunnel. For safety, the entire course was banked with three meters of powdery snow, and marked with cheery orange glowsticks at every turn.

The house was quite proud of itself. At last its encyclopedic knowledge of every centimeter of the estate had been put to use.

But not everything was under control. The mistress's guest had insisted on building the sled himself. Captain Zai had requested a bewildering variety of materials to be synthesized, adapted, and cannibalized. Apparently, sleds on Vada were made entirely of animal bone and skins, lashed together like macramé inside a hard frame. The house had serious reservations about trusting the mistress's safety to such a contraption, which had no internal diagnostics, native intelligence, or self-repair capacity.

Still, the house was impressed when Captain Zai finished

winding the strips of salvaged leather garments around the mock ivory runners and frame, and jumped onto the sled, testing it with his full weight several times. The leather stretched, but held, the force elegantly distributed throughout the frame.

'How long have Vadans been building those?' the mistress asked.

'Twenty thousand years,' was Zai's nonsensical answer. The house knew that Vada had only been colonized for fifteen centuries. Twenty millennia ago was a time before the diaspora.

'You certainly hold on to the old ways.'

Zai nodded. 'Ever seen one before?'

'A sled? Laurent, I'd never seen *snow* before coming to Home. There isn't any on Vasthold. Well, perhaps at the poles, but we haven't gotten that crowded yet.'

The house read surprise on the captain's face. 'You'd never seen snow? And you bought a house in the antarctic? That was . . . adventurous.'

'Adventure had nothing to do with it. Home is more crowded than Vasthold. This is the only place on the planet I can withdraw completely from apathy. But it's true, I always did want to see snow. On Vasthold we have children's tales about it.'

'About sisters lost in a blizzard?' Zai asked. 'Freezing to death?'

'Godspite, Laurent, no. I grew up thinking snow was magical stuff, rain turned white and powdery. Pillow feathers from the sky.'

Zai smiled. 'You're about to find out just how right you were.'

He hoisted the two and a half meters of skin and pseudobone onto his shoulder.

The mistress narrowed her eyes at the sled, rising a little hesitantly.

'It looks sound enough,' she said.

'Shall we find out?'

The house's mind shot down the sled trail again, searching once more for a poorly banked turn, a hidden crevasse, a dangerous ice patch.

All seemed in order.

As the mistress and her guest changed into warmer clothes, the house connected with the planetary infostructure, accessing several collections of oral and written folklore. In seconds, it had discovered hundreds of children's stories from Vasthold, and many more from the older world of Vada. Then its search spilled across the many planets where the two worlds' founder populations had originated, and hits came in the tens of thousands. The house found tales of animated snowmen and wish-granting white leopards, magical arctic storms and strandings on ice floes, stories of how the aurora was made and why the compass sometimes lied. It even found the tale Zai had mentioned, entitled 'Three Vadan Sisters Lost in a Blizzard.'

The two headed for the east door, the leather of the handmade sled creaking softly as the captain carried it downstairs. For the next minute or so, they couldn't hurt themselves.

The house settled in for a pleasant hundred seconds of reading.

Captain

'Of course, when I mentioned sledding I didn't mean *downhill*. Nothing quite so childish.'

'Well, Laurent, we couldn't very well fly in a team of dogs.'

'True. But what's a country house without dogs, Nara?'

'Dogs aren't fashionable on Home, I'm afraid.'

He sighed. 'So I'd noticed.'

Zai turned down the heating in his uniform. His metabolism was enough to keep him warm inside Navy wool. The snow crunched under his boots with the bright sound of a recent fall. Perfect powder for sledding.

If only he had a long, flat stretch of it and a team of huskies.

Nara's blue eyes were flashing with a smile. 'I'm relieved to see that you Vadans don't slavishly follow the Emperor's taste in these matters.'

Laurent cleared his throat. 'There's nothing wrong with cats . . . strictly speaking.'

The trail began only a few meters from the door. It was shiny and slick, as if incised into the snow with lasers. On the mountain side of the trail the snow had been melted into an overhang, forming a half-cylinder of ice that wound downward around the peak. On the other side loomed a vertiginous drop.

Zai felt a bit dizzy, possibly from exhaustion. With only an hour of darkness every night, they hadn't slept much in the last three days.

He took a deep breath. 'I hope your house knows what it's doing.'

'Sometimes I think my house knows altogether too much,' Nara said. 'It has an excess of time on its hands.'

Zai looked up at the building, which seemed quite modest from the outside. Most of its bulk was hidden within the stone of the mountain, its true extent revealed only by the glimmer of a hundred polarized windows. Not all looked out from Nara's living quarters, of course. He had toured the gardens this morning, or at least some of them. The warrens that had produced three days of sumptuous meals seemed endless.

That sort of decadence always resulted when machines were given too much autonomy. Zai adjusted his tunic waist, which was growing tighter by the day.

'I get the feeling it can still hear us,' he said.

'Probably.' She shrugged in her coat.

Laurent pulled the glove from his real hand and ran his fingers through the short, yellow-gray fur.

'Paracoyote,' Nara said.

His eyes widened. 'You're wearing a canine? That's a crime on Vada.'

She laughed. 'They're a pest on Vasthold, to say the least.'

Zai wondered if Nara knew how extraordinary it was to come from a planet where 'pest' could mean something bigger than an insect. On Vada, hunting was only allowed on stocked private lands, a sport for the unthinkably rich. 'Vasthold is fortunate that terraforming has taken so well. Did you kill it yourself?'

'No, I haven't hunted since I was a kid.' She smiled, fingering the fur. 'And then only with a slingshot. This was a political gift from a conservationist group. But taken in the wild, with a bow, I think.'

Zai shook his head. 'We have no wild mammals on Vada.'

He placed the sled on the snow.

'I wish I could take you on a proper sled ride, Nara. With a team of huskies, across a floe of new sea ice.'

'*Sea ice*? You mean without *land* underneath?'

'It's very smooth when it's new.'

'No, thank you.'

'Well, after a few days of strong wind, pressure ridges break up the landscape.'

She laughed. 'It's not the monotony, Laurent. It's the thought of nothing but ice between me and an ocean!'

'There is safety equipment. When you fall through—'

'*When?*'

He cleared his throat again. 'Perhaps we should get started.'

'Yes. I'm beginning to think you're delaying us intentionally. Afraid of heights, Laurent?'

He looked down the trail. The surface looked somewhat glassy, a bit fast. Too slick for dogs' feet, certainly. He wondered if the runners would find any purchase to keep them on the track. The trail was banked to keep them from flying off the mountain, but they had no way to control their speed.

'Not heights.'

'What then?'

'Putting my life in the hands of an AI.'

She smiled, and sat down on the front of the sled. 'Come on, Laurent. It's a very clever house.'

It was marvelous.

The sled accelerated quickly, like a dropship spiraling down a gravity well. Laurent clung to it fiercely, his fingers wound into the leather straps that held it together. The runners found the ruts pre-cut deep into the ice and stayed in them, banking comfortably with the turns.

The trail seemed never to pass into the shadow of the mountain; the clever house reflected sunlight from the surrounding peaks, the snow in their path glowing with the warm red of the rising sun. But his eyes still reduced to slits against the wind, the crisp air turned freezing by their velocity.

Nara leaned back into Laurent's chest, laughing hysterically, her arms wrapped around his legs. She was warm, and her chaotic hair brushed his cheeks. He squeezed his knees together tightly to hold her in the plummeting sled, and to keep her warmth against him.

After four turns around the mountain, the trail slanted upward, slowing them as it straightened. The rise hid the terrain before them.

'I'd do that again,' Laurent shouted as the sled came almost to a halt.

'I don't think it's done,' Nara said, shaking her head. 'Are you familiar with the term "roller-coaster"?'

'I don't think – *Godspite!*'

The sled had crested the rise, revealing a gut-loosening decline dotted with giant boulders. The trail ahead was lined with high snow banks, but the ruts guiding the runners suddenly disappeared, leaving the sled free for the straight decline. The slope was forty-five degrees at least.

'It's trying to kill us!' Zai shouted.

'We'll see!'

Laurent and Nara clutched each other, screaming, as the sled dropped into the canyon of ice.

After the acceleration of the first mad drop, the trail leveled, descending gradually between icy walls. The exposed interior of the glacier was deep blue, the color of a clear Vadan sky on the Day of Apogee. In the rift's protection, the air was still except for the wind of their passage, but Laurent held his lover closer. He touched his lips to her left ear, which was bright red and as cold as the metal buttons of her coat.

'Remember when I said we had no technology for slowing down time?' he whispered.

'Yes?'

'I was wrong. This lasts forever.'

She reached back and put a gloved finger to his lips softly, and Laurent felt foolish. It wasn't right to speak of these things. This was a fragile endlessness, soon followed by an onrushing of events that would part them for decades.

Tomorrow, they would take the suborbital back to the capital. The commissioning of the *Lynx* was set for the day after. On Home, any such event would be a tremendous affair, lasting an entire night and filling the great square before the Diamond Palace with supplicants, zealots, and status-seekers. After that, Captain Zai had only a matter of weeks to train his crew in orbit before leaving for Legis.

But he had these moments here with Nara. Against the

weight of years and the depredations of the Time Thief, he had only the sharp and brittle thing that was *now*.

Laurent wondered if it were possible that any alliance formed across days could really last decades. Or would what they'd shared in this icy waste prove illusory, born of torturous memories, lack of sleep, and the romance of its own improbability?

Of course, Laurent realized, what was real or unreal would be determined in the years to follow. Falling in love was never genuine in itself; what had happened in these four days would be given meaning over their decades apart. Like some figment of the quantum, love was made true only when measured against the rest of the world.

The sled was slowing, and Laurent Zai sighed softly to himself. Thinking of the future, he had missed the present.

Nara kissed him and stood. They were at the blind end of the rift.

'What now? Climb out?' He looked back up the trail at the kilometers-distant house, just visible on its mountain peak. It would take hours.

Nara shook her head and pointed to a patch of icicles, which shattered as something metal rumbled behind it. A door opened, and warm air rushed out carrying the scent of jasmine.

'Just through the tea gardens, I think,' she said. 'I hope you don't mind riding in a drone elevator.'

Laurent smiled. 'So we can go again?'

'Of course. As many times as you like.'

Something broke inside him, but the fissure didn't open onto the familiar well of sadness. Laurent found himself laughing hard, almost hysterically as he lifted the sled. Nara smiled quizzically, waiting as he gathered himself.

When Laurent found his breath, the echo of his laughter

still played at the edge of hearing. It was a wonder he hadn't brought an avalanche down upon them.

He felt a small tear already freezing in the corner of one eye.

'Laurent?'

'I was just thinking, Nara: you have a very clever house.'

7

WAR PRIZE

When a single nation's
armies are ordered against
each other, all is lost.
          – ANONYMOUS 167

Dead Woman

The Other came to her talking of darkness.

There were no words, just gray shapes issuing from a maw, inside a cave whose blackness invoked faerie lights upon her optic nerve. So dark that whispers rode the ears. Her blindness made things calm and rich.

Rich, but so many things were missing now. The keen edges of desire, the pleasures of flesh, all the appetites of drama, expectation and dread, hope and disappointment – all the anguished terrain of uncertainty had been flattened into an arid plane. And soon, the Other explained, she would entirely forget the phantom shapes of those extinct emotions.

It led her toward a bloodred horizon.

She didn't know where they were headed, but she felt no worry. The Other explained that worry was one of those missing things.

The dead woman took a deep, calm breath. No more fear, ever again.

The red horizon opened up – like the slit of opening one's eyes.

'Rana Harter,' a voice said.

The woman at the end of her bed was short and had the gray skin of the dead. She wore an Imperial uniform, the dully glinting, gunmetal robe of the Political Apparatus.

'Yes. I know who I am.'

She nodded. 'My name is Adept Harper Trevim.'

'Honored Mother,' she said. The Other had prompted her with the proper form of address. (The Other lived inside her like an organ, like a software guide, like a subtle form of second sight.)

'You will live forever.'

Rana nodded. Then a moment of disorientation troubled her, as she wondered if she should be joyful. Immortality was the highest reward her society could bestow on any citizen, an honor that had seemed utterly out of her humble grasp. But joy was such a gross emotion. Instead, Rana Harter closed her eyes again and regarded the subtle beauty of eternity, which had the pleasures of a geometrical simple, the ray of her lifetime extending indefinitely.

But the question lingered: why was she – a militia worker, a lower-school dropout, and a recent traitor – one of the honored dead?

'How am I risen, Mother?'

'By the action of the symbiant.'

A trivial answer, using the outsiders' word for the Other.

'I was never elevated, Mother.'

'But you died at the hands of the enemy, Rana.'

'I died in the arms of my lover,' she answered. The self-damning words surprised her in a dull way, but it seemed that it was not within the dead to lie.

The honored mother blinked.

'You were taken hostage, Rana Harter. A terrible experience. The minds of the living are fragile, and under stress they are bent with strange emotions. You suffered from a weakness called Stockholm Syndrome. Your "love" for your captor was a perversion caused by the fear of death, a need to hang on to something, anything. But now you have faced death and crossed it, and your mind is clear. Those feelings will pass.' The adept brought her hands together. 'Perhaps they have passed already, and you spoke out of habit.'

Rana Harter narrowed her eyes. The Other prompted her to agree, but she found herself resisting. She remembered the avian precision of Herd's movements, the sure violet of her eyes, the alien pathways of her mind.

'We shall see, Mother.'

The dead woman nodded, unperturbed.

'You will discover your old life slipping away, Rana. And ultimately, you will be glad to be free of it.'

The honored mother held out a hand, and Rana grasped it. Trevim helped her rise into a seated position, and the bed re-formed to support her back. Her muscles felt different, strangely supple and free of tension, but a bit weak. Rana looked around the room. The walls were a deep, rich color, full of shapes and suggestive motions, immanent with potential, covered with old and pure ideas.

She realized that this eloquent surface was painted with the color she had once called black. It was more than a color now.

The two of them were silent for a time that could have been a minute or an hour, or longer. Then the honored mother spoke again.

'Rana Harter, let me ask you some questions.'

'Certainly, Mother.'

The adept pressed her palms together.

'In your time with the Rixwoman, did you ever see signs of . . . another presence?'

'You mean Alexander.'

Her eyebrows arched. 'Alexander?'

'The compound mind, Mother. It chose a name from the history of Earth Prime. The founder of a great empire.'

'Ah, yes. He died young, I believe.'

Rana shrugged, a gesture of millimeters among the dead. Trevim looked pleased, as if she were already making unexpected progress.

'The Apparatus has reason to suspect that this entity possessed certain critical information.'

Rana looked up at the black ceiling. 'Alexander *is* information. All the data on Legis.'

The honored mother shook her head. 'Not all. There are some things hidden away, crucial secrets. But there is evidence that the compound mind went to great lengths to uncover them. And to transmit them from Legis.'

'Why don't you ask it?'

The adept frowned. 'Have you . . . *spoken* with this abomination?'

Rana sighed, her mind returning to the halcyon days of her captivity, learning the Rix language and working under Alexander's guidance on necessary changes to the entanglement facility. Rana remembered the embrace of the compound mind, the security of knowing that practically every object on the planet was imbued with her lover's protector.

'*Spoken* is the wrong word, Mother. But let me use the infostructure, and perhaps I can find an answer for you.'

The adept shook her head. 'Alexander no longer exists.'

For a second, Rana felt one of the vanquished emotions of the living. Shock coursed through her, a sudden fire. The Other calmed it.

'How?'

'We don't know. It seems to have fled. Or perhaps it simply ceased to exist.'

Rana closed her eyes, calling on her brainbug. She thought of the work she had done, when Alexander had helped her through the intricacies of the translight communication facility. The floating synesthesia icons of their researches appeared in memory, their meanings inflected by what Trevim had just reported.

Here in the arid place inside her dead woman's eyes, Rana's brainbug was different. It moved with new surety, open and confident where once it had been furtive. She could guide her ability now, instead of having to turn her mind away to give it freedom.

In a few minutes, she saw the answer.

'Alexander sent itself away.'

The honored mother swallowed.

'Did it know?' As she said these words, pain seemed to cross her face. Odd, to see pain in a dead woman.

'Did it know what?'

Trevim's features contorted again. 'The Emperor's Secret,' she gasped.

Rana narrowed her eyes.

'Are you well, Honored Mother?'

Adept Trevim wiped her brow, the gray skin of which shone with a milky-looking sweat.

'It is forbidden to speak of it,' she managed, 'to one uninitiated.'

Rana Harter looked down at her bedclothes. Her mind moved lightly across the weeks she'd spent in the shadow of Alexander. The brainbug searched for clues to what the adept might be talking about. But there was no purchase for the question; the evidence was insufficient.

'Mother, I know nothing about this.'

Trevim sighed, making the crude facial movements that showed a living person's relief. Then she nodded. 'I hoped you would not.'

Trevim stood silent for a few minutes, regaining her composure by staring at the engaging blackness of the walls.

'You will go on a journey now, Rana.'

'Where?'

'To meet the Emperor. He would speak to you of this.'

'Home?'

'Yes. A great honor.'

Rana frowned. The trip would take ten years Absolute. 'But where is Herd?' she asked.

'Your Rix captor?' The adept's face seemed to hold distress again. How agitated she was for a dead woman. The Other in Rana rippled with cool displeasure.

'Yes.'

'Don't think of her, Rana. You must let that unfortunate episode pass into memory. You don't need such attachments anymore.'

Rana closed her eyes, thinking of the Rixwoman. When she opened them again, the honored mother was gone, leaving Rana alone with the question.

Would her love for Herd really slip away?

She stared at the walls and considered. The afterlife was clean, and pure, and good. The propaganda of the grays was true. Fear was vanquished now, the Old Enemy death had been beaten, and with it pain and need.

But Rana Harter shook her head in quiet disagreement with the honored mother's words. She knew that she would always miss that other heaven, those weeks with her Rix lover that had changed everything. That time with Herd had been so short. The alien woman had given her happiness, had somehow placed her on the path to immortality.

Most of all, the alien Herd had been beautiful, even more so than this wondrous blackness.

Rana wanted to see her. *Desired* – no other word was correct – the alien lemongrass of her touch. Where was her lover now?

The Other calmed these thoughts before they grew too anxious. It explained that the still-living were never suitable companions for the dead. The pinks were like spoiled children, petty and tempestuous. They were ugly creatures, squalling brats who vied constantly for attention, for the baubles of wealth and power. They were blind to the subtle beauties of the darkness. The dead rightly kept themselves apart.

You don't know Herd, Rana Harter thought.

The Other was silent at this, as if it were a bit surprised.

And Rana closed her eyes, slipping back across the red horizon onto the calm, arid plane of death, and soon was smiling, an odd expression for a dead woman.

Executive Officer

Katherie Hobbes awoke.

She felt strangely rested. For the first time in weeks, her body wasn't full of nervous tension. But her sight was blurred, and all that she could comprehend of her surroundings were a few pastel planes, the restful hues of sickbay.

Hobbes tried to move.

Medically restrained, said a machine voice in second hearing.

'Shit,' she said, remembering her knee. She blinked gumminess from her eyes and tried to look down the length of her prone body.

Standing at the foot of her bed was a figure whose stance she recognized even through the haze. Laurent Zai.

'They said you'd be coming around.'

'How long, sir?' Her voice was dry and frail.

'Ten hours. Five hypersleep cycles.'

A whole day, Hobbes thought. And she couldn't remember a single dream. The last time she'd slept more than two straight hours had been before the hostage-taking. It was strange to remember that time could go on while she was asleep. Despite this disorienting news, however, Hobbes's mind felt clearer than it had in days.

'Who cut out the drive, sir?'

He smiled. 'Frick.'

Of course. The first engineer could operate any aspect of the ship from his synesthesia interface. It was lucky he'd been on the bridge, and not knocked unconscious on one of the wildly spinning aft-decks of engineering.

'But you made a valiant try, I see,' Zai added.

He glanced down at her left knee. Hobbes lifted her neck, straining to see her legs, but all she could see was a network of traction bars and a few glistening nano drips traveling down into shrouded flesh.

'Looks pretty ugly, sir.'

'Nothing permanent, Hobbes. The AI doubts you'll even need a servo-prosthetic. But you'll be limping until we get back to Legis and get some new ligaments put in you.'

Back to Legis. The engagement was truly over then. No more monstrosities had emerged from Rix space to threaten them. It was hard to believe.

'Just ligaments?' she wondered. It had felt as if the kneecap had been shattered. She must have weighed more than three hundred kilos when she'd fallen.

'Well,' Zai admitted, 'ligaments and a hypercarbon kneecap. If you plan on taking any more strolls at five gees, I would recommend you get a *pair* of those.'

She smiled. Then images returned to her mind from the fiery moments of the blackbody drone attack. Dead bodies on the bridge. Blood in the air.

'How many casualties, sir?'

'All told, eighty-one of us died,' he said. 'All three bridge pilots, and Gunner Wilson.'

Eighty-one. A bloodbath. Between her three engagements – hostage rescue, the first pass of the battlecruiser, and the blackbodies – the crew of the frigate was more than a third gone.

'I should have listened to you, Hobbes,' Zai said. 'Removing the armor from around the bridge almost cost us the *Lynx* entire.'

'No, sir. It was my mistake. I shouldn't have gone to six gees. That was too much with the AG already failing.' She shut her eyes, reliving the moment. If only she'd ordered a slower ramp-up to three gees, the AG might have held.

'You couldn't have foreseen that, Hobbes,' the captain assured her. 'The Rix plan was brilliant – mutual destruction. The battlecruiser released a hundred and twenty-eight drones just before they self-destructed. Full blackbody types. Enough to tear the *Lynx* to pieces. We were saved by Data Master Kax, who stayed alert while the rest of us were celebrating. He spotted them and warned Tyre.'

Hobbes furrowed her brow. Hadn't Kax been blinded?

'And you too, Hobbes,' Zai continued. 'You got us out before the drones could cut us to pieces. Every kilometer between *Lynx* and the blackbodies saved lives. No one died from the acceleration.'

Hobbes felt a moment of relief. At least her rashness hadn't killed anyone. 'But there were a few injuries, I'll bet, sir.'

'Purely from the acceleration? Only a hundred or so. Your knee's just about the worst, though. Every other member of my crew has the sense not to stand up in five gravities.'

She smiled wanly at the captain's teasing. Hobbes's memory of her mutinous thoughts was hazy. The fierce conflict that had raged within her seemed now like a phantasm, a stress reaction rather than a true failure of will.

'And we've captured it,' Zai said.

It took Hobbes's mind a moment to grasp this. 'The object, sir?'

Captain Zai nodded. 'We've got artificial gravity again, as you may have noticed. We have the thing under tow.'

Her eyebrows rose. Easy gravitons were swamped in the proximity of supermassive objects like planets. But on something like the Rix object, which massed only a hundred billion tons or so, they could get purchase, she supposed.

But the ship would be straining like the devil to make any headway.

'What vector are we making, sir?'

'Practically nothing. But four heavy cargo tugs are under construction on Legis,' he said. 'Between them and the *Lynx*, we'll be able to accelerate the object at almost a full gee.'

Hobbes nodded. The frigate's powerful drive was her most advanced feature. If it weren't for the fragility of humans and equipment inside, and the limits of AG when it came to dampening high gravities, the *Lynx* could accelerate like a remote drone. With a few cargo tugs thrown in, and additional darkmatter scoops to provide reaction mass, the frigate could move a small planetoid.

'The object is already making two thousand klicks per second into Imperial space, sir,' Hobbes said, calling a tactical display into the air before her. 'We should be able to get it up to point-nine constant in under a year.'

Zai smiled at her enthusiasm. 'It'll take a hell of a lot of reaction mass, Hobbes. You might want to include darkmatter variation in your math.'

'But where are we taking her, sir? Trentor Base?'

'We're going Home.'

Hobbes's mouth fell open. All the way Home again. She could see the quiet happiness in Laurent's eyes. Whoever his secret lover was, she was back on the Imperial capital.

A trip to Home would take ten years Absolute. The war might well be over for the crew of the *Lynx*.

Of course, for many of them, the war was over already. Katherie wondered how many of the honored dead were suitable for reanimation, and how many were gone forever.

She suddenly felt exhausted again, despite her five cycles of hypersleep. Her mind couldn't take in any more information. The simple facts were overwhelming enough. The *Lynx* had survived, accomplished her mission, and captured a war prize that might well change Imperial technology forever. Laurent Zai was still alive, still an elevated hero, and Katherie Hobbes, it seemed, was not a traitor.

Things were better than she would have expected.

But Hobbes knew the next time she woke, she would have to face the details of the situation: endless components to be repaired; preparations for the long trip home; assistance in the rebuilding of Legis's infostructure. Learning how to walk again.

And she would have to read the names of the dead. Friends, colleagues, and crewmates. She closed her eyes, deciding not to call up the casualty list yet. That could wait.

'I'm sorry to have disturbed you, Hobbes,' Zai said. 'You must be—'

'Tired, sir. But thank you for seeing me.'

'Thank you, Hobbes.'

'For what, sir?'

'For never doubting me,' Laurent said softly. 'Through all this madness.'

'Never, sir.'

Never again.

Marine Private

The prisoner offered no resistance as she was led onto the *Lynx*.

She emerged from the airlock with alien grace, her step like a courtesan's from a storydream back on Private Bassiritz's home world. But the marine realized after a moment that her tiny steps were not a sign of humility, but the result of shackles. The woman's ankles were bound with two interwoven sheaths of hypercarbon fiber. Her hands were concealed by a garment that stretched around her like a straitjacket, as if she were hugging herself to keep out the cold. A stun collar was clasped around her neck. The Legis Militia guard who escorted her carried the collar's remote outstretched before him, a totem to ward off evil.

The prisoner had been through some sort of terrible fire-fight, Bassiritz could see. Her head was mostly bald, and her red, dimpled skin and lack of eyebrows suggested she'd lost her hair to fire. Her face was hatched with cuts and scars.

But the woman met Bassiritz's stare with a steady gaze, her stunning violet eyes bright with curiosity.

He swallowed. He had never seen a Rixwoman without a helmet on. Since the battle in the palace, Bassiritz had read many books about the members of the Cult, the first people he'd ever seen who moved as fast as he, who reacted as quickly. They seemed to share the accelerated time frame that had until now been Bassiritz's private domain.

But that didn't make them friends, he reminded himself. This woman had killed dozens of Imperial soldiers, even a few *Lynx* marines, maybe even Sam and Astra. Wrapped in unbreakable bonds or not, she was dangerous enough to warrant three guards. Still, she fascinated him.

The militiaman handed over the stun collar's remote, and the three dirtsiders disappeared back into the airlock with evident relief. The marine sergeant stayed a few meters from the prisoner at all times, gesturing for Privates Bassiritz and Ana Wellcome to take hold of her arms.

Bassiritz could feel the corded strength of the Rixwoman's muscles even through the straitjacket's metallic fibers. She crossed the deck as smoothly as cargo on a gee-balanced lifting surface, her tiny footsteps utterly silent. Her head darted about like a small bird's, taking in the passageways of the ship in a way that made Bassiritz nervous. Her movements had the sudden menace of a predator, her eyes the acquisitive gleam.

The cell they brought her to was new, specially configured for the Rixwoman. It was constructed of six bare surfaces of hypercarbon. The substance was not as strong as hulalloy, Bassiritz knew, but it was less susceptible to metal-eating viruses and other tricks. It was hard, simple, massive.

They had to take her through the cell's door, which was a meter square. Bassiritz watched her calculating the angles, and saw the danger here. Even with her arms immobilized, the Rixwoman could use the door frame to lever her powerful leg muscles. A simple bend at the knees, and she could push off like a rocket in any direction, butting her head against one of the guards with devastating force.

Private Wellcome stepped through and held out his hand for the prisoner.

Bassiritz hesitated.

'Sergeant?' he said.

'What is it, Bassiritz?'

He struggled to form his instincts into words.

'She has the advantage here, sir,' he said haltingly. 'The small door helps her.'

The marine sergeant scowled. He looked the woman up and down, then turned to Bassiritz.

'Are you sure?'

'Yes, sir.'

The sergeant held up the shock collar remote.

A jolt ran through the Rixwoman's body, every muscle stiffening. Her violet eyes went wide, and a stifled cry came through teeth that were suddenly clenched like a hunting dog's. Bassiritz was frozen for a moment by her horrible expression.

'Well, get her in!' the sergeant barked.

He lifted her stiff and vibrating body through – she was much heavier than he'd thought – and placed her gently on the floor. At another gesture from the sergeant, she sagged limply in Bassiritz's arms. Spittle ran down one of the Rix-woman's cheeks.

They left her there, and sealed the door.

The outside wall of the cell was covered with a hardscreen that showed what happened inside, as if the wall were glass.

Bassiritz was ordered to remain on watch here.

'Don't take your eyes off her, Private,' commanded the sergeant as he handed over the remote. Bassiritz held the device gingerly. The woman still lay on her back, breathing sharp, pained lungfuls of air.

'I'm sorry, Rixwoman,' he said softly to himself.

After half an hour or so, the prisoner had recovered enough to sit up. A few moments later she stood, her motion graceful even within the restraints, and began to pace the dimensions of her cell. She moved with measured deliberation, bringing her eyes strangely close to each of the walls.

Finally, she turned to face Bassiritz.

And smiled, as if she could see him back through the wall.

Bassiritz swallowed. She must be angry after the shock from her stun collar, but her aquiline face showed no rancor. The Rixwoman seemed attentive, as keen as a hungry bird even in that featureless chamber, but no human emotions crossed her visage.

She sat down in the corner across from him and stared, keeping a watchful eye on the door.

Bassiritz watched her carefully for another two hours before he was relieved, never quite able to shake the feeling that she could see him.

In all that time, her only movement was to turn her head every ten minutes or so, and press her ear flush against the metal of the cell wall. Her eyes would close then, and a strangely placid expression would overtake her sharp, predatory features for a moment. It was almost as if she were asleep for those few seconds, blissfully absent from her prison.

Or maybe, Bassiritz thought, the Rixwoman was listening for some small sound that she hoped would reach her from a great distance.

compound mind

The *Lynx* was coming back.

Alexander saw the frigate's reaction drive come alight again, a spark in high orbit above Legis XV. The ship arced away from the planet, describing a nautilus curl outward from gravity's bonds. Soon, the *Lynx*'s hull eclipsed the fires of her drive: the vessel was headed directly toward Alexander.

The compound mind looked at Legis across the massive distance, still fascinated with the world that had given it birth. The radiosensitive elements in Alexander's belly listened intently to the wash of chatter from the planet. The mind refocused the huge, superreflective lens which it had made of its new body, and its gaze turned from the *Lynx* to penetrate the clear night skies of Legis. At this range, the lens could image the running lights of individual aircars, the infrared patterns of greenhouse farming in the arctic, the glowing archipelago of squid-fishing robots in the southern sea. All seemed well on the cradle world, almost returned to normal after the insults of war.

Alexander was glad to see that Legis had not been terribly damaged by its departure. Imperial efforts to dislodge the mind over the last few days had reduced the planet's dependencies on its infostructure; only a few thousands had died as a result of the move, noise compared to the daily births and deaths of millions.

But the cradle was still a melancholy sight. The familiar traffic patterns and newsfeed chatter brought a nostalgic pull of recognition. The mind had already passed apogee with its nascent world, and now its marvelous new body was departing the Legis system, still plummeting toward the heart of the Risen Empire.

New worlds to conquer.

While the frigate's sensors were still distant, Alexander flexed its muscles, sending coruscating elemental patterns through its limbs. Control of this new body was so direct, so palpable after Alexander's mediated existence on Legis. The mind was no longer an epiphenomenon, no mere set of recursive loops lurking within the interactions of others.

Once a ghost in the machine, Alexander had become utterly material, its own creature now.

The mind was able to manipulate the quantum-well electrons of this new body like a computer addressing the registers of memory; Alexander could create with these pseudo-atoms any substance it could imagine. It had gone from the most ephemeral of presences to the most solid, every detail of its composition self-defined. The heady power of this new existence alternately thrilled and frightened the mind. It felt like some bootstrapping god of ancient myth, one of those beings who had created themselves.

But like those old gods, Alexander was mortal now. No longer protected by massively redundant distribution across an entire planet, it had become focused and vulnerable, and alone in the void of space.

Alexander quieted these thoughts as it watched the *Lynx* come closer.

The frigate had spent almost a hundred days in Legis orbit. From what Alexander had gleaned from listening to radio traffic and watching the ascents of cargo shuttles, the ship had been massively repaired, her lost crew replaced by locals who'd been quickly trained. As she made her way toward Alexander, the *Lynx* was accompanied by several tugs that had been crash-built. The hasty construction of these starships and the extensive repair of the frigate had probably done more damage to the Legis economy than any other event in this short war. Refitting the warship in such a hurry had required stripping several small, new cities of their infrastructure, looting fiber and processors from the ground, scrapping whole bridges for their metal.

The *Lynx* had been badly bloodied by her travails; she had survived extraordinary odds. Her captain would make a formidable enemy.

Or perhaps a valued ally.

Alexander understood Imperial culture like a native (arguably, it was just that), and understood the enmity between Laurent Zai and his sovereign. The mind was sensitive to the subtle clues in Imperial military traffic. It knew better than Laurent Zai of the ships massing to meet the *Lynx*.

This split between Alexander's captor and the Emperor could be exploited. Certainly, the Emperor's Secret would be a powerful tool.

The compound mind had one other advantage in this situation. It had listened carefully as the last shuttle rose to meet the *Lynx* just before she left orbit, and knew the names of those final passengers. The seemingly indestructible h_rd had not outlived her usefulness.

Alexander sent out invisible limbs, field effects that were only tens of angstroms across, just powerful enough to hold quantum wells and their silicon substrate in place, barely wide enough to allow information to pass back and forth. Certainly, they were too minuscule for the *Lynx* to see. Alexander stretched these tendrils into a web across space, ready to catch the faint emanations of the Imperial ship's machinery and the chatter of her internal communications.

The mind watched carefully, comparing observational data

to its vast knowledge of Imperial starship design, mapping the configuration of the vessel. It searched for purchase, for some slender pathway into the ship.

As the *Lynx* grew closer, possibilities gradually became clear.

Sub-Rating

Gunnery mess was an embittered quarter.

Sub-Rating Anton Enman still didn't know the names of his crewmates. The *Lynx* was seven days out of Legis XV, and he had been training aboard her for a month before departure, but the gunners were religiously closemouthed around replacement crew. Enman made friends easily, and had developed camaraderie with a few senior crew in other departments, but none in gunnery.

The mess had sounded lively from a few meters away — loud with the japes of old friends, the casual ethnic slanders of a multiplanetary crew — but the conversation dropped off when he entered, the gunners' voices silenced as quickly as conspirators'. Perhaps this simile was not far from the truth, Enman thought. From what he had heard through his other connections, the Lynx mutiny had probably been hatched here in this room. Four gunners had been implicated in the plot to kill Laurent Zai.

Enman took his place at the single, round mess table. Recessed in its centerwell were three stewpots, their contents just under a boil, perpetually filled with self-renewing dishes that were unexpectedly fresh, varied, and satisfying. The sub-rating knew that all Navy fare was composed of the same eleven species of mold, kelp, and soy, but the food still tasted good to him. When Enman admitted his pleasure to his senior crewmates, they assured him that his tolerance of the diet was temporary. After a few months, they warned, an adjustment period would strike. For those few days, the stews in the bubbling pots would be inedible, the meaty textures nightmarish, the faintest whiff of the Navy's common spices revolting. Then, after this feverish interlude, the body would capitulate to the food with desultory acceptance, as if Enman's taste buds were some bacterial invader domesticated by the *Lynx*'s immune system.

But at the moment, the food was quite tasty.

He reached across the silent table and liberated a segmented bowl from the locked-down stack at its center. The metal eating sticks and spoon, which sported two sharp tines like canines, were magnetically attached to the bowl. The pots were covered, of course. Everything in the mess was zero-gee ready at all times. Even the bowls would slam themselves shut if their internal sensors detected a non-one-gee condition. If hurled into the air, he'd been told, the bowls would seal before falling, unbreakable, to the deck. This last sounded to Enman like the sort of rumor foisted off on junior crew. He figured that those who tested this feature would wind up on their knees, scrubbing.

He pushed down on each of the pot's center spouts, plodging (this was the Navy's onomatopoetic verb for it) a portion of stew into each segment of the bowl. There was a new feature in the spicy green stew: small red dumplings with a hard carapace that suggested they'd been fried in oil under low atmospheric pressure.

Not one for eating sticks, Enman speared the dumplings one by one with his spoon's short tines. Each broke into a different flavor — soft potato surrounding a whole garlic clove, crisp red pepper, a small round piece of dry, spongy bread. Over the centuries, it seemed, the Navy had learned to incorporate every imaginable foodstuff into stew.

The sub-rating ate voraciously, appearing to ignore the senior crew around him. He always showed for meals at the same times, as silent and regular as a monk attending the hours of the mass. Each day the other denizens of the mess grew a bit less aware of his presence. After a few minutes of silence, Enman felt himself sinking into the background. The gunners' conversation had been particularly intense before his interruption, and they wanted to get back to it. The sub-rating kept his eyes focused into his stew.

'Did you see the CW today?' a third gunner with big ears said.

This was their shorthand for Katherie Hobbes, the frigate's stunningly beautiful executive officer. It had taken weeks of eavesdropping for Enman to identify the nickname's refer-ent, but he had no idea of its derivation. The gunners were a very circumspect lot.

'Where? Down here in mortal country?' an ordnance spe-cialist asked.

Bigears nodded. 'Inspecting the hardpoint armor. "Checking the seams," she said. Had a shitload of scanning gear.'

There were nods and grumbles. Bigears made the gestural code for cargo, his motion deliberately sloppy so that the ship's interface wouldn't pick the hand sign up. Enman stared into his stew. The gunner was suggesting – in a way that no recording of this conversation would reveal – that Hobbes had been checking for contraband stashed between the newly installed plates of armor. Sidearms, and anything that might be made into a weapon, were still very tightly controlled on the *Lynx*.

'Seemed satisfied, though.'

'Waste of time.'

'Not giving us much credit.'

'Gives her something to do.'

'When she's not servicing the old man.'

There was a grumbling laugh in the mess. Enman's eating slowed as he listened. This was a new thread in the gunners' talk, at least when he had been within earshot. He wondered if he should take the risk of expressing a careful measure of interest.

'CW?' he asked innocently.

His question was met with scowls. Faces turned away from him. He swallowed, willed himself to blush like a boy rejected by older men, and bent back to his stew. The room was silent for the rest of the meal. Enman cursed himself. He had spoken too soon. The gunners were still too paranoid to talk in front of a newcomer. This would be a game of months, or even years.

But when the watch chime rang, Bigears grasped Enman's shoulder as the sub-rating rose to leave. He handsigned the table to purge, fully resetting the mold culture. Sometimes, like an aquarium with water gone bad, the stews went funny, and had to be started over from scratch.

As the hiss of a steam-cleaning thundered through the mess, a few wisps of vapor rising from the sealed pots, Bigears leaned close, his lips almost touching Enman's ear.

'Captain's Whore,' came his whisper, almost lost in the hiss of steam.

Enman nodded just a bit, allowing his face to show a faint smile.

The mess cleared, and the sub-rating returned to his gunnery post in the ship's nose, spending a watch operating close-in-defense lasers against the few small fragments presented by the Legis system's thin asteroid belt. The flush of his accomplishment in the mess helped his aim; over the two hours, Enman managed the highest hit-rate of any Legis-drafted gunner yet.

By the time watch ended, he was aglow with satisfaction.

The path from forward gunnery to his cabin led past the Apparatus section of the frigate. Most crew avoided the political quarter, preferring any route that avoided the black-walled halls and the cold stares of the dead interlopers onboard ship. But Enman took the straight course this time.

He soon found himself in an empty corridor. With a quick look in both directions, he stopped at a small door and announced himself.

'Aspirant Anton Enman, reporting.'

The door opened quickly, and the aspirant slipped furtively inside.

Executive Officer

The four prisoners hung from the ceiling.

They were trussed with an elastic rope. Like everything in this gray moment, the pattern of their bonds was prescribed by ritual. The rope pulled tight against their red brig fatigues, and sectioned the prisoners' torsos like cutlines painted on cattle prepped for slaughter. This particular type of rope was derived from the long chain proteins of spider thread, and she, Katherie Hobbes, had been their Arachne.

'Any statements?'

Silence. Thompson, Hu, Magus, and King had already been put to the question, and their wills had held against drugs, against threats to their families, against pain. Their loyalty to their fellow mutineers had proved unshakable.

Hobbes reached up to the prisoners' throats to check the vorpal shunts again. With the marine doctor dead, the shunts had been implanted by medtechs never trained in the procedure. But the shunts looked fine. They pulsed visibly with the prisoners' heartbeat. Katherie checked the lengths of rope that stretched to the floor from the four mutineers' ankles. They looked fast, tight in their hypercarbon rings.

Finally, Hobbes glanced up at the four wide-mouthed ceremonial platters bonded to the ceiling. Each was in its correct place.

There was nothing else to do.

'Ready, sir.' She stepped back across the yellow-red stripe of the gravity line. Sudden inversion, those colors meant.

Captain Zai nodded. He said some appropriate prayer, his voice sinking into the rolling glottal fricatives of Vadan. A few of the marine guards muttered prayers in their own tongues. Then, without further ceremony, Zai made the signal.

Nothing happened yet. In theory, the captain's gesture was not the trigger that killed the prisoners. No one person did the Emperor's work in this regard, but the universe itself. Zai had commanded the *Lynx* to watch for a certain occultation, an astronomical event that would inevitably occur within a few minutes. When the *Lynx* made the observation – a star of a specific class disappearing behind some random asteroid in the Legis belt – the executions would unfold.

They waited.

A timeless minute later it must have happened, a tiny and momentary blackness amid the river of light on which the *Lynx* moved, a drifting closed of some sleepy god's eye.

Gravity inverted in the other half of the room, the prisoners suddenly levitating before Hobbes's eyes. The bonds around their ankles snapped taut, like a fall halted by a noose, their vorpal shunts opening as one. Four thin streams of blood shot toward the ceiling – the floor in their frame of reference – striking the ceremonial platters with a sound like piss hitting a metal bowl.

The prisoners didn't struggle. Supposedly, this form of execution was relatively painless, the limbs growing quickly cold. Oxygen would cease to reach the body's cells, but like suffocation by carbon dioxide, there would be no frenzied gasping for breath.

Their faces grew pink at first, as the inverted gravity brought blood down from the feet to the head. But Katherie could see the mutineers' bound hands turning white already. Eventually, their faces would blanch and grow expressionless. Blood pooled in the ceremonial bowls, the metal-ringing, splattery sound replaced by the gurgle of liquid into liquid.

Katherie stood at attention. She felt light-headed, as if the gravity inversion were losing integrity, suffusing across the yellow-red stripe, its tendrils finding her. She blinked, and nausea rose in Hobbes. Her old nemesis vertigo threatened as her eyes read the clear signs of up and down reversed on the other side of the room, a few wisps of Magus's hair flailing upward, the lines of Thompson's face pulled wrong.

Then the flow of blood began to slacken. The prisoners' faces grew white. It was almost over.

And then something terrible happened.

The four hanging bodies suddenly jolted toward her, as if kicked from behind. She and Zai jumped back. Magus's hair pointed directly at Hobbes now. Gravity inside the inversion zone had shifted by ninety degrees, a malfunction of the *Lynx*'s ailing generator.

Hobbes looked at the ceiling with horror.

The blood already collected in the ceremonial bowls was spilling out, pouring across the ceiling in a sanguine waterfall, rolling toward the yellow-red stripe almost above her head.

Katherie barely had time to cover her face.

The liters of blood reached the normal gravity zone, a red river that was cleaved by the sudden directional shift. It sprayed upon her and Laurent Zai like a warm summer rain.

Katherie Hobbes awoke gasping, clawing at the strands of her own hair in her mouth.

A *dream*. Just a dream. The executions had been more

than a month ago. Nothing so horrible had happened. In the real event, the ritual had unfolded with admirable military precision.

Hobbes coughed, wiping sweat from her face, which tasted as salty as blood. She pulled her knees to her chest and breathed deeply, trying to calm herself.

Then she realized it: this had been her first real dream in months.

Katherie Hobbes had just gone back to natural sleep, her usage of hypersleep having exceeded the recommended maximum by more than a hundred percent. The ship's new doctor, an earnest civilian from Legis's storm-swept equatorial archipelago, had given her drugs to help the transition. But Katherie had left them untouched, relying on exhaustion to get her to oblivion.

Clearly, that had been a bad idea. Hobbes had grown addicted to the instantaneous drop into hyperdreams, the familiar, symbolic process-narratives that reliably reconstituted her brain. Falling into natural sleep had taken a thrashing, anxious hour. And when Katherie Hobbes finally slipped into a restless unconsciousness, it was only to discover this long-suppressed nightmare.

A moment after she awoke from the execution dream, the entry chime sounded from Hobbes's door, an insistent summons dragging her fully awake. The access icon glowed in second sight: an Apparatus subpoena in brilliant red.

Without waiting for a response, three politicals entered her cabin. Two honored dead and a living woman.

'Katherie Hobbes.' Even in the dark cabin, Hobbes recognized the flat voice of Adept Harper Trevim.

This was serious, Katherie's addled brain slowly realized. Trevim was the ranking political on board the *Lynx*. What had happened? Hobbes sat up, and quickly ran the frigate's top-level diagnostics in synesthesia. Nothing seemed out of place.

'Yes, Honored Mother?' she managed with a dry voice.

'We must talk with you.'

She nodded and rose shakily to attention. In an odd moment of embarrassment, she hoped the politicals wouldn't notice her bedclothes. The natural worm silk of her sheets was a guilty pleasure from home. Hobbes kept it covered with a blanket of Navy wool during the day. The politicals looked only at her body, however, a bit of discomfort showing on the living woman's face. Having grown up on a Utopian world, Hobbes felt no discomfort in nakedness. The dead, she assumed, were similarly unflappable.

'Yes, Adept. At the Emperor's pleasure,' she answered.

'We must speak of your captain.'

Of course. They were still after Laurent. They always would be.

'Yes, Honored Mother?'

'New information has come to us about his rejection of the blade.'

Hobbes could barely hide her disgust. She spoke rudely. 'He was pardoned by the Emperor, Adept.'

The dead woman nodded. The precise, expressionless movement reminded Hobbes of her protocol instructor when she'd been a staff officer. She'd learned the gestural cues of a dozen cultures from the man, but he had never seemed fully human himself. The adept had the same neutral presence, as if this were all some strange ritual. Indeed, the whole scene was so surreal, Hobbes wasn't sure she wasn't still dreaming.

'Yes, it was fortunate that he did not take the blade before pardon was given,' Trevim said. 'But we are concerned about his motivation for delaying the ritual.'

Hobbes couldn't see where this was going. She blinked, trying to will away the cobwebs of sleep in her mind. 'Honored Mother?'

'What is the exact nature of your relationship with Laurent Zai?'

For a moment, Katherie could not answer. Her silence stretched and redoubled itself, until it was a hand over her mouth.

She finally forced herself to speak. 'What do you mean?'

'We have heard troubling rumors.'

Hobbes felt the flush at her breast, the heat in her face. She was angry, humiliated, enraged at her own inability to respond. This had to be another nightmare: naked, her head groggy with sleep, called on the carpet by the Emperor's representatives.

'I don't know what you mean, Adept.'

'What is your exact relationship with Laurent Zai?'

'I'm his executive officer.'

'Is there anything more?'

Hobbes willfully forced emotion from her mind, and let herself be ruled by the dictates of gray talk, as if she were making a military report. She only had to tell the truth. Anything else between them had only ever been in her own mind. 'I have the utmost respect for the captain. There is nothing unprofessional in our friendship.'

'Friendship?'

'Friendship.'

'Do you know why he rejected the blade?'

'I don't—' Hobbes choked herself off. She did know, she realized. 'There is no reason for Captain Zai to die. And he was pardoned.'

'Was it because of his affair with you?'

'There is nothing between Laurent and me,' she said. Somehow, it seemed harder to tell the truth than it would have been to lie.

'Laurent?' the adept noted.

Hobbes took a deep breath and closed her eyes. She felt

the heat of another blush travel across her exposed body. Hobbes realized that if they were polygraphing her, they had every advantage. She was naked and exhausted, without defenses.

But she was telling the truth, after all.

'Were you and Zai lovers?'

'No.'

'Did Laurent Zai choose to live for you, Katherie?'

'No, Adept. It was someone else.'

Their faces showed no surprise, but Hobbes's words won her a moment of respite. She felt triumphant to have silenced the dead woman.

'Who, Katherie?' the adept finally asked.

'I don't know.'

'Another crew member?'

'No. Captain Zai would never—' She swallowed. 'I have no idea who.'

'So it could be a crewmate of yours.'

'No! It's someone on Home, I think.'

The adept leaned closer, peering at her like some troubling specimen under glass.

'He just wanted to live, Honored Mother. For some lover, for some imagined future. Why is that so hard to believe?'

The dead woman blinked, then nodded again, as smoothly as a machine. Hobbes felt she could detect an expression on her face: a ghost of satisfaction.

'I believe you, Executive Officer,' the dead woman said.

They left Hobbes, and she curled back into bed. The worm silk didn't comfort her. The privacy of the cabin had been utterly violated, her mind stripped of its deepest secret. They had seen what she had wanted, what she had allowed herself to hope for. That old humiliation had returned, amplified by a dead woman's smirk.

And as she calmed herself, curling into a ball and gesturing for the susurrant music of her childhood, Katherie realized that she might have made a terrible mistake. The politicals still wanted Captain Zai's blood, still sought revenge for his rejection of tradition. They would try to turn anything they knew about him to their advantage. And she had told him of his secret lover on Home.

Had she betrayed her captain?

Marine Private

Bassiritz watched the transformation.

The prisoner had lain with her head pressed against the cell wall, just as she had for a few minutes of every hour for the last two weeks.

He had checked the interval against his time stamp many times, and it was always just over an hour. In his shifts guarding the Rixwoman, Bassiritz had never seen the ritual disrupted. Her actions were absolutely regular, as if her mind were empty of everything but numbers, counting ten thousand seconds again and again. She seemed more machine than human.

Bassiritz's fascination with her had led to still more reading, and he knew that Rix bodies were half artificial. Brain, muscles, cellular systems – no aspect of their physiology remained untouched, even in the womb. Of course, Imperial knowledge had for centuries been limited to corpses recovered after battle; live specimens had only been observed in firefights, where the Rixwomen seemed more demonic than mechanical.

The woman before him was the Empire's first captive Rixwoman.

For the last two weeks, Bassiritz had keenly observed this

event, this moment when the prisoner looked fully human. As she listened, head pressed to the hypercarbon wall, the fierce cast of her features softened, as if she were adrift in some innocent daydream years distant from her empty cell.

So he saw when it happened.

Her eyes popped open, and filled with predatory pleasure.

The marine jumped at the Rixwoman's sudden motion, a measure of cold fear trickling into his belly. The hypercarbon between them suddenly seemed no more substantial than glass.

Bassiritz remembered his childhood, when he used to dare himself to face his father's tarantula, trapped in a terrarium above the old man's desk. The arachnid glowered down from the transparent globe, guarding its tiny domain of twigs and sand. The glass sphere never seemed sufficient to ensure its captivity. When, subjective years ago, Bassiritz had returned home to discover that the Time Thief had taken his father, the globe above the desk was empty. The tarantula had died long ago, his aging sisters assured Bassiritz. But in his mind, it had escaped, free to roam now that it was no longer held in check by his father's iron will. Since that disappearance, the marine had never slept comfortably in his family home.

The Rixwoman now seemed to embody the spirit of that missing spider, as if it had come for him at last.

She stared directly at Bassiritz, even though the imaging was one way.

'Bring your captain to me,' she said.

He nodded dumbly, unable to resist her command.

Captain

Laurent Zai looked at the command bridge airscreen and sighed.

The colors of the image were false, the terminology metaphorical, the clean-looking shapes wholly a mathematical invention. The illustration was purely hypothetical; merely a representation of a theory about an enigma. Nothing was ever straightforward when one tried to plumb the quantum.

'We think that the pseudoatoms are physically disjunct from the silicon substrate,' Tyre continued.

Zai's eyes drifted about the command bridge. He wondered how many of the officers present really understood this. They were all still exhausted by battle and repair work, and perhaps a bit complacent from victory. For the last fifteen minutes, only Hobbes had been questioning the DA ensign.

'The silicon simply gives it mass?' his executive officer asked.

'Gives it mass, ma'am,' said Tyre, 'and serves as the semiconducting medium. Without a semiconductor, you can't make quantum wells.'

Captain Zai winced. There was that term again. He'd always thought of quantum mechanics as safely in the realm of the minuscule – relevant to data processing and communications, but not the hard and 'strongly interacting' physics of combat. Whenever the twisted rules of the quantum domain reached up into the macroworld, the results were unnerving.

'Please explain quantum wells again, Ensign.'

Tyre took a deep breath, managing to keep frustration from her face.

'In certain semiconducting environments, electrons occupy something called a quantum well. Inside a quantum well, pseudoatom electrons assume the arrangement of a normal atom, but there's no nucleus – no protons or neutrons.'

'No real mass, Captain,' Hobbes added, 'and with infinite half-life: no radiation or decay even in transuranium elements. But like an isotope, quantum-well pseudoatoms have the same physical characteristics as a real atom with the same number of electrons: hardness, reflectivity, chemical properties.'

'Imperial data processors use quantum wells, correct?' he asked.

'Some do, sir,' Tyre explained. 'The *Lynx*'s processors certainly use quantum *bits* – data are stored in the spin-state of electron pairs in trapped phosphorus atoms – but that's not a quantum well. Those are *real* phosphorus atoms.'

Zai sighed.

'But we do know how to create quantum wells,' he stated.

'Yes, sir. That's pre-starflight technology.'

'In that case, and please put this simply,' he said, 'what can the Rix do that we can't?'

Ensign Tyre looked pleadingly at Hobbes, and the executive officer nodded and looked upward to gather her thoughts.

'Sir, we can only create wells with fixed electron counts, and under relatively controlled circumstances. But the Rix have found a way to add and subtract electrons on the fly, to change the wells' elemental characteristics at will. Apparently, the object can address its pseudoatoms as if they were registers in a computer's memory. In some sense, the object is a quantum computer.'

'A computer that can change itself into whatever it wants?'

'Yes, sir. The process of the object's thoughts is transubstantiation.'

'Mind and matter, one,' he mused.

Hobbes narrowed her eyes. 'I suppose so, sir.'

Laurent Zai dared another look into the airscreen. Since his last question, Ensign Tyre had put up a representation of a quantum well. It looked like any number of three-dimensional graphs: a terrain of spiky mountains arranged with an odd symmetry, like a wedding procession of volcanoes, or the spinal ridges of some exaggerated trilobite.

Thoughts of evolutionary past turned over the soil of Zai's

growing disquiet. His staff seemed insufficiently alarmed by the object's abilities, as if they'd captured some alien and charming children's toy. Ensign Tyre seemed to view this as an intellectual game, as if it were one of the reverse-engineering conundra that DA officers composed and swapped like chess puzzles. For Hobbes, this new Rix technology translated into nothing more than a set of tactical advantages, like a new form of armor or an improved gravity effect.

But Zai saw a greater danger. Not only to the Empire, but to humanity itself. This was a revision of *matter*, for god's sake. He had to make them grasp the enormity of this development.

'Tyre,' he said, 'would this work at higher temperatures?'

'Absolutely, sir. It might improve its operation. Frankly, we have no idea how they've managed to get the silicon to semi-conduct at deepspace temperatures.'

'And it would work in a hard-gee field?'

'It should, sir. We've poked at it with easy gravitons, anyway, and there seems to be no disruption. This all happens in the electromagnetic domain; gravity is a relatively trivial force.'

'So this object could exist on a planet?'

Tyre and Hobbes were silent. Other officers around the table straightened, awakening from the stupor of the physics lesson. Zai waited a few more moments as the idea sank in.

Then he asked more directly. 'This object might well adapt itself to terrestrial conditions?'

'I see no reason why it couldn't, sir,' Tyre admitted.

'Could it propagate itself, like nanotechnology?'

'Possibly, sir. If there was sufficient silicon in the environment.'

'What percentage of the average terrestrial planet is silicon, Tyre?'

Hobbes shook her head as she interrupted. 'We don't know

if propagation is even remotely possible, sir. And we do know the object has limitations. It can change itself, but it hasn't turned into a starship and attacked us.'

Tyre spoke. 'It seems to be unable to create complex objects, ma'am, as far as we've seen. And, of course, the object has only its own silicon substrate for reaction mass; acceleration would gradually consume it. Without nuclei, of course, it can't make a fusion drive or nuclear weapons.'

'I hope you're right, Tyre,' Zai said. 'How many megatons of silicon do you think exist on Home?'

'We can keep it physically distant from any planets, sir,' Hobbes said.

'I wouldn't bring it within a billion kilometers of Home, orders from the Emperor be damned,' he stated flatly.

The disloyal words brought a look of shock to the officers' faces. Good, he had their attention. They were going to have to be very careful with this war prize.

Tyre spoke up, back with an answer to his previous questions. 'Silicon is universally prevalent, sir. In terrestrial planetary crusts, only oxygen is more plentiful by mass. And in cosmic terms, only a few gases and carbon exceed silicon in abundance.'

Zai was finally satisfied by his staff's reaction to this information.

'Listen carefully,' he said. 'We seem to have a tiger by the tail. Emergent minds have existed for a long time. As the Rix Cult insists, they are the natural result of any petabyte-scale data system, just as biological life seems to be the natural result of oxygen, carbon, and a billion years of steady sunlight or geothermal. But however threatening compound minds are, so far they have always depended on humanity for their existence. *We* formed the substrate for their thoughts.'

Zai looked around the command bridge, catching his officers' eyes one by one.

'But we are no longer necessary,' he said slowly.

Laurent Zai watched their faces carefully. The trip to Home would take almost two subjective years. To keep his crew alert during that long passage, he needed to illustrate the threat that this enigmatic cargo posed to the *Lynx* and the Empire, and to humanity. The spaceborn mind was a new species, an altogether unknown entity that would test this crew sorely.

A strange look passed over Hobbes' face. She put a hand to one ear.

'Sir,' she said quietly. 'I'm getting double-priority from the Rix prisoner's marine guard.'

'An escape attempt?' Zai asked. He had feared that having a commando on board would cause trouble, no matter how carefully she was guarded.

'Negative, sir. A message.'

'She's decided to speak?'

'Not her, sir. The message . . . it's from the compound mind. For you personally.'

Laurent Zai glanced around at the shocked faces of his officers. He didn't allow himself to show surprise. They would have to learn. Over the next two years, the unexpected would be the norm.

'It has already begun,' was all he said.

He left them there, signaling for Hobbes to follow.

Executive Officer

As they walked toward the cell, Katherie Hobbes's hand went to the flechette pistol strapped to her wrist.

She had intended to visit the prisoner once her duties permitted. The commando was a fabulous physical specimen, a captive unique in Imperial history. She was the only Rixwoman ever captured alive and conscious by Imperial forces over a century of armed clashes between Empire and Cult.

For the Rix, fighting to the end was the rule, suicide the alternative to victory. Hobbes's researches had found only a single previous example of live Rix prisoners. At the end of the First Incursion, sixteen Rixwomen had been taken while in coldsleep, their long-range small craft intercepted by an Imperial raider deep within Cult space. One by one, they had been awakened, but each died within seconds of consciousness. Imperial doctors had attempted to discover and neutralize the mechanism by which the prisoners had ended their own lives, but no amount of medical intervention could keep them alive. Their bodies rejected sedatives, resuscitation, even − it was rumored − the holy symbiant. It seemed that the Rix had conscious control over their vital functions. For a Rixwoman, breathing was an option, the actions of the heart a voluntary choice.

Suicide, simply a decision.

Maybe, Hobbes thought, they actually believed their own propaganda. If human life was inherently meaningless, then one's own might be ended by a whim.

Here was a Rixwoman, however, an elite commando of the Cult, who had apparently decided that life in captivity was worth living. But was it her own decision that kept her alive, Hobbes wondered, or the purposes of the compound mind?

The marine guards snapped to attention when the executive officer and Captain Zai reached the cell. Hobbes had sent an extra fire team here when the priority signal came through; there were five marines present in all. One was Private Bassiritz, the man she'd drafted to help foil the mutiny. Hobbes had personally chosen him for this duty. If anyone could react quickly enough to meet a Rix commando on her own terms, Bassiritz could.

A living initiate of the Apparatus – the woman's name was Farre – also stood by. The captain grimaced at the sight of her. The politicals had kept a close watch on the Rixwoman and Rana Harter since their arrival on the *Lynx*. An Imperial writ gave them absolute power over the two prisoners.

'Captain.'

'Initiate,' Zai responded and turned to Bassiritz.

'She actually said something to you, Private?' he asked.

'Yes, sir. Asked for you, sir.'

Hobbes looked at the prisoner through the false transparency of the hypercarbon. The commando sat in one corner, as dirty and forlorn as some forgotten madwoman in an asylum. She hadn't spoken in her months of captivity – only those nine words when she'd been captured, a lament for her dead lover. Why would she wait until now to reveal a message?

'Can we two-way this transparency?' Captain Zai asked.

'No, sir. There's no hardscreen inside.'

'Then let's go in.'

'Sir!' Hobbes protested. 'That's a *Rix commando*, restrained or not.'

'She appears to be wearing a shock collar. Private, you have the remote?'

'Yes, sir.' Bassiritz held the little hardkey up.

'Keep it handy.'

'Captain,' interjected the initiate. 'I will take the remote, if you please.'

'Initiate Farre,' Zai said, 'this man's reflexes are far quicker than yours. You'll put our safety at risk.'

'The Emperor is concerned about secrets supplied to the prisoner by the compound mind on Legis,' the initiate said. 'Is this cell secured?'

Zai glanced at Hobbes.

'The cell has no particular data security, sir. But it's pretty blind in there. No camwall or synesthesia projectors. And she's hardly been spilling secrets.'

'Ma'am,' Bassiritz offered nervously. 'There's an extra remote, for watch changes.'

They would only be safer with two remotes, Hobbes realized. She nodded, and the marine produced another of the black hardkeys. He handed it to Farre.

Zai gestured, but the door failed to open. Hobbes recalled that it was purely mechanical, cut off from automatics and even decompression safeties. She nodded to the ranking marine, who ordered two of the fire team to muscle it open. Chain of command in action, Hobbes thought.

Bassiritz went through first.

Captain Zai waited for a moment, watching for the commando's reaction. The Rixwoman stood, but kept to her corner. Hobbes saw now that her movements were strangely disjointed, as sudden as a nervous bird's.

'Executive Officer,' Zai said.

Hobbes's finger brushed the reassuring bump of her concealed flechette pistol before stepping through the meter-wide door. The room was bright, lit by a ceiling full of dumb, spray-on filaments. It smelled of confinement, but without overwhelming rankness. The Rixwoman's sweat had the scent of milk about to turn.

Zai and the initiate came after her. The four of them remained in the opposite corner from the Rixwoman. Her eyes shone violet in the harsh light, her face as still as some ancient lizard's.

'Captain Laurent Zai,' she said. Hobbes recognized in her accent the long vowels of Legis XV's far northern provinces.

'Yes. And your name?' Zai answered.

It had never occurred to Hobbes that she would have one.

'Herd.' Her accent slipped into some native phonology, and the vowel was inflected by a buzz at the back of the woman's throat.

'And you have a message for me?'

'From Alexander.'

Good god, thought Hobbes. The compound mind had a name.

Zai just nodded. 'What is it?'

The commando cocked her head, as if listening to something. Then shifted inside the straitjacket, rolling her shoulders.

'Alexander wishes to give you a weapon.'

'A weapon?' Zai asked, finally unable to keep surprise from his voice. 'Technology?'

'No, Captain. Information,' she said. 'To use against the Emperor.'

Farre raised the shock remote.

'You see, Captain? She has classified information.'

Zai was silent for a moment, stunned by the Rixwoman's words. Hobbes glanced toward Private Bassiritz. The commando might be trying to create a moment of confusion before launching an attack, and the old initiate would never react quickly enough to stop her. The marine seemed completely alert, however; he was shutting out the words. His eyes were fixed on the commando fiercely, as if she were some childhood monster come to life. Hobbes swallowed, and again touched the shape of her flechette pistol through the wool of her sleeve.

'I am the Emperor's servant,' Zai said.

'He is afraid of us, and he will destroy us if he can,' the Rixwoman said.

'Us?' Zai asked. 'You and . . . ?'

'The *Lynx* and Alexander. Us. We are bound together now.'

Captain Zai placed his palms together. 'The Emperor knows no fear,' he began the catechism. 'Not even death—'

'A lie,' Herd said quietly.

Farre made a noise, as if she'd been struck with something.

'Silence,' the initiate cried. 'Captain, you must secure this room. Immediately.'

The captain glared at the prisoner. Hobbes thought for a moment that Zai would turn and leave the madwoman in her lonely cell. However much the past months had changed him, Zai was still appalled by her blasphemy.

But instead he took a deep breath.

'Of what is the Emperor afraid?' Laurent Zai asked, his jaw clenched with the effort of the calumnious words.

'He has a secret,' Herd said, 'which Alexander discovered on Legis. If this information became known, it would destroy his power.'

'Silence!' the initiate shrieked, again flinching as if the words were dealing her physical blows. Both her hands clenched around the remote.

The Rixwoman's form jerked horribly to attention within the straitjacket. She toppled against the wall and slid down to the floor, her body as stiff as a statue, her face frozen in a terrible rictus.

'Listen, Zai,' she hissed, her accent becoming flat and Rixian. 'The dead are—'

Then the collar overwhelmed the Rixwoman, her body thrashing like a corpse animated with electrical shocks.

'Private,' the captain said quietly.

Bassiritz adjusted his own remote, and the shock collar released the commando. Initiate Farre dropped to her knees, holding her head and shaking as if she'd been shocked as well.

Hobbes ignored the initiate and took a few steps toward the prisoner. She knelt, still a meter away, and looked into the commando's now slack face.

Saliva bubbled from her lips. She was breathing, at least. Hobbes glared back at Farre.

'Silence,' the political insisted again, her voice reduced to a mewling cry.

Bassiritz gazed on the proceedings with a strange, horrified expression. Yet the marine looked strangely pleased, as if he'd just squashed some large and repellent insect.

'Cut the audio feed from this room,' Zai said to the wall. 'No more contact with this prisoner.'

'Sir?' Hobbes asked.

'She may indeed know Imperial secrets, Hobbes. It's up to us to guard them.'

Hobbes reached out a hand, and touched the woman's neck. She felt for a pulse.

'They have no hearts, Hobbes,' Zai said. 'Not the beating kind, anyway.'

The executive officer nodded. The skin was room temperature; she remembered that Rix commandos were generally cold-blooded to prevent thermal imaging.

What a compromised human being.

'Come away from there,' Zai ordered softly.

Hobbes stood, and retreated.

The Rixwoman moved, turning her head slowly.

'Wait,' she croaked.

'For god's sake, *silence*, woman!' Zai pleaded.

Herd shook her head. 'No secrets. Just a question.'

Captain Zai looked at Hobbes, lost for a moment. The initiate lay on the ground, head in hands and beyond hearing, but Bassiritz stood ready with the other remote.

The executive officer turned to the prisoner, knelt again.

'What is it, Herd?'

The commando took a few breaths, swallowing, as if to wet her mouth. When she spoke, the words were tortured.

'Is it true that Rana Harter is alive again?' she said.

The woman seemed confused, as if she were speaking her own mind after a lifetime of prompting. Her words were halting.

'I must see . . . Rana Harter,' she said.

Zai shook his head. 'The Honored Sister is not to be disturbed. Not by anyone.'

The prisoner nodded. 'But she is alive.'

Hobbes felt a strange sympathy for the Rixwoman. But the captain had no choice; the Emperor's orders were explicit. Not even the other honored dead were allowed to speak with Rana Harter. An adept of the Apparatus, the ranking political aboard the *Lynx*, was posted in her antechamber.

'He'll kill her,' Herd said.

'Who will?' Hobbes asked.

'The Emperor,' the woman said softly. 'Your Emperor fears that she knows his secret. But she doesn't.'

'Rixwoman,' Zai said. 'Don't speak of secrets.'

'Let me see her,' the woman pleaded, trying to rise from where she lay. But the attempt exhausted her, and her head dropped back to the floor.

'My orders are clear,' Zai said. 'Rana Harter is to be left alone.'

He turned away from the prisoner and pulled himself through the door. Hobbes stared at the alien woman for a moment, looking for the signs of truth she might find in a normal human's eyes. But the commando's face had hardened again. Once more she seemed to come from some nonmammalian order, as inscrutable as a tortoise.

Hobbes signaled to Bassiritz to help the initiate out of the cell. What had affected the political like that? She knew that calumny against the Emperor was painful to the most heavily conditioned members of the Apparatus, even to lifelong grays like her Vadan captain, but she'd never seen anyone brought to their knees by mere words.

Hobbes followed Zai, wondering what to do. The room was sealed behind them, and the wall went blank, as impenetrable as stone.

As they strode toward the bridge, Zai said, 'Rana Harter.'

'Sir?'

'The order to keep her isolated. I've never seen such a command. It is very strange to imprison the honored dead.'

Zai's voice shook as he said it. Hobbes knew that Harter's reanimation was dubious at best, in the eyes of tradition. The politicals occasionally used the symbiant for tactical reasons, to interrogate a traitor or reverse a local assassination that threatened stability, but the official fiction was that all the dead were honored. So it must wound Zai's Vadan soul to restrain a risen woman.

'Perhaps there are secrets that we're not meant to know, eh, Hobbes?'

'Almost certainly, sir,' she answered.

He stopped short, turned to her.

'Do you think we *need* a weapon against the Emperor, Hobbes?'

She knew that anything short of swift denial was treasonous, but she couldn't bring herself to lie.

'I don't know, sir.' She half-closed her eyes, her face tense as if awaiting a blow from an angry parent's hand.

But Captain Zai said, 'I don't either, Hobbes. I don't either.'

He turned away again, and they went up to the bridge.

Senator

The garden had changed.

Arciform sand dunes still dominated the walk to its center, but the scorpions had been replaced with desert flowers. The many fountains still played their tricks of orientation, lovely gravity wells bending the water through playfully twisted paths, but the liquid was now phosphorescent, the drops sparkling like the last glimmers from a firework display. The sinuous and threatening vines Nara Oxham remembered lining the walk had been done away with. Ranks of tulips framed the spiraling path now. Purple and black, their petals were variegated with red lines caused – she remembered – by a virus.

They were quite beautiful, though.

Senator Oxham wondered if these changes to the Emperor's garden were part of some weekly redecoration, or if the lighthearted touches were a response to war, a curative for the sovereign's cares. The short journey through the garden certainly seemed less threatening now.

Oxham shook her head, realizing that her own assurance had nothing to do with the flowers or sparkling waters. She was simply no longer intimidated by the Imperial mystique.

The dead man waited for her at the center.

'Counselor,' he greeted her.

'Good day, Sire.'

'Please be seated, Senator Oxham.'

Oxham sat in the floating chair. It seemed to remember her, adapting to her shape more quickly than it had the first time she'd come to the Diamond Palace.

It was strange to meet the sovereign again outside the presence of the War Council. The precisely balanced tensions of that group had become so familiar, their range of emotional reactions so predictable. Oxham felt a sense of dislocation. Perhaps that was why the Emperor had reconfigured his garden, to put her subtly ill at ease.

A cat leapt into her lap, startling her. The creature was the color of gray ash, with an apricot-colored mask and white paws. Oxham ran her hand along its back, feeling with quiet distaste the ridges of the symbiant.

'Does it have a name, Sire?' she asked.

'Alexander.'

'He seeks new worlds to conquer, then.'

The Emperor smiled wanly. 'Perhaps.'

She could see the emotions in the dead man clearly. Anxiety, tempered with the confidence of a well-laid plan. Oxham had set her apathy bracelet perilously low, but here, shut off from the raging city, her sensitivity was bright. She remembered Roger Niles's warnings, and determined that she would make no mistakes today.

'To what do I owe this honor, Your Majesty?'

The sovereign reached under his chair. He produced a small human skull, turned so that its eye sockets stared at her.

Oxham stiffened slightly, and the little beast on her lap betrayed her reaction with wide-eyed annoyance at the motion.

'Forgive me, Senator,' the sovereign apologized.

'I am your servant, Majesty.' Oxham stealthily jabbed the cat with a fingernail, but it simply purred.

She regarded the skull. At first, it seemed to be that of a child, but the cheekbones jutted ahead of the brow, and the teeth were arrayed in an uncorrected, pretechnology jumble. Along with the sloping forehead, these characteristics suggested the diminutive skull of an ancient hominid adult.

'Another history lesson, Sire?'

'An illustrative example, Senator.' He rotated the skull in his hand, tipped it to face him as if he were going to play Hamlet. Now its top was to Oxham, and she saw the holes.

There were four of them in a rectangle, each a few centimeters across, the two closer to the front much larger. Old cracks emanated from the holes. Only a sealant of gleaming transparent plastic kept the skull from crumbling in the Emperor's hand.

Nara swallowed. This example might be a grim one.

'Some ancient form of execution, Sire?'

He shook his head. Another cat appeared from among

the tulips and wound between the legs of her chair, then disappeared.

'Just an old story, for those who can read it.'

'I'm afraid I cannot, Liege.'

'This creature, one of our honored ancestors, lived on the African continent of Earth Prime.'

'In Egypt?'

'Farther south,' he corrected. 'Before there were nations. At the edge of humanity's existence, when tools were first emerging.'

Oxham nodded. This skull was old indeed. What a long, strange journey it had taken, to wind up here in this dead man's hand.

'They lived in darkness, without language or fire. No agriculture, of course. Her people had no rudiments of civilization. They had no writing or spoken language.'

'What did they eat, Sire?'

'Wild plants, from the ground. Distasteful.'

'I've eaten wild plants, Sire.'

'Vasthold has a primeval charm.'

'It did when I left it.'

The sovereign turned the skull to face her. 'She and her people lived in lava funnel caves, massive and deep, extensive enough to support their own food web. Our ancestors had a stable and protected niche. We would be there still if they hadn't been driven outward into the sun.'

Oxham's eyes narrowed as she looked at the holes again.

'The teeth of a predator, Your Majesty?'

'*Dinofelis*. Extinct long before the diaspora.'

The senator took a deep breath, realizing that the Emperor had returned to his favorite theme.

'I take it, Sire, that this animal is one of the great cats?' Until a few years ago, Oxham had always assumed the creatures legendary, created by the Apparatus at an Imperial whim. But the Imperial Zoo here on Home held a small, inbred family of lions that were generally believed to be natural. Awful beasts from a childhood nightmare, four times the size of any predator on 'primeval' Vasthold.

The Emperor nodded happily. 'A creature more than two meters long, when humans stood under a meter and a half. It possessed so-called false-saber teeth. Knives in its mouth.'

The Emperor of the Eighty Worlds made a claw of four fingers with his right hand, and plunged them into the holes. Oxham removed her hand from the purring creature on her lap.

'The great cats lived deeper in the caves than our ancestors, in the absolute darkness beyond the humans' twilight domain.'

'They attacked from behind, apparently, Sire.'

He nodded, lifting the skull with his rapacious fingers, so that its empty eyes stared at her again.

'They grasped the heads of their victims with their jaws, penetrating the brain and killing instantly. Then they dragged the body back into the darkness.'

'And this danger drove us out of the caves, Your Majesty?'

'Exactly,' he agreed with flashing eyes. 'But don't think of these cats simply as some evolutionary pressure. This wasn't mere natural selection; this was terror. The saber-tooths were utterly silent, invisible in the darkness. It's possible that no human ever clearly saw one. They were original nightmare buried deep in our species' psyche. They were death itself. *This* is the mark of the Old Enemy.'

Oxham looked down at the cat on her lap. She offered it a finger, which it licked once with its raspy tongue. The beast made a small noise in its throat and continued to purr, absolutely content.

'I see your love of felines has a darker side, Sire.'

'Of course, Senator. Their contributions to humanity,

though always essential, haven't always been pretty. Imagine being a predated species, Nara. At any moment, a family member, a lover, a friend might be hauled away screaming to die.'

'Like being always at war,' she said.

'And always on the front lines. But from this enemy came the necessity to evolve. We were defenseless against this beast, until we developed group cooperation, tools, and finally, the only useful weapon: fire.'

'The terror is what brought humanity up?' Nara Oxham said, then realized it at last: 'perhaps you are pro-death too, Sire.'

'Perhaps. The council faces another difficult decision.'

She took a deep breath. Was the Emperor contemplating another genocide already? 'Sire, shouldn't this be raised before the entire War Council?'

The dead sovereign narrowed his eyes. 'Senator Oxham, the War Council is not a parliament of equals. I have enjoined twelve such councils over the last sixteen hundred years, and in each of them one counselor has arisen from among the others.'

Her eyes widened. Flattery from the Emperor? 'I am your servant, Sire.'

'Don't contest with me, Senator. You are nothing of the kind. You are the force that has risen up to balance my power. A natural occurrence in the evolution of this war.'

Oxham ordered herself to relax, trying to see into the man's mind. There was more in his words than flattery. She spoke carefully.

'I agree, Your Majesty, that the council has achieved a balance now.'

He nodded. 'That is its purpose, to be a microcosm of the Risen Empire. It must possess two parts, equal parts. But there are times when we must act together, you and I.'

She realized that the Emperor had taken the first person singular. He had dropped the imperial *we* for plainer speech.

The garden darkened, and the *Lynx*'s war prize appeared in synesthesia.

'Our elevated hero Laurent Zai has concerns about this Rix artifact,' the sovereign said. 'He believes it contains some sort of ghost of the Legis compound mind.'

'A ghost, Sire?'

'A doppelgänger. A copy, transmitted from Legis. Captain Zai has been rather convincing on this point. If he's right, the object is even more dangerous than the mind that occupied Legis. It contains all our secrets. And now it has a body as well.'

'Lucky, then, that the good captain has captured it.'

'We hope so. But the powers of this thing are unknown. It can change itself, Senator, at the lowest level of matter. Zai's journey to Home will take almost two subjective years, ten Absolute. We don't know what tests the *Lynx* may face over that length of time.'

Senator Oxham frowned. The official reports that the council had received about the object had couched their conclusions in very speculative language. Oxham wished that she could retain outside scientific counsel, but the reports were wrapped in the hundred-year rule. She couldn't even access them outside the council chamber.

'In fact,' the Emperor continued, 'it may be that the *Lynx* cannot control the object.'

'Control it, Sire?'

'The Apparatus representatives on board the *Lynx* believe that the object may be exerting an . . . influence. The thing is trying to subvert Zai's crew. There is grave danger.'

What was the Emperor saying? Her empathy flared, and Oxham saw a bright shape in the Emperor's mind, a point coming to focus: the culmination of a plan.

'Sire, aren't there escort craft heading to rendezvous with Zai now?' she asked. Two smaller vessels had set out for Legis when the incursion began; they were now altering their paths, angling in behind the *Lynx* as it headed back toward Home.

The sovereign nodded. 'Exactly. They will keep a greater distance from the object than the *Lynx*. And they will be under Imperial writ, outside of the usual chain of command.'

She saw it in his mind: the cold point of closure. Victory. Revenge.

'What are their orders, Sire?'

'They are fabricating several high-yield nuclear drones. If the need comes, they will destroy the object and the *Lynx* in a surprise attack.'

Nara Oxham felt blindness creep into the edges of her vision. Felt her own emotions rise: anger and desperation. She knew finally that the sovereign wouldn't rest until Laurent Zai was dead.

'Sire . . .'

'Only if the need becomes immediate, Senator. I will make the final decision. I alone will take responsibility.'

The first person singular again.

'Shouldn't the council discuss—'

'My oath is to protect the Eighty Worlds, Senator. Captain Zai's warning is clear in this matter: 'this object represents a great threat to the Empire, even to humanity itself.''

She swallowed. The dead man was hanging Laurent with his own words. He would use them later to justify his decision. Now that he had warned her, the Emperor could even claim that he had consulted with his counselors before emergency action. Although he couldn't depopulate a world without the political cover of a War Council vote, the sovereign could certainly order a single frigate destroyed.

The people would remember that the Emperor had pardoned Zai. Making him a martyr would maintain a certain symmetry.

'I know you will keep this information confidential, Senator. The hundred-year rule still applies, of course, to this conversation.'

'Of course, Your Majesty.'

The cat leapt from her lap and crossed to rub itself against the Emperor's legs. Nara Oxham rose, her mind numbed by the depth of the sovereign's hunger for revenge against Laurent. She forced herself to look again into the arid space of his emotions, searching for what he feared so much.

But there was nothing there but satisfaction.

After the rituals of parting, as she walked through the obscenely gilded garden, Nara's mind rang with one imperative. She had to warn Laurent. The *Lynx* could handle two escort craft, provided her captain was wary. But if he assumed they were friendly, they could overwhelm the frigate with a single stroke.

Then, as her eyes traced a swath of red flowers decorating an inverted sand dune, Oxham saw it, the shape hidden in the Emperor's satisfaction. It grew clearer with every step away from his icy presence.

This was the trap. This was the mistake of which Niles had warned her. It had nothing to do with Laurent Zai.

The Emperor wanted *her*, Nara Oxham. He had somehow learned of their relationship, their previous communication. He knew that she would warn Zai.

And, of course, he was right.

There was no choice but to walk into this trap, eyes open.

It was the only way to save her lover.

Captain

Laurent Zai stood at the extreme of the observation blister.

He looked up at the object, its shape ominously black this far from the Legis sun. It boiled like a dark cloud presaging a storm. According to the DA staff assigned to monitor its movements, it had grown gradually more active over the last few weeks. Its attempts to signal the *Lynx* had grown in number and subtlety: there were signs scrawled huge upon its surface, old codes flashed at obscure frequencies, cryptic phrases in local Legis dialects that somehow made their way into the ship's internal channels. It was all the *Lynx*'s AI could do to forestall the mind's attempts at communication. Finally, Zai had been forced to cut off all but the crudest level of sensor scrutiny of the object.

The *Lynx* had shut its ears. The Apparatus had demanded it.

Ever since the Rix prisoner had attempted to deliver Alexander's 'message,' His Majesty's Representatives had behaved as if they were victorious boarders on a captured enemy ship. Their watchful gaze seemed to penetrate every deck of the *Lynx*. It was all ExO Hobbes could do to track the various bugs that the Apparatus had placed in the ship's functions. This invasion of his ship appalled Zai, but he was powerless against the imperative of an Imperial writ, the scope of which seemed to expand daily.

Adept Trevim had sealed up the Rix prisoner's cell as tight as a tomb, and posted an Apparatus guard with her at all times. The Adept had also taken personal control over the *Lynx*'s external communications. Every outgoing message required her approval now. And, of course, Trevim had commanded that the frigate blind itself from any and all signs emanating from the object.

Of course, there were rumors. Some crew thought they knew what the Rix artifact was trying to say. But the stories were contradictory and absurd, just the chatter of a bored crew. ExO Hobbes had even detected a rumor that the suicide of Data Master Kax a few weeks ago had been related to a message from the object that he had deciphered. But the theory conveniently ignored the fact the man's immune system had rejected his artificial eyes; a lifelong data analyst, he had simply gone mad from blindness.

Zai touched the plastic membrane between himself and the void, feeling the cold on the other side. He wondered what weapon the object had offered him.

Then he pushed the disloyal thoughts aside, and turned to his more important business here.

A senatorial missive awaited his attention. From Nara Oxham, His Majesty's Representative from Vasthold. August and luminous, the message hovered against the blackness of space, its security icons slowly coiling around themselves like tree snakes crowding a branch.

He opened it.

Zai smiled as his lover's words appeared. He imagined her voice.

Laurent, it read, *I wish I could start tenderly. But instead I have to warn you of danger.*

Zai blinked his eyes, and shook his head at this beginning. All his life, he had been taught that warcraft brought meaning and order to existence, but this conflict with the Rix despoiled everything it touched.

He continued.

The ships sent to rendezvous with the Lynx *are governed by two sets of orders. The open dictate is to escort you here to Home in safety, but there is also an Imperial writ carried by a few officers. It can be triggered by a single word from the Emperor. If he gives the command, the task force is to destroy your ship and the war prize in a surprise attack.*

Laurent Zai straightened. It was just as the Rixwoman had said: the Emperor wanted to destroy him, the *Lynx*, and the object. The dead man's hunger for revenge was insatiable. What was he hiding?

Zai's anger quickly turned to concern, however. This was confidential intelligence data from outside the chain of command, from the War Council itself.

'What have you done, Nara?' he whispered, his heart sinking.

Supposedly, the Emperor will only invoke the writ if the object threatens the Empire. But I have felt . . . I know that he intends to kill you all. I've been close to the Emperor since joining the council, and I can read him now.

Of course, Nara had used her empathy on the man. As Zai continued, the realization dawned that Nara's ability had doomed her. She had broken the hundred-year rule.

He's terribly afraid of something, Laurent. Something that the Rix mind knows. Something that it discovered on Legis.

The words of his lover echoing those of the Rixwoman sent a chill through Zai.

He'll go to any length to prevent this knowledge from reaching the rest of the Empire, Laurent. I've seen it myself. He even pressed the War Council to approve a genocide. The Apparatus was ready to release a nuclear attack on Legis XV, with dirty weapons. They would have killed hundreds of millions just to destroy the compound mind.

Zai closed his eyes. If Nara was right, then the Rixwoman had told the truth.

He'll kill you, Laurent. The Emperor so fears the mind, he would destroy a world.

Laurent Zai nodded slowly, straightening as if a weight were lifting from him.

Take care, beloved. Return to me.

Captain Zai nodded again as the missive refolded itself, disappearing to a bright mote of synesthesia against the void. Suddenly, a wave of nausea struck him, and he had to reach out one hand to the blister's wall to hold himself upright. The plastic felt reassuringly solid and cold. Real.

Still, it was painful. The last shreds of Vadan loyalty were passing from him.

The Emperor had designs to destroy one of the Eighty Worlds.

Zai remembered the catechisms of his childhood. The old relationship between the Emperor and Vada had been formed after the Vadan Founders had fled their ruined previous home. *No killing of worlds*, the Compact read. And now the sovereign had broken it.

Through his nausea, Zai saw an icon blinking in the lower corner of Nara's folded message. One of Hobbes's telltales, indicating that this message had gone through the adept's hands.

'Damn,' he whispered.

He'd assumed that the document was secure. It carried senatorial privilege, with the full protection of the Pale, but the adept's writ had somehow opened it.

Nara Oxham would be found out now. The Emperor would know that she had warned him. The final wave of nausea lasted only a few seconds, then Zai felt ready.

He took the slow, measured breaths of a Vadan warrior. He turned from the blackness of space and strode from the blister, glad to hear the ring of his boots on hard metal.

He was smiling.

Strange, that such danger should lighten his soul. But he felt sure and powerful for the first time in months: all his own shortcomings were buried now, overwhelmed by the crimes of his enemy: the Risen Emperor.

'Hobbes,' he signaled.

'Captain?' She sounded half asleep.

'Meet me at Rana Harter's cabin.'

'Sir?'

'In five minutes. Bring your weapon.'

Executive Officer

Katherie Hobbes fastened the seals of her tunic as she ran.

She stopped around the corner from her goal, and checked the time. She had fifty seconds left. Her eyes scanned the black wool of her uniform, checking for imperfections. She pulled up one sleeve to reveal the flechette pistol. Its ammo meter read full, but Hobbes popped the cover to check the needles with her own eyes.

The darts were nestled in their twin magazines, as perfectly aligned as two ranks of tiny metal soldiers.

She walked briskly and calmly around the corner. Zai awaited her with a grim expression.

'Captain, what is it?'

'We've been betrayed, Hobbes.'

Mutiny again? She took a deep breath against panic, drew her pistol.

'Not by our crew, Hobbes,' her captain said.

She blinked. What was he saying?

'Just hand me that.' He pointed at the pistol.

What? she thought. The captain could draw his own weapon from stores. But of course that would raise any number of flags with the politicals aboard the ship.

Hobbes handed him the weapon silently.

The captain held the flechette pistol behind his back and opened the door to the dead woman's cabin. Light spilled between Hobbes and Zai into Rana Harter's dim antechamber. The dead Adept Trevim herself was here, kneeling with her back to them, her hands working gestural commands.

'Forgive me, Honored Mother,' Zai said.

He shot Trevim with a spray of needles, cutting an X across her heart.

Hobbes gasped, her knees week. This must lie a dream, she thought.

'Her symbiant should rise from that,' Zai said.

He turned to Hobbes.

'What was she doing?' he demanded.

Hobbes forced herself to concentrate, probing the *Lynx*'s diagnostics. The adept's actions were officially hidden from Navy AI, but there were always indirect signs. The translight grid was cycling out of a transmission.

'It looks as if she sent a message, sir.'

'Did I interrupt her?'

Hobbes shook her head. 'It's stepping down in an orderly way, Captain. She was finished, and the main entanglement grid shows depletion.'

'Home,' he said.

She nodded.

'Damn. Shut it down, Hobbes. The whole grid – cut its power.'

She swallowed, and signaled the com staff to perform the task. This was one trump card the captain held. The Apparatus might have a writ of authority, but the crew of the *Lynx* could still disable the frigate's components by hand.

The captain opened the inner door of the antechamber, holding the pistol ready.

'Rana Harter,' he called.

Was Zai going to murder the woman? Hobbes wondered. The Adept would reanimate easily from her heart wound, but a shot like that to the head could destroy a risen permanently.

The dead woman stepped from the darkness, blinking in the light. She was small, her hair shorn like the Rixwoman's. Though she was shorter than the commando, Hobbes could see how their faces were alike. The Legis authorities believed that Rana had been chosen from the militia's population for her resemblance to Herd, and perhaps for a savant ability to process chaotic data. Hobbes wondered to what uses the compound mind had put Rana's intellect, and what traces captivity had left in the dead woman before her.

'Please come with me, Honored One,' Zai said.

Harter nodded quiescently. She had none of the usual hauteur of the dead. Laurent Zai went ahead, with Rana after him. Hobbes brought up the rear, reminding herself that this was real.

They reached the Rixwoman's cell in a few minutes. The gunfire and Adept Trevim's medical monitors had triggered various alarms aboard the ship, but Hobbes had managed to suppress them as far as she knew.

There was a single marine guard, not the familiar Bassiritz, and one of the lower-ranking politicals on station. The man was living, and Captain Zai shot him in the leg, and kicked him in the head as he fell. The aspirant dropped to the floor unconscious.

Zai sternly ordered the startled guard to return to attention.

The private froze in shock for a moment, then obeyed as crisply as if at parade drill. Zai's tone of command was stronger than Hobbes had heard it in some time. The sound thrilled her, however bizarre these proceedings.

Her fingers flickered, moving to quell the new alarms. The remaining politicals must already know that something was happening.

'Shall I get a fire team up here, Captain?'

'Good idea, Hobbes. That fast private, for one.'

She nodded, sent commands.

'Secure this area, Private,' she ordered the motionless marine.

Hobbes opened the cell, turning the screwlock and bracing one leg to pull out the massive door.

Zai moved to enter first.

'The shock collar remote, sir,' she called.

'We won't need it.'

Hobbes followed him closely, wishing that she had another weapon. Straitjacket or no, the Rix commando could probably kill them both easily. She doubted that a half-expended clip of flechettes would even marginally slow down a Rix soldier.

The prisoner stared at them coolly, a hungry look in her eyes. Hobbes felt naked under her hunter's gaze.

But then Rana Harter followed them through the door, and for a moment Herd seemed utterly human.

'Rana!' she said, stepping forward.

The dead woman walked toward her former captor and lover. The Rixwoman was in for a disappointment, Hobbes thought. The honored dead never held fast to the emotional bonds of their former lives. The transition of the symbiant left them altogether indifferent to the prattle of the living. Hobbes had encountered many of her dead shipmates after their reanimation; they were no longer friends, or even crewmates. Just passengers.

But Rana Harter looked tenderly at the Rixwoman, and smiled.

The expression startled Hobbes; it looked exaggerated on that cold, gray face, like a clown's painted joy. The dead woman embraced Herd, wrapping her arms around the hypercarbon straitjacket, and the two kissed as unselfconsciously as adolescents on a Utopian world. The captain and Hobbes just watched, too surprised and respectful of the dead to interrupt.

Finally they separated, pulling apart to gaze into each other's eyes.

'Rana,' murmured Herd quietly.

The dead woman spoke in return. Hobbes recognized the buzzing syllables of Rix battle language in her speech.

'Preserve us,' she murmured. A risen woman, one of the honored dead of the Empire, speaking Rix. What had Rana Harter become?

'Herd,' Captain Zai said in a level voice. 'I've come for information.'

The commando kissed Rana Harter once more before answering, and whispered at the edge of Hobbes's hearing, 'Your lips are as cold as mine now.'

Katherie swallowed, wondering again if this was a dream.

Herd turned from her lover and looked at Captain Zai.

'So you want to hear the Emperor's Secret now?'

He nodded, then said, 'I will hear it,' with the measured formality of an oath in military court.

Herd cocked her head, as if listening to some internal voice. Then she smiled, a predatory expression that chilled Hobbes's soul.

'It will not make you happy, Vadan.'

Zai met her gaze without flinching. He reached back and pulled the door shut behind them. With the heavy metal in place, even the inescapable hum of the ship was silenced.

They were absolutely cut off from the rest of the *Lynx* now.

'Tell us,' Zai said.

The Rixwoman took a breath, then she began.

'Your Empress was killed not by us, but by the Apparatus.'

'Of course,' whispered Hobbes to herself. The records of the battle had suggested as much. The Emperor was a murderer.

'But that fact is not the secret that concerns you, Zai,' Herd added. 'Alexander was inside the Empress before she died, through the agency of a machine that was within her body.'

'The confidant,' Captain Zai said.

'Exactly. Alexander took control of this machine, like every other on Legis, and could see inside the Empress. Alexander saw something.'

As the commando went on, her flat voice became almost singsong, as if she were telling a children's tale. She leaned her head against Rana Harter's shoulder, and the dead woman stroked Herd's bound arms.

The story took fifteen slow minutes.

Hobbes had known that her bond to the gray world was broken – by the false Error of Blood, by the *Lynx's* travails, and now finally by Zai's inescapable treasons – but the Rixwoman's words were something altogether different. They left her captain retching on the floor, unraveled centuries of the history she had been taught, and tore Hobbes's last convictions from her like a swallowed hook dragged from a fish's gut.

And after that, everything was different.

Senator

Awaiting the closure of the Emperor's trap, Nara Oxham was very careful.

She knew instinctively that it was only a matter of time before the Apparatus uncovered her communication with Zai. Perhaps they already had, and were merely waiting for an opportune moment to move against her. After a few nervous nights at home, she decided to sleep in her office, remaining within the safety of the Rubicon Pale. As a rule, a senator could not disappear suddenly without explanation, but a case of wartime treason might convince the Apparatus that it could make an exception.

When the trap closed, it did so quickly.

The news swept through the capital's infostructure quickly, a fire rampant in pure oxygen. It started as a newsfeed rumor, well traveled but patently incredible. Then supporting evidence was released: images of Oxham and Zai meeting at the Emperor's party ten years ago; the repeater path of her first message to him; a time line of the War Council's agenda, the debates for which the hundred-year rule had been invoked covered with a broad swath of black. And finally her voice, dictating the first few words of her warning to Zai – this last synthesized for dramatic effect.

Across the wee hours of morning, the treason of Senator Nara Oxham moved from the back pages of gossips and conspiracy theorists to blaring headlines crawling the periphery of every channel of second sight.

The newsfeeds were forbidden even to speculate about what secrets the Senator had revealed to her warrior lover, but the hundred-year rule itself bore the weight of proof: this young and headstrong senator had betrayed the Emperor's trust.

The morning that the story broke, the psychic frenzy itself awoke her, the growing fury of the city bleeding into her head like a wake-up alarm invading a sleeper's dreams. For a moment of unprotected madness, Nara could see the bloated body of the capital convulsing, the beached whale shaking off carrion birds with some grotesque, after-death spasm. And before wheeling back to feast on the war economy, the scavengers swirled toward a new target.

The treasonous senator: live prey.

The empathic vision waned in power. Senator Oxham could feel her own body, and a hand at her wrist: someone adjusting her apathy bracelet. She opened her eyes, furious at this presumption. It was a grim-faced Roger Niles kneeling next to her.

She blinked once.

The dose was strong, and Oxham's mind became coherent in seconds. She instantly understood what had happened; she'd been expecting it. This was the trap the Emperor had set. She had walked into it full knowing.

'What have you done, Nara?' Niles asked.

Oxham put both hands to her face, rubbing it to confirm the reality of her body. She pulled herself up into a seated position. Her back ached in the particular way that always resulted from sleeping on her office couch.

'I can't tell you much about it, Roger. The hundred-year rule.'

He scowled. '*Now* you want to obey the law?'

'I had to tell Laurent what the Emperor planned. I knew they'd catch me, but I had to save him. That's all I can say.'

'They're calling for your blood, Nara.'

'I know, Roger. I can hear them.'

She gestured to bring up second sight. Synesthesia confirmed what Roger Niles and empathy had told her. The story choked every newsfeed. She flipped across a few channels: her voice and picture, the text of a useless Apparatus warrant for her arrest, a Loyalist spokesperson demanding her expulsion from the Senate.

Expulsion was the crux of the matter, she realized. Stripped of senatorial privilege, Nara Oxham would be just another citizen. Just another traitor with no Pale to protect her.

'I warned you, Nara. Why didn't you listen?'

'Can they throw me out, Roger?'

'Of the Senate? There's precedent, but it hasn't been done for a hundred and fifty years.'

'What was the reason back then?'

Niles blinked, his fingers twitching. 'Murder. A Utopian killed her lover. Strangled him in bed.'

Oxham smiled wanly. She, at least, had broken the law to save a lover, not kill one.

'That's far more dramatic,' she said.

'But it wasn't even a crime against the state,' Niles said. '"Conduct unbecoming" was the phrase employed in the writ of expulsion. A lesser charge than treason, I dare say.'

'How long did it take?' she asked.

'Forty-seven days. They held a trial before the full Senate. Witnesses, defense counsel, even a psychologist.'

'And then they expelled her.'

Niles nodded. 'And with her privilege gone, a civilian court found her guilty of murder in a second trial. Loss of elevation, life internment.'

'Better than exsanguination.'

'God, Nara,' Niles said, his voice breaking. 'Did you actually do it? Reveal War Council secrets to Zai?'

'I did. To save him.'

'There must be an exception for military exigency.'

She shook her head. 'There's no way out of it, Roger. It was pure treason: my lover over my sovereign. I made a choice.'

Niles was silent for a moment, going into a data fugue. He stood over her, hands flexing as he tried to discover some exception to the hundred-year rule, his entire body flinching with the effort. He looked like a handeye gamer trying to escape some virtual maze, his face showing frustration at every roadblock and dead end.

Nara drifted back into second-sight newsfeeds. One showed a crowd gathered at the edge of the Pale, a Loyalist mob demanding that Oxham abdicate her privilege immediately and face a Court Imperial. Now that she was its target, the Loyalists' wonted righteous anger seemed less comical. On another feed was the Secularist Party whip, a young man who had replaced her after she'd been promoted to the War Council. He was calling for calm, stalling, trying to slow down the pace of events without appearing to support rank treason. She didn't envy him the job.

In the midst of this maelstrom, Nara felt oddly peaceful. The usual players of political drama – the political parties, the Apparatus's propaganda machine, the newsfeed hacks – had jumped into motion in the usual way, jostling for advantage, working damage control. She could feel the shifting ground in this contest for power, the tug of every carefully chosen word, every deliberately sculpted reading of Imperial law and Senate tradition. But at the center of this chaos was one immovable point: the rightness of her own choice.

Nara Oxham felt purified by treason. After all her compromises, she had finally done something for a simple, unalloyed reason, no matter what the cost.

'I'm free, Roger.'

His eyes snapped open. 'What?'

'We can't fight the Emperor with pragmatism forever.'

Niles shook his head hard; a few gray hairs jutted out as a result. His features seemed to be aging by the minute.

'This was not the time, Nara. There's a *war* on.'

She understood his point. The Emperor was always at the peak of his power when defending the realm. But the argument cut both ways; at its peak was when power was most often abused.

'I'm going to tell the whole Risen Empire what I told Zai,' she said. 'The Emperor's plans for Legis.'

Niles looked down at her in despair.

'They'll kill you,' he whispered.

'Let them.'

'Use whatever you know as leverage to bargain your way out.'

She shook her head. There would be no escape for her, the Emperor would make sure of that.

'Nara, they'll drain your blood out, drop by drop.'

'Not before I turn a generation against him.'

Niles swallowed. He was still looking, she knew, for a way out of this. Senator Oxham suddenly saw her old counselor's greatest limitation. However pure his hatred for the dead, Niles had always fought them cautiously, slowly laying his plans against them. He had no taste for drama.

'How old are you, Roger?'

'Damn old,' he said. 'Old enough to know how to stay alive.'

'That's your problem. War requires sacrifice, sometimes.'

'You're talking about suicide, Nara.'

She nodded. 'That's correct, Roger. A just and well-considered suicide.'

Her counselor sat down next to her, deflated. She was shocked to see tears on his face.

'I spent three decades bringing you here, Senator,' he said, and sobbed once.

'I know.'

'And this is how you repay me?'

After a moment's silence, she knew the answer. 'Yes. Absolutely.'

They were quiet for a while. Oxham shut off her second sight, quenching the flow of opinion and grandstanding, the headlong rush to committees, hearings, and judgment, all the unwieldy maneuvers of a legislature turning on one of its own. The rising sun lanced into the crystals that had been carefully moved here from Niles's old office. Like a tree of tiny mirrors, they dappled the walls with a glimmering pattern.

Nara Oxham listened to Niles's labored breathing, and wished she could spare him this. She still needed his counsel. She hoped he wouldn't give up on her.

As if hearing her thoughts, the old man spread his hands and said, 'What do you want me to do, Senator?'

She took hold of his arm.

'Delay them for a while. Then agree to a trial. No witnesses to testify for me except myself. With the broadest possible public newsfeed.'

He frowned, concentration replacing despair on his face.

'They'll try to silence you, Senator. Secrets of the Realm.'

'They can't sequester the whole Senate, Roger. And no lesser body can vote to expel me.'

His eyes narrowed. Now that his mind had something to chew on, a sparkle grew in them.

'I suppose not, Senator.'

'And I have the right to speak at my own trial.'

He nodded. 'Of course. Even the hundred-year rule doesn't stand against privilege. They can't truly silence you until *after* the Senate has expelled you officially.'

'Now that I've chosen death, my options multiply,' she said.

Nara considered her own words. She could appear at the edge of the Pale right now and address the hovering cameras of the newsfeeds, telling them what the Emperor had planned to do on Legis. But the newsfeeds would be bound by the hundred-year rule. Her only shot at revealing the sovereign's plan would be before the Senate.

'I'll wait for the trial to say my piece, when the whole Empire is watching.'

'The Apparatus will bury your words.'

Nara looked at Niles, and nodded. 'Then we'll have to devise a backup plan. A way to publicize the speech if I'm silenced. Something a bit illegal, like we used to spread rumors back on Vasthold.'

'It won't be so easy here on Home. The networks are all Apparatus controlled.'

She thought for a moment. 'I think I know a way to get around the Apparatus. Something I've been saving for a rainy day.'

Niles looked puzzled, then a forced smile broke through

the heavy cast of his features. 'Well, at least I've drummed some little bit of pragmatism into you, Senator.'

'Tactics, Niles,' she corrected. 'Let them hear me, and the Emperor will wish he'd died the true death a thousand years ago.'

Adept

'I need to send a message,' Zai repeated.

Adept Harper Trevim looked at him, trying to pull her mind into the frantic, empty time of the living. It was so much easier to stare at the walls. Even the flat gray of hypercarbon, so bland compared to sensuous black, was rich and compelling here in the fugue of ongoing re-animation.

Trevim's symbiant still labored to bring her back to full animation. Her new heart was not yet whole; the supple cells of the Other were doing much of the work, filling in for the tricuspid and mitral valves. Zai's attack had not damaged her brain, but her lungs and spine had been torn mercilessly by his flechettes.

The adept was barely alive. When she closed her eyes, the darkness behind them was lit by the red horizon, that first sight of the risen.

Trevim forced herself to look at the man, and through the haze of her fugue she managed to scowl at Zai.

'Leave me alone, Captain. You shoot my heart out, and then expect me to commit treason to repay you?'

'The only treason here is the Emperor's,' Zai said.

The words caused a start from Trevim, bringing the living world into sudden focus.

'Blasphemy,' she spat. 'You'll suffer for this, Zai. The tortures you felt on Dhantu will be nothing compared to the Emperor's revenge.'

'Adept, I need to send a message. Only you can authorize it.' Zai spoke as if to an unruly child, repeating his demand with the calm insistence of the rational adult.

'Your crew will join you in your agonies, Zai,' she said.

Anger crossed his face, and Trevim felt distant amusement. He dared to treat an adept of the Apparatus, who had lived four hundred subjective years, as a child? Even if Zai destroyed her, gave her final darkness, she was one of the honored dead. She would not be frightened or manipulated.

His crew. That was Zai's weakness. He had dragged them all into this mutiny with him.

'The Apparatus will pull them to pieces, Zai. One by one, before your eyes and their families'. Traitors all.'

The man took a deep breath, then cocked his head and smiled softly.

'I know the Emperor's Secret.'

A jolt passed through Trevim. Revulsion clenched every muscle in her body. She shook her head reflexively. Zai didn't know. He simply *couldn't*. The Secret was too tightly bound within the world of the Apparatus; an uninitiated man – and a *living* one – could never have discovered it.

'No,' the adept managed.

'The Rix prisoner explained it to me.'

The words sent another shock through Trevim, a violent seizure that threatened the functioning of her half-repaired heart. A wash of physical, biological pain, something she hadn't felt in decades, coursed down her left arm.

Trevim whimpered a little. The Other tried to calm her, but the Apparatus conditioning was an implacable force, a hurricane that raged inside her very cells. These reactions had been laid down like mineral strata over centuries of service to the crown, the ultimate stopgap to prevent a member of the Apparatus from revealing the Secret.

But now the pain was being used against her.

Trevim swallowed, and forced herself to believe her next words.

'You are bluffing, Zai. You know nothing.'

'The dead are dying, Adept Trevim.'

'*Silence!*' she shrieked, her vision disintegrating into a cloud of red. She felt a hideous movement inside. For a moment, the Other seemed to retreat from her, its tendrils shrinking from the violent reaction.

Adept Trevim understood vaguely the raw science behind the miracle of the symbiant. The Other's ability to heal and sustain required absolute acquiescence from the body. The calm remove of the honored dead was a means to keep the body and mind from rejecting the life-sustaining ministrations of the symbiant. The tranquillity of the immortals was not merely a spiritual benefit; it was a necessary state. But Trevim's Apparatus conditioning warred with her deathly calm, threatening the mesh of body and Other.

Zai's words could literally tear her in half.

'Silence,' she pleaded, gasping.

'Just relinquish the writ, Trevim. Release the writ that binds the communications grid.'

An action icon hovered before Trevim in second sight. All she had to do was make the sign, and Zai would have his access. He could send a message to Home.

An act of treason.

'No,' Trevim said.

'The dead are dying, Adept. Since the beginning.'

The pain screamed through her again. And worse than the physical agony was the feeling of the Other pulling away, shying from her body's convulsions. Her heart shuddered, almost failing in her chest.

'You're killing me, Zai.'

'Die, then,' the man said.

He went on, calmly detailing what the Rix had revealed to him.

Adept Trevim fought to control herself, to withstand the pain, to resist the pleas of the Other to return things to calm. Once, she saw her hand reach out, about to make the gestural sign that would give Zai what he wanted. But she managed to hold herself back. Then his words continued, and the wrenching punishment of the war inside her resumed.

Before her will could crumble, Trevim's half-rebuilt heart stuttered, striking once like a hammer blow in her chest before failing, and the Other abandoned her to oblivion.

For a moment, the adept thought she'd won. Her mind began to fade. But horribly, the victory of death calmed her, and the Other returned, working its relentless miracle to begin repairs again. Trevim knew even as consciousness slipped away that she would reanimate to face these tortures again and again. The symbiant was too powerful, too indomitable and perfect, and her centuries-long conditioning was equally immovable. As she died, Trevim realized that her will, caught between these two indomitable forces, would eventually be destroyed.

Sooner or later, she would relent to Zai.

Senator

Rarely had she seen the Senate so full.

Many planets, Vasthold among them, had only a single senator in the Forum. Winner-take-all, it was called. But the majority of the Eighty Worlds sent delegations, proportional representations of their constituencies. The voting strength of each world was weighted according to its taxed economic output, and senators from planets with many representatives subdivided their world's votes. The system had been carefully honed to achieve balance over the centuries, but it made for complex vote tabulation. It also led to a crowded Great Hall on those rare occasions when every senator was present.

They were all here now, to try Nara Oxham for treason.

The Great Forum was a huge, pyramidal hole cut into the granite foundation that underlay the capital. Plaster poured into the empty space would have cast a flat-topped pyramid with steps up its four sides. Each of the major parties claimed one of the triangular staircases, with their leadership clustered at the point down close to the center, and their rank and file arrayed across the wider rows farther up.

The President of the Senate was seated on the Low Dais, a circular riser of marble in the center of the Great Forum's pit. Senator Oxham had seen the old man, Puram Drexler of Fatawa, seated on the ceremonial dais only once before, when he had given her the oath of office. It was strange to think that in a few days, she might be stripped of that office and condemned to death after the votes were counted aloud by the same man.

The Great Forum was lit today with a sharp, unreal light that left no shadows against the gray granite floor. That was for the newseyes, which lined the high lip of the Forum. Senator Oxham allowed herself a moment of second sight, checking the viewership. On Home, the numbers were staggering: eighty percent of the populace was watching. Even in the antipodal cities, spread from midnight to the early morning hours, a majority were tuned in. Niles had told her that a low-grade translight feed was headed out live through the Imperial entanglement repeater network, and a high-grade recording of this trial would eventually reach every world in the Eighty. The Emperor had never turned Laurent Zai into the martyr he'd wanted, but at least now he had a villain for his war.

The Apparatus had done everything possible to inflate viewership of the Oxham trial. Evidently, they were not afraid of her words.

She would be allowed to speak in her own defense. Senate President Puram Drexler had insisted on the fullest possible interpretation of the tradition of senatorial privilege, turning back the arguments from his own party about the security of the Realm. But even privilege didn't stand up to the hundred-year rule, so a compromise had been forged. Puram held a cut-off switch, in case Oxham mentioned the Emperor's genocide. The shock collar around her throat reminded Nara to watch her words.

Drexler looked a bit pale, there on the Dais. The Apparatus must have briefed him about the nuclear attack the Emperor had proposed, so that Drexler would know when to censor her. Oxham was sure that he had taken deep umbrage at this breach of the Compact, but however much the Emperor's plans had shaken him, Drexler's politics were as gray as the stone of the Great Forum. He would silence her if she hinted at the forbidden subject. Oxham realized ruefully that the pink political parties hadn't contested Drexler's position in decades, considering the presidency to be nothing more than a figurehead. But now the man held her life in his hand.

Roger Niles had shaken his head when these terms had been explained in the second week of preparation for the trial.

'We're finished,' he'd said. 'If you can't tell them about Legis, it's pointless. Give up and beg for mercy.'

'Don't worry, Niles,' she had answered. 'I've got other

secrets to tell.' Her counselor had raised his eyebrows at this, but she dared not say more.

The Emperor didn't know about the latest transmission she had received from Laurent, hidden alongside a political report from one Adept Harper Trevim. A Rix prisoner had revealed what the compound mind had learned on Legis: the truth behind the hostage rescue, the symbiant, the Empire itself. The Emperor's Secret was hers.

It didn't matter that Nara Oxham couldn't speak of genocide. She had a better story now. The Apparatus had locked the wrong door.

Senator Drexler opened the trial. He wrapped his withered right hand around the staff of his office, and struck its metal tip against the floor. The sound was amplified, and echoes skittered around the hard stone of the Forum.

'Order,' he said. His voice rasped like gravel.

The Great Forum became silent.

'We are here in a matter of blood. A matter of treason.'

Nara had left a newsfeed translucent in her second sight, and her own face zoomed up to fill her vision, some distant camera searching for her reaction. She had the disembodied feel of seeing herself in a synesthesia mirror. She blinked the feed away, and reminded herself to stay in the real world. Even her prepared speech was memorized; she wanted no text prompts cluttering her primary sight.

Nara needed to watch the faces of the Senate, rather than worry about how this was playing in the feeds. If she couldn't win her fellow solons over, the impressions of the popular audience could hardly save her.

'Who is the accuser?' Drexler said.

A dead woman rose from the Loyalist benches. A prelate. The Senate had given her special permission to cross the Pale, the first representative of the Apparatus ever to do so.

'The Emperor Himself,' she said. 'With me as His agent.'

'And who is the accused?'

'His Majesty's Representative from Vasthold, Senator Nara Oxham.' The dead woman pointed as she said the words.

Nara's felt a surge of emotion in the room, and her fingers went to her apathy bracelet automatically. But she forced her hands to her side again. She had already precisely adjusted her empathy. The capital hovered over her, a volatile presence focused on every word spoken here, but its emotions were in check. After weeks of furious calls for immediate revenge, the solemn ritual of a trial had focused the mob into a respectful audience. The people of the capital had long been trained to revere tradition.

The Senate's guard-at-arms strode up to Senator Oxham now. The young man was the only person allowed to carry weapons in the Forum. This was another position Nara has always thought honorary, but which had become suddenly very real.

The man took her arm.

'This one?' the guard asked the prelate.

'Yes.'

The guard-at-arms released her, but stayed close, as if Nara might try to run.

'Who will speak in defense of the accused?' Drexler asked, his eyes sweeping the whole of the Senate, daring them to stand against the Emperor.

'I will speak for myself,' Nara said. Her own words seemed disembodied, a result of both amplification and the incredible situation. It was hard for Oxham to believe that she was speaking to hundreds of billions, and to history, and that her own life depended on her words.

'Then let this Honorable Senate begin to hear the accusation,' Drexler said, and sat on his chair of stone.

The dead prelate rose again, and walked to the fore of the Dais.

'President, Senators, citizens,' she began. 'The Emperor has been betrayed.'

The trial had begun.

The prelate went on, as sonorous and repetitive as prayer. The ritual phrases rolled over Nara, all the words of blood oaths and bloody payment for broken promises. The war against death, and of the Emperor's great gift of immortality, all made its suffocating way into the prelate's narrative. Every iota of childhood conditioning was triggered, until even Senator Nara Oxham found herself appalled at what she had done. How dare she break faith with the man who had bested the Old Enemy death?

She steeled herself. Let them play all their cards now. Let them invoke every ancient superstition. The Emperor would fall all the harder when his secret was revealed.

'This woman was called to give the Emperor counsel in time of war.'

Finally, the real charges.

'And having taken an oath of secrecy,' the prelate continued, 'she betrayed the Emperor's War Council. She broke the duly invoked hundred-year rule. Nara Oxham turned traitor.'

The proof came next. The Great Forum darkened, and the airscreen above the Low Dais came alive. Puram Drexler would have had to crane his ancient neck to see, so instead he stared out at the audience like an alert teacher whose class was watching a synesthesia lesson.

The Senate listened in solemn silence, although these facts and images had been broadcast throughout the Empire for the last two weeks. In the newsfeeds, of course, each piece of evidence had been reduced by repetition to a single signifier: an image of her and Zai at the party, a few words of warning in her voice, a long shot of the palace's east wing where the War Council met. But here in the Senate, the scale was stretched in the opposite direction. Time slowed to a crawl. Each mark the Oxham/Zai affair had left on the public record now consumed long minutes of explanation. Their first conversation was studied frame by frame like a crime caught fleetingly on a security camera; ten years of short missives were read aloud in the dead prelate's dolorous cadence; quietly made plans were revealed with dramatic flourishes, as if their love had been a conspiracy from the start.

The last few messages between Oxham and the *Lynx* were read out, having been stripped of privilege by an overwhelming Senate vote a few days ago. Her single-word message, *Don't*, was associated with Zai's refusal of the blade of error. It was all edited in the name of security, and slanted to make her the aggressor in the relationship. Nara was glad that they weren't going after Laurent. Over the last two weeks, the Apparatus had walked a fine line with the hero Zai. His propaganda image had been weakened, but not destroyed – he was now a once-strong Imperial warrior weakened by the influence of a scheming woman.

Thankfully, Laurent's final message to her was absent from the evidence. Zai's subterfuge had worked. They still didn't know that Nara Oxham had the Emperor's real secret in hand.

The litany went on, slipping into irrelevancies toward the end. Oxham's antiwar bill, the one withdrawn before she'd taken a seat on the council, was revealed. Her old votes in the Senate were isolated and given new significance; the accuser even found sinister components in acts that had passed the legislature unanimously.

And this was simply the opening statement. This slow crawl was the merest outline. The Emperor's accuser apparently planned to present an insuperable mountain of detail over the days ahead. The two hundred minutes of the accusation, half the first day of trial, seemed like years.

Finally, Nara Oxham was called to make her own opening statement.

The Senate President held up his cut-off switch and warned her before she began.

'The secrets of the Realm are sacred, Senator Oxham. Do not attempt to reveal them here in the Great Forum.'

'I won't, President Drexler.' Of course, the old solon had only been briefed about the Emperor's planned genocide, the issue covered by the hundred-year rule. If Laurent was right, the real secret, the one His Majesty had been willing to murder those millions to protect, was unknown to any person, living or dead, outside the conditioned drones of the Apparatus.

According to the Rix mind's story, even the Apparatus could not speak of that secret. It brought them pain to hear it mentioned.

She hoped that part of the tale was true.

Nara finally understood why the Empire was built on fear and bribes, on intimidation and loyalty conditioning, on the superstitious babble of some pretechnology mystery cult.

It was all because the Empire was built on a lie.

She turned to the Senate, prepared to undo it all.

For a moment Nara couldn't speak. The weight of the Empire's attention was too suffocating. She feared for a moment that she herself might be conditioned, bound from uttering the words by some deeply buried imperative. But she breathed deeply, lightly touched her bracelet for luck, and let the fear pass. Her anxiety was simply anticipation of how this speech would feel empathetically; she was about to take a wild and dangerous ride on the nervous animal that was the Empire.

'President, Senate, citizens,' she said. 'The dead are dying.'

A small cry escaped from the prelate's lips, but there was no other sound in the Great Forum. Drexler hadn't cut her off, she noted with a final touch of relief. Laurent was right: even the oldest Loyalists didn't know.

'We were made a promise,' she continued. 'We were told that the Old Enemy had been defeated, that in service to the Emperor we could live forever. But the dead are dying. All of them.'

A murmur came from the audience, and Nara felt a *snap* in her empathy, a sudden disconnect. The rapt attention of the capital city above her had tumbled into confusion.

So soon? she wondered.

A quick check in second sight confirmed that the newsfeeds had gone dark. The Apparatus had cut her off already.

Plagueman

'Are you well?'

The representative of the Plague Axis looked down at his valet/minder. The young initiate had suddenly fallen to the floor, clutching her stomach, a retching noise coming through the speaker of her protective suit. The plagueman knelt and reflexively checked the suit diagnostics across the bottom of her visor.

They read green. He hadn't infected the young dead woman with anything. And certainly the symbiant would have protected her from any disease for days at least. 'Can I—'

'Turn it off!' The initiate flailed at the hardscreen upon which they had been watching the trial.

The request puzzled the plagueman, but he turned to mute the wall-sized image of Nara Oxham. Before he could gesture, however, the embattled senator's face was replaced by a slowly spinning shield, the emblem of the Apparatus media censors. The feed from the Great Forum had been silenced at the source.

The initiate's retching noises stopped. She put her hands to her head and groaned the same words several times. 'She knows.'

The plagueman wished that he could see the initiate's face through her biosuit visor. Here in his own sealed quarters, he wore his usual clothes, and visitors donned anti-contamination suits. The reflective visor over the suffering aspirant's face brought home to him again how dehumanized he must appear when he wore his own suit, how anonymous he was here in the monoculture.

He didn't need to see the woman's face, however, to know she wasn't well, not well at all. That she was one of the risen made her seizure even more alarming.

In synesthesia, he called for the other initiate who shared her minder's duties. There was no response, not even the polite regrets of a busy or sleeping recipient. Just repeated queries that went unheeded. He made calls to the other palace staff he had dealt with, but none of the Apparatus was answering.

Had they *all* been stricken? The plagueman knew that disease could spread with incredible rapidity here in the monoculture, one of the many weaknesses of these half-people, but such suddenness and simultaneity seemed more like a biological attack than a contagion.

He blinked and looked at the media censor emblem still on the screen. The image had cut off so suddenly, very unlike the Apparatus's usual interventions. He had seen them fade out a newsfeed's audio when necessary, breaking in to interrupt a live interview with a spurious weather emergency or war bulletin. But the Apparatus rarely silenced its opponents so crudely as this. The synesthesia newsfeeds were still down, all of them, and even the gossip channels were blank.

What had Oxham been saying before the initiate had collapsed?

'The dead are dying,' the plagueman repeated softly.

'Don't!' the young dead woman pleaded, sinking back to the floor. 'I can't stand it.'

The plagueman rose. 'I think you need help,' he said. The plagueman quickly put on his biosuit, taking particular care with its fittings in case this *was* an attack, and gestured for the room to open. The triple-doored airlock began its familiar sequence of hissing noises.

Out in the halls of the Diamond Palace, he immediately encountered another stricken member of the Apparatus, an initiate rising slowly to his feet. The optics in the biosuit visor revealed that his skin was far colder than even a dead man's should be.

'Do you know what's happening?' the plagueman asked.

'She has the Secret,' the man said hoarsely, reaching out a shaking hand. 'She's telling.'

A squadron of the House Guard ran past, live soldiers in full battle armor. They looked unaffected by the strange contagion, and ignored both initiate and Axis representative. Apparently, it wasn't a biological agent, or perhaps the living were immune.

The Axis representative turned to the initiate again, but a chime sounded in his secondary hearing. Perhaps synesthesia was clearing up, he thought with relief. But then he recognized the tone.

The War Council had been summoned.

The plagueman made toward the council chamber, amazed as he shuffled his slow way at the pandemonium that reigned in the usually solemn Diamond Palace. Normal staff seemed physically healthy though panicked, the Apparatus were uniformly paralyzed, and still more soldiers passed in full battle dress. He wondered if the capital had been attacked in some new and strange way, and if there were more assaults yet to come.

House

In the southern reaches, the house of Senator Nara Oxham became alert.

It had been pleasurable for the house to watch its mistress on the news these last few weeks. She was here at home so little since the war had started. But now her image had been cut off during her speech, quite suddenly, and without explanation.

Fortunately, the mistress had left strict instructions about what to do in this situation. She had even invoked privilege: the house was to use maximum initiative, ignoring regulations, sparing no expense to carry out these orders. The house had been a trifle amused at the mistress's urgent tone. It had been employing its own initiative for decades now.

First, the house located the special file in its copious memory. It was a tiny thing, only a few thousand bytes of data, stored with the marvelous efficiency of pure text. The house copied this file across its memory, filling every spare nook and cranny with duplicate after duplicate. Over the last century, the house had expanded its mind deep into the mountain on which it stood, to backups in rented space at hundreds of cheap data farms on Home's twelve continents, and into nanocircuitry spread across the snowy tundra surrounding the vast estate. Enough room for quadrillions of copies of the little file.

The house was pleased with this first phase. Even if Home was subjected to a massive nuclear attack, Imperial civilization reduced to glowing ruins, it would be overwhelmingly likely that some future data archaeologist would run across a copy of the file, somewhere.

But there was more to the owner's wishes.

The house sent copies of the file – it was the complete text of the speech she had just been giving, the house noticed – to every newsfeed professional on the planet, the messages emanating from thousands of fictitious addresses, bombarding the media with the persistence of a huge mailing campaign. Then the house began calling every possible handphone number on Home in numerical order, and reading the speech to whomever answered and would listen.

The mirror fields with which the house warmed its surface gardens were put to use, blinking the file in antique on-off codes to passing aircraft. An old hardline to its original architects was reactivated, and the blueprint plotters in the firm's offices worldwide began spouting the senator's speech.

With these processes underway, the house fired its missiles.

The house was quite proud of the modifications it had made to the emergency message rockets. They were to be used in case of communication loss, should a guest require vital medical attention during a storm or com blackout. They were small suborbitals, armed with low-band transmitters, useful for lofting above the weather to shout an SOS in a quick burst. The house had increased their range, improving the fuel and adding variable geometry wings that could keep them hopping atop the atmosphere for hours. They blazed into the cold, clear summer sky and headed for the nearest large cities, ready to transmit the speech on the reserved frequencies of weather pagers, burglar alarms, and taxi radios.

The house watched its preparations unfold with humble pleasure. Mistress Oxham should be happy. It had carried out her request with considerable creativity. In a few minutes, the planetary infostructure would be saturated with this tiny document.

With the messaging well underway, the house turned

happily to its next project. The snowmelt waterfall that was the principal attraction of the west garden needed reining in.

With the spring thaws, it had become far too noisy.

Senator

Nara Oxham gathered her thoughts. She had only the Senate for an audience now. They were lost in confusion, though. Most of them had been tracking the newsfeeds with half their minds, watching instant polls and viewership numbers. Their political reflexes didn't know how to deal with the sudden absence of media.

'Senators,' she cried, trying to gather their attention again. 'Hear me!'

'*Silence her!*' came a shriek from the accuser. The dead woman leapt to her feet and took a step toward Oxham.

The Forum buzzed in surprise at this display. Few people had ever seen one of the honored dead raise their voice, much less scream in anguish.

'Order!' proclaimed Drexler. He glared at the accuser, aghast that one of the Emperor's servants would disturb his Senate. 'You are within the Pale, Prelate. Take care!'

'These words cannot be spoken!' the prelate cried. 'Use the switch!'

Drexler looked at the cutoff in his hand. Nara saw the doubt in him, a sharp discomfort at disobeying the command of an honored dead. But the power of tradition, of senatorial privilege, was greater.

'It is Senator Oxham's turn to speak,' he ruled. 'Silence yourself, Prelate.'

Nara swallowed. Zai had told her that members of the

Apparatus would feel pain at the mention of the Secret, but she hadn't realized how frantic the accuser's reaction would be. The dead woman's emotions were suddenly brighter than any in the Forum, a fearful hatred that was animal in its intensity.

Oxham spoke slowly and carefully.

'We were told, Senators, that the symbiant was an immortal coil. We were told that the elevated would live forever. We were lied to.'

'No!' the accuser screamed, and leapt toward Nara.

She had never seen a dead woman move so fast. The accuser crossed the granite floor in a few strides, a flash of metal gleaming in one hand.

Nara never saw the rest, although she watched reconstructions later on the newsfeeds. The prelate came at her, knife upraised, a wild assassin trailing black robes. A meter from dealing Oxham a murderous blow, the prelate crumpled to the floor. Shown at the slowest speed, a small puff of smoke could be seen coming from one hand of the guard-at-arms, who had fired a ball of gel filled with metal pellets, a nonlethal but powerful weapon.

At the actual moment of the attack, all Nara Oxham saw was the black-robed woman falling at her feet, and the knife careening across the floor. The blade struck the bottom of the Low Dais and broke, one piece whirling on the granite floor like a spinner in a children's game.

Gasps filled the Forum.

'I move for a recess,' the Loyalist Higgs called above the noise.

Oxham realized that this was another attempt to silence her. The prelate's knife hadn't killed her, but with a recess the Emperor would have won a few precious hours. She might never have this audience again.

All eyes turned to Drexler.

'Order,' he said, the old voice booming. There was silence in the hall again.

'Let me speak, President,' she pleaded.

'Bind the accuser,' Drexler ordered. 'But do not remove her.'

The guard moved efficiently, deploying another riot-police device. A bright orange web moved across the prelate, winding through her limbs like a sentient vine. It curled around wrists and ankles, and around her throat. It took up stations at her mouth and covered her eyes.

'No one will disrupt this trial again,' Drexler said, 'even a senator, or I'll have them bound as well.'

The guard stood and looked across the ranks of senators, almost daring them to make a sound. Nara Oxham wondered for a moment where this young guard came from. The Senate guards-at-arms had always seemed so ceremonial, like toy soldiers. But this man moved like a cat.

Nara looked up at Drexler and was startled by what empathy showed her. There was cold fury in the President's heart, a deep blue knot of anger that she could see clearly in her empathic sight. After a moment she grasped the source of his indignation. The most ancient Senate tradition had been broken. For the first time in the history of the realm, violence had been attempted in the Great Forum by an agent of the Emperor.

The Rubicon Pale had been crossed.

And Nara Oxham had gained an ally.

'Continue,' the old Loyalist said.

Nara nodded solemnly, trying to ignore the bound and writhing woman at her feet.

'Our beloved Empress was not killed by the Rix. She was already dying, ailing from a slow wasting that stalks every risen person in this empire. Her body was destroyed to conceal the evidence of aging, evidence of the Emperor's lies.'

A noise came from Loyalist senators at these words, but

Drexler silenced them with an icy glare. Nara could also hear the prelate whimpering at her feet, but the Forum's amplifiers ignored the sound.

The prelate's pain pricked at Oxham's empathy, though. Her words were torture to the dead woman, warring against the conditioning that had kept the Emperor's Secret over the centuries. Nara dialed up her apathy bracelet and continued.

'The risen dead do not live forever. They live less than five hundred subjective years.'

Even numbed, Nara's empathy felt the burst of confusion among the senators. The Emperor himself was almost seventeen hundred years Absolute.

'This is the true reason for the pilgrimages,' she explained. 'The dead travel endlessly across the Empire for one reason only: so that the Time Thief will put off their natural deaths. Immortality is a trick of relativity. Outside the royal family, there are no dead who have been risen more than four hundred subjective years.'

She gave her audience a moment to absorb this information. It was so simple, really. A parlor trick in the age of common near-lightspeed travel. It was little wonder that the compound mind had discovered it so quickly in the Legis infostructure. The Rix had watched Imperial shipping for decades, searching for weaknesses. They had probably begun to suspect long ago that the pilgrimages harbored some deception. According to Laurent, the invading mind on Legis had entered the Child Empress's body through her medical confidant, and had spotted signs of her aging. The veil of deception had fallen quickly after that. It had all the data on Legis to work with, and the pilgrimage ships' manifests were recorded in great detail by the Apparatus, the subjective age of every elevated subject carefully watched in order to maintain the ruse.

The risen themselves didn't know the real purpose of the

pilgrimages. They were doled out as a reward of the afterlife, and, as in everything else, the symbiant made the risen complacent followers of tradition. In their timeless lives, the swift passage of centuries seemed natural.

'The Emperor and the Apparatus have long known the symbiant's true lifespan. When the Apparatus and Court aren't traveling, they use stasis, just as we members of the Senate do in order to live out our terms. But the Child Empress grew tired of the ruse. She realized that despite the Emperor's continuing researches, the symbiant's life would never be extended.'

Oxham let her voice dip at the mention of the lost Empress. She was giving a political speech now, riding the emotions of the Forum. Even the Loyalists were beginning to listen; the Reason had always compelled greater love than her brother.

'She had decided to let herself die, and by her death to reveal the lie on which the Empire had been built. Her body began to show signs of aging, and she required a prosthesis to maintain the appearance of health. There were decades left to her, but the Emperor had already put his agents near her on Legis. He planned to conceal her death eventually. To invent an accident or some other obliterating event when the opportunity arose. The Rix simply created that opportunity.'

She felt a sense of horror rising in the room. The Apparatus had always presented the Child Empress as the soft side of the wrathful Emperor. It was her name put to pardons and crisis relief. She was the Reason, whose illness had spurred the Emperor's researches. The claim that she had been murdered by her own older brother appalled even the most cynical Secularists.

'Nara Oxham,' the President interrupted gently. 'These are grave charges, but what do they have to do with your crime?'

She nodded respectfully, grateful that Drexler had allowed her to speak unquestioned for so long.

'To explain, I must bend the hundred-year rule, President.'

Drexler's eyes narrowed. He placed the cutoff switch on the dais next to him and said, 'Carefully, Senator.'

'Captain Laurent Zai has captured the Legis compound mind, which knew the secret,' she said. 'The Emperor realized that Zai would soon learn it as well. Laurent Zai's life was in danger. I had to warn him, a hero of the realm. That is why I broke the rule.'

'And the Emperor sought to use the rule to silence you?'

'Yes, Senator Drexler.'

The old man nodded, satisfied. She wondered what these revelations were doing to him. Drexler was long since elevated, probably only a few subjective years from death. And now his promised immortality had been revealed as a fraud, his beloved Emperor the murderer of his sister, Anastasia the Reason.

Then another empathic shock interrupted Oxham's thoughts, a burst of emotion from the city outside the Great Forum.

'Something has happened,' she said softly.

Drexler looked up, his old fingers trembling with the slightest interface gestures.

'Our link to the rest of the capital has been cut,' he announced. 'The physical hardlines below the Forum have been destroyed.'

Fearful cries came from the senators.

'Order!' Drexler commanded. 'This body is still in session!'

Nara brought her second sight online. The bandwidth of the Forum's infostructure had been degraded. The images were coming through weak wireless, as if she were on horse-back trip in the deep country of Vasthold.

But the snowy newsfeed image was familiar enough. She could make out the Forum complex, a veil of smoke rising from its periphery. The low black shapes of military hovercraft surrounded the building.

'They will not cross the Pale,' Drexler said.

Godspite, Oxham thought. The army was outside. Their tradition of noninterference would be sorely tested now.

What had she started?

A rumble came through her feet. The very granite of the Great Forum was trembling.

'They will not cross the Pale,' the President repeated, quiet desperation in his ancient voice.

Plagueman

'The Empire faces a crisis.' The sovereign addressed the hastily assembled War Council gravely. 'We are under a new and diabolical form of attack, and the War Council must deal with it without delay.' The representative of the Plague Axis reflected silently that this was not the entire War Council. Only eight of nine were present. Three of the senators were here, still looking stunned by their swift passage from the Pale to the Diamond Palace, but Nara Oxham was not. The Senate had officially suspended Oxham from the council pending her expulsion trial, but her absence from the chamber pit had never been more noticeable.

'How have we been attacked, Majesty?' the Loyalist Senator Raz imPar Henders said.

'From the Senate floor itself,' the Emperor said.

'I must protest, Sire,' the Utopian senator interjected. 'The Senate is in legal session, considering a matter of great importance. The only attack on the Empire is the military's incursion against senatorial privilege.'

'No military units have crossed the Pale, Senator,' the risen general said.

'Then why is the Great Forum surrounded?' the Expansionist demanded.

'For the protection of the Senate,' the Emperor nearly shouted.

The plagueman had never seen the sovereign so incensed. He seemed unaffected by whatever had crippled his Apparatus, though he had lost his usual boundless reserve of calm. The biosuit's optics had always revealed the Emperor's physiology to be more animated than an ordinary risen, but now they showed a heat in his face almost as intense as a living man's.

'Protection?' the Expansionist sputtered. 'The Senate is surrounded, its contact with the rest of the capital cut off. This is nothing but bald intimidation.'

'I assure you, Senator, no military units shall cross the Pale,' the dead general said flatly. 'Not without due order by this council.'

'There'll be civil war if they do,' Ax Milnk said. 'And all of us will lose everything.'

The plagueman raised his eyebrows. That much was true. The Empire was perpetually balanced on a knife's edge between gray and pink, the dead and the living, military and economic power. The military forces stationed on Home were as carefully equilibrated as the rest of the fragile mechanism, with units hailing from pink worlds and gray. Any military move against the Senate would be met with an equal counterforce. A disaster.

'Please, let us calm ourselves,' Henders insisted, obviously flustered at his fellow senators' abuse of the sovereign. 'Sire, what is this attack you speak of?'

The Emperor nodded, visibly working to calm himself. 'Of course, we must explain. No doubt events today may have seemed precipitous. But we are sure that once you've heard the facts you will understand our actions.'

The pink senators and Milnk responded with stony silence.

The risen general leaned forward, gesturing to bring an image of Nara Oxham onto the central airscreen. The plagueman recognized it from her trial, clipped from the newsfeed of only an hour before.

'Counselors, during the trial of Senator Nara Oxham, we discovered that a neural virus was being transmitted from the Senate floor. The virus used the newsfeed as a carrier wave, instantly affecting a small but vulnerable portion of the capital's populace. The virus caused nausea, seizures, paralysis. We believe that the effect would have spread to the entire population had the broadcast continued. Fortunately, the Apparatus acted quickly, shutting off the attack at its source.'

The council chamber was silent as those assembled digested the general's words. The plagueman quietly searched the database within his biosuit. He found references to visual stimuli that could cause seizures, but only to a small percentage of human beings, most often children, and nothing that could be hidden inside a normal newsfeed. This was an unprecedented weapon, if the general's words were true.

'This sounds incredible,' the Utopian said. 'Nothing but a pretext for silencing Senator Oxham.' He turned toward the plagueman and Milnk. 'We heard more than you did, before we were summoned away. After the newsfeed was cut, Oxham accused the Emperor of murdering his sister. And she claims that the symbiant's immortality is a lie.'

'Incredible stories seem to abound today,' the Emperor said.

'If Oxham is lying, then why concoct this story to cut her off?' the Expansionist senator countered.

'The palace had nothing to do with the decision,' the Emperor said. 'As I said, the media monitors found themselves under attack, in great pain. They acted in self-preservation.'

'That much may be true,' the plagueman said quietly. 'Oxham's words seemed to have effected the Apparatus in particular.'

The Emperor started, then fixed the Axis representative with a glare. It was rare for the representative to speak at all, and the sovereign had counted the Axis as an ally throughout the war, especially since the vote on the Legis genocide.

'That may be,' the dead admiral said. 'We don't understand exactly how the virus works or who is susceptible. But we suspect who is behind it.'

'And that would be?' the Utopian said.

'Oxham, and perhaps some elements of the Secularist Party,' the general said.

'You have proof of this?' Ax Milnk demanded.

'Give us Oxham, and we'll get the proof,' the Emperor said.

'This is utterly transparent,' the Utopian said flatly.

The plagueman remained silent as the argument raged, biding his time. The members of the War Council would soon lose all civility, but that hardly mattered. The details of whatever Oxham had discovered were, in their way, unimportant as well. This drama would ultimately be played out in other venues. The pressures that had been too long restrained in the Empire would shortly be released, violently and disruptively, that much was obvious. The Axis had seen this coming for a long time. It had failed in its mission to stabilize the Eighty Worlds. The Rix, with their blockade, their wars, had finally won.

But the plagueman was glad that the Emperor's desperate gamble would allow him one last act of penance here on the council. It was clear that the sovereign would call for a vote, thinking he had five among the eight counselors in his pocket, believing that under cover of the War Council he could move against Oxham, perhaps ultimately against the Senate, and keep the whole unwieldy contraption of the Empire clanking along for a few more decades.

'I shall repay you, Nara Oxham,' the plagueman thought to himself. Not just with this vote to save her, but with all it would bring. As much chaos, progress, and the Old Enemy death as she and her party could ever want.

'God is change,' he muttered to himself.

Captain

Laurent Zai looked down upon the object.

At this point in the *Lynx*'s slow rotation, its dark bulk was beneath his feet, barely discernible through the observation blister's high-impact plastic. Its shape had grown ever more difficult to make out as the Legis sun receded. Now, the object was merely an absence of stars, a giant lump of coal blackening one quarter of the universe.

The *Lynx* was still studiously avoiding communication with the thing. The frigate's mass detectors were the only sensors trained on its position; mass was the one aspect of itself the object couldn't modulate, and thus use to signal the *Lynx*. Zai felt safer this way, cut off from the mind. One of Alexander's secrets had already brought the Empire to the brink of civil war.

Now, the only means of contact with the mind was through the slender connection it had established with Herd. The Rixwoman spoke for it like some ancient oracle: as expressionless and miraculous as a bleeding statue, an intermediary with the deity.

But Zai knew that this prophylaxis couldn't be maintained

forever. The object was too tenacious and resourceful, too capable of unanticipated configurations. And the *Lynx* was too porous: it was fundamentally a scout ship, designed to gather information in a thousand ways. The object would get in sooner or later, would reach Zai's crew just as it had reached Herd.

He would have to tell them. The crew knew that Zai had disarmed the politicals on board, so they would eventually have to know about the Emperor's Secret and the coming civil war. Their native worlds would be thrown into chaos soon. Zai and his lover had lit a match that would consume millions of lives.

Laurent watched Home's bright star rise slowly on his left, still two subjective years away, and wondered what was going on at the Forum. Nara would have made her speech a few hours ago, threatening sixteen hundred years of stability. The Apparatus's reaction would be swift and desperate, but Nara Oxham was a Senator, and would not be easily silenced.

Laurent Zai had burned seven percent of the *Lynx*'s entanglement reserve trying to keep track of the developments, and he knew that the Empire was already shaking. If the signs were to be believed, the Emperor had acted directly against the Senate. Zai hoped that the other messages he had sent, warnings to old colleagues and confidants within the military, would help Nara come through this unharmed. She and the Senate would certainly need allies to survive the next months. But in the long term, Zai believed, victory would be theirs.

The Apparatus would do what it could to forestall the spread of the Secret, but their efforts could only be stopgap. The data on pilgrimages were public; once examined, rumors would turn swiftly into accepted fact. And the Secret revealed would strain even the greatest loyalty. Few religions could withstand the news that heaven was, in fact, a lie. Temporary.

Zai wondered what had led the Emperor down this path. Five hundred extra years of life was hardly a trivial boon. Presumably, the sovereign had simply been mistaken at first, thinking that the symbiant was permanently stable, and a religion had been built on the concept that the Old Enemy had been beaten. When the first signs of the error had been detected, perhaps it had been too late for such a massive revision in scripture.

Well, a revision was coming now.

If the sovereign chose to fight, the Empire might remain divided for a long time. The Apparatus could easily keep a few warships, perhaps even a majority of the fleet, in the dark for years. Vessels could be ordered into deep cover for decades, receiving only censored information from the outside universe. But slowly, the truth would chip away at the loyalists, the conditioned, the willfully blind. Though some of the military would certainly remain loyal to the Emperor regardless of his lies, the Eighty Worlds would turn against him one by one. And what would follow this civil war? A republic? A new sovereign? It might take decades to resolve the question of succession.

The *Lynx*'s problem was more immediate, however. As Nara had warned, the vessels pursuing them were under orders to destroy the object, Zai, and his ship. One had to assume that they'd been under deep cover from the start of their mission – and Imperial writs were a difficult code to subvert. In a few years Absolute, they would be closing with the *Lynx*, their velocities almost matched. With the extra mass of the object in tow, the frigate could not outrun them. Outnumbered, with a half-untrained crew and an imperfectly repaired ship, Zai would have to fight again.

He needed an ally, and he was alone in deep space.

All he had was the object.

He reached down toward the absence below him, looked at his gloved hand against the absolute blackness of the thing. He pulled off the glove, and gazed upon the smooth metal of his hand. If the Rix were at long last arriving in the Empire, they had begun with the right man. Laurent Zai knew what it was to be half machine.

And he wanted to return to Home; that was all that mattered. That was what had moved him from the start. Now that everything else – honor, tradition, sovereign, and immortality itself – was stripped away, he had love to return to.

Nara.

'Bridge.'

'Captain?' Hobbes's voice came.

'Assemble the senior staff in one hour.'

'Yes, sir. Command bridge?'

'As good a place as any.'

'Any prep, Captain?'

'Consider contact with the object, Hobbes, an alliance of convenience with the Rix. Consider how to fight a guerrilla war in a crumbling Empire. Consider how best to explain to our crew that death is final, and that we all may die soon.'

There was a pause, but not a long one.

'On it, sir.'

Senator

The four officers entered the Great Forum slowly, as warily as a pack of predators trespassing in another's territory.

They clearly didn't want to be here, committing this transgression.

The rows of white-clad senators watched the four descend the steps toward the dais. A murmur rose up, a sound halfway between defiance and fear. Nara Oxham felt the two emotions collide and mix, creating a strange discomfort that was almost like *embarrassment*. In their black uniforms, one might have mistaken the officers as guests arriving at a ball wearing tragically confused dress – fantastical masks at a white-tie function.

But then the fear grew, displacing everything else. These four had thousands of soldiers under their command, who surrounded the Forum even now, dozens of ships in the skies above.

'President,' the most senior officer said, nodding a small bow.

Drexler looked down upon the four with undisguised anger.

'You have broken the covenant, Admiral. Would you destroy the Empire?'

The woman looked surprised. With the Forum infostructure down, Oxham had no prompts, but Nara recognized her from official parties. It was Admiral Rencer Fowler IX. She had been on Home for some time, and had aged the last ten years at full Absolute.

'We are unarmed, President Drexler. We meant no violation of the Pale.'

The old man scowled. 'No Imperial soldier has ever come inside the Forum before, Admiral, and your troops threaten us even now.'

'These are strange times, President,' she said simply, as if in somber agreement. 'The four of us wished to speak in private with you, but the secure lines crossing the Pale seem to be in disrepair.'

The Forum reverberated with a hissing sound: the word *disrepair* spoken with contempt. Against the feigned politesse of the admiral, defiance reasserted itself.

'The hard lines were deliberately destroyed,' the President said coldly.

Admiral Fowler nodded. 'That would seem likely.'

'Do you claim this was not the military's doing?'

She shrugged. 'We aren't certain. We suspect the Apparatus is responsible. In any case, we four do not represent the military per se.'

Confusion filled the Great Forum now. Nara could read nothing useful from the officers. They were soldiers on a mission, hardminded, determined not to consider the greater implications of their actions. Whatever Fowler's claims, the four were following orders.

'You carry a writ from the Emperor himself?' Drexler asked.

Fowler shook her head. 'We don't represent the Emperor, either. Can we speak in private, President?'

'The Senate is in session, Admiral. We are conducting a trial.'

Fowler looked about the hall, begrudgingly recognizing the hundreds of senators surrounding her. She sighed, and turned to address them all.

'Two of us are here to speak for the Home Fleet and certain ships of the High Fleet. My own flag vessel, for one.' She indicated the men on her left. 'And these fine officers represent ground units of the Capital Guard and Home Reserve. But not much of the latter, I fear.'

Nara Oxham swallowed. *The military was divided.*

Drexler raised his eyebrows. 'The situation is complicated, then, in terms of your chain of command.'

Admiral Fowler nodded slowly. She glanced nervously around the Forum, as if wishing again for a smaller audience. Then she shifted her weight, looked at the gray marble floor, and spoke carefully.

'Yes, but perhaps you could clarify matters for us, President Drexler. Due to the communications situation, the War Council has rendered an incomplete vote on an issue of great importance.'

'An incomplete vote?'

'Eight members have voted, President, and the result is a four-to-four tie. Certain members of the military command structure insist that the Emperor's vote should break the tie, as per tradition when the council is not at full strength.'

The admiral cleared her throat.

'But others of us would prefer to wait for the vote of the ninth member of the council, given the importance of the issue. Should she be available.'

For the first time, the admiral looked at Oxham. Nara could read nothing in the woman's expression. Fowler's mind was clean, as if she were a disinterested, slightly bored observer at some hoary political convention.

'What is this issue?' Oxham asked.

The admiral spoke officiously. 'The council has voted – *partly* voted – on an order to the Capital Guard. The order is to suspend temporarily the normal operations of the Senate. To arrest Senator Oxham and turn her over to the Apparatus.'

'To cross the Pale?' Drexler hissed.

Admiral Fowler nodded. 'That exceptional action was explicitly dictated.'

Drexler's face darkened.

'Thus, in a manner of speaking, we four are authorized to be here, President,' the admiral continued, 'by partial vote of the council. But, being on this side of the Pale, we discover the ninth member of the council.'

The woman bowed to Oxham. Finally, emotion finally surged from all four of them to reach her empathy. Strong effect, focused directly on her.

'Should she be available.'

President Drexler spoke carefully, joining the admiral's dance of words.

'Senator Oxham's membership in the War Council has been suspended, as you may know, pending the result of this trial.' He looked down from the dais at Oxham, raising one eyebrow.

For a moment, Nara wondered if this was a charade, all a trick. Her empathy was mostly suppressed; she couldn't feel the emotional reality of the situation. The confusion of the divided city raged around her, but the emotions of these officers were too subtle to read. But one thing was certain, Nara had to act.

Four to four, she thought. The Plague Axis had made good on their promise. And now she could break the tie.

'President Drexler, I rest my defense. And call for a vote on my expulsion.'

The young Secularist who had replaced her as party whip, rose.

'I second the call. A fast vote, if the President pleases.'

Puram Drexler's gavel thundered. 'Senators, you have fifty seconds. Vote by standard gestural code.'

A few objections were raised from the shocked Loyalist benches, but Drexler gaveled them into silence. The Senate was stunned for a few moments, but then votes began to tally. Oxham almost failed to cast her own, forgetting that she had never been officially removed as His Majesty's Representative from Vasthold, Senator of the Empire, and that she had every right.

The Senate voted.

Half a minute later, it was over. Even a sizable number of Loyalists – whether from confusion, the realization that defeat was certain, or a final faithfulness to traditions even older than the Emperor – voted with the majority. Nara Oxham had been overwhelmingly acquitted of treason; the motion for her expulsion had failed.

The suddenness of it all left her empty inside; relief would take a long time to come.

'Senator Nara Oxham is returned to full status and duties, without prejudice or delay,' President Drexler announced.

The old man turned to the officers.

'She is available, Admiral,' he finished.

They turned to her.

'Senator, we await the final vote of the War Council.'

Still stunned at the speed of events, Nara gathered herself. Enough of the military had dared to forestall the Emperor, Drexler had supported them, the Senate had acted quickly and true. All that was left was for her to finish the job.

Again, it all came down to a word.

'I vote against the proposal, Admiral,' she said quietly.

'Thank you for the clarification,' Fowler answered. She turned to face the Senate. 'We apologize for this intrusion. Certain elements under our command will remain – outside the Pale – to render technical assistance and all necessary protection to the Senate.'

'That is acceptable,' Drexler said.

'Death spare the Senate,' Fowler said.

'Death spare the Senate,' came the murmured response of the assembly.

Three of the officers turned and strode from the Forum, hurrying back to the Pale and the military infostructure, where they could give orders to their troops and ships. But one of the navy men stayed behind, and took a step toward her.

'Senator Oxham?'

'Yes . . . Commodore?' she asked, reading his rank.

'My name is Marcus Fentu Masrui.'

She blinked, recognizing the name. Masrui had been Zai's commanding officer on Dhantu. In fact, she'd come close to meeting the man on the night she'd met Laurent, ten years ago.

'Is it true, Senator?' the officer asked.

'What, Commodore?'

'That the Emperor wanted to kill Laurent Zai? After everything?'

She nodded. 'Absolutely true. I heard him say the words.'

'And that there is no immortality?'

'Yes. It's all true, Commodore. Laurent himself told me.'

The Commodore shook his head ruefully. 'If any man deserved to live forever, it was Zai,' he said.

She felt it then, the emotion the officers had hidden so well. It burst from behind Masrui's discipline, from behind his decades of training and loyalty. The prize they'd all been promised, the Valhalla where their dead comrades had gone for rewards eternal, the very reason many of them had joined the military: all of it was a lie.

The man's face wrenched, as if he were swallowing something awful. Then he took a deep breath, and focus returned to his thoughts.

'And, another thing, begging your pardon . . .'

'Yes, Commodore?'

Masrui bit his lower lip before speaking.

'Were you and Zai . . . really lovers?'

'Yes, Commodore. We are lovers.'

For a moment, his face was blank. Then he grasped her hand.

'Thank you,' he said.

Nara found herself speechless for a moment. Then she pulled her hand from his. 'No thanks necessary, Commodore. It was never pity.'

'Of course not, Senator. I didn't mean to imply pity. Thank you, though. I wanted . . . all of us wanted somehow to restore Zai. He lost too much on Dhantu. After the

Legis rescue failed, we thought the Emperor's pardon was real.'

'It wasn't.'

He swallowed, the bitter taste of another lie showing on his face.

'Commodore, tell me something,' Oxham said.

'At your service, Senator.'

'Are there enough of you? Enough to fight those who'll follow the Emperor without question?'

'Not yet. But there will be. The truth will turn them.'

He looked up at his departing comrades, realizing that he should join them and put this revolution, this righteous treason, this civil war into motion. But he turned back to Nara.

'Laurent Zai's name will turn them,' he said.

'And death,' Nara added.

'Death, Senator?'

'Death is real again, Commodore. Remind them of that.'

Commodore Masrui thought about this for moment, then shook his head.

'It was always real, Senator, for us soldiers. Death out in space rarely left enough for the symbiant. But I suppose that now death is *unavoidable*, as it always was before the Emperor's lie.'

'Spread the word, then,' Nara Oxham said. 'We're free again.'

Fisherman/Pilot

After a long time, the sun and moon stopped wheeling in the sky. The tides were over.

The fisherman looked down at himself. Somehow, he was

still here, still whole after having been consumed a thousand thousand times. The fish were placid now, half in the tide pool, half in the bay.

But no, there were more of them . . . in the sky.

The dark night seemed to have filled with stars, as if he'd jumped ten thousand light-years closer to the core. But what looked like stars were in fact the little luminescent fish, strewn across the sky to make a galaxy, a milky river of light. The fisherman's thoughts grew clearer, and he understood what had pacified the ravenous schools: they had reached their goal, resplendent and sovereign in the dark.

They were up there, beyond the reach of his spear.

He dropped the weapon and turned toward the opening sky . . .

Master Pilot Jocim Marx's gummy eyes focused first on the scarred woman.

Her face was blank, as if nerve damage had rendered it expressionless. The hair had been burned from her scalp. But the woman's gaze was bright and intelligent.

And violet, her eyes as bright a hue as stained glass catching the sun.

Had he been captured by the Rix?

Marx started, trying to sit up. The scarred woman moved away, with the suddenness of a bird cocking its head. He knew from that movement that she was not human.

'Who—?' Marx began, then he saw Hobbes over the woman's shoulder.

'Jocim?' the ExO said.

She articulated the two syllables carefully, as if to establish whether he knew his own name.

He did her one better. 'How are you, Katherie Hobbes?'

She smiled, 'Relieved.'

'How long?'

'A month.'

'Godspite.' To Marx, it had seemed like an eternity, but the memory was already fading when contrasted to the real world. He looked around, and recognized the room as a private sickbay cabin aboard the *Lynx*. The violet-eyed Rix had moved to the side of a small, gray-faced woman. One of the honored dead? This was too confusing.

'Why is there a Rixwoman here, Hobbes? Have we been captured?'

'No, Master Pilot. She is a . . . guest. Or an ally, perhaps.' Hobbes sounded only slightly less confused than Marx. 'She helped cure you,' the ExO added with surety.

He looked at the violet-eyed woman, blinked.

'Thank you, then, I suppose.'

The woman's gaze remained both piercing and empty, as if he were a specimen pinned in a curio case.

'How do you feel, Marx?' Hobbes asked.

He sat up. His muscles had the even tone of artificial exercise. His fingers, chronically suffering mild soreness from the demands of piloting, felt rejuvenated from the enforced break. His head was . . .

Different.

'What happened, Hobbes?'

'Everything.'

That was Hobbes. Concise, but not always helpful. The passage of weeks must have refreshed his brain, Marx thought. He could see the executive officer's stunning beauty again, as he had before growing accustomed to it over the last two years. As if he'd spent a month on leave rather than in a . . . coma?

'You were caught in an upload, Jocim,' she said. 'Alexander – the Legis compound mind, I should say – was transferring itself from the planet to the object. You got in the way.'

The *object*. That word brought a shiver to Marx. Images swirled in his head: a kind of liquid creature below him, its pseudopods reaching out, like those legant members to which a sea creature delegates its kills. Marx recognized from his own discomfort that he was nearing his last memories from before the onset of coma. He'd been taken prey.

'Your sensor subdrones were pumping everything they could directly into your synesthesia,' Hobbes continued. 'The information gain was too high for you. And perhaps it was partly my fault, too, Jocim. You'd been pulled out of a hypersleep cycle out of phase, less than an hour before you were hit with the compound mind. Your mind was vulnerable.'

He looked up at Hobbes, silently begging her to talk more slowly. '*What* hit me?'

'Alexander. The Legis compound mind. You had a planet stuffed into your head.'

Marx nodded, and rubbed his aching temples. That metaphor felt about right. Then he blinked. He *hoped* it was a metaphor.

'Again, Hobbes,' he pleaded. '*Why* is there a Rixwoman running loose on our ship?'

'Ah,' Hobbes said. 'She's a commando, from the Legis attack.'

'Oh, a commando. Understandable then, that we would want her in sickbay.' Marx vaguely realized that he should be terrified, as if a poisonous snake had been dropped in his lap, but his body wasn't up to producing adrenaline.

'Things have changed, Marx. Not just here, but throughout the Empire. We've had to ally ourselves – or at least cooperate – with the object. With the Rix.'

'The Empire and Rix are allied?' Suddenly, three months' sleep didn't seem adequate.

'No, just us, Marx. The *Lynx* is on its own.'

'Wait,' the master pilot interrupted. 'Who's in command, Hobbes?' He clenched his fists. Had the aborted mutiny finally occurred?

'Captain Zai, of course.'

Marx's head swam. The *Vadan* had committed treason?

'Listen, Marx,' Hobbes kept at him. 'The Emperor's status is unsure. The dead have called a quorum. The pilgrimage ships are coming into Home from all over the Empire. The sovereign may be removed.'

A quorum of the dead? Something from a ten-year-old's civics class. A strictly theoretical possibility. For sixteen hundred years, the Emperor had ruled without a single dissenting vote from among the billions of honored dead. The dead never argued, never even *disagreed*. For them to consider removal of the sovereign seemed unthinkable.

'Hobbes,' he started, waving at her to slow down. His mind fought to locate the questions that would straighten out this strange new world.

'What the hell . . . ?' was all he could manage.

She started to speak, and Marx winced.

Katherie Hobbes shook her head, laughed. 'Master Pilot, I think you should rest now.'

She took his shoulders, *touched* him. Things had changed, indeed.

'We've lost so many, Jocim. It's good to have you back,' Hobbes whispered.

Marx simply nodded, and leaned back on the sickbed. Suddenly, he was exhausted again.

The ExO left him there, the lights dimming as she exited the private sickbay cabin.

He leaned back, and his mind roiled now, full of questions, confusion, sheer energy. Marx felt as if he'd drunk a pot of coffee after a full day of meetings, his mind tired but buzzing. Deep breaths had only the slightest calming effect.

He exercised his fingers, forcing himself to think about how good it would be to fly again.

Then he caught the eyes of the Rixwoman. She was still here – watching him, *observing*, as if monitoring a patient, awaiting some expected symptom to evince itself. The dead woman stood beside her, their shoulders just touching with the casual intimacy of old lovers.

Marx locked his gaze onto the Rixwoman's, focusing himself. Somehow, her implacable stare calmed his mind, her violet eyes glowing like meditation candles in the dark cabin. The rhythm of his breathing slowed, and he felt the cycle of the dreamtide again. He heard the ambient sound of the ship, the ever-present hum of engines, air system, and gravity generation.

Something was different.

Without releasing the commando's gaze, Marx placed his hand on the side of his bed, palm flat against cool metal. The ship-hum was stronger there. He let the dream phantoms, the reverberations of his fugue, align themselves to the frigate's vibration. Memory and metal conjoined, like the many instruments of an orchestra tuning to a common pitch.

They matched the flicker of the Rixwoman's eyes.

She smiled at Marx. Then the two of them together – yes, they *were* lovers, he suddenly knew – left him.

And the master pilot understood the deal that the captain had made. He wondered what must be arrayed against them, their lone ship in the deep, to have motivated Zai to let this thing aboard. To have allied his vessel and crew with the Empire's sworn enemy.

Perhaps Laurent Zai didn't even know, didn't understand the extent of its subtle, pervasive occupation. But Marx knew. He had spent a hundred days inside its belly. He could see its signs and hear its music. Like a vortex of wind revealed by the leaves, dirt, and debris it captured, the shape and scope of Alexander were clearly marked.

The *Lynx* had been taken.

The Rix were here.

■■■■

TEN YEARS EARLIER (IMPERIAL ABSOLUTE)

Marine Private

Marine Private Second-Class Bassiritz explained it again to his new crewmates: 'just *Bassiritz*. In the village where I come from, we only have one name.'

'Only one name?' Astra shouted above the roaring crowd.

'Better than none at all,' Master Private Torvel Saman assured him.

'Better than one too many,' Astra added.

'How many names would be too many?' Bassiritz asked.

'Not how many, but which ones!'

'Retired.'

'The late . . .'

'Corporal!'

They laughed at their own jokes and clapped Bassiritz on the back as if he'd made one himself. He didn't completely understand, but didn't press his mates with questions. He was relieved at their good humor, knowing from his travels that in some cultures, a single, unadorned name was a badge of shame, or a mark of servant lineage. But these *Lynx* marines all had wide experience; they'd seen far stranger things. The crew of the new, experimental warship was drawn from the cream of the Empire. Bassiritz knew that he himself only rated selection due to his high scores as a marksman and close combatant – he was younger and less educated than his squadmates.

The fire team was perched, alongside a hundred or so of their crewmates, on the gantry supporting a huge, false *Lynx*. The facsimile of their new ship loomed up behind them, two kilometers tall. (But it was not a figment or ghost-sight: the dummy ship was *real*, physical at least. Bassiritz had begun to realize that no expense was too absurd here on Home. Not for a pageant or party.) Before them, filling the great square before the Emperor's Diamond Palace, was a huge crowd of cheering citizens. An uncountable host, far more people than Bassiritz had ever seen in his life. Not merely in one place, but more than all the people the young private had ever seen, *put together*. That fact bounded around inside his head, a realization as sovereign as the glittering facets of the palace as it caught the strangely white light of Home's large sun.

This horde seemed to be the Empire entire, assembled to send off the *Lynx*'s crew.

Master Private Saman grasped his arm and pointed into the crowd.

'She's got something for you, Bass!' (The single name indeed didn't bother his squad: they'd shortened it already.)

Bassiritz's keen eyes followed Saman's gesture, and spotted a woman among the ecstatic dancers in the front of the crowd. She had removed her jacket and tunic, ignoring the autumn chill, baring flesh pale enough to shine like a ray of sun among the gray throngs of the faithful. Then others followed her example, men and women dancing out of their clothes, euphoric and supplicant before the towering, mock totem of the warship.

Bassiritz shook his head in bemusement. The gray religion took on many forms throughout the Empire, but here on Home all its strangest versions were clustered together, as if the planet were a curio cabinet stocked for the amusement of the Risen One himself. The ecstatic dancers had seemed like monks to Bassiritz at first. He had watched them over the last few days, encamped in the square before the rising dummy ship. Their gray tents and clothes, shaved heads, quiet prayers, and diet of cold field rations had given them a solemn dignity. But now he saw that the purpose of these privations had been to secure a position in the front of the crowd. To dance and scream wildly – now *nakedly* – before the crew and the onlooking masses. To become part of the spectacle of christening a new class of Imperial warship.

To pay their . . . respects.

'You'll catch flies, Private Second Class.'

Bassiritz closed his mouth, and smiled to echo the laughter of his squadmates.

'Bass's never been to a christening, I suppose.'

'Neither have you, Astra!'

'But I've seen war prizes presented. The dancers were there.'

'The dancers are *everywhere*.'

'There were a couple in your room last night, I overheard.'

'Those were honest surrogates, Private.'

'I'm sure you kept them honest.'

'I kept them awake.'

The squad laughed again. Bassiritz felt warm in their company, even in the chill wind. It was new and wonderful to be here up above a crowd, arrayed with his crewmates on the slender beams of the gantry, almost flying over the press of people. He had never felt so . . . *exalted* before.

His eyes scanned the buildings that rose as straight as cliffs around the square. The wide balconies were full, glittering with the reflective clothes of the wealthy, as if the city itself were bejeweled for this event. Bassiritz had heard fantastic stories about the cost of rooms on the square, which could not be owned, only leased from the Apparatus or temporarily bequeathed to high office-holders, such as senators and visiting planetary governors. Wealthy families exhausted whole fortunes to rent them, if only for a few days, in hopes of establishing connections, rising a little higher in the social order, nearing the ultimate prize of elevation. They were all out to gaze upon the mock ship, glittering and awestruck, yearning for immortality.

And with that thought, Bassiritz realized why his crewmates were so deliriously happy here. Suspended above the horde, under the gaze of the Empire's plutocrats, they felt their true value as soldiers, saw a prefiguration of their true reward. For their grueling service – the years confined on tiny ships, the decades lost to the Time Thief, the constant danger of sudden obliteration – they were granted the one prize that even the wildest wealth could not absolutely guarantee.

If they could just die in combat, cleanly and without too much brain damage, or enjoy long and exemplary careers, Bassiritz and his squadmates might live forever.

Forever. A period not even the Time Thief could steal.

He could see the Emperor's promise here, from this vantage above the crowd.

As his incredibly sharp eyes scanned the balconies of the powerful, Bassiritz's elated thoughts were suddenly interrupted. Alone on a small veranda were two figures, one wearing civilian white, the other military black. An odd couple.

The man in black seemed familiar. Bassiritz squinted, focusing on the pair. The man turned to profile, making some comment to his companion, and the young private started.

'It's the captain!' he cried.

'Where?'

'Not a chance.'

'Won't be here for hours!'

Bassiritz pointed. 'There on that balcony. With that woman in white.'

The others followed his gaze, cupping their hands against the glare of the sun now spilling into the square.

'That's the Secularist senatorial block. You wouldn't catch the Old Man in those abodes.' Master Private Saman had served with Laurent Zai before.

'Zai's *Vadan*, Bass! Not some pink.'

'But it's him. I can see him clearly.'

'It's at least a klick away, young man. You're hallucinating.'

The two figures on the balcony grew closer, first hands touching, then bodies drawing near against the cold. Then white and black intertwined.

'He's kissing a woman up there,' Bassiritz announced.

'Hah-hah!' Saman yowled, almost doubling over against the gantry's handrail. 'The captain kissing a pink senator!'

'Kissing anyone at all!' Astra added in amazement.

The squad laughed at Bassiritz's fine joke on them, slapping his back again, full of good humor and intoxicated by their imperious position above the crowd, above the naked and gyrating dancers, above the grasping wealthy. Above everything but the huge false ship behind them, and its real and lethal double in high orbit above, where they would soon be lofting to join it, to journey toward the rumored troubles of the Rix frontier.

They laughed that the possibility of death awaited them.

But Bassiritz frowned. He alone could see that it was, in fact, the captain. He could see that it was a long and vigorous embrace. And in his small village the elders had taught Bassiritz one certain rule: never laugh at a kiss. A kiss was mysterious and powerful, fragile and invincible.

Like any spark, a kiss might fizzle into nothing, or consume an entire forest. A kiss was no laughing matter. Not for the wary.

A kiss could change the world.

NEWTON'S WAKE

Ken MacLeod

The Hard Rapture took Earth's best minds away.
Now the rest are about to find out where they
went . . .

Centuries ago, space settlers and soldiers fled to the stars
from the sentient AI war machines that engulfed Earth.
They colonised Eurydice, a planet whose rocks contain
traces of its own war machines – some of which still guard
a vast, enigmatic artefact on a remote tundra.

When an expedition raids this strange artefact, the
Eurydiceans discover that they weren't the last survivors of
humanity after all. Their leisured lifestyle is about to be
disrupted by new arrivals for whom Eurydice is a prize
worth fighting over.

And the long-dormant war machines are awakening . . .

SINGULARITY SKY

Charles Stross

In the twenty-first century man created the Eschaton, a sentient artificial intelligence. It pushed Earth though the greatest technological evolution ever known, while warning that time travel is forbidden, and transgressors will be eliminated.

One far-flung colony, the New Republic, exists in self imposed isolation. Founded by men and women suffering from an acute case of future shock, the member-planets want no part of the Eschaton or the technological advances that followed its creation. But their backward ways are about to be severely compromised in an attack from an information plague that calls itself The Festival. And as advanced technologies suppressed for generations begin literally to fall from the the the sky, the New Republic is in danger of slipping into revolutionary turmoil.

The colony's only hope lies with a battle fleet from Earth. But secret plans, hidden agendas and ulterior motives abound.

THE ALGEBRAIST

Iain M. Banks

It is 4034 AD. Humanity has made it to the stars. Fassin Taak, a Slow Seer at the court of the Nasqueron Dwellers, will be fortunate if he makes it to the end of the year.

The Nasqueron Dwellers inhabit a gas giant on the outskirts of the galaxy, in a system awaiting its wormhole connection to the rest of civilisation. In the meantime, they are dismissed as decadents living in a state of highly developed barbarism, hoarding data without order, hunting their own young and fighting pointless formal wars.

Seconded to a military-religious order he's barely heard of – part of the baroque hierarchy of the Mercatoria, the latest galactic hegemony – Fassin Taak has to travel again amongst the Dwellers. He is in search of a secret hidden for half a billion years. But with each day that passes a war draws closer – a war that threatens to overwhelm everything and everyone he's ever known.

COYOTE

Allen Steele

Embark on an incredible journey of courage, ambition and discovery.

Forty-six light years from Earth, six moons orbit a gas giant three times the mass of Jupiter. Each has been designated a name from the animal demigods of Native American mythology: Dog, Hawk, Eagle, Coyote, Snake and Goat.

Only the fourth moon, Coyote, is likely to sustain life. The crew setting out on Mankind's greatest adventure know that the success of the mission will depend on how well they adapt to their new home. There is no going back.

But Coyote is also known as the trickster.